Aunt Margaret,
I hope you enjoy
your nice gift.
Enjoy!

CONFEDERATE GOLD AND SILVER

D1290184

"War at the best, is terrible, and this war of ours, in its magnitude and in its duration, is one of the most terrible."
President Abraham Lincoln

"What a cruel thing is war …."
General Robert E. Lee

"Let us have peace."
General Ulysses S. Grant

CONFEDERATE
GOLD *and* SILVER

A STORY OF THE LOST CONFEDERATE TREASURY AND
ITS MISSING GOLD AND SILVER

PETER F. WARREN
(A fictional piece of work)

WESTBOW
PRESS
A DIVISION OF THOMAS NELSON

(http://www.readpete.com)
petesbooks63@yahoo.com
See the author's Facebook page for additional information.

Author's photo – Peter Warren's photo was taken at the Caledonia Golf and Fish Club, in Pawleys Island, South Carolina, where he works. In the photo is one of the many Southern Live Oak trees which grace the property. (Photo by Marc Guertin)

This fictional story, while including some accurate historical facts, also includes conversations, writings (in the form of letters), and dialogues which take place between characters in this book; they are not intended to be real or historically accurate. They are a product of the author's imagination and are intended solely to enhance the story line. Some scenes, events, and locations within this book have also been created for the same reason.

WestBow Press books may be ordered through booksellers or by contacting:

WestBow Press
A Division of Thomas Nelson
1663 Liberty Drive
Bloomington, IN 47403
www.westbowpress.com
1 (866) 928-1240

ISBN: 978-1-4497-4278-2 (sc)
ISBN: 978-1-4497-4279-9 (hc)
ISBN: 978-1-4497-4277-5 (e)

Library of Congress Control Number: 2012905738

Print information available on the last page.

WestBow Press rev. date: 03/12/2015

To My Father
Frank G. Warren
We Miss You.

Chapters

Acknowledgements

Like all of you, the successes I have had in life, if any, are ones which have been influenced by the support I have received from family and friends. Fulfilling my dream of writing this book was one of my successes, and it was accomplished, in part, by the support I have received along the way.

After developing the storyline for this book, I first proposed my thoughts to perhaps one of the least interested persons in American History that I know. From that first conversation, and through the many early mornings and late nights I have spent writing, typing, and finally editing this book, the support I received from my wife, Debbie, has been amazing. *'Debra Lynn, I could not have done this without your help, without your support, and without your understanding! Thank you so much!'*

During the time it took to write this book I lost my father to Huntington's disease; a terrible disease he fought and struggled with for several years. My mother, a hero in my eyes, gave up so much of her life to support and care for my father in his final years. A retired Irish Catholic nurse, my mother was unwavering in her dedication and determination to properly care for my father. Despite the round-the-clock care she gave to him, she always found the time to call me and to support my efforts in completing this book. She, along with Debbie, served as my first two "editors". *'Mom, Thank you for the love you have shown to dad and me, and to all of your family. Thank you so much!'*

Many of the characters in this book I have named after family and friends. I have done so both out of my respect and fondness for each of them. To our special group of Southbury friends (some who now live in Florida and one who sadly now lives in heaven), friends like Jane and Steve White, Pete and Kathy Francis, Chuck and Karen Mann, and JD and Sue McAulay, and with a special thanks to one of my closest friends, Stephen T. Cochran, Debbie and I extend our sincere thanks for the friendship and support we have shared with each of you over the years. We have shared so many Friday night dinners together, shared so many vacations and holidays together, shared so many family moments together, and now we share a book together. *'To my friend Pete Francis, who we all miss terribly, I know somewhere in heaven you are enjoying this book.'*

To my many other personal and professional friends, especially those from the CT State Police Department, and those from NASDEA, I thank you for being part of this book. I also want to express my thanks to Marc Guertin for his assistance with my website.

And, finally, to the two people who mean the most in life to my wife and I, our sons Brian and Sean. I thank you both for being such a big part of my life. You both will always hold special places in my life. I am so proud of both of you.

I hope all of you who read this book have children, parents, family, and friends in your lives who mean as much to you as they do to Debbie and me.

Enjoy your reading!

1

The Move.

"I am a Connecticut State Trooper, a soldier of the law,
to me is entrusted the honor of the Department ..."
Connecticut State Police Department's Code of Honor

Many people spend their entire adult life working in careers they do not enjoy. Having such a job has to make your outlook on life not quite as rosy as it should be. Life is tough enough; not being excited about your job as you climb out of bed and put your feet on the floor each morning has to make facing the world much more difficult. For Paul Waring that was never the case. Paul loved his job and for most of his career as a Connecticut state trooper he enjoyed the various challenges a trooper faced each and every day. It seemed to him the public, in their good moments, but especially in their bad ones, always made his job interesting. He never could have survived a career hiding behind a desk.

Paul did well in his career and had been promoted several times, the last being to the rank of Major. During his career he had the opportunity to command several different investigative units and earned a reputation as an excellent investigator. His reputation was also that of being a fair, but a demanding boss. He was someone who had proved he could be trusted to do the right thing for those who worked for him as long as they did what was expected of them. For those who did not perform up to the standards he had set for himself, or to the standards he had set for his subordinates, he was known as someone who quietly could put a boot in someone's rear end to motivate them. His staff knew when they walked away from such an occasion, not only were they just more motivated but they often times walked away looking forward to the next time he gave them the boot. He had that way with people as he always left them with the feeling he was looking out for them. As cops held the public accountable when they broke the law, Paul held his detectives accountable when they were not performing well. On most occasions he looked at it as something that just had to be done. One of his favorite sayings described his feelings about having to address problems at work. "It's just business, it's not personal." The troopers and detectives who worked for him knew he had their backs and this was just one of his ways of looking out for them. They knew a boot in the ass sometimes kept the rats from Internal Affairs off their backs.

Paul was the type of boss who saw the potential in so many of the troopers who worked for him. As two of his sergeants had done for him early in his career, he often did the same for those he supervised. He spent hours and hours of his own personal time helping them to develop their skills so they could be successful in their careers. He was happy to help anyone. When a kick in the pants was needed he was not afraid of doing so, but it was always done in private, never in front of others. As Paul was not bashful about telling someone they had screwed up, he was often the first one to pay a compliment to a member of his staff who had accomplished something significant. He always took the time to publicly praise his staff when they solved a particular case and often stepped to the rear so his troopers were the ones who received the recognition from the state police command staff for a job well done. The troopers and detectives who worked for him knew he often did that for them and they appreciated him for those gestures.

Giving a kick in the pants to someone was something which sometimes had to be done, and most times it got the desired result. But after Paul had done it to you twice and you had not responded accordingly, he wrote you off and you soon found yourself back on the road, writing tickets and investigating accidents instead of working in an investigative assignment. As a lifelong New York Yankee fan, work was unlike baseball. When it came to work you had two strikes with him and then you were out. Three strikes was never an option for him as he did not have the patience or the inclination to give you that third strike. In his world after the second strike it was over and you had struck out with him. He had the juice to transfer his few problem children back to the road and he occasionally did so without regret.

While Paul sometimes needed to motivate certain members of his staff to get them refocused on what they should be doing, no one ever had to motivate him to get back on track. He was often handed some of the most complex cases that needed addressing, such as a murder needing to be solved, a bank robbery to investigate, an underachieving command to take over, or even a complex narcotics wiretap to run; those were the matters which were never a problem for him to take on as they were issues he excelled at. He looked forward to issues and problems; it was the mundane police work which bored him. The problem assignments which were handed to him always had the problems resolved by the time he was done. Those assignments were always thoroughly completed as Paul's work ethic was beyond reproach; so were his ethics in dealing with others. Well, at least most of the time they were.

Sometimes he stepped on people's toes, sometimes egos got ruffled, and sometimes it even got physical, but the job always got done. "Get it done; I don't care how you do it, just as long as it's legal, ethical, and moral. Just get it done." That had been the motto he lived by. Whatever the assignment was, Paul and his troops always got it done very well.

One of the last investigations Paul conducted was an Internal Affairs investigation which the Commissioner of the Department of Public Safety personally directed him to handle due to the sensitivity of the matter at hand. He argued with the commissioner over being handed this assignment, but he had lost the fight. He was now forced to take on an investigation he wanted no part of. This investigation involved the Governor's office, the media, and a fellow member of the state police department who was alleged to have been involved in some minor criminal activity. To make matters worse, the subject of this investigation had come up through the ranks with Paul. While not close friends, they had developed a mutual respect for each other.

The allegations made against this fellow command staff member were suspect from the beginning, but by the time the investigation was handed to Paul they really stunk. They continued to stink the entire time he investigated the case as the media whipped the sensational allegations onto the front page of several Connecticut daily newspapers for weeks. When his lengthy investigation was completed he had justified enough of the facts, which others had summarily dismissed early on, that his investigation helped to clear the false allegations made against his friend. But as he had done so many times before, Paul had not been content enough to just clear his friend; he kept investigating when others would have been content enough to stop there. His persistent efforts at digging at the other facts of the investigation led to new evidence being discovered. This evidence resulted in another senior command staff member and two other state employees being charged with several criminal violations, as well as with several administrative violations. The investigation had been an unpleasant one to conduct as no cop likes to have to investigate another cop, but for Paul it had been *"just business"* as usual, even though his thorough investigation had brought him some personal satisfaction in the end.

During the criminal trial following his investigation, Paul was present as often as his scheduled allowed. During the trial's closing arguments, and later during the sentencing phase, he listened as the presiding judge, and the Senior Assistant State's Attorney who had prosecuted the case, both made strong comments publicly criticizing the state police commander Paul's investigation had identified as being complicit in a variety of serious criminal activity. To make matters worse, when Paul's report was obtained under a Freedom of Information request the media had made, the report identified Major Thomas Barlow as the person directly responsible for conducting unauthorized criminal investigations on several state employees. Part of those unauthorized investigations also included Barlow illegally accessing state police computer files for personal use and falsely obtaining copies of the employees' financial records. Barlow had also participated in a variety of questionable off-duty activities during the same time these unauthorized investigations were being conducted. Paul's reports detailed all of these transgressions in significant detail. Both the criminal conduct and the administrative violations were clear violations of the *State Police Administrative and Operations Manual* regarding personal conduct.

Barlow then made the additional mistake of commenting publicly on the results of the investigation. In doing so he lied to the media, blaming others for the crimes and violations he had been accused of. Paul knew there would be hell to pay over the investigation's findings because of Barlow's close relationship with the governor, but he did not care as he knew it would be well worth it. Plus it had been the right thing to do. Sitting in Hartford's Superior Court, Paul had a thought about Barlow just before he was sentenced. "Payback can be a bitch!" He then listened as an obviously upset Judge James Washington berated Barlow in open court for his criminal conduct and falsehoods. While Paul had never cared for him as he thought he was a two-faced publicity hound, he did not gloat when Barlow was found guilty of the charges against him. He did allow himself to take a little pride in his own work when Barlow was finally dismissed from the state police a week after the criminal trial had concluded. It was really more personal satisfaction than gloating, but whatever it was he was pleased Barlow was finally gone from the ranks of the state police.

Paul's efforts in investigating this matter received many favorable comments from within the state police and from several Connecticut newspapers as the investigation had shown that cops can police themselves. However, because the governor did not like his association with Barlow being mentioned in police reports or in the newspapers, Paul was soon transferred to an administrative assignment that he was totally unprepared for. It was a transfer he never saw coming.

The one thing Paul could never tolerate in his career was administrative bullshit. Now his new assignment, one which required him to attend the same boring and repetitive meetings each and every month listening to the ass-kissers who agreed with every decision or with every new worthless program the commissioner and his civilian staff dreamed up, gave him heaping doses of administrative bullshit. During these meetings he often found himself daydreaming and wondering what cases his detectives were working. When he did pay attention it was not for long. "No wonder nothing ever gets done at headquarters. All of these morons are sitting in meetings all day instead of being in touch with the troopers in the field. They are the ones who are doing the real work." Paul had always tried not to invoke the mentality others in the field had when they referred to headquarters types of people, but now he found himself mixed in with them. "Guilty, but through association only and not for much longer!"

Paul tried every way possible to cope with his headquarters assignment. He gave it a new chance every month or so, but after several months of trying, and after he had met with the state police commissioner for a second time to try to get back to the field, he realized the commissioner was simply a political hack of the governor. Even though he had just completed a long and difficult sensitive investigation, one the commissioner personally selected him for due to his acquired investigative skills, it seemed as if his hard work did not matter. Despite his requests to be reassigned back to his previous assignment, one the state police had spent thirty years training him for, his requests fell on the commissioner's deaf ears. He now knew the commissioner would only do what he thought was best for his own career and would do only those things which would keep him out of the governor's dog house. The commissioner, who he had openly defended in the past from previous criticism, was someone who now proved to be a person who did not have the spine to do the right thing, not only for Paul, but for the department as well. He now not only lost Paul's confidence, but also started to lose the confidence of many other senior command staff members as well. On the day he left his second meeting with the commissioner, he knew the end of his run had come. He went home that evening and told his wife, Donna, he was done. "They're trying to fit a round peg in the proverbial square hole and it's not going to be me. I've tried talking to Commissioner Cagney and I've tried reasoning with him, but it's no use talking to him about something he won't do anything about. Men with principle and conviction stand up for what they know is right, but he won't ever stand up. I'm getting out as it's time for me to do something else in life."

During the last week of Paul's thirty-plus years in law enforcement, few people learned of his decision to retire and many never knew he had left until after he was gone. Even the day before he retired, when he treated one of his former secretaries to lunch to celebrate her birthday, he kept news of his retirement quiet even from her. He wanted it that way and he jokingly threatened those he had told about his retirement plans with bodily harm if they told anyone else. He had joined the state police department without any fanfare and now he wanted to leave the same way. Pomp and circumstance had its place, but he always detested it being directed at him. He quickly nixed any mention of a retirement party.

As he wound down the last couple days at work, Paul finished up the few loose ends which remained. This included turning in most of his gear and his assigned undercover car. "I guess I'll have to go and buy a car now. I haven't owned one in over thirty years," he told Michael Smarz, manager of Fleet Operations for the state police when he turned in his Chevy Impala. Turning in his assigned gear, he only kept two souvenirs from his career; his state police badge and his Connecticut State Police ID card. "I might need these someday,"

Paul thought as he signed off on paperwork at the Quartermaster's Office. Without anyone noticing, he slipped both items into his jacket pocket.

While Paul had one of his detectives drive him home after his last day of work, it was a difficult ride for him to experience. As he stood in his driveway watching his detective drive away, tears washed down his face. It was difficult for him to realize his dream was finally over.

* * * * * *

While the ride home on the last day of work was difficult, the really difficult part was just beginning. Paul and Donna had wrestled for months over whether she should also retire when he did. While it took a couple of more weeks for her to make the decision to do so, somewhat reluctantly she retired as well. Paul had spent the past several years laying the seeds, dropping regular hints to his family that he wanted to retire to the Pawleys Island area of South Carolina. Now it was time to make the move.

For the past twenty-two years, Paul and his family had vacationed in the greater Myrtle Beach area with family members and friends. It was during those trips that Paul's idea of retiring to a warmer winter climate had grown. The beautiful Grand Strand, with its great beaches, warm weather, plentiful restaurants, and numerous golf courses, helped to convince Donna this was the time to make the move. They looked forward to starting a new chapter in their lives together and being able to do so when they were still relatively young and healthy enough to enjoy it.

Donna Waring had been a somewhat reluctant supporter of the move to South Carolina as she also had a career she loved. She had looked forward to spending many more years at her career and to developing her skills even further in the financial field. Her financial skills had allowed her to work her way up from a part-time teller's position with the Newtown Bank and Trust to a branch manager's position at one of the bank's busiest branches. As much as she loved her position with the bank, the bank administrators loved her even more. In her they had found someone they could trust to train new managers and someone who could be counted on to resolve the most complex financial problems some of their customers had encountered during the market's downturn. When they learned she was retiring, they knew she would be difficult to replace.

Donna's somewhat reluctance to move south also was due in part to the fact she liked the stability of her life in Connecticut. She had a beautiful home, her career was flourishing, she had a wide variety of friends, and most importantly their two children, Brian and Sean, lived close by. While her two boys were now up and out on their own, and while both were doing well for themselves, they were still her babies. Brian had recently purchased a home in Southbury, had a nice career at Costco, and was active in the town's volunteer fire department. Sean was living nearby in Waterbury and was teaching physical education at a nearby local elementary school. He had recently surprised Donna when he told her of his engagement to a fellow teacher. This news made it even tougher for her to leave her boys. While she knew her boys no longer needed them to manage their daily lives, deep down Donna always wanted them to need her. She was a mother who truly loved being a mother to her two boys.

A few days after Donna retired they made the decision to put their Connecticut colonial style home in Southbury up for sale, believing it would not sell for several months in a depressed housing market. Mistakenly they thought they would have plenty of time to find a home in South Carolina. However, soon after putting their house up for sale they found a buyer and within two days of receiving the initial offer a deal was finalized. It happened all too fast for Donna's liking. Now they had the pressure of not only having to move out of their home and moving away from their boys, but they also had the added pressure of trying to find a new home to live in eight hundred miles away.

In the weeks after reaching a deal to sell their home, Paul and Donna made three trips to South Carolina to look for a new place to live. Paul had found a Century 21 real estate agent to work with, and between emails, phone calls, real estate books, virtual home tours, and visits south, they looked at many homes. After looking at over one hundred homes in one manner or another and not finding anything which interested them, they resigned themselves to the possibility of having to delay their move. Then, on the last day of their last visit, they found the one they had been looking for. They quickly signed off on a home they would soon come to love.

Their new home, within the Blue Dunes Country Club in Murrells Inlet, sat on a quiet cul-de-sac within a private community. It had a great view of both the golf course and a large nearby pond. Within minutes they could be sitting at the community pool or lounging on the beach. During the process of buying their new home, they soon learned several families living on the street where their home was located were also retirees from Connecticut. Life was going to be good.

Paul was an avid golfer, but had not played very much over the last three years because of work and family commitments. With his retirement came plans to play more often and far better. When he finally told friends back home where they were moving to they kidded him about moving to a golfing community, but the real reason for moving had not been for golf, it was about the weather. He had grown tired of the cold New England winters and the many years of having to work and drive in the snow. The weather was the real reason Paul wanted to move, he hated the cold.

Besides the warm weather and the golf he looked forward to playing, Paul also looked forward to fishing again. He also wanted to learn how to hunt for crabs in the salt water marshes that lined the shores in and around Murrells Inlet. He planned on putting a big dent in the crab population as soon as he got settled.

Paul had also developed a strong interest in the Civil War several years prior to his retirement. During that time, he read many books on the war, and had visited several Civil War battlefields. With his move south, he now hoped to visit many more battlefields in and around North and South Carolina. Accumulating many books on the war, he now looked forward to reading them as he sat at the beach enjoying his new life. He never could have foreseen what his interest in the Civil War would soon involve him in.

After finding what they had been looking for, Paul and Donna soon started the process of buying their home. Donna's banking connections led them to start working with the Murrells Inlet National Savings and Loan to secure a mortgage. After finally signing all of the necessary paperwork with the bank, they spent the remaining part of their last day at the beach enjoying the sun before flying home the next afternoon. During an early lunch, a walk on the beach, and later during dinner at one of their favorite restaurants on the Grand Strand, they talked about their upcoming move to South Carolina and the dreams they had for their new life.

While Paul had been the driving force behind the move to South Carolina, Donna had been a somewhat reluctant partner. She became even harder to convince this was the right move for them to make when she received a phone call as they drove home from Bradley International Airport, in Windsor Locks, Connecticut. The call had come from one of her brothers and he sadly told her their father had suddenly succumbed to the cancer he had been fighting for the past two years.

Over the next five weeks, a distraught Donna coped with the loss of her father, helped to plan his funeral, dealt with the closing of his estate, and retired from her job at the bank. While all of those issues were difficult to deal with, the really hard part was mentally preparing for the move away from her two boys, selling a home she had dearly loved, and moving away from her tight circle of good friends. It was almost too much for one person to bear. She spent the weeks which followed both in tears and doubting whether she should have agreed to help Paul fulfill his dream.

But by late June, just after her fifty-fifth birthday, Paul and Donna, accompanied by Sean and his fiancée, Lauren Nester, and by a large moving truck which held the sum of their thirty-five years together, slowly moved south on Interstate 95 to begin the dream Paul had imagined for them.

The discovery Paul would soon make after they arrived in South Carolina would change their lives in several ways. They just had no way to see it coming.

2

War Begins.

"I am loathe to close. We are not enemies, but friends. We must not be enemies ..."
President Abraham Lincoln in his first Inaugural Address

The original thirteen of us started out so well together. Despite the usual differences between us, differences sometimes caused by the actual geographic distance between some of us or because of differences caused by our different ways of life, we still managed to rally together to fight a common enemy. Despite our differences, we fought together and we fought well, and despite fighting a giant who many others thought we could never beat, we did. We won because we were united in our cause and because we were we became the United States of America.

Then a few scant decades later, with several new members being added to our original group, and despite developing a constitution which provided for so many of the individual freedoms we had fought hard to win, we now grew at odds with each other. Now we threatened to go to war against each other, against our very own constitution, and against our own beliefs that defined who we were. While it was not a constitution everyone thought was perfect, it was one far better than anything else we had lived under. Most importantly, it was ours. The arguments over the wording of our constitution, as well as the arguments between the states, would last for years.

Looking back it seems like we began arguing about several issues and collectively agreeing on very few of them. We argued about what our constitution did and did not allow for regarding the rights of the individual states, and we argued about the power of the federal government and what control, if any, it had over the individual states. Then we began arguing over whether states could secede or simply resign from the Union. As the rift between the North and South grew wider, many Southern states began interpreting the constitution as merely being a type of compact between the states and not an actual binding document which had created a centralized federal government. If that was not enough, then we argued vehemently about the slavery issue and whether states had the right to maintain the institution of slavery or not. Then to complicate matters even more, we argued about whether new states admitted to the Union could or could not be considered a slave state. While the arguing over the slavery issue existed for many years, it soon would become an issue that many men would die fighting over. We argued, it seemed, about everything.

With all of those issues and others being argued about, as well as the states threatening each other with force to defend their individual rights and beliefs, it was easy for many people, then and now, to question how we ever had gotten together to fight for our own independence.

When the arguing became too strong to settle with negotiations and compromises, we then banded together regionally. The Northern states, determined to keep the Union together, threatened the Southern states with sanctions. The Southern states, most decidedly at first the states in the Deep South, threatened the Northern states with talk of secession, partially because of their belief that slavery was an issue, and a way of life in the South, which the federal government had no jurisdiction over. We argued with each other some more, threatened each other some more, and talked about a war between the states, but early on it was just that, just talk. While each side had hawks who wanted war, each side also had doves who tried to avert war from occurring and who urged for cooler heads to prevail. Early on, if war was to occur, it also appeared that each side wanted the other side to fire the first shot as they knew it would help their cause if they were drawn into a war where they had not been responsible for firing the first shot. Political posturing had occurred even back then.

But the arguing continued too long and like a family reunion gone bad the arguing soon led to clear threats of violence being made against each other. Then the threats led to actual acts of violence and, sadly, acts of violence led to war between the various factions of our family. It was a family of individual and separate states who had valiantly fought alongside each other to achieve a common goal, our freedom from an overseas monarchy.

Now it was up to the individual states to either fight against or to defend our own monarchy, the federal government we had created. The arguing started well before President Abraham Lincoln was elected to office in November 1860, but now his election accelerated the talks of secession and of war. What had started as talk, talk about secession from the Union, now became a reality in February 1861 when several Southern states passed secession ordinances. Among those states leading the way was South Carolina. Soon other Southern states followed her lead. The states that had not seceded soon did after South Carolina and the Confederacy clashed with the federal government over a small island where an even smaller Union military fort was located. When Major Robert Anderson, the commanding officer of Fort Sumter, surrendered his post to the Confederacy, after far too many hours of angry cannon fire between his troops and the young and inexperienced troops of the Confederate army, the war was on. Turning back was no longer an option.

Fort Sumter sits in Charleston Harbor, guarding the entrance to Charleston, South Carolina, and sits close to where the Ashley and Cooper Rivers meet along the banks of the city. Charles Towne was initially created as a colony in 1670 and then, as a city no longer tied directly to England due to our victory in the Revolutionary War, changed its name to Charleston in 1783. Despite its rich history, its busy harbor, and its success as a thriving colonial era city, Charleston, as was the rest of the South, was active in the slave trade. It had even faced down a slave uprising in 1822 that became known as the Denmark Vesey rebellion. Perhaps prior to as well, but certainly after the rebellion was quelled, the issue of slavery in Charleston and across the rest of the Southern states became a very hotly contested issue.

Despite that issue, Charleston was a bustling Southern city with a deep port, successful businesses, and many large prosperous plantations. Several of Charleston's sons had been framers of our country as they had been signers of both the Declaration of Independence and the United States Constitution. Another son, Francis Marion, the 'Swamp Fox', was legendary for his feats against the British, tormenting them with his daring raids during our fight for independence. For war to come amongst us was difficult to comprehend, for it to start in a city with such a strong role in our fight to establish ourselves as a free and independent country was even more difficult to comprehend.

Both sides, at least in principle, and depending on your interpretation of their efforts, tried to avert war. But their actions in attempting to avert war from occurring often seemed to push the other side closer to it. At times it almost seemed like they dared each other to start the war.

The South had tried to avert war from occurring by sending delegates to a Peace Convention, in Washington, in February, 1861. But the convention accomplished little as none of the states which had seceded by then sent any delegates to attend; nor had several Northern states. When further efforts to meet with President Lincoln were ignored, with Lincoln sending only Secretary of State William Seward to meet with them instead of doing so himself, the South viewed the meeting with Seward as a snub by the North. While the two sides still tried to avert war, the first unofficial act of the war had already occurred. It occurred when Confederate guns fired upon the *Star of the West*, an unarmed merchant ship trying to resupply Fort Sumter with much needed supplies.

The North had tried to avert war as well, to some degree, when they promised South Carolina Governor Francis Pickens their efforts to resupply Fort Sumter would not include providing the fort with additional troops, ammunition, or weapons, but merely with food. When the South later learned of the North's plans to send a total of eight ships to Fort Sumter, ships containing both additional cannons and soldiers, the South viewed the act as a direct threat and they prepared themselves for war. The fact that a federal fort sat in Charleston's harbor had long been a point of irritation for the South, especially to South Carolina. That irritation helped to make Fort Sumter the logical place for war to start.

As the South viewed the Union's attempt to resupply Fort Sumter with additional soldiers as a direct threat, correspondence which occurred between Washington and the fort's commander, Major Anderson, seemed to indicate Washington was certainly expecting war to occur. A Union loyalist despite being born in Kentucky, and despite having a wife who had been born in Georgia, Anderson also knew war was soon to come. A line in a letter to Anderson seemed to reveal Washington's position on the expected conflict. *"Whenever, if at all, in your judgment, to save yourself and command, a capitulation becomes a necessity, you are authorized to make it."* While it is quite unlikely Washington wanted the fort to fall into the hands of the newly formed Confederacy, history will always question whether Washington wanted the fort to fall to aid their position in declaring war against the South.

To the credit of Governor Pickens, and to others in the South who sought to avoid war, he allowed visits to the fort to occur so officials from Washington could meet with Major Anderson. Pickens later did deny permission for a United States warship to enter Charleston harbor, a ship whose alleged mission was to evacuate the personnel assigned to the fort.

Even with the efforts of both sides to avoid war, it was easy to see war was looming on several different fronts. The South, after learning of the approaching federal naval warships headed towards Fort Sumter, did attempt one last time to negotiate the peaceful surrender of the fort through Major Anderson. Remaining loyal to the North despite his strong Southern ties, Anderson refused to surrender the fort to the South. His reply to their final offer of a peaceful surrender was a simple one. In summary, it simply said, *"I will await the first shot."* As Anderson knew war was imminent, he also knew the South would have to be punished for the aggressive act they would soon undertake.

Despite the strained relations between the two sides, negotiations to avoid war were often polite and cordial, and often done in face to face meetings. When the final attempt failed to avert war from occurring, during the negotiations between the South and Major Anderson, he was advised by Southern negotiators when the first shot would likely be fired at the fort. It was perhaps due his friendship with Confederate President Jefferson Davis, and with Brigadier General Pierre G.T. Beauregard, which caused Anderson to walk the Southern negotiators to their boat as they prepared to leave Fort Sumter. Before they departed, Anderson spoke to them. *"If we never meet in this world again, God grant that we may meet in the next."* It is still hard to imagine such civility, demonstrated at times from both sides as they met during last ditch efforts to avoid a war, could not have prevented it from occurring. It was a war which could have been avoided by men who should have worked harder. It would soon prove to be a war that lasted far longer than anyone could have predicted. In the years that followed, the war would have terrible results. While it would soon devastate both sections of the country in many different ways, its impact would hurt the South the most.

Charleston's motto *'She guards her buildings, her customs, and her laws'* would prove to be true in very short time after the Southern negotiators left Fort Sumter. Soon the Confederate Army, at around 4:30 a.m., on April 12, 1861, fired what is thought to be the first official shot of the war, a shot fired upon the garrison of Union soldiers stationed at Fort Sumter. Over the next many hours, approximately five thousand rounds of cannon fire would be traded between the two sides. When the firing slowed down, and as many of Charleston's citizens still stood on the roofs of homes close to Charleston Harbor watching the exchange of cannon fire between the fort and the Confederate artillery batteries which lined the harbor, the flagpole at Fort Sumter saw a flag soon replaced by a newly created one. The flag of the Confederacy would fly there for some time before the flag of the United States was again raised there. On April 14th, with supplies running low, Major Anderson surrendered Fort Sumter to the Confederacy. Nearby, two other smaller Union pieces of property, Fort Moultrie and Castle Pinckney, sat off in the harbor, having already been seized by the Confederacy. Having lost Fort Sumter to the Confederacy, the Union would soon lose another important asset as well. Six days later Colonel Robert E. Lee would resign his commission in the United States army; a resignation that would cause him to be remembered by the ages.

Almost five weeks prior to the first hostile shot being fired, the Confederacy had called for one hundred thousand volunteers to help wage war against the North. Now Lincoln would do the same. The day following the fort's surrender, he would call for seventy-five thousand volunteers to help put down the Confederacy. Neither of those first two calls for volunteers would be the last each side would make.

After Brigadier General Beauregard's troops had fired on the fort, the Confederacy, at first comprised of South Carolina, Mississippi, Georgia, Alabama, Louisiana, Texas, and Florida, soon would be joined by several other Southern states. In short order, the states of Arkansas, North Carolina, Tennessee, and Virginia would join the Confederacy. As the Confederacy grew, they would continue to seize other federal property in the South. Among those properties was the United States Mint in New Orleans. Within the mint was a large amount of Union gold and silver. That gold and silver would also be seized by the Confederacy to help finance their war efforts.

The gold and silver would soon be moved from New Orleans across the Confederate States of America. It would take another one hundred and fifty years for most of it to be found.

3

A New Friend.

*"In my mind I'm gone to Carolina, can't you see the sunshine,
can't you just feel the moonshine ..."*
James Taylor - Lyrics to 'Carolina In My Mind'

The move to Murrells Inlet had gone as smoothly for Paul and Donna as any move could go when you pull up stakes and move over eight hundred miles away from your family and friends and the world you knew. All in all it had gone fairly well. Despite the usual problems associated with such a move, such as trying to find the essentials they needed to live with, much of which were still packed away within the moving boxes stacked in their garage, they were settling nicely into their new home. They had found no matter how well the boxes had been marked before they were packed away in the moving truck, trying to find the items they needed after they reached South Carolina had been difficult. Despite those small bumps they managed to survive the move. Now they only had to try and remember the names of their new neighbors who popped in to welcome them to the neighborhood.

In the first few days in their new home, even as hard as she tried to put on a good face for Paul, Donna's heart was still back home with her boys. She also continued to mourn the recent loss of her father. Still, she tried hard to adapt to their new life.

Neither of them had planned on returning to work after moving to South Carolina, at least not right away, but that plan was soon changed. Stopping at the bank to open their new checking and savings accounts, the bank's branch manager, Kristi Thomas, who had helped them secure their mortgage, introduced Donna to her regional manager. As the three of them talked, Donna told them about her career as a banker back in Connecticut.

Karen Tracy was the regional manager for sixteen branch offices of the Murrells Inlet National Savings and Loan in the greater Myrtle Beach area. She immediately took a liking to Donna as they chatted in Kristi's office for several minutes. Surprisingly, Karen was a native South Carolinian who had received her degree from Central Connecticut State University. Due to her outstanding academic performance in high school, she had accepted the school's offer of a full scholarship as it also had given her a chance to see a different section of the country while obtaining her degree. Majoring in finance, just as Donna had done during her college years back in Connecticut, she had completed her studies in less than four years. During their conversation, Karen talked about still managing to maintain ties with several of her friends from college despite her many family and career obligations in South Carolina.

As they spoke, Karen encouraged Donna to submit an application to the bank as they were constantly looking for experienced people to staff their branches. Donna had not been interested in starting to work again, but when she was told the bank was having difficulty in filling a branch manager's position in nearby Garden City, a branch consistently ranked as being their most non-productive office, her interest in returning to work quickly returned. As she listened to Karen talk about the position, Donna initially thought about taking her up on the opportunity for a formal interview, but then elected to decline the opportunity at first. However, later that same afternoon, after thinking over the offer which had been given to her, Donna called Karen on the phone telling her she had succumbed to the opportunity of a new challenge. By late afternoon she had her resume emailed to Karen's attention at the bank.

Earlier when they had talked, Karen told Donna to make sure she wanted the position as the previous three managers at the Garden City branch all failed to meet the bank's expectations. Karen had told her this as she did not want Donna to have a negative experience so soon after moving to South Carolina. However, when told part of the problems at the branch seemed to also include internal problems caused by some of the staff members, she felt even more challenged to seek this new position.

Donna's previous employer had determined one of her strengths was she could quickly identify root causes of operational problems within their branches. They soon assigned her to evaluate several of their branches in hopes of making them run more efficiently. Donna never had a problem identifying who the problem employees were, and when she did they were often quickly terminated. Her efforts made all of those branches perform higher than they ever had. Now she had an opportunity to face another similar challenge. When it came to running a tight ship at work, Donna ran a tight ship. Everyone who worked for her quickly learned the inmates no longer ran the show when she was in charge. The employees at the Garden City branch would soon learn the same thing.

On the other hand, Paul had no interest in returning to work full-time as the thirty years he had spent as a state trooper had been enough of the work world for him. He was ready for a much quieter lifestyle and that meant little, if any, work in the foreseeable future. However, just like Donna had, he also soon found a job. It was actually a job which found him and it was the result of a good deed he had done for a stranger.

Paul was out running errands and was returning home from Pawleys Island one afternoon during a heavy rainstorm when he saw a car partially blocking traffic northbound on busy Highway 17. Running along the Carolina coast, Highway 17 has two heavily travelled lanes of traffic running in each direction. It serves as one of the main arteries between Myrtle Beach and Georgetown. The elderly male operator of the disabled car was partially blocking traffic where the highway forks in Murrells Inlet. The operator had turned his four way emergency flashers on and was attempting to change a flat tire on the left rear of his Mercedes Benz when Paul first saw him struggling to get the spare tire out of the trunk of his car. Because of the heavy rain, as well as the traffic moving both too fast and too close to the disabled car, he could tell the elderly operator was not having too much success at fixing the flat tire.

"If I don't stop to help this guy somebody is either going to run him or his car over and then nobody is going to be getting home." Paul thought as he got out of his vehicle. As he did, he noticed none of the other passing motorists had stopped to help. "Just like back home, everyone is in their own little world, too busy to lend a hand to someone in need." Soon he had the tire fixed and the flat tire put away in the trunk of the Mercedes.

As he closed the trunk, the elderly male operator attempted to hand Paul a twenty dollar bill as a sign of his appreciation for the service rendered to him. "This won't do much for the wet clothes you have on, but please accept this as a token of my appreciation. You were the only one to stop in the fifteen minutes I struggled with the flat." Steve Alcott then extended his right hand as another sign of his appreciation.

"That's not necessary, I was glad to be of help. I'm sure you would have done the same for somebody else," Paul said as they shook hands.

With no success, Steve tried one more time to hand Paul the twenty again. "Tell you what, if my money is no good, how about letting me buy you a drink to settle the debt I owe you. It's the least I could do to show my thanks."

More interested in getting home so he could change out of his wet clothes, Paul knew Donna was being interviewed that afternoon for the position with the bank. She would not be home for another two hours. "OK, sounds like a plan. Where are we going?"

"Great! Just follow me down the road and we will stop at my favorite watering hole."

Within a few minutes, Paul found himself seated at the bar within *The Grumpy Sailor*, a restaurant located along the marshwalk in Murrells Inlet. Both the bar and the adjoining dining area were decorated with beach and golf related themes. Sitting there, he still had his wet clothes on, but was somewhat drier than he had been after first changing Steve's flat tire. Paul had driven by the restaurant one afternoon with Donna when they had been out exploring their newly adopted hometown, but they had not yet stopped in for a drink.

Paul was somewhat surprised when the barmaid quickly placed a Dirty Martini, complete with two olives, directly in front of where Steve sat at the bar. She had done so before they could even order their drinks. When she addressed Steve by his first name, Paul guessed she had done so as he was likely a regular at the bar.

"Hey, what's your wet friend drinking?" Looking at both of them sitting there in their wet clothing caused her to ask Steve the next question. "You boys been riding the surf out back or what?"

Steve explained to Kathy Comer, the lone bartender on duty, the events of the afternoon. He told her how Paul had been the only person to stop and help him with his flat tire. He also told her his reward, besides a frosted mug of cold Coors Light, were the wet clothes he was still wearing. They both had gotten soaked from the typical late summer afternoon thunderstorm which had run along the coast as they struggled with the flat tire.

Kathy was a long time employee of Steve's. He had liked her from the first day she started working for him and had liked her enough to help her financially make ends meet on a couple of occasions. Working at the bar off and on for the past twelve years, she often struggled to make ends meet for her and her three children after two tough divorces. In her late forties, she was still a very attractive looking woman. Paul watched her as she playfully flirted with several of the other customers sitting at the bar. She seemed to know each of their first names as she set drinks down in front of them. Kathy soon set Paul's frosted mug of beer down on the bar in front of him.

"Thanks for helping him out with his flat tire. Even though he's the owner of this dump, he's a great guy. I appreciate what you did for him. If he had to do it by himself he probably would have died of a heart attack as the most work he ever does is counting his millions." Steve could not help but laugh at her comments as he knew she was one of his few employees who really did care about his health. She had been the only employee of his who had occasionally looked in on him when he had recovered from two heart attacks a couple of years back. As she walked away from where they now sat on two bar stools, Steve tossed a sarcastic comment back at her. It caused her to laugh as she started mixing a drink for another one of her customers.

Taking a long hit on his cold beer, Paul saw he had not gotten all of the grime off of his hands from when he changed the flat on Steve's car. Using some of the drink napkins on the bar, he managed to quickly get most of it cleaned off his hands. As he finished cleaning his hands, Paul asked Steve if he really was the owner of *The Grumpy Sailor*.

"Yes, I am. I'm lucky enough to own a few other places as well." Pressing him some more, he soon learned Steve's family had been among the early settlers of Murrells Inlet. Steve described how his family had set up a trust fund for him many years ago and further described how the fund had allowed him to invest in several real estate ventures in both Murrells Inlet and in nearby Pawleys Island. Besides the bar they were now spending part of the afternoon in, Steve spoke of the other properties he owned, including a nearby strip mall, a family friendly water park which the tourists flocked to each summer, and a small strip of land along the ocean in Litchfield, the next town south of Murrells Inlet. "I've had several offers for that piece of property, but I'm not interested in selling it. I do pretty well with what I own, considering the current economy and all, but of everything I own that dang water park makes me a ton of money every year. Those tourists are some of my favorite people." Steve was not bragging as he spoke to Paul, he was just still amazed after all of these years how well his small theme park managed to provide for him.

At first, Paul thought he had heard all of what Steve owned, but then he learned he was partners with three of his friends in a good size marina down on the southern tip of the Inlet. He also learned Steve and his partners were the owners of *The Links at Pawleys Island*, one of the premier golf clubs along the Grand Strand. "We got the marina up and running about twenty-four years ago. After a few years of giving it a go, we finally started making some money. At that point, we decided we needed a new challenge so we formed a partnership called *Bogey Free*. We soon built a golf course which has become one of the most challenging courses around. Without a doubt, it certainly is one of the most scenic courses along the Grand Strand. That's doing pretty well for us also, despite the many other places folks have to play golf down here. But we treat our golfers well, that's why they keep coming back."

Steve had not planned on telling Paul about all of his real estate holdings, but when Kathy stopped to check on their drinks she took it upon herself to fill in a few of the missing pieces. It was only because of her comments that he reluctantly spoke about the golf course and marina he owned. As he did, he shot her a disapproving glance. Seeing the look he gave her, she realized she had crossed over into an area she probably should not have spoken about. Almost immediately, she disappeared out of sight for several minutes, hiding in the bar's nearby kitchen.

Paul was now somewhat taken back by who he was sitting with. He was just not having a drink with just some retiree from New Jersey, but rather it was with an obviously wealthy descendant of one of the first settlers of the area. He had severely underestimated who Steve really was.

"I'm impressed," Paul said after polishing off the rest of his cold beer. He then told Steve about briefly visiting the marina on one of his early house hunting trips, seeing the size of the marina and the volume of business it did on the weekend day he was there. He further described how amazed he had been at the number of boaters who were buying gas, beer, snacks, and other supplies at the marina's store. "I knew someone had to be making some money down there. That's a busy little place you have during the boating season. You must be doing well!" He also told Steve he had been amazed during his visit at the many different sizes of boats he had seen docked at the marina. The watercraft had ranged from jet skis, small personal fishing and pleasure boats, to the larger and more impressive yachts which travelled up and down the east coast during warm weather.

"You're involved with two of the things in life I have an interest in. I've always dreamed of owning a pontoon boat, but I'm afraid that's going to remain a dream for a few more years. I also love playing golf. I hope to start playing more than I've had the chance to do over the past few summers back home. What a life you must be leading, I'm envious!"

They spent the new few minutes talking more about the marina's operation and about the highly respected golf course that Steve was the majority owner of. As they talked, Paul spoke about his recent move to Murrells Inlet and about his career as a state trooper.

As they sat talking, and after noticing Kathy had finally felt it safe to come out of the kitchen, Steve motioned for her to come over to where they sat at the bar. As she did, Steve interrupted his conversation with Paul by asking her to bring him his briefcase. "I left it on the floor in my office next to the filing cabinet. Don't bother trying to open it; I locked it when I left last night. I know you thieves like to steal my stuff when I'm not paying attention." Kathy shot him a smirk as she turned to fetch his briefcase. The smirk caused Steve to quickly chuckle at his own joke as she walked away. As Paul and Steve resumed talking, their talk soon turning to other topics of conversation. They were topics any two strangers sitting at a bar might have with each other as they enjoyed an afternoon cocktail with each other.

After being handed his briefcase, and after putting pen to paper, Steve handed Paul two pieces of paper. "Besides today's drinks, as another sign of my appreciation for your help this afternoon, here is a gift certificate for you and your wife to have dinner on me here at the restaurant. I'm sure she will enjoy it as the food is quite good. We have a couple of the area's best chefs working for us. Treat her to a nice night out, it's all on me. This other piece of paper has Willie Tegeler's name and cell phone number on it. Willie is the golf pro at *The Links*. I'll call him in the morning to let him know you have a summer's worth of free golf coming. That's my welcoming present to you for moving to Murrells Inlet. And, if you want, tell Willie you are looking for a part-time job at the course, you know a few hours a week, and I'll make sure he finds something for you to do. Keep the job and you will have free golf as one of the perks. It won't pay much, but the free golf is worth it, at least that's what I've been told. Your new neighbors will love being able to play the course with you at a discounted rate. You will soon be the hero of your neighborhood!"

Struggling to find the right words to express his appreciation, Paul momentarily sat quiet as he was not sure what to say or how to say it. He had only known one other person in life who had been as generous to him, but that had come from a long time friend, not from a total stranger. He tried to protest that this was far too much for just changing a tire for someone in need, but Steve would hear none of it. "I'm an old man with tons of money. You helped me out when no one else did, and I've always respected people who have gone out of their way to help others. From what you have told me about your past career, I doubt too many people went out of their way to show you their appreciation, even if you were just doing your job. So let's just call these tokens of my appreciation and paybacks for all that you have done for others over all of those years. How's that sound?"

Again, weakly perhaps because he was still taken back by Steve's generosity, Paul attempted to decline the gifts he had been given, but Steve quickly cut him off, waving his hand at the notion of his new friend not accepting his thanks. "When I give something to someone, I expect them to accept it. Give it back and we aren't friends any longer." While he knew Steve was joking, at least he hoped he was, he placed the papers on the bar and simply thanked him the best he could.

"Paul, one more thing, let me have your cell phone number. I want my foreman, Chubby, that's what we all call him, to call you in the morning. He might be able to help you with your dream of owning a pontoon boat. It's nothing special mind you, but I have one I want to sell. He'll explain it to you when he calls you. Now, seeing as we finally have business out of the way, how about another beer?"

Wanting to leave so he could get home and tell Donna about the events of the afternoon, Paul realized he could not say no to Steve after what he had just been given. Quickly, he agreed to have another beer. "How about I pay for the drinks? How's that sound?"

Steve couldn't help but laugh, as did Kathy who was standing nearby pouring Paul's second beer. "Pretty ridiculous, don't you think? I own the place so why should you have to buy a drink for the owner? I appreciate the thought, but the drinks are on me. I think I can afford it."

It had been a pretty foolish statement to make and Paul quickly admitted it had not made much sense as soon as he said it, but it had been too late to take back. "Well, perhaps another time then and perhaps at another place."

"Sounds like a plan. Let's make sure it happens."

Raising his second mug of Coors Light, Paul thanked Steve for the beer and for his other generous gifts. After a few more minutes of continued small talk between them, they finished off their drinks. Standing up from his bar stool, Paul put a ten dollar bill down on the bar for Kathy's tip and again thanked Steve for his generosity, assuring him they would get together again soon. Walking outside, Paul was quickly greeted by the high humidity brought on by the afternoon thunderstorm. Making the short walk to his car, he managed to avoid the large puddles of water still remaining in the parking lot. Driving home he could not help but smile at the good fortune he had encountered that afternoon. "Thank goodness for thunderstorms and flat tires!"

What he could not possibly realize was what the events of the afternoon would soon lead him to. The phone call from Chubby would soon start to make it all come together.

* * * * * *

Donna had just gotten home from her job interview and was getting some groceries out of her car when Paul pulled into the driveway. "How on earth did your clothes get so wet?" She asked as he got out of his car. Closing his car door, Paul was still smiling over his good fortune. "OK, what's so funny? I see the smirk you're wearing."

"Not a hello or a 'Hi Honey'? Just a comment about my wet clothes, is that all you have to say?" Paul knew Donna's question had been the obvious one for her to ask as his clothes were still wet despite sitting at the bar with Steve for a couple of hours, but he also had to tease her as well. "My clothes got wet when I was being interviewed for my new job."

His statement made absolutely no sense to her as she had no idea what he had gotten himself into during her absence that afternoon.

Soon Paul told her about the events of the afternoon as he stripped out of his wet clothes inside their now closed garage. As Donna listened to what her husband was telling her about his afternoon, she made sure he was taking off all of his wet clothes. She was not about to let her new carpet get stained by his dirty wet clothes. As he got deeper into the events of the afternoon, Donna realized something special had happened. She then felt foolish about making an issue over his wet clothes.

"Hey, it's no big deal. I was going to take them off anyhow."

She stood silently as Paul finished telling her about meeting Steve, and about his generosity in thanking him for being a Good Samaritan. Standing there with her mouth open, she did not know what to say about his new good fortune.

"Honey, you can close your mouth now," an almost naked Paul told her. "Oh, yeah, and by the way, tomorrow some guy named Chubby is going to call me about a pontoon boat Steve wants to get rid of."

"He wants to give you a boat as well? Just for fixing a flat tire?" Donna asked incredulously.

"Sounds something like that. I don't think he's going to give it to me, but maybe there is a deal or something we can work out. I guess I'll just have to wait and see." Deep down Paul hoped his good luck would continue.

After hearing about the boat, and while pleased to hear what he had been up to, Donna's shoulders slumped as he finished talking. "I thought I had a good afternoon as I got a new job which pays good money, but you won, you had a great afternoon." Paul could not help but smile at her as he knew she was amazed at what had happened for both of them that afternoon.

Later over dinner, and after the excitement of his day had been talked about, Donna told Paul about the interview she had gone through, and of the subsequent job offer she received. It was not nearly as exciting as the news he had brought home, but for her she knew having a new job would be a great way to help her get settled in her new life in Murrells Inlet. While her new job would keep her busy; more importantly, it would also keep her from missing her boys more than she already was.

* * * * * *

Late the following morning, Paul received the phone call he was expecting from Chubby. After speaking for several minutes, they agreed to meet around 2 pm at the marina. "Sounds great, I look forward to seeing you." After hanging up the phone, Paul realized he had a new problem to deal with since moving south. He realized it as soon as he listened to Chubby talk on the phone. While he had understood most of what had been said, Paul realized he would be meeting many people, folks like Chubby, who spoke with that distinctive Southern drawl he found so hard to understand at times. "I'm going to have to train these Northern ears to a whole new way of listening." It was a challenge he had waited for years to do.

Chubby was waiting outside by the marina's main office when Paul pulled into the parking lot. Like many others in the area, the parking area was a combination of dirt, beach sand, and broken oyster shells that car and truck tires had ground up into small pieces over the years. Pulling into the lot, Paul heard the shells crunching even more under his tires.

Even before they introduced themselves to each other, Chubby started ragging on Paul. "The old man told me about the help you gave him yesterday when he got the flat tire. Got to admit that was a right neighborly thing for y'all to do, especially for you. You know, being a Yankee and all."

Paul just smiled as he shook Chubby's hand.

"Hey, partner, I'm just having some fun with y'all. But that was a right fine thing you did for Steve. He's a good man. I'll tell ya, he will never forget what you did for him. He's like that, just remembers everything."

As they started walking down the wooden walkway to the marina's main set of docks, Paul now saw he had pictured Chubby pretty well. It was easy to see how he had been christened with his nickname as Chubby, a friendly man of about thirty-five years of age, was someone who likely carried close to three hundred pounds on his six foot plus frame. He was a bear of a man in size. His denim blue bib overalls, with one strap unbuttoned, were covered with both work and food stains in several spots. They likely had been worn for several days since they were last washed Paul thought as he followed his new friend down the walkway. With a nickname of Chubby, and with the clothes he was wearing, he was just as Paul had pictured him. He was someone he took an immediate liking to.

Chubby led Paul to a section of the marina where several small white-colored wooden rowboats bobbed in the Inlet's gentle tide. Located just off the main dock, they were tied up along one of the wooden walkways. From the looks of the rowboats, they were obviously ones used by boat owners when they needed to ferry supplies out to their larger boats, ones moored off the marina's largest dock. Nearby, behind one of the outbuildings the marina owned, various supplies were piled up. They were supplies needed to keep a busy marina in operation.

Stopping for a moment as they reached the end of the first wooden walkway, Paul saw the walkway was one of many that had been firmly secured with long cables to several large concrete blocks which sat at the edge of the parking lot. He knew this had been done so they did not float away during the severe storms which occasionally hit the South Carolina coast. He then followed Chubby as they walked down another walkway which was connected to a series of several smaller wooden docks. Each of these docks and walkways had been bolted to one another in a way so they could each rise and fall with the passing tide. The docks and walkways floated on large pieces of Styrofoam and on large blue plastic barrels. The gentle low tide that was present made it easy for them to walk on the docks without having to use the handrails.

Looking back over his left shoulder, Paul could see they had walked almost two hundred feet out from shore. From where he was on the dock, he saw the adjoining set of docks held the marina's gas pumps. Over the top of the pumps was a faded red and blue wooden sign which read 'Alcott's Marina, Murrells Inlet, South Carolina'. The lettering had been neatly stenciled some time in the past as the large white lettering was now starting to fade. Despite its age, Paul smiled when he saw his new friend's last name displayed on the sign.

"Well, there she is. Not much to look at, but she still has some life in her. What do ya think?"

Paul turned to see Chubby pointing at the old pontoon boat sitting moored at the end of the walkway. On both sides of the boat hung smaller wooden versions of the sign he saw displayed over the gas pumps. The pontoon boat was one the marina's employees used for the operational needs of the marina. From that use it was easy to tell the boat had not been cared for as well as it would have been if it had been privately owned.

As Paul stepped onto the last section of dock before climbing onto the boat, Chubby, whose real name was Earl Jensen, chose to remain on the dock. It was obvious Chubby's years of feasting on far too many of the Inlet's delicacies, both seafood and cold beer, prevented him from doing anything too strenuous. Even the short walk down the several sections of walkways had winded him significantly.

Chubby explained to Paul the variety of use the boat has seen since the marina purchased it seven years earlier, describing how it was primarily used to ferry boat owners to and from their boats when the marina's row boats were not practical to use. Looking around and not seeing anyone nearby, Chubby told him of another way the boat had been used. "I have to tell you I have also used it on more than a few occasions to satisfy the personal needs of many female tourists after they have visited our restaurant or one of the other nearby bars. The boat, like its secluded location, has come in quite handy after they've had too much to drink. You know what I'm talkin' about, right?"

Not wanting to hear anymore about Chubby's alleged romantic escapades, and also wanting to quickly erase the ugly mental picture he now had in his head of a naked Chubby frolicking on the boat with an inebriated female, Paul put a quick end to this part of the conversation. "I've got the picture, I've got it!" The brief mental picture of one of Chubby's naked escapades lingered far too long in his mind. Quickly he quickly sought to erase it.

Examining the boat, Paul could see it was a twenty-two foot Sylvan Signature series pontoon boat. The boat's original burgundy color was now faded for the most part from its constant exposure to the sun and salt air. While Paul's first impression was that it needed some work, he could see the boat still had some life left in her. Even to his eye, it was obvious it needed some cosmetic work done to it, along with a few minor repairs, and then a real good cleaning before it would be something to have some pride in. The boat also had a minor dent in the outside edge of the left transom, but it was not large enough to repair at this time. As he studied the boat further, it was easy to see the boat's original carpeting had been replaced with a more durable dark green Astroturf style of carpet which was now both faded and in need of replacing. Paul could not help thinking the boat's carpeting reminded him of the putting surfaces at several of the Mini-Golf venues his family had waged friendly competitions at during their summer vacations in Myrtle Beach. He also could not help wondering if this was the same carpeting Chubby and his 'dates' had used during their romantic one-night stands. Even with its constant exposure to the elements, he hoped it was not the same carpeting Chubby had frolicked on. "One thing for sure, the carpeting has to go," Paul thought to himself.

Inspecting the boat further, Paul noticed the captain's seat had a small tear in the upholstery, a tear which had been poorly repaired with grey duct tape. After inspecting most of the boat, he asked Chubby about the condition of the black sixty horsepower Mercury engine.

"We just serviced it about two weeks ago. It's only two-years old and I think it's still under warranty for another six months or so. We've never had a problem with it. The engine runs fine."

Paul knew he was being shown the boat on orders from Steve, and while he knew it was likely being offered to him to buy, he played along by looking at it some more until Chubby broached the topic about buying it. "Why do y'all want a pontoon boat anyhow? Don't y'all want something better than this old slow tub? It's already ten years old."

"Well, I guess it's because I've always wanted a pontoon boat or a party boat or whatever they're called. I don't have a need for a fast boat as I'm not in a hurry anymore in life. I just want something to fish off, to set a grill up on, and to enjoy some good times on with my wife and friends. I told Steve I've always wanted a pontoon boat, so I guess if you are taking the time to show it to me, I guess it's up for sale. This boat does have some repairs which need making, so it all depends on the price he is asking."

"Sounds like you've been thinking on this for some time now." Chubby said as he stood next to Paul. "Listen here, Steve wants me to do two things and he always wants me to do them his way. At least that's what he told me on the phone last night. He wants me to get moving on buying a new pontoon boat for the marina, and he wants me to sell this old tub to you. That's if you're interested and all in it." Chubby further explained that Steve's style was to always treat the customers at the marina fairly. As he spoke, he described how Steve had recently begun to feel the aging pontoon boat was a poor reflection upon the marina; instructing him to start looking for a newer one.

"So this here boat is yours if ya want it. Well, not exactly like that, free and all I mean. Steve told me you can have the boat and the trailer for one thousand dollars. The trailer is over yonder there in the parking lot. That's not too bad a deal, I guess. He also told me to tell ya everything works on the boat, including the navigational lights. The deal also includes a small anchor and that large Igloo ice chest sitting right there. Part of the deal he is giving ya includes mooring it here for the rest of the summer if ya want. He ain't gonna charge ya for that."

Paul bent over and opened the large white colored Igloo ice chest to see what kind of shape it was in. "A cooler this size could come in handy for storing cold beer and sandwiches in on future river trips," he thought to himself. As he opened the lid, besides noticing the cooler's white interior was no longer remotely close to being white, a strong foul smelling fishy odor emanated from the inside. The cooler was partially full of warm rancid water. The odor, coupled with the heat of the day, was strong enough that it made Paul gag. It almost caused him to lose the lunch he had eaten about two hours earlier.

"Guess it needs cleaning, huh?"

"Chubby, that's a slight understatement as it needs more than a cleaning. Burning it would be a good idea. You're not getting the smell out of that thing."

Inspecting the boat a little bit more, Paul saw it had been properly registered in South Carolina and had also been inspected earlier in the year by the South Carolina Department of Natural Resources. A DNR 2013 sticker was properly displayed near the bow section of the boat.

Paul then walked over to where the boat trailer sat in the marina's parking lot. As he inspected the Load Rite trailer, which was painted a deep red, he noticed Chubby had climbed onto the boat and had unfurled the boat's blue canvass top. He was not sure if Chubby had done so to stay out of the afternoon sun or if he had done that so the canvass top could be inspected while he was there looking at the boat. Either way, he took his time giving the trailer a once over to make sure it was in decent shape. Inspecting the trailer, he noticed one of the rear tandem tires on the right side had gone flat, likely from having sat unused in the parking lot for so long. Overall, the trailer proved to be in good condition. Paul was pleased it had been included in the offer with the boat.

After taking the time to inspect the boat's canvass top, Chubby motioned for them to walk over to the steps outside the side door of the marina's office. The steps also led to the marina's showroom area. The steps were out of the sun and by now Paul welcomed the opportunity to sit in the shade. Sitting there, they talked for several minutes about the condition of both the boat and the trailer. While they talked, Paul outlined the repairs he would have to make if he purchased the boat. Besides the torn seat, the non-functioning engine tachometer, the one thing they found that did not work, would also need repairing. Using the list of repairs he mentioned, he made a counter offer on the boat.

"Chubby, it's got a few dents and so on, but it's worth buying and fixing up. Tell Steve I'm grateful for the offer. I think his price is a fair one, but tell him if he comes down to eight hundred and fifty dollars he's got a deal."

"Sounds like a fair price. That cooler was in nasty shape, wasn't it? I'll call him and see what he says. I'll be right back."

Having left his cell phone in the office, Chubby got up and walked up the steps to call Steve. In a few minutes he was back, telling Paul that Steve was good with his offer. "He even agreed to throw in a new cooler as part of the deal. I've got to go to Costco this afternoon so I'll fetch one of those big Igloo coolers they've got there. It will be here for you in the morning if you want to come fetch it. If not, it will be here when you come to get the boat. I'll have the flat tire looked at as well. It won't be a problem to get it fixed right."

Paul thanked Chubby for his efforts and told him he would be back in two days with the cash to pay for the boat and trailer. By then, Chubby promised, the boat would be cleaned up some by the time it was ready to be picked up. "Please tell Steve I appreciate his generosity. I'm fortunate to have met such a nice guy. I'm looking forward to having some good times on the boat." After being assured his message would be passed on later in the day, the two of them exchanged the necessary information needed to complete a *Bill of Sale* for the boat. After doing so, Paul spoke one last time. "Before I head out, I'm just going to look at the boat again for a few minutes if you don't mind."

"Be my guest. I'll see y'all on Thursday morning."

After briefly inspecting the boat again, Paul drove home to tell Donna about his purchase. As he did, he could not help but to again think of what a generous person Steve was. "I wonder what he has done for other people he has met? I hope I can somehow repay him for his generosity."

What Paul would soon realize was by buying the boat he would soon help someone else. Someone who had not seen home in almost one hundred and fifty years.

4

Gold On The Move.

"The war is commenced, and we will triumph or perish."
Governor Francis Pickens – South Carolina –
After the Confederacy had captured Fort Sumter.

The war had started with cannons being fired in anger at each other; the South's cannons firing defiantly at the North and the North's cannons angrily responding back at the South's attempt to leave the Union. Behind the loud roar of the cannons it was now countrymen fighting against each other and, in some cases, brothers fighting against brothers. The two sides were made up of their many different states, their militias and armies, and for the South, their ragtag armies that were preparing to fight against a seemingly far better trained and equipped Union army. In many cases, especially in the Confederate army, soldiers who had served in the Union army prior to the war now fought against their family and friends who had remained loyal to the Union. Many Union soldiers now found themselves fighting against family members and friends who pledged their allegiance to the newly formed Confederacy. A war between our country's own individual states was something no one ever expected to occur, but now it had. It would rage for four long years. The war would cost the nation over 600,000 of our countrymen before it was over.

The anger behind the cannon fire, anger fueled by both sides being committed to their respective causes, caused the war to last far longer than anyone could have imagined. After the war had started, many people on both sides predicted it would be over by the end of the first summer. The Confederacy, committed to defending the rights of each state, and their institution of slavery; and the Union, committed to keeping the country intact as it had been prior to the start of the war, and to ending the practice of slavery, as well as being committed to punishing the South for trying to leave the Union, kept the war raging. Each side was convinced their beliefs were the right ones. As the war reached the end of its first summer, no one could predict when the killing of our nation's young men would end.

Here the legend began. Two years after the war started at Fort Sumter, the war visited many other places, places where peace, family, farming, religion, and even local politics should have been the issues, not visits by soldiers fighting a war killing each other. The war between the two large armies stopped in places called Chancellorsville, Spotsylvania Court House, Vicksburg, and in many other places, places where the tragedy of war robbed families of their husbands, fathers, brothers, and sons. In places where battles were being fought, the war robbed everyone of their right to the pursuit of happiness.

In many of the war's early battles, the Confederate army, seemingly more organized and more determined than the larger and better equipped Union army, won more of the battles than they lost. Then both sides came to Gettysburg. Here the two sides fought a three-day battle which many people soon believed caused a turn in the South's fortunes to occur. It was a turn which saw the Union army finally start to fight with much more conviction. That conviction came to the Union army, in part, because Lincoln and his generals finally realized in order to win the war they had to defeat the Confederate army itself; trying to conquer their land, like some of the early Union generals had tried to do, would not lead to the end of the war. Devastating the Confederate armies with huge losses of men, as well as interrupting their supply and communication lines were among the keys to securing a victory. Soon President Lincoln and his new commanding general, General Ulysses S. Grant, along with some of Grant's most trusted generals, would employ that tactic in their future campaigns against the Confederacy.

The Confederate army fought well at Gettysburg, but decisions which had been made to attack the Union army at times during this battle, especially when the Union army held the high ground, proved to be poor ones. Attacking an army who was continually being resupplied with more men and with more equipment as the battle went on was also among the poor decisions which were made. Those decisions, influenced in part by other factors, such as poor communication at times between General Lee and his generals, as well as the South's cavalry unit being elsewhere during a significant part of the three-day battle, doomed the Confederate army at Gettysburg. These failures would rob them of one of their most precious resources, one they could never replenish as easily as the Union army could. That resource was their men. Unlike the South, the North had a much larger portion of the nation's population to draw from and finding replacement troops was far easier for the North during the war. The poor tactical decisions which were made, coupled with the sheer strength and size of the Union army, as well as the terrain which the Confederate army had to fight on, all proved too much for the Confederacy to overcome at Gettysburg.

The Confederate army lost far too many men during this battle as over twenty-three thousand soldiers were either killed, wounded, captured, or missing by the time it was over. While the Union army lost a similar number of men, just like the other needs of war, such as food, weapons, and horses, the Union absorbed those losses far better than the Confederate army could. Perhaps those losses might have been less, and perhaps the poor decisions might have not been made if General Robert E. Lee, the commanding general of the Confederate army, had not lost his 'right arm'. General Thomas 'Stonewall' Jackson had been killed earlier in the year, having been accidentally mortally wounded by his own men. But many factors turned the tide in this significant battle and Jackson could not have controlled all of those factors which in the end worked against the Confederacy at Gettysburg during that hot July in 1863. While Lee would accept the responsibility for all that went wrong, it was not the fault of one man they had been turned back. It was far more than that.

Despite their courage, and despite their desire to stay and fight another day, the decision was made to begin an orderly withdrawal south, back across the Potomac River, and back into the relative safety of the Shenandoah Valley. As the Confederate army withdrawal took place, the long gray line of the Confederacy stretched for miles and took weeks to complete before they reached safety. As they withdrew, and despite the best effort of the Confederate army to protect their rear guard, both armies clashed in several small skirmishes and battles.

As Lee's wounded army moved south through Maryland after crossing the Potomac River, the Union army continued to inflict losses on the Confederacy. Among those losses was the death of Brigadier General J. Johnson Pettigrew. Despite surviving Pickett's Charge at Gettysburg, Pettigrew was killed during the Battle of Falling Waters. His death was another the Confederate army could not afford.

At the Battle of Manassas Gap, at Fairfield, at Boonsboro, and in other places, the Confederate army would lose another five thousand soldiers. Their losses at Gettysburg, of both the battle and of men, and their additional losses of men during their withdrawal, did not directly lose the war for the rebel army. Their losses also did not cause them to lose their will to fight, but those continuing losses did have a significant adverse effect on their ability to sustain an army large enough to fight in many future battles.

After their withdrawal from Gettysburg, the Confederate army would again fight bravely despite being ill-equipped in many battles. They would fight at the Second Battle of Fort Sumter, at the Battle of Chickamauga, at the Battle of Five Forks, at the Battle of Atlanta, and at over one hundred and fifty other locations before they agreed to surrender at Appomattox Court House in 1865.

* * * * * *

As Lee's army moved south, the President of the Confederate States of America, Jefferson Davis, soon learned of the defeat of his army at Gettysburg. Davis would then learn of another devastating loss to the Confederacy when news of General John Pemberton surrendering his troops in Vicksburg to

General Ulysses S. Grant reached him. The additional news of Port Hudson, on the Mississippi River, also falling to the Union army contributed to the bad news that would reach Davis. The news of those losses was crippling to both the South and to President Davis. He, like others, soon began to fear Richmond, the Confederate capitol, would be next to fall to the advancing Union army. The pressure placed on him to protect Richmond, and to protect the assets of the Confederacy, was enormous. Among the principle assets he took steps to protect was the treasury of the Confederacy. Money needed to continue their fight against the Union.

In the early days of the war, the Confederacy had seized the United States mint in New Orleans and had taken possession of a large amount of gold and silver coins. Those coins were estimated to be worth in excess of six million dollars at the time they were stolen. Additionally, the Confederacy also seized bonds and bank notes which led to approximately twenty million dollars in total assets being seized from the mint and from a nearby state bank depository. That money, first taken to Columbus, Georgia after being seized, was later shipped to Richmond to help the South finance their war efforts. President Davis now had to take drastic steps to protect that money and the rest of the Confederate treasury.

After meeting with Confederate Secretary of the Treasury Christopher Memminger, a Charleston, South Carolina native, and explaining his concerns to him, President Davis drafted a letter to General Lee. After several more conversations with Memminger, Davis sent two army captains assigned to his staff to deliver his letter to Lee. The captains were also directed to discuss with him the concerns Davis had regarding the safety of the Confederate treasury. "Tell General Lee he must act fast. We cannot afford undue delays in starting this mission as I fear the Union army will soon be on the outskirts of Richmond."

It took the better part of eight days for Captains John McAulay and Steven White, both native Mississippians, to finally locate Lee as he moved south through the lower part of the Shenandoah Valley.

The difficult withdrawal, during the hot humid days of July, coupled with the additional burdens of responsibility Lee faced as his injured army moved south after their defeat at Gettysburg, had begun to take their toll on him. He had eaten little, and slept even less, despite the protests of his aide, Major Walter Taylor, and others. Finally, as they moved into the southern part of the Shenandoah Valley, Lee relented and agreed early one afternoon to halt the army so they could rest. As his men began to make camp, Lee finally had an opportunity to relax and to eat his first good meal in several days. Before he did, he made sure kitchens had been set up to feed his men their first real meal in days. Once he had been assured steps were being taken to feed the men, Lee finally sat down to eat. It had only been out of sheer exhaustion, both mental and physical, that Lee had consented to stop and rest. Now knowing his men were being taken care of, he sat and enjoyed his meal.

Sitting alone as he finished his meal under the shade provided by a canopy of large maple trees, Lee heard sentries announce the arrival of Confederate messengers. Major Taylor, assisted by other staff members, intercepted the messengers before they could reach Lee. As he spoke with them, Taylor quickly realized the importance of their assignment after learning they had been sent personally by President Davis to meet with Lee.

If they had arrived in camp without being sent by President Davis, they would have been denied access to Lee until after he had gotten some rest, but after being briefed on why they had to see him, Taylor had no choice but to interrupt a very fatigued Lee as he finished his meal.

"General, please forgive me for interrupting you as I know how tired you are, but these two messengers were sent here to meet with you by President Davis. I could not refuse them this opportunity to meet with you. Sir, it is very important that you see them. I would not have bothered you if it was not a matter of grave importance. General, please forgive me."

As he eyed the messengers sent to meet with him, Lee dismissed his aide's anxiety. "Major Taylor, do not be concerned about interrupting me. I know you would not have done so if it was not important. You may escort them over to my table. Please join us when you are finished with your other duties." Lee set his fork down on his plate, too tired to completely finish his meal and too polite to do so in front of the messengers sent to meet with him.

As Taylor escorted the two officers to Lee's table, they both stopped before reaching it. First coming to attention, they then saluted the commanding general of the Confederate army. Lee stood, returned the salute, and walked to where they had stopped. The captains stood several feet away, respecting the privacy Lee's rank demanded as he sat at the table.

As he shook hands with the two captains, Lee told them to relax and extended his hand towards chairs which had been brought over for them to sit down on. Even though they had been invited to sit down, neither of them moved until they saw Lee take a seat first, knowing it would have been disrespectful for either of them to sit down before he did. As Lee sat down, they both took notice of how slowly he moved, his fatigue far too obvious to miss. Despite his lack of sleep, Lee was still sharp as a tack. He quickly recognized Captain McAulay from meetings President Davis had hosted during the early days of the war. Lee warmly greeted him, addressing him by his first name.

"General Lee, I am honored you remembered my name." The fact that Lee had spoken to him by using his name, and not his rank, made McAulay feel important.

Then Lee looked at Captain White. "Forgive me, captain. While I am quite certain we have met, I cannot remember your first name or where it was we first met, but I know we have. Perhaps it is because of my fatigue, but I am having trouble recalling where we have met. Please forgive me."

"General Lee, I also am honored you remember me. We met briefly on two occasions in Washington prior to the present conflict we are currently engaged in. I am humbled to be in your company again."

As Major Taylor and other staff members set up a small folding table next to the table Lee had been eating at, one of Lee's aides brought over a pitcher of cold water. Now playing the role of host, Lee poured cups of water for his guests and for himself. "Major Taylor, please see to it that our guests have some food ready for them after we are done here. They will also need a tent so they can rest. I am sure they are quite tired from their journey from Richmond." Taylor, who had already detailed the staff to take care of these needs, briefly left to make sure the tasks were being completed.

Captain McAulay was the first to speak. As he did, he extracted an envelope from within his uniform blouse; handing it to Lee to open. Examining the envelope, Lee saw it was addressed to him, and that it had been done so in the same unique style President Davis had used in the past. He also observed the envelope bore the wax seal of the Confederate President's office. The presence of the two captains seated before him, having been sent personally by Davis to meet with him, as well as the sealed letter, indicated that whatever was contained in the envelope was of grave importance.

Breaking open the wax seal, Lee took out the letter and quietly read it.

General Lee,

The news of Gettysburg has reached me. While I am saddened by the loss of so many of our fine young men, I do not view the losses at Gettysburg to be fatal ones for the cause that we are fighting for.

However, as news of our defeat at Vicksburg has also reached me, I must take the necessary precautions to protect our assets here in Richmond as I fear the Union army will soon attempt to advance upon us. Out of my concern that this letter might be intercepted by the enemy, I have given my instructions to Captains McAulay and White to personally deliver to you. Please know they speak for me when they meet with you. I am confident that you will understand my reasons for doing so. Take the steps necessary to immediately complete the orders I have relayed to you through them.

Despite the results at Gettysburg, I still have the greatest confidence in you, and in our army. I trust this letter finds you well and in good health. I look forward to seeing you soon.

Affectionately yours,
President Jefferson Davis

After reading the letter from Davis, Lee reached for his glass of water. He sat quietly for several moments before speaking. Looking at the two nervous captains seated near him, he finally spoke. "While I believe I understand what President Davis is saying in his letter, perhaps you should tell me exactly what he wants accomplished regarding our assets."

"Sir, as his letter states, President Davis was concerned that if his letter fell into the hands of the Union army they would know not only learn what our assets are, but they would also learn what steps he is directing you to take to protect them. That is why he personally gave us his orders to give to you. His concern regarding the safety of our assets is also another reason he sent us to personally deliver his orders to you. He did not want the Union army intercepting such a sensitive message being sent to you."

Lee sat quietly, his legs crossed, while a nervous Captain White had summarized what he already knew from reading the letter. He patiently waited for more information to be presented to him. As White began to speak again, Major Taylor, attending the meeting as Lee's witness for the discussion taking place, interrupted him. After doing so, Taylor ordered a nearby sergeant, who was performing sentry duty by Lee's tent, to move further away from the discussion taking place.

"General Lee, as Major Taylor has just correctly done, President Davis has directed us to tell you this mission is not to be discussed with anyone else. The sole exception is the officer whom you choose to lead the mission. The other members selected for this mission are not to be told the full details until they reach Richmond. Sir, President Davis is directing you to select someone you hold in the highest regard, someone you can personally vouch for, to lead this mission. While President Davis insists this officer be of the rank of major or captain, he is not mandating who that officer is; he is leaving the choice of that officer up to you. He does insist this person be in Richmond within seven days to personally meet with he and with Secretary Memminger. Secretary Memminger will then provide the specifics, such as the mission's details and its final destination, to whomever you choose. General Lee, the purpose of this mission is to move the majority of our treasury to a location south of Richmond. We must keep it out of the hands of the Union army. President Davis does not want to wait until the Union army is advancing upon

Richmond to move the money to a safe location. Sir, the President is obviously very concerned about this situation."

Lee sat back in his chair as White finished speaking; pondering the additional responsibility Davis had just thrust upon him. The responsibilities he shouldered already were enormous. While he knew President Davis only wanted him to select the proper personnel for the mission, he also knew Davis, and likely others, would hold him accountable if the mission failed. Quietly sitting in his chair, he wished he knew the exact locations of all of the Union armies that might threaten those men who would soon be moving the Confederate treasury further south.

Captain McAulay then brought Lee back from his thoughts of what the ramifications would be if the Union army seized the treasury. "Sir, we have more for you to consider as well. Because our treasury includes funds which have been raised from each of our glorious Southern states, as well as money we've seized from the Union, President Davis demands each of our states be represented when the treasury is moved south, preferably a soldier at the rank of sergeant. He believes the entire Confederacy should be represented to keep an eye on the money and to have a role in protecting it. Therefore, he is directing you to have a detail put together which is to be comprised of four sergeants from the Army of Northern Virginia, and one sergeant from each of the armies of North Carolina, South Carolina, Georgia, Florida, Louisiana, Mississippi, Alabama, Arkansas and Tennessee. Sir, because no Texas units are currently fighting in the region, he is not making it a requirement Texas be represented in this mission. President Davis wants you to have the final say in who those fourteen soldiers are, but he begs you, and these are his words, 'Sir, please pick the fourteen bravest and honest men who are at your disposal'."

Lee sat silent for a couple of minutes, digesting what they had told him. Then he simply asked, "Is that all?" Nervously, McAulay and White answered in the affirmative. As he slowly rose from his chair, so did both captains. "Captains, it was good to see you both again. You have completed your assignment very well. As you can see, I am very tired from our forced march from Gettysburg. I will sleep on what you have told me; we will meet again in the morning after breakfast. I hope you will find our meager accommodations to your liking and I hope you both get some rest. That will be all for now."

That said, Lee turned and walked slowly to his nearby tent. The fatigue he felt earlier was now even more pronounced due to the additional responsibility which had been placed upon his shoulders. Sensing he was being pushed to his limits, he knew only sleep would make things look better. As he turned to walk back towards his tent, the two captains gave an awkward salute to their general, but a tired Lee never saw it. He was already focused on another responsibility given to him. Walking to his tent, Lee yelled for his aide without looking over to where Taylor now stood with McAulay and White. "Major Taylor, quickly see to the needs of our guests and then join me in my tent."

As quickly as he could arrange for another staff member to see to the needs of McAulay and White, Taylor walked to Lee's tent. By now, Lee had removed his uniform jacket and was starting to remove his boots. "Major Taylor, where is Captain Francis? Captain Judiah Francis that is, from the Virginia Fourth Cavalry Regiment. Is he still in the hospital or has he recovered from his wounds? Do you know?"

"Sir, I saw him just this morning. He has been released from the hospital. While he's still recovering from his injuries, he seems to be doing well for having lost two fingers on his left hand. His days of being a cavalry officer may be in jeopardy, but that's yet to be decided."

Sitting in a small wooden rocking chair, Lee looked up at Taylor. "Major, knowing Captain Francis as I do, I doubt the loss of two fingers will stop him from serving as a cavalry officer. As you likely know, he's an excellent soldier. Major, I'm curious, how do you regard Captain Francis?"

"Sir, I believe Captain Francis is indeed one of our finest officers. He is a unique combination of a Southern gentlemen and an excellent cavalry officer. I also believe him to be above reproach. He is, at least I hear he is, a fierce fighter who will not back down from a fight, no matter what the odds are. I know his men seem to have a great deal of respect for him. Sir, if you are thinking of him to lead this assignment, I would, respectfully of course, concur with your decision. Missing two fingers or not, with his experience and proven leadership skills, I believe he would be a sound choice."

Lee sat quiet for a moment, reflecting on the comments his trusted aide had just offered. "Major Taylor, I hate to have you do this for me, seeing it is both hot and late in the day, and I know you are as tired as I am, but I need you to find Captain Francis immediately. And, Major, as you know, this has to be kept quiet. I apologize for having to tell you this, but I need to know you understand the importance of this assignment and the importance of it being kept quiet. Now go find Francis and tell him he is to meet with me for breakfast tomorrow morning at seven. He does not need to know why, nor does he need to know any of the other details at this time. After you speak with him, please make sure you personally speak with General Stuart and advise him Captain Francis has been assigned to my staff until further notice. General Stuart simply needs to know that and nothing else for now."

Without hesitating, Taylor acknowledged the orders given to him by Lee. He then left to go find Francis.

* * * * * *

The following morning was like a rebirth to Lee as he sensed he had gotten his first good nights sleep in well over a month. While not totally refreshed, he felt significantly stronger than he had when he went to bed. As he washed his face with water from a small bowl within his tent, he sensed the high humidity his army had endured on their march south through Virginia had finally broken. As he finished dressing, fresh coffee was brewing nearby.

Stepping from his tent, Lee spied Captain Francis and his heavily bandaged left hand. He was seated at a nearby table awkwardly attempting to eat his breakfast. Major Taylor, joined by Captains McAulay and White, stood off to the side of Lee's tent talking as the Confederate camp began to come to life that morning. As he walked to the table, Francis saw Lee approaching. Quickly standing to salute, Lee waved him off, motioning for him to remain seated. With too much respect for Lee, Francis stood and saluted him sharply. It was one that was returned with a warm smile.

"Captain, good morning, I am pleased to see you again. I do hope the doctors have done well for you. I also hope you are indeed on the way to a quick recovery." Lee said rather warmly.

"Good morning, sir. Yes, and thank you, they have done their best for me. I am most grateful for their skills."

"Very good! I am pleased to hear you are on the mend. Please, be seated and please continue eating your breakfast."

Lee had known of Captain Francis and of his daring military exploits for just over two years, first taking real notice of him after hearing of a cavalry ride he had made one night through Union picket lines. With only a handful of other cavalry officers, Francis had almost single-handily rescued General John Legg who had been injured and then captured by Union forces during the Battle of Big Bethel. This daring ride had earned Francis the nickname of *'Bull Rider'* as he had bullied his way through thick brush and Union picket lines to rescue Legg.

In his earlier years, Lee was close friends with Judiah Francis' father, Major Peter Francis, when they had served together in the Union army. Peter had sustained a severe back injury in early 1861 after being thrown from his horse; an injury which occurred just months before the war had broken out. Lee knew it pained his good friend not to have an active role in defending Virginia during the war.

From their friendship, Lee learned Peter's father, James Peter Francis, had disgraced his family many years ago due to his problems associated with alcohol. The problems also included him taking up with several of his female slaves. Peter talked little about his father to others, but he had with his friend, Bobby Lee. He called Lee by that name when no one else had dared to, but they had been good friends for many years. Lee had long known about the story of Peter's father's problem with the slave women and with alcohol. As little as Peter had spoken about his father, he spoke plenty about his great-grandfather, William Peter Francis. As a young man, William had bravely fought with George Washington's troops at Yorktown when they defeated the British at the end of the Revolutionary War.

It had been two years since Lee had seen his old friend, but when he had, in a brief encounter during the summer of 1861, Peter had proudly compared his son to his great-grandfather. He had told Lee he knew his son would live up to his great grandfather's reputation. Partially because of his close friendship with Peter, Lee later had taken a liking to Judiah the first time they met.

"General, please excuse me for starting my breakfast before you arrived, but Major Taylor insisted I eat as soon as the food was served. As you can see, I am somewhat handicapped at the time due to this bandage on my hand. I . . . well, I just need a little more time to eat these days. I need to work through this injury I have sustained, so please forgive me for being so clumsy. Sir, I am reporting to you as ordered. I can assure you I will not allow this injury to stop me. How may I be of service to you?"

As Francis spoke, Major Taylor, followed by Captains McAulay and White, moved closer to the table where Lee and Francis sat. Sitting at the table, Lee noticed the pause Francis had taken when he was speaking to him. He knew from the pause the injury to his hand was one which greatly bothered Francis. Lee soon realized it was more than just a physical injury. He now sought to address the injury head-on, comforting Francis as he did. "Captain, to start with, I know the circumstances of how you were injured; I want you to know you have my appreciation for your service. While I am grateful for your service to the cause we are fighting for, I am also saddened by the injury you have sustained. Secondly, I know your father would be proud to know how well you have conducted yourself during our recent campaign. Please do extend my greetings to your father the next time you may write to him. I miss having him here with us."

Lee's comments comforted Francis. He was also pleased Lee had taken the time to mention his father. "Thank you, sir. I will indeed tell my father you have sent your regards to him. I expect he is likely still moaning about both his injury and about missing the action of this war. He would have done the South proud with his service." Francis had wanted to ask Lee more about why he had been summoned to meet with him, but knew it was not his place to ask. He knew when Lee was ready he would tell him.

Lee smiled and then briefly nodded his head in agreement to what Francis had just said.

Getting comfortable at the table, Lee was served his breakfast by a rather overweight corporal who, amongst other assignments, served as his cook.

Major Taylor then sat down at the table next to Lee, quickly briefing him on a few unrelated matters. Captains McAulay and White, who had not been invited to sit, stood respectfully off to the side. Standing behind where Francis sat, they quietly listened as Lee and Taylor spoke.

"Major Taylor, have you made arrangements to contact the commanding generals of the respective states we discussed last evening? Have you advised them to provide one sergeant each for this assignment?" Lee asked his aide after taking his first taste of his morning coffee. The warm tin cup brought warmth to Lee's hands.

"Yes, sir. I have personally dispatched couriers to each of them. The orders were sent out early this morning. The instructions directed the generals to make sure their sergeants were in Richmond within a week's time, by August 4th in fact, to meet with Captain Francis at the Richmond train station."

"Very well." Lee took a moment to again sip the coffee he had set on the table before speaking to Francis again.

As he sat quietly, Francis overheard Major Taylor mention his name to Lee. As Lee drank his coffee, Francis wondered why he was being sent to Richmond. Patiently he waited to be told what his assignment was going to be.

Putting his cup down, Lee looked at Francis for a moment before speaking. "Captain, I have an assignment for you. I hope your injury will not prevent you from accepting this assignment, but if you feel you cannot accept what I am about to ask of you due to your injury, nothing will be said about you declining this assignment. Before I tell you more about what is involved, I must ask you a question. Do not take offense with this as you know of both my fondness and respect for your family. This assignment, if it is not properly kept in complete secrecy, could spell catastrophe for our cause. Captain, for the time being, can I trust you to keep this conversation secret from everyone except for those who are present here right now?"

As he looked up at the others who were present around the table, Francis could not figure out what else to expect from Lee regarding the assignment he was being given, but realized it was something very important. "Sir, you have not offended me or my family as we have the same respect for you. My entire family is proud to be from the South. We are here to serve you and the cause we have taken up arms for. Sir, as you can trust my family, you can also trust me."

Lee smiled at the answer Francis had given to his question as it had been the one he expected to hear. "Very well! Now I must tell you one other important requirement for this assignment, and I must know you fully understand the seriousness of what I'm about to tell you. Unless you find yourself in significant trouble, and I stress it has to be significant trouble, under no circumstances are you to tell anyone, other than those who are here right now, as well as

President Davis and Treasury Secretary Memminger, of your movements. Do you understand what I am telling you?"

Judiah was now more intrigued than ever. He now knew whatever assignment Lee had planned for him was obviously a very important one. As he listened to Lee speak to him, he could only guess what the assignment might be. "What could be so important that he needs to be assured complete secrecy will be maintained by my men and me?"

"Sir, I promise you I will keep my orders to myself. My men will only know what they need to know unless something arises which may prevent me from completing my assignment. With your permission, and only after I know which of the men I can trust, I would like to tell one man what our final objective is, just so someone knows what has to be done in the event I am injured or killed."

Francis' response pleased Lee. He quickly responded to his young captain's thought. "You have my permission to do so, but only after you know for sure who you can trust. You must select someone you can trust and someone who the other men will follow; I suggest you select this person wisely. Do you understand that?"

"Sir, I do."

Lee remained quiet for a few moments before asking his next question. Before doing so, he told Francis something about his grandfather's past. It was an issue that Francis had no idea he knew about. "Captain, I know of your grandfather's problems with alcohol. Do you use alcohol at all?"

"Sir, I do not. General Lee, please, and with all due respect, if I am to be compared to anyone in my family, I wish to be compared to my great-grandfather or to my father, not to a rogue member of my family, but I do understand why you have asked the question. My family is still embarrassed by the past conduct of a family member. I know my grandfather had a problem with alcohol, but I do not. When my two fingers had to be amputated recently the doctors offered me alcohol to help kill the pain I felt. They made this offer both before and after the surgery. I refused their offer as I would rather not succumb to the same vices as my grandfather did. Sir, if you check with those doctors they will verify my words to you, but I truly hope you believe what I have said."

"Captain, that is a fair answer to perhaps an unfair question, but one I had to ask. You will soon understand why. And yes, I believe you. If I did not trust your words I would not have sent for you. Fair enough?"

"Sir, that is fair enough for me. I am honored by the faith you have in me."

Satisfied by the brief interrogation he forced Francis to endure in front of the others, Lee then gave him the details of his new assignment. He soon finished by telling Francis he was to immediately meet with President Davis and Secretary Memminger after arriving in Richmond. Then Lee concluded the meeting by telling Francis he needed only to report back to his command to collect his personal belongings as Major Taylor had already taken care of contacting his commanding officer. As Lee stood up from the table, so did Taylor and Francis. "Captain, I wish you well in your new assignment. It is safe to say the future of the Confederate States of America rests, to a large degree, in the success of your mission. God speed to you! When you have completed your assignment you are to report directly back to me." After answering a couple of minor questions Francis had regarding his new assignment, Lee dismissed him.

As Francis walked to where he had left his horse, he was momentarily overwhelmed by the responsibility given to him. Gathering himself, he mounted his horse and began the short ride back to his tent so he could collect his few personal belongings. Looking down at his injured hand, he hoped it would soon heal so he had one less problem to be concerned about.

After Francis left, Major Taylor motioned for Captains McAulay and White to join Lee at the table. As they did, Taylor poured them each a cup of coffee. "Gentlemen, you can now report back to President Davis that I have made my choice. Captain Francis has proved himself well in battle and in previous administrative tasks he has been given. Despite the injury to his hand, I'm confident he will do well. Please tell President Davis I trust him completely and that I know his family very well. I would not have chosen him if I did not have a strong degree of faith in him. He is an excellent officer to lead this assignment. Do you each agree?"

Neither captain had known of Francis before they heard his name first mentioned by Lee, but they knew if he was Lee's choice to lead the assignment, then he was their choice as well. Lee, even with his rank as the Commanding General of the army, was an easy man to speak with, but they also knew captains did not challenge decisions made by generals. "Sir, we will advise President Davis of your choice of Captain Francis to lead this assignment. We will recommend final preparations begin so we are ready when he arrives in Richmond." Rising from the table, they thanked Lee and Taylor for their hospitality, saluted Lee, and soon began the ride back to Richmond.

* * * * * *

It was just before noon when the four sergeants selected to represent the Army of Northern Virginia located Francis as he was finishing up packing his saddlebags with his personal items. As they walked towards his tent, they all eyed his heavily bandaged left hand, but no one said anything to him about his injury. After a few brief introductions, he advised them they had been selected for this assignment because of their loyalty to the army and because of their fighting skills. "Most importantly," Francis told them "you have each been selected because your commanding officer has deemed you to be one of the most trustworthy men within his command. This is not going to be the easiest assignment you have had, so I need to know each of you are committed to this assignment. I expect you men will work the hardest to make sure we're successful. Being Virginians and all, I have to be able to trust you more than I trust the others who are being selected. Speak now if you have any issues."

Hearing none, Francis and his four new men soon mounted their horses and started their ride to Richmond. As they started out, he eyed each of the sergeants riding with him. As he did, he realized at twenty-eight years of age he was probably at least three to four years older than they were. Francis was young for a captain, but had risen in rank because of his father's reputation as a soldier, and because of his own fighting and leadership skills. He had quickly demonstrated these skills soon after the war had broken out, showing an almost lack of fear in battle. He had gained the attention of others because of that lack of fear. It was a trait most men did not possess. While the South had at least one other brilliant cavalry officer in J.E.B. Stuart, what Francis may have lacked in reputation, he was certainly Stuart's equal when it came to fighting.

Beginning the ride to Richmond, they soon left the protection of the Confederate camp and its surrounding area; Francis pushing his men hard over the first few hours as he wanted to arrive as early as possible so he could properly begin the planning of his new assignment. As he rode with the others through the countryside, he could not help thinking of the significant amount of money he would soon be responsible for protecting. He could not imagine what a great deal of money really looked like. While he had come from a well-to-do family, he had never really seen much money as his family often traded and bartered for many of their needs. His father never spoke about how much real money the family had, and he had never given too much thought about it as he had been far more interested in being the typical country boy growing up.

As they rode south, Francis prayed he and his men would perform well together as he feared embarrassing those who had chosen him for this mission. Nor did he want to disgrace his family.

* * * * * *

In the weeks to follow, Captain Francis and his men would face several challenges during their assignment. It was his job to complete the assignment and to bring his men back alive. One of the tasks would be somewhat completed, the other would not. Despite the many difficult challenges he would face, Francis would not disgrace his family or his uniform.

5

A Tree Reveals Her Secret.

"When the sun's at his back and the winds in his face, it's just him and the wheel;
He wouldn't take a million for the way it makes him feel ..."
Kenny Chesney - Lyrics to his song 'Boats'

The day after he agreed to purchase his new boat, one which was everything but new, Paul also purchased a used truck so he could tow the boat to and from a storage facility close to his home. He appreciated the offer Steve had given him, one which allowed the pontoon boat to be moored at the marina for the rest of summer, but he had declined the offer. He planned on mooring it at one of the marinas situated along the Waccamaw River as the water in the river was generally not as rough as the constantly changing tides were inside Murrells Inlet. For now though, he decided he would keep the boat at the storage facility until he found a marina he liked along the river.

The truck he purchased was a used 2002 Chevy V-8 Silverado four door. Besides its four-wheel drive capability, it was also equipped with a tow package. Pewter in color, the truck had just over 72,000 miles on it. While the front hood had a couple of small dents, the rest of the truck was in very good condition despite it being close to ten-years old. Paying only $2,500.00, Paul purchased it from a widow who had recently lost her husband. She had priced it on the low end so it would sell quickly as she wanted one less sad memory of her late husband being around the house. As he drove the truck out of her driveway on the morning he purchased it, he could not help thinking his good luck was still continuing.

After buying the truck, Paul stopped for a late breakfast at the Waccamaw Diner on Frontage Road, just off Highway 17 in Murrells Inlet. With Donna having started her new job earlier in the week, he had already made the diner his new place to grab a quick breakfast and to read the paper.

After ordering his breakfast, and after opening up the sports section of *The Sun News*, a local newspaper in the Myrtle Beach area, Paul glanced out the diner window at his newly purchased truck. He caught himself smiling at the excitement of soon picking up the pontoon boat he had dreamed about owning for years. Drinking his coffee as he looked out the window, he had one other pleasant thought. "Retirement life is working out pretty well so far!"

"Here you go, sweetheart," Betty Repko said as she placed Paul's breakfast of scrambled eggs, home fries, and sausage down on the table. "You're becoming a regular here, ain't ya? I've seen ya here three times this week." Paul introduced himself to Betty, telling her he had just recently moved to the area from Connecticut after retiring.

"Well imagine that, another Yankee moving to South Carolina!" Betty quickly laughed at her own good-natured joke. He could tell from her demeanor she had just been joking with him when she called him a Yankee. "Let me tell ya something, if y'all are going to become a Southern gentleman we are going to have to teach ya to eat grits with your breakfast, not home fries," Betty again joked. Paul made a face to show his lack of interest in the creamy cornmeal Southern delicacy. The expression caused Betty to laugh at her suggestion regarding the grits. "If ya are going to become a regular here, ya also need to be sitting on the other side of the diner, that's where those old fools who have lived here for years sit. All they do is complain about you Yankees moving here, complain about not catching enough fish, and generally lie to each another about how much sex they are having. The way they describe it, their women are always pissed off about something, so I know for a fact they aren't getting any. Besides being a bunch of complainers, they're all lousy tippers too!" Betty had just told him far more than he cared to know. She soon left the booth where he was sitting and walked back behind the diner's lunch counter, carrying a tray of dirty dishes she had cleared from the booth next to his.

Outside of her rough language, Betty reminded him of many of the waitresses he had known in diners back home. They were often cheerful hard working single moms who were trying to earn a living by being nice to their customers. From the friendly banter they had with their customers, they hoped to be rewarded with enough tip money to help them pay their bills and to care for their kids. For some of them, they also held out hope of finding someone decent enough to care for them. Betty was only different than the other waitresses he had known back home because she was a bit older and because she talked with the Southern drawl he loved to hear these days.

Starting to eat his breakfast, Paul glanced over towards the section of the diner where Betty had told him the diner's regular morning customers tended to sit. As he did, he saw Chubby sitting in one of the booths with a couple of his friends. Next to their booth sat four other guys who looked to be part of Chubby's group of friends. Seeing them sitting there, Paul thought the guys with Chubby fit his description of Southern rednecks. They all wore baseball hats, all had work pants on, and some of them were wearing shirts that were either ripped or torn. Most of them had not shaved for a few days. As he continued to look at them between bites of his breakfast, he could not figure out why but those were people in life he always had an appreciation for. Southern rednecks or Northern rednecks, it did not matter, they were the hard working guys in life who spent their down time just enjoying the simple pleasures that life offered, pleasures like hunting and fishing. Chubby's friends all appeared to be going fishing later as they all seemed appropriately dressed for it. From where he sat in the diner, he could also see several different types of fishing boats on trailers in the parking lot. The trailers were hitched up behind several different model Ford and Chevy pickup trucks. The rear windows of two of the trucks had a variety of *NASCAR, Ducks Unlimited*, and *America – Love it or Leave it!* stickers displayed on them; a third truck had red and white window tinting in the form of a Confederate flag filling up most of its rear window.

As he sat finishing his breakfast, Paul heard Chubby's voice yell out to him as he was walking to the door. "Hey, partner, y'all coming by for the boat this morning?" Nodding his head, he gave Chubby a thumbs up to indicate he would be there. With his mouth too full of the last few bites of his scrambled eggs, Paul was unable to answer him. "Alright then, we'll be ready for y'all when ya get there," Chubby replied as he gave a wave at the same time. As Paul looked up from his plate, he could not help noticing one of the guys Chubby had been sitting with now stood in the diner's doorway for several moments glaring at him before walking out to the parking lot to get into Chubby's truck. For a moment, he wondered what the glare had been about, but soon returned to finishing his breakfast. As he cleaned his plate with his last piece of buttered rye toast, he watched Chubby and his friends as they drove off in the direction of the marina. As he watched them, Betty saw Paul staring out the window as she stopped to refresh his coffee.

"Who was the guy sitting next to Chubby, do you know? He kind of glared at me for a few moments, almost like he was mad at me. I don't even know the guy."

"Oh, that fat son of a bitch is known as Swamp. To tell you the truth, I don't even know his real name. He's a local and a real pain in the ass. He spends most of his days fishing in the Inlet and in some other areas over on the river. He likes to drink and fight with his friends, but I don't know much more about him. He's got a big mouth to go with his big belly, but I think he is more talk than anything else. What I do know is when he comes in here, I'm not going to get much of a tip from him cuz he's also a cheap son of a gun as well," Betty sarcastically sighed.

As Paul finished his coffee, he made sure he left a fair tip for Betty as he did not want to earn a reputation as being a cheap tipper with her. Then he went out to his truck and drove off to get his new toy, the pontoon boat he had dreamed of owning for years.

* * * * * *

Pulling into the marina, Paul was pleased to see Chubby had pulled the boat out of the water and now had it secured on the trailer in the parking lot. His first impression in seeing the boat was that it did not look like Chubby had put much of an effort into cleaning it as he said he would, but it wasn't enough to get upset over. "Doesn't really matter, I'm going to clean it my way anyhow." He was even more pleased when he saw Steve was there talking to Chubby as they walked around the boat, apparently giving it a final inspection before selling it to him. Getting out of his truck, he could see the two small signs had already been removed from the sides of the boat.

"Steve, good morning! I wasn't expecting to see you here," Paul yelled as he walked to where the boat sat on the trailer.

"Well, Chubby told me you were fetching the boat, and I have business here in an hour with a boat dealer, so I thought I'd stop to make sure you like what you are buying. I'm glad you decided to buy it. We've had great luck with it and I hope the luck continues for you."

Paul again thanked Steve for the deal he had offered him on the boat and trailer. Then he told him about the good deal he had gotten on his truck. It was a truck he had recently seen parked on Highway 707 with a red and white plastic *'For Sale'* sign taped to the front windshield.

"I'm glad to hear about that. It seems like you are doing OK for yourself as I hear you are also meeting with Willie Tegeler later today to take that part-time job I offered you."

"I am," Paul replied, "I'm seeing him around five this afternoon. I might even play nine holes afterwards just to see part of the golf course. You know, between what you have done for me, and me finding this truck, along with my recent move down here, my dreams are all coming true. Good luck seems to have found me since I moved here. Perhaps I should stop at one of the Kangaroo Express gas stations I see so many of around here and buy a lottery ticket or two." Steve laughed at his joke, but Chubby nodded his head several times, seriously thinking Paul had a great idea on how to continue his streak of good luck.

"Steve had me buy a new cooler to replace the one which stunk so badly. I have it in the office for you before you go. Oh, and I also told him when we pulled the boat out of the water yesterday we found a chip in one of the propeller blades, so we replaced that as well. One of the idiots who work for us likely did it when he backed the boat up by the boat ramp one day. No matter, it's fixed. We even filled the gas tank for you, so you should be good to go." Chubby offered as he stood sweating in the hot sun.

"Steve, you have been too good to me, and I appreciate what Chubby has done as well, at least let me pay you for the propeller and the gas."

Shrugging him off, Steve joked that Paul could not afford the labor rate they charged their customers to replace broken propellers. As they continued to talk, Chubby took the keys to Paul's truck and backed it up so he could hitch the trailer to it. After doing so, he secured the trailer's safety chains to the truck's hitch and then plugged in the lights so the trailer's brake lights could be tested before Paul left. They worked fine. Then Chubby went and fetched the new cooler he had picked up at Costco.

As they talked some more in the parking lot, Steve recommended to Paul that he should consider buying a marine radio and a compass; both of which he suggested could easily be mounted on the boat's dashboard. "Storms sometimes come up quick out on the river. Not knowing the river too well, you will be glad you have them if you get in a jam. With all of the bends and turns in the river it is easy to get lost, especially when the weather is lousy." Steve's recommendations were well taken and Paul thanked him for his good ideas. "We also called the Department of Natural Resources about the sale of the boat and gave them all of your information. They will mail you your new registration when they send you your two tax bills, one each for the boat and for the motor. You should have them in the next couple of weeks."

Wrapping up the sale of the boat, Paul and Steve agreed to meet the following Friday night with Donna at *The Grumpy Sailor* for dinner. Waving a quick goodbye to Chubby, Paul shook hands with Steve and then drove out of the marina with his pontoon boat safely secured to the rear of his pick-up truck. He was in his glory. As he turned onto the local section of Highway 17 in Murrells Inlet, Paul started thinking perhaps he should play it safe and buy the lottery tickets he had joked about. He stopped at the first Kangaroo Express gas station he came to and purchased four South Carolina Education lottery tickets. He felt foolish doing so, but deciding he should not close the door on Lady Luck, he purchased the tickets, along with a Coke, just in case his good fortune continued.

After leaving the Kangaroo Express, Paul's next stop was at The King's Highway Car Wash, in Murrells Inlet. Almost fanatical about his cars always being kept clean and running well; his pontoon boat would be no different. He spent the better part of the next hour feeding quarters into the meter at the self-service car wash so he could use the high pressure water hose to wash off the combination of salt, algae, and mud stains which had accumulated primarily on the boat's transoms. He also took the time to do the same across the entire boat, even taking the time to unfold the boat's canopy to get rid of some mold which was starting to grow on the canvass top. Between the high pressure hose, some soap and bleach, and some elbow grease which he applied with a steel brush and with a large sponge, the boat soon looked far better than it had two hours ago.

Not planning on mooring the boat immediately at any of the nearby marinas along the Waccamaw River, Paul wanted to first explore the numerous inlets and rivers around Georgetown and Horry counties before he gave any thought of keeping it at one location. With the driveway of his house already crowded with their two cars, and with his recent addition of a pickup truck, he rented space for the boat at a nearby storage facility. Less than two miles from his house, the storage facility sat between Highway 17 and McDowell Shortcut Road in the Inlet. *Shapiro's Indoor and Outdoor Storage* had space available for the boat and trailer underneath their covered canopy. The large open air storage space, which had a heavy duty corrugated metal canopy, had been built for people who wanted their boats and recreational vehicles stored there. The canopy had been built to house twelve vehicles or boats underneath it. Currently it protected a combination of eight boats and campers, and one large recreational vehicle, from the sun and other elements. *Shapiro's* had surveillance cameras mounted around the storage facility and the secured parking lot. He was pleased to have been assigned his own electronic pass code for 24 hour access to the facility. After thoroughly cleaning the boat, Paul towed it to *Shapiro's* and parked it in his designated spot under the canopy. The owner of the storage facility, Ed Shapiro, a retired cop from Clinton, New Jersey, had given him a special *'cops'* discount when he signed the six-month rental agreement.

After parking the boat and trailer under the canopy, Paul drove up to *Bonner's Discount Carpet* located on Highway 17 in Murrells Inlet. There he picked up a large roll of indoor/outdoor carpet so he could replace the boat's torn and ripped deck carpeting. The same carpeting Chubby had bragged about having his romantic adventures on. Just the thought of those occasions occurring was enough of a reason to replace the old carpeting. Over the course of the next two days, the old carpeting would be ripped up and replaced with the nice new green colored carpeting.

After he finished that chore, Paul took the stencils he had purchased at a nearby arts and crafts store and taped them to the side walls of the pontoon boat. Carefully he painted *'Donna Lynn'* in navy blue lettering on each side wall. For letting him fulfill his dream of moving to South Carolina, he figured the least he could do was to name his boat after his wife. Finishing up his stenciling job, he gathered up his tools and prepared to head home. Having to meet Willie at *The Links* later in the afternoon, he had just enough time to get home and get cleaned up. Before leaving the storage facility, he again took a moment to take a look at the *'Donna Lynn'* he had painted on the boat's side walls. He could not wait to take Donna out on the Waccamaw River.

Just before 5 pm, Paul arrived in Pawleys Island to meet with Willie Tegeler, the PGA Golf Professional at *The Links Golf Club*. Steve had previously told him *The Links* sat alongside the Waccamaw River and had been built on the site of a former rice plantation. As he drove down the long driveway towards the clubhouse, a driveway which ran between the perfectly manicured first and tenth fairways, it was easy to see why the golf course was so highly rated as a great golf facility. Even while driving down the driveway it was easy to see how lush the fairways were. The myriad of colorful flowers in several different flower beds gave the impression they were as well-maintained as the fairways were. The Spanish moss hanging from the large Southern Live Oak trees, which lined the length of the mile long driveway, gave Paul the impression he was visiting a special place. The view of the golf course was spectacular.

Parking his car in the parking lot near the Pro Shop, Paul walked inside to meet Willie. As he entered the clubhouse, Willie Tegeler, fairly tall and slender in his stature, was just coming down the hallway from the clubhouse's *Bogie Free Grill Room* when he saw Paul. "If you're Paul Waring, you're looking for me, I'm Willie," extending his right hand to shake hands with Paul. "Thanks for coming in to see me. Steve told me how you helped him with the flat tire the other day, and about your recent move down here. He also told me he wanted to repay you for your help by giving you a part-time job so you could play some free golf at our great course. So if the boss says to make it happen, let's do it. Come to think of it, Steve even told me he sold you an old boat. Boy, you two must have really hit it off."

Paul started by thanking Willie for his time and then acknowledged the points he had brought up. "Yeah, I guess by performing a simple act of kindness you can say I have made a new friend, someone you can also say is very generous. I still cannot believe the luck I have had."

Walking outside, they climbed into Willie's *Club Car* golf cart. The golf cart had *'PGA Professional'* neatly painted across the front of it. Above the *Club Car* logo, Willie's name had been nicely stenciled in dark blue lettering. The golf cart was by far the nicest one Paul had ever seen. Driving towards the course's practice area, Willie gave him a quick tour of the facility. As they toured the scenic golf course, he told Paul his job was going to be as a ranger on the course, making sure the golfers moved along in a timely manner so play did not get backed up. As they drove along the beautiful 18th closing hole, Willie explained the job only paid ten dollars an hour, but golf was free, as was the use of the facilities. Paul was surprised to learn the facilities included a private boat launch on the property. Willie then described how the waters around the boat launch had been manmade. Priding himself in learning all there was to know about the property's previous use as a rice plantation in the mid-1800's, Willie further described how the waterway had been first used for various needs in the old rice fields. "In fact, take a moment to visit the large meeting room we have on the second floor of the clubhouse before you leave, Steve commissioned an artist to paint the walls with a rendition of what the property looked like when it was an actual rice plantation. They used some really old photos to recreate what the property looked like back then. It's a great painting."

"I'd like to see that. I'll make sure I take a look at it." Paul could not get over how beautiful the facility was and how pretty the marsh grass looked where it was growing in the waters where the rice had grown many years ago.

"Well, if you're good with what we've discussed, I guess I will see you on Tuesday morning. Be here around 7 a.m. and we'll get you started with your retirement job. One thing about this job, besides the great golf, you'll soon realize you have friends you never knew about as once your neighbors find out you work here they'll want to be your new best buds." Paul laughed at the remark as he thanked Willie for the tour.

"Free golf, working outside driving around in a golf cart a few hours each week, and being able to use the private boat launch, not too bad. The perks alone are worth the job." Paul thought on the drive back home.

* * * * * *

The next morning Paul was up early. He started the day by reading the previous day's newspaper as he sat at his kitchen table eating breakfast. Far too busy from picking up his boat, cleaning it, and then meeting with Willie, he had not found time to read it before now.

He had also taken Donna out for dinner and afterwards took her to *Shapiro's* to see the boat for the first time. She was a little disappointed in its condition at first, but when he told her about what he still planned to repair on the boat, she had warmed up to it. Earlier, Paul had left the sides of the boat covered up when he left to meet with Willie. When he pulled the tarps off the two areas where he had stenciled '*Donna Lynn*', Donna got a kick out of the gesture he had done for her. She giggled as she asked him a question after seeing her name painted on the boat. "Does this mean we can stop and buy those silly boat captain hats I have seen at all of those tourist trap stores in Myrtle Beach?" Paul laughed with her when she saw her name on the boat, and laughed even harder about her hat idea, but he quickly assured her the captain hats were definitely out of the question.

After a quick morning read of the paper, Paul drove the short distance to *Shapiro's*. After hitching the boat to his truck, he headed down the By-Pass section of Highway 17 to Wacca Wache Landing, located off of Wachesaw Road in Murrells Inlet. The boat launch was an easy fifteen minute drive from the storage facility. Once there, he slowly backed the trailer down one of the two ramps at the boat launch. It was one of several small boat launches along the river that the South Carolina Department of Natural Resources maintained for the public's use. Adjacent to it was a small private marina and restaurant.

Nervous about backing the trailer into the water for the first time, Paul was greatly relieved when he saw no one else was using the boat launch when he arrived. He was even more relieved when he saw that none of the nearby marina's employees were standing on the dock watching him back the boat down the wet ramp. Backing up a truck with a trailer attached to it was not the easiest task for anyone to accomplish and he was pleased to see he did not have to do so in front of an audience.

It took Paul three attempts to back the trailer down the wet ramp, but on his third attempt he succeeded. He backed just far enough into the water so he could unload the boat from the trailer. As he exited his truck, proud of his accomplishment of backing the trailer into the water without an incident occurring, he slipped on the wet concrete ramp and landed on his butt in ankle deep water. Standing up, his bathing suit now soaking wet, he quickly looked around to make sure no one had seen him slip. Embarrassed, but smiling to himself, he had but one thought. "That was rather graceful!"

In took him only a few minutes to unfasten the straps that held the boat to the trailer. Then he slowly let the rope out from the trailer's winch and allowed the boat to float free of the trailer. Grabbing the rope tied to the bow, Paul tied the boat to the nearby dock so he could pull the trailer out of the water. In a matter of moments he had the truck and trailer parked in the nearby parking lot. "So far, so good!" He thought to himself, relieved his first trip to the boat launch had gone fairly well.

Paul returned to the boat carrying a plastic bag containing a few bottles of water, a couple of Cokes, and some snacks. In his other hand he carried a large bag of ice. The day's warm temperature was causing the bag of ice to already start melting. Climbing onto the boat, he placed the drinks and ice inside his new Igloo cooler.

Starting the engine up for the first time, Paul sat listening as it hummed very quietly. "It sounds as good as Chubby said it would." Untying the rope, he pushed away from the dock and slowly steered the boat out of the small boat launch area, heading southwest on the Waccamaw River towards Georgetown. Paul could not have been happier. As he slowly motored down the river, he had another thought. "Now I can cross this off of my Bucket List of things to do."

Heading down the Waccamaw River, which he knew was part of the Inter-Coastal Waterway running along the Atlantic seaboard, he passed several small inlets and streams running off in many different directions from the main part of the river. "I'm going to have plenty of time to explore those areas to see where they come out. I wonder if they lead to another part of the river or if they just kind of peter out?" With these thoughts he then realized he needed to buy a detailed map of the river to keep on the boat so he could explore those areas and to have in the event of an emergency. "I better get an emergency kit as well and stow it along with the map in one of the storage seats." With that thought, Paul started to make a mental list of things he needed to acquire for the boat.

Proceeding further down the river, Paul passed several marinas with boats moored there which were much larger, and in far better shape, than the *Donna Lynn* was. But none of that mattered to him as he knew he finally had what he had dreamed about for years. The sights of those fancier boats did nothing to dampen his feelings about his boat. He did not need anything big or fast, he just wanted what he now had. He found himself smiling as he reflected back on the good fortune which had come his way recently. His good fortune reminded him of the words to Kenny Chesney's song *'Boats'*. For a few brief moments, he hummed the tune to the song as he moved further south on the river.

Passing other marinas along the river, as well as remnants of several old rice and indigo plantations which had lined the river years ago, Paul tried to guess where places were that he knew. Places such as *The Links*, or the *Caledonia Golf and Fish Club*, and the beautiful *Brookgreen Gardens*, all of whom lay between Highway 17 and the river, but the thousands of trees lining the river obstructed his view in many places. He could not find any landmarks he recognized.

Driving the boat slowly and cautiously his first time out, Paul took almost two hours since leaving the marina to reach the entrance of Winyah Bay. There the brackish water of the Waccamaw River meets the waters of the Atlantic Ocean outside of Georgetown. He was somewhat awed by the size of the bay as he guided the small pontoon boat under the huge L.H. Siau bridge, a bridge carrying traffic to and from Myrtle Beach to Georgetown. As his boat entered the main section of the bay, he saw the waves in the bay had increased in size from those on the river. Despite it being a beautiful sunny day, it had gotten somewhat windy down in the bay. Turning his boat around as he reached navigational buoy number eight, he began to head back up river, deciding he would challenge the waves on another day. Today he was content to just enjoy his first day on the river with his new boat. As he steered the boat back up river, Paul grabbed a cold bottle of water from the cooler and toasted his good fortune.

As he headed back into calmer waters, Paul decided he would try to see if he could take a different route back to the marina. Checking the boat's gas gauge, he saw he still had enough gas left in the boat in the event he got lost. He knew if he got lost he could turn around and then double back to the marina the same way he had first come. Heading north, he noticed a small peninsula sticking out into the bay. Not having a map of the area, he decided he would steer to the right side of the peninsula to see where this section of the river led him. He was in no hurry as he wanted to enjoy his first boat ride for as long as he possibly could before returning to the marina. Proceeding north, he saw where several other rice and indigo plantations had once sat along the river. Moving up river, he waved to the other boaters who passed by and took in the many different types of birds who made their homes along the river. The pelicans and the egrets he watched kept him amused as they hunted for their next meal.

It took Paul about ninety minutes to get a good distance back up the river. As he began to navigate a bend in the river, he saw a large sandbar extending out into the water. Nearby a large sign was posted on adjacent land which identified the property where the sandbar was located as being the *Sandy Island Wildlife Management Area*. Needing to stretch his legs, and to make a nature call to relieve himself, he cut the engine to the boat. Slowly he ran the boat up and onto the sandbar's east side. Jumping onto the sandbar, he tied the boat to a tree limb hanging several feet out over the water.

As he stretched his legs, Paul noticed that no other boats were in the area. He also could not see or hear any hikers walking within the wildlife area. Walking inland a short distance off the river, he wished Donna had been along to enjoy the day with him. He took consolation in knowing many more days like this one would soon come along for them to enjoy themselves together on their boat.

Paul was soon captured by the isolation he quickly felt after being in the woods for only a couple of minutes. As he walked a bit further into the woods, he could not help but wonder if anyone else had ever walked on the same ground he was now walking on as the area seemed to have been untouched by human hands. Walking further inland off the river, he noticed several massive Southern Live Oaks in the woods. Unaccustomed to seeing trees this shape and size; he walked closer to inspect them. As he moved closer to the trees to answer the call of Mother Nature after drinking a large bottle of water, Paul made sure no one was nearby watching as he unzipped his pants amidst the huge Live Oak trees.

As he zipped his pants back up, Paul's eyes caught something shiny in the base of one of the nearby Live Oak trees. It caught his attention as it reflected the sun's early afternoon rays. The reflection he saw had been brief and he was about to dismiss it, but then the object reflected the sun again. Now curious, he walked closer to the tree to investigate.

Approaching the large Live Oak, clearly the biggest of the six Live Oak trees present, he saw the reflection again. It came from inside the base of the tree. He now also saw the tree had apparently grown with a deformity in its base. At first, he could not tell if the tree had been struck by lighting years ago, or if the tree was starting to die, but either way he saw the base of the tree had a large opening in it. It was an opening which he estimated had to be over three feet wide and almost four feet high. Looking at the size of the opening, Paul first wondered how the tree still stood, but then realized the Live Oak was probably at least sixteen to eighteen feet in its circumference. From its massive size he figured out how the tree still stood. It was simply a huge tree. Like most Southern Live Oaks, it was also a beautiful tree to look at.

Looking into the base of the tree through the large opening, Paul saw the tree's interior was partially filled with small branches, leaves, and strangely, with a medium size rock which was about two feet in height. The rock was easily three feet wide. As he stood there, he wondered how the rock had gotten so far into the tree's base. "Could the tree have simply grown up around the rock?" It was the first of many questions he would pose to himself. He would have answers to none of them.

His eyes then strained to see what caused the reflection he noticed. Kneeling down near the opening in the tree, Paul noticed a long thin piece of metal, partially obscured by a small dead tree branch, leaning against the back of the tree's interior. "How in heck did a piece of metal get inside this tree?"

Moving closer to the opening so he could reach into the tree to grab the piece of metal he saw, Paul hoped he was not about to be bitten on the hand by a raccoon or a skunk, or, even worse, by a snake who now called the tree home. Slowly at first, he reached inside the tree and carefully put his right hand around the piece of metal, hoping not to get bit, or to cut himself on the piece of somewhat rusted metal. Clutching the object, he quickly withdrew his hand from inside the tree, grateful he had not suffered an animal's bite during the process. It took Paul a couple of moments to finally realize what it was that he had found. Looking at it, he finally realized it was a long bayonet, rusty in several spots, but still in fair condition. The bayonet had been found with its tip partially stuck in the ground.

As Paul inspected the bayonet, he could not help but wonder how it could have found its way into the base of the tree. "Perhaps kids playing here years ago forgot about it and it got left here?" As his eyes examined the bayonet, they also darted back and forth to the opening in the tree. He then noticed what he had thought were dead tree branches were not branches at all. Reaching back into the opening of the tree, he grabbed the objects and pulled them out from where they had rested on the ground. After withdrawing them, Paul immediately recognized the objects as being human bones. His years as a state trooper had given him many opportunities to see dead bodies and human remains. After examining the bones for several minutes, he was confident they were too big to be from any animal that had died there. At first, his discovery caused him to move quickly away from the tree as the bones had caught him totally off guard. Soon composing himself, he moved back closer to the tree and to the bones he found. "What have I just found?" he silently wondered.

Again kneeling in front of the opening in the tree, Paul used his hands to carefully rake out the accumulated leaves, twigs, and small tree branches the wind had blown inside the tree over the years. As he did, his right index finger caught on another object, one which had been obscured from his view by the layers of dead leaves. Using both hands, he reached into the poorly lit tree base and grabbed at the object, pulling it and a large number of dead leaves around it towards him. Finally able to clasp his hands around the object and the leaves, he set them on the ground so he could see what he had found. Clearing the leaves from around what he had found, he was again startled by this new discovery. It was a human skull. "What the hell is this?" It was his only thought as he again moved back away from the tree. His next thought was a logical one for a seasoned state trooper to ask. "And who the hell is this?" Startled by what he found, Paul had not yelled or screamed, but in his somewhat perverse cop humor he did have the thought he was glad he had relieved himself prior to making the discovery of the bones and skull.

Composing himself, he again moved back towards the base of the tree. Doing so, he questioned whether he should continue looking for other items, or whether he should put everything back inside of the tree and call the sheriff's office to report his findings. "The bayonet is pretty rusty, and the bones and the skull have been here for years. I'll just keeping picking and see what else I come across; then I will call them if I have to." Again using his hands, Paul began raking out the remaining leaves, twigs, and small branches from inside of the tree. As he did, he found a couple of smaller bones which looked to be ones animals had chewed on some time ago. Then he found pieces of shredded and decayed cloth, and also found what appeared to be the partial sole of a long ago worn shoe or boot. His experience as a trained investigator caused him to have additional thoughts about his discovery. "If the skull and some of the bones are here, where are the rest of the bones? I wonder if animals have dragged them off?" His eyes briefly scanned the surrounding area for any other remains, but he was too focused on the tree's opening to pay any real attention to anything else for now.

Now Paul refocused on the medium size rock within the tree. It seemed strange to him a rock that size could have gotten inside the tree's hollow trunk without it having been intentionally put there. It also did not seem logical that the tree could have grown up around it. As he started to clean out the leaves and branches which had accumulated around the back of the large rock, his eyes caught something hanging down within the tree just above his head. Fearing it was an animal now trying to escape while he was there, he instinctively swiped at the object with his right hand in an attempt to protect himself. As he did, and fearing an animal was about to fall on top of him, he quickly extracted himself from within the tree.

The object Paul swiped at fell upon him before he was able to completely free himself. Still on his knees, but almost free of the tree, he grabbed the object in his left hand and tossed it a few feet away. He prayed he had done so before he could feel a painful bite on his hand from some upset animal. Rolling away from the tree, and realizing at the same time he had not been injured, he looked to see what had fallen on him. As he saw what it was, and what now lay only a few feet away on the ground, Paul received the shock of his life.

What Paul found would be talked about for years to come.

6

Instructions.

"Our march yesterday was terribly severe.
The sun was like a furnace, and the dust thick
and suffocating. Many a poor fellow marched his last day yesterday."
Lt. Col. Rufus R. Dawes, USA

Captain Francis and the four sergeants of the Army of Northern Virginia finally made their way to Richmond without encountering any Union troops or by being challenged by any Confederate troops. The only troops they had encountered were those posted at the outskirts of the city. The trip had taken a day longer than expected, but it had been an uneventful one to make. Now they were in need of a hot meal and some sleep.

During the ride south to Richmond, Francis had the opportunity to get to know each of the four sergeants better. Besides learning their names, he also learned of their backgrounds and why they had joined the army. Collectively they told him they had done so out of their loyalty to Virginia. Two of the men told him they had joined the army to protect their way of life from what they and their families perceived to be an attempt by the Union to take away the rights of the individual states. He found it interesting that little mention of the slavery issue had been brought up during their talks. From these talks, each of the sergeants began to develop a sense of respect for their new commanding officer. Unlike many before him, they saw he had a respect for their feelings and opinions about the war. While they respectfully kept their distance from him, they did notice Francis was different from the other officers they had served under.

Sgt. Blake Stine was a tobacco farmer from outside of Manassas, as was Sgt. Frank Griffin who hailed from Winchester; both were twenty-two years of age. Sgt. Harrison Charles Davis, better known to his family and friends as 'H.C.', was dirt poor, had never received any formal education, and had barely been eking out an existence as a hired hand. He had been barely making a living doing odd jobs at several farms near where he lived along the James River when the war had broken out. Davis had seen an opportunity in the war. The army would give him a chance to do something other than the menial jobs he had been doing. He hoped by joining the army he would get fed on a regular basis and, perhaps most importantly, it would give him an opportunity to fight for Virginia. Like Stine and Griffin, Davis was still a young man, barely twenty-three years old. Sgt. Franklyn Banks was the oldest, at twenty-four years of age, and had seen the most action in the war of the four sergeants. Banks had already been involved in several battles against the Union army and had received high praise from several of his superiors for his bravery on the battlefield. Prior to the war he had been working in his father's blacksmith shop in Augusta County. When the war broke out, and despite his father's early protests, Banks had joined to fight the hated Yankees. As he learned parts of their pasts, Francis told them parts of his as well, but not everything, and certainly not the embarrassing parts about his disgraced grandfather.

After arriving in Richmond, Francis and his men took the time to scout the area in and around the train station. He was not sure at first why he had them spend the time doing so, but a strong feeling told him the start of his assignment would likely involve a trip on the railroad. Whether he was going to be right on that premonition or not, Francis still felt better getting a feel for the area around the station as neither he nor his men had ever been to Richmond before now.

Feeling good about the time he spent surveying the area, Francis made arrangements for his men to get a hot meal and to get cleaned up from their weeklong ride. Before he left them to go meet with Secretary Memminger, he pulled his pocket watch out from inside his uniform blouse. After checking the time, he instructed his sergeants to meet him at the train station's platform in three hours. As he stood with his men, Francis noticed their presence, despite the difference in their uniforms, drew little attention from other nearby soldiers and passersby.

After the sergeants had eaten their meal, and had gotten cleaned up somewhat, they returned to the train station to wait for Francis. While waiting for him to return, the men passed the time taking turns sleeping and watching the pretty girls of Richmond who passed by. They also passed their time watching the open rail cars and boxcars being loaded and unloaded with the various supplies that were needed by the Confederate armies to fight the war. For farm boys from the country, the bustle around the train station was captivating to watch.

As his men watched the activity around the train station, Francis waited patiently for Secretary Memminger to meet with him after his presence had been made known to the treasury secretary. As he waited, Francis soon saw Captains McAulay and White enter the outer room where he sat. They were closely followed by an older man who he assumed was Memminger. He first shook hands with McAulay and White, and then with Secretary Memminger, after McAulay had introduced him to the Secretary. As they did, the treasury secretary spoke to him.

"Captain Francis, it is indeed an honor to finally meet you. I have received several positive reports about you and your abilities. I trust that you and the other men with you had a safe trip down here."

"Yes, sir. We did. We had no problems at all. My men are enjoying a hot meal and are getting cleaned up as we speak. I will be rejoining them soon."

"Very well, very well! I have been advised of your selection for this assignment by General Lee himself; your fellow captains here have also told me many good things about your sterling reputation. I have a sense General Lee has made the right choice in you for this assignment. I hope you are up for it. I also hope that injured hand I see you have will not have an adverse impact on your ability to complete this assignment."

"No, sir. My hand is recovering nicely. It should not be a problem at all."

"Fine, just fine! Captain, this is a very important assignment. It is safe to say the future of the Confederacy rests with your ability to complete this most sensitive mission. I'm afraid our future also rests with the ability of two other men to complete two similar, but smaller assignments as well."

Memminger then took Francis by the arm and escorted him into a large office on the second floor of the Confederate capitol building. They were joined by both McAulay and White. After a few moments of pleasantries, Memminger excused himself for a few minutes and left the room. While he was gone, the three captains took the brief time that was available to renew their friendships which had started back at Lee's camp.

As they talked amongst themselves within Memminger's office, the large double doors leading to a larger office opened. As they opened, Francis expected to see Memminger returning to rejoin them for a further discussion. Instead, he saw that not only was Memminger coming through the doors, but so was Confederate President Jefferson Davis. Quickly coming to attention, Francis saluted President Davis as he walked across the office to greet him.

"Captain Francis, it is indeed an honor to meet someone I have recently heard so much about. I am pleased to tell you everyone speaks glowingly about your abilities." The President kindly offered.

Never having met President Davis before, Francis was somewhat awed to be in the presence of someone he had heard so much about. Nervously he responded to Davis' comments. "Sir, I assure you, the honor is indeed all mine. As I have been humbled to have been selected for this assignment; I am equally as humbled to be in your presence. I shall indeed remember this day for many years to come."

"Captain, I have also heard of the recent injury to your hand. I trust you are recovering well and will soon be back in good health. I am in your debt for your service to the Confederacy."

"Sir, I am doing fine. I appreciate the interest both you and Secretary Memminger have shown regarding my injury. I assure you it will soon be healed quite well."

President Davis then motioned for Francis to follow him towards three large chairs sitting within Memminger's office. "Judiah, please allow me to be informal while we briefly speak on the matter at hand. Please, be seated." After they had each taken a seat, President Davis spoke again. "I have the fear, a fear Secretary Memminger and others now share with me, that Richmond soon will be a target for the Union. As such, I must take immediate precautionary steps to protect our government and our ability to continue to fight this terrible war we are now engaged in. I must, as Secretary Memminger has correctly pointed out, take the steps necessary to protect our assets, that being the money in our treasury. We must move our treasury to a safer location so it does not fall into the hands of the advancing Union army. As a result of an order I have sent to General Lee, you have been chosen by him to move these assets to a safer location. You must understand the importance and the seriousness of the situation we now face. Do you, captain?"

"President Davis, I again say to you that I was humbled several days ago by being in the presence of General Lee. I am equally humbled to be here now with Mr. Memminger and with you. I am honored by the faith and confidence each of you have shown in me to serve our country. I promise I will never give you cause you to question your faith in me. Sir, I do understand the importance of the assignment you are giving me and I also understand the seriousness of the situation we are facing."

President Davis stood and shook Francis' hand, wishing him well with his assignment. As Lee did, he now also directed Francis to report directly back to him after he completed his assignment. Then he left Francis with Memminger so he could return to his office and to the other affairs which awaited him.

As the doors to his office were closed, Memminger now gave Francis some additional information. "Captain Francis, as both President Davis and General Lee have already expressed to you, I also have the utmost confidence in you. I will pray for your safe return. As they have already done, I also wish you well in your assignment. Now back to the matter at hand. I am preparing three copies of a letter that I will have delivered to you at the train station. Another letter from President Davis will also be delivered to you at the same time. These letters are sealed and are not to be opened. You will be given one copy of each letter for your needs as you travel. They are letters directing you to escort our assets, which President Davis has spoken to you about, to Atlanta. The letters are only to be opened in the event you are challenged by anyone, including any officer of the Confederacy, who attempts to impede your delivery of the assets to Atlanta, or who attempts to challenge your authority to pass unmolested throughout the South. You must guard these assets with your life and with the lives of your men. You must not fail us. Sir, we cannot function as a government, nor can we convince our potential overseas allies to join us, if we cannot sustain our own cause." Memminger paused briefly to collect his thoughts before continuing. "Captain McAulay and Captain White will accompany you to the train station. Once there they will give you further orders. Captain, if problems occur, significant problems mind you, you are to telegraph my office with your concerns. I must know you are well and that our assets are safe. If I do not hear from you, I will trust that all is well. Remember though, the Union has spies amongst us, including at our telegraph offices. Be careful with the messages you send me as you will not know who might be intercepting them. Now, captain, I bid you a successful mission."

Francis had closely listened to what Memminger said to him. As he listened, he noticed the anxiety and concern in Memminger's voice. Francis equated it to the same concern and worries a parent might have in the middle of the night when a child was terribly sick, fearing and wondering if the child's life would see the light of day the following morning. Saying goodbye to Memminger, he sought to assure him that all would be fine. "Sir, I will not fail you."

* * * * * *

The short ride back to the train station was done in silence as McAulay and White both allowed Francis time to absorb what had been thrust upon his shoulders. They knew what they would soon tell him would add to the burden he now faced. They let him ride in peace, collecting his thoughts as they rode.

While he had met with President Davis and Secretary Memminger, the other Confederate sergeants assigned to the detail started arriving at the train station during the afternoon. They had all arrived by the time he returned, except for the sergeant from South Carolina. As Francis approached, the sergeants from Virginia saw him and walked to where he now hitched his horse to a railing near the station's main office. As they did, the sergeants from the other states followed their lead; walking to where Francis had dismounted.

After dismounting from their horses, McAulay and White led Francis to an area of the rail yard where four boxcars sat at the end of a rail spur for the Richmond, Fredericksburg & Potomac Railroad. Stopping before they reached the boxcars, McAulay told Francis that what he was going to be told by them was to be considered sensitive. They also told him that he was to post a guard around the boxcars as they were now his responsibility. McAulay further suggested to him that he should post the guards a short distance away from the rail spur as they were concerned about prying eyes, meaning Union spies, seeing what was contained within the boxcars. McAulay then made one last suggestion; recommending that one of Francis' sergeants be with him while he was briefed on the contents of the boxcars. "Captain, I suggest you do so in the unlikely event you are seriously injured or killed during this assignment. Someone will have to know what is expected of them. I'm sure you can understand why this is being suggested to you." Francis had somewhat discussed this very need with Lee already, but had not planned on telling any of his sergeants the details of their assignment so early in the mission. Reluctantly, he decided to follow McAulay's suggestion.

Francis nodded his head and excused himself for a moment, walking over to where his men had gathered. After briefly introducing himself to the newly arrived sergeants, he explained the need to have a guard posted around the perimeter of the boxcars. "I want it done quietly and discreetly." As he started to assign his new personnel to the posts he wanted them to take, Sgt. Douglas Vane, a Georgia boy from outside of Athens, through tobacco stained yellow teeth challenged him on the need to post them on guard duty as the boxcars had not been guarded prior to this.

Stepping close to Vane, Francis could feel his blood begin to boil. "Sergeant, if you ever challenge my authority again I will have you court-martialed, if not shot first. If you survive those two indignities, then I will recommend that you be severely disciplined. When that's all over with, you will wish that I just had you shot! Do you understand me?" He now glared at Vane, waiting for him to answer, but he was not yet finished dressing him down. "Someone picked you to represent Georgia for this assignment, but right now I'm thinking they could have made a better choice, and I don't care who it was that picked you. Do you understand what I am saying?" Francis had just faced down the first challenge of his assignment and he had done so very strongly. He knew doing so would likely lessen the number of any future challenges to his authority.

The rebuke Sgt. Vane received was one delivered with a fierceness, and with such a strong air of confidence, that he immediately knew he had challenged the wrong person. He had all he could do to muster a weak reply to Francis. "Yes, sir, I understand. Sir, I regret my comments."

Francis then looked at the rest of his men who were gathered around him, warning them never to question his ability or authority. He also told them if they did they would incur his wrath worse than Vane had just received. Collectively they simply nodded their heads to show they understood what he had told them. Now he looked at Vane again. "Sergeant, for what it's worth, if you had taken the time to notice what was going on in the area, and I hope you other men have done so, you would have noticed there were at least seven other soldiers already guarding these boxcars and the train station when we got here. Look up at the station's water tower and you will see there is someone on the roof; he's a soldier not a worker. Look up at the opened window near the top of the church steeple. Can you see the soldier on the right side of the window looking down on us? And what about those two men standing in the shadows of those trees over yonder? Those are rifles leaning against the trees, not rakes or shovels. Our boys have been guarding the train all along, so don't tell me we have not had a guard on it. They have been guarding the train just like you are going to do from this point on." He watched as his men looked to find the sentries he had pointed out to them. Unlike Francis, they had not seen any of the sentries before now.

Francis eyed his men closely before selecting two of them. "Sgt. Banks, post the men around the train and the station. Sgt. Hatfield, come with me." His orders sternly given to his men, Francis turned and walked to where McAulay and White had watched him deal with his authority being challenged.

The observations made by Francis of the soldiers guarding the boxcars and the train station itself, not only caused all of the sergeants assigned to his command to be impressed at what he had detected, but also caused McAulay and White to be impressed as well. They had been responsible for setting up the guard around the perimeter of the boxcars, but had not yet told him about it. Francis' detection of the soldiers before they could tell him about them, as well as how quickly he had handled a challenge to his authority would later be relayed to Secretary Memminger. It would confirm to all of them that Lee had selected the proper person to lead the move of the treasury further south.

Opening one of the boxcars, McAulay and White explained to Francis and Sgt. Hatfield that President Davis had elected to move the majority of the treasury in three separate moves, each to three different locations. White explained further that two days prior a smaller detachment of soldiers had moved almost one million dollars in gold and silver coins south to Meridian, Mississippi. He then told Francis of another plan already in place. It was a plan to be executed in another two days, and it involved a similar size shipment of gold and silver being shipped to Louisiana. The last shipment, in due time, White further explained, would also be sent to Meridian; the rail lines running through the city would make it easier to transfer the treasury to a new Confederate capitol if Richmond fell to the Union army. But for now, White continued to explain, the money would sit in three different cities until President Davis gave further orders on where it was to be consolidated. The money being moved in two days was also being shipped by rail. It would be protected by a group of soldiers disguised as wounded soldiers returning further south to recuperate from their wounds.

Captain White then told Francis his assignment involved the largest amount of money of the three shipments. It was a shipment of several million dollars, mostly in gold and silver coins, destined for Atlanta. Once inside the boxcars, Francis was shown how the gold and silver had been concealed. The boxcars held a total of four large Conestoga wagons and nine large buckboard wagons, several of which had been secretly modified. While two of the Conestoga wagons simply held supplies and provisions for their trip, the other two, as well as each of the nine buckboards, had been outfitted with special compartments to hide the money. The wagons also carried several large wooden barrels with false bottoms that contained gold and silver coins as well. Most of these barrels, Francis was told, also contained flour, sugar, salt, and water in a further attempt to give the appearance they were simply what they appeared to be.

As Francis listened to White talk about the various hidden compartments, he saw one of the Conestoga wagons had a small painted star on each side of the wagon's canvass top. "Excuse me, captain, but the wagon with the two stars on the canvass; do those stars have any significance?"

White walked them to the wagon with the stars painted on the canvass top. "Captain, I'm impressed. Your powers of observation are again very good. Those stars were painted on the canvass so you could easily identify this wagon from the other three like it. Look here."

After they moved closer to the wagon, White showed them this wagon, like the others, also carried some provisions so it would look like any other wagon. But then White opened a hidden compartment, one of several built into the wagon by some of Richmond's finest cabinetmakers. The opened hidden compartment revealed to Francis and Hatfield a total of ten gold and silver bars of assorted sizes. "Captain, there are a total of five hidden compartments within this wagon, plus the barrels with their false bottoms. Each compartment holds gold and silver bars which have been made from some of the South's finest gold and silver jewelry. Some of the bars have been made from silverware as well. All of which has been donated by our citizens to help fund the fight for our cause. Also inside one of the compartments is a large cloth bag which contains some expensive jewelry. It is jewelry many Southern ladies have only just recently donated to help fund our cause. The stars have been put on this wagon so you know, in the event of trouble, that this is the most important wagon for you to protect. It must be protected at all costs."

Listening to what White told him, Francis quickly realized his mission had been well planned out. It was not a mission which had been pieced together overnight. "Very impressive! I can see the wheels on these wagons also appear to be built differently than the wheels on the other wagons. They give the appearance of being built stronger, perhaps to handle the weight of the gold and silver bars better?"

"Captain, you are correct. They were purposely built just for that reason. We also have had two extra wheels placed in one of the wagons in the event you should experience a problem with one of the wheels during your trip. Hopefully you will not need them." As they closed up the hidden compartments, and then the side door to the boxcar, Francis was told the train would also have three additional boxcars on it for the teams of horses needed to pull the wagons. Those additional cars would also have space for his men's horses and for other supplies they would be taking with them. Francis was then told the final piece of information he needed to know. The train was scheduled to leave at 6 pm.

Captain McAulay then spoke the words Francis had earlier privately raised with himself when he thought about the trip south. "Captain, as much as possible you should be travelling by rail as it will get you to Atlanta in the shortest amount of time. However, you need to be ready to adapt to the problems you may face when you are confronted by acts of Union sabotage to our rail lines or from equipment failure that may stop a train you are riding on. Regardless of what you encounter, you must get these wagons, and the precious cargo contained within them, to Atlanta as soon as possible. Captain, we wish you good luck and a safe trip."

As the three officers shook hands and said their goodbyes, White reached inside his uniform blouse and pulled the letters from President Davis and Secretary Memminger out of his pocket, handing them to Francis. Memminger had instructed White to hand them to him after he knew for sure Francis was up to the challenge of this assignment. White now knew he was. Leaving him standing alone on the train station's platform, McAulay and White walked back to their horses so they could report back to Secretary Memminger.

Remaining on the railroad platform, Francis watched as his two fellow officers rode away; standing there until he could no longer see them. He was now alone with a large sum of money and a group of men he did not know. As he walked down the steps from the station's platform, he had but one thought as he eyed his men who were now posted around the boxcars. "I hope these men are up for the challenge that awaits them. God knows I will need their help to complete this mission."

After motioning to his men, Francis gathered them near one of the rail cars. He then told them some of the particulars of the mission they were about to start. "Men, we have been charged with a most sensitive assignment, one which must be completed as it has been planned. If we fail, well that will likely mean the end of our way of life I am afraid and we will be governed, again I'm afraid, by the laws of the Union. I will tell you more as we move south, but what I will tell you right now is our destination is Atlanta. I will also tell you this train is leaving at 6 pm. So right now, I need you to get your horses and your gear onboard one of those three boxcars being coupled to the other cars. Be prepared to leave very soon." Pausing for a moment to think a thought out, Francis then looked at Banks. "Sgt. Banks, pick two men and have them stay with you guarding the boxcars until we are ready to leave. Sgt. Griffin will make sure your horses are put onboard the train."

"Yes, sir!"

"Steele, you and Rickert come with me. Just bring your rifles and leave the rest of your gear here. Frank will see it is taken care of for y'all."

After detailing Sgts. Steele and Rickert to complete a task for him, Francis stood off to the side watching as the other sergeants started to load the train with their horses. His men were working together for the first time. Over the coming weeks he hoped they would mesh well with each other, forming a hard working unit. Their success depended on it. The South needed them to succeed so they could continue to wage their fight against the hated Yankees. Unfortunately for this group of men the fight would not go quite as planned.

7

Clues Uncovered.

"Never take counsel of your fears."
General Thomas Jonathan 'Stonewall' Jackson, CSA

It all took place so fast that Paul was not sure what had happened when the object fell on him, but now as he examined himself he saw he had not been bitten or injured by what had fallen. At first, he thought it had been an animal or a wasp's nest, but it was neither. Now as he got up off the ground, he saw what he was looking for earlier.

As Paul moved closer to what he had tossed away when it fell on him, he saw the rest of the bones he had been thinking about earlier. It was not the bones that now shocked him; what shocked him was what was lying there with the bones. Lying on the ground was a frayed and tattered Confederate soldier's uniform which apparently belonged to a soldier who had hidden himself within the tree many years ago. Shocked to think he had just found the remains of a long dead Confederate soldier, he stared at what was on the ground in front of him. As he did, he quickly did the math in his head; calculating what he found had likely been inside the massive Live Oak for almost one hundred and fifty years. It would take weeks for him to put all of the pieces of his discovery together, but he quickly made a connection between the tattered clothes and the rusted bayonet; they had all belonged to this soldier. As he looked at the collection of bones, some of which were still partially entangled within the old uniform, he also saw within the base of the tree a piece of rotted rope, a saber, and what appeared to once have been a hat. Paul quickly looked around to see if anyone else was now present in the woods with him, but saw no one.

Stunned by what he just found, Paul began to question what had occurred and how a body could have possibly remained hidden within a tree for so many years. His law enforcement experience told him this was not possible, especially after a body's skin and muscle had decomposed and deteriorated. "How the heck did this soldier stay hidden for so many years? And how come animals and humidity did not do more damage to the clothes and bones?" Not having any immediate answers for the questions he asked himself, Paul then tried making sense out of what he found.

Crawling into the base of the large Live Oak on his hands and knees, Paul cautiously looked up into the dark interior of the tree. Summoning his courage, as he was still afraid of being bit by an animal hiding within the dark confines of the tree, he reached up and grabbed onto the first object he felt. Tugging on it, he pulled down two sections of rotted rope that appeared to have been tied to something inside the tree. Two more similar attempts of reaching into the interior of the tree turned up nothing else. "I bet something else is up there, but I just cannot see, it's too dark." The tree's cavity easily extended upwards for at least eight feet, but Paul could not see past the first few feet due to the lack of light. His last two attempts at trying to find anything else hidden inside the tree produced little except for a long scratch on his right forearm. Looking at the scratch caused him to have a thought as to why the soldier may have stayed hidden for so long. "I bet some of the clothing, perhaps the bones as well, got hung up on the inside of the tree as it is obviously splintered pretty bad in there." Reaching into his back pocket, he used his handkerchief to wipe the small amount of blood off his arm.

Sitting back down on the ground, Paul began looking at the tattered Confederate uniform and the rotted pieces of rope he found. It took him several minutes of thinking about what the rope had possibly been used for, but then he theorized the soldier had perhaps used it to somehow hide himself inside the tree. "It's almost like the soldier may have been hiding from someone. Sounds kind of crazy, but who knows. Maybe he put the rock inside the tree so he could climb a little higher. Who knows, but it's very weird though."

As he continued to inspect the items he found, items the tree had previously refused to surrender for almost one hundred and fifty years, Paul continued to search for answers to the many questions racing through his head. While the clothing was tattered, he easily identified the items as being a shirt, a pair of badly ripped pants, and a blouse. The blouse was easily identifiable as part of a Confederate uniform. "Perhaps this soldier was a Confederate officer? I doubt too many regular soldiers wore this type of blouse." Then, despite the many dead bodies he had handled at the various crime scenes he had supervised, Paul felt a chill run down his back as he began to inspect the items even closer.

Starting with the pants, besides noticing one of the pant legs had been slit open from the bottom of the leg to almost up to the knee area, Paul found nothing except for one long bone which had gotten caught inside one of the legs. Reaching inside the pant leg, he simply pulled the bone out and set it off to the side for the time being. After realizing the pants had no pockets to them, he placed them next to the bone he found. Then he picked up the tattered remains of a shirt, one which still had two buttons sewn on it. After looking at it for a couple of moments, he set the shirt aside as well.

As Paul placed the shirt down on the ground, he then remembered as these items had fallen on him something fairly hard had struck his head when he was attempting to back out of the tree. Looking around on the ground he tried to identify what had struck him, but he could not tell for sure what it was.

Now turning his attention to the uniform blouse, Paul saw it was in relatively good shape except for three small holes in the left shoulder area. Over the years it had become stained from insect droppings and was covered to a large extent with bits of tree bark and dead insects. Looking at the small holes gave him the impression they likely had been caused by insects eating away at the cloth. As he picked the blouse up off the ground, besides seeing it was also covered with almost one hundred and fifty years of windblown dust, he sensed it weighed far more than what it should. He quickly realized the blouse was about to reveal items which had been hidden within it since the day the soldier climbed up into the tree. Reaching into the partially torn left exterior pocket, one still fastened shut by a button; Paul found three ten-dollar gold coins, each of them minted in 1861. The shock of the discovery stunned him. The coins were in excellent condition, but obviously dirty from their time being hidden in the blouse. Carefully he placed the coins in the left front pocket of the beige cargo shorts he was wearing. "What else could be hidden in the other pockets I wonder? More coins perhaps?" Checking the right front exterior pocket he found nothing.

Reaching into the left interior pocket of the blouse, Paul removed a dirt-stained brownish colored liquor bottle. Briefly examining the bottle gave him the thought it looked to be one that had once held about a pint of liquid. Remarkably the flask style bottle still had the cork in its neck. Shaking the bottle caused him to hear something inside of it, but he made no immediate effort to open it. Carefully he placed the bottle on top of the pants lying on the ground by his feet. Resuming his search of the blouse pockets, he found another bottle inside the right interior pocket. This bottle was slightly larger than the first one. While stained and faded from time, it appeared to have been bluish green in its original color. Looking at the bottle, he saw it had some type of cloth stuck into its fairly wide neck, apparently replacing the original cork that likely had been lost. As with the first bottle, Paul also detected something was inside the second bottle when he shook it, but again made no attempt to look inside it.

Next Paul picked up what appeared to be the remnants of the soldier's hat, but it was in such bad condition that he was not even sure it was a hat he was looking at. "I want to say it looks like a kepi hat. I know Confederate officers wore them during the war, but it's in terrible shape. I'm really not even sure if this is a hat or not." He placed the hat on the ground and then picked up the pants again. As he looked at the pants, Paul saw there was no belt that went with it. "Had some of the rope been used as a belt I wonder?"

The object he immediately took an interest in was the soldier's saber that now lay on the ground near the base of the tree. As he picked the saber up, he saw it had remained in very good condition. Paul's first impression, due to the size of the saber, was it appeared to be the type a cavalry officer would have used during the war. "When I first knelt down I did not see this saber, I only saw the bayonet. So where did the saber come from? Was it hanging inside the tree or was it stuck inside the soldier's pants?" Then he realized the saber did not have a scabbard with it. He again felt a chill go down his neck. "If this saber had been hanging somehow inside this tree it could have fallen at anytime and gone through the back of my neck when I was kneeling inside the tree. Then what would I have done?" That scary thought stayed with him for several minutes as he counted his blessings over his continued good fortune. As he counted his blessings, he wondered if the saber had been the object that had hit him on the back of the head when the bones and clothing had fallen on him. He quickly realized how close he had come to possibly suffering a serious injury.

Finished examining what he found, Paul sat back down on the ground to think about his discovery. As he did, he again briefly wondered if he should call the authorities to report his findings. Pushing his thought aside, he realized this had been a chance discovery which many people, including himself, would never have believed was possible. His thoughts then turned back to the soldier whose skull and bones were now lying on the ground around him. "Who was this soldier and why did he hide inside this tree? I wonder what unit he was with and what he was doing out here in what looks to be the middle of nowhere?" As he pondered his many thoughts, he realized he had found a bayonet and a saber, but had not found any type of firearm or any parts of one. "Could it still be inside the tree or did he discard it before he took refuge within the tree?" As he sat there pondering his many questions, his eyes focused on what he thought was one of the soldier's femur bones, the bone he had pulled out of one of the pant legs minutes earlier.

Picking up the long bone, he casually inspected its two ends. As his hands cradled the bone, he felt a smooth object stuck in the middle of it. Turning the bone over to look at what his hands had first detected, Paul could see a small round object had penetrated the bone before becoming lodged in it. Around the object he saw several small radial fractures in the bone, each approximately one inch in length. As he looked closer, he could only see the top of the round object as the majority of it was embedded deep within the bone. His first thought was to try and pry the object out of the bone, but then his law enforcement training kicked in and he resisted the urge to do so. "If this really is a Confederate soldier, could this object be a minie ball he had been shot with so many years ago? Was the reason he was resting, or possibly hiding inside the tree, was because he had been shot?" The totality of his discovery continued to raise more questions than he could logically deal with in one afternoon.

The loud exhaust sound made by a large boat moving quickly nearby on the river snapped Paul back into a clearer mindset from the thoughts he had been having regarding the dead soldier. Now he realized he needed to make a decision on what to do with what he had found. "Should I just keep a few of these items for myself and then put the rest of them back inside the tree?" It was a question he immediately felt guilty about asking himself. Just as quickly as he asked himself the question, he was kicking himself for even thinking along those lines. He knew that was not what he was going to do with the items he had found. Believing for some unknown reason he had been selected to find these remains, Paul knew he had to do the right thing. That meant telling someone about what he found. But he also knew he was now curious about what he had found. The thought of uncovering something special from the past tickled his still keen investigative instincts. He just needed time, and some of the clues he had found, to help him find the answers to the thoughts he was now just starting to put together.

Picking up the skull and the bones, he placed them all, except the bone with the apparent minie ball still stuck in it, back inside the base of the tree. Along with those items, he also placed a piece of the rotted rope, the decayed hat, and the apparent sole of a boot. Paul then covered them with leaves to make it look like he had never been there.

Paul decided he would return the following morning with a flashlight to investigate the inside of the tree even further. He was sure the tree had not yet given up all of her secrets. After that he would decide who to call to report what he had found. As a Civil War buff, he wanted to make sure this soldier finally received a proper burial. Leaving the soldier's remains within a hollowed out tree was totally unacceptable. He did not yet know who he would call, but he knew he would make sure this soldier was properly laid to rest.

As he gathered up the bayonet, the sword, the femur bone, and the soldier's other belongings, including the two bottles he found within the blouse, Paul started to make his way back to his boat. As he did, he looked over his shoulders several times to make sure no one had been watching him. He could sense that his heart was beating almost as fast as his brain was racing. Both were trying to process what he had stumbled across. "What the hell have I found?" It was a question he repeated to himself several times during the afternoon.

As he walked to where his boat was tied up, he found himself repeatedly checking his pocket to make sure he had not dropped any of the gold coins he found. Climbing onto the boat, Paul feared someone at the marina might see what he had found. As he tried to figure out how to hide the items he had found, he spied his new Igloo cooler. After draining the ice and water from his cooler, he placed the items inside the cooler to keep them from being seen. Not wanting any moisture to further damage the blouse, he took the time to wrap it inside the plastic bag he received when he purchased his drinks at a nearby Kangaroo Express Mini-Mart that morning. He did his best to hide the saber from view by wrapping it in the beach towel he had brought with him. Satisfied he had done his best to hide everything from view, and now perspiring heavily under the hot summer sun, he grabbed a cold bottle of water and sat down under the boat's canopy, relaxing for the first time in a couple of hours.

"Hey, boy, whatcha all doin' over there?" A loud voice nearby yelled out.

The gruff voice startled him as he sat relaxing on the boat, his eyes closed as he drank the cold bottle of water. Quickly sitting up, Paul saw the small green and brown camouflaged colored *War Eagle* fishing boat first; then his eyes focused on the male operator. The operator was standing up as he steered the small fishing boat closer to his. He could see no one else was in the small boat. In his haste to hide what he found, Paul had not taken the time to see if any other boats had been present and now one was. He quickly became upset with himself for not taking the time to look. As the boat got closer, he recognized the operator to be the same guy who had been with Chubby at the diner, the one who had glared at him. "Great, just what I need. Some pain in the butt poking around seeing what I'm up to. I need to get rid of this jerk real quick."

"What's that?" Paul yelled back at Swamp. It was the name Betty had referred to him as.

As the small boat drifted closer to his, Paul saw Swamp had been trolling along the shore with two fishing lines running off the back of his boat. He was using his electric MotorGuide motor as he fished and not the Yamaha 50 horsepower motor mounted on the back of the boat. The electric motor allowed Swamp to troll without scaring the fish. It had also allowed him to approach Paul's boat without being heard. Swamp then hollered to him again, asking him if he was having problems with his boat.

"Nope, no problems with either the boat or the motor, it's running just fine."

As Swamp's boat drifted closer to his, Paul saw Swamp was sizing him up. "Well, y'all ain't hunting then in there is you? That's illegal you know."

"Nope, I'm not hunting or fishing. I'm just relaxing on the boat, enjoying a bottle of water and having something to eat. That's not a problem for you, or is it?" The last part of Paul's response was meant to be as sarcastic as it sounded. Now he turned away, hoping Swamp would get the message that he did not care to prolong the conversation any longer. Paul also could not help but think Swamp was someone who really did not care what the laws were when it came to hunting and fishing. Silently he thought, "Like you've never broken the law regarding fishing or hunting too early, or too late in the season, you fat bastard."

"Well, alright then."

Swamp slowly began to move his boat back down the river and away from where Paul's boat was still tied up. As he did, Paul chuckled at his thought of

Swamp's likely disregard for hunting and fishing laws as on the right rear of his unwanted visitor's boat he saw a South Carolina DNR sticker displayed. The *'Stop Game and Fish Violators – Call Operation Game Thief'* sticker was a nice touch he thought, but by the looks of him Paul's impression was he likely fit the mold of being one of the area's bigger violators rather than that of an enforcer of the South Carolina hunting and fishing laws. As he watched Swamp move away down river, Paul's law enforcement training kicked in again. "Call it profiling or call it whatever, but that guy is bad news." He now knew Betty had been right when she referred to Swamp *'as a pain in the ass'*. He had been all of that for sure.

After waiting a few minutes to make sure Swamp had left the area, Paul untied the boat and headed back to the marina. As he did, he started to put a game plan together for the following day when he planned on returning back to where he had found the soldier. "First thing is to head home so I can look over the items I have in the cooler. Then I need to head over to Wal-Mart and get a good flashlight, or maybe even a portable spotlight, so I can have something to look up into the tree with tomorrow." Still having the feeling the tree might be hiding other items inside of it, and not wanting to leave anything behind, Paul continued to wonder if he had missed any other items which might have been hidden under the layers of leaves accumulated in the tree and on the ground. As he steered towards the boat launch, he had another thought about what he needed to bring with him the following morning. "Perhaps I also need to bring a metal detector with me."

* * * * * *

On a blanket that covered the top of a small folding table in his garage, Paul laid out the items he found. Deep in thought as he sat by the table examining the gold coins, he was startled by the noise that came from his Stanley garage door opener. The garage door opening signaled Donna's arrival home. Looking up at the battery operated clock on his garage wall, he realized he had simply lost track of time as he looked over the femur bone and the other items. "This is the second time today I have been spooked. I hate when that happens." As Donna got out of her car, he quickly covered the items on the table with two beach towels which had been drying on a rack in the garage.

Between the many unpacked moving boxes that remained in the garage, as well as the folding table which was now set up there, Donna was forced to park outside. Waving to him as she exited her car, she soon entered the garage carrying her belongings. Donna had barely gotten into the garage when Paul already had the garage door going down. Now he walked over to the refrigerator running near the folding table and grabbed two cold cans of Coors Light.

Donna was surprised Paul had been in the garage when the door opened and was even more surprised when he closed it so quickly. "Why did you close the garage door so quickly? Are you afraid of the neighbors seeing us having a beer together?"

"No, not really, just thought we could use a little privacy right now." Pain said as a grin creased his face.

Putting her pocketbook and the rest of her belongings down on a couple of cardboard boxes, she asked Paul about his first ride on the boat. "So tell me, how was the first day out on the boat? Did it go OK? Did you have any surprises?"

Paul's somewhat sarcastic reply followed his first swig of beer. "Surprises? Yeah, I guess that's what I had today. Surprise is definitely a good word for what happened to me today."

"So what happened? Tell me." Then Donna saw the towels covering up the objects Paul had found earlier in the day. "Hey, what's on the table under the beach towels?"

Telling Donna he had a surprise for her, Paul made her close her eyes; instructing her to hold her hands out in front of her. As she did, he turned over one of the beach towels and picked up the gold coins he had found. After placing a coin in each of her hands, he told her to open her eyes. Paul held the third coin in the palm of his opened left hand.

"Are these real? Where'd they come from?" Donna asked as she looked at each of the coins in her hands before taking the third coin from Paul's hand. Quickly she bombarded him with questions as she looked over each of the coins, but each time he attempted to answer one of them she would ask him another one. Growing frustrated by the number of questions being asked of him, and not being able to get a word in to answer any of them, Paul grabbed two plastic lawn chairs and placed them next to the folding table.

After taking another long swig on his beer, Paul placed the can down on the garage floor. He then told Donna to just sit and listen to what he had to say. "Honey, the coins are only part of what I found today. To be honest, I still don't know what it is I've found, but it's already becoming a great story." He spent the next several minutes piecing together what had occurred earlier in the day. As he told her what he had found, Donna sat quiet, just listening as the events of the day were told to her. Stunned by what she was hearing, she sat in the chair with her mouth wide open at times as she digested what Paul was telling her. When he finished telling her the story, Donna placed the coins down on the table and took the biggest gulp of beer she had ever taken.

Reaching over to the table, Paul pulled the two towels off the other items they had covered. While Donna was taken back by the sight of the minie ball that was lodged in the bone, she found the other items fabulous to hold and touch.

"Donna, think about this while you are looking at these items. Besides me, you are the only person who has seen and touched these items in almost one hundred and fifty years. Kind of freaky, huh?"

"Kind of? It most definitely is that."

Paul then told her of his plans to go back to the site the following day so he could inspect the area for any other items he may have missed. When he finished, he swore her to secrecy about his plans and jokingly threatened to place her within the same tree if she gave up his secret. Laughing at his threat, Donna promised not to tell anyone about what he had found.

"I can't wait to see what you find tomorrow, and to see how all of this plays out. This is fascinating stuff!" She then asked him the obvious question surrounding the discovery of the two bottles. "Something is definitely inside these bottles. What do you think it is?"

"I don't know. I haven't really had time to think about it. Good question though, but that's going to have to wait for now." Paul was beyond tired from the events of the day. While he was tempted to try and open the bottles, he knew they would have to wait until he was ready to open them properly. Securing all of the items he found during the day, Paul placed them inside one of the moving boxes that had already been unpacked. Hidden away from the other items, the saber was placed inside a large coat box that had yet to be unpacked. The only items he did not pack into the boxes were the gold coins. Sealing the box up, a box which had been marked as '*Kitchen items*', he mixed it within the other boxes they still had to unpack. As he did, he had one last thought. "No one's going to find these items in all of this mess."

Later that evening, Paul and Donna took a ride to the Wal-Mart in nearby Surfside Beach. It was one of several in the area, but it was the closest one to their home. Once there, Paul picked up the few items he needed for his return trip back to mystery tree the following day. After getting what he needed, they stopped and picked up the pizza they had ordered from a Pizza Hut restaurant on Highway 17. As they drove home, with the three gold coins still in his pants pocket, they could not stop laughing when they thought about the pizza and beer they would be having for their dinner. With the three gold coins in their possession, they realized they should have been able to afford a couple of steaks for dinner, but neither of them had the energy to cook. Pizza and beer would work out just great for them. As they pulled into their driveway, Paul jokingly asked Donna what the change would have amounted to if he had paid for their pizza with one of the ten-dollar gold coins.

* * * * * *

The three gold coins were just the beginning.

8

The Mission Begins.

*"I am willing to serve my country, but do not wish to
sacrifice the brave men under my command."*
Major General John Buford, USA

Captain Francis watched from the train station's platform as his men loaded the
rail cars with their horses and gear. As he watched them work, he reached into
one of the pockets of his uniform blouse and pulled out the pocket watch his
father had presented to him three years ago as a Christmas present. Turning the
watch over before checking the time, he ran his right thumb over the initials
'JF', initials his father had engraved on the cover. He often found himself
rubbing the initials and he knew he did so to remind him of his parents back
home. It had been almost two years since he had last seen them. He longed to
see them again. Opening the watch he saw it was 5:15 pm. "Forty-five minutes
to go before we move out." As he closed it, Francis went over the details of the
trip in his mind, hoping things would go as planned and hoping the money
would be delivered to Atlanta without incident.

After he closed his watch for the third time within the last hour, Francis
reinspected the contents of the rail cars to make sure they had been properly
secured. He wanted no last minute problems holding up their departure.
When he first inspected the Conestoga wagons, making sure they had been
tied down properly so they would not move when the train pulled out, he had
not attempted to open any of the hidden compartments as he feared some of
the gold would fall out. During this inspection he noticed the bottoms of the
wagons, which in some cases were actually the bottoms of some of the hidden
compartments, had pitch placed between all of the wooden joints to protect the
gold and silver from the elements they would be facing. He now took note of
the ample supply of provisions the Quartermaster's Office had provided them
with. "All we will seem to need is beef. It looks like they have us well-supplied
for the start of our mission with everything else." Finishing his inspection, he
silently wondered how well the Quartermaster's Office had done supplying
them with extra rifles and ammunition, but then he saw they had even taken
care of that need as well.

Francis knew the Conestoga wagons, from the precious cargo, as well as
from the supplies they each carried, were likely at their weight capacity for
what the wagon's axles and wheels could carry. While they had been built to

carry several thousands of pounds, he wondered how the horses would hold up pulling these heavy wagons on the rough and muddy roads they would have to travel over when they experienced problems with the railroads. As he completed his inspection, Francis prayed both the wagons and the horses would hold up to the demands of the difficult trip they were about to make.

As part of his preparation for the ride on the train, Francis made sure his men had watered and fed their horses. Earlier, he had made sure his men had eaten a meal before the train moved out. Now it was his turn to do the same. Sitting down in the railroad stationmaster's office, he looked over the meal Captain White had sent over for him. Before eating his meal of fried chicken and baked potatoes, Francis bowed his head and prayed for the safety of his men. *"Lord, I hope these men, men whose names I barely know, have the courage to face the unknown that is about to confront us. I pray for their safe return, and of mine, so we may be reunited with our families when this terrible war is over with."* As he finished his short prayer, he had one final thought before he ate. "I cannot let President Davis, General Lee, or my father down. I must not fail them." Quietly eating his meal, he read the letters Davis and Memminger had written in his behalf. Soon finished with his meal, he placed his copies of both letters into an inside pocket of his uniform blouse, and then placed the rest of the letters back into his haversack. Leaving the small office, he walked to the front of the train and spoke with the engineer about the route they would be taking.

As the train slowly began pulling out of the station, its wheels slipping at first on the tracks, but then finally gaining both traction and speed, it moved out of the rail yard and began the first leg of their journey south towards Atlanta. As the train soon crossed over the James River, Francis knew there would be no turning back. With the train gradually increasing its speed, he gathered his men in one of the boxcars as he wanted to briefly speak with them. He did so as he wanted them to know what their assignments were going to be in the event they had to move the wagons off the trains and start moving over land. Now he carefully advised each of the men what their assignments would be. Some would be wagon drivers, some would be scouts, and some would ride alongside the wagons protecting the gold and silver in the event a problem occurred. With the assignments soon made, he now deployed his men so the entire train was under guard. Outside of the precious cargo they now were responsible for, the train carried only mail and other war materials southbound from Richmond.

As his men moved out to the positions they had been assigned, Francis was approached by a very remorseful Sgt. Vane. He again expressed his regret to Francis for his earlier conduct. "Sergeant, as long as you have learned from your mistake, and you assure me your conduct will be exemplary for the rest of the mission, then I will accept your apology. I will consider the matter closed and we will not speak on it again. However, and remember this, I will not tolerate any kind of challenge to my authority again. Understood?"

"Yes, sir. Captain, I ain't looking for any problems. I'm truly sorry, sir."

As they continued to talk, Francis learned Vane had worked on one of the railroads in Georgia before the war. Taking advantage of his previous railroad experience, Francis deployed Vane to ride with the train's engineer so he could get word back to him if a problem occurred. As Francis explained this to him, he also told Vane he wanted him to ride up front with the engineer and the brakeman so he could also keep an eye out for any sabotage efforts done by the Union army to the tracks.

"Don't worry none, captain. I'll keep a close eye out." Vane confidently offered as he began moving to his position in the front of the train.

The train had moved slowly south along the tracks for almost two hours when Francis finally was comfortable knowing everything that had to be done had been. Climbing from one slow moving rail car to the other, he reached an open rail car with one of the Conestoga wagons on it. As he jumped down into the rail car, he saw Sgt. Edward Odom, a tall and lanky Alabama country boy from outside of Mobile, standing guard. Even though he had only known his fellow sergeants for a few hours, Odom had already acquired the nickname of 'Big Ed' due to his stature. He was at least six inches taller than most of the other men. After briefly speaking with Odom, Francis climbed up into the wagon, found a blanket and then sat down, preparing to take a brief nap while he could. Before falling asleep, he again pulled his pocket watch out to check the time. As he placed the watch back into his pocket, his thoughts returned to the trip they were taking down the rail lines. "Hopefully we can stay on schedule. I want to get back to the army and to the men in my unit so we can help win this war." As his thoughts played out in his head, his mind began to race. "Should I be planning an alternate route of travel in the event we have problems with the train, or with Yankee sabotage, or should I just deal with problems as they arise?" Realizing these were issues out of his control, and that he would have to deal with problems when they arose, he tried falling asleep. "I will just have to adapt to the problems as they occur. I'm praying we can just make our first connection with the East Tennessee & Georgia Railroad, that would at least get us started off well." Closing his eyes, Francis soon fell asleep on top of the gold and silver hidden below him in the wagon.

As he slept, the early evening sky displayed a bright red sun as it started to go down for the day. The red sun gave every indication the following day would be just as hot as this day had been. Soon the sun faded out of view; the sky gradually giving way to total darkness. As day turned to night, Francis still catnapped in the back of the wagon as the train moved through the Virginia countryside under a full moon and a sky full of bright stars.

Then, without the slightest bit of warning, the peaceful ride they had been enjoying abruptly ended. As the train made its way down a slight grade and then began to navigate a turn, the train's engine, *The Lady Richmond*, jumped the tracks that had been sabotaged earlier in the day by Yankee troops. Despite the brightness of the full moon there had been no time for either the train's engineer or brakeman, or even for Sgt. Vane, to see the tracks had been damaged. The sharp curve in the tracks had given them little chance to see what lay ahead as they approached the damaged rails. The Yankees had picked the perfect spot to inflict their damage.

As the train derailed from the sabotaged tracks, its speed from going down the grade of the small hill caused the out of control engine to strike several large trees as it continued off the western edge of the tracks. As it struck the final tree, the train's engine and fuel car came to a vicious and abrupt stop. Stopping abruptly caused the train's fuel car, filled with wood for the trip, to violently slam into the rear of the engine. Wood from the fuel car now flew forward into the engine car. Despite leaving the tracks, and despite both cars striking each other, the train's engine and fuel car both managed to remain upright.

The derailment caused the rest of the rail cars to separate from the train's engine and fuel car. It also caused both men and horses to be knocked off their feet. At first, the only injuries were thought to have been a broken left leg and a broken left wrist that were sustained by Sgt. Edward Hatfield. He was from Florida and had been in the army for over two years without suffering a scratch during the several battles he had fought in. Now he was seriously injured after riding in the relative safety of a rail car. After Francis and his men finished checking on everyone who had been in the rail cars, they moved to check on the three men in the train's first two cars. As they did, they quickly located the crushed and mangled bodies of Sgt. Vane and the train's engineer. Both had been killed instantly when wood used to fuel the train had flown forward into the engine compartment. Both men had sustained significant injuries to their head and chest areas. As Francis found these two men, his men soon found the brakeman's body. He had died after being thrown from the train when it struck the last tree. The mission was barely three hours old and Francis already had his first casualties. It would prove to be a sign of things to come.

As Francis had checked on Vane, some of the others already started to spread out in the woods around the train in the event Union troops were preparing to attack them. They had done this even before they were given the order to do so. The Virginia sergeants, who had already seen enough fighting in the war, had learned what to do from listening to stories told back home. They were stories which had been handed down through the generations regarding the fighting done during the Revolutionary War. They now reacted to what had to be done without being told. When Francis saw the steps they were taking to protect the others, he gave them each a nod of approval for knowing what had to be done.

Out of fear that Union troops might still be in the woods around the wrecked train, Francis kept his four Virginia sergeants on alert in the woods. They would be his eyes and ears, sounding the alarm if they saw any suspicious activity. He then ordered the others to start off-loading the train as he knew they would have to move over land until he could find the next train station.

It took over three hours to fell the trees needed to make ramps so the wagons and horses could be carefully off-loaded from the train, but they did so without any further problems and without any signs of Union troops. As the train was being off-loaded, Francis silently wondered about the damage that had been done to the railroad tracks. "Was this done because they wanted to just disrupt the railroad from being able to move supplies along the lines or do they already know about the gold and silver we are moving? The Union has spies everywhere. Could they have been at the Richmond train station? If they do know what we have, why have they not attacked us while we're so unprepared to repel such an attack?" These thoughts and many others like them would race through his mind for the rest of the night.

There was no time to bury Vane and the other two men, but Francis saw to it their bodies were wrapped in blankets and then placed inside one of the rail cars. He identified Vane's body with a brief note he left in one of his shirt pockets. After saying a quick prayer for Vane and the other men, Francis gave the order to move the wagons south and away from the wrecked train. As they moved out, he hoped somewhere close was a doctor they could find so the injuries sustained by Hatfield could be treated properly. For now he would have to endure the pain he was experiencing with his broken leg. While he was concerned about Hatfield's injuries, Francis' main concern now was putting distance between them and the wrecked train. As they moved south, each bump the wagon hit that carried the injured Sgt. Hatfield caused him to cry out in pain.

As soon as Francis knew they were out of immediate danger, he deployed Sgt. Stine and Sgt. Griffin to be his eyes and ears out in front of the wagons. He also deployed Sgt. George James, a Louisiana lumberman by trade, to do the same in the rear of the wagon train; one now formed out of necessity. Knowing the wagon train was being protected somewhat by the three scouts, Francis then sent Sgt. Micah Steele, a twenty-one year old Mississippi fisherman, to ride out in front of the others, instructing him to find a doctor or a plantation where they might find some medical care for Hatfield. "If you find help, I want you to report back to me immediately. Do not approach anyone about Hatfield's injuries without me being there."

"Yes, sir!" Steele was quickly out of sight as he rode off into the darkness of the Virginia night.

Riding his horse in front of the lead wagon, Francis decided he needed to get word back to Memminger to tell him about the train wreck and the change to his plans. Locating Sgt. Davis, he instructed him to ride back to Richmond and to personally tell Memminger what had happened. "Make sure you tell him we are moving south over land for now. Most importantly, assure him the gold and silver is safe, but tell him about Vane and the others. Tell him I would consider it a personal favor if he would see to it that Vane was buried properly. After you tell him what has happened, get back to me as fast as possible. I am relying on you Virginia men to help me complete this mission."

"Sir, I will be back as soon as I can. I promise I will find you. Make no mistake about that. Them Yankees got me upset now for what they did to that Georgia boy back there. I'm afixin' to get even with them." With that, Davis rode off to Richmond to tell Memminger what had happened.

It was close to midnight as the wagons moved south under a bright full moon. As they did, each man reacted to the noises they heard in the woods, fully expecting the noises to be made by Union troops riding out to attack them. It took some time, but finally these country boys who made up Francis' unit settled down and their years of living in the woods back home allowed them to easily identify the noises emanating in the night.

They moved south for another hour, moving slowly along a narrow country road at times and at other times through open fields before Francis had them stop to rest. As the men rested, he tried to get his bearings from a map he had been given back in Richmond. They had only been stopped for about ten minutes when the alarm was spread that riders were heard approaching from the south. As they took up defensive positions around the wagons, a voice they recognized as belonging to Sgt. Steele could be heard. "Boys, don't do no shootin'! It's just me, Micah! We're coming in!" Sgt. Griffin had returned with him.

Dismounting his horse, Steele advised Francis he had located a small plantation with several outbuildings and three barns about four miles southeast of where they were stopped. "I was real quiet like, no one heard me. I got so close to the house, I could even see a candle burning in one of the upstairs windows." The news pleased Francis as now something positive had happened. He hoped Hatfield would soon be treated for his injuries as he knew it had been a tough ride for him to have endured with a bone protruding from his broken leg.

* * * * * *

Francis signaled the wagons to come to a halt when they had gotten to about three hundred yards away from the small home. It was obviously the home of the plantation owner. As he approached the home on foot, accompanied by Sgt. Steele and Sgt. Gerald Rickert, Francis saw through an open window that a candle softly illuminated one of the upstairs bedrooms. The house was quiet and they could see no movement from within as they approached near the front door.

Instead of trying to wake the occupants by knocking on what appeared to be the main door of the house, Francis elected to call out to them instead. He did so as he thought it was safer to wake them up from a distance than to be standing on the plantation's front porch and being shot at by a startled homeowner, woken in the middle of the night by strangers. He woke them after only two loud calls to the house.

After getting the attention of the sleeping occupants, Francis identified himself to them and told them of the injuries sustained by one of his men. In a few moments the front door opened and he was greeted by a woman who appeared to be in her late forties. "Ma'am, thank you for helping us. One of my men is hurt real bad and needs more help than we can give him. Is there a doctor nearby?"

A widow for several years, Mary Charles was the owner of the small plantation; living there now with just her young daughter. She had become a fierce supporter of the Confederate cause over the past two years. Her husband had died years earlier and now she carried the pain of only recently learning of the death of one of her three sons. He had been killed during the Battle of Funkstown, during Lee's retreat south from Gettysburg. Her other two boys were serving in the Army of Northern Virginia, but she did not know where they currently were. As Francis talked to her, he brought a smile to her worn face when he told her he and four of his men were native Virginians.

"Captain, you bring that boy in the house. I will have the parlor table cleaned off. No sense carrying him upstairs, him being hurt and all. If the damn Yankees did this to him I want to help!" Seeing the late night commotion had woken a couple of her slaves, who were now standing in the yard near the front door, Mary quickly barked orders to 'Big Richard' and his wife, Tika. "Big Richard, come in here and help me move the parlor furniture. Tika, get some water boiling and get some bandages ready. Rip those old sheets up that we've got stored in the closet." As Mary turned to walk back into the house, Francis heard her mutter three words. "Damn Blue Bellies!"

After Hatfield had been carried into the house and placed on the parlor table, Francis again asked Mary about a doctor. "Captain, I've worked this plantation with my dear departed husband, with my three boys, and now with just my daughter, for many a year. With the help of our slaves, I've done so for over twenty years, started it from nothing. At one time or another they all have had broken legs, arms, fingers, and, Lord knows, much worse. With Tika's help, and with the help of the good Lord, I have always got them back on their feet somehow. Didn't need a damn doctor then and I don't need one now. Now listen here young fella, I'm sure you are an important man and all, but right now you and your men are in our way. Y'all need to get out of our way so we can take care of this boy. Now scat!" As he turned to leave, Francis could not help but smile. They had found the help they needed in Mary Charles.

With Hatfield being tended to, Francis focused on his other men and the sleep they needed. After Big Richard showed him the insides of each barn, Francis had the wagons brought into the barns as by now the sky had clouded over. Off in the distance lighting could be seen in the sky. After the wagons had been secured inside the barns, and the horses secured within two adjoining fenced in corrals, Francis went back to check on Hatfield.

Keeping his distance from Mary, Francis saw Hatfield's broken leg had already been placed in a crude splint. She was just finishing tending to his broken left wrist. As she continued to treat Hatfield's injuries, Francis spoke to her. "Mrs. Charles, my men need a meal and some sleep. They are likely not going to be enjoying a good hot meal for several days. We have the rations and provisions to make a fine meal with, which we are pleased to share with you, but we need to use your kitchen. If we …" He was cut off in mid-sentence by her.

"What kind of a host do y'all think I am?" She did not wait for Francis to reply. "I already have Tika and my daughter in the kitchen starting to cook. Give her whatever food y'all can spare and they will get it cooked for you. I ain't having our boys leave my home without getting a good home-cooked meal. Lord only knows when their next one will be." Directing her attention to two of Francis' men, she barked her next orders at them. "Now you boys do what you can to set up a place to eat in the backroom off the kitchen. I ain't having y'all eat in the barn, but mind my clean floors, ya hear?"

Francis again smiled as he knew Mary was more than likely a lot less gruff than what she showed to them. Her feelings for his men gave away how her heart felt for the strangers who were soldiers just like her sons.

When the meal was finally ready, Francis had his men rotate in from guard duty in the barn so they could eat. As they enjoyed their meal, they could now see rain and lighting was moving into the area, cooling the night off as it did. After they had eaten, they took turns sleeping on the floors within Mary's home. As they slept, the rain grew harder and harder.

Sgt. Mark Foster, who had been a teacher in the hills of Tennessee prior to the war, was woken up by Francis around four in the morning so he could relieve Sgt. Steele. He had been on guard duty in the barns while the others slept. After putting his boots back on, Foster grudgingly walked the short distance to the barns through the rain, leaving behind the comfort of the warm dry place he had found in Mary's parlor. In minutes, he was running back to the house.

"Captain! Captain Francis . . . the wagon . . . one of the wagons is gone . . . and Steele . . . he's hurt right bad!" Waking up from the alarm Foster had sounded, Francis and his men were out the door and into the barn in no time.

Inside the biggest of the three barns they found the wooden slat they had secured the large double barn doors with now lying on the ground. Nearby they found Steele unconscious and lying in a pool of his own blood. The back of his head had been partially caved in by a piece of wrought iron which now lay on the ground next to his almost lifeless body. It was a horrible injury for the others to see. It was one Steele never saw coming. By now, Mary had come into the barn; kneeling down, she carefully inspected the injury to Steele's head. Seeing the extent of it caused her to start crying as it was obvious how bad the injury was. Her tears confirmed to the others the seriousness of Steele's injury.

"Captain, look here!"

Sgt. Banks, who was standing outside of the now opened barn doors with a lighted torch in his left hand, was the first to see them. "Look here! There are at least four, maybe five sets of footprints in the mud." Pointing to the muddy ground, he showed the others what he also saw left in the mud. "See here, there's the tracks left by the wagon."

Staring at the muddy tracks, Francis tried remembering what was in the stolen wagon, but his mind had trouble focusing on anything except for the terrible injury that had been inflicted upon Steele. Looking around, he saw the Conestoga wagon with the stars painted on it was still in the barn. He quickly realized whoever had stolen one of the other wagons had likely done so for the food provisions stored within it. While the stolen wagon had gold and silver coins secreted within it, it fortunately did not have as much as the one Francis knew was the most important one. He quickly breathed a sigh of relief after realizing the wagon with the stars painted on it had not been the one stolen.

"Captain, we's going after them, ain't we?" Banks anxiously asked as he continued to stare at the muddy tracks that had been left for them to follow.

The question brought Francis' mind back to full attention and he soon had Steele carried into Mary's parlor so she could do whatever she could for him. After posting a guard on the barns, he had the others saddle up their horses to go after the stolen wagon. He kept a guard on the buildings as he did not know if whoever had stolen the wagon would be greedy enough to come back for another one. "If they come back, don't kill them unless you have to. I want to speak to them first!" The look his men now saw in his face caused them to realize that whoever had stolen the wagon would soon wish they had not.

His men were forced to address this new problem from the deep sleep they had all been enjoying, and they were now somewhat slow in getting their horses saddled. The exception had been Sgt. Stine who had his horse saddled and ready to go in moments. When Francis saw he was already mounted, he instructed him to follow the tracks of the wagon through the mud. He also told him he and the others would be right behind him. "Wait for us before you do anything!"

As Stine raced off, Francis quickly checked on the conditions of both Hatfield and Steele. Unaware of what had happened to Steele, Hatfield was peacefully asleep. Unconscious next to him, Steele was being tended to by Mary. As she looked up to see Francis enter her parlor, the tears in her eyes told him her newest patient would likely not make it to daylight.

It did not take long for Francis and the others to locate Stine as he had been riding back to find them after locating the stolen wagon. "Captain, I ain't sure of what to make of it, but I think there are five men out there. They is just sitting around the wagon in the rain, just talking and laughing, almost as if they did not have a care in the world. It don't make sense, does it, captain? Why you gonna steal a wagon and then stop and sit around talking so close to where you stole the wagon from? It's like them boys don't care if they is caught."

After tying their horses up in a stand of trees a short distance away from where Stine had found the stolen wagon, Francis and the others walked the remaining distance. As they made their way closer to where the wagon sat, the rain that had been falling for the past couple of hours came to a stop. As they got closer, they saw the men who had stolen it were sitting around a small campfire, laughing and joking with each other just as Stine had described. As he watched them, Francis wondered if they were Confederate deserters or Yankee soldiers who had been probing the area before the main body of the Union army proceeded south. It really did not make a difference to him about who it was that had stolen the wagon as he knew he was going to get it back no matter who had taken it. As they stood in a small group of pine trees less than one hundred yards from the wagon, Francis pointed to a stone wall sitting between them and the men who had stolen it. In a low whisper he spoke to his men. "Maybe they needed the provisions that were in the wagon, but whoever they are they have something that belongs to us and we're getting it back. I don't take kindly to folks stealing from me!"

As he looked back towards the wagon, Sgt. Roy McKinney, a twenty-three year old cooper's apprentice from New Bern, North Carolina, softly told Francis what he needed to know. "Captain, I count five men over yonder and there are only four of us. Looks like the odds are in our favor." Even though the night was still partially overcast, Francis could not help but notice that McKinney was grinning at him. He knew McKinney and the others were not only looking to settle the score with the men who had stolen the wagon, but more importantly they were looking to settle the score with those who had nearly killed a fellow soldier of theirs. Despite having one less man than the group of men who stolen the wagon, McKinney and the others did not care that they were outnumbered. His men were fired up over what had happened and they were now ready to exploit the advantage they had. It was an advantage of taking the fight to a group of soldiers who were unaware of what was about to descend upon them. As he looked back at the stolen wagon, Francis had one more thought. "McKinney's right, the odds are in our favor."

Just as he was about to tell his men where he wanted them, and that he did not want them to fire their weapons until they heard him fire first, a deep and unrecognizable voice came from out of the darkness behind them. The unexpected noise the strange voice made startled them and they wheeled from where they knelt by the stone wall, pointing their guns in the direction of where it came from. Despite being seasoned hunters, as well as experienced soldiers, they had not heard anyone approach them from behind.

"Six men, theys six men down there. Don't shoot, boss, please don't shoot! I ain't with them white folks."

With his pistol in his right hand, Francis crept closer to the large black man who was behind them. He was down on all fours watching the men around the campfire. "Them men dun stole dat there wagon a short time ago from a barn. I dun seen them do it. Boss, is dat your wagon theys dun stole?" Afraid of being heard by the men who had stolen the wagon, Francis was forced to listen closely as the black man whispered softly to him. As he did, he also had to try and figure out some of the words this man used as he was difficult to understand at times.

Francis quickly learned from this man, a run-away slave by the name of Samuel, of a horrible incident he had witnessed. He told Francis that two days prior the six men had shown up at his master's plantation, one roughly twenty miles northwest of Mary's. He described how he and some of the other slaves had been returning to their cabins after working in the fields until late in the afternoon when they heard gunshots. Now crying as he described the incident, Samuel told of seeing the six men riding off after the shots had been fired within the plantation's main house. He then described running up to the main house to investigate what the shooting was about and how he had found his wife dead on the kitchen floor. He had found her with her dress pulled up around her face. "They dun had their way with my wife and then dun killed her." With the plantation owner and his family gone for the day, Samuel's wife had been alone in the kitchen preparing dinner when she was attacked by the men.

Samuel described to Francis how he had tracked these men for the past two days. He then spoke of wanting to kill them for what they had done, but feared doing so even though he knew he would have been right to do so. Samuel knew a black man who killed a white man in the South would be quickly hung for doing so, no matter how justified he was.

Already enraged by the theft of the wagon, Francis now was raging with anger from the story he had been told. "Samuel, we will take care of these men. You stay here until we are done and then you can come down to where we are. You understand me?"

"Yes, boss. Thank you, suh."

As quiet as possible, McKinney crept up to where Francis and Samuel were kneeling on the ground. Now he questioned Samuel as to where the sixth man was as he could still not see him. Samuel pointed his finger towards another small stand of pine trees that were about seventy feet away from where the wagon was sitting. "Boss, sees him right there in them trees. Looks real close, boss, I think dat man is smoking a pipe or maybe it's a cigar, buts I can sure smell dat tobacco." McKinney now looked at the trees Samuel had pointed to. As he did, he could now make out the outline of the sixth man as he appeared to lean against a tree while smoking. As he watched the man Samuel had pointed out to him, he now smelled the tobacco being smoked.

"We'll get that son of a bitch too!" Looking at Francis, McKinney told him he would take care of the soldier smoking in the tree line when they approached the stolen wagon. Quietly, Francis nodded his approval.

With his men deployed as he instructed them, Francis now crawled closer and closer to the campfire, getting to within twenty feet of the wagon. Raising his rifle, his pistol securely fastened inside his waistband, he dropped the soldier closest to him with a shot to the soldier's upper chest. The soldier who was shot had been sitting on a log near the fire and had not seen Francis until it was too late. As promised, McKinney snuck up on the sixth man and knocked him out with a savage blow to the back of the head from his rifle butt. In the brief chaos that followed, three of the men who had stolen the wagon were killed. The others were seriously wounded. All of them were soon determined to be Union deserters. When Francis had his men account for the six men they had first seen, they then realized one of the Union soldiers had gotten away in the confusion of the moment. Immediately they located a small trail of blood leading away from where the deserters had sat near the fire. It was obvious the missing soldier had been wounded during the exchange which had taken place. Francis quickly sent two of his men to search for the missing soldier.

Questioning the two deserters who were still alive, Francis learned they had jumped Steele from behind; deciding to steal the wagon after finding it contained food they desperately needed. A quick check of the wagon determined none of the secret compartments had been tampered with.

Cautiously keeping his distance, Samuel walked close to where Francis and his men stood with the two remaining deserters. Seeing him, Francis again spoke to the Union deserters. "You men have deserted your army, and you have stolen our wagon and our food. You have also crushed the skull of one of my men and I fear he shall soon die from his injury." Pointing his finger at Samuel, Francis spoke again to his prisoners. "This man here has also told me that two days ago you killed his wife after you had your way with her. What have you to say about that?"

As expected both men quickly begged for their lives while at the same time pleading for mercy as they accused their dead friends of both raping Samuel's wife and injuring Steele. "Captain, sir, we were just hungry, we just needed food. We ain't hurt no one, it was them other fellas who done all that." His eyes flashing anger, Francis scoffed at their responses.

As he finished questioning the two deserters, Sgts. Foster and Davis returned from looking for the injured soldier who had gotten away from them. "Captain, that Yankee soldier ain't gonna be stealing food from anybody else in this here life." Francis nodded to Foster that he understood what he was being told.

Following his orders, and despite their pleas for mercy, his men tied the hands of the two remaining Union deserters behind their backs and placed them on two horses. After selecting one of the pine trees present, two ropes were thrown over a sturdy limb; both were soon tied to the tree's base. Each of the other two ends of the ropes were quickly fastened into nooses and placed around the necks of the deserters. Without saying a word, Francis then smacked the backsides of both horses and the two deserters were left dangly in the early morning air, soon to be dead from broken necks. "May God have mercy on each of these Yankee bastards!" There was no need for anyone to say anything else. While it was the first hanging a couple of his men had ever witnessed, it would soon prove to be one of several they would witness. For a slave who watched from off in the shadows, it was not the first hanging he had ever witnessed. It was, however, the first time he had seen white men hung. It did not bring him any satisfaction or joy.

With the horses hitched to the wagon, Francis and his men made their way back to the Charles plantation. While he rode, Francis wondered what would have happened if they had not located the Union soldier who had gotten away. He knew that would have likely brought him a whole new host of problems. What he did not know was the dead Union soldiers would soon be found by other Union troops. That subsequent discovery would cause Union troops in the area to intensify their push south to cripple the Confederate cause.

9

The Discoveries Continue.

*"Find out where your enemy is, get at him as soon as you can
and strike him as hard as you can, and keep moving on."*
General Ulysses S. Grant, USA

The following morning Paul again put his boat into the river at the Wacca Wache Landing boat launch that he had used the previous day. As he did, he saw the only other people present were two elderly men who had just put their small aluminum fishing boat into the river. He was pleased no one else was in the area as he did not want anyone asking him why he had a metal detector on his boat that morning.

After he made his way to where he had tied his boat up the previous day, Paul waited several minutes before walking into the woods. He did so to make sure no one else was in the area. Collecting his gear, he walked to where he had made his discovery the previous day, stopping only once to again make sure no one was watching him. After reaching the tree where he found the soldier's remains, he set the metal detector and the portable battery operated spotlight he had purchased at Wal-Mart on the ground. After doing so, he checked to make sure the bones and skull remained as he had left them the previous day. After seeing they had not been moved, he carefully removed them from within the tree and placed them off to the side. After briefly taking the time to sweep away some leaves, and to make sure he had not missed anything the previous day, he went to work.

Grabbing the spotlight, Paul inched his way into the base of the tree so his back rested on the large rock. In this position he could easily see up into the hollowed section of the Live Oak. After finally getting into position, he turned the Brunkman spotlight on. It lit up the interior of the tree so he could easily see the inside of it. The interior of the massive tree was easily almost four feet in diameter in places near the base of the tree. Lying there as he moved the spotlight from side to side, his first thought was about the observation he was making. "There's plenty of room in here for someone to hide if they wanted to." As he continued to inspect the tree's interior, he could not tell if the cavity had been caused by a deformity when the tree had grown or if it had been damaged by lighting, but he easily noticed the inside was significant in size. He also noticed how rough and splintered the interior was. As his eyes scanned the now lit interior, they confirmed what he had been thinking. "Perhaps I was right yesterday; perhaps the rope and clothing had gotten hung up on some of this splintered wood. If they had gotten caught it would explain, at least to some degree it would, why the clothing had remained in decent condition for all of these years."

Paul's eyes soon noticed other pieces of frayed and rotted rope still fastened to the tree's interior. As he maneuvered his body up higher into the tree, he now looked closer at the frayed rope. "How on earth could someone have done this to make it stay here this long, especially when it's so dark in here? Could someone really have done this when they were as injured as this soldier apparently was? Remarkable!"

Scanning the rest of the tree's interior, his eyes saw only pieces of frayed rope and small swatches of cloth fibers at first, but then, partially hidden by a small piece of frayed cloth, he noticed something else. It was something hanging above where the rope had been attached to the tree. Paul started to reach for it, but then stopped. Before he did anything else, he reached into the left front pocket of his denim cargo pants and pulled out his small Sony digital camera. "If I don't take pictures of what I find, no one will ever believe that I found them inside of this tree." Slowly moving his right arm above his shoulders, he took several pictures of the rope and cloth fibers still hanging from the tree's interior. Somewhat blindly, he then took three additional pictures of the object hanging above his head. With that done, he now tried to get his right arm extended high enough to reach the object. At this point inside the tree the space diminished in size, but after two failed attempts to grab the object he finally succeeded.

Even before his eyes could tell him what the object was, his hand told him it now held a pocket watch. Slowly he crawled out of the tree to examine what he had just found. Sitting on the ground, Paul saw he had found a gold pocket watch. It had been suspended in place within the tree by the chain still affixed to it. A quick look at the watch showed it was still in relatively good condition despite the number of years it had apparently been hanging in the tree. Examining the watch closer, he could see moisture had rusted shut the hinge. The rust now prevented him from being able to open it. As he wiped away some of the grime, his fingers told him the watch had some type of engraving on its exterior. Not wanting to damage the watch, he made no further attempt to clean all of the grime off of it. As he continued to examine it, he knew the soldier had put it there but wondered why he had. "Was this put there so he knew what time it was? Was he supposed to meet someone at a particular time? Was it put there for sentimental reasons because he knew he was dying from his bullet wound? Will I ever know why it was hanging there?" He could only guess at what the answers to his questions were.

Setting the watch on the ground, and after placing the skull and other bones around it, Paul took a few additional photos for documentation purposes. After he finished, he took his handkerchief out from the right rear pocket of his pants and carefully wrapped the watch inside of it. He placed the watch into the right front pocket of his pants for safekeeping.

Picking up the White's metal detector he had rented from a local pawn shop in Murrells Inlet, Paul threw a quarter down on the ground to make sure the metal detector was sensitive enough to detect the coin. His only other experience with a metal detector had been using a friend's while looking for coins on the beach years ago. He chuckled to himself that he was again using one for the same reason, but now he was searching for coins far more valuable than the dimes and nickels he had found on the beach. After assuring himself the metal detector was functioning properly, he slowly swept it over the ground hoping the area around the tree would give up additional treasures his eyes had not detected. As he swept the ground near the base of the tree, the metal detector chirped, indicating he had found something. Another pass over the same spot had the same result, another chirp. As he looked at the metal detector's electronic display screen to see what had registered, the screen indicated the presence of a coin buried roughly three inches below the surface. Kneeling down, he first used his hands to move away some of the fallen leaves. Then, carefully using a small gardening trowel he had brought with him, he scraped away the accumulated layers of sand, soil, and mulch which years of fallen leaves had left. Carefully scraping away the soft soil, he found the first coin. Moments later, he found four others. All were identical to the previous ones he found the day before, except two of the coins had been minted in 1862. "Are there more? Could these have been in the left front pocket of the blouse I found yesterday and they fell out when the pocket's seam finally gave way?" He was again asking himself questions he had no answers for.

Moving the rock out from inside the base of the tree, in the event something had been hidden under it by the Confederate soldier, Paul swept the metal detector over the area where it had sat. The metal detector gave no indication of anything metallic being hidden there. For one reason, he then placed the rock back within the base of the tree. As he did, he continued to ponder questions he simply had no answers for. "If he did place this rock here so he could hide up in the tree, who was this soldier hiding from and who was chasing him? Could it really have been Union soldiers?"

Already calculating what needed to be done, he then placed several items, including one gold coin, back into the base of the tree. From his previous career, Paul knew crime scenes were often staged to fool the police; now he staged the scene within the base of the tree for the same reason. Knowing he was going to call the authorities regarding this find, he knew the discovery of a gold coin amongst the items he had placed there would make the scene more likely to be considered real and untouched by the detectives handling the investigation. While he was confident the likelihood of anyone asking him any really hard questions was pretty remote, he still took the time to carefully stage the scene to minimize any questions being asked of him.

For now, Paul decided he would keep the watch, the coins, and the items he had previously discovered as his instincts told him there was still more to this story that needed uncovering. Until he had the answers to his questions, he could justify keeping what he had found. At least to himself he could. How he would later explain to the authorities why he had kept them was another matter he did not have an answer for as of yet.

* * * * * *

Several years earlier Paul had attended a law enforcement management session at the FBI National Academy, in Quantico, Virginia. Held four times a year, these sessions teach law enforcement executives management skills they might not learn elsewhere. One of the benefits in attending one of these sessions is it allows attendees to establish working relationships with other cops from across the country, and from across the world. However, like many others, after being at the National Academy for just a couple of weeks, Paul quickly realized the NA had actually stood for *'Never Again'* as the time spent away from family and work was a true hardship to endure. Even the massive quantities of beer that was consumed nightly in *The Board Room Bar* did little to make his time away from home bearable. But like the others in the 183rd Session, he also made several good contacts and one especially good friend. Bobby Ray Jenkins had been in law enforcement for almost twenty-eight years and now was a captain with the Georgetown County Sheriff's Department, serving as the commander of the department's Major Case Squad. Like Paul, he had been promoted twice since graduating from the National Academy.

Over the years since they attended the NA together, they had become the best of friends and so had their wives. They all had become as close as friends can be. Their families had visited each other's homes, had vacationed together, and they had also shared far too many beers and bourbons together. Perhaps when Paul's soldier had been alive a Northern boy and a Southern boy may not have stood much of a chance at becoming such good friends, but times were different now.

Bobby Ray had just left a monthly regional law enforcement meeting in Little River, South Carolina, when his cell phone rang. Picking up the phone, he saw the phone number displayed and immediately recognized who was calling him. "Y'all better not be telling me that you ain't coming to dinner on Friday night. Judy and I have been looking forward to seeing y'all, especially your lovely wife!" Paul could not help but laugh at how his friend had answered the phone, but then he knew Bobby Ray was different than most people.

"Nope, we're still coming. We wouldn't miss it for the world! How are you and my girlfriend both doing?"

Laughing at Paul's joke, Bobby Ray followed up with a sarcastic comment of his own. "OK, whatcha bothering me for then?" After hearing Paul laugh, Bobby Ray told him where he was. "I'm southbound on Highway 17, just leaving Little River. I'm headed back to my office as we speak. Where y'all at?"

"Bobby Ray, I'm down near the Inlet. I need some help. Can you meet me down here?"

"Sure, you bet I can. Paul, you OK?" Bobby Ray could sense some anxiety in his friend's voice.

"Yeah, thanks, I'm fine. But you're not going to believe what I've found. I don't want to talk about this on the phone though. Meet me at the boat launch at Wacca Wache Landing, OK?"

"Be there in less than thirty-five, that quick enough?"

"Sounds perfect, it will give me just enough time to get back there. See you then."

Headed in the direction of Georgetown, Bobby Ray disconnected the call as he entered the southbound on-ramp for Highway 31. He was confused about the tone in his friend's voice and wondered what was so important for Paul to call him about. Entering the highway's southbound lanes, he punched the accelerator down on his black Dodge Charger and quickly had it up to 95 mph. Bobby Ray did not do anything in life slow, especially when a friend called and needed his help.

* * * * * *

Paul had just finished tying up his boat to the dock when he saw Bobby Ray drive into the marina's parking lot. "Hey, Johnny Reb, over here!" Paul said, waving to his friend as he climbed out of his unmarked police car. As Paul had an interest in the Civil War, so did Bobby Ray, and they had spent many hours talking about whose side had been right and whose had been wrong. Despite their differences, they both shared an appreciation for those who had served in the *War of Northern Aggression*. That was a term Bobby Ray, and many other Southerners, often referred to the war as. Paul never had argued with them on that point.

Carrying his assigned Motorola portable radio, Bobby Ray walked the short distance from the parking lot to Paul's boat. He playfully smirked as he stood on the dock staring at his friend's boat for a few seconds. Bobby Ray was someone who could never pass up an opportunity to jab someone; this time it was his buddy's turn. "Partner, forgive me for asking, but that thing y'all got tied up there to the dock, does that piece of junk float?" Paul laughed as he nodded back at him. He had learned over the years on most occasions Bobby Ray always started their conversations with an insult. When he had not, Paul knew he was mad at someone or something. After a few more moments of good natured insults between the two of them, Bobby Ray got them back to the reason why they were meeting at the marina. "OK, Yankee boy, what's this here mysterious phone call all about? What did y'all do, find a dead body or something?"

"Yep."

At first, Bobby Ray laughed at Paul's answer, but as he did he immediately could tell his friend was serious. "What are you telling me, partner? Did you really find a dead body?"

"I wouldn't have called you if I had found a live one. You wouldn't have shown up. Hop on and I'll tell you more. You're not going to believe what I'm about to tell you."

While Paul drove the boat back to where he had made his discovery, he filled Bobby Ray in with what he found. After tying the boat up for the third time in the same spot in two days, he showed Bobby Ray the digital photos he had taken. Paul had given a lot of thought as to whether he should tell his friend about the items he had kept, but decided for now he would keep that a secret from him. He hoped after Bobby Ray had seen the actual site that he would not challenge him on whether or not he had kept any items for himself.

Bobby Ray was still not convinced Paul was not playing a joke on him until he saw the remains of the soldier inside the base of the tree. "Damn, boy, what have you found? I don't believe this?"

"So what happens now?" Paul curiously asked.

Bobby Ray thought about Paul's question for a minute before raising his Motorola radio to call into the Georgetown County Sheriff's Dispatch Center. But then, just as quickly as he raised the portable radio to speak into it, he lowered it. "You know what's gonna happen if I call this in on the radio, right? We're gonna have every damn television station's mobile news van, and every damn newspaper reporter, and every other dang fool who listens to the police and fire scanners, at the marina before we even get back there. We don't need that problem to deal with right now. No, sir, I ain't having that happen. Get me back there and I'll call this in on a land line. I ain't even gonna use my damn cell phone to call this in. Now I understand why you did not want to tell me about this when y'all first called me."

On the boat ride back to the marina, Paul asked Bobby Ray how the investigation would unfold. Carefully he reminded his friend that all of the indications seemed to point to the remains belonging to someone who had been dead for almost one hundred and fifty years. "You need to tell your folks this appears to be someone who had been killed in an act of war and not murdered during a crime. I hope they don't come flying up here with their lights flashing and with their sirens wailing as there is no need for all of that."

"When I call this in I'll make sure that does not happen. One thing for sure though, I bet this is gonna get a whole bunch of attention in the news. Dead Confederate soldiers don't turn up too often anymore, even in these parts. Another thing you can bet the ranch on is I'm guessing my boss will play this up for sure. He's someone has who never met a television camera he did not like. I believe he thinks every time his face is on the damn television it gets him more votes in the next election."

"Bobby Ray, what I'm trying to get you to see is you, or I, we need to make sure folks know this is an historical find of great significance. We need to make sure the South Carolina Historical Society, or the Sons of the Confederacy, or whoever it is, know about this. This soldier needs to be properly buried and the artifacts found with him need to be preserved for others to see. Don't let it get pushed to the side. Make sure the right thing gets done here."

Bobby Ray, whose interest in the Civil War was as great as Paul's was, thought for a moment about what his friend had just said. "You're right, partner. I'll make a couple of calls after I call the office; don't worry, we'll make sure the right folks find out about this. I don't care if my boss gets upset over this or not. Anyone stuck in a tree for that long deserves a proper burial. I'm on it, don't worry."

Planting another seed in Bobby Ray's head, Paul then suggested it would be a good idea for the area to be looked over by someone using a metal detector. "Hey, who knows, maybe they'll find something I missed. Perhaps some old minie balls or some gold coins."

Bobby Ray jumped off onto the dock next to a wooden walkway as his friend eased the boat up against the marina's day dock so it could be tied up there for now. As he shut the engine off, Paul saw Bobby Ray entering the marina's office door.

After notifying his office of what Paul had found, Bobby Ray walked back to where his friend now sat on a wooden bench. The bench sat under a badly painted wooden canopy which protected it from the hot sun. Handing Paul one of the two Cokes he purchased at the marina's restaurant, Bobby Ray advised him the Georgetown County Sheriff's Crime Scene Processing Unit and a local coroner would soon be arriving to process the scene. After taking a long sip on his cold soda, a smiling Bobby Ray gave his friend a wink. "I would not be surprised to see a couple of folks from the Georgetown Historical Society show up here also. Funny how those folks find out about these things so fast."

Without even looking up at his friend, Paul smiled as he knew Bobby Ray had *dropped a dime* to the historical folks. "Yeah, that is funny. I wonder how they found out about this so fast?"

Then Bobby Ray told Paul his boss was also en route to the marina. "The three-ring circus, with Sheriff Leroy William Renda as the ring master, will soon flood this parking lot, bringing with it a total loss of dignity for the soldier whose remains you have found. Sheriff Renda likely has zero interest in what you have just found. All he cares about are television cameras and votes. As I have already told you, for him those two things go hand in hand."

As Bobby Ray predicted, the marina's parking lot soon filled up with satellite trucks from several local television stations, newspaper reporters and their requisite photographers, and other media types. Soon more cops, curious onlookers, and as Bobby Ray had correctly predicted, the sheriff of Georgetown County, jammed the parking lot full. As they did, the various media representatives all clamored for ten minutes of Paul's time; it was time he reluctantly gave them. Within the next few days, news of the discovery of the Confederate soldier's remains would spread across the country. Those stories would all credit Paul for the discovery he had accidently made. The only good news was the promises he heard made by the governor of South Carolina and by the president of the South Carolina chapter of the Sons of the Confederacy. Both promised they would see to it that Paul's soldier would receive a proper military burial.

* * * * * *

Over the course of the next two weeks, the media attention given to the discovery of the Confederate soldier would temporarily renew interest in the Civil War in many parts of the country, especially in the South. For Paul, his interest in this story would intensify after he finally opened the two bottles he had found with the soldier.

10

Troubles Continue.

"Major, tell my father I died with my face to the enemy."
Colonel Isaac E. Avery, CSA, at Gettysburg, 2 July 1863

On the ride back to the Charles plantation, Captain Francis knew the chances of Sgt. Steele still being alive were going to be slim as the blow to his skull had been severe. Upon entering the front parlor of the Charles home, he saw a sheet was now draped over the lifeless body lying on the table in the parlor. He had lost another of his men.

As the sun began to make its presence known, Francis' men prepared to move out. Having lost two men already he knew he could not afford to lose any more, so despite the risk involved he decided to bring the injured Sgt. Hatfield with him, broken leg and all. He also told Samuel he was coming with them as well. Francis prayed Sgt. Davis would rejoin them soon.

Thanking Mary for her help, Francis now moved his wagons towards Petersburg, Virginia, hoping to get back to the railroad so they could move south at a faster pace. As they moved along that afternoon they met up with Confederate cavalry troops who were tasked with attacking Union troops who had been creating havoc with the railroads in southern Virginia. From them, Francis learned Union troops had recently blown up two other trains. They had also damaged several nearby sections of railroad track in their attempts to disrupt the flow of supplies to the Confederate army in northern Virginia. From what he now knew, Francis decided he would continue to move south by land, but would do so as close as possible to the rail lines in the event they could locate a still functioning train.

They had been on the move for three days since leaving the Charles plantation and during this time Sgt. Davis had returned from Richmond. He was shocked by the news of Steele's death. "I hope you fellas gave them Union boys what they deserved, and then some for killing Micah." When he heard Francis had ordered the deserters hung, Davis knew they had gotten what they deserved.

Despite the return of Davis, problems continued to occur as Hatfield's leg injury grew worse from enduring long hours riding over bumpy roads and fields. On their fourth day of travelling one of the wagons sustained a broken axle, but Samuel showed his ability to repair things and he soon had the axle fixed. To everyone's surprise, he had also proved to be a fine cook.

Then the small problems got bigger fast. On the sixth morning since leaving the Charles plantation, and with little warning, they were attacked by a small Union cavalry unit of twenty-five soldiers. This small cavalry unit was part of the larger compliment of Union troops who had been charged with destroying the railroads in southern Virginia. Hidden from view in a large grove of pine trees, and patiently waiting until Francis' wagons had passed their location, the Union cavalry attacked the wagon train from the west, first firing their rifles as they moved closer to the slow moving wagons. They then charged through Francis' men with their sabers drawn. As Francis and his men turned to address the attacking Union troops, Sgt. George James immediately fell from his horse, dead from a minie ball striking his right temple. Sgt. Gerald Rickert, an Arkansas Razorback, and a two-year veteran of the war, also fell to the ground as a result of being shot in his right leg by the advancing Union cavalry. His wound would prove to be far less serious than the fatal wound James had sustained.

After the Union cavalry's first pass through them, Francis attempted a daring dash into a clearing in the woods he saw off to his left. As he urged his men towards the clearing, the wagon Sgt. James had been driving overturned as it now had no one controlling the team of horses pulling it. The wagon had run through a small ditch just before it overturned. Seeing the rest of the wagons would make it safely into the woods before the next Union charge at them, Francis gathered Sgts. Davis, 'Big Ed' Odom, and Foster to protect the contents of the overturned wagon.

Despite being caught off guard, and despite the loss of another man, his men reacted well to the Union attack. While outmanned and outmaneuvered by the swift moving cavalry unit, they beat off the next charge, killing two Union soldiers who had tried to capture the injured Sgt. Rickert.

To Francis' surprise the Union cavalry then rode off to a clearing east of where his men now readied themselves in the woods. Even though they had the protection of the woods, they were at a clear disadvantage to the swifter and stronger Union cavalry. Francis knew the cavalry unit could easily finish his men off with a coordinated attack, but for now no attack came. Seizing the opportunity the stalled Union attack gave him, he had his men utilize two teams of horses to right the overturned and damaged wagon. Quickly they moved it into the woods near the rest of the wagons. As they did this, Francis waited and waited for the Union cavalry to attack, yet they did not.

With his men and wagons safely in the woods, Francis prepared them for another attack. He deployed Stine and McKinney, the two self-proclaimed *'best here shots in Bobby Lee's army'*, forward of the others. He told them their sole purpose was to shoot the officer in charge of the Union attack, an officer displaying the insignia of a lieutenant. "He likely will be the one leading the attack. Shoot him and their attack will quickly fall apart!"

Sgts. Stine and McKinney had both honed their skills with a rifle prior to the war, but now the war had given them the opportunity to become even better shots than they already were. In their respective units, Stine with the 12th Virginia Volunteer Cavalry Regiment, and McKinney with the Army of Northern Virginia's 10th Volunteer Infantry Regiment, they had routinely awed many of their officers and fellow soldiers with their marksmanship skills. Each of their units had often bragged about having the best shot in the army serving with them.

Soon news of each others marksmanship abilities had become well-known. During a period of rest for both of their regiments a few months back, their commanders had arranged for a friendly shooting match to take place between the two of them to decide who the best shot was. Stine and McKinney matched shot after shot during their friendly competition that spring afternoon in 1862, but McKinney had been declared the eventual winner. His last shot had struck dead center in a wooden canteen being used as a target at almost four hundred feet away. Stine's last shot had hit the target, but only grazed the right side of the canteen.

The two sergeants became friends that day, but had not seen each other since the shooting contest until they both showed up to meet Francis in Richmond when the mission began. Now they stood side to side with each other, each partially shielded behind a pine tree, Stine with his Springfield rifle and McKinney with his Richmond rifle. Raising their rifles, they now took careful aim at the Union cavalry officer advancing upon their somewhat protected position, his horse kicking up dust from the dry field as it led the charge towards them.

The two shots they fired hit next to each other as they struck the lieutenant's upper chest. Later both men would lay claim to having fired the shot which soon caused the lieutenant's death. It did not really matter who fired what shot as either of the two shots would have caused his death to quickly occur. The well-placed shots would later cement their reputations as being amongst the finest sharpshooters within the Confederate army. In the heat of the moment, Francis was just pleased they had hit the target he identified for them.

Just as he had positioned his other men, the Union cavalry attacked again, splitting into two groups in an attempt to cause confusion within the ranks of Francis' men. That move, coupled by McKinney's and Stine's well-placed shots which knocked the lieutenant out of his saddle, failed miserably for the Union. The men Francis now commanded were veterans of several battles before they had been assigned to him. They had learned long ago that staying calm while under fire often proved key to staying alive.

During the attack, Sgt. Daniel Sturges, the South Carolinian who had been the last to report to Francis in Richmond, and who at twenty-five was the oldest sergeant in the group, had received a minor gunshot wound to his left forearm. Sgt. Odom had sustained a minor slash across his back from a Union saber, but he and Sturges would survive. The Union cavalry unit lost six more men senselessly attacking a somewhat fortified position, and an experienced group of soldiers. Francis still was at a loss as to why the Union cavalry had not attacked them when they had been out in the open, but his thoughts quickly turned to the welfare of his men. As he did, he saw Banks and Stine dragging the seriously injured Union lieutenant back into their line. Francis knew they likely would not be attacked while they held him as a prisoner. The capture of the Union lieutenant at first drew much hooping and hollering from his men as they celebrated the capture of their first prisoner, but now they taunted the Union soldiers over the loss of their commanding officer. They had gotten the best of the Yankees in this skirmish.

"Lieutenant, I am Captain Judiah Francis of the Army of Northern Virginia. You have attacked me and my men; in doing so you have killed one of my men. Sir, you have done what you were charged to do, but we had no desire to fight you as we have far more important orders to complete. Despite your unprovoked attack, and because you are an officer of the United States Army, I will accept your word if you swear to me you will not attack us again. In return, we will provide you with the medical care your wounds need. If you do not give me your word, I shall let you die. After you are dead, I promise you we will not run if your men decide to attack us again; it is they who will die here today with you. Promise me your men will not attack us again and my men and I will ride away. There is no further need for anyone else to die here today; the decision is yours alone."

Lt. Kevin Casey, of the Connecticut Volunteer Cavalry Unit's First Regiment, lay bleeding profusely from the gunshot wounds he sustained to his upper chest. While he did not know if he would live or not without the promised medical care Francis offered to him, Casey had grown fond of living in this world and he immediately sought to prolong that experience. "Captain, I give you my word. No more attacks." Francis then fulfilled his promise and had him treated as best as he could be. The sip of water Casey soon requested would become his last one as his wounds had been that severe. Soon he was dead.

Just before Casey died, Francis walked to the edge of the woods and yelled to the Union troops, telling them their lieutenant had agreed to call off the attacks. As he did this, he knew his prisoner was dying, but he also knew he needed time to put some distance between his men and the remaining Union cavalry soldiers. As he yelled again, Francis sought to buy himself that time by playing a risky bluff. "Your lieutenant is being treated by my men. We are moving out soon, but I am leaving at least one man behind to care for him. You can fetch him back in one hour's time. Any earlier and we will shoot him dead." As he turned back towards his men, he saw Casey was already dead. Francis knew the Union troops would now likely want to seek vengeance on his men for Casey's death.

"Men, we need to move out quick. I need a volunteer to help bide us some time so the rest of us can move out." He was moved when the four Virginia sergeants did not hesitate, each stepped forward to volunteer. Before he could select one of them, Davis spoke up.

"Captain, this here fight is on Virginia soil and I'll be dammed if I'm gonna let somebody else fight our fight for us. I'll stay behind and watch them Yankee boys. I'll make sure y'all have time to get away."

Francis quickly gave Davis his instructions. "Get up to the tree line so those Yankee soldiers see you as we are moving out. After we leave, move in and about the trees so they can see you for another thirty minutes or so; then come join us."

"Don't fret none about me, captain. I'll be fine. It's them dang Yankees who need to do some worrying, not me!" With Casey's revolver stuck it in his waistband for added protection, Davis had barely moved off to his position when the next issue was brought to Francis' attention.

"Captain, we got us another problem!"

Francis turned to see Sgt. Banks pointing at Samuel. He was looking at the damaged wagon they had rescued after it turned over when Sgt. James had been shot. Samuel watched as gold and silver coins from one of the damaged hidden compartments began to drop onto the ground through the wagon's cracked floorboards. Seeing little money in his lifetime, what Samuel saw drop from the wagon seemed like a fortune to him.

Knowing he did not have time to repair the wagon, Francis ordered the coins to be thrown into an opened barrel of flour on another wagon. He had the rest of the wagon's contents transferred to the other wagons. Then he ordered the wagon to be set on fire. "Hurry men, hurry! We need to get away from these Yankees!" As the men moved as fast as they could, Francis and Samuel hastily buried Sgt. James in a shallow grave amongst the pine trees where they had made a courageous stand against the Yankee cavalry charge. After they finished their task, Francis said a few quick words over his body. They were soon on the move.

Francis had thought for a brief moment of what to tell Samuel about the gold and silver coins, but soon decided not to tell him anything. Telling him about the money would accomplish nothing, and doing so might upset his men even more as they had not been all that pleased to have him travelling with them, even if he had proved to be a good cook.

With the damaged wagon set on fire so the Union troops could not put it to use, they moved out as fast as the other wagons would allow. Joined by Stine, Francis rode at the rear as the wagons moved along, waiting for the Yankees to attack them again. As they rode, they soon could hear the shouts of Sgt. Davis as he raced towards them while riding low in his saddle. He was already ducking rifle shots from the pursuing Union cavalry who had found Casey dead.

The wagons had been steadily moving through several large open fields when they were alerted by Davis' warning calls. Reacting to the warning he heard from the fast approaching Davis, Francis tried to get the others organized into a defensive position behind a waist high stone wall which had once been part of a farmer's field. As they moved towards the stone wall, Davis passed them at a full gallop, dismounting on the far side of the wall. As Francis and the others quickly moved into position, Davis took his first shot at the charging Union cavalry. Quickly the others prepared to do the same. As they did, they then heard gunshots off to their right; collectively turning to face the threat they had not seen approaching. To their relief, they quickly realized the shots were coming from a Confederate cavalry unit; a unit now approaching their position at a fast gallop. The sight of the Confederate cavalry unit now caused the Union cavalry, already depleted by the loss of their commander, and others, to turn away and retreat. Briefly they were pursued by the rapidly advancing Confederate cavalry soldiers until a bugle call ordered the pursuit to end. Francis and his men now slumped to the ground against the stone wall to catch their breath. Pleased to know they would live to see another day.

From his position, Francis watched as the Confederate cavalry called off their pursuit of what was left of the Union cavalry unit. Then he watched as the officer in charge started to ride up to where he had sat down on a large rock adjacent to the stone wall. As he sat there, Francis heard his men let out a large cheer for the cavalry soldiers who had saved them.

Francis stood up and walked the few steps to greet his fellow officer. It was someone he had never met before. "Captain, you and your men are indeed a welcome sight. That group of Union cavalry had already charged us twice and they were getting ready to come at us again. We held them off the first two times, killing their lieutenant and a couple of others, but I'm not sure how we would have done this time. Sir, we are in your debt."

"Captain, the pleasure is all ours. I'm pleased we were close by to help you. My name is Captain Kenneth H. Kirschner of the North Carolina Second Cavalry Unit. This is my second in command, Lt. Robert Moniz, also a proud North Carolinian, his friends call him Bobby."

Standing next to Kirschner, who was still mounted on his horse, Francis shook hands with both men. "Captain, again my thanks to Lt. Moniz, to your men, and to you for your timely arrival. My name is Captain Judiah Francis of the Army of Northern Virginia. My men and I are moving south towards Atlanta on orders from President Davis and General Lee."

Awkwardly, Francis then looked up at Lt. Moniz who was still mounted on his horse. He had just started to light a cigar when Francis spoke to him. "Lt. Moniz, with entirely no disrespect to you, may I have a moment with Captain Kirschner?" With a nod of the head, and then a salute, Moniz moved away so the two captains could speak privately.

After dismounting, and after quickly checking on the status of his men, Kirschner joined Francis where he had again sat down on the large rock. As Kirschner took a drink from his canteen, Francis stared at him as he spoke. "Captain, my men and I are grateful for your help. I promise when my assignment is over with, I shall be pleased to advise President Davis and General Lee of the invaluable assistance you and your men have given to us today. However, on orders from both of those two men, I cannot tell you anything more about what we are doing. I can tell you if you are to challenge me on what my assignment is I am prepared to show you a letter from President Davis, one which authorizes me and my men freely move about the South uncontested. It is my hope, as an officer of the Confederate army, that you will accept my word and will not formally challenge me as to what I am doing." Francis paused for a moment as a loud noise momentarily got his attention. Looking back at Kirschner, he spoke again. "Captain, while I don't know what your orders are, I would be most grateful if you would give us an escort to Petersburg. We need to get to the railroad there and we cannot afford to encounter another skirmish with any other Yankee cavalry units."

Standing up from where he sat, Kirschner was somewhat taken back by the forcefulness of how Francis had delivered his message to him. Sensing Francis had indeed been selected for a special assignment by those men who now led the Confederacy, Kirschner knew they would have likely chosen someone like him, someone who was confident, bold, and, perhaps, someone who had a touch of arrogance or self-confidence about him. He decided he would not challenge Francis on his assignment. "Captain, if you tell me you have been selected by General Lee and President Davis for some type of assignment, I believe you. You do not have to justify your presence or your orders with me. As for my mission, I have orders to sweep the area northeast of Petersburg for Union cavalry who have been creating havoc with our railroad supply lines. We are returning to Petersburg in the morning for supplies. I would be most happy to provide you with the assistance you need."

Pleased to learn what each other had to say, the two captains quickly shook hands. Without showing it, Francis also breathed a sigh of relief. He now knew he and his men would be much safer over the course of the next few days as they travelled with a well-armed escort.

That evening, as their men shared a dinner together, Kirschner and Francis, joined by Lt. Moniz, enjoyed their meal away from the others. As they ate, they shared their personal experiences from the war. Earlier when they talked, Kirschner had noticed Francis' bandaged left hand. He had not asked him about it until now. "Judiah, it is easy to see this war has inflicted some type of injury upon you as your bandaged hand looks quite painful. I hope you are recovering well."

"I am doing much better now, thank you for asking. An unlucky shot fired by a Union soldier has cost me two of my fingers, but my injury is far less than what so many others have either lost or had to endure during this terrible war. My only real fear is how my mother will react when she sees my injury. I have not told her about it as I would rather wait and tell her in person as I don't want her worrying about me after reading about my loss in a letter."

In short time the conversation turned to other topics, including Kirschner speaking of what he hoped to do after the war. As Kirschner spoke of returning home, Francis repeatedly tried to clench his injured hand several times through the bandages he still wore. As he did, he tried feeling for his fingers which were no longer there. Focused on his injured hand, he only heard parts of what his new friend had said. Francis hoped he could soon remove the stitches and then learn how to use his hand all over again.

* * * * * *

Over the course of the three-day ride to Petersburg, the two Confederate captains developed a quick friendship and a mutual respect for each other. For one of them it would be a friendship which would last in his memory for many years to come. For the other, the friendship would soon die with him.

As they entered Petersburg, Francis and Kirschner both saw to the needs of their men. After Francis secured passage on the next Richmond, Fredericksburg & Potomac train moving south, both men shared a meal together at the Petersburg Hotel before they parted company later in the afternoon. After eating their meal, they walked back to the train station together. For a short spell, they sat there talking about the war and their families. Then wishing each other well, they promised they would meet again after the war. It was a promise they would not be able to keep.

11

Filling In The Pieces.

"I was too weak to defend, so I attacked."
General Robert E. Lee, CSA

The long day had finally come to an end for Paul after telling his story to both the Georgetown County Sheriff Department investigators and, reluctantly, several more times to the various media representatives who had gathered at the marina. Despite being physically and mentally tired from the strain of the past two days, he called Donna on her cell phone during her ride home from work. They were able to spend a couple of quiet moments together when she stopped at the marina to witness the sideshow which was occurring there. She was amazed at the commotion Paul's discovery had caused.

As they stood off to the side of the marina talking for a few minutes, Donna asked Paul if he had told Bobby Ray about the gold coins. Taking a moment to walk her to the back of her car so they could have some privacy, he reached into his pants pocket and showed her the five gold coins he had found earlier in the day. "Do you mean these gold coins or the gold coins I found yesterday?" He was grinning as he watched her open her eyes wide at the sight of the additional gold coins. Not saying a word, Donna elected to just stare at them as he held the coins in his hands. "To answer your question, no I have not, nor am I going to tell him about them. At least, not yet I'm not."

As they talked, Bobby Ray walked over to where they were standing in the parking lot. While he had spoken to Donna on the phone, it was the first time they had seen each other since her move to South Carolina. Bobby Ray gave her a quick kiss and a long hug. She was pleased to see Bobby Ray, even if it was for a brief few minutes, and she laughed when he joked about her living with an old retired guy. After only a few minutes of talking, Bobby Ray began to walk back to the boat launch so he could get back to work. As he did, they told each other they were looking forward to getting together for dinner on Friday night. "Try to find a new date if ya can, I'm already tired of seeing this guy." Bobby Ray's joke made both of them laugh and Donna waved a quick goodbye as he walked back to where the Georgetown County Sheriff's Crime Van was parked. It was where Sheriff Renda was conducting yet another interview. This time it was with a reporter from the *Georgetown Times*.

After Donna left, Paul answered a few more questions for Bobby Ray's partners regarding his initial find of the bayonet and the soldier's clothing. He also spent a few more minutes with the media, answering the same questions he had already answered several times earlier in the day. Finished answering questions, Paul walked over to the Wacca Wache marina's small restaurant, *The Waterway Cafe*, for a couple of cold beers.

Paul barely had time to get inside the door to the small restaurant when he was loudly greeted by the bartender. "Hey, ain't you the guy who found the Confederate soldier? You're him, ain't you? Hey, my name is Jed, but my friends call me Bubba." Bubba, the marina's part-time bartender, looked to Paul like a stereotypical *Southern Bubba* should. He was a big man in not only his height, but in his weight as well. His shiny bald head seemed to reflect the light from the various lighted beer signs hanging on the wall behind the bar. As he moved back and forth behind the small wooden bar, Paul could see the reflections as they bounced off of Bubba's shiny head. He noticed Bubba's once white tee shirt was now stained with grease from the burgers he had either cooked or eaten during the day.

"Whatcha drinking? Charlie told me if you stopped in your drinks were on him. Them TV folks, and them reporters, they've been buying sodas, snacks, and burgers all afternoon. Charlie is real appreciative of what you've found, and for all the business y'all have given him today, so he's buying your drinks. What can I get for you, buddy?" Bubba asked as he wiped a section of the bar off where two previous customers had sat.

"Two Coors Light please. No glass."

As Bubba walked to the nearby cooler to fetch his two beers, Paul let out a sarcastic chuckle. "What a great day for South Carolina! A Civil War soldier is finally coming home to be buried, a sheriff is posturing for votes in front of the television cameras, and I'm being offered free beer for finding the soldier. Obviously the owner of this place cares more about making a few bucks than he does about the historical event that is unfolding outside his joint." Thirsty from the long hot afternoon, Paul quickly drained the first cold beer as he sat down on a stool by the restaurant's side window. His seat gave him a view of the marina's parking lot and of the activity occurring there. He could see several news reporters frantically running around as they prepared the finishing touches to their news stories before they went live with their broadcasts from the parking lot. "What a zoo this is turning out to be!" Finishing off his second beer, he threw a few bucks down on the bar and walked outside. As he did, Bubba quickly followed him. In his left hand he was holding the money Paul had left on the bar.

"Hey, mister, I told ya Charlie was buying your drinks for y'all." Walking to his truck, Paul did not give a look back at Bubba. He was not interested in capitalizing on his new and unsought fame by quaffing a couple of free beers.

After finally getting home, and after filling Donna in with the rest of the details of the day over dinner, including finding the soldier's watch, Paul closed the plantation style shutters in their kitchen as she cleaned up. After spreading a couple of bath towels over the kitchen table, he went into the garage and gathered up the tools he thought he would need. After placing the tools on the table, he walked back to the garage one more time, returning with the two bottles he found in the soldier's clothing. Then he went to find his camera equipment that he had temporarily stored in one of the guest bedrooms.

After setting up the camera equipment, Paul described each bottle in detail to Donna so she could write down the descriptions on a yellow legal pad. He wanted a description of each bottle for both posterity reasons and in the event they broke as he was trying to open them. When they finished that task, he held each bottle up so she could take digital pictures of the bottles with their Nikon camera. Moments earlier, Paul had placed his Sony camcorder on a tripod next to the kitchen table. After giving a brief introduction, including the date and time, he allowed the Maxwell eight millimeter tape to record what occurred as he handled the bottles. He had learned redundancy was something that often proved to be important when processing crime scenes during his career as a state trooper; now they took both still photos and a video recording of the bottles for similar reasons. He did not want a photograph or an angle for a photo to be lost if he needed to show his findings to others. Paul knew he soon might be doing just that.

First they started with the pint sized flask style bottle that was brownish in color. As Paul closely looked at it, he noticed a double ring around the neck's opening, one apparently designed to help seal the bottle. He made sure Donna included that observation in her description of the bottle. Using a soft soapy sponge, he carefully wiped away some of the accumulated grime on the bottle's exterior. As this was being done, he could hear the faint whirl of the tape in the camcorder as it recorded his actions. With the bottle somewhat cleaned off, he noticed one exterior side had been embossed with an eagle on it. Inspecting the bottom of the bottle, he saw it had been made by the Willington Glass Company, in West Willington, Connecticut. "Well, I'll be. Hon, this bottle, it was made back home in Connecticut. This is getting weirder by the moment!" Paul then took notice of the interior portion of the bottle's neck. He described to Donna the apparent partial remains of some kind of cloth that had been likely used to replace the bottle's missing cork many years ago. For now, he let the piece of cloth remain in the neck of the bottle.

After he finished inspecting the first bottle, and after making sure the camcorder was still recording their efforts, Paul inspected the second bottle, describing it in detail to Donna as he had with the first one. The second bottle was slightly larger than the first one, and had what appeared to be the original cork still stuck in the neck. Further describing the bottle to her as being bluish green in color, he estimated it likely had also held about a pint of liquid at one time. As he slowly cleaned the exterior of the second bottle, he was careful not to get any water inside of it. With the exterior now much cleaner, he saw the bottle had raised lettering on both sides, as well as the raised outlines of two faces, one on each side. Cleaning the bottle off even more, he quickly recognized the first person to be George Washington. Under the outline of Washington's face was the wording *'Father of our Country'*. Turning the bottle over, he did not immediately recognize the second face, but after reading the inscription under it, *'General Taylor Never Surrenders'*, he then believed it to be a likeness of General Zachary Taylor, who he remembered as being one of the country's earliest presidents. Looking at the bottom of the second bottle, while holding a magnifying glass in his left hand, he could see it had been made by the Dyottville Glass Works, in Philadelphia, Pennsylvania. "Donna, why would a Confederate soldier have two bottles made in the North on his person? Did the South not have companies that made bottles? I wonder why he kept these in his blouse? Kind of strange, isn't it?"

"Can't help you with that. You know more about that stuff than I do." Donna said with a shrug of her shoulders.

Donna had put her pen down and was looking at the first bottle they inspected. "If these bottles are that old, and were found with the remains of a Confederate soldier, they have to be worth something, right?"

Paul could now see that both bottles had accumulated some grime and dirt inside of them. He paused from his inspection of the bottles to think about what Donna had just asked him. "They're likely worth something to someone who collects old bottles, but your guess is as good as mine. One thing for sure, we need to Google the names of these glass companies later and see what we can find."

With the exteriors of the bottles now cleaner, and despite the thin layer of grime which still coated the interiors of both bottles, Paul alternated between using his kitchen ceiling lights and a flashlight as he held each one up in the light to see what was inside of them. While he could not tell for sure, it looked as if each bottle appeared to have some type of rolled up papers inside of them. Focusing on the papers inside the bottles, he muttered a thought out loud. It was one he did not expect Donna to answer. "Tell me how to get these papers out as they're sure not coming out the way they went in without me ripping them to pieces?"

"I don't know. Why don't you try to drill them out if you just don't want to break the bottles?"

At first Paul gave Donna a sarcastic look. He was about to say something smart to her for what he had first perceived to be a ridiculous idea, but before he could say something to her he caught himself. He thought for a moment about what she had just said to him. "Perhaps I could drill a few small holes in the bottom of the bottles, perhaps forming a small rectangle and then I could tap that piece of glass out. If it works I would at least save the rest of the two bottles."

It took several minutes to find the still packed box which contained some of his tools, but he soon did. In moments, he had his Black and Decker drill plugged into an extension cord in the garage. As he did this, Donna carried the bottles into the garage and placed them on the folding table Paul previously used when he first had found the bottles and the other items. After searching through his box of drill bits, Paul selected a very fine masonry drill bit to try drilling the bottoms of the bottles with. Before starting on the bottles, he moved his video camera into the garage so he could film what he was trying to attempt. As the video camera was set-up, Donna retrieved their digital camera from the kitchen so she could take some additional photos as the bottles were being drilled.

"You know I have never tried drilling holes in glass before. This may not work, but what the hell, if it does it does, and if doesn't it doesn't. Either way we'll find out what's inside the bottles. They probably just have a note inside of them telling us a genie will soon appear to grant us three wishes." Donna rolled her eyes at Paul's weak attempt at humor.

Wrapping the first bottle in a towel so only the bottom was exposed, Paul placed it between his knees as he sat on a stool. He hoped the towel would protect his legs from being cut if the bottle broke while he was drilling it. Proceeding very slowly, and using the drill at a low speed, he began drilling a hole in the bottom of the first bottle. As he did, Donna made sure the camcorder was recording properly. Satisfied it was, she began taking a few more digital photos, hoping at the same time not to see either the drill or broken glass pierce her husband's legs.

When the drill bit went through the bottom of the bottle for the first time, Paul expected to see the bottle break, but surprisingly it did not. Over the next hour, he carefully drilled and chipped a series of holes close to each other in the bottoms of both bottles, holes which formed small crude rectangles. Finished drilling the last hole, he placed the drill and the safety glasses he had been wearing on the garage floor next to the table. With his right thumb wrapped up in the towel, he then pressed against the drilled out section of the first bottle, hoping the glass would break and fall inside it. It did not. "As my father would say, if I did not want the glass to break it would and if I wanted it to break it wouldn't."

Grabbing a small rubber mallet, Paul gently tapped on the small rectangle. It took three taps, but on the third tap the drilled out section of glass broke.

The broken glass fell into the bottom of the bottle as he had hoped. "Wow, it actually worked!" Grudgingly he complimented Donna on her suggestion about drilling holes into the bottles. The smile he saw on her face made him realize she would be rubbing this in his face many times in the future. He knew she was savoring the moment. Focusing on the second bottle, he tapped out the glass just as he had done to the first one. Like the first time, on the third gentle tap the bottom gave way and the broken glass fell inside the bottle.

Paul grabbed two small plastic shopping bags and dumped the broken glass from each bottle into separate bags, looking up at Donna as he did. "Just in case we need to prove we opened the bottles this way to someone else later on." She nodded back at him, realizing he had thought of everything.

Using a pair of needle-nose pliers, due to the sharp edges of glass lining the broken hole in each bottle, Paul gently grabbed the papers in the first bottle and moved them closer to the opening he had made. Finally able to grab the papers between two of his fingers, he removed them from the bottle with great care. As he laid each of them down on a towel Donna had spread out on the table, he could see sections of the paper had been stained, possibly from condensation that had gotten into the bottle or from moisture having been in the bottle when the papers were placed inside it. Remarkably the papers appeared to be in great condition. As he placed them on the table, Donna continued to click away with the digital camera.

As Paul carefully unfolded the first set of papers, the ones that had been in the smaller of the two bottles, an impatient Donna asked the obvious question for the moment. "Well, what is it? Is it a letter or what?"

Paul was slowly unfolding the three pieces of paper that had been folded first and then rolled up so they would fit into the neck of the bottle. "Patience, young lady, patience. I don't want to rip the papers. Is the video camera getting this?"

Sarcastically, Donna answered her husband. "No, Paul, I shut it off just before this important moment! Of course it is. You're killing me with the suspense; tell me what you are looking at!"

The three pieces of paper were faded from their original off-white color. As Paul carefully finished unfolding them, he saw they were actually two letters which had been folded together. Sitting down after laying the papers out on the table, it took a moment for his brain to register the significance of the signature he was looking at. When it finally did, he quickly stood up. Stunned by what he was now looking at, he quietly whispered the name out loud.

Standing near the opposite side of the table, Donna was startled by her husband's quick reaction after seeing the signature; backing away from the table so quickly she nearly fell to the floor as she tried to avoid tripping over a box on the garage floor. "Paul, you idiot, you scared the hell out of me. I almost fell avoiding that stupid box of yours on the floor. What did you see that caused you to react like you did?"

As she walked back around the table, she was about to take the papers out of his hands when Paul told her not to. "Donna, whatever you do, do not touch these papers with your bare hands. This is amazing!"

Donna was not a history buff like her husband was, but when she saw the signature on the bottom of the second page, a signature written over one hundred and fifty years ago by President Jefferson Davis, even she knew the importance of the papers found within the bottle. As she put her hands up to her face, she weakly mumbled a surprised reaction to seeing the Davis signature. "Oh, my God!"

At first, Paul did not completely read the Davis letter as he was too interested in seeing whose signature was on the second one-page letter. The second letter had been neatly folded over the Davis letter. Looking at the signature on it, he saw only a partial one as part of the first name appeared to have been damaged by moisture. Not recognizing the last name he was now looking at, he did not know at first who *Ch Memminger* was. Silently he guessed at the first name. "Was it Charles, or could it be Christopher, or is it some other name?"

A question Donna asked interrupted his thoughts about the smudged signature he was looking at. "Paul, I know this is another of my stupid questions, but these are real letters, not fakes, right?"

"I guess . . . I mean sure . . . I mean . . . well, I guess what I mean is I don't know, but found in a bottle, and in the clothing of someone who we believe to have been a Confederate soldier, I guess they have to be real. Look how the first name in this second letter has been damaged by moisture. I don't know if a signature on a reproduction of a letter would run like that when the ink became wet. I think they have to be original letters."

Paul then read the letter out loud so Donna could hear what President Davis had written so many years ago.

August 3, 1863
Richmond, Va.
To Whom It May Concern:

Please extend to Captain Judiah Francis, of the Army of Northern Virginia, and to all who travel with him, free and unobstructed passage through our Confederate States of America. This includes the use of any rail lines that Captain Francis deems necessary to use. He is to be granted priority use of any railroad at anytime he deems it prudent.

Captain Francis has been selected for an assignment by both General Lee and me. This assignment is both secret and sensitive to the needs of our cause and must not be interrupted, or delayed, for any reason. His orders come personally from me.

> *With Warmest Regards,*
> *Pres. Jefferson Davis*

With the letters still spread out on the table, Paul quietly reread the letter written by President Davis. Afraid of damaging them, he kept his hands away from the pages of the letters. Still shocked at what they found, Donna remained silent for several more minutes as her eyes darted from page to page, trying to comprehend the historical significance of the letters at the same time. As he read the Davis letter for the second time, Paul used a magnifying glass to decipher a couple of words as the pages appeared to have been folded and then refolded a few times in the past. For the most part, he was amazed at the letter's condition.

Paul then turned his attention to the second letter. He read it to himself the first time and then twice out loud so Donna could hear what had been written.

August 3, 1863
Richmond, Virginia
Sir,

The fate of our cause, and the survival of our Confederate States, rests with the ability of Captain Judiah Francis to complete a mission for my office, and most importantly, for all of us.

Please extend to him the courtesies you would expect a Confederate officer deserves while on assignment from both the Office of the President, and from my office.

> *Affectionately,*
> *Ch   Memminger*
> *Secretary of the Treasury*
> *Confederate States of America*

After reading the letters Paul knew a great deal more than he had, but still he could not figure out what the soldier's assignment had been about. Donna then verbalized the same thoughts he was having. "Well, I guess it's safe to assume, and I know you do not assume anything, but in this case I bet it's safe to assume our dead soldier is Captain Judiah Francis who the letters refer to. We at least now know who this Memminger fellow was; he was the Secretary of the Confederate Treasury. But what is this mission, this assignment, the two letters are referring to I wonder? Neither letter tells you much about that. What do you think they are referring to?" Her husband was as equally confused by the contents of the letters as she was.

"At first blush, and I am just guessing, these letters seem to be written for the sole purpose of giving this Confederate officer, this Captain Francis fellow, and whoever is travelling with him, special permission to move unmolested about the South, especially south of Richmond. The Davis letter clearly authorizes him to use any of the Confederate railroads that he might need to use. Right now I have no idea why, but it's obvious, because of the signatures on the two letters, that something important was happening."

They both stared at the letters for the next several minutes, looking closely at the somewhat faded writing on the yellowish pages. They did so for another ten minutes or so when Paul, regaining his focus, looked at Donna with a wrinkled smile. Pointing to the second bottle, he asked her, "So what's in the second bottle?" Like Paul, she had been so taken back by the discovery of the first two letters that she had also momentarily forgotten about the second bottle.

Without answering his question, Donna simply picked up the towel and handed it to him. "Let's find out!"

As Paul wrapped the towel around the second bottle, whose glass bottom had not broken as cleanly as the first one, he again used the needle-nose pliers to move the folded up papers closer to the hole so he could grab them with his fingers. As he did, he could not help but notice the enthusiasm Donna now displayed. It was totally out of character for her to get excited with anything related to history. As with the first bottle, she now took several digital photos to document what was being done with the second one.

After removing the folded papers from the second bottle in the same manner as he did with the ones in the first bottle, Paul gently unrolled the papers on the towel laying on top of the folding table. As with the first set, he noticed they comprised two separate letters. Like the first two they had just read, they were ones once written on white paper which had faded over time. However, unlike the first two letters, another smaller piece of paper was folded up between these letters. As he compared the two newest letters to each other, Paul noticed the penmanship appeared to be from the same person. He also noticed the writing on one of the letters appeared to be much neater. His first thought after seeing the difference between the penmanship was a logical one. "It's almost as if the writer was not as rushed, or as hurried, as he possibly had been when he wrote the second letter."

Paul first read the letter with the neater penmanship of the two. He saw the letter had been written on November 10, 1863. It appeared to have been written in Charleston, South Carolina.

Dear President Davis,

It is with great regret that I must advise you I have failed in my mission. It is my hope to tell you the details of our struggle in person, but in the event of my death, I have instructed my men, of which only three are still alive with me, to deliver this letter to you. Please know we have tried our best to fulfill the orders you personally gave me.

My men have died defending our assets and they have died both tragically and heroically. I am very proud of their gallant efforts to help further our cause. Be proud of their sacrifices as I have been.

It is due to attacks from Union forces upon us since we left Richmond, as well as a couple of other unfortunate accidents, which have resulted in the deaths of some of my men. Due to problems with our railroads, and with the wagons we hauled our assets in, I have been forced to bury some of our assets in a shallow grave outside of a farm near Maple Hill, North Carolina. My men who survive with me, and I, know where that location is. I have marked the location with a large cross made of wood from one of our wagons. I have had one of those boards inscribed with the initials C.S.A. on it. The assets lay close by to that cross, in a shallow grave that contains the remains of three of my men. Four large rocks mark the location of the grave.

Now, despite being pursued by superior Union forces, I have attempted to get the remains of our assets to Charleston, South Carolina, so they could be moved further south by our boats, but the Union naval blockade has prevented this from occurring. With dwindling resources, I have secured the remains of our assets within one of our army warehouses along the King Street Road. I am told our assets will never leave from here, and while battered and broken, these strong solid black friends of ours, who have served us well since Fort Sumter, while <u>even</u> in number, remain loyal protectors of our 'C.S.A.' assets. I am confident you will find them in excellent shape, <u>even</u> in years to come.

We are now forced to ride north into South Carolina with my saddlebags filled. Our black friends, while strong and solid, are limited to twelve and I could not force them to protect what they could not. What we have left with our strong black friends is similar to what we have already left in South Carolina with the resting children of Governor R.F.W. Allston. Those assets were secured within their compound for safe protection. They rest comfortably (NW) with the money. It is my hope to retrieve that money and to move it here to Charleston if the Yankees do not threaten us again.

It is also my hope to soon obtain more men so we can complete our mission to some degree.

> *Respectfully, Your Servant,*
> *Captain Judiah Francis*

With still one more letter to read, Paul took a moment to digest the one he had just read. He could not believe what he had just read in the first three letters. Silently he wondered why he had been the one to find them after all of these years. "Did I really find these letters or are they part of a dream I am having?" He also could not help replaying in his mind everything that had happened to him since changing the flat tire for Steve a few days earlier. "This is tantamount to finding the buried treasure chests everyone thinks pirates like Blackbeard and Stede Bonnett left hidden along the North and South Carolina coasts years ago."

While Paul read the letter written from Francis to President Davis, Donna read the other letter that had been with it. As she did, the tears which formed in her eyes now turned to soft sobs. Still focused on the letter he was reading, Paul had been blind to her tears and now was confused when he saw her crying. It took him a couple of minutes to finally calm her down so she could speak.

"You read the letter and you will see why I am crying. The letter confirms who the soldier was and how alone he must have felt when he died horribly in that tree, all alone by himself in the woods." Donna managed through her sobs.

As his eyes fixed on the letter that had upset his wife so much, Paul hoped it would fill in some of the pieces of the puzzle which were still missing. On the stained and faded yellowish paper, he again saw the handwriting was not as neat as it was in the first letter. Now he concentrated on reading it.

Dear Father,

Please know I have done my best to serve my country, and my family, as well as I could. I am afraid my best was not good enough.

Despite my best efforts, and those of my men, to complete an assignment that both President Davis and General Lee selected me for, I have failed. While the assets of our united Confederate states have been protected, the vicious, and unrelenting Union attacks upon us will likely stop me from ever seeing you, mother, Patricia, and Rita Margaret again.

Two days ago I was struck in the left leg by a Yankee minie ball and I fear that I shall not see another day as I have not the strength, or means, to seek assistance for my wound.

Please know I have done my best. Please give my warmest regards to mother and to my dear sister. In my final hours you are all here with me. The watch you gave me as a gift brings back fond memories of my family and of you. It is my hope that my last conscious thought will be of all of you.

Do not cry for me as I shall always be with you.

Affectionately, Your Loving Son,
Judiah

Paul did his best to hold back his tears as he read the letter twice. Hugging his still upset wife as they stood in the garage, the soft whirl of the Sony camcorder was all that could be heard. Shutting it off, they sat down on two lawn chairs in the garage, each quietly sipping a glass of wine as their minds processed what they had just found in the two bottles. After a few minutes, Paul broke the silence as he wanted to see his still upset wife smile again after she had cried so hard while reading Judiah's letter. "So what do you want to do tomorrow night for excitement?" His comment made Donna laugh briefly, but tears still filled her eyes.

Waiting a few more minutes, Paul turned the camcorder back on and unfolded the small piece of paper which had been with the letters in the second bottle. As he did, he saw it was a roughly drawn map. "Donna, look at this. This looks like a map that someone has drawn. Like the letter mentions, it makes reference to a spot on the map as being a wooden cross. It also has a spot marked with some stones, but it doesn't give us any clue as to where the location actually is or who is buried in what I assume to be a grave."

Donna finished drying her eyes as she looked at the small map for the first time. "Well, someone drew it for some reason. It must one of the locations he mentions in his letter."

"Could be, could be just that, but who knows right now."

As they silently stood in the garage looking at the map, something clicked inside of Paul's head. He realized dinner with Bobby Ray was still on the schedule for tomorrow evening, as was dinner with Steve. "With all that's been going on, I screwed up and scheduled two different dinners on the same night. How did I do that?" As Donna read for the second time the letter Francis had written to his father, she barely acknowledged what Paul said about tomorrow's dinner plans. She was simply too engrossed in the letter she was reading.

Grabbing his cell phone, Paul made a quick phone call to Bobby Ray. He had just gotten home after finishing a very long day at work. After a few moments of small talk, Paul begged him to change their dinner plans to Saturday night.

"Yeah, no problem. Everything OK?"

"Oh, yeah, no problems at all. Donna and I are just enjoying another boring and quiet night here at home with a couple of glasses of wine. Not much of anything happening here."

"That's good. OK, we will see y'all on Saturday night, say around 7 pm? See y'all then. Bye!"

After Paul had rearranged their dinner plans for the following evening, they tried figuring out how they could use the newly found letters to help clear up some of the missing pieces of the puzzle that they knew still existed. The biggest piece that still needed figuring out was trying to determine what Captain Francis had been sent to do by General Lee and President Davis. "Of all the letters we just read, I have to think the one Francis wrote to President Davis definitely has some hidden clues within it. We figure some of those clues out and we will know the whole story about what he was sent to do." Then they decided Donna would hit the computer and try to answer some of their questions by researching certain points the letters brought up. As they put their camera equipment away, Paul told her he would have working copies of the letters made the following morning. The originals would later be placed in their safety deposit box for safekeeping until they decided what to do with them.

* * * * * *

The next day would be one of many interesting days Paul would soon experience. The upcoming days would take him back in time so he could solve one of the greatest mysteries of the Civil War.

12

Tough Decisions.

"Bully for old K! Give it to them, boys!"
Major General James Ewell Brown 'JEB' Stuart, CSA
Battle of Yellow Tavern, 11 May 1864

After saying goodbye to Captain Kirschner, Francis returned to his men at the Petersburg train station. They had waited for him at the far end of the platform while he talked with Kirschner. He was greeted with the news that the Confederate officer in charge of all train movements in and out of the station had changed his mind about allowing them to move south on the train. This officer now refused to empty three rail cars of cotton which was being shipped south to Savannah. While his men had been able to secure some space on the train for their needs, they needed the other three rail cars for the rest of the wagons and horses.

With Sgts. Griffin and Davis in tow, Francis walked to the station master's office to seek the space he needed on the train. As he walked into the small office, Captain Arthur Bevens, of the Confederate Army Quartermaster's Office, was busy with the train's engineer. They were finalizing the tasks needed to get the departure of the southbound train underway. He barely raised his eyes from the paperwork he was looking at on his desk when Francis and his men entered the office.

Somewhat distastefully, Bevens now advised Francis he had no room on the train for their needs. "Captain, as I have told your men I cannot make anymore room for you on this train. I have my orders, and my priorities, and right now you are not a priority for me. The next train is scheduled to depart from here sometime around eleven tomorrow morning. You will simply have to wait until then."

Less than pleased by Beven's attitude, and by his refusal to accommodate their needs, Francis did his best to stay calm. "Captain, what you're telling me is unacceptable. We have to have those rail cars off-loaded so my men and I can move out when the train is ready to leave. You are going to have to change your priorities, not mine. We must get moving south."

Sensing tempers were about to start flaring, the train's engineer, Walter Worden, a short and rather skinny man who wore thick glasses on the tip of his nose, tried leaving the office but found his path blocked by the two Virginia sergeants. Not looking to add to the problem that was already occurring, Worden quietly moved off to a corner of the office.

After a moment or two of tension and stares between the two officers, Bevens again tried to state his position. He had barely started to speak when Francis quickly cut him off.

"Bevens, my men and I have personally been assigned a mission by both General Lee and President Davis, a mission of the utmost importance to our cause. We must move south immediately and without delay. I have already lost time, and I have already lost some of my men, I will not be delayed any longer. Are you going to clear the rail cars for me and my men or should I just have them burn the cotton where it sits?" Francis had tried keeping his temper under control, but he now found himself dealing with a bureaucratic idiot who would rather move cotton than men assigned to a specific mission.

"Captain, I resent the tone you have taken with me. I shall warn you that if you persist with your threats, I shall report you to the Quartermaster's Office, who will then contact your commanding officer. I sincerely doubt that General Lee or President Davis, or anyone else in command of our armies, has ever even heard of you, yet alone assigned you to a mission for them."

Francis saw Davis take a step towards the still-seated Bevens, likely to reinforce to him whose authority they were really acting under, but he stopped him before he could reach the desk. Reaching inside his uniform blouse, Francis threw the envelope containing the letters written for him by President Davis and Secretary Memminger down on the desk for Bevens to read. "Captain, after you read the two letters feel free to walk over to the telegraph office with me. You can telegraph President Davis to make sure the letters are authentic. Be my guest!" Francis had lost his patience with Bevens; now he dared him to send a telegram to Richmond.

Opening the envelope, Bevens quickly read the two letters. After noticing whose signatures were on them, he placed them back into the envelope. Standing up from the chair he had been sitting in, he handed the envelope back to Francis. "Captain, I apologize for doubting you. Please accept my sincere apologies for not believing you. Please excuse me so I can make arrangements to have the rail cars emptied so you and your men will have the room you need."

Francis had gotten what he needed, but now he had one more point to make with Bevens. "Captain Bevens, before you leave I must tell you what you have just read is not to be spoken about with anyone. This mission is of particular importance to President Davis and to the entire Confederacy. I am giving you an order; it's the same one that was given to me by the President. You are not to speak about what you have read to anyone, for if you do, you will have to answer to President Davis directly. Do you understand?" Nervous and now sweating profusely, Bevens simply nodded his head to show Francis he understood what he had been told.

After Bevens left the office to clear room in the rail cars for Francis, the train's engineer, who chuckled out loud as Bevens left the office, finally got up the courage to speak. "Was that letter really from Ol' Jeff himself?" The wink he received from Francis let him know that it had been.

"Well, I'll be! Captain, this here train ride is gonna be the best one ya ever had. Tell me what y'all need and I'll get it for ya. I like that Ol' Jeff, he's a good man."

It took over two hours to change out the rail cars, but shortly after it was done, and under a hot summer sun, the train moved south out of Petersburg towards North Carolina. As it moved along the tracks, the heat and humidity were quickly forgotten by most of Francis' men as they had fallen asleep wherever they could find a comfortable spot.

They had been travelling for only three hours when trouble struck again, but this time it was not caused by the Yankees. Shortly after crossing into North Carolina, one of the steel bars connecting the two sets of the engine's wheels to each other cracked and the train soon lost traction on the rails. In moments, it soon came to a slow stop. After the problem had been identified, Francis learned it would likely take days to repair the damage. The repairs would shut down the rail line until the repairs could be made.

Out of concern that his men, and the precious cargo they were transporting, could become easy prey for any Union troops who might come upon the stalled train, Francis ordered them to unload the wagons from the train and to prepare to move south over land. Looking at a map Worden had on the train, Francis now hoped to move south to Hillsboro, North Carolina. "Hopefully we can link up with the North Carolina Railroad which runs through there." He thought as he studied the worn old map.

* * * * * *

Outside of Hillsboro they encountered a small group of Confederate replacement troops who were headed northeast towards Richmond. From them, Francis learned Union troops had recently probed the area northeast of Raleigh and that another small Union cavalry unit had also been seen off to the southeast. He also learned other Union troops had conducted a few small raids near Lincolnton, North Carolina, mostly damaging crops and setting fire to a few small buildings. As an experienced cavalry officer, he knew if these Union troops moved to join up with each other, and possibly with others in the area, they would likely target the rail lines first. Getting back on another train was a risk Francis knew was not worth taking. For now, they would have to move over land.

Gathering his men, Francis told them what he learned about Union troops being seen in the area. He also told them of his concern about using the railroad to move further south towards Atlanta. "If we can push south over land and get close to Lexington then I believe we will have a better chance of completing our mission and staying alive. Once there we can put the Yadkin River between us and any Yankee troops that might be in the area."

Over the next four days they slept little and ate simple cold meals as they moved slowly towards Lexington and to safety. But the men, whether they were scouting out in front of the wagon train, or driving one of the wagons over the bumpy terrain, never complained. Francis had grown impressed with their efforts to move the wagons south without a lick of any complaining. As they were earning his respect, he also was earning theirs as they saw he worked just as hard as they were. Unlike others they had served under, he also ate the same simple cold meals they were eating. He showed them, without trying to do so, that he was a different type of a leader than those they had previously toiled under.

After safely reaching the Lexington train station, their only problem came when it was time to load the train with their horses, wagons, and other supplies. Every available space on the station's platform was now crammed with war supplies, cotton, injured soldiers, lumber, and much more, all waiting for future trains to move them to assist in the war effort. Francis and his men now had to improvise a way to load the rail cars with the heavy wagons and their precious cargo.

From lumber stored on the station's platform, they crudely built ramps that ran from the ground up to the sides of the now empty rail cars so they could load the wagons onto the train. With Francis supervising the work, and with help from other railroad workers and from other Confederate soldiers who had been waiting to move out on another train, they pushed and pulled the first few wagons into place without any problems. But then, as they pushed and pulled one of the last wagons up the ramp, one of the ropes being used to pull the wagons onto the train snapped, and the heavy wagon rolled backwards. Despite their best efforts, it was too heavy for the men to hold in place on the ramp. As the wagon rolled off the side of the ramp, it crashed to the ground and landed on its left side. It was the wagon with the stars painted on it.

Standing on the edge of the rail car, Francis looked down to see the damaged wagon had spilled several gold bars on the ground; no longer hidden from sight within their secret compartments and flour barrels. As he saw them scattered on the ground, so did his men and the others who had been helping them load the wagons onto the train. At first they all just stood there staring at the gold bars, but then a Confederate soldier, a sergeant from North Carolina who had been helping them, quickly followed by another soldier, moved to pick up a couple of the gold bars.

"Not another step or you shall not live to see the end of this beautiful day!" Immediately the strong command tone in Francis' voice caused the two soldiers to stop in their tracks. Looking up, they saw Francis standing there pointing his pistol at them. Acting quickly, and before any other men could get up the courage to challenge him, three of his men grabbed their rifles. Quickly they moved the others who had been helping them away from the gold bars. As they did, they barked at those who had been helping them.

"Don't do it boys, don't try it! It ain't worth dying fer! Go on, get!" As they moved the others away from the damaged wagon, the rest of Francis' men collected the remaining gold bars on the ground; stacking them at his feet on the edge of the rail car.

As his men did this, Francis again spoke to the others in an attempt to try and diffuse their thoughts of trying to steal a gold bar. "Men, we appreciate the help you have given us today, but this gold belongs to the people of the Confederacy. It belongs to you and to wherever you are from, be it North Carolina, Virginia, or wherever, but it belongs mostly to our cause. This gold is what helps us fight the Yankees. It buys us food, it buys us weapons, and it buys us whatever else we need. My men and I are protecting this gold on orders from General Lee himself, so do not challenge me or my men here today, for if you do you will have to answer to your maker very soon and we do not want that. If you talk about what you have seen here today to others, you're a traitor to our cause and you will have defied the orders of our leaders. Now move along and forget what you have seen here today."

As the others moved away from the train station, Francis had his men, who like him were men who also had never seen this amount of gold before in their lives, off-loaded the rest of the gold and silver from the damaged wagon and place it on the rail car where he stood. In total, they took eight bags of silver and gold coins, as well as several more gold bars from the damaged wagon. They also placed the bag containing the jewelry on the floor of the rail car. It was the first time Francis had seen it. After taking the remaining provisions, harnesses, and two wagon wheels from the wagon, they dragged it off to the side of the rail yard and abandoned it.

When the train's engineer saw Francis' men had finally completed the loading of the train, and after checking with Francis one last time to make sure his needs had been completed, Worden moved the train slowly out of the station, heading it further south. As it moved out of the station, Francis had his men consolidate the gold and silver, and the other items they salvaged, amongst the other remaining wagons.

Before closing the last hidden compartment in one of the Conestoga wagons, Francis showed his men the contents of the cloth bag. It held the jewelry so many ladies from across the South had recently donated to the Confederate cause. The fine jewelry, especially two sets of diamond earrings, drew comments from all of them. "Men, your sweethearts would love to have any one of these pieces. I don't know much about jewelry, but these pieces look very expensive. It was generous of some of our ladies to give up this fine jewelry for the cause. Let's just hope we can put it to good use."

As they stood together looking at the jewelry, Stine, speaking for the other men, asked Francis about their precious cargo. "Captain, begging your pardon, but what's this all about? I mean . . . these here gold bars, the bags of silver and gold coins, and this here fine jewelry . . . why are we moving all of this in these here wagons? Early on y'all told us some news, and while we all know our place in this here army, and while we'll always do whatever you and General Lee asks of us and all, but with all due respect, ain't we got some right to know the story about this here money and all?"

Over the past two days, Francis had thought several times about telling his men more about their mission. He had wanted to be able to trust them just as they had shown their trust in him. Now he knew the time had come to tell them everything.

"Men, first I want you to know all of you have earned my confidence in a short period of time. Until just recently I had to keep our mission a secret from even you as I had to know that I, and the Confederacy, could trust you. I now know that we can." Over the course of the next half-hour Francis told his men about their mission, about the money they were protecting. He also told them President Davis wanted each of the Confederate states represented in the mission as the money belonged to the entire Confederacy and not to one state. Most importantly, he told them why keeping this money out of the hands of the Union army was so important to the Southern cause.

After he answered a couple of questions his men had, Francis surprised them with his last few comments. While he told them his original orders were to get the money to Atlanta, he then told them he expected to receive new orders after they got there. He believed his new orders would instruct him to move the money to Mississippi. He then shocked the men by telling them he believed they would not live to see that happen. "Men, if I am wrong in my premonition I will be a happy man. If we should live, but fail in our mission it will be my fault alone that we do. I will never allow any of you to be blamed for our failure; I simply will not allow that to occur." Upset by his own thoughts, Francis walked to the other side of the rail car to be alone. His men were left wondering why he thought they would all be killed. No one, not even Stine, had the courage to ask him about his premonition.

After speaking to his men, Francis returned to his daily routine of inspecting the wagons and the horses. His routine never varied at the end of the day as he believed in what one of his early commanders had told him about fighting a war. *"Proper planning prevents problems!"* So he always checked and rechecked the wagons, the horses, and, most importantly, upon his men every night. His men had grown to appreciate both his concern and his thoroughness. They now appreciated him even more for one piece of news he had just told them. That news was he would take the blame if things went wrong during their mission. After posting the guard for the evening, Francis climbed aboard one of the wagons, checked his pocket watch to see what time it was and then fell asleep. As he slept, the train moved further south and away from Lexington, passing through Salisbury, and then on towards Charlotte where it would stop to take on more wood for fuel.

When the train stopped in Charlotte, Francis and his men gladly took the opportunity to stretch their legs. As they did, they also took on some additional water for their horses. They had just finished doing so when several young boys quickly rode into town on their horses, yelling news of Yankee troops being seen less than an hours ride from town.

At first, Francis did not know what to make of the news, or whether he could trust the information the boys had excitedly brought to town, but soon the train station's telegraph operator came running out of his office with similar news he had just received. With that news also came other news about Union troops being seen further south in Chesterville. They had seriously damaged rail and telegraph lines running through there. The telegraph operator then gave Francis more bad news. His line had gone dead part-way through the last message he had just received. Francis knew he had to act fast.

Summoning his men, he told them they could not risk staying on the train and running into a Union ambush somewhere along the train's route. Knowing it would take time to unload the wagons, to get them hitched, and to move southeast away from the rail line, Francis ordered his men to do so quickly. As they did, he studied a map in the telegraph office for a route of travel. After finding one, he then checked with the minister of the First Baptist Church about the route he intended to take. He had been speaking with him when the boys had ridden into town with the news of the Union troops being close to Charlotte. He hoped Minister Hartman would know if any rail lines were still in operation. Francis knew if they were not, the rest of his trip would be that more difficult to complete. No longer did he have Atlanta as his final destination, now he was focused on making it to Charleston, South Carolina. He no longer cared how they got the gold and silver there; he just wanted to get the treasury someplace where it would be safe, even if only for a few days. He also knew if he was to get the precious assets of the Confederacy safely to Charleston, they probably would need his prayers to the almighty to be answered. Francis counted on his prayers being answered as he knew whatever luck he still had it was running out fast.

Minister Elijah Hartmann, a devout Baptist preacher, and an almost equally devout member of the local militia, told Francis that as far as he knew the train was still running to and from Charleston. "Twice a day I still believe." The news brought a smile of relief to Francis. Silently he thanked the almighty for blessing him with some good news.

As soon as the horses had been hitched to the wagons, Francis moved them out, heading southeasterly towards Charleston. Once there, he hoped to either find a train that would take them south towards Atlanta or a ship that would do the same. As they moved out, he silently processed his one other option available to him. "If I have to, I will hide the money with our friends in Charleston until it is safe to move it further south, but where would I leave it and with whom?" As he thought more on the options he had, he also knew they first had to make it to Charleston.

With the Yankees now close to Charlotte, Francis and his men pushed the horses hard so they could put distance between themselves and their enemy. As they did, they continually looked over their shoulders to make sure no one was gaining ground on them. There soon would be.

13

The Investigation Starts.

"Tell the General I can hold my ground."
Major John Pelham, CSA

Paul was not much of a computer guy, but he knew enough to spend part of the morning on Friday searching for answers on the Internet while he sat with his laptop at his kitchen table. Donna had found some information on the computer for him, but he was desperately trying to find answers to the many questions his brain had raised before shutting down for the night only five short hours ago. Sitting at the table, he soon drank several cups of black coffee in an attempt to stimulate his thought processes as he searched the Internet for answers to his many questions.

He spent the better part of the morning looking for information on the two bottles he had found. He also spent time seeking answers to why valuable gold coins might have been found on a Confederate soldier. In doing so, Paul sensed the coins seemed too valuable and too many for a soldier to have been carrying. "Had he stolen them, or won them playing cards, or had he simply just been paid in gold coins?" He knew the latter was not the case as even a Civil War novice knew about the financial problems the Confederacy had long endured during the war. He quickly realized they would not have paid a soldier in gold. He even spent time seeking out information on 'CH' Memminger and Judiah Francis. Paul had wanted to find out more about the watch he found, but for now he chose not to force open the slightly rusted watch. Not knowing who the maker of the watch was, and with little information to go on, he elected to deal with it at a later time. "I'll leave the watch be for now. If the other clues I have don't lead me to anything then I'll come back and look at it closer. I need to focus on the other clues first."

As he Googled information on the Internet, Paul soon found what he was looking for regarding the two makers of the bottles. He was especially interested in the information he found on the Willington Glass Works which had been located in Connecticut at the time of the war. "I worked a few investigations in Willington, I wonder how close I had been to where they were once located?" While he learned more about the two bottle makers, he still did not know how the bottles had come to be in the possession of Judiah Francis.

Continuing his search on the Internet, Paul quickly learned more on Confederate Treasury Secretary Christopher Memminger, but in his quick initial search for information on Captain Judiah Francis he found nothing. As he sat at his kitchen table with his computer, he took a sip from his fourth cup of coffee, realizing he had just drawn a blank on learning more about his soldier. "That was a disappointment," he thought as he shut down his HP Pavilion laptop. While he knew he needed to try and find more information on the Internet, he had hoped to find some quick answers as to what type of assignment President Davis and Secretary Memminger selected Captain Francis for, an assignment they both referred to in their letters. As he stood up from the table, he knew he probably had little chance in finding specific information on the Internet regarding the actual assignment. Doing so would require a significant amount of time and research going over Confederate documents to find that kind of information. Paul hoped he would not need to spend any significant amount of time doing that type of research as doing so would likely stall the progress he was trying to accomplish with the clues he had.

From his interpretation of the letters he found, Paul began to believe Francis had been responsible for moving some amount of Confederate money, but was not sure if his thought was a correct one. Earlier that morning, he had run several other thoughts through his mind regarding the gold coins, but they were just that, thoughts and guesses more than anything else. "Was he moving money to help pay for war materials? Could it have been destined for England to show them the strength of the Confederate economy? Or was it simply being moved to keep it out of the hands of Union troops before they invaded Richmond?" As he struggled to find the tiniest piece of useful information, he wondered if he would ever know the answers to his questions. The one thing he wanted to know more than anything was if Francis had been charged with moving money of some kind "what happened to that money?"

As he washed his coffee cup out in the sink, Paul continued to ask himself questions. "Had Francis hidden the money like his letter says or did he finally deliver it to its destination? And what happened to the money he had supposedly buried in North Carolina and the money he talked about being left in South Carolina? Did he ever recover it or is it still buried in those locations?" The questions he raised were far too many. It was the answers to the questions which were far too few at this time.

As he dressed to leave the house, Paul realized some type of crisis must have occurred, or was likely going to occur, for President Davis to authorize the movement of the Confederate treasury from Richmond.

* * * * * *

His first stop after leaving his house was at the Socastee Public Library, on Highway 707, in the small community of Socastee, South Carolina. Paul had visited the small library on two other occasions and had found the staff there fairly friendly. He went there today as he knew he would need their assistance to search for some of the answers to his many questions.

After spending some time looking through several Civil War reference books, Paul quickly found the information he had been seeking on Treasury Secretary Memminger. What he found, while interesting to him as a Civil War buff, did little to answer any of his questions regarding the assignment Memminger had a part in giving to Captain Francis. Like all amateur history buffs, Paul knew the Confederate capitol had been located in Richmond, Virginia, but when he read a couple of articles about Memminger's role in the Confederacy, one of the articles spoke about the threat the Union army had posed to Richmond. The same article later detailed the fierce and prolonged battles which had taken place in and around Richmond, a battle eventually won by Union troops. "So perhaps I am right about this assignment given to Francis by Memminger and President Davis. Perhaps they were concerned about the threat Union troops posed to Richmond, and perhaps they had assigned him to move the Confederate treasury, or part of it, to another location. Perhaps that money was the assets he talked about in his letter to President Davis?"

As Paul continued to read about the Battle of Richmond, he formed dramatic mental pictures in his head about the siege that had taken place there. The pictures he created were obviously not totally accurate ones, but they were ones which allowed him to generate both an understanding and an appreciation for the battles that had been fought there. Paul's brain had always allowed him to form these vivid mental pictures and it was this ability to form those pictures which helped him to develop an appreciation for the Civil War. These vivid pictures were present with him during the several visits he had made to the battlefield sites at Gettysburg. They were also with him during his walk down the Sunken Road at Fredericksburg, and they had been with him when he had stood at Marye's Heights looking down at the field where the Union army had been slaughtered by the Confederate army. As he had questioned the wisdom of the Confederate army attacking the high ground at Gettysburg, he had also questioned the Union's decision to attack the high ground at Fredericksburg. These same vivid pictures were also with him during one of his favorite visits, a visit to Appomattox Court House.

During his visit to Appomattox Court House, he had stood along the same path the Confederate army walked along that fateful morning when they finally surrendered. Paul had pictured Union General Joshua Lawrence Chamberlain sitting on his horse adjacent to the path, surrounded by his victorious men, watching the defeated, but still proud Confederate army pass by them as the Union army ceremoniously accepted the formal surrender of the Confederacy. On that particular day, Paul had even thought he heard Chamberlain's voice as he ordered his men to salute the brave Confederate soldiers who passed by them. Those vivid mental pictures of the Civil War also caused him to shudder at the carnage that had occurred during those battles when brave young men, both Union and Confederate, were often murdered by their blundering generals. It was many of those officers, perhaps more so in the North, who had simply been promoted to their ranks to curry political or ethnic support back home for the needs of the war. Many of those officers had known little about military tactics. Paul had always held those officers in contempt for their actions in wasting so many young lives. He had often thought how happy he was that his two boys did not have to fight in such a terrible war.

As he snapped back from his mental pictures of the battles fought in and around Richmond, Paul now looked for information on the gold coins he had found with the remains of Captain Francis. He wanted to know where the coins had been minted, and what their approximate value was, as he thought knowing that information might give him a clue as to why Francis had them in his possession at the time of his death. After searching unsuccessfully for several minutes for such a book, he went to the Reference Desk for assistance. When his turn came, Paul explained to Caren Mullaney, the Head Reference Librarian, what it was he was looking for. After checking her computer files, she guided him to where several books on coins had been placed on the shelves. After finding a couple of books for him to review, he thanked her for her assistance.

"If you give me a couple of minutes, I'll check the computer again to see if the library in Conway has any others you might be interested in."

"OK, thanks. If it's OK with you I'll wait for you at the table I was working at. It will give me a couple of minutes to look at these books we found."

"Fine, I'll be right back." She gave Paul a quick smile and then headed back to her computer.

Paul went back to the table he had been working at and started looking through the coin books to see if he could find any references to the coins he had found, ones he now had secreted within his garage. He had only been able to look at the coin books for a few minutes when Caren reappeared by his side. She then told him the Conway library had two other books on coins for him to look at besides the ones he already had. Telling Paul this, she happened to notice he had one of the books opened to a page that showed pictures of several old gold coins.

"I hope you have a box full of those gold coins. You'd likely be a very rich man."

At first, Paul only had a silent response for her. "If only you knew, if only you knew." He had yet to look up at her as he had just found a picture of one of the coins he found.

Caren's next comment was simply meant to be a joke, but it caused Paul to put the book he was looking at down on the table. "With all of the books you have here on the Civil War, and on gold coins, what are you trying to do, find the lost treasure?"

She now had his attention. "I'm sorry, guess I was kind of focused on a picture of a gold coin. What did you say about a lost treasure?"

Caren gave Paul a quizzical look at first, but then realized he really did not know what she had been referring to. Over the next several minutes, she told him about the legend of the lost Confederate treasury. He listened carefully as she described the legend that had been passed down for generations since the Civil War about the missing gold and silver; money which had been shipped out of Richmond during the war. "It's a widely accepted fact that the money was moved south out of Richmond by Confederate solders, but no one knows what happened to it after that." Caren then told him that ever since the money disappeared Southern folks had speculated for years over what had happened to it. She then told him about the various theories that had existed for years. In doing so, she explained the theories included some people believing those soldiers tasked with moving the money had actually stolen it; that some people thought crooked politicians had stolen it during the final days of the war when all hope had been lost for the Confederate cause; that some folks believed the gold and silver had been captured by Union troops and they had kept it for themselves, and that others simply believed the money had never existed at all. "I don't know what to believe myself, but I'm telling you one thing, if you ever find it you had better share some of it with the gal who helped you out this morning!"

What Paul had just learned about the missing Confederate money sent a cold chill down his spine. As he sat there digesting what Caren had just told him, the news caused him to silently generate additional questions. Like his previous ones, these were questions he did not have any immediate answers to. "Were the coins I found part of the Confederate treasury, that missing money? Was Francis the person who had been charged with moving that gold and silver? Was that what Davis, Memminger, and Francis were referring to in their letters? Is this money the assets Francis vaguely described in his letter?" Paul thought of the Francis letters and began to wonder if they contained any hidden clues which would lead him to where the money had been buried.

"Sir, do you need anymore help?"

Caren's question brought Paul back from the thoughts he was having about the letters. "What? Oh, yes, I'm sorry. Your story about the missing money caused me to daydream there for a minute. I'm terribly sorry. Your story about the missing Confederate money, do you have any books on that? Oh . . . one more thing . . . if you don't have anything on this I'm sure I can probably Google it when I get home . . . but do you have any books or information on R.F.W. Allston? He was governor of South Carolina near the time of the Civil War, but I'm not sure of his exact term of office."

Caren smiled when Paul asked her about books on the missing treasury as she knew she had piqued his interest in this legend. "Give me a bit. I'll let you know what I find."

As she left to find the information Paul had asked her to look up for him, and to email the Conway library so they could send down the other two coin books for him to look at, his attention returned to the letter Francis had written to President Davis. "Was the letter actually giving us veiled clues about the missing Confederate money when we read it?" He also could not help thinking, as he tried recalling the wording of the Francis letters, "that one of the letters actually talked about money being buried in three separate locations; two in South Carolina and one in North Carolina. But where?"

The events of the past several days had certainly captured Paul's attention. Far too much, such as meeting Steve, buying the boat and the truck, and then finding the soldier's remains and artifacts, had taken place in a short a period of time. Now after being told of the legend of the missing Confederate money, his instincts took over. He knew he possibly might have the clues needed to find the missing gold and silver. He hoped his acquired investigative skills would help him find what others before him could not. He also had one other thought as he sat in the library waiting for Caren to return. "With all that has happened to me over the past several days, am I destined to be the person who finds this missing money?"

After a few minutes, Caren returned to where Paul was still sitting. She was carrying several pieces of papers, some of which had answers to a few of the questions he had asked her to look up for him. "OK, I emailed the Conway library and they will have those two coin books here by tomorrow afternoon. When they get here, I'll mark them with your name and you can pick them up at the Front Desk late tomorrow. Now, here is some of the information I was able to find for you when I Googled the name of Governor Allston, this should get you started at least. You know, I learned something today doing this for you as I did not know he was a governor of South Carolina, but I guess that explains why the Allston name still exists to some degree in Pawleys Island. Well, good luck with whatever you are doing, and don't forget to share some of the gold with me when you find it!"

Thanking her for her assistance, Paul promised he would bring her a gold coin when he found the missing money. His promise made her laugh. "I've had a lot of guys promise me things over the years, but never a gold coin. I won't hold my breath on that promise!" Caren gave him a smile and then returned to her desk to help her next customer, an elderly man interested in researching his family tree.

* * * * * *

Donna and Paul arrived a few minutes early at the restaurant that evening so they stopped at the bar for a drink before Steve showed up to meet them for dinner. As they settled onto their bar stools, Paul looked to see if Kathy was bartending, but saw no sign of her. After ordering their drinks, he began to tell Donna about what his research at the library had uncovered. He was beginning to tell her about the bombshell Caren had revealed regarding the missing Confederate treasury, but just as he started to do so Steve was standing next to them as they sat at the bar.

Before Paul had a chance to introduce Donna to Steve, he took her hand and introduced himself to her. "When I met your husband I could tell he was a good guy as he helped me with my flat tire, but what I didn't know was that he had such a beautiful wife." Now blushing, Donna thanked him for his compliment. After spending a few minutes talking at the bar while enjoying their drinks, they were escorted to their table for dinner.

Pulling out Donna's chair for her as they sat down at the table, Steve commented on Paul's recent discovery. "I'll tell you one other thing also. I did not know your husband was going to become such an instant celebrity in these parts for finding an old bag of bones in the woods. That was an amazing discovery, just wonderful. I'm happy for him."

Paul smirked at the good-natured shot Steve had given him for having his picture in the papers, and for his face being all over the local television news recently as a result of discovering the Confederate soldier's remains. "That must have been quite the exciting first boat ride," Steve said as the waitress took their drink orders. Steve and Donna elected to share a bottle of Kendall Jackson Vinter's Reserve Chardonnay, while Paul decided to stay with Jack and Coke. As she took their drink orders, Paul asked the waitress for a small favor. "Please tell the bartender I'd like a little more Jack and a little less Coke in the next one." Handing her his empty glass, he thanked her for her assistance, hoping it would result in a stiffer drink than the first one.

Steve joked with Paul about his first drink, asking him if he was disappointed with it. "Yeah, kind of, but I understand the guy who owns this place tells the bartenders to water down the drinks so the booze lasts longer. You know, more drinks out of one bottle equals more money." While Paul's comments were meant as a joke, and while Steve took them as they were intended to be, Donna's face showed her embarrassment. Even though she knew Paul was joking, she thought his comment was a bit harsh, especially to someone they barely knew.

Sensing Donna was uncomfortable with the comment Paul had made, Steve quickly assured her he knew it had been made in jest. "Owning a bar, I hear these jokes all the time. Please don't think I was offended as I like being able to laugh with friends. Besides, I'll just mark up the drink prices next time he comes in so I can get even with him. He'll never know what hit him." Donna and Paul quickly laughed at Steve's comments. His comments made her feel more relaxed as she knew he had not been offended. Quickly, she made Steve promise to live up to his threat of charging her husband more for his future drinks.

Over the next two hours they talked like old friends do when they share drinks and a meal together. They laughed and joked about their lives, learned more about Steve and his interests, and Paul shared with him some additional details on how he had found the soldier's remains. While he told Steve most of what he had found along with the remains, he intentionally left out a few of the details. During dinner, when he thought the time was right, Paul told Steve about hearing of the legend of the lost Confederate treasury. When the time was right, he asked him what he knew about it. Real or imagined, Steve confirmed it was a story most true Southerners knew about. He also told Paul it seemed as if almost everyone had their own version of what had happened to the money. As he talked about what he knew about the Confederate treasury, he also told Paul something totally unexpected. "Unlike most people, I don't really have an opinion on what happened to it. I guess it's because I never really thought about it too much. I'm like your wife in that regard as in school history never really interested me much."

Steve then surprised Paul again by telling him one of his best friends, and his sometime golfing partner, Chick Mann, was an American History professor at the University of South Carolina. He also mentioned that Chick was somewhat thought of as a Civil War expert by many people. Surprising him again, he offered to call his friend so Paul could talk to someone about what he had found. "He teaches history and he knows his stuff. I know from talking to him that people often call him when they find something related to the war, so I guess he would be a good guy for you to speak with. I'm sure he would love to hear what you have found."

"Fine," Paul replied, accepting Steve's offer to call Chick for him. "I'd be happy to speak with him."

During two more rounds of after dinner drinks, the conversation returned to other local topics and issues. After they finished their drinks over dessert, they chatted for almost another hour before saying their goodbyes. As they walked to their cars, Donna promised Steve they would soon call him to invite him over for dinner. "I just need to do a little more unpacking first. We need to have you over for a nice meal on my good plates. I'm certainly not serving you your first meal at our house on paper plates."

Steve warmly accepted the invitation, telling Donna he looked forward to hearing from them soon. After opening the car door for her, Donna got into their car. For a brief few moments, Steve and Paul stood near the rear of Paul's car and shook hands while they said their goodbyes. As they did, Steve held the handshake for a few moments longer than normal. Staring at Paul, who had now made eye contact with him, Steve spoke to him about the gold coins he had found. "I hope you find the rest of that gold. You call me if you need anything or if anyone tries to get in your way." Then he walked away and got into his Mercedes.

As Paul watched him walk to his car, he thought about Steve's last comment to him. "Does he know about the gold coins I found or is he just guessing?"

Driving home in silence from the restaurant, Paul and Donna were savoring thoughts of the meal they had just enjoyed, as well as Steve's company, when the quiet was broken by the country music ringtone on Paul's cell phone. Answering it, he learned Steve had remained back in the restaurant's parking lot so he could reach out to his friend.

"Chick's very interested in meeting with you about what you've found. He wants to know if you can meet him at Coastal Carolina University on Tuesday morning, say around ten or so. He has a meeting there at nine, but expects to be done just before ten. He said to meet him in the small courtyard out in front of the Kimbel Library. The school is just off of U.S. 501; it's probably only a twenty minute drive from the Inlet. Is that OK with you?"

"Shouldn't be a problem. I'm actually looking forward to speaking with him. Thanks for setting the meeting up for me. Hey, we had a great time tonight. We'll do it again soon, I promise."

"I'm looking forward to it. Give your pretty wife a kiss good night for me. Take care."

* * * * * *

The following morning was a lazy one for Donna and Paul as they each had been flat out the entire week. They slept late and spent a good part of the morning reading the newspaper as they drank their morning coffee.

Late in the afternoon after unpacking a few more of their belongings, which had been neglected by the recent purchase of the boat and the finding of the soldier's remains, Paul took out the soldier's watch from the cardboard moving box he had hidden it in. He wanted to try and clean it as he hoped it might contain a few more clues for him. After examining it for a few minutes, he began to gently clean away the rust and grime from the watch's exterior.

Using a soft piece of cloth and a fine brush, he carefully took his time cleaning away some of the rust from around the hinge and clasp.

Cautiously applying some pressure to the clasp area, Paul was surprised when the watch opened relatively easy. He was again surprised when he found the interior of the watch to be in very good condition. Only a small stain on the bottom of the watch's interior marred its face. It had likely been caused by moisture getting under the glass face. He was pleased to see the face of the watch was still in excellent condition.

Paul had hoped to find a picture of someone, perhaps the soldier's sweetheart or his mother, on the left side of the watch when he opened it, but none were there. Looking at the watch, he saw it had long ago stopped running. It had stopped running at 7:58. "I wonder if it was a.m. or p.m.?"

Afraid he would harm the watch by trying to wind it with the small key he found in one of the pockets of the blouse, Paul did not try to wind it. He feared doing so might permanently damage the watch and that he might never get it to run again. As he looked at the time displayed on the watch, he noticed the name *Waltham* on its face. He made a mental note to Google the name of the watchmaker to see what he could find out about them. Carefully closing the watch, he now focused his attention on the front of it. Gently he cleaned the outside so he could see what had been engraved there. As he did, he saw the initials he hoped to see. They became easier to read once most of the grime had been cleared away. The simple engraving read *'J.F.'*.

By simple deduction, Paul was fairly confident the initials were likely those of Captain Judiah Francis, whose letters, to both his father and to President Davis, he had found in the bottles. "Another part of the puzzle has come together."

After carefully securing the watch back in its hiding place, Paul went to his computer and Googled *Waltham watches* on his laptop. The Waltham Watch Company had been a fairly large maker of watches for a period of time in the 1800's and, as their website showed they had even been the maker of a pocket watch, a Model 1859 – a *William Ellery* pocket watch - which President Abraham Lincoln had been the owner of. Lincoln's watch had a recorded serial number of 67673. Reading about Lincoln's watch, he wondered about the specifics of the one he had found. "I don't dare open it, but I wonder what year it was made in and what the serial number is. I will have to find that out somehow."

As he continued to read about the Waltham Watch Company, Paul could not help but to realize the irony that existed regarding a pocket watch which had been made in the North, in Waltham, Massachusetts to be precise. It was a watch that had been carried by an officer of the Confederate Army. He quickly realized it was likely due to the fact the industrial North was further ahead of the South at that time in our country's history when it came to making items like watches.

After making a few notes about what he found on the Internet regarding the watch, Paul shut down his computer. As he did, Donna hollered to him that it was almost time to take a shower and to get dressed for the cookout at Bobby Ray's home. Later, as he started getting dressed, Paul caught himself smiling. He knew he had been looking forward to spending an evening with his good friend. Enjoying the night with good friends, laughing over a few drinks, and sharing a great meal was all he needed. It was what life was supposed to be all about.

As he finished getting dressed, Paul pondered whether he should tell Bobby Ray about the gold coins, the watch, and the other items he had found. While he wanted to tell him, he realized this was not the right time. Having more leads that needed following up on, he did not want any distractions stopping him from learning what he needed to know about his secret collection of items. "I'll tell him, but not right now. He's going to be mad at me for not telling him, but I'll make him understand why I didn't. At least, I hope I can."

* * * * * *

In the coming days and weeks, as he worked on the few leads he developed, Paul could never have guessed where those leads would take him. It was a journey that was just beginning to address a Southern legend which had existed for almost one hundred and fifty years. It would be a remarkable journey for him to make.

14

The Race to Charleston.

"That man will fight us every day and every hour till the end of the war."
Lt. General James Longstreet, CSA, describing Union General U.S. Grant

Francis and his men pushed their horses hard to put distance between their precious cargo and the Union troops who would soon be arriving in Charlotte. Forgoing food and rest, they pushed on; fearing Union troops would soon begin to pursue them. Francis knew they still had at least six more days of hard travel before they reached Florence and, hopefully, the still operating North Eastern Railroad. But he knew if he pushed the horses too hard they would die and then he would never get his precious cargo to where he needed to get it to. Pushing the horses was a risk he was not willing to take as the chances of finding replacement horses were few. Horses strong enough to pull the heavy wagons were harder and harder to find these days because of the demands of the war. Now he began to slow their pace.

As he slowed the pace of the wagons so the horses could rest to some degree as they moved south, their pace grew even slower when they were forced to travel over difficult terrain. The ground had been made soft by two days of steady rain and during that time several of the wagons had sunk up to their axles in the mud they encountered. Still they pushed on, with Francis only allowing them to pause for brief spells so both horses and men could be fed.

As the horses always did, now his men did the same. The men ate cold meals for several days as Francis, out of fear that a campfire would alert Union troops to their whereabouts, refused to allow them to cook a hot meal. The men ate what little food they could prepare in a short amount of time before pushing forward again. His men grumbled about the meager amount of food they were being given, but they knew Francis had eaten even less than they had. They grumbled like all soldiers do when they are not fed well, but even they knew the risk had been too great to start a fire.

As they travelled into the early evening hours of their fifth day since leaving Charlotte, Francis sent out scouts in different directions to determine if any Union troops could be seen. When the last of his scouts reported back to him that they had found nothing in the way of any pursuing Yankee troops, Francis ordered a halt for the day. The wagons were soon moved into a small clearing within a lightly wooded area. They were now only five miles northwest of Monroe, North Carolina when they stopped for the evening. As a reward for their efforts in pushing hard for the last couple of days during heavy rain and over bad terrain, and because he finally felt they were safe from any Union troops, Francis allowed a fire to be built. That evening the men enjoyed their first hot meal in several days.

For the next four days the wagons again moved slowly south, with Francis choosing times to push the horses hard when the terrain allowed for a quicker pace. Pushing on, they moved through Wadesboro and Sneedsboro stopping only for water and food for both the men and the horses. Each time they stopped, Francis tried learning news of any Union troop movements in the area, but he learned nothing of any importance. The lack of news worried him. As they moved out towards Darlington, a five-day ride from Sneedsboro, he fully expected they would be attacked by Union cavalry at any time. "Where are they? Someone surely has told them about us and our wagons? Why have they not attacked us yet?"

But then, as luck would have it, disaster struck them. This time from the hands of Southern sympathizers and not from Union troops. While the people of Wadesboro and Sneedsboro had yet to hear of any Union troop movements in the area, other citizens west of those two towns had and they had organized themselves to attack any Union troops they saw marching towards Charleston. It had been injured Confederate soldiers, sent home from the front to recuperate, who were joined by old men and young boys, as well as a few ill-trained local militiamen, who gathered their guns and courage to fight the Yankees. This group of misfits was determined to halt the Yankees advance south.

In the early evening hours of the tenth day of traveling since they had left the rail yard, Francis pushed his men to make a few more miles before halting for the day. As they moved through a large meadow, Sgt. Gerald Rickert, who was riding out in front of the wagons, was suddenly shot and killed. He had been mistaken for a Union soldier by a member of the group of Southern sympathizers who were determined to fight the Yankees.

The shot had been heard by both Sgt. Sturges and Sgt. Foster who also were riding away from the wagons. As they arrived to investigate the shot they had heard, they rode into a deadly crossfire and Foster fell dead. He was shot twice by two injured Confederate soldiers who had mistaken him for a Union cavalry officer. Sturges had also been shot, but his wound was at first not thought to be serious. It had been his screams which caused this ragtag group of men to finally stop firing.

As soon as Francis saw the carnage that had taken place, he quickly knew his chances of completing a successful mission had just been crippled with the loss of Foster and Rickert. As he sat on his horse looking at the bodies of his two men now dead on the ground, senselessly killed by friendly fire just as

General Thomas 'Stonewall' Jackson had been killed, he felt a rage boil inside of him. He quickly sought a victim to extract his revenge on. Drawing his saber, he spurred his horse forward, charging directly at a man about his own age so he could punish him for the loss of his two men. But as he did he saw a young boy, a boy too young to be out fighting a war, run to his father, the intended target Francis had sought to seek his vengeance on. Whether it was out of fear for his own safety, or to protect his father, the actions of the young boy caused Francis to pull up on his reins. His horse stopped directly in front of the man and his frightened son. As he glared at the man who had helped kill two of his men, Francis dropped his raised right arm to his side. As he did, his saber harmlessly scrapped the side of his right boot. The anger he felt, anger which had raised the saber to harm someone, quickly left him.

As he dismounted from his horse, Francis saw the rest of the wagons had come up to where they were. With Griffin's assistance, Samuel tended to the injury Sturges had sustained. Sturges had sustained what appeared to be a through and through minor gunshot wound to the left side of his chest. As he sat on the ground being treated for his injury, he cursed a streak of profanity at those men who had shot him and killed his two friends. While not a person who used profanity much as he thought the use of it showed one's shortcomings in life, Francis did nothing to stop Sturges from cussing out those who had shot him.

Francis then collected the ragtag group of men who had mistakenly fired upon his men. As he told them their actions had seriously harmed a mission of great importance to the Confederacy, he could feel his anger return and his blood again starting to boil. As he berated them for their actions, the man whose son had saved him moments earlier from being on the receiving end of Francis' saber, dropped to his knees crying, begging for forgiveness.

"Sir, I beg you to forgive me for what I have done. I have done a terrible thing, something which shall live with me for the rest of my time here on earth. I have sinned terribly here today. Please forgive me!"

Rising from where he had knelt, the man walked to a large nearby rock and broke his rifle against the rock, the wooden stock splintering into several pieces. Tossing the broken rifle to the ground, he then removed a cartridge box of ammunition from his belt and dropped it to the ground. Gathering up his still frightened son, he started the long walk home; one arm around his young son and the other wiping tears from his own face. The anger Francis felt in his body again left him. After ordering two of his men to run the Southern sympathizers off towards their homes, Francis walked to where Foster and Rickert lay on the ground. Kneeling down next to them, he began to cry over the loss of his two men. He also wept over what the young boy had witnessed and would carry with him for the rest of his life.

Soon regaining his composure, Francis realized with the loss of two more men, plus the injury sustained by Sturges, he did not have enough men to drive the wagons and to serve as scouts when he needed them. He now was forced to make a hard decision.

Still fearing they would soon be attacked by Union cavalry, Francis made the decision to empty the provisions, as well as the gold and silver, from one of the wagons. As this was being done, Odom and Samuel dug a large hole in the ground. "It needs to be big enough to bury our two friends and a large wooden barrel." Everyone momentarily stopped working when they heard the order he gave as they now wondered why Francis was planning on burying a barrel in the grave that would be the final resting place for Foster and Rickert.

As some of the men worked on moving the provisions from one wagon into another, and while others stacked the gold and silver on the ground from the wagon being unloaded, Francis called to Sgt. Banks. Having shown his ability to whittle during their journey, Banks was directed to make a large wooden cross out of the floorboards from the wagon which was being left behind. "Use whatever you need from the wagon, but make the cross a good size. When you are done, I want you to somehow whittle C.S.A. into the cross or into another board you are to attach to it. I don't care how you do it, but make it big enough to be seen from a distance."

Francis had a large wooden barrel emptied of its small amount of remaining flour and then had it dragged into the large hole Odom and Samuel finished digging. He then explained his intentions to his men. He told them they were now forced to lighten their load as they did not have enough men to drive all of the wagons. He further explained how he intended to bury the gold and silver which had been in the wagon they just emptied. "We're going to bury it inside the barrel. After we cover the barrel with dirt, then we'll place the bodies of Foster and Rickert directly over the top of it."

Understanding what he wanted to accomplish, the men quickly loaded the barrel with the bags of gold and silver they unloaded from the wagon. Sealing the end of the barrel as best they could, they then covered it with a thick layer of dirt. Then the blanket wrapped bodies of Foster and Rickert were gently laid in the hole directly over the top of the barrel. Then the hole was back filled with dirt. When the grave was finally filled, it almost looked as if the ground had never been disturbed. Francis then had his men find four large rocks. The large rocks were then placed directly over the grave which now held the bodies of his two men and the flour barrel filled with gold and silver.

After helping to bury Foster and Rickert, Francis inspected the wooden cross Banks had constructed. Using boards from the wagon, as well as nails and bolts he had been able to salvage, Banks constructed a cross almost seven feet in height and roughly five feet in width. In large letters, he had whittled

C.S.A. into the boards running the width of the cross. Francis was pleased by what he saw and took the time to pat Banks on the shoulder for what he had put together. "Franklyn, I know our friends would be proud to have this cross displayed over their grave. You have done a fine job!"

Francis then surprised his men again by having them carry the cross not to the grave, but to a nearby stone wall which stood less than fifty feet away from it. Pointing to where he wanted it, Francis said, "Put the cross in the ground here. This way we know where the grave is and no one else does. I don't think anyone is going to be doing any digging around it, but if they do, we certainly don't want them to find the gold." His men quickly realized the cross, as well as the stones on top of the grave, would serve as reference points for them when they could come back and retrieve the gold and silver.

After planting the cross in the soft North Carolina soil, with his remaining men following him, Francis walked back to the grave which now held the bodies of two of his soldiers. Taking off his hat, he dropped to one knee. "Men, let us pray for our departed friends." The others, some standing, some kneeling, several with tears now on their faces, took off their hats and joined him around the grave as he offered a prayer for their two friends. As the sun began to disappear in the sky, no one moved or said a word for several minutes. They were still numb from the events that had occurred during this hot late summer evening.

After several minutes of silent mourning, Francis told his men to make camp for the night as he knew trying to make up any lost time now would be a wasted effort. His men needed time to grieve, to eat, and to rest after a difficult day. But staying true to his routine, and before he allowed them to rest, the ever cautious Francis ordered two of his men to ride the perimeter around where they were making their camp for the night. He had already lost two men today and wanted to make sure he did not lose anymore. His two men rode the perimeter together, making sure they were not being watched by Yankees or by anyone else. As this was being done, Francis retrieved a pencil and a small piece of paper from one of his saddlebags. Under the last remaining light of day, he drew a map of where the grave had been placed, of the four stones marking it, and of the cross which had been placed a short distance away. As he drew the map, he had but one thought. "I can only hope my men will guard this money for me until I can come back to get it." He then prayed his roughly drawn map would someday soon guide him back to where the money had been buried.

By the time he finished his map, the men had the campfire already started and Samuel was beginning to cook them a hot meal. After finishing their meal, and with their horses already cared for, Francis told them all to sleep. Climbing onto his horse, he rode out into the night as his men had done so many nights before. Tonight he would be the sentry on duty so they could sleep. He would stand guard during the night, making sure the Yankees did not disturb their sleep.

Francis had ridden around the northern perimeter of the camp for the second time, keeping a sharp eye out for any movements which would cause him to sound the alarm to wake his men, but the night had been a peaceful one. As he stopped his horse for a few moments, he pulled out his pocket watch. From the light the full moon displayed on this beautiful summer evening, he could see it was just past three in the morning. As he placed his watch back into his uniform blouse, he saw the silhouette of one of his men riding out to meet him. Sgt. Roy McKinney, the short stocky North Carolinian, who had been such a big help during their mission by always being ready to care for the needs of their horses, rode up to where Francis had stopped his horse near a small stand of pine trees.

"Morning, captain. I thought you could use some sleep. I'll stay out here until we get moving in the morning."

"Thanks, Roy. I could use some sleep. I appreciate the consideration."

"Captain, I'm sorry to tell you this when you're so tired, but I checked on Sturges before I rode out here. He's dead, likely been so for about an hour. I think he bled to death as I could see his shirt and bandages were soaked in blood. I had checked on him earlier . . . so had Odom . . . he was fine both of those times, but he must have bled to death from his wounds as he slept. I liked that boy, he's one I'm gonna miss." McKinney turned his head away so Francis would not see him wiping away the tears starting to form in his eyes.

As tired as Francis was from being up all day, and for most of the night, upon hearing Sturges had succumbed to his wounds, he now felt exhausted. He knew he had to get some sleep, but as he rode back to where the others now slept he also knew without Sturges he would have to figure out how to finish his mission with only six healthy soldiers, one injured soldier, and a slave.

Before attempting to fall sleep, Francis knelt down and pulled back the blanket covering the face of the now deceased Sgt. Sturges. He had been the quiet one of the group. While he fit in well with the others, especially when they played card games by the campfires at night, perhaps because he was older and more mature, Sturges had kept his distance at times. As he looked down on Sturges' still youthful face, a face his parents would never see again, he bowed his head and prayed for him. After finishing his prayer, and despite knowing Sturges was dead, Francis softly spoke to him, not knowing if he was comforting himself or Sturges' spirit, a spirit he believed was still present. "Later this morning we shall bury you near your friends, Sgts. Foster and Rickert. You have each served our cause so well together and now you shall sleep near each other for eternity. I shall miss each of you." Pulling the blanket back over Sturges' face, he then went to lie down. He knew it would likely prove to be a wasted effort as he could not possibly fall asleep after three of his men had just died.

As he thought about his men who died that day, his thoughts turned to others who had also lost men in battle. "How had so many generals been able to sleep at night after they had ordered thousands of men to their deaths in some battle? I have lost only three men today and I wonder if I will ever be able to sleep again or be able to clear their faces from my mind." Lying on his blanket, Francis knew his troubles would likely continue. He also knew the chances of his mission being a successful one was now in trouble.

If he knew how much more trouble they would soon face he might have been able to plan for it, but Francis was just a soldier and on most occasions soldiers do not know the trouble that lays waiting for them. He would just have to deal with it when it confronted him, just like so many other soldiers before him had done.

Amongst those thoughts, with his blanket spread out on the ankle deep and dew covered North Carolina grass, he finally fell asleep. It would not be a restful sleep.

* * * * * *

The men had already risen and taken care of their horses before Francis woke a few scant hours after falling asleep. They had made themselves some coffee and were preparing to move out for the day by the time he started to stir in his blankets. They appreciated his efforts last evening in riding guard duty while they had slept and now they tried to quietly complete their morning chores so he could sleep as long as possible.

It was Griffin who saw Francis starting to stir. After bringing their small campfire back to life, Griffin began making the second pot of morning coffee for all of them to share. "Morning, captain. I set a cup of coffee down by you a couple of minutes ago; it should still be plenty warm. I know you heard about Sturges. We dug a grave for him this morning near where we buried Rickert and Foster. We got him wrapped in a blanket, but we ain't yet buried him as we knew you'd want to say some words over him." It was not the type of a greeting Francis normally started the day with.

Propping himself up on his elbows, Francis saw the still steaming cup of coffee which had been set down next to him. Picking up the cup of hot coffee, he nodded his thanks to Griffin. Drinking his coffee, he saw the others huddled around Sturges' blanket wrapped body.

As he stared at this scene, he then saw the injured Sgt. Hatfield climb down out of the wagon he had been riding in. He watched for a moment as

Hatfield started hobbling to where the others had gathered. As he hobbled along, Francis easily caught up to him.

"Good morning, Sgt. Hatfield, how's the leg this morning?"

"Captain, good morning to you, sir. I am making it, but not too well I'm afraid. This leg splint is an evil device. I know it's supposed to help my leg get better, but to be honest, it ain't working. My leg hurts real bad. Sadly, I'm afraid as much as my leg hurts; I'm doing better than Sturges is this morning. He and I became good friends in a short period of time. He was a good man, a real Christian man."

"That he was . . . that he was." Francis said, agreeing with Hatfield's assessment of their departed friend.

As they walked the short distance towards where Sturges was to be buried, Francis saw the pain in Hatfield's face with each step he took. "Edward, I know you are having trouble with your leg, but I need you more than ever now that Sturges is dead. This is going to be difficult for you, and while I'm still holding out hope we can jerry-rig something to help ease the pain you're feeling, I need to know if you can drive a wagon for us. Can you do it?"

"I guess we will know soon enough, won't we, captain?"

"I guess we will."

Francis now knew Hatfield's leg was hurting him more than he had previously let on as each step brought a grimace of pain to his face. The grimaces told Francis he now needed to find proper medical care for him. He knew the ride in the back of the wagon for the past several days had been painful for Hatfield to endure, but now the ride on the hard seat of a wagon would offer no comfort at all to his broken leg.

After burying Sturges next to where they had buried their other two friends, they broke camp and started the ride south for the day. The men tried rigging a contraption to try and ease the pain Hatfield would feel from each bump his wagon hit, but before they had gone very far he let out the first of several screams. Hatfield's painful screams told the others their efforts had failed to make the ride any easier for him. Still they pushed on.

Moving south towards Darlington and the North Eastern Railroad, Francis surveyed the looks on the faces of his men. He sensed the deaths of their friends, and the screams of pain Hatfield let out, were taking a toll on his men. They were struggling to finish their mission with far fewer hands than they had when they left Richmond.

Francis had grown to admire his men not only for how they handled themselves when faced with adversity, but how they had done so despite the loss of several of their fellow soldiers. While others selected these men for this assignment, and while they now were his men, he knew those who had selected them had picked the right soldiers for this mission. He was grateful to them as well.

As they moved along, Francis could also not help but smile when he saw the irony which now existed. The irony involved Samuel. As the wagons moved south and deeper into the Confederacy, a slave now drove one of the wagons, one loaded with gold and silver needed to help keep the Confederacy alive. He shook his head at this sight as he knew many a Southerner would be appalled over this, but times were different now and Samuel drove his wagon as well as any other man could.

Under the hot North Carolina sun they slowly moved along. As they did, they purposely skirted the few homes and villages along their route of travel to avoid being detected by anyone. As they did, a tired Francis, still fatigued from being up most of the night, dozed at times in his saddle. The slow pace helped to keep him upright. It was a shout from McKinney that woke him up and got his attention back. The shout alerted him to a new problem. Francis quickly realized the wagons had come to a stop. As he stared at them, McKinney was waving at him to come over to where they had stopped.

The rough ride had damaged the hub on the right rear wheel of one of the wagons and now it was threatening to fall completely off. Again they were forced to waste time unloading the contents of the damaged buckboard wagon; redistributing the provisions, as well as its hidden gold and silver, to the remaining Conestoga wagons. After the tasks were completed, Francis had the damaged wagon and its team of horses tied behind two of the other wagons. While having little time to make repairs to a wagon he really did not have a driver for, Francis hoped the wagon would stay together until they made camp that evening. They would then try to make the necessary repairs to it before dinner.

Before moving out, Francis allowed the men time to rest and to drink from a nearby stream. As the others made their way to the stream, Francis, assisted by Odom and Stine, helped the injured Hatfield down from the wagon he had been driving. After being helped down, he started to limp to a nearby fallen tree to sit down, but quickly his injured leg gave out. After falling, Hatfield screamed out in pain when his leg struck the ground. As the others did, Francis also rushed to Hatfield's side. "Sergeant, can you continue? Or do I have to make room for you in one of the wagons? Tell me the truth as I shall not feel any ill will towards you. You have already done an admirable job despite your injured leg. I know the pain you are in, and I don't care to see you suffer any longer."

Waiting for the pain to subside, Hatfield finally answered. "Captain, it hurts real bad, but I ain't gonna let y'all down. Let me keep going, at least until we stop this evening and then we can decide what to do about my leg. Y'all have other things to be worrying about besides me. Just get me back up into the wagon, I'll be fine." Reluctant to let Hatfield continue on, but needing him as a driver, Francis soon had him helped back onto the wagon. They were quickly on the move again.

Francis knew he needed to get medical help for Hatfield if he had any chance of saving his leg for him. As they moved along, he called for Odom. Telling him they would continue to move in a southeasterly direction for another five hours or so before making camp for the evening, he instructed Odom to ride off to try and find medical help for Hatfield.

* * * * * *

They had just made camp for the evening, settling down under the fading sun, when Banks sounded the alert. Performing sentry duty a short distance away from the others, he saw two riders approaching their position. Grabbing their weapons they prepared for the worst, but then Odom's familiar voice called into camp, alerting them that he was one of the riders Banks saw approaching.

"Captain, this here is Doc Brede from outside of Darlington town. I stumbled upon him by accident; told him about Hatfield needing help. Even though he's a Tar Heel, he seems to be a good man!" Odom laughed at his own joke as he climbed down from his horse, but the others were too tired to laugh. Even Doc Brede did not find humor in the good-natured joke which had been directed at him.

Dusting himself off from his ride, Doctor Kenyon Brede watched as Francis approached him. "Captain, I can assure you, despite your sergeant's comedic protests about the fine state of North Carolina where I reside, that I'm a true patriot to the Confederate cause. I'm more than pleased to assist you. Now, where is your injured Sgt. Hatfield I have been told about?" Brede shot a quick look of mild disdain at Odom before following Francis to where Hatfield had been resting near the fire.

Hatfield's boots had already been taken off by the time Doc Brede arrived. After briefly speaking to him about his injury, Doc Brede removed the wooden splint that had been in place along the broken leg. As he ripped open Hatfield's pant leg, the foul smell of his infected leg gave the doctor the first clue that his patient's condition was serious. The light from the campfire, and from a torch Davis held in his right hand, showed the horrible discoloration which had settled in Hatfield's broken leg.

"Captain, this man is in bad shape. He is losing blood into his leg from the broken bone. That is what is causing the discoloration. The open wound also appears to be infected. The wound has caused gangrene to set into his leg. He may lose his leg if he is not stabilized immediately; the wound needs to be cleaned much better than it has been. I'm afraid the situation is very bad." Francis saw the worried look on Hatfield's face. He also saw the same look of concern in Brede's face. From the looks he saw, Francis now knew Hatfield was in serious trouble. He could also tell from the doctor's brief examination that Hatfield losing a leg was probably the only good news they would hear. The bad news was that he might possibly succumb to an infection or to blood poisoning.

After Doc Brede had done what he could to make Hatfield comfortable for the night, he walked to where Francis now sat by himself. Francis was reading his bible near one of the two camp fires which had been started for the evening. He had always found comfort in reading the bible and he cherished the one his mother had given him as a gift just before he left to fight in the war.

"Captain, excuse me for disturbing you, but I thought I would let you know Sgt. Hatfield is asleep now. I cleaned his leg wound as best as I could, but what I really need to treat his broken leg with is back in my office. I will clean it better tomorrow when I get him back there, and then I'll set his leg if I can. I'm afraid it may be too late to do what I would like to do to try and save his leg, but we'll see tomorrow if it is or not. I will at least try to save his leg, but I'm not too optimistic I can. The high temperature he has seems to indicate the infection is too far along for me to be able to do much of anything, but I'll certainly try. My main focus will be trying to save his life, but I'm afraid it may even be too late for that. I expect he will lose his leg, if not more, in less than a week. His condition is very serious now. I'm sorry to give you such bad news." Brede said as he cleaned his hands with a wet rag.

Francis bowed his head momentarily after listening to what Brede told him. Now he looked up at him before speaking. "Doctor, I also have the same fear, this is why I am sitting here with the Good Book. I'm praying for a miracle to happen for such a fine young man. At the same time, I'm also praying the worst that happens to him is he just loses his leg. It saddens me to pray for a man to just lose a leg, but I hope the Lord understands my prayers are meant as prayers of hope for Sgt. Hatfield."

Tired from a long ride that day, and upset by the condition of Hatfield's broken leg, Brede sat with his head down, staring only at the small campfire in front of him for several long moments. "Captain, I commend you on your concern for one of your men. I will pray that someone hears your prayers for help. I am afraid divine intervention is the only real hope he has now."

Francis could see Doc Brede was tired and likely very hungry from his long day. He sought to thank him for his assistance with Hatfield's injuries. "Doctor, thanks for your help today, we are blessed that you were kind enough to come out here this late in the day. I know all of my men appreciate what you have done for their friend. I only wish we had found you sooner than we did, perhaps Sgt. Hatfield would have had a better chance of keeping his leg." Sadly, Brede nodded his head at Francis' comment.

Captain Francis and Doc Brede sat in silence for several minutes by the campfire, each of them thinking of Hatfield's serious medical problems. The doctor was the one who soon broke their silence. "Before I join your men for some dinner, I need to see one more patient of mine."

"Doctor, I beg your pardon, but I'm confused. Who is it you are referring to?"

"You, captain. Let's take that bandage off so I can see exactly what you are recovering from."

Unwrapping the bandage caused even the seasoned doctor to be taken back by the sight of Francis' left hand missing two fingers. Doc Brede held Francis' hand in his own hands as he carefully inspected the injury that was now healing very nicely. "For such a traumatic injury, it looks like your hand has healed very well. Your surgeon did a remarkable job amputating your fingers as I do not see a hint of any type of infection. His skills have obviously saved the rest of your hand. I suggest when this war is over with you need to find him and thank him for what he's done for you. While you have the bible open, you also might want to give some thought to thanking our Lord for blessing the doctor with such great skills."

"Doctor, I assure you I'll do both. For now, I just want to get rid of these stitches so I can start using my hand again." Francis said as he stared at his now deformed hand.

Doc Brede walked back to where he had left his medicine bag by the sleeping Hatfield, and then returned to where Francis still sat. "Hold your hand up so I can work on it. Just hold it steady and I'll remove the stitches for you. Your wounds have healed nicely so the stitches can come out now. Just make sure you're careful using your hand for the next few days."

As Brede began to remove the stitches from Francis' left hand, Sgts. Davis and Banks walked over to see what was happening. Watching as the stitches were being removed, the two sergeants now saw for the first time the seriousness of the injury Francis had sustained. The sight of his injured left hand missing two fingers was almost too much for them to look at, but they did. Realizing what he endured since his fingers had been amputated, and realizing all he had accomplished during their mission, gave them an even better respect for Francis as he never once complained about his injury. Neither was sure if they could have accomplished what he had done since losing his fingers. After removing all of the stitches, and after sharing a meal with Francis, Brede again checked on Hatfield.

Early the next morning, Hatfield was placed in the back of the same wagon he had been driving the previous day, its damaged wheel fixed during the night. As Doc Brede prepared to move out, his horse now tied to the rear of the wagon, Francis climbed into the back of the partially covered buckboard wagon where Hatfield lay. Shaking hands with him, Francis briefly spoke to him. "Sergeant, if we succeed in our mission, it is partially due to your efforts. Please know I am personally grateful for your help and know that I shall make mention of your efforts to both General Lee and President Davis. God bless you." Then Hatfield was driven to the doctor's home some fifteen miles away. Once there, Brede would further try to treat his injured leg. Unfortunately it would be treatment which would neither save the leg or the life of a brave young Confederate soldier.

With Hatfield taken away by Doc Brede, Francis now was down another man. As much of a concern this was to him, the news the doctor had given them last night of Union cavalry recently being seen to the north and west of their current position caused him even more concern. They still had two more days of travel before they would reach the Darlington area and then at least two more days of hard travel before they would reach Florence and the railroad connection there. As he moved the men out, Francis had but one thought. "Surely the North Eastern Railroad has to be still running, it has to be!"

Despite the hardships caused by almost two more full days of hard travel, they finally reached the relative safety of Darlington. There they enjoyed their first real hot meal in several days. There they were also able to obtain some additional provisions, but they had little time to rest. As hard as it had been on the men to reach Darlington, it had been just as hard on their horses. Between Darlington and Florence they lost three horses because of the heat. They had simply been overworked.

After reaching Florence, they had a chance to eat another hot meal and to get cleaned up for the first time in many days. After taking care of both their horses and themselves, they moved the wagons and their precious cargo into a large barn which sat close to the train station. Next to this barn they found room for their horses in a smaller adjoining barn which also had an attached corral. Both barns sat just east of the train station. After obtaining the information he needed at the train station, Francis returned to where his men had just finished their chores at the barns. He told them of learning that it would likely be hours before the train would arrive back at the station. The news pleased his men as they realized they would be getting their first nights sleep indoors in several weeks.

Before allowing himself to fall asleep, Francis went back to the railroad station's telegraph office in an attempt to send a message to Secretary Memminger in Richmond. But as he learned in the previous telegraph offices he had found along the way, the lines here had also been experiencing problems with Union sabotage. "Captain, I guess it's up to you, but these here lines have been unreliable the past few days. The damn Yankees keep cutting the lines.

When the lines are working, I suspect they are listening in to as many messages as they can. I wouldn't trust these here lines if ya want to send anything too important. No sense lettin' them know what you boys are up to, if ya know what I mean." Francis knew William McGuire, the railroad's telegraph operator, was right about what he should and should not risk sending over the lines to Richmond.

Tired after another long day, Francis sat down on a wooden chair outside the telegraph office. Relaxing for a moment, he wondered if he should risk sending a telegram. "I cannot risk sending a message to Secretary Memminger and then have the Union army intercept it. Our problems would be even worse than they already are if the Yankees knew what we had in the wagons and then came after us." Francis continued to ponder his next steps as he sat outside the window to the office where McGuire was busy trying to send another telegraph message. "Mr. McGuire, are you confident these lines have been tampered with by the Yankees or is that what others have told you because they are afraid of the Union army possibly being headed this way?"

Looking at Francis through his wire rimmed glasses McGuire tempered his words as he knew he was dealing with a Confederate army officer. "Son, I been doing this far too long to be guessing about my lines. I know when they have been tampered with and when they haven't been. As far as listening to talk about when them Yankees are coming, well I guess when I see them coming down the tracks that's when I know they are here. Now, and with all due respect, ya gonna send a message or not? For what it's worth, I'm suggesting ya don't, especially if it's anything too important." McGuire stared at Francis for a couple of minutes before returning to what he had been doing.

Francis was not sure what he would have told Memminger, but he wanted to let him know some of the problems he had encountered. They were now too far south for him to even consider sending a messenger back to Richmond, plus he could not afford the loss of another man. Deciding to risk it, he wrote down a brief message to send, one he hoped only Memminger would understand. After he read what he had written, making sure it would not jeopardize the rest of his journey south, Francis handed the message to McGuire. "Send this out as soon as you can!" Looking to see who the telegraph message was being sent to, McGuire saw it was addressed to the Confederate capitol in Richmond. Pushing aside the other messages which still needed to be sent, he quickly transmitted the important message Francis had written.

Walking back to the barn, Francis spent time trying to figure out how to get the gold and silver to Atlanta, but again realized he would have to make it to Charleston first before he gave any thought of moving the money further south. "Perhaps I can get some more men in Charleston to help us. If I can, then things might look better, but right now I'm worried." Arriving back at the barn, he was still determined to complete his mission. He knew whatever the coming days would bring, with or without any additional help, the gold and silver was not going to leave his sight.

After making sure his men and the wagons were safe, and the barn doors had been properly secured, Francis finally fell asleep. He had only been asleep for a short time when he was woken from his deep sleep by his nightmare, the same nightmare he had first experienced two nights earlier. In his nightmare he again heard the voice of Sgt. Hatfield calling for him as his injured leg was being amputated. It was a dream which caused him to wake up in a cold sweat. It would also be a dream which would revisit him on several more occasions in the coming days.

15

Whom To Tell.

"My plans are perfect, and when I start to carry them out,
may God have mercy on General Lee, for I will have none."
General Joseph 'Fighting Joe' Hooker, USA

On Tuesday morning, before Paul was to meet with Chick Mann at Coastal Carolina University, he stopped at the diner to settle the craving he had for their blueberry pancakes. The diner was little more than a greasy spoon, but they made pancakes like nobody else. He had not been back to the diner since discovering the remains of the Confederate soldier.

As Paul walked through the diner's front door, the bell above the door announced the arrival of another customer. Wiping down the lunch counter where an earlier customer had sat, Betty saw him as he walked through the door. "Well, well, look who it is, our own world famous South Carolina discoverer of dead Confederate soldiers himself!" She had announced his arrival loud enough for everyone in the diner to hear; her doing so made Paul cringe. He had not sought the media attention his discovery had brought him, nor was he interested in being the focus of Betty's attention or that of anyone else. He just wanted to have a quiet breakfast so he could enjoy his blueberry pancakes in peace.

As he made his way to the booth he always sat in, Paul gave a brief wave to a couple of men who were seated at the far end of the lunch counter. They had interrupted their breakfast to clap their hands for him when Betty announced his arrival. Sitting down in the booth, he heard a familiar voice yell out a comment. It quickly brought a smile to his face.

"That's what happens when you get a boat, Yankee boy!" The good-natured jab was from Chubby, who had helped him purchase his boat from Steve. Looking over to where Chubby sat eating his breakfast, he gave him a wave. As he did, he saw Chubby's idiot friend sitting there with him. As he ate his breakfast, Swamp angrily stared at Paul.

"Y'all told me that you weren't up to nothin' the day I seen you in the boat. You lied to me boy!"

Even from where Paul was sitting on the other side of the diner, he could still see the anger in Swamp's face and the flecks of food which spewed from his mouth when he yelled at him. Chubby hollered at Swamp to shut up, but he just continued to glare at Paul for a few more seconds before returning to his grits and eggs.

"Don't mind that stupid old jackass. Like most ignorant fools he's got a big mouth that opens before his brain engages." Betty gave a nod of her head in Swamp's direction as she poured Paul's coffee for him.

Betty asked Paul a few questions about his discovery, but he deflected them as best as he could. "You been busy I bet, making that discovery and everything. That must have caused you to about pee in your pants when you found that ol' boy in the tree, huh? You gonna tell me about it?"

"Not today, Betty, but I will. I have to meet somebody across town and I just have time to eat this morning, but I promise I will tell you about it soon. Can you get me some of your blueberry pancakes and some bacon? I don't have much time."

Waiting for his pancakes to arrive, Paul gave the day's *USA Today* a quick once over. Leafing through it, he saw a follow-up story to the feature article the paper had written just after he had found the Confederate soldier's remains. He was pleased to see the background work the reporter had obviously done regarding the discovery and on him. He was also pleased the reporter had gotten all of the facts correct. Reading the article reminded him of several newspaper articles back home that had been poorly written. Those articles had failed to accurately report the facts related to several major cases he participated in. Those articles, regarding several brutal murders and a few high profile narcotic cases, had numerous factual mistakes in them. He often bristled at the poor quality of many news stories some reporters had written. On one occasion, he had called one of the Connecticut newspapers to complain about the numerous mistakes an article contained, but the editor he spoke with could have cared less about a cop calling to complain about one of his reporters. In this particular story, he was pleased by what he had just read. Finishing the article as he dug into his fresh blueberry pancakes and the generous side of bacon, Paul thought about some of the people he had worked with back in Connecticut. "I wonder what the guys back home are thinking about this story?"

After paying for his breakfast, Paul waved a goodbye to Betty, promising her he would be back soon for their talk. Then somewhat out of character, but with a specific purpose in mind, he yelled a goodbye to Chubby. In doing so, he made sure he got Swamp's attention. Turning in the booth to look back at Paul, Swamp was greeted with the middle finger salute and with four words. *"Up yours fat ass!"* The message he sent to Swamp was to let him know he was not taking his crap any longer. The gesture caused Chubby to let out a big laugh from his oversized belly. Betty, as well as two men sitting at the lunch counter, also got a laugh out of the message. Swamp did not find the gesture quite as funny as everyone else did.

Paul's drive to Coastal Carolina University took less than twenty minutes. As he followed the signs to the Kimbel Library, he could see two people apparently waiting for him as they sat on a bench in the library's courtyard. Chick Mann, who wore his long grayish hair in a ponytail, was someone who Paul guessed to be in his mid-seventies. Soon he learned Chick was an American History professor at the University of South Carolina and had been for almost fifteen years. After they exchanged greetings with each other, Chick told him about his passion for the Civil War. As he talked about his passion, Chick made sure he mentioned that he did not consider himself to be an expert on the war. He told Paul while he felt he knew more than most people about the fighting and the politics which had taken place in North and South Carolina, he knew others were well more versed than he was about the events which had occurred in Washington prior to the war. "My focus has always been more about what occurred at the local and regional levels. The war's political stuff never really interested me enough to focus on it too much." Paul quickly read Chick to be a down to earth person who he got a good first impression of. He was not the stuffed shirt '*know it all*' academic type he thought he might be meeting. The fact that Chick told him his other passion in life was trying to regularly reduce his golf score did not hurt the first impression he had of him either.

Standing quietly off to the side as they talked was Jayne Ewald, Chick's graduate assistant. She was nearing the completion of her doctorate degree in American History at the University of South Carolina. Paul's first impression of her included a thought that she was likely in her early to mid-thirties. She was short and slightly overweight, but still an attractive looking woman with long black hair that she also wore in a ponytail. While his early read of her also included that she seemed to be an extremely focused person, she gave Paul the impression she was someone who was a bit of an introvert. For some reason he also thought she was perhaps a little naive. While he tried, he could not figure out what had caused him to have such a strong early read of her this way. He would soon find out his early evaluation of her was a very accurate one.

After introducing Jayne, Chick explained how she had researched her family history a few years ago; learning that one of her great-grandfathers had served in the Union army during the Civil War. Her research had shown he had been captured during the war, and was later held in a Confederate prison camp in Wilmington, North Carolina for a period of time.

Jayne then told Paul about reviewing Union army records and finding that her great-grandfather, Private John Kinsella, had served with the 7th Connecticut Infantry Regiment, being assigned to Company D. From other documents her family obtained, she learned Private Kinsella's real name, Kenseller, had apparently been misspelled along the way, possibly by some Union army clerk when her great-grandfather reenlisted in the war. Her research determined just after reenlisting, in Danbury, Connecticut, his unit had moved south to fight. "He was later captured at the Battle of Bermuda Hundred, in Virginia, on June 2, 1864." She then described how her great-grandfather had died from Chronic Dysentery. His *Record of Death and Interment,* which she had obtained a copy of, documented he had died on April 7, 1865, at the Wilmington General Hospital. She had also found on his *Record of Death and Interment* form that he had been buried in a mass grave with other Union soldiers. As far as she could tell from her research, he had likely been buried in the Wilmington National Cemetery in North Carolina. "The only other things I know about him is he had grayish colored eyes, light colored hair, and a light complexion. All of that I got from a copy of his *Volunteer Re-Enlistment* form. Probably a form some clerk likely filled out when he reenlisted. There is more to find out about him and I will. All it takes is time."

It was from this research she conducted on her family tree that an interest in the Civil War had been sparked. Her continued research, along with her studies in American History, now fueled her passion for the Civil War. She also told Paul that she had even gone as far as petitioning the National Park Service to have a tombstone for her great-grandfather placed in the military cemetery in Wilmington. They had initially denied her request, but her persistent efforts, supported by her findings of her great-grandfather's service in the Union army, finally resulted in the Park Service granting approval of her request.

As they finished talking about her great-grandfather, Jayne also told Paul about visiting the cemetery where his tombstone had been placed, and about participating in a few historical digs in the area. It was her hope these historical digs would continue and would someday further document what life was like for those Union soldiers who had been confined in the Confederate prison camp in Wilmington.

"I'm impressed by your determination to learn more about him. I hope you stay with it until you find what you are looking for." It was obvious to Paul that Jayne was very dedicated to learning as much as she could about her great-grandfather.

As the three of them got to know each other better over small talk, Paul also sensed Jayne had a strong respect for Chick. It was more than what one would expect to see in a teacher –student relationship he thought, but he was not sure he was correct in that assessment as yet.

The talk then turned to Paul's discovery of the Confederate soldier's remains. As they sat on the front steps of the Student Center, Chick asked him questions about the condition of both the soldier's uniform and his remains. As they talked, Paul began to feel more comfortable with Chick. Slowly starting to believe he could put his trust in him.

As they talked, the courtyard began to fill with students and teachers wanting to enjoy a few minutes of morning sunshine before heading off to their classes. Not wanting others to hear what they were discussing, Paul sought to move the conversation to a quieter location. "Chick, let's take a walk. Jayne can certainly join us, but could we talk some more in private, perhaps over by my truck for a few minutes?"

Walking to his truck, Chick told Paul more about the studies Jayne was completing. "Paul, Jayne is working on her doctorate as we have told you. Do you have any objections if she takes notes while we talk? It might help her with a paper she has to write during the upcoming semester."

"Yeah, sure, but if I want something discussed privately she has to put the pen down and nothing gets written about that part of the conversation, understand?"

"No problem." Concurring with Chick's statement, Jayne nodded her head in agreement to the ground rules Paul had just laid out.

Paul had allowed Steve to set this meeting up with Chick as he realized he needed someone he could trust and work with. While he likely had the clues to find the missing treasury, Paul knew having someone else helping him decipher those clues might lead to other ideas about what they meant. He knew early in their conversation he had found the person he needed to help him. Now he was about to reel Chick in without him having a chance to say no. As they walked to his truck, he asked Chick if he had ever heard the story about the missing Confederate treasury.

"Oh, sure, I think most people have heard about that legend. In fact, I think it's probably a true story and not one that's been made up. I think the money . . . actually most of it was gold and silver coins . . . is still hidden and probably buried some place just waiting for someone to find it. In fact, I actually did some research into the legend several years ago. From what I could tell after reviewing a few Confederate documents, and from reading some letters which had been written by both President Jefferson Davis and his Secretary of the Treasury, a guy by the name of Memminger, I believe the documentation I reviewed proves the money actually did exist. My feelings are the same ones many others have. Like they do, I believe the money was being transferred from Richmond to some place further south so it did not fall into the hands of the advancing Union army. It was during the time it was being moved when the treasury went missing. Who had it and what happened to it is the mystery which exists to this day. I can't help you there."

"So what's your best guess on where the money might be, if in fact it did exist?"

"Like I said, I have no doubt it existed. Whether it still exists, or if it was stolen, or lost, or captured by the Union army, I can't tell you. That's a tough question to answer, but if it still exists my guess would be the money is likely buried along the eastern shore area of either North or South Carolina. The Union army was advancing south and had focused a great deal of their efforts along the rail lines in both of those states. They were ripping up tracks and destroying railroad equipment to hurt the Confederacy's efforts of being able to resupply their armies in Virginia. So my guess is whoever had it likely steered clear of where the Union army was operating. That's why I believe it's probably buried somewhere along the eastern edges of either of those two states. It probably will turn up in Texas or in some other location which makes no sense, but I don't think so. One thing I do believe is that I doubt the Confederacy would have chanced shipping it south by boat. Trying to ship it to Atlanta or possibly to either New Orleans or Mississippi by boat would have been a big risk to take because of the Union blockade. The money would have been lost forever if their boat was either sunk or seized. The South would not have risked losing it like that. My guess is the money was being shipped by rail, or by wagons, or maybe both, and likely it was disguised as it was being shipped to cut down on the chances of people trying to steal it. War and money makes people do crazy things at times, even to people on your own side."

Having listened intently to Chick's thoughts on the missing money, Paul stood quiet for a several moments in the parking lot as he digested what Chick had told him. As he did, he mentally compared the opinions Chick expressed to the contents of the letters he had read. Letters he had not yet told Chick about.

"Chick, we don't know each other very well yet, but I'm here because our mutual friend told me I can trust you. I hope I can trust you. I also hope we can become friends."

"Well, I guess it will have to depend on how many strokes you are going to give me when we play golf, won't it?"

Paul smiled as he knew Chick had attempted to bring some levity into their conversation. "That's a good answer, but I'm probably the one who will need the strokes. My game is terribly rusty; it's been on the back burner far too long."

Deciding it was the right moment, Paul took his conversation with Chick a bit further, teasing him with pieces of information others had yet to learn. "What if I told you I found several more items besides the soldier's clothing and his remains, items the authorities don't know about yet. Would that interest you? And, if I do decide to tell you about them, can I trust both of you to respect my decision about keeping them for myself for now?"

Chick had not yet responded to Paul's questions when Jayne dropped the pen she had been taking her notes with. Bouncing off the asphalt parking lot, it landed near her feet. It was obvious that what she had just heard took her completely by surprise. Her other reaction was to cover her mouth with the hand which had held her pen. She then uttered two words very softly. "Oh, my!"

"Paul, I think you probably know the answer to your question already, but the answer is obviously yes. I will tell you friends and I have talked about the discovery you made after we read about it in the paper. We did discuss whether you might have kept a souvenir or two, if any were found with the remains. If you did, then you have to decide whether you should have them or whether they should be shared with others who also have an interest in the Civil War. It's a moral issue you have to wrestle with. But the answer to your question is yes; you can trust us to keep your secret quiet. It sounds like you might be interested in doing some digging, both literally and figuratively perhaps, on the items you have found. If that's the case, then I certainly can understand why you kept them. One thing though, if it's me who has those items in my possession, when I'm done with them I would turn them over to the soldier's relatives . . . that's if they can be found, or to the South Carolina Historical Society, or to some other historical group, or perhaps even to some school." Chick paused for a moment to get a read on how Paul took what he had told him. "Now, if you care to show us what you've found, I would be very interested in looking at whatever it is you have. Until you tell us we can talk about the items, I promise neither of us will tell a sole about what you've found."

Any doubts Paul had about whether he could trust Chick were a memory after he heard the answers to the questions he asked of him. While not having any intention of keeping the items he found, he planned to do just what Chick had suggested when he was done with them. He just wanted them for his own while he looked into the mystery of the lost Confederate treasury. Then he would decide what to do with them.

Feeling confident he could trust both of them, Paul reached into his pocket and pulled out a handkerchief he had wrapped two of the gold coins in. As he unfolded the handkerchief, they saw it protected an 1862 gold dollar and an 1862 three-dollar coin. He placed them in the palm of his right hand for Chick and Jayne to see.

"May I?" It was all Chick asked before taking the gold coins to examine closer. After examining them one at a time, he handed the coins to Jayne so she could look at them. Handing them to her without looking at Paul, Chick asked him if the coins had been found in the soldier's clothing or on the ground near the remains. Before Paul could answer Chick's question, Jayne nearly dropped one of the coins in the parking lot. She had been examining the coins and taking notes at the same time. After already having dropped her pen, and now nearly dropping one of the coins as well, Paul's first impression of Jayne now included the thought that she was a little clumsy as well.

"Chick, to answer your question, yes and yes. One I found on the ground and one I found in some clothing, but not in the clothing the authorities have in their possession."

"So you did find more clothing! Most likely the soldier's uniform I'm guessing or at least parts of it, correct? What else did you find?" Chick anxiously asked.

Paul took the coins back from Jayne, wiped off any oils which might have been transferred onto them from being handled, and then wrapped them back up in his handkerchief. Then he placed the coins back in his pocket. By this time the section of the Student Parking Lot where his truck was parked was beginning to fill up with students arriving for their summer semester classes. "Tell you what, walk over to the corner of the parking lot and I'll bring my truck over there. We can talk some more over there. That way the whole world is not seeing what is going on."

Backing his truck into the corner of the lot, Paul could not help thinking it looked like the three of them, with their somewhat furtive movements, were consummating a drug deal in the parking lot. As he got out of his truck, he heard Jayne giggle as she spoke to Chick.

"This is so exciting!" They both shot her puzzled looks, but the looks did little to dampen her excitement. "Well, at least to me it is!"

Paul reached around the back of the truck's front seat and pulled out a folded up blanket. Placing it on the hood of his truck, he unfolded the blanket so it revealed the objects he had carefully hidden from view. After unfolding it, he then stepped back so they could look at what had been hidden within the blanket. Lying there was the saber and bayonet he had found with the soldier's remains. Chick examined them without touching either of them at first, simply asking where they had been found.

"They were with the remains. To be precise, I actually found them inside the same tree where I found the soldier's remains. As you can tell, the bayonet has likely been exposed to the weather for a longer period of time. I'm guessing that's why it's in a somewhat poorer condition, but its condition could also be from the quality of the steel it had been made from. You can see the saber is in far better condition."

Paul then surprised Chick by pulling out a pair of white lightweight cloth gloves from his truck. He handed them to Chick so he could put them on before picking up the two items. "Just to be safe, I hope you understand."

"No problem, it's a good idea actually."

After handling both items, Chick commented on their conditions, agreeing the saber was in far better shape than the bayonet. "Two real nice finds.

Especially when you . . . and not to be morbid . . . but when you have a body to put them with, if you know what I mean. You know whose they were is probably a better way of phrasing it, I guess. They both are definitely Civil War period items and likely would fetch a few hundred dollars if they were up for sale; especially the saber, that's in very good condition. Any collector or any museum would be proud to own these two items. Nice find!"

After Chick had set both of the items back down on the blanket, Jayne went to write down a description of the items, especially the manufacturer's name that was still clearly visible in the saber's blade, but Paul blocked her from doing so. "Chick, you have to understand, and I'm certain you do, that until I get done investigating certain things, these items included, I need to be protective of them. I still don't know why I'm showing them to you, but you two are the only ones to have seen these items besides my wife and me. These items, along with a few others I have in my possession, are being kept away from my house so no one can steal them from me. I know that thought may have already entered some people's minds, especially those people, like you and your friends, who may think I have found some items which I have not yet turned over to the authorities. What I'm trying to do, possibly with your help, is to unravel some clues. So I guess what I'm trying to say is if I let Jayne take some more notes, what is it you two . . . that's if you're interested in helping me . . . can bring to the table to help me unravel some clues I might have?"

Chick understood completely the hesitancy Paul had in trusting him regarding his discovery of the soldier's remains and with these artifacts. His answer to the question was an honest and simple one. "At this time I don't know how I can help you as I think there's more to the story than what you're telling us, but I'm honored by what you've shared with us so far. I can tell you that my background is in American History, and apparently like you, Jayne and I both have a strong appreciation for preserving the history of the Civil War. One of our interests is researching the history of specific points of the war. If you need research done, and if you want some help doing field work, then I guess we're here to work with you. We both know this is your show and that you make the rules. This is a self-serving statement, but as I told you earlier, you can trust us. I hope Steve told you that as well. I would suggest you let Jayne take down a few notes on these two items . . . let her take a couple of photos as well . . . then give us a couple of days and we'll get back to you on what we find. That should prove to you we can be trusted."

Paul thought about what Chick had said for a moment, weighing the pluses and minuses of having them help him with his needs. "OK, that sounds reasonable."

"But Paul, I'll tell you if you want our help, then I want two things in return. One is that I may want your permission to write a paper on what we'll be doing with you, as writing such a paper will give me some additional standing in the historical community I work within. Secondly, as I've mentioned Jayne is going to need to write a paper for school next year so she will need your OK to document our involvement in this with you. This is a rare opportunity for her to show her direct involvement in such a historical find. Her writings, supported by photographs and videotape, would help her complete her course requirements. I would appreciate your approval for that need she has. We would even go as far as to give you some editorial control on the papers we write. For now, I just want your OK for us to proceed with those needs we have. Certainly we would give you full credit for the discovery you've made. Does that sound acceptable to you?"

"That sounds fine. I guess as I'll have to trust both of you, you'll also have to trust me to some degree. Is that OK with both of you?"

Without looking at each other, Chick and Jayne both nodded their heads at what Paul had just said. "Paul, I promise, and I know talk is cheap, but neither one of us will ever cross you. This means too much for our careers to jeopardize your trust in us." Paul just nodded his head at Chick's comment.

With Paul's blessing, Jayne copied down the markings she observed on the saber. The markings had apparently been engraved into the saber when it had been made years ago. They were simple ones and were found in two places on the saber. One marking, found on the blade near the handle, read *'B.G. & M'*. The other marking, also near the back end of the handle, displayed the number *38*. Looking at the saber as she took her notes, Jayne estimated the blade's length to be approximately twenty-two inches long.

The bayonet, crude and rough in its appearance, had apparently been made for a musket of some sort as it had a locking ring on one end of it. Chick believed the ring had been used to fasten it to the end of a musket when it would have been needed. Unlike the saber, the bayonet had no manufacturer's markings on it. Looking at it as she took her notes, Jayne estimated the bayonet, which was slightly shorter in size than the saber's blade, to be twenty to twenty-one inches in length. After she finished taking her notes, Paul wrapped the items back up in the blanket.

Closing her notebook as Paul secured the two items behind his seat; Jayne asked him a follow-up question regarding the bayonet. "You didn't find a musket or a rifle when you found the soldier?"

"Nope, not even the hint of one. Strange, huh?"

Paul and Chick then made plans to meet again in a few days so Jayne could take some additional notes on the other items he found and to photograph them as well. Chick then asked him if he would allow them to see the area where he had found the soldier's remains so they could document the location. At the same time, Chick also presented a new thought for Paul to consider. "We have a lot of things going on here, but I'm already thinking this story could make a great documentary. Paul, just think about that over the next couple of days and we'll talk about it some other time. Just so you know, I have a friend who has made a couple of short films. He has a wealth of experience with video equipment. We could be onto something here. Just think about it, OK?" Chick's comments received no immediate response back from Paul.

Agreeing to soon take them to where he had found the remains, they then exchanged cell numbers with each other and agreed to meet in a few days to talk further. After talking about matters other than his discovery, Paul and Chick decided they would meet on Friday morning at *The Links* to play a round of golf. Without speaking about it, they each knew this would be a way for them to get to know each other a little bit better.

As they were preparing to go their separate ways, the three of them paused to shake hands with each other. As they did, Chick looked Paul in the eyes before asking the question he had waited for the right moment to ask. "Are you going to tell me what else you found that day?"

Paul feigned a mock sense of hurt to the question Chick had asked him. "What? You think I found more than what I have already shown you?" Chick did not respond to Paul's rhetorical question, choosing instead to just smile back at him. Then he and Jayne turned to walk back towards the Student Center.

After making sure the items he placed behind his seat were secure, Paul started his truck and drove towards Chick and Jayne as they walked across the parking lot. Approaching them, he drove slowly in order to give himself time to open the console between the two front seats. Then he gave the truck's horn two quick beeps to get their attention. As they turned to look at him, he slowly drove by them as he dangled the soldier's gold pocket watch from his right hand, teasing them with another item he had found. Despite their attempts to wave him down so they could look at the watch, he did not stop. He knew he had gotten their attention and that was all he wanted. From their reaction to seeing the watch, Paul was pleased it had worked so well.

* * * * * *

Over the course of the next couple of days, Paul spent time relaxing, trying to get the all-consuming thoughts of the missing Confederate gold and silver out of his mind. To do so, he played golf a couple of more times, including a second time with Chick so they could continue to get to know each other a little more. For Paul to feel comfortable with him, he needed to know he could trust him.

On Saturday afternoon, Paul took Donna for her first ride on the boat. On the way to the marina they stopped and picked up a couple of grinders from one of the several Subway Restaurants along Highway 17. Besides towels, sun tan lotion, and other necessities for the day, they brought along a cooler of drinks for them to wash their food down with. Once on the boat, they slowly cruised north on the Waccamaw River before turning around to head south. As they headed south, they did so the point where U.S. 501 crosses over the river. Even from where they were on the river, they could hear the traffic on the bridge as it passed high above them. This day was like many other summer days as today the bridge again served as a main artery for visitors coming and going to Myrtle Beach. Seeing the bridge from a different viewpoint for the first time caused Donna to marvel at its size.

The lazy day on the river was proving to be a rare treat for them as they had been so busy since moving to South Carolina they really had not spent much time together just relaxing. Donna did not want this day to end. Relaxing in the afternoon sun, she hoped they would spend many more days cruising on the river, just the two of them. Paul's boat was turning out to be a treat even for her to enjoy.

During the time Paul spent over the next couple of days with his discovery, he spent much of it trying to interpret the hidden meanings he thought were contained somewhere within the four letters he found. His concentration was especially focused on the one Captain Francis had written to President Davis. "What is he trying to tell Davis in this letter? It's obvious he hid some of the gold and silver in North Carolina, at least that's what I think he's saying, but he's so vague as to where he hid it. It could be almost anywhere. And why did he leave some of the gold and silver with Governor Allston's children and not with the governor himself? If he did leave it with the children, what did they do with it and where is it now?" The questions which raced through his mind were many. Again, it was only the answers to the questions that were few. The more he read, the more questions he had, but still he could not crack what it was that Francis was trying to explain in his letter. He even spent a few hours one evening just sitting in his garage trying to put some logic together in his thought process to help him have a sense of where the money could possibly be buried in North Carolina. But the more he worked at the clues, the further his mind seemed to push away any logic he mustered from the letters he read and reread a countless number of times.

Three days after Chick and Paul played golf, they all met for breakfast to talk about what information Jayne had found on the bayonet and the saber. By now, Paul had spent several hours pouring over the letters in his garage. After meeting them at the Waccamaw Diner for breakfast, Paul was planning to show them the location where he had found the soldier's remains.

Arriving before the others did, Paul sat in his favorite booth waiting for them. While he was by himself, Betty came over with a pot of coffee and tried to squeeze a few tidbits of information from him regarding his discovery. As she poured his coffee for him, he only gave her back answers to her questions based on information which had already been contained in the newspapers. She soon realized her curiosity was not going to be satisfied that morning.

"OK, OK, I get the message. When you are ready you will tell me, right? But remember, you promised!"

Paul nodded to her and then took his first sip of coffee to help him start the day. Waiting for the others to arrive, he moved the other coffee cups off to the side of the booth and then spread out the day's *Myrtle Beach Times*. It had been left on the nearby lunch counter by a previous customer. Casually he looked to see how the Yankees had done against the Red Sox the night before. He was pleased to see the Yankees had beaten Boston for the second night in a row. They were now four games up in the division standings over the Sox. He was almost finished going through the Major League box scores when Chick and Jayne sat down in the booth.

After placing their orders for the blueberry pancakes Paul highly recommended, Chick asked the question which had been bugging him for the past few days. "OK, when we played golf the other day I promised myself I would not ask you this, but today is different. Was that the soldier's gold watch you were teasing us with the other day when you drove off?"

"Might have been, but you know the ground rules by now. I give you some information, like I did the other day with the coins and the other two items, and then you tell me what you've found out about them. Then I decide if I'm going to tell you more." Paul knew for now he held the high cards in the deck. He also knew Chick, likely for no other reason than to satisfy his own curiosity, wanted to know more about his discovery and what those cards were that he was holding.

"Alright, alright, I understand. I'll let Jayne tell you what we know. But you better tell me more about that watch!" Despite being frustrated by Paul's position, Chick nodded to Jayne. It was a nod telling her to let Paul know what they had found out about the saber and the bayonet. As she started to describe what they had learned, Chick momentarily lost interest in the conversation as his eyes settled on the large stack of hot blueberry pancakes that Betty placed down in front of him.

Momentarily ignoring her stack of pancakes, Jayne told Paul what they had learned. "Surprisingly, I think we have found out quite a bit about the two items. While we still have some other resources to check, we have a good feeling about our findings so far. The gold coins are another story in themselves."

Through a mouth full of pancakes, Paul responded back to her. "Well, so far so good. Tell me more."

"The saber was made by a company called *Boyle, Gamble & MacFee*; they were suppliers of arms to the Confederacy. The model you found is one we believe they called their Type 1 saber bayonet. It was made to be twenty-one and a half inches in length, the blade that is. The number you saw on the brass hilt, the number thirty-eight actually, we believe that number identified the saber as being the thirty-eighth saber they produced. They were a Richmond based company that operated on South Sixth Street for a period of time. Now for the better news. While it will need to be appraised, our guess is it's likely worth around $2,400.00 or so. Good news, huh? As you likely know, appraisals are based on the conditions items are in and how many of the same item still exist, and so on, but we think we're in the ballpark with our estimate of its value."

Wiping his mouth with a napkin, Paul surprised Jayne with his next comment. "You know, I really hadn't even thought about its value so I guess I'm surprised . . . maybe I'm not . . . at what you say the saber is worth. To be honest with you, I don't care what it's worth as that's not what this is about for me."

As Chick continued to eat his breakfast, he could not help but smile when he heard how Paul had responded to Jayne's comment about the value of the saber. He now knew Paul was motivated solely by the hunt for information regarding his discovery. He sensed his new friend, while likely interested in knowing what the value was of the items he had found, was far more interested in other information. What the saber and bayonet were worth was secondary in its importance to what he was trying to accomplish. Knowing this now caused him to be even more interested in working with Paul. Now he sat quietly, more intrigued than ever, trying to figure out what mystery his friend was trying to solve.

Jayne barely had time to start her breakfast when Paul interrupted her second forkful of pancakes. "So what else do you have for me, Miss Jayne?"

Putting down her fork, she looked back at the notes she had spread out on the table next to her pancakes. "As we've discussed, the bayonet was somewhat crudely made. It was likely one that was mass produced, at least mass produced for that period of time you understand. We think it was also likely manufactured by another Richmond based company. It fits the description of bayonets which had been made by the *Richmond Armory*. They were designed to be used with a musket known as a Richmond Musket. The bayonet's design, with the off-centered locking ring, is why we believe it was made by them. For what it's worth, at the time it was manufactured the bayonet's length was around twenty-one and one-sixteenths in size. We don't even have an educated guess on its value yet, but we hope to soon. I have some feelers out there with some Civil War dealers I know and I hope to have an estimate on the value in the next couple of days." Not knowing how much time she had before Paul peppered her with more questions, Jayne quickly dove into her pancakes again.

"Looks like you have done your homework. I'm impressed with what you've found out so fast. But I want you to stop. I don't want to know about the gold coins or their value or how rare they might be, at least right now I don't." Paul stopped to collect his thoughts before he said anything else. Sipping his coffee, he thought about what Jayne had just told him.

"What the saber is worth, what the coins are worth, really is for others to be concerned with, but not me. Those items I've shown you are not mine to keep as I really have little interest in profiting in any way from what I've found. I also have zero interest in any of the media attention which has been directed my way as that's not what I'm about. What I have an interest in, perhaps because I was a cop, and perhaps because of my interest in the Civil War, is digging at the facts and clues that I have in my possession. Above that, I could care less about what these items are worth. You may not believe me, but that's how it is. If you want to continue to working with me, you both have to agree we will not profit personally from anything we find. That does not include the papers you write, or a book you and I may write together. That's how it's going to be. It's up to you whether you're in or out."

Chick finished his breakfast as Paul had spoken and was enjoying his second cup of coffee as Jayne was finishing her breakfast. "Paul, it's refreshing in these times to hear your thoughts on whether we should be able to profit from such an historic find. We both share the same position you have. Being a teacher myself, Jayne as a future teacher, and certainly you as a cop, none of us chose our professions expecting to get rich. I don't expect to get rich because we're in this with you, even if we find a few more coins or some other items of value from the war. For the two of us, this is a unique experience which will help us become better teachers. I hope you will let us be a part of this with you." Jayne did not say a word, choosing instead to finish the last few bites of her breakfast. As she did, she nodded her head emphatically at Chick's comments.

Previously having made the decision to trust them with the details about his find, Chick's comments now caused Paul to realize he had made the right decision. As they sat in the diner's small booth, Paul sat opposite from his two new partners. Now he pushed an unused coffee cup towards them. The cup had been placed upside down on a saucer like all diners do when they set their tables. "Either of you need a clean cup for your next cup of coffee?"

Grasping the hidden meaning of what Paul was saying to them, Jayne reached for the cup first, pulling it closer to her. Picking it up, she saw the gold pocket watch that had been hidden under it.

"Jayne, please be careful with the watch. It opens now because I cleaned it somewhat, but don't force it open or close the face too hard. I still need to have it professionally cleaned. Listen, if you want to make some notes about the watch, that's fine with me." Paul said as he smiled at the astonished look on Jayne's face.

Chick and Jayne both carefully examined the watch for several minutes. As she did, Jayne took some notes regarding her observations so she could research the name displayed on the watch's face. She hoped she would be able to find out more about the watch than what they knew so far. As they both continued to examine the gold watch, Paul told them about finding it still hanging inside the same massive Live Oak where he had found the soldier's remains. The fact that it had remained hanging in the tree for so long astounded both of them as the watch had remained in such good condition.

As they finished looking at the watch, Paul showed them the digital photos he had taken during his second visit to the tree. "Of course anything can be staged to make it look real, but this photo shows you where the watch was hanging in the tree. If you look closely at several of the photos, you can even see some of the rope fibers I told you about. The fibers were still attached to spots inside the tree."

"Simply amazing!" It was Chick's only comment as he studied the photos.

After talking a few more minutes, Paul then suggested they should head out to the marina so they could talk more freely once they got on the boat. His two new partners quickly realized Paul was being careful about discussing details of his find in the diner as he was protecting what was being discussed from others who sat nearby eating their breakfast. Handing the pocket watch back to him for safekeeping, they readily agreed to his suggestion.

Starting from the time they climbed aboard Paul's boat, until they returned to the marina almost four hours after shoving off, Paul talked to them about what he had found in the tree. As they visited the location where he made the discovery, Jayne made a rough sketch of the area, took numerous photos of the Live Oak tree which had hid the soldier for so many years, and took several additional photos of the surrounding area. She did so utilizing two Canon cameras. She also videotaped the same areas with her Canon eight millimeter video camera. As she shot her footage, she stopped short of filming the inside of the tree as she feared an animal would jump out and bite her. With little choice, Paul somewhat volunteered to complete that task for her. They did everything they could to document the area in and around the tree, even measuring the tree's circumference with a small tape measure Chick had brought with him. Jayne and Chick even took the time to measure the size of the opening in the tree, the same opening which both the soldier and Paul had crawled into. After they were done taking those measurements, Chick crawled into the opening so he could get a proper perspective of what the tree's interior looked like.

On the return trip to the marina it was Jayne who again brought up the idea of making a documentary. "You know this would be a great story to tell, a story many others would probably enjoy seeing. We need to give this some strong consideration."

To their surprise, Paul told them he had given serious thought to making the documentary since they had last met. He now told them he felt they should put a plan together to move forward with that idea. "I actually like the idea of a documentary as I think we have the start of a great story that needs to be told. I also think we should give some consideration to including the story about Jayne's great-grandfather in it. That's a part of the war we should include in the film. The only request I have is I want to meet the guy who Chick spoke about the other day. I want to make sure he understands what the rules are. I need to feel comfortable around him. Sound OK?"

"That's fine with us. We already knew you'd want to do that." Chick said, pleased that Paul liked his idea regarding the documentary.

Paul could tell from the look on her face that Jayne was touched by the comment he had made about her great-grandfather's story being included in the film. He had not made this suggestion to just make her feel good; he had simply suggested this as part of his idea for the documentary's storyline. It was part of a story he thought would mesh well with the discovery he had made.

After Paul got the boat back on the trailer at the marina, he offered to buy them both a cold beer at the marina's small restaurant. Soon they were enjoying their cold beers on the outdoor patio. Sitting at a small wooden table, they had a great view of the river as they discussed what they saw earlier while visiting the tree. They spent the next hour relaxing and talking until Paul announced he had to go. Standing up to leave, he suggested Jayne should shoot a couple of pictures of the pocket watch he had left in his truck. "This way I can put it back in my safety deposit box tomorrow and not have to worry about it."

As Jayne took her photos and a short video clip of the watch, Chick asked Paul if he had given any more thought to the legend of the missing Confederate treasury.

"Actually I have given it a lot of thought."

"Think the treasury will ever be found?" Chick curiously asked.

"Yes, I do. All someone needs to do is figure out a couple of the clues which were left behind. But then, when you know the clues, and you know some of the other details, you should be able to figure it out. Yes, I expect to find it."

Chick was stunned by what Paul had just said. "Are you telling us that …"

Paul cut Chick off in mid-sentence. "Yes, I am."

Standing only a few feet away as she packed her cameras back in their cases, Jayne quickly spun around towards Paul and Chick. Her expression revealed the shock she heard from the news Paul had just given them.

Still momentarily stunned by the magnitude of what Paul had told them, Chick stood silent for a few moments. "Paul, are you telling us you know where the missing Confederate gold and silver is hidden? Are you telling us you know what others have tried to figure out for almost one hundred and fifty years? People have dedicated significant periods of their lives trying to unravel this mystery and now you're telling us, from an accidental discovery you made, that you know where the money is?"

"Yep. Care to see it? That is the clues I mean."

"Damn straight we want to see them!"

The loud and bold response from Jayne caught Chick off guard. Almost immediately, he and Paul laughed at her quick aggressive response. It had been so out of character for her to talk so loud, but now she was caught up in the excitement of the moment just as Chick had been moments earlier.

Paul made plans for them to meet him tomorrow morning at his house so they could talk further. The excitement of what he told them caused the three of them to talk in the marina's parking lot for almost another hour. As they talked, Chick did his best at trying to pry more details from Paul about the clues, but he held him off, telling him to be patient. "Chick, let's wait until tomorrow before we talk further on this. We'll have more time then. I need to get going and I'd rather tell you about them went we aren't so rushed for time." Now more eager than ever to move on with the hunt, those hours they would have to wait would seem like a lifetime.

As they prepared to leave, Paul reminded them about their promises to him. "Remember, I have your word, this does not get discussed with anyone!"

They could do nothing except to nod their heads in agreement to what he had just told them. They both wanted to be a part of the entire ride, all the way to the end, no matter how it ended.

16

Ambushed.

"Tell General Hancock for me that I have done him and
you all an injury which I shall regret ..."
Brigadier General Lewis Addison Armistead, CSA, at Gettysburg

The war had raged along the east coast for over two years and during that time so many men had died. Often their lives had been wasted in battle due to the poor military tactics employed by some of their inept commanders. Despite their many years of military service, despite their experiences in previous military conflicts, and despite the lessons learned in earlier battles in this Great War, far too many generals, as well as many of their subordinate commanders, had continued to slaughter their men using frontal attacks upon the enemy, even when the enemy held the secure and fortified positions. It was a waste of a generation of men. The waste of lives would be no different for those men, both grey and blue, who wasted their own lives trying to steal the gold and silver from Captain Francis and his men.

Francis had been asleep for only two hours when he was woken by the voice. It was the voice in his nightmare, the voice of Sgt. Hatfield screaming out his name as a doctor was amputating his broken leg. Waking up startled, his head drenched in sweat, he sensed his heart beating loud and fast. He was terrified, believing it was real and not a dream, then relieved, but still somewhat panicked when he realized he had only been dreaming. As he sat there in the dark barn calming himself down, the only light present was what the cracks in the sides of the barn allowed in from the full moon. Sitting there as he calmed down, he wondered if he had woken any of his men when he was startled out of his sleep by his reoccurring dream. Looking around, he saw his men were still fast asleep.

Lying back down on his blanket, he was thankful for the hay which had been present in the barn as it gave him his first soft cushion to sleep on in weeks. He had almost fallen back to sleep when he heard the first noise. Seconds later he heard it again. At first he thought the noise was probably caused by mice foraging for food, but then as he lay there he saw the first figure creep across the barn's hay loft. Clouded by the still present thoughts of his dream, and of his lack of sleep, Francis' tired mind was slow to process what it was he was seeing. Confused, he wondered why one of his men was up in the loft. "Who is that up there and what could he possibly be doing?"

Then he saw the second figure creep across the hay loft directly above where he had been sleeping. The light from the full moon now also shown through the open hay loft door off to his left, fifteen feet above the barn's dirt floor. It was the open hay loft door which brought Francis to his senses as he realized he had closed the door when he inspected the barn before lying down for the night. Now he realized the men he was watching were not his, but likely men who had come to claim the gold and silver for themselves. Absorbing what was unfolding above him, Francis realized he likely had only a couple of minutes to react to the threat they were now facing. He did not know who these men were, nor did he care, but he knew what they had come for.

Holding his saber in his injured left hand, and with his pistol stuck in his waistband, Francis crept closer to where Sgt. Davis was asleep, only a few feet away from where he had been sleeping a few moments earlier. As he slowly moved towards Davis, the snoring of some of his men masked the sound he made as he moved across the dirt floor. As he did so, he could see one of the intruders trying to peer down at them in the dimly lit barn. The light from the moon allowed him to see the men as they crept across the hay loft, but the moonlight only illuminated the loft and not the barn floor. It had given him a tactical advantage, one he was about to exploit to his benefit.

As he crept closer to where Davis still was fast asleep, Francis saw two more men slowly creep across the hay loft above him. In moments they joined the first two men near the top of the stairs, stairs which led from the hay loft to the barn floor. "They're likely gathering their courage to come and get us," Francis thought as he finalized his plans for defeating the intruders' attempt to steal their precious cargo. Knowing he had to act quickly, he reached out and firmly placed his right hand over the mouth of the sleeping Sgt. Davis.

Whispering into his right ear, his hand still covering Davis' mouth, Francis woke him up. "Davis, it's me Francis. Do not make a sound, just look up at the top of the stairs. Do you see them? There are four of them. They came in through the hayloft door." Now he took his hand off of Davis' mouth. "I think they're coming to get the gold and silver; we need to be ready. We only have a couple of seconds. Is your musket loaded?"

"Yes." It was the only word Davis softly uttered.

Francis then whispered his instructions to him. "Let them start down the stairs. When they do, I want you to shoot the last man in line. Make it count!"

It only took a moment before they saw the four men above them slowly start to move. Seeing them start down the stairs, Francis first, and then Davis, slowly positioned themselves so they could fire their weapons. As they did, and as the last of the four men had started to come down the stairs a couple of steps, Francis sprang to his feet. With the faint light of the moon as his only available light, he fired his pistol at the third man in line. His shot struck the intended target and the intruder immediately fell dead, his lifeless body tumbling down the stairs.

Within a moment of Francis firing his weapon, Davis did the same, striking the last man in line with a well-placed shot to the chest. Like the intruder Francis had shot, he also fell forward down the stairs. The chaos caused by the two unsuspecting shots, coupled by the two men falling down the stairs upon them, caused one of the two remaining men to be knocked off the stairs onto the barn's dirt floor. The first intruder in line, distracted by the shots fired by Francis and Davis, momentarily turned around to look at his comrades. When he turned back to see where the shots had come from, he quickly realized the fatal mistake he made. In looking back at his comrades, he had taken his eyes off the barn floor. Doing so had allowed Francis to quickly be on top of him.

Now on his feet, Francis charged at the last man on the stairs. Reaching him, he ran his saber clean through the man's stomach, catching him off guard and with no time to react to the saber's thrust. Now gasping as the saber was pulled back out of his stomach, the first intruder dropped his musket and fell down the final two steps to the barn's dirt floor. Almost immediately, he clutched his stomach in agony. The intruder who had been knocked off the steps by his dead friends falling on him was now crying out in pain from a strong kick to his face. By kicking him hard, Davis had made sure this intruder was no longer a threat.

The gunshots fired by Davis and Francis quickly woke the other men from their deep sleep. As experienced soldiers would, they immediately reached for their muskets; reacting to the gunshots they had heard. Their next reaction was to respond to any threats still present. As they did, Francis loudly yelled to them, ordering them not to fire their weapons. Seeing his men responding to his order, he realized it was only through the Lord's blessing no one else was shot in the panic of the moment. Now in the darkness, Samuel lit two lanterns, bringing more light into the dark barn.

Ever alert for danger, Francis then made sure no one else was present in the barn. "Stine and Griffin, both of you get up into the loft and check for anyone who might be hiding, but be careful!" Checking the loft they found no one else hiding there. Looking out the hay loft's open door, they saw no other trouble lurking outside.

After the loft had been checked, Francis grabbed the long hair of the intruder whose face had been partially rearranged by the kick from Sgt. Davis. He now sought to know if others were lurking outside the barn waiting to ambush them. Through a busted lip, and now minus several teeth, the intruder first spit out a mouthful of blood onto the dirt floor before answering. "No, sir, ain't no others out there, Captain Francis."

Francis was momentarily taken back by the answer he heard. Then he asked more of the injured soldier. "How can I believe you? How do you know my name? Do I know you?" Still clenching the intruder's long hair in his injured left hand, he was stunned by the injured soldier calling him by his name. Now he bent over to look closer at whom it was he was interrogating. The injured man looked vaguely familiar, but he could not recall where he had seen his face. It quickly became clear to him.

"Captain, look at these two dead boys here!"

Francis turned to see Davis standing next to two dead intruders. "These here boys are them North Carolina boys. You know, them soldiers who helped us load the wagons onto the train the other day. Remember? The wagon fell off the ramp and broke, and the gold spilled out onto the ground. These are them same two boys y'all told to stay away from the gold or you'd shoot them. Well, I guess ya gone and fulfilled that promise. Not like you'd thought you'd do, but ya dun shot them as y'all said ya would. These Tar Heels boys . . . just like them other two with them . . . they musta likely thought they could catch us sleeping and get some easy money. Guess they didn't think y'all was gonna be awake in the middle of the night. Too bad for them, I guess."

Francis quickly scanned the faces of the dead soldiers who now lay nearby on the barn floor. He vaguely recognized one of the two when he held one of the lanterns close to their faces. He then turned to look back at the soldier he had run his saber through. The dying man wore the tattered remnants of a Confederate soldier's uniform. Now curled up in a fetal position as he screamed out in pain, the soldier's stomach burned due to the internal laceration caused by the saber. The dirt floor was now stained with the dying soldier's blood. Francis looked at the other dead soldier lying nearby; strangely he was wearing the uniform of Union soldier.

"Captain, it hurts real bad! Please, please help me. We didn't mean no harm to y'all. We just wanted some gold and some food. We ain't ate much lately!"

Francis stood silently over the dying soldier, his pleas for help falling on deaf ears. "Tell me what I want to know and perhaps I may get you some help. Whose idea was this? How did you know where to find us?"

The soldier's pain was intensifying from the internal damage done by the saber, but Francis stoically stood there, showing no remorse for what he had done. Impatiently he waited for a response from the dying soldier. Through his painful gasps for air, the soldier tried to answer him. "Captain, I swear to you, it were not my fault this all happened. It was all Smitty's idea, I was just hungry. I swear to you. You dun killed him it looks, but I swear it were his idea, the whole thing. Ain't nobody else outside waiting on y'all. It was just us. We been following y'all for a couple of days since we dun seen them gold bars fall out of the wagon. We just been waiting for the right time, that's all. I suspect we dun guessed wrong. I'm real sorry for the trouble we caused y'all. Captain, can y'all please help me with the pain? It hurts real bad now!"

Sergeants Stine and Griffin, who had called into the barn after checking the area outside, were let back inside through the barn's two main doors. After glancing at the dead bodies of two intruders, they told Francis what they had found. "Captain, them boys got up into the loft using a ladder we found leaning against the barn. Likely stole it from someplace close to here. We also found four horses tied to a tree just the other side of the railroad tracks. Ain't nobody else out there though." Finished telling Francis what they had found outside, and with a look of disgust on his face, Stine spit a mouthful of tobacco juice on the shirt of the soldier curled up on the barn floor. Like the others, he had little use for traitors.

Francis then noticed the railroad stationmaster, as well as William McGuire and four other men, standing in the barn's open doorway. They had all been woken from their sleep by the sound of shots being fired. He could tell they were all far too afraid to venture further inside the barn.

Standing off to the side of his men, an angry Francis yelled loudly for all to hear as he pointed at the soldiers lying on the ground. "These men were soldiers once. Three were once our brothers-in-arms; one was our enemy. No longer are they either our brothers or our enemy, they are now just simple thieves and traitors. They have tried to kill me and my men, and they have tried to rob the Confederacy of what is needed to sustain our cause. They have tried to rob us of what we desperately need to fight the damn Yankees with. Damn each of these men to eternity!" Still seething anger, Francis strode to one of the side walls of the barn and grabbed a long length of rope hanging nearby. Throwing it to the ground where the two injured soldiers now lay, he yelled to his men. "Hang them damn it! Hang them right now from these very rafters. They do not deserve our mercy!"

The two injured soldiers had less time to cry out in protest than they had to react when they had been injured by Francis and Davis. Ignoring their pleas for mercy and forgiveness, they were brusquely grabbed off the barn floor by Francis' men. Within moments, they each were placed on a horse with their hands tied behind their backs. With quickly tied nooses placed around their necks, and without any ceremony or additional words being spoken, they were hung from two rafters in the barn. Rafters which helped to support the hay loft they had crept across before their ill-conceived plan went bad. At first, their feet danced in the air; desperately trying to grab at something that was not there. In less than two minutes, they were both dead.

Looking back at the men standing near the opened barn door, Francis hollered to them. "You men there, know these soldiers are traitors to our cause.

Let them hang here for others to see what happens to traitors. Then do as you please with their bodies, but shed no tears for them as they are not brave soldiers like my men. They are just traitors! I care not what happens to them."

Francis had just done what was expected of him. It was something he had long ago taken an oath to do. He had protected his men and he had helped to protect the future of the Confederacy. While he knew he helped to kill four men who had tried to kill them, and despite reacting as he should have, he found no pleasure in killing these men. "When will this terrible war, one which makes men do such crazy things, be over with?" It was a question all of his men would ask themselves many more times in the coming weeks.

* * * * * *

Shortly after the sun rose, the lifeless bodies of the two soldiers still hung from the barn rafters. They hung there in full view of those townspeople who came to see what had taken place during the night. While the bodies still hung inside the barn, the train finally arrived at the Florence train station. Soon Francis and his men were again focused on their mission. They began the process of loading the train's rail cars with the wagons, horses, and with the small amount of remaining supplies they could still carry.

With the train's arrival, Francis learned new information regarding the movements of Union troops in the Carolinas. News first came from the train's brakeman, James Reilly, a disabled soldier from Georgia who had lost most of his right leg earlier in the war during fighting in the first battle of Bull Run. Reilly spoke of Union troops being seen both west and northwest of Florence. He also told Francis many people were now speculating that Union troops were planning to attack Confederate strongholds in western South Carolina, including Columbia. It was speculation that could not be confirmed as most of the telegraph lines have either been cut or damaged. "Captain, them Yankees are coming soon. My boys and I gave them hell at Bull Run; I hope you boys can do the same if y'all get the chance. I'd like to come with y'all, but this dang leg just don't work right any longer." Francis was glad to hear the news Reilly gave him as it helped him know where units of the Union army had been recently seen. The news also told him their presence posed a serious threat to the success of his mission.

As he thanked Reilly for both the news he brought them, and for his service to the Confederacy, another soldier who had been on the train, Captain William Baldwin, from the 15th South Carolina Infantry Unit, brought more news concerning Union troop movements. Baldwin claimed three days ago, while in Richmond seeking much needed supplies for several of South Carolina's infantry units, he heard news of a Union army telegraph message being intercepted. "From what I was told, part of the telegraph documented

Union cavalry movements south through eastern Tennessee. I heard they were being supported by some unknown infantry divisions as well. Supposedly they were headed to Columbia from there. The guess was they were going to give their armies free reign in creating havoc there as payback for starting the war. I'm not sure everything I was told was factual or if it was a rumor, but they're coming, that I know to be a fact."

As he had done with Reilly, Francis also thanked Baldwin for the news he brought him. "Captain, I cannot speak to you about our mission, but I can tell you the news you have told me is most distressing. I fear what the future will bring, not only to my men and me, but to the Confederacy as a whole. If these Union troops are soon to be as far south as you have told me, and if they are not challenged by our troops immediately, we may soon be doomed as a nation."

Now more than ever Francis knew he had to get to the relative safety of Charleston. Once there, he could either gather additional help to move the money to Atlanta, or he could possibly ship it south by boat, but he had to get to Charleston before the presence of Union troops threatened the area around him.

The train pulled out of the station as soon as the wagons and horses had been loaded. Slowly the train, one of the few still operating for the North Eastern Railroad, began to move them south towards Cades, South Carolina. As the train moved along the tracks, Francis prayed it was also moving them further away from the Union army. As his men rested from their ordeal back in the barn, and from loading the train under the already steaming South Carolina morning sun, Francis and Baldwin stood together by the side of one of the rail cars. They spent time talking of the war's progress and of what they both had experienced. Homesick by now, the two Confederate officers expressed frustration to each other about the war lingering for far too long. Both were in agreement about the end of the war. It was an ending which was not yet in sight.

The small talk between Francis and his new friend included Baldwin, the son of a wealthy South Carolina rice planter, talking of his life prior to the start of the war. His life was vastly different from the one Francis had lived, but as Baldwin told him his father's wealth allowed for special privileges, it was easy to tell it had been a life with some unhappiness in it. Baldwin talked about falling out of favor with his father due to an incident which occurred during his senior year at the Virginia Military Institution. The incident had resulted in him being expelled from school over an allegation of cheating; an allegation later proven to be false. Despite that, the allegation created a deep rift between them as his father had not stood by him during the time the matter was being investigated. Later, again to his father's ire, Baldwin had joined the Confederate army instead of returning to school. In doing so, he had chosen to simply enlist in the army, choosing to advance on his own instead of using his father's wealth and influence to buy an officer's commission. Enlisting had caused an additional strain on his relationship with his father.

"I do hope the pride we carry in our own lives, and the pride we have in each other, will allow us to mend our past grievances when the war ends. But for that to happen, he will have to apologize for thinking I would dishonor his reputation by cheating. I would never tarnish our family name like that." Francis sensed Baldwin truly regretted what had come between him and his father.

Unlike Baldwin, Francis never received any formal education. He received his education from his mother, Bertha, who had been a school teacher for a few years after completing her own schooling in Baltimore. She had been his only teacher, and it was from her he learned how to read. Her interest in reading carried over to him as she had exposed her son to the outside world through her small collection of books.

Bertha Elizabeth Bland had been the only daughter of John Bland. He had sent her away to a finishing school in Baltimore so she could receive not only an education, but to hopefully meet someone else to marry besides the boy who tried courting her back home. The boy who lived only four short miles from the Bland plantation was Peter Francis. Bertha's father had not liked young Peter early on, but finally consented to allow her to marry him after he received his first promotion in the Union army.

Despite having been taught at home, Judiah Francis had become an enthusiastic student. After learning the basic educational skills, he pushed himself to learn more, especially in mathematics. From the books he borrowed from nearby friends, he read whatever he could get his hands on. Despite his lack of a formal education, he had become much more than just a young uneducated man from the back country of Virginia. He had proved that to others every day since joining the Army of Northern Virginia. Deep down, as he listened to Baldwin talk about VMI, he wished he could have experienced some form of a formal education.

As their talk continued, and as the train slowly plodded along the tracks, Baldwin tried to learn more about the mission Francis was on. "Judiah, it is apparent to me, due to both your silence on what your mission is about and from what I perceive to be a somewhat increased level of alertness among your men, an alertness I would not normally expect to see from soldiers riding on a train, that you are doing something far different than what most other soldiers are doing in the war. Am I right?"

Growing tired from his lack of sleep, and from his self-reflection over hanging two traitors earlier in the day, Francis looked at Baldwin for a moment without speaking. A couple of moments later he gave Baldwin a simple response to the assessment he had made about his mission. "You are correct in your assumption."

Fearing Baldwin was going to likely ask him more questions about his mission, Francis tried to steer the conversation in another direction. Pointing out one of his men, Francis spoke before he could be asked another question. "You see the soldier grooming the horse over there? He is from North Carolina, the New Bern area if I remember right. He is representing North Carolina very well during our difficult mission. In fact, all of my men are performing very well. They all are enduring many hardships without complaining. I am proud of all of them. Those who are higher in rank than I am chose these men to be part of this mission. I must admit, they chose very well."

But Baldwin did not see what Francis had attempted to do with the conversation, and he again asked about the mission his new friend was leading before he was cut off. With a touch of frustration in his voice, Francis sternly spoke to him. "Captain, my mission is not to be asked about again. As a military officer and as my new friend you need to respect the position I have taken in not talking about my assignment. I cannot speak on it, nor will I. I can only tell you that I must get as far south as soon as possible."

Finally realizing he had pursued his interest in Francis' mission too far, Baldwin apologized. "Judiah, out of no other reason than my mere personal curiosity, I have asked you questions I now realize I should not have asked. I respect your orders and I respect you. I offer a sincere apology to you. I hope I have not offended you." Smiling, Francis patted his new friend on the shoulder to indicate the apology had been accepted.

"Judiah, I'm a proud South Carolinian, born and bred, and a soldier just like you. I know many routes of travel south from where we now are. Tell me where you want to get to and perhaps I can suggest some way for you to get there so harm does not fall upon you and your men."

While Francis knew he could not tell Baldwin what their mission was, he also knew he needed help getting to Charleston. He would be foolish not to accept the recommendations of someone so familiar with the roads in and around South Carolina.

"William, my immediate goal is to get to Charleston safely. I had hoped to get to Columbia or Chattanooga, and then on to Savannah, but train problems in North Carolina have changed my plans. Now the presence of Yankee troops no longer allows me to risk trying to get there, especially since I have recently heard that Chattanooga is under frequent attacks from Union troops. Now I must get to Charleston. Once there, I'll decide if I should move further south by boat or by the Charleston Savannah Railroad. I can only pray the train will still be running by the time we get there. Now, what do you suggest? And please, while I cannot tell you specifics of our mission, know it is an important one. I shall be in debt to you for your assistance. If I had not received a direct order from General Lee regarding this mission, I would have been glad to speak with you about it. As an officer in the Confederate army, I cannot ignore the order he has given me or the trust he has shown in me. I hope you can understand my position. Sir, please . . . tell me how to get to Charleston safely with these wagons."

Francis had played a hunch when he intentionally mentioned General Lee's name to Baldwin. While Baldwin's opinion of Lee was not important to Francis, mentioning Lee's name now signified the importance of his mission. He hoped by playing his hunch Baldwin would tell him the safest route to Charleston. He would soon find out he had played his hunch very well.

"Judiah, I understand the tacit message you have just given me. Please extend my best to the good general when you see him. My father and the general are good friends from their times spent together earlier in their careers. You do not have to mention my name to him as someone who has rendered you some assistance, simply send him my regards. Hearing you mention his name gives me a sense of the importance of your mission."

Francis then walked to where his haversack sat on the floor of the railcar. After briefly checking on his men, he returned to where Baldwin still stood. Unfolding a map for them to work with, he looked at Baldwin. "Show me how to get there."

Fearing the Union army would likely be targeting the railroad they were on, as well as others in the area, Baldwin surprised Francis by suggesting he leave the safety of the train before they reached the Santee River. He suggested Francis lead his men towards the relative safety of Georgetown and then south towards Charleston. "The train will get you further south quicker, but if I were you I would go to Charleston over land. The Union army likely wants to disrupt rail service so we cannot resupply our armies in a timely fashion. Your mission appears to be an important one. If it's as important as you are leading me to believe, I suggest you go by land. You will have to cross a few rivers along the way, but you will also find pockets of Southern sympathizers who can supply you with food and information."

Always the well-prepared and cautious Confederate officer he was, Francis wrestled with the advice he was given, but soon agreed with Baldwin's recommendation to disembark from the train. As he thought more about doing this, his military training told him the decision to leave the train was the right one. Silently he gave his friend's recommendation serious thought. "Plus, if I do leave the train, the Santee River will afford me some protection as I move east to Georgetown. Hopefully the river will slow any Union troop movements towards Charleston."

Soon gathering his men to tell them what would be occurring, Francis saw Baldwin climb up and over the end of the rail car they had been talking on. He then saw him beginning to make his way over and through the other rail cars. He knew Baldwin would soon be telling the train's engineer where to stop the train for them.

In less than two hours, the train neared the location Baldwin had recommended to Francis. As it neared the location, the engineer braked the train to stop. It came to a long slow stop alongside a narrow rough trail. As it did, Francis immediately ordered the train to be unloaded of the wagons and horses.

"Judiah, I would like to accompany you to your final destination, but I must get back to my men as I have been away from them far too long. I have been gone so long I suspect they likely believe I have joined up with the Yankees!" Francis shook hands with Baldwin, laughing at the improbable thought of him wearing the uniform of the Union army.

"Captain Baldwin, it was indeed an honor to meet you. I thank you for your valuable assistance. I shall indeed let General Lee know of your help, and of your high regard for him."

That said, and with the wagons now unloaded from the train, they again shook hands. In moments, the wagons slowly started their move east towards Georgetown. As he watched them move away, Baldwin signaled for the train to start moving. Holding onto the side of the open door of one of the boxcars, he braced himself as the train lurched forward as it started moving. He watched as Francis moved out of sight, partially obscured from view by the many pine trees along the side of the rough trail he now travelled on. As he stood there on the straw covered floor of the boxcar, Baldwin reached down and picked up a single gold coin, an 1861 Quarter Eagle. He had seen it mixed in with the straw on the floor of the boxcar. Fingering the almost new gold coin, he finally realized what Francis' mission was about. "I hope he makes it. We need that money to fight the damn Yankees with!" Silently he stood there for a few minutes, wishing his new friend well. He hoped they would see each other after the war.

* * * * * *

The war would continue to rage for well over another year, but Baldwin would not see the full year unfold. The gold and silver coins would last for many more years. It would only take someone smart enough to finally find it.

17

Looking For Gold.

"When Johnny comes marching home again, Hurrah! Hurrah!
We'll give him a hearty welcome then, Hurrah! Hurrah!"
Lyrics to 'When Johnny Comes Marching Home', a Union Civil War song.

Like it is for most people the night before they get married or the night before they start a new job, it was the same for Chick the night before he was to meet with Paul and Jayne to learn the clues his new friend had uncovered regarding the missing Confederate treasury. The excitement of what the following day would bring denied him any chance at sleep, and he spent most of the night tossing, turning, and thinking of what he would learn in the morning.

As he lay in bed, Chick ran many questions through his head. "Does Paul really have the clues needed to find the missing gold and silver? Is the legend of the missing money really true or are we just chasing a myth? What are we going to find?" As Paul had no answers to the many questions running through his mind, Chick also had no answers to the many questions he asked himself during his sleepless night.

Just before 6:00 a.m., he gave up any hopes of falling asleep. After getting dressed, Chick made a pot of coffee and sat down at his kitchen table with his books, hoping to find some answers about the missing treasury.

Before trying to fall asleep, Chick picked through a small mountain of books he had piled in his den. From the pile, he pulled out three books. Each contained information on the legend of the missing Confederate treasury. Now over several cups of coffee, he read what he could find on the missing gold and silver. He hoped to find some innocuous clue about the missing money which could help them. He found nothing.

Four hours later, Paul greeted Chick and Jayne as they walked up the steps to his front door. "Are you excited, nervous, or both?"

"I'm both, but surprisingly I slept like a baby last night!"

Chick was jealous of Jayne's response as he had tried everything to fall asleep during the night, but counting sheep, and even gold coins, had brought no success. He was working on adrenaline now and was not sure how long it would last, but he knew the suspense would keep him going for as long as it took Paul to tell them what he knew about the missing money.

After ushering them into his kitchen, Paul turned on his *Keurig* coffee maker. Soon they were sitting at his kitchen table, talking over their coffee.

"Look, I have a couple of items I want to show you before I let you read the letters I found. I think it's important for me to show you how I found them so you have a mental picture of the scene as I found it."

With coffee cups left behind on Paul's orders, they both followed him into the garage. Patiently they waited as he unpacked a cardboard moving box containing some of the items he had yet to tell the authorities about. First, they were shown the Confederate tail coat, the blouse which held the coins and bottles Paul had found. It was a coat with several of its original buttons still sewn in place.

Handing them each a pair of white cotton gloves he picked up the previous afternoon from the Dollar General Store not far from his house, Paul gave them some simple instructions to follow. "Before you touch anything you need to put these on. We don't want the perspiration from your hands damaging the items I'm going to show you." Chick and Jayne both donned the gloves without saying a word as they continued to stare at the blouse that had been carefully laid out on a blanket. The blanket had been spread out on top of a sheet of plywood which rested on two wooden sawhorses.

"For being in a tree for so long, exposed to all types of weather, as well as insects and whatever else, this is in amazing condition." Jayne barely took her eyes off the blouse as she unpacked her Nikon camera from its case.

With Paul's permission, Jayne took photos of the blouse from all angles and from all sides. She even had Chick carefully hold the blouse up so she could photograph the backside of it for documentation needs. After she finished, Paul directed their attention to the bottles he had set up on his work bench; ones that had held the letters for so many years. "These bottles contained four letters and a small map. You can see I drilled the bottoms out so I could get the letters out." The click of Jayne's camera was the only noise in the garage as they all stared at the bottles and at the holes which had been made in them. Paul then showed them copies of the photos Donna had taken as he drilled the holes in the bottom of the bottles. "My wife took these photos to document the finds we made when we took the letters out of the bottles. We also ran a video camera at the same time. I have the video ready to show you later when we're done in here. If we do decide to do a documentary on this, I was thinking the video we took, and possibly these photos as well, could easily be incorporated into our finished product."

Setting her camera down on a nearby folding table, Jayne complimented Paul for having the foresight to document what he had done with the bottles. "Taking the video and the digital pictures was a wise idea as it showed not only what you found, but it also shows how your soldier had packaged the letters so many years ago to protect them. I agree with you, the pictures and the video are things we should definitely think about including in our documentary."

While he appreciated the compliment Jayne directed at him for documenting what he found, Paul had done so without even thinking about it. From the crime scenes he worked at, documenting those scenes with both photographs and videotape was a routine task which needed to be done. Looking at Jayne as she held the pictures Donna had taken, Paul gave her a zing. "Thanks for the compliment, but it's not my first rodeo!"

Grasping the meaning of his somewhat sarcastic comment, and then remembering what Paul had done previously in life, Jayne's face turned a somewhat embarrassed shade of red. Chick smiled at Paul's comment, but remained quiet as his eyes slowly scanned the photos he was looking at.

"Amazing stuff, just amazing."

"What about ....."

Paul cut Jayne off in mid-sentence. "I know, I know. You want to see the letters. I would too."

Moving back into the kitchen, Paul refreshed their cups of coffee as they again sat down at his kitchen table. "Don't get upset with me, but we're going to do all of this in piecemeal fashion. I'm only going to show you three of the letters today. I promise I'll show you the fourth one very soon, but not today. However, I will tell you that letter is perhaps the best of the four of them. Again, I promise you will see it sometime very soon. You have to trust me on this, just like we talked about when we first met, OK?"

Obviously disappointed, Chick asked the same question Jayne had poised on the tip of her tongue. "If we're going to find the missing gold and silver, and who knows what else, don't we need to know what the contents of the fourth letter are?" It was a question Paul had anticipated they would be asking.

"I understand your point, and you're absolutely correct, but you have to trust me on this. It will all make sense very shortly, I promise. And one more thing, while I'm going to show you the other three letters, when we're done they stay with me. When you leave, they go back under lock and key again. Don't ask me if you can take them with you as it's not going to happen. One more thing as well, no pictures get taken of the letters today. Deal?"

Frustrated by the conditions placed on them, but still eager to see what clues the letters contained, Chick and Jayne were forced to accept Paul's conditions. "OK, deal." It was a reluctant response, but it was one they both knew they were forced to accept.

The conditions understood and agreed upon, Paul had them clear the table of their coffee cups. Then he wiped the table down to make sure it was completely dry. Confident it was, he then covered the table with a large blue table cloth before spreading out a white towel down on top of the tablecloth. Retrieving a small gold colored metal lock box he had hidden in one of the kitchen cabinets, Paul set it down on the kitchen table. After unlocking it, he carefully placed down on the white towel the original letters which had been signed by President Davis and Treasury Secretary Memminger. Next to those letters he placed the letter written from Captain Judiah Francis to his father. "Please be careful around these letters as they're the originals. Don't even think of touching them without wearing your gloves."

Chick and Jayne jockeyed for position around the table for several minutes in complete silence as they slowly read the letters. Previously having the opportunity to view several other letters written and signed by President Davis, Chick told Paul these letters appeared to be original documents, especially the one written and signed by Davis.

"Paul, these two letters, the ones signed by Davis and Memminger, they are clearly talking about the missing Confederate treasury. They are referring to the money without actually calling it what it is, gold and silver, but that's what they are talking about. I have no doubt about it. Wow, what a find!"

Jayne had focused her attention on the letter written by Francis to his father and now started crying as she finished reading it for the second time. As she finished reading the letter, her fingers were poised on her lips as tears streamed down her face. Seeing she was crying, her tears both scared and confused Chick at first. Paul gently calmed her down by patting her on the back. "Donna had the same reaction when she read the letter. It's obviously a very emotional letter." Handing her a napkin, Jayne wiped away her tears as best as she could, but she was still upset from reading the letter a dying Judiah Francis had written.

Having been lost in his own concentration as he read the Davis and Memminger letters, Chick now read the Francis letter. Quickly he understood what had moved Jayne to tears. "Simply amazing! A piece of history no one has ever seen or even knew existed. Paul, if the fourth letter is the best of the bunch as you say it is, I cannot wait to see it!"

After the letters had been read and reread a countless number of times, and talked about even more, Paul secured them back in the metal lock box until he could place them back in his safety deposit box later in the day. As he finished doing this, Chick and Jayne sat at the kitchen table sipping their lukewarm coffee in total silence. After a few more minutes of silence, Chick was the first to speak. "Paul, these letters, you said you know where the gold and silver is from reading the letters, but from what we've read they give no indication of where the money is. It has to be the fourth letter which told you where the money is."

"Somewhat."

"Somewhat? What kind of an answer is that? You told us you know where the money is. Either you know or you don't know. What is it?" The tone in

Chick's voice demanded an answer. Before Paul could respond, Jayne gave her interpretation of where they now stood with him.

"My guess is Paul has an idea or two as to where the money may be, but he still needs to figure out, possibly with our help, how to decipher a clue or two from one of the letters so the money can be found. Is that a good guess?"

Paul nodded back at Jayne, smiling as he did as she had been pretty close in her estimation of what was still needed to find the gold and silver. "Not bad, not a bad guess at all."

"Say, what is this," Chick asked, "an Indiana Jones movie or what?"

His comment made Paul laugh as they sat around his kitchen table. "Pretty much that's exactly what it is, Chick. You still in?" As he waited for his answer, Paul laughed again as he liked the analogy Chick had used.

"I guess I am. I mean, I guess we still are." Chick was now somewhat disappointed from not being able to see the fourth letter and from not learning exactly where the gold and silver was buried. His disappointment now caused him to feel his fatigue from not being able to sleep. Needing another cup of coffee to keep him going, he stood up from the table and dropped in another pod of *Green Mountain* coffee into the *Keurig* coffee maker.

Now they all exchanged weak, but excited smiles with each other. Paul then surprised them by giving them one final piece of information for the day. As he spoke to them, he referenced the fourth letter in his comments, doing so caused Chick's earlier disappointment to be pushed to the side for now. Quietly he moved his chair closer to the table as Paul was talking to them.

Paul then told them the missing treasury appeared to have been buried in at least two places. "From the fourth letter, I know some of the gold and silver was separated from the original shipment and was buried in North Carolina, but I'm not exactly sure where that is. However, I do know what markings our Captain Francis gave to the area where the money was buried. He marked the area to make it easy to be found when he went back to retrieve it at a later time. Unfortunately for both he and the Confederacy, he never made it back there. If we can find this location, then we'll find some of the missing treasury; gold and silver coins that have been buried for over one hundred and fifty years. Besides the historical significance of finding the money, the gold and silver is obviously worth many times over what it was worth when it was buried by Francis and his men."

Chick and Jayne were now smiling as they at least knew where they would be starting their search for the missing treasury.

"Oh, I told you he buried it in two places, didn't I?" Paul jokingly asked. "Well, from the fourth letter I think he may have hid some of it in a few places just to keep it safe, but I don't think he buried all of it. I think he just hid it for us to find."

The excitement in Chick and Jayne's eyes was easy for Paul to see. He could almost hear the wheels spinning in their heads as they tried figuring out a way to locate the first spot where the missing gold and silver had been buried. After several minutes of listening to his two excited partners talk about ways of finding the missing money, a grinning Paul calmed them down so he could speak. "If it's of any interest to you, I already have a plan on how to possibly find the money."

Paul then shared his plan with both of them. After he finished, and without a moment to reflect on what he had told them, they both quickly agreed it was a great way to try and find the missing money.

* * * * * *

Now all they had to do was to implement Paul's plan. Praying at the same time that no one had placed a ten-story apartment building or an interstate highway where Francis had carefully buried the money so many years ago.

Summer, 1863

18

The Cemetery.

*"To move swiftly, strike vigorously, and secure all the fruits
of victory is the secret of a successful war."*
General Thomas Jonathan 'Stonewall' Jackson, CSA

After disembarking from the train, Francis rode out to scout the area in front of them as they moved further south. As he did, he continually looked over his right shoulder to make sure the wagons stayed together as they slowly proceeded down the rough dirt trail. It was a trail the local residents referred to as the Georgetown Turnpike. "It's hardly worth being called a turnpike," Francis thought as he again turned to check on the wagons. He was pleased they were still in line, and still staying close to each other in the event they were surprised by a Union attack of some sort.

They had been travelling over the rough road for almost five hours when he saw one of his Virginia sergeants, Franklyn Banks, who he had sent out in advance of the wagon train, riding back towards him. Francis reached for his pocket watch and saw the time was close to six pm, still too early to call a halt for the day.

"Captain, the road ain't no better as far as I've ridden, it gets even worse in some spots. I ain't gonna be surprised if one of them wagons don't throw a wheel seeing how bad it gets up ahead. You might want to give some thought to having us move out into the fields. The ground ain't as hard, but it seems to be a lot less rugged than this here road is. Might be worth thinking on." Banks suggested as he wiped the afternoon's dust and sweat off his brow.

"Alright, I'll give it some thought. We need to keep moving for a spell as we still have plenty of daylight left. What else do you see up ahead?"

"Not much, but y'all already knew that didn't ya, captain? Seeing we is in South Carolina now and not in the beautiful state of Virginia." Francis smiled at the comment Banks had made, knowing it was an attempt at humor and a way for both of them to spend a quick moment thinking of home.

"This is pretty country too, Franklyn, but you're right, it isn't home."

As Banks started to ride towards the wagons to get a drink of water before heading back out, Francis yelled to him. "Sergeant, tell the men we'll ride for another two hours or so, then we'll make camp for the night. Tell Samuel we're having a hot meal tonight." Banks waved to let him know he heard him before

188

giving his horse a gentle nudge with his spurs, riding off towards the wagons and the drink of water he badly needed.

They had moved along for two more hours when Banks rode back to where Francis was still riding out in front of the wagons. "Captain, I found us a good spot to spend the night. It's only about another five-minute ride from here. There's a small brook running nearby; it's a good spot to water the horses, and for us to get cleaned up a bit."

Francis nodded his head in approval to Banks. "OK, I'll tell the men. When we get there, keep an eye on us until you see we've made camp. I want you to scout the surrounding area so we know we're not going to have any unwanted visitors. We'll get you some dinner later on."

After finally stopping after a long hot day of travelling, Samuel cooked them a dinner consisting of beans, salt pork, and some vegetables they obtained back in Florence. For life on the road, it was a feast they had not enjoyed in some time. As they finished their meal, it was nearly dark and little time existed for the men to talk. The thought of a good nights sleep took precedence over campfire stories which had already been told several times over amongst them.

After eating, and then sleeping for only four hours, Odom, still tired from a long and hot day, rode out to relieve Banks. Like the others, he was tired and hungry from several long days of being in the saddle. Remaining on sentry duty as the others had eaten and grabbed a few hours of shut eye, now it was his turn to do the same. While Banks and the others slept, Odom spent the rest of the night slowly riding around the camp making sure unwanted Yankee guests did not spoil their sleep. As he kept a sharp eye out for unwanted guests, he failed to keep an eye out for someone fleeing the camp.

As dawn broke the following morning, one by one the men woke up and began to stir. Soon they started preparing to move out for the day. On most mornings the smell of both the morning campfire and brewing coffee would greet them as they started moving about, but today it took a couple of minutes before Sgt. McKinney noticed this was not the case. It took him several more minutes to realize Samuel was not in camp. Almost immediately, he let the others know what he had realized.

"Captain, I saw him here late last night. He had kept some food warm for Franklyn until he could be relieved by Big Ed. I even saw him when he sat down on his blanket under the mess wagon. You know . . . like he usually does." Francis then had Stine and Davis search the area around the camp to see if they could locate Samuel. As they left, a somewhat embarrassed Sgt. Odom now worried he would soon incur the wrath of his captain, but it did not happen.

The two sergeants had just left camp when McKinney yelled to no one in particular. "It looks like we're missing some food and a couple of blankets. I hope we ain't missing any gold!"

Francis and the others quickly scrambled to check the wagons to see if any gold or silver was missing, but soon determined their precious cargo was still secure. Nothing else was found to be missing. While pleased the gold and silver was safe, Francis now realized he had one less man to help them drive the wagons. More importantly, he realized they had also just lost their most experienced cook.

"OK, men, let's get ready to move out, we leave in ten minutes. When we do, we need to keep a sharp eye out for Yankee cavalry. If Samuel is caught, he knows what we're carrying in the wagons. Who knows what he might tell them blue bellies. Mind the wagons as well as we cannot afford to lose anymore of them."

Over the next three days, Francis and his men pushed closer to Georgetown. Despite the unusually hot weather, they moved without incident. As they moved along, Francis steered them east and closer to the South Carolina coast. Moving closer to the coast, they passed north of Georgetown, an area where Clifton Plantation was located. There they watered and rested their horses while Francis learned the best route to take. From the plantation's owner, he learned they would soon have to cross both the Waccamaw River and the Great Pee Dee River, as well as a couple of other smaller streams, in order to make it to the northern part of Georgetown.

The crossing of the Waccamaw River proved to be a fairly easy task as a well built, but narrow wooden bridge spanned the river. The bridge easily allowed for even the heavy Conestoga wagons to pass over it without incident. Francis had the heavy wagons move over the bridge cautiously, allowing only one wagon to move across at a time. He did not want the weight of several wagons causing the bridge to buckle as spilling their precious cargo into the fast moving water below would deal a devastating blow to the Confederacy. It took some time, but soon the wagons were all across the river.

Shortly after crossing the Waccamaw River, they arrived at the northern bank of the Great Pee Dee River. As they did, Francis sent Griffin out as their advance scout so he could scout the banks of the river for the easiest place to cross. It took some time, but Griffin located a private ferry operating on the river. Riding back to the wagons, he advised Francis of what he found. Now the wagons moved to where the ferry operated. It was late afternoon when Francis, after briefly scouting the area himself, realized they would have to use the ferry to cross the river as it was far too deep to cross on their own.

The operator of the ferry, Joseph Sullivan, was huge in size and as strong as any man living in the parts north of Georgetown. Pulling ferry barges across the river for years had made him famous in these parts for his strength; winning many foolish bets from strangers who challenged his almost legendary strength. Besides being a man who liked to take a drink, Sullivan was also a man who never said no to making a dollar. But when Francis told him he was moving south on orders from General Lee, he refused to take any payment for moving the wagons across the river.

"No, sir, I ain't taking no money from the Confederate army. General Lee himself moved across this here river on my ferry a couple of years back when the war was first starting. A right neighborly type of man he was. He even shook my hand when he thanked me for pulling him across the river. Nope, I ain't taking no money from you soldiers. Enough said about that, let's get moving!"

As much as Francis had warned Sullivan about his concern regarding the weight of each of the wagons, the wagons and one team of horses soon moved across the river without incident. Then, on the second to last trip across the river, with the ferry now loaded with three teams of horses, and with McKinney and Odom tending them, one of the ferry's two ropes worked free from the pulley assembly on the south side of the river. The ropes were used to guide the ferry across the river in a straight line. Soon the pulley assembly broke completely. Even though the river's current was not terribly strong, the broken pulley caused the ferry to spin momentarily out of Sullivan's control. The sudden movement caused the horses to panic, and almost immediately they jerked free of the reins McKinney and Odom had been holding onto. As McKinney struggled to regain control of the reins for one team of horses, he was violently kicked in the head by one of the horses. Immediately he fell down onto the ferry's wooden deck. As he lay there unconscious, he was repeatedly stepped on by the agitated horses. In a matter of moments one team of horses spilled into the river, pulling with them the unconscious Sgt. McKinney. His nearly lifeless body had gotten tangled up in the reins of one team of horses. Just seconds after that, Odom, who was also attempting to regain control of another team of horses, was also knocked into the river by another team of horses. A second team of horses soon followed Odom into the river as they now had no one trying to calm them down. The horses had lost their footing on the ferry's slippery wooden decking before they fell into the river. Forced to momentarily let go of the ropes he had been holding, Sullivan quickly managed to calm down the third team of horses.

Standing on the southern bank of the river, Francis saw this all unfold. Like his men who now stood on both sides of the river, he was helpless to do anything. Soon both teams of horses were able to regain their footing in the river. Despite struggling against the slow moving current, they reached the southern bank of the river without further incident. With the help of Francis and Sgt. Davis, who waded into the river to reach him, Odom made it out of the water with only a sprained ankle. He was soon distraught over the loss of his good friend. Over the next couple of hours they all searched the river's muddy water for McKinney, but despite their efforts they could not locate his body. He had likely drowned after being kicked in the head by one of the horses.

After all of the horses had been retrieved, the ferry was quickly repaired and the remaining horses and supplies were moved across the river. Devastated by the accidental death of McKinney, Francis sensed his men needed a rest and he quickly ordered a halt for a couple of hours. Now down another man, and battling to hold back his own tears, Francis rode off to grieve in private. The loss was especially hard on him as he had come to lean hard on the dependable McKinney over the last couple of weeks.

Riding along the banks of the Waccamaw River as he grieved over the loss of another of his men, Francis tried to figure out how he could move more wagons than he had men to drive them. As he slowly rode, he came across a small inlet which led inland off the river. Riding along the shore of the Inlet, he came across a clearing that held a small cemetery within it. After dismounting, he led his horse to a small brook which fed into the river. From the slow running brook, he and his horse drank the cool fresh water. As his horse rested, Francis walked the short distance to the small cemetery. It was surrounded on all four sides by a chest high mortared red brick wall. The front wall had two large black wrought iron gates that served as the entrance to this family cemetery. Nearby several large massive Live Oak trees, each draped in Spanish moss, stood guard outside the rear wall, their large limbs hanging over a section of the back part of the cemetery.

Francis had barely pushed open the wrought iron gates when a voice hollered out to him from the edge of the Inlet. "Those are some important folks buried in there!" Whether it was due to the loss of McKinney or because he was lost in his thoughts about the elaborate cemetery he was standing in front of, Francis was completely taken by surprise by the voice he heard. He sensed his heart had skipped a beat as he had been taken so off guard by the voice calling out to him. Turning to face what had startled him, he saw a man climbing out of a small flat bottom boat not more than thirty yards away from where he had left his horse to drink from the brook. His horse briefly watched as the stranger climbed out of his small boat. Quickly losing interest, his horse returned to drinking from the brook and feeding on the soft green clover growing nearby.

"How did I not see this man or his boat? Am I that upset about losing McKinney I let my guard down that much?" Francis knew doing so could have led to his demise if someone, such as Yankee soldiers, had wanted to hurt him.

"This here is the Allston family cemetery, ya heard of them?" Asked the elderly white man who had been in the boat. Francis stared at the stranger as he slowly walked towards the entrance of the cemetery. The old man looked to be about seventy years old. To Francis, it appeared to have been a tough seventy years of living as the man's face was heavily wrinkled, almost weather-beaten, from years of living outdoors. As the elderly man walked towards the cemetery, Francis could easily see he walked stooped over.

"Is this the same Allston who I know was governor of this fine state at one time?"

"Yep, that's him alright. This here cemetery goes back quite a spell as ya can see. The governor's family has been burying their kin here since just after we beat them redcoats many years ago. This here piece of land, for almost as far as ya can see, is called Turkey Hill Plantation as it once was a spread that thousands of wild turkeys called home. Good eatin' ones they are too! Still got plenty of them runnin' around this spot, ya just got to find them. Ya seen any, soldier boy?"

"No, sir, I have not. I just rode up here before you called out to me. I saw the cemetery and the brook over there. Thought I'd let my horse take a drink while I stretched my legs."

"I seen ya from the river, wondered what y'all were doing." The old man paused for a moment to look over the uniform Francis was wearing. "Seems this Allston family they got them kinda ties, not sure what the real name is for them, but sees they knew that King George fella, you know from England, and he dun give them a whole lot of land to settle. The way I heard it, after they got the land they dun soon forgot about the old king. Even helped fight against them redcoats themselves; same folks who gave them the land. Kinda peculiar, ain't it? Seeing how they got the land and then fought against his soldiers and all."

"I believe it is just that. My late Aunt Alice would have called it ironic."

"Ya call it what ya want. I don't know nothing about them fancy words and all, but its dang funny to me. Ya know what I mean?"

"I do, sir. I do."

"Well, this here cemetery property has a bunch of the Allston kin buried here, including a couple of young children. They's direct kin to the governor, ya know, R.F.W. Allston himself. Too bad them young folk ain't had a real time to live, ain't fair, ain't fair at all. Never met the man, but I seen him here visiting his kin a few times. Folks around these here parts speak right fondly of the man. Right good fella, I guess. I still call him governor, but he ain't governor no longer. Doing something else these days I suspect. Still a good man though."

"I'm sure he is. I also have heard many good references regarding Governor Allston. I hope to meet him someday, perhaps soon." Francis said as his eyes inspected the area around the cemetery.

"Hey, we been talking a spell and I ain't yet learned your name. My name is Johnny Lincoln. Mostly folks call me Old Johnny or Johnny. You like my last name? Kinda strange a Southern boy having the same name as the President of these here United States, but I ain't no kin to him. Is that what y'all might call that fancy term ya used before?"

"You mean ironic? Yes, you might call it that." Extending his right hand to Old Johnny, Francis introduced himself, telling him where he was from and where he was headed. They talked for another several minutes before Old Johnny started moving back to his boat. After saying a brief goodbye, he was back in his boat and soon down the river out of sight.

As Old Johnny moved down river, Francis walked back to the cemetery and pushed open the wrought iron gates the rest of the way. Standing inside, his thoughts drifted back to McKinney drowning, to Samuel running away, and to how much harder the mission was going to be to complete with two less men. As he struggled with his thoughts, he found himself staring at grave markers where two young infant children had been buried.

"How hard it must have been for their parents to bury these two young children. Buried forever; their young faces never again to be seen by their parents. How sad that must have been for them." As soon as he had run the thought through his head, he replayed the thought one more time. "Buried forever . . . but why does it have to be forever?" As he ran his thought through his head a third time, he concentrated on just the first two words of his thought. "*Buried forever* - but it doesn't have to be forever!" Quickly his eyes scanned the cemetery plot. Then, just as quickly he was on his horse and racing back to his men. Once back with them, Francis told them his idea. It was one that would allow them to get to Charleston much quicker and much lighter than he first expected they would.

"Sgt. Stine, the rest of us are taking one of the wagons back to the cemetery. You are staying here with the other wagons. We are not going to be too far away, so if you see anyone approaching I want you to fire two shots into the air and we will come back to you. Make sure you have two muskets loaded and ready to fire."

"Yes, sir, captain. Not to worry, I'll be fine."

"Good! Sgt. Odom, make sure we have at least three or four shovels with us in the wagon, the same one you've been driving. When we get to the cemetery, you're going to be our eyes and ears while the rest of us are working. Make sure no one is watching us . . . get back to us if you see trouble. But be close to us, because if we see trouble we'll fire one shot to let you know we need your help. If you hear that shot, come running back to us as fast as you can as we'll be needing your help."

"Don't worry none, captain. I'll have y'all covered. No one is going to bother y'all."

"Sgt. Banks, tie up Big Ed's horse to the back of the wagon in the event we no longer have any use for it when we're done. Griffin and Davis, you're both riding your horses back with me. Does everyone understand what they're to do? I want to get this done as fast as possible."

"Yes, sir, but why are we going to a cemetery and why are we bringing a wagon with us?" Banks asked as he tied Odom's horse to the wagon.

"Franklyn, no time for questions right now, just trust that I know what I want to do. You will understand real soon."

In the short ten minutes it took to get back to the cemetery, Francis and the others kept a constant vigil, making sure they were not being watched by either friends or foe. After reaching the cemetery, Francis gathered the men by the gate. "Men, we've been pushed hard these past few weeks and we've lost some of our friends along the way. Today we lost McKinney and I'm sick over his passing; just like I was when the others died. Because they have died, I now fear we cannot properly protect the gold and silver as much as I would like. For that reason, we're going to take one of the flour barrels we have in the wagon and bury it here in this cemetery with some of the gold and silver. Burying the money like we did back in North Carolina will allow us to move to Charleston with at least one less wagon. After we've had time to rest there, and perhaps get some new men to help us, we'll come back and retrieve the money. I doubt anyone is going to suspect we left some of the money in a cemetery. How does this sound to you?"

"Captain, I've always respected you," Odom replied before riding off to make sure no one disturbed them as they worked, "but now I fear a man who disturbs the dead. I do agree with your thinking as I also doubt that any god-fearing man would look for gold in a cemetery, at least not a god-fearing man like me!"

The others shook their heads in agreement with what Odom had just said. Francis only chuckled at his comments as he realized many people, apparently Odom included, had certain fears about death and cemeteries.

After Odom rode off to keep watch over them, and after only a few minutes of digging in the soft sandy soil, the men had a good size hole dug. In the minutes which followed, they quickly completed digging a hole that would easily consume the size of the flour barrel they were soon to bury in this handsome cemetery.

It took far longer to unload the heavy bags of gold and silver coins from the wagon, as well as the gold and silver bars, and to carry all of it to where the barrel had been placed in the ground, than it took to dig the hole. But as quick as possible, they got it done. Francis had Davis climb down into the hole they dug and carefully place the heavy bags of coins in the barrel so the bags did not tear when they were placed inside it. After the bags filled the barrel almost halfway, the men handed Davis several of the gold and silver bars so he could place them on top of the bags of coins. They then filled the rest of the barrel with bagged and loose coins, leaving just enough room for the barrel's lid to fit snuggly in place. A large rock was then placed on top of the closed wooden lid. Francis had the rock placed there just in the event if someone dug in the area they would hit the rock first and not the lid of the barrel. After the hole was filled in, Griffin scattered the remaining dirt outside the grounds of the cemetery while the others did their best to make it look like no one had disturbed the area inside the cemetery where the barrel was buried.

As they finished picking up the shovels, Banks saw Odom approaching. "Captain, look yonder. Here comes Big Ed in a hurry. I'll bet something's up!"

As Francis looked to see where Odom was, he saw him riding his horse hard towards them. "OK, men, expect the worse. Let's get moving back to where Stine is waiting for us."

As they started to move out, Odom galloped up to where Francis had just mounted his horse. "Captain, you need to come take a look at this. We've got company coming up river by boat and also coming south on horses on the far side of the river. Not sure if they're gonna meet each other or not, but I knew you'd want to know about this."

Francis first had Griffin and Banks take the wagon back to where Stine was waiting for them. "Take everything we might need out of the wagon. Be ready to leave as soon as I get back. We might burn the wagon, but don't do anything to it until I get back there." With Odom leading the way, Francis and Davis went with him to check on the two groups of men he had warned them about.

After tying their horses up in a small stand of pine trees just off the river, Francis, Odom, and Davis, protected from view by a thicket of bushes, watched as a medium sized flat bottom boat was rowed up river. In the boat were three men. Francis could see at least one of them was holding a musket.

On the opposite side of the river from where they were hiding, they also saw a group of five men on horses headed south towards Georgetown. Watching as the two groups closed the distance between themselves, it became evident they knew each other as several voices called out to one another as they drew close to each other. From their hiding spot, Francis and his men watched as the boat was rowed to shore to where the men on horses had come to a halt. For several minutes, the two groups talked to each other, but from where Francis watched he could not hear what was being said. Soon the two groups moved away from each other. Despite being satisfied the men were not Union soldiers or others after them, Francis still had his men wait in the bushes until the others were out of sight. After waiting several minutes, they rode back to where Stine and the others were waiting for them.

Once back with the others, Francis saw the wagon had been emptied of everything they might need. Next to it, another wagon had also been emptied of its remaining provisions. The men had consolidated everything in the other remaining wagons.

"Captain, we don't need these two wagons any longer, you want us to burn them?" Stine asked.

"No, just leave them be. We don't need the attention smoke might bring. Just disable them as best you can. Make it look like they broke down in case someone finds them. That way it won't look too strange for them to just be sitting here and all. Whatever you do, just make it look good. Then tie up one team of horses to the back of one of our wagons. Unhook the other team, someone will find them soon enough. But hurry, we need to get moving."

Within several minutes they were underway, headed again towards Georgetown. They still had some twenty miles to travel before reaching the outskirts of the small town. Once there, Francis knew he wanted to keep the wagons out of town as he did not want to risk the gold and silver being seen by anyone. His plan was for only one wagon to accompany him into town so he could obtain some much needed provisions for their move towards Charleston. As they moved along, he finished his plans for getting to Georgetown. Looking at his pocket watch, he decided they would try to make another ten miles or so and then spend the night camped fairly close to town. Riding on his horse, Francis continued to think about Georgetown and the Union army. "Tomorrow I'll ride into town and see what provisions I can find for the trip to Charleston. I also hope I can find out some more news about any Yankees being seen in the area."

For the rest of the ride the men rode in silence as their collective thoughts reflected back on the loss of McKinney earlier in the day. He had been well-liked by all of them, Francis included. As Francis thought about what had happened, he spurred his horse to move out in front of the others as he did not want his men to see the tears which now filled his eyes. He had always found it easier to shed them in private.

19

One Down – Two To Go.

"I don't believe in Secession, but I do in Liberty. I want the South to conquer, dictate in its own terms, and go back to the Union."
Sarah Morgan Dawson

The historical discovery Paul made when he found the remains of the Confederate soldier remained a story in the news for several weeks. When the story finally started to fade in Northern newspapers, those newspapers in the South, especially the newspapers and local magazines published in the Carolinas, Virginia, and Georgia, continued to run stories on his discovery. Media outlets from across the South continued to contact him for interviews and comments. Initially sidestepping as many of these requests as possible, now he took every opportunity he could to use the interviews to his advantage. Initially he had wanted the newly found Confederate soldier to be the focus of the media's stories, but now he knew the media would be his way of trying to find some of the missing Confederate treasury. Money he believed was still buried in North Carolina. The gold and silver which had been buried somewhere in South Carolina was a secret only he really knew about at this time as no one else yet knew about the clues Francis included in his letter.

After putting their collective thoughts together, Chick and Jayne crafted a press release which had Paul's name all over it. Soon they faxed, emailed, texted, and snail mailed the press release to every television station, newspaper, magazine, and historical society they could find in Virginia, Georgia, and the Carolinas. After this was done, Paul called each of the media outlets who had left messages for him. As he called them, he simply told them he had been too busy since making the discovery to return their calls before now. With Chick and Jayne's help, they tickled the media with news of a press conference that was soon going to be held regarding new information concerning the discovery of the Confederate soldier. They even went as far as telling the media that several additional items from the discovery would be put on display during the press conference.

The press release stated that Paul's orchestrated media event would be held on Thursday, August 18th, at ten in the morning, at the Wilmington Convention Center, in Wilmington, North Carolina. After he finished calling the media representatives on his list, Paul called Chick's home. Chick and Jayne had been faxing and emailing a few additional news releases from there.

Tired from a long day of finishing up the details for the media event, and from dealing with several reporters on the phone, Paul briefly gave Chick an update on where they stood. "Well, I've done what I can do to get everyone there. Let's hope it all works as we planned it."

"Did you get any feedback from them?"

"Several newspaper and magazine writers said they were going to be there, so I guess we'll have to wait and see. I promised several of them I would do one-on-one interviews after the presentation. I figured that might motivate them to get there. Let's get together at my house on Friday, say around eleven, and we'll talk more on this then, OK?"

"Sounds good. See you then."

* * * * * *

On Friday they finalized their plans for the *'Dog 'N' Pony Show'*. This was the name Paul had taken to calling the press conference. After finishing up a few last minute needs, they decided they would drive up to Wilmington the night before the event to have dinner and to get settled.

* * * * * *

The morning of the press conference, Paul let Chick and Jayne handle the logistics of the event as he stayed out of sight in a back room of the convention center protecting the Confederate uniform blouse and the two bottles he was using as his main props for the day. As they got the media settled in the large conference room and satisfied their needs for seats, electrical outlets, and other similar requests, Paul sat in the small back room rehearsing what he was going say.

Precisely at ten o'clock, Jayne came to where Paul had been rehearsing and told him they were ready. "Paul, the response is even better than we hoped for! We have at least fifteen television stations here, at least eighteen different newspapers, and several magazine writers are also here. We even had a few folks show up from several different Confederate historical groups as well. To accommodate the needs of several television stations, Chick set them up on one side of the room, and put the folks from the Southern historical groups in seats in the front row as you wanted. We know you want to treat those folks well. So let's go do this and let's hope it works!"

As Paul opened the door in the room he had been waiting in, a door which led to a small hallway off the back of the main conference room, he was confronted by the presence of two large uniformed security guards. Jayne quickly explained their presence. "Paul, Chick thought last night, because of the uniform blouse being displayed here today, that it wouldn't hurt to have some security here. You never know who might try to do something stupid. I hope you aren't mad he didn't tell you, but he thought it was a smart thing to do. He just wants it to go well today."

"Nope, not at all. It was a good idea in fact." Paul smiled as he answered her as he knew the presence of the two armed security guards would only contribute to the effects he hoped the *'Dog 'N' Pony Show'* would have with the media.

As Paul walked to the podium carrying the box containing his props for the day, a voice yelled out from the back of the room. "What's in the box?" It was a question that did not get an immediate response.

After introducing himself and after laying out the ground rules for the press conference, Paul walked those present through the events of his discovery. He told them almost every detail, including most of what he had found with the soldier's remains. During the presentation he also introduced Chick and Jayne to the media; introducing them as friends who he was now working with to properly document the discovery he had made.

Paul spoke confidently to those who were present as his years of speaking to groups of fellow workers, civic groups, and others during his career as a state trooper had made him comfortable speaking in front of large crowds. As he spoke, his eyes scanned the room looking for familiar faces, but he knew there would likely not be anyone present he would know except for a few television reporters whose faces he had seen on the news a few times. Then his eyes focused on one familiar face. He could tell it was a face that was not a happy one.

Winding down the first part of his presentation, Paul acknowledged the assistance several South Carolina agencies provided since the soldier's remains had been discovered. Singling him out, Paul acknowledged the presence of Captain Bobby Ray Jenkins of the Georgetown County Sheriff's Office. He thanked him, as well as Sheriff Renda, for their assistance when the soldier's remains were first discovered. Even with the recognition he directed at his friend, he could tell it had done little to change the scowl on Bobby Ray's face.

After finishing the first part of his presentation, Paul moved over to the box he had placed on a small table next to the podium. "I have been a cop for over thirty years so I know when there's more to a story than what the obvious clues are telling you. I want to start this part of the presentation by telling you that neither I, nor my friends, seek any benefit, any fame, or any personal gain from the discovery I have made. I may be retired from being a cop, but I still possess my investigative instincts. The discovery I have made is not just that of a long forgotten Confederate soldier finally being found; it is much more than that. Because of what I have found, and because I was paid in my past career to dig for facts, I've intentionally kept a couple of items I found from the authorities. I did so because I realized a bigger picture existed within this discovery and that it was more, and excuse me for saying it this way, but it was a discovery of more than just the bones of this dead soldier. Whatever I've kept, like whatever I find from this point on, will be turned over to the rightful owners or to the authorities after we've sifted through the clues I have. I have meant no disrespect to anyone by keeping these items, but no crime was committed by the soldier as we believe he was killed during an act of hostility at the time of the Civil War. I also have committed no crime. I just happened to find his remains. I promise you when I am done, all that I find, rather what we find, will be turned over to the people of this country to see and enjoy. It is not ours to keep or to profit from. None of you know me, so none of you know if you can trust what I've just told you about turning over the items I've found when I'm done with them. I want you to know that's exactly what I'm going to do. If any of you elect to write your stories with any hint that we've done anything wrong or that we're using this discovery to make a fast buck off, you will not get another ounce of cooperation from us. This is simply a story about the discovery of a Confederate soldier's remains being found by a retired cop who believes this soldier still has an important story to tell."

Then he dropped the first bit of new information on those present. As he did, the click of cameras and the intensity of the reporters' concentration intensified.

After taking off the lid of the box, Paul reached into his pants pockets and pulled out a pair of white cotton gloves. With a planned purpose, the purpose being to play up the moment for the media, he painstaking put the gloves on before withdrawing anything from the box. Finished donning the gloves, the Confederate Tail Coat was carefully removed from the box. "This Tail Coat, which I commonly refer to as a uniform blouse, belonged to the soldier I found. I found it still hanging within the tree where I found the soldier's remains. In fact, some of his remains were still within this very blouse. As you can see, this blouse still bears the Confederate symbols for the rank of captain. Inside the blouse I found the soldier's first initial and his last name sewn into one of the pockets. As many of you know, soldiers on both sides often did this. They did this so in the event they were killed in battle their remains could be positively identified. From the name sewn inside the blouse, and from other evidence I found at the site, we believe we now know who this soldier was. The other evidence matches the initials sewn into this blouse. But because I've told you we are going to dig into the clues which were left behind, we are not going to identify the soldier's name at this time as we want to make sure we know who he was." A collective groan then went up in the room as the reporters wanted as much information as possible from Paul that morning.

"I realize you are all interested in knowing this soldier's name; I would want to know that as well if I was doing what you do for a living. However, as

I did when I worked on significant investigations, I never release information before it can be verified and corroborated. As you all know, anyone worth their own salt never prematurely releases important information. When we know for sure who he is, you will also know, but not before."

Paul then held up the blouse so it could be photographed and videotaped by those present. Then handing the blouse to Jayne, she carefully laid it out on the table so it could be photographed again after the press conference was over.

After reaching back into the box, Paul held up the two glass bottles, explaining they had been found within the soldier's blouse. After telling the media about them, he placed them down on the table next to where the blouse had been laid out. In fairly quick succession, and with brief comments on each, as he had done with the blouse and the two bottles, he held up the bayonet, the saber, and the soldier's gold pocket watch for those present to see.

"Folks, the items on the table have all been photographed by me and by others. We have also documented the locations where they were found. They all were found within the same tree which hid the remains of the soldier for so long. You can come up here and photograph them when we are done, but please do not touch any of the items we have set out on the table as they are very fragile. Everyone will have time to ask questions and to photograph them, so please respect the historical value of each item and the desire we have to preserve them for others to see."

Paul then dropped the second piece of new information on those present. "I also want to tell you that besides the items we have already discussed, I also found letters the soldier had apparently written to his father and to Confederate President Jefferson Davis. They were secreted within these same two bottles. We also found one other letter and one other piece of paper in the bottles as well. We believe these letters will help us verify who this soldier was. Based on what we already know, we are currently searching for any military records which might exist before we release his name to you."

From the back of the room came the obvious question everyone present wanted an answer for. "We understand your need to be accurate, but if you've learned so much about him already what's the harm in releasing a dead soldier's name?"

"Because we simply are not ready to do so. Out of respect to this soldier, someone who time had apparently forgotten about, I will not release his name until we are certain who he is. If we can, we would like to have the opportunity to notify anyone who might still be family of some sort to him first. If we find any living kin of his, I promise we will notify you of that. Perhaps we will set something up so you can be there with us when we tell them what we've found. I'm confident when the time comes to notify you of his name, you all will have an appreciation for why we are not releasing it now. All I can do is to ask you to trust me for now. I promise you there will be a great finish to this story!"

Standing up from where he was seated in the third row, a writer directed a question to Paul. "OK, I'm still of the opinion that you should be releasing his name to us, but for me personally I'll give you some slack on this for now. However, if I find out you are trying to pull a fast one on us, I'll expose you as a fraud, as a con artist, or whatever the term is that fits you. You need to know that." Greg Masterson was a North Carolina based freelance writer who had many written articles regarding the Civil War, primarily selling his stories to magazines whose audiences were Civil War and military buffs. Paul knew who he was as he had read several articles Masterson had written over the years.

"Greg, as an amateur history buff I've had the pleasure of reading some of your work. Most of it I've enjoyed very much. While I appreciate you giving us some slack on this, I would expect you to discredit us if you found we were misleading you, but I promise you have nothing to worry about. We are also promising you and everyone else here today, when we finally release the soldier's name to you, we'll also release copies of the letters I found within the bottles. On the table next to me is a sign-up sheet, just write your name and contact information down before you leave today and we'll send you a copy of those letters when we're ready to release them. All we are asking for is a little bit of time to follow up on a few leads we think we have and then we'll be back in touch with all of you." Paul paused from speaking for a couple of moments to finish completing a thought he had. Then he spoke directly to Masterson. "Greg, before you leave this morning, please stop and see me so we can talk for a moment."

Finished with everything else he had to say, Paul finally gave his audience the biggest piece of news he had for them. It was the bait he hoped the writers would take; bait he hoped they would write about to help him move forward with the clues he was trying to solve. He also hoped the television reporters would talk about it when they did their segments on the evening news regarding the day's press conference. What he told them was not entirely the complete truth.

"The last piece of information I would like to tell you about is we know this Confederate soldier fought his way through North Carolina during a part of the war before entering South Carolina. We also know while he was in North Carolina he had to bury three of his soldiers along the way; we believe that occurred in the eastern part of the state. When he did, he had a wooden cross made to mark the spot of these three graves. As Civil War buffs, like some of you are, we hope when you file your stories or write your articles you will mention this grave site. We would simply like to have the opportunity to examine this site for possible connections to our soldier. We'll be happy to work with the authorities so we can give those three soldiers a proper burial. We realize these graves may not exist any longer as they may have already been discovered. They also may have been disturbed when a highway, a road, or when a new neighborhood was being built, but it's our hope we can still find the site. It's also our hope one of your viewers or readers might have seen, or know of, a crudely made wooden cross which marks this site. If they do, we hope they would call me so we can work with the local historical society, and with other local authorities, to have the remains exhumed. We would like to have those remains then reburied with those of the soldier I found."

From the back of the room another reporter yelled out a question to Paul. "Why should someone call you about this? Shouldn't they just call the authorities, perhaps their local medical examiner, and not just you?"

"They could certainly do so, but it's our hope if someone knows of this grave they have an appreciation for the sacrifices these young soldiers made during a time when our country fought such a terrible war against each other. That grave, if it still exists, is a historical site and we would like an opportunity to connect it to the soldier I found. We would also like to make the gravesite a part of an independent documentary film we are considering making. The soldier I found and the three soldiers buried in North Carolina were once Confederate soldiers who served together during the war. We believe it would be a nice gesture to reunite them together again and to properly bury them next to each other. They deserve at least that for the sacrifices they each made."

Off to his left a television reporter asked another question. "So what else did the soldier's diary tell you?" Paul smiled at the question at first. "Good guess, not a totally accurate one, but a good guess nevertheless." Quickly he had a follow-up thought to the question which had just been asked. "OK, let them think it's a diary I found. That works for me."

"OK, folks, that's about it for the day, but I just want to reinforce to you one thing. I'm a retired state trooper, but more importantly for this matter I'm simply a history buff who has stumbled onto some clues about our soldier's past. My previous career trained me to dig for facts and that's what I am going to do with the help of my two friends who also have a passion for the Civil War. None of us are interested in making names for ourselves, or making a buck off the remains we've found, or off the clues we think he left behind. As I've already mentioned, we're considering making a documentary about this discovery. If we do, and if it becomes a film which turns a profit, we'll donate every cent back to a cause that preserves the history of those who fought in the Civil War."

With this last statement, Paul concluded his presentation to the reporters and writers. Chick and Jayne, with help from the two armed security guards who stood nearby, closely guarded the items spread out on the table. The artifacts were photographed and videotaped over and over by several of the news photographers and video camera operators to help complete the stories their colleagues would later file on this event. As that happened, Paul spent the better part of the next two hours giving one-on-one interviews to reporters from several local and regional television stations. He soon did the same for those newspaper reporters, magazine writers, and others who were present from area historical societies. As he patiently did so, he made sure he gently reinforced his request for help in finding the gravesite of the three Confederate soldiers he mentioned during his presentation. He gave each reporter and writer his personal cell phone number and email address, hoping they would include them in their stories and articles. Paul knew the wooden cross would be key to being able to find at least part of the Confederate treasury. Finished speaking with the last of the reporters, he silently prayed someone would see this story and would then call him with the location of the wooden cross.

During his presentation, and during each of the interviews he did, Paul failed to tell the reporters the gravesite of the three soldiers was also likely the same spot Captain Francis had chosen to bury some of the Confederate gold and silver he had been charged with moving south. The same gold and silver Southerners had talked so much about over the years that it had become a legend. He had not failed to tell the reporters about what other secrets the gravesite held. It had been his plan all along not to do just that.

* * * * * *

After the media finally left, Paul went over and sat down next to Bobby Ray. He had waited patiently until the interviews had been completed. From the facial expressions he displayed, it was obvious Bobby Ray was still upset. Now Paul did his best to calm him down. "Look, I know you think I should have told you about finding these items, but I didn't tell you about them because I didn't want to put you in a situation that would have made you feel uncomfortable. I didn't want you to feel obligated to have to tell your boss about these items if he asked you any questions. Besides, I just found these items, I didn't steal them and I am going to turn them over to some historical society or to someone else when this is over, I promise!"

"What is it that you want, Paul? What do you expect to find from these items you kept? I just don't understand why you couldn't tell me about them!" Bobby Ray was still upset with his friend, one he thought he could trust.

"Like I said, I didn't want to put you in an uncomfortable position with your boss, OK?"

"No, that's not OK!" The tone of Bobby Ray's voice reflected the displeasure he was now feeling towards Paul. "I appreciate y'all looking out for me, but I've been a cop a long time, so why don't you just stop jerking my chain and just tell me the real reason you didn't let me know what was going on! What do you think you are going to find from this big mystery of yours? Perhaps another saber, another bayonet or two, or maybe even his musket, or is it the bones of three dead soldiers your morbid curiosity wants to find? Wow, big deal!"

Paul looked around the large conference room to make sure no one else was still in the room before he responded to his friend. Seeing no one except Chick and Jayne, he calmly spoke to his friend. "Bobby Ray, any of that would be nice to find, but I expect to find at least ten million dollars of buried Confederate gold and silver."

"Yeah, sure." His friend scoffed at him.

Before he spoke again, Paul stood up and reached into his pants pocket. Withdrawing the gold coins he found near the soldier's remains, he sat back down and handed the coins to Bobby Ray. "Well, here's part of it. Ten million is what I expect to find on the low end, but I hope its worth much more than that when we find it all. I believe I've found the clues we'll need to find it. This is the same gold and silver you Southerners have talked about for years, the same gold and silver from the missing Confederate treasury." He paused for a moment as Bobby Ray examined the gold coins. The next question was one Paul already knew the answer to, but he still asked it anyways. "You coming to help me find this money? I could sure use your help or are you still that ticked off at me?"

"You ain't joking with me, are you?" The anger Bobby Ray had previously allowed to fester inside of him was now spent. He was stunned by both the gold coins he was now holding in his hands and by what his friend had just told him.

Paul then explained the press conference had been a staged event; one done with an ulterior motive. "I had to pull some kind of stunt to try and find the wooden cross we know existed at one time. I didn't tell you about that either as I didn't want you getting in trouble with your boss."

Looking up from the gold coins he had been examining, Bobby Ray asked only one more question. "You think you can find it?"

"Bobby Ray, the question is not *if* I'm going to find it, but rather the question should be *when* am I going to find it. I don't know what ten million dollars in gold and silver coins looks like, but it has to be one big pile of coins. I will tell you that I'm not pulling your leg about this. Just one thing though, if you're coming to help me, you need to promise me you will not mention this to anyone, not even to your lovely wife. You promise?"

"Ten million dollars … wow! Yeah, I promise, and you bet I'm tagging along on this here hunt. I ain't letting some damn Yankee dig up the whole dang state of North Carolina looking for gold without me being there. Damn straight I'm gonna be there!"

Paul laughed at what Bobby Ray just said. He knew his friend had gotten over being mad at him. "Bobby Ray, I promise, no more secrets. Now listen, your first job is to follow me to the bank. I want you to help me put some of these items in a large safety deposit box I've rented so they are under lock and key. Too many people will soon know about them and I don't want them to go missing. Do that for me and then I'll buy you a beer or two back at my place. OK?"

"Let's get it done. I need a beer already!"

"Good. We still friends?"

"Not right now we ain't. Perhaps when you buy me that beer we will be, but right now we ain't."

Bobby Ray's answer made Paul laugh again. Then with Chick and Jayne in tow, the four of them, along with their precious artifacts, started back to Murrells Inlet so they could lock up whatever they could fit in the safety deposit box.

* * * * * *

After securing those items they went back to Paul's house for a few cold beers. Then they sat and waited for the phone to ring. They hoped it would be someone telling them where Captain Judiah Francis had buried the gold and silver.

20

Georgetown to Charleston.

"Well, it is over now. The battle is lost, and many of us are prisoners, many are dead, many wounded, bleeding and dying."
Major General George Pickett, CSA, Gettysburg, 4 July 1863

The warm gentle rain had fallen on them during most of the night, but dawn brought clearing skies and the clean fresh feeling in the morning air gave a nice start to the new day for Francis and his men.

Sgt. Odom had been out scouting the area around their camp to make sure they were not being watched or about to be ambushed by Union troops, but now he returned to camp to report that nary a sole was in sight. The men knew the day was going to be a day of rest for them as Francis was soon to leave them so he could scout the area around Georgetown. They also knew he would try to obtain some fresh food for their journey to Charleston as little was left in the wagons in the form of provisions. They all enjoyed the rare lazy start to the day by drinking their morning coffee and hanging their still wet clothing, wet from the previous night's rain, from every available space they could find on the wagons so it could dry in the sun.

Before he left for Georgetown, Francis spoke with his men, telling them Odom was coming with him. He would be driving one of the wagons so the provisions could be brought back to camp. Francis warned the others about being too lazy during the day, telling them to make sure they kept a close lookout for approaching Yankee troops and other strangers. "Enjoy the easy day y'all have in front of you, but make sure someone is out riding around the camp. I best not come back to find the gold and silver missing, for if I do y'all better be dead from defending it. Y'all hear me?" His men knew he was joking with them, but they also knew he was serious about someone being awake and protecting their precious cargo the whole time he was gone.

After a short morning ride, Francis and Odom entered Georgetown. They stopped at Wood's General Store, on Front Street, to obtain provisions for their journey towards Charleston the following day. They had already stopped at a small Confederate Quartermaster's Office in town, but the shelves were bare of provisions.

"Captain, I ain't got much left, but what I got you certainly can have for a fair price. I know you soldier boys got it tough. I doubt you boys are likely eating too well these days. I got some corn meal, a small amount of flour, some dried beans, a few onions, and some carrots, but that's about all the food I can spare at a fair price. Will that do?"

"If that's all you have, then that will do fine. My men and I appreciate your help. As you guessed, we have not had much to eat recently so anything you can spare is a blessing. Write the bill up and I'll sign for it. You can get reimbursed down at the Quartermaster's Office. I was able to get a couple of new blankets from them this morning, but what they had left in food had been shipped out in wagons two days ago. Pickings are getting slim, I guess."

"Yes, sir, that they are. Say, you know we got us a bunch of wild pigs running around on the outskirts of town, folks will show you where they are. Perhaps one of your men can shoot one and you can have a right fine meal tonight. They's good eating, I hear."

"OK, thanks." Francis gave the suggestion about shooting one of the wild pigs a brief thought, but for now his main interest was getting back to his men outside of town.

As Francis turned to leave, James Wood, the proprietor of the store stopped him. "Captain, wait a moment, I've got something for you!" Wood then disappeared into the store's back room. As he returned to where Francis had been waiting for him, he set two bottles of liquor down on his wooden counter. In appreciation for his service to the Confederacy, Wood graciously presented them to Francis. "Captain, I don't see much money these days, mostly folks trade their goods with me for food or supplies. Fella from town traded me these two bottles of spirits for some things he needed. I'd like you and your men to have them."

"Thank you, Mr. Wood. I'm most grateful to you for your kindness."

As they had spent a few more minutes talking, Francis noticed a change had quickly come over James Wood. He noticed sadness had quickly appeared in Wood's face.

"Captain, this life we're all leading these days, you know with the threat of war coming further south every day, well that's no way for decent folks to live. Life has already been too unfair to me personally. I don't need the war to stop at my doorstep and neither do the folks who live in these parts. I'm already a broken man in life, a sad man really, been that way since my wife passed away. Her name was Susan. Susan Schilling it was before we were married. I always loved the way her name sounded when I spoke it. She's been dead almost nine years now, she died during a difficult childbirth; so did our infant son. We had chosen Michael for a boy's name. You know, I have somehow managed to live without them, but the pain of losing them is still with me. I think of them everyday, her especially, and still talk to them each night when I finally put my head down at the end of the day. That likely sounds corny to you, but it helps me stay sane somehow. The pain I still feel is different than the pain I likely would have felt if I had sent a son out to fight against them Yankees and he had gotten killed in some type of fight. Don't know if I ever could have gotten over that kind of loss. My wife and my son dying like they did, well that I can deal with as I figured the good Lord just brought them home to the Promised Land a little earlier than I expected, but losing a son in a war, well that's just a damn waste of a life. Too many folks, Northern and Southern families alike, folks just like us, are grieving these days over the loss of a loved one, lost in this terrible war. Personally I don't care if they are Yankees or Southern folks like us; I just feel for them. I hate to say such a terrible thing, but in some perverse way I am glad my son did not live to see this war. Who knows how long it's gonna last, but him gone off fighting some place would have scared me to death; news of him being killed would have likely killed me also."

As he finished speaking, Wood paused for a few moments before he spoke again. As he paused, Francis could see the tears which had welled up in Wood's eyes, tears clearly caused by the painful memory he lived with every day. As he put his hand on the shoulder of James Wood to comfort him, Francis had no way of knowing this was the first time he had spoken to anyone about the loss of his family in almost five years. He had done so to a total stranger.

"Captain, please forgive me as I should not have put the burden of my loss on your shoulders today. I'm sure you have far too much on your mind already. Sir, please forgive me."

"Mr. Wood, I assure you that you have nothing to apologize for. Sometimes we need to talk about matters like these to others. I'm honored you did so with me. I'm truly sorry for the loss you've had to carry for these past many years. I' not sure I would have been able to endure such a loss as well as you have."

Wood shrugged and offered a weak smile to the compliment Francis had given him. "I'm not so sure I have coped with my loss very well. I have often felt that I have just carried on as best I could, just as my wife would have wanted me to do."

An uncomfortable and awkward silence then existed briefly between the two men before Wood spoke again.

"Captain, your men are likely the type of men I would have hoped my son would have become, so give these bottles to your boys and tell them Georgetown appreciates what they are doing for us. Let them all have a drink on me tonight, ain't gonna harm nothing. That one bottle there has got a picture of George Washington himself on it. Pretty fancy, don't you think?" Wood finally smiled again, free of the sadness he had just felt.

Placing the two bottles inside his uniform blouse, Francis shook hands with James Wood, thanking him for his generosity. "Mr. Wood, I know the men will appreciate your kindness. I will make sure they know you were thinking of them. They will indeed enjoy a taste of your spirits tonight with their meal." Then, as Wood walked with him to the wagon Odom was loading the supplies into, Francis asked him what he knew about any Union troop movements in the area.

"We ain't seen any Yankees down this way yet, but we heard about some Union cavalry being seen up north in Cherokee County. Heard they burned down a few barns up there also. Best y'all be keeping a sharp lookout though as they likely will be upon us soon enough."

"What about Charleston? Heard of any problems down there with Union troops or with the Union blockade?"

"I haven't heard about any Yankee troops being there, but a while back one of our soldiers told us the Union boys were going to try and seal the city off. You know, try to starve them into a surrender and all. Ain't happened yet, but it might. From what I've heard the city gets a few shells thrown at it once in a while from them Union navy boats, but nothing too bad from what I dun been told. I hear our boys fire right back at them. We got the whole harbor surrounded with our guns so I doubt them Union boys are gonna risk having their ships sunk right out from underneath themselves. I know I wouldn't risk it!"

"How about the railroads? Any still running?" Francis asked, hoping to finally hear some good news.

"Not that I know of. Between train and track problems, as well as sabotage by either the Yankees or their supporters, I dun heard our folks are too afraid to run them out of fear of losing more train engines. Costs too much to fix them and ain't no one skilled enough to be working on them when they do break down these days. Them regular train people are out fighting the war and working on trains in other places I've been told. Heard Chattanooga, you know where a great many of them trains run through there on their way south, heard fighting is fierce up there. Dun disrupted a great many of them trains running through there. Damn shame too, we need them trains to be running. Damn shame, that's what it is!"

Shaking hands with Wood again, Francis climbed up on his horse and gave him a wave goodbye. He then started riding alongside the wagon which Odom had already turned back towards their camp and to the men who waited for their return.

They had been riding for about twenty minutes outside of town, Francis reflecting upon the sad story James Wood had told him, when Odom, who had been staring down at the ground on the right side of the wagon, turned and looked at Francis. "Captain, you may not be able to see this, but look over here. Some riders have been through here recently, looks like maybe four, maybe five sets of fresh horse tracks." As Francis moved to see the tracks which had been left in the soft soil, he immediately felt an uneasy feeling enter his stomach. The tracks led in the direction of where his men were waiting for them back in camp.

"Sergeant, take the wagon west and into the line of trees up there above the camp. But stay on the backside of the hill so you are less likely to be seen. I'm going to ride up ahead. I'll meet you in the tree line. Do what you can to keep the horses quiet."

By the time Odom arrived in the tree line, Francis had confirmed his worst fear. Looking down at where they were camped, he saw his men had been surprised by four strangers on horseback, strangers who now had his men seated on the ground and away from the wagons. As his men sat on the ground, they each held their hands behind their heads. What Francis and Odom looked down on was not a good sight to see.

"Captain, look over near the campfire, I think that's Griffin laying face down on the ground." Francis had been too busy making sure he counted the right number of strangers within the camp to notice Griffin was down on the ground and likely dead. He momentarily bowed his head over what the loss of another man would mean to the success of his mission.

Francis then told Odom what he wanted done. "We need to move off to our left so we can put the wagons between us and those men. After we get closer to the wagons we need to make a run at them before they see us coming. When we reach the wagons you go for the two men on the left and I will go after the two others on the right. Take your time, but make sure you get at least one of them. It looks like they are too concerned about what is going on down there as they have yet to look up here or anywhere else for several minutes. Go quickly as possible, but be as quiet as you can, we need to catch them boys off guard. You ready?"

"As ready as I've ever been!" Odom was itching for the fight to start.

Carrying a musket he retrieved from the wagon and with his Remington revolver stuffed in his waistband for easy access, Francis moved slowly into position. His revolver was a souvenir he had taken from a dead Union officer on the battlefield at Bull's Bluff. Followed closely by Odom, Francis stepped quietly from the tree line. Moving slowly at first at the pace of a fast walk, they then began to run down the hill as quietly as they could. As they ran, they kept the wagons between them and the strangers who had invaded their camp. Reaching the wagons, Francis first, and then Odom, each dropped one of the strangers with well placed shots. As the other two men turned to fire back at them, they were quickly tackled from behind by Stine and Banks. In short order, they were beaten to a whisker of their lives.

As soon as the threat was extinguished, and with his men now in control of the two severely beaten intruders, Francis ran to the nearly lifeless body of Sgt. Griffin. He had been ambushed by these four men while riding around the perimeter of the camp and had been shot in the right temple when he attempted to fight them off after getting back to warn the others. As he knelt on the ground next to Griffin, Francis soon heard him take his last breath.

"Captain, look at these boys here." Stine hollered, almost out of breath from the beating he had given to one of the men. "On the outside they're wearing our shirts, but under that they is wearing Yankee uniforms; Yankee pants and all. Who are they, our boys or Yankees?"

"Yankee spies more than likely," Francis quickly answered as he looked at one of the bodies lying dead next to him. "Damn Yankees!"

Francis stood up and walked back to where the two seriously injured Union soldiers lay on the ground. Without saying a word, he drew the revolver which had once been owned by a Union cavalry officer and then shot each of the two men once in the head. He shot them with bullets issued to the Union officer who had once owned the revolver. The revolver was one he now claimed as his. Angrily he yelled to no one in particular. "We still shoot spies, don't we?"

"Damn right we do," replied Stine. "Shoot the bastards again!"

Francis thought about it for a moment, but despite the urge he refrained from doing so. "They are already dead. Shooting them again will not bring Griffin back to us I'm afraid. For if it would, I would surely shoot them many times over to get him back with us." Of the five men shot and killed that afternoon only one was buried. The others were left lying on the ground under the hot South Carolina sun.

Soon after they buried Sgt. Griffin, Francis knew he had to move his men away from the area. They moved another ten miles south before he allowed them to make camp for the night. Along the way Stine rode up to Francis and kept him company for part of the ride. "Captain, we hope you know we weren't being lazy when you were gone. We all took turns riding around the camp. Them fellas who bushwhacked Griffin, they just got the jump on him, that's all. Likely he saw them wearing Confederate uniforms and thought they was with us. What happened to Frank could have happened to any of us. We all feel bad we kinda let you down."

Knowing any anger he displayed would have been misplaced, Francis calmly assured Stine he knew they had been doing what was expected of them. He told Stine he did not hold them responsible for Griffin's death. "We're at war and bad things happen to soldiers who fight in wars. I just wish I had been there to help him. We all likely feel that way. Tell the men I'm not angry with any of them."

In camp that night, as the men quietly ate their dinner, Francis brought out the two bottles of spirits James Wood had given him earlier in the day. They had been intended for the men to have a pleasant evening with, but now they drank to forget what had happened to Griffin earlier in the day. For Francis, the alcohol only served to make the pain he felt feel worse, not better.

Soon his men were asleep under a sky full of bright stars. Nothing disturbed the quiet of the South Carolina evening. Francis was still so upset over the loss of Griffin that he did not even bother to post a guard as they slept. "What's the point?" he thought as he finally drifted off to sleep while trying to remember the names of his men who had died during the mission. Remembering each of their names made their faces appear in his mind. Seeing them only increased the pain he felt as he finally closed his eyes. It would be a night in which Francis would not see much sleep.

21

Gold in North Carolina.

*"Mine eyes have seen the glory of the coming of the Lord: He is
trampling out the vintage where the grapes of wrath are stored; He
hath loosed the fateful lightning of His terrible swift sword ..."*
Lyrics to 'The Battle Hymn of the Republic'

Several days had passed since the press conference was held in Wilmington. Outside of a couple of reporters contacting Paul with a few follow-up questions and a couple of others calling to see if he had found the gravesite of the three Confederate soldiers, not much had happened to give him any hope of finding the grave. He knew it was still early, but each time the phone rang he prayed it was the call he had been waiting for. Paul spent the days following the press conference doing what he expected to be doing in his retirement life. Playing golf, working a couple of shifts at his part-time job, and taking the boat out on the river was what he thought would keep him happy in retirement, but now he just went through the motions. His focus was on waiting for the phone to ring to tell him what he needed to know. Even helping Donna unpack a few more boxes from their move did not stop him from thinking about the whereabouts of the wooden cross or the treasury that had likely been buried near it. Several boxes still had sat untouched in their garage since being left there by the movers. Hoping he would soon be receiving the phone call he was waiting for, Paul used two cardboard moving boxes to pack some tools, pads and pencils, some batteries, a flashlight, and a few other items in. They were items he thought he would need when he went hunting for the missing Confederate treasury. He wanted to be ready to roll when he received the phone call telling him where the gravesite was. It was a site he was anxious to find.

During the same time, Chick sought out the help of a part-time guest instructor he knew at Coastal Carolina University. Pete Cater was a former video technician who had worked at a couple of local South Carolina television stations before venturing out on his own, filming weddings, graduations, and other local events for those who could afford his prices. Besides running his own business, he was also an occasional instructor at the school's Video Production Unit, helping students to edit and produce their required projects in several film classes. Chick and Pete had gotten to casually know each other from several school sponsored events they had each attended. From talking at those events, Chick learned Pete had a passing interest in American history.

From his time working at several television stations, Pete knew everything about video production techniques, and knew a great deal more than most people about video cameras and other related equipment. His technical expertise was the main reason Chick sought him out for the film project they wanted to undertake; it certainly had little to do with his passing interest in history. While knowing Pete's other interests in life excited him far more than his token interest in history did, he cared little about what those other hobbies and interests were. He just wanted Pete's help due to his acquired skills and experience.

On the afternoon Chick sought him out, he tried learning of Pete's possible interest in helping them produce their Civil War documentary. After listening to what Chick presented to him, Pete initially told him he was not interested in doing that kind of work anymore.

"Chick, I've been there and done that. Those kinds of projects require a great deal of work, and a huge commitment of time from many people. Many times the reward doesn't equal the effort you've put into projects like the one you want to try and put together. These days I kind of like working by myself." Pete was even less interested when he heard the opportunity did not come with a guarantee of making any money until after the documentary got sold.

As they talked, Pete asked more about the film's subject matter, but Chick was forced to give him a vague answer. "I'm sure you've read about the recent discovery of the remains of a Confederate soldier down in Murrells Inlet. Well, the guy who found him is a friend of mine and we're working on an idea which has grown out of this discovery of the soldier's remains. I'm sorry, but I cannot tell you anything more about this right now. I can tell you this is one of those once in a lifetime opportunities we hear about. Pete, I' not going to make you any false promises, but I can promise you if you help us we'll pay your expenses and we promise you'll receive full credit as our video producer if the documentary gets sold. Plus, I know you'll also get a couple of thrills out of this as well. I'll also tell you on a couple of occasions you might have to get your hands dirty, but it's nothing like having to clean out a sewer or anything like that. You interested?"

"Gees, I don't have to clean out any plugged sewers! Where do I sign up for this gig? Chick, I don't know about this offer, I like having a regular paying gig. You know what I mean?"

Beginning to feel a little frustrated by Pete's lack of interest, Chick let him know it with a dose of sarcasm. "Yeah, I do. I can see how you wouldn't want to pry yourself away from filming those exciting weddings and kid's birthday parties every weekend. Sounds like your life is really packed with excitement these days, I don't know how one person can stand having so much fun."

Pete understood the sarcasm being directed at him. He knew it was part of the recruiting effort to get him to join Chick and the others with the documentary they were working on. "OK, OK, I surrender. I'm sure I'm going to regret this, but what the heck, you're probably right. Your gig has got to be better than filming those weddings every Saturday. OK, sign me up. Call me when you want to get together."

"Great! But one thing, Pete, this is not for the world or for anyone to know about. You need to keep this to yourself for now. OK?"

Intrigued to hear about the degree of secrecy, Pete wondered what it was all about, but knew Chick would fill him in soon. "I'm sure you will tell me what the big secret is about when you're ready, but OK, mums the word for now."

* * * * * *

Paul had gotten home late in the day on Sunday afternoon after taking Donna for a boat ride. He finally felt comfortable enough with the boat to make the leisurely ninety minute trip down the Waccamaw River to Georgetown. After enjoying their ride down the river, they docked the boat along the river walk on historic Front Street. After seeing the sights along Front Street, they enjoyed a casual lunch at the Crazy Mermaid, one of the many waterfront restaurants located along the river. Eating outside on one of the restaurant's sun-drenched wooden decks allowed them to enjoy their lunch while they watched the boat traffic on the river, and the tourists walking up and down the river walk.

It was a beautiful sunny day and they had taken full advantage of it by enjoying a leisurely ride back to the marina. Paul had purposely taken his time getting back as he wanted the quiet afternoon to last as long as possible. They had left their cell phones at home so they would not be interrupted as they enjoyed the day together. Neither of them missed the interruptions their phones often seemed to cause.

After arriving back home, Paul began putting some of their gear away in the garage. As he did, Donna came back into the garage carrying his cell phone. She had heard his cell phone beeping when she first went into the house to throw their beach towels into the washing machine. "Paul, your cell phone is beeping. Looks like you have a couple of messages on it."

"That's a shock," Paul sarcastically responded, "probably just some more crank phone calls generated by some of the articles which have been written, but let's see." As he took the phone from her, he asked Donna for a favor. "Hey, would you bring me a Coors Light from the kitchen? The refrigerator out here is tapped out of beer. I'm just going to put the rest of this stuff away and then listen to the messages here in the garage. I'll get the grill fired up for dinner in just a few minutes."

After putting away the two life preservers they had used and after emptying out the small cooler they had taken out on the boat, Paul grabbed one of the plastic lawn chairs he had stacked in the garage. Sitting down, he took a long swig on the can of beer Donna had brought out to him. Then he began listening to his messages.

The first two messages were follow-up calls from writers he had previously spoken with. They had called about a few needed clarifications for articles they were about to publish. The third call had simply been a wrong number. As Paul deleted the third call, he took his second swig of Coors Light. Then the fourth message played. It was the call he had waited several days for.

"Mr. Waring, my name is Joseph Johnson, my friends call me Duke. I've been following your story about finding the Confederate soldier and I've got to say its one heck of a story. I own a hog farm, almost two hundred and fifty acres in size, up here in Maple Hill; it's a small community in Pender County, here in rural North Carolina. The reason I'm calling you is I think I might have what y'all are looking for. Listen here, I'm reading the story in our local paper about what y'all have found and I see this part about the gravesite you're looking for. Well, like I already said, I think I just may have what y'all are looking for. Call me when you can and we will talk on it. My number is 910-623-...."

When the message finished playing, Paul stood up so fast he forgot about the can of beer he had placed between his legs as he sat in the chair. In his excitement from listening to what Duke Johnson's message told him, he sent the partially full can of beer flying onto the garage floor when he stood up. Ignoring the mess he made, he scrambled to find something to write with so he could jot down Duke's phone number. Replaying the message a second time, he was still so excited he wrote Duke's number down wrong. He had to hit the button on his phone so he could play the message again. Finally calming down, he wrote the phone number down correctly on one of the cardboard moving boxes still stacked in the garage.

The phone rang three times before Duke Johnson answered his cell phone. "Mr. Johnson, good day, sir. This is Paul Waring returning your phone call. I appreciate you calling me."

"Well, thanks for calling me back, Paul. My friends call me Duke, please do the same."

"I will, thanks, Duke. From your call it sounds like you believe you may know where the gravesite is for the three soldiers who once served with the soldier I found. Is that right?" Paul anxiously asked.

"Based on what I've read in the local paper, yeah . . . I might know where the gravesite is. My family has owned our property forever, since before the Civil War. It's actually been in our family since the late 1700's. Some of the property, like where I believe the gravesite might be, is as pristine as it ever was. We've kept over fifty acres of meadows just for hunting. We also fish in one of the ponds on the back of the property, but we've never used it for our hog business or for anything else. We kind of use it to relax on, if you know what I mean."

"I do, it sounds beautiful. I'd like to see it someday. Duke, let me ask you, why do you think you know where the gravesite is? I can't imagine a simple wooden cross which was made almost one hundred and fifty years ago to mark the site is still in the ground today, or is it?"

"No, it's not. After the cross broke apart some in a windstorm many years ago, my granddaddy had it repaired; then he put it in one of our barns for us to enjoy. It's still hanging on the barn wall just like it has been for years."

Paul was stunned by what Duke told him about the wooden cross. "What? You still have the cross? Wait, so how would you know where the graves are after all of these years or would you just be guessing where they are?"

"Paul, folks here still have a deep respect for the dead. When the wooden cross broke apart, my granddaddy made another cross, made it out of scraps of metal and steel he had lying around. Then he placed the new cross back in the very same hole the wooden cross had been in. Did so out of respect for 'Old Charlie', least that's what we've referred to the gravesite as."

"That's a tribute to whoever is buried there. It's also a wonderful act of kindness which was done by a special person. Your granddaddy must have been some kind of man. Duke, help me out here. Why did you refer to the gravesite as 'Old Charlie'?"

"Well, the original wooden cross had the initials CSA carved into it so we figured the man buried there might have been named Charles, so we started calling the gravesite 'Old Charlie'. Just as a family joke, I guess."

"The cross has CSA carved into it?"

"Sure does. It even has holes carved into it to resemble periods after each of the three letters. Amazing stuff, huh?"

"Duke, I would have to agree with you on that."

As he listened to Duke, Paul realized CSA did not refer to anyone by the name of Charlie or any other name. Instead, the letters stood for the Confederate States of America. As Duke spoke more about his property, Paul only heard parts of what he was saying. His mind was concentrating on the letters carved in the wooden cross. "That was a clue he left behind. It would have helped Francis find the gold and silver he buried there. Only he never made it back. But I bet he had those initials carved in the cross in the event he could not make it back there. They were meant to help him, but it was also a clue he was leaving for someone else as well. Pretty ingenious of him to plan ahead like that." Paul's thoughts excited him as they ran them through his head.

Back from his thoughts about the cross, Paul caught the last few words Duke said in describing his property. "Duke, I'd like to come up with a couple of my friends and look at your place. Is tomorrow too soon?"

"Tomorrow sounds fine to me. I'll be around most of the day."

"Duke, just out of curiosity, does anyone else know about this site?"

"Just a few folks, mostly my kin and some of my employees, that's about all."

Paul was pleased to hear Duke had not called any reporters to tell them what was displayed in one of his fields. "Duke, I look forward to meeting you tomorrow."

"Likewise. Tell you what, better make it tomorrow afternoon. I just remembered I have some business out of town early in the morning, but any time after 1 pm is fine with me, I'll be here. You know, thinking about what you asked me a minute ago, I'd have to say outside of my family and perhaps a couple of my friends who have seen the gravesite when we hunt back there, and maybe a couple of my hired hands, no one else knows about it. Not sure why anyone else would be interested in it to tell you the truth."

"Sounds good! Duke, I appreciate the call. I look forward to meeting you tomorrow afternoon some time. Before I let you go, I guess I'd better get some directions from you."

After jotting down the directions Duke gave him, Paul again thanked him for calling. The phone call barely had time to disconnect when he was punching the numbers on his phone's keypad. Excitedly he made a phone call to Chick.

"Hey, Paul, any news yet?"

Still too excited from talking to Duke, Paul did not bother with any small talk. After Chick answered the phone, he got straight to the point. "Chick, get in touch with Jayne and your film guy, what's his name? Oh, yeah, Pete. Tell them I just spoke with a farmer in North Carolina. He has the spot we are looking for!"

Paul's news caught Chick by surprise and he sought to make some sense out of it. "What makes you so sure we're not heading out on some wild goose chase?"

"Chick, he owns a large hog farm which sits on property his family has owned since before the war. Guess what his granddaddy found on the property years ago and guess what this farmer still has hanging in one of his barns?"

"If you're joking with me, don't tell me it's a wooden cross." Paul could tell he now had Chick's attention.

"A wooden cross! Want to guess what's carved into it?"

"I don't know, perhaps 'Dig here and find gold'?"

"Funny, Chick, real funny, but it's even a shorter clue than that. Carved into the cross are the letters CSA. What do those letters mean to you?"

The silence was brief as Chick quickly made the connection between the letters and what they stood for. Now excited, he loudly answered Paul's question. "Confederate States of America! That's a clue someone left behind. It's just that I bet, it's a clue!" Chick was almost screaming into the phone by now.

"I'm going to North Carolina tomorrow to meet this farmer. I'm leaving at eight in the morning." Then adding a tease to the conversation, Paul asked Chick a question similar to the one he had asked of Bobby Ray after the Press Conference in Wilmington. It was a question he already knew the answer to. "You thinking of tagging along?"

"Damn straight I'm coming along. So is Jayne and Pete, they just don't know it yet. I'll get in touch with them. We'll meet you at the Dunkin' Donuts up on Highway 17, the one in Garden City. I'll make sure we're all there by eight. I'll need a cup of coffee for the ride. You can fill me in with the rest of the details then, OK? You bringing Bobby Ray along?"

"I imagine I will. We'll need at least two vehicles, perhaps three with all of our gear. Bring your van if you can. Better make sure everyone packs for a couple of days, maybe three. I'll see you at DD in the morning!"

Before calling Bobby Ray, Paul walked into the kitchen and grabbed another beer to replace the one he spilled in the garage. As he closed the refrigerator door, Donna walked into the kitchen after just getting out of the shower. As she continued to dry her hair with a large blue towel, she asked him if any of the phone messages had been important. Trying to suppress his excitement, he did his best to nonchalantly answer her question as he opened the can of beer. "Just a few from some writers who needed a couple of points cleared up for articles they are writing. Oh, and one was from some hog farmer in North Carolina who basically told me the missing Confederate gold and silver is buried on his property."

Standing there with only a towel wrapped around her, Donna shrieked at the news Paul had given her. When she did, she jumped into the air due to the excitement of the moment. Landing on the kitchen floor caused her towel to fall to the floor, but she did not care as she knew Paul had gotten the phone call he had been waiting for. "Nice butt!" Paul smirked at the picture of her standing there naked in the kitchen. Bending down, he picked both towels up off the floor. He was happy to see her as excited as he was. Grabbing a roll of paper towels off the kitchen counter, he headed back out to the garage to clean up the mess he had made. He also had to call Bobby Ray.

After speaking with Bobby Ray on the phone, Paul could tell his friend had tried to suppress his excitement upon hearing the good news regarding Duke's call. "He's too much of a Civil War nut not to be excited about this. He may not have sounded too excited, but I bet he's already stuffing clothes into an overnight bag." He sensed his friend was looking forward to seeing what they could find in North Carolina. Before hanging, they made arrangements for Paul to pick him up at his house at seven-thirty the following morning.

* * * * * *

The following morning after meeting at Dunkin' Donuts, and with Paul leading the way, they started the drive up to Duke Johnson's farm on a beautiful summer morning. Along the way, Paul and Bobby Ray talked about what they expected to find buried on the property. As they often did when they got together, they also spent time arguing with each other over the strategy the Confederacy had employed at Gettysburg. It was arguing that had lasted for years. After driving for almost two hours, Paul pulled off Highway 17 before driving the short distance through Wilmington to I-40. Pulling into the parking lot of a Kangaroo Express Mini-Mart, he parked his truck near the right side of the building. The brief stop was going to fill two immediate needs as Bobby Ray needed to use the bathroom and they both were ready for their second cup of coffee. Getting out of his truck to stretch, Paul could see Jayne was sleeping in the reclined right front seat of Chick's van. She had a navy blue blanket wrapped around her. Parked nearby in his Jeep, Pete was pounding away on his steering wheel as listened to some type of music playing on his Apple iPod. Paul laughed at the picture of him enjoying his music. The dark red tinted sunglasses Pete was wearing only added to Paul's amusement as he watched him keep up with the beat of the music.

Shortly after they had gotten back onto the highway, with his second cup of coffee only halfway gone, Bobby Ray was fast asleep. It always amazed Paul how fast Bobby Ray could fall asleep, and that he could do so almost anywhere. Now he was fast asleep, his head leaning against the passenger window as his friend drove north towards Maple Hill.

The rest of the ride took only took another hour and fifteen minutes to complete. Paul spent the hour Bobby Ray was asleep rehearsing what he was going to tell Duke when they met. He knew he had to be upfront and honest with him from the beginning as he could not violate the trust Duke had shown by calling him. Misleading him would likely have tragic consequences in trying to find the Confederate treasury.

Arriving too early to meet with Duke, they stopped in town first as Paul wanted to get a sense of what Maple Hill was like. While in town, they grabbed an early lunch at a small barbeque restaurant on North Carolina State Route 53 before driving to Duke's farm.

After eating lunch, they drove the short distance down S.R. 53 to Duke's hog farm. As they pulled into the entrance of the farm, Paul and Bobby Ray could not help but laugh at the large sign hanging on one of Duke's barns.

The large colorful sign greeted visitors to the hog farm. The animated sign, which had a smiling red pig's face on it, read *'Our pork products will make you squeal for more!'* A good old boy himself, Bobby Ray could not help laughing uncontrollably when he first saw it. "I wonder who the brain behind the sign was. I like it though; it's a simple country kind of sign."

Duke Johnson was just getting out of his Ford Expedition when Paul's caravan; comprised of Chick's Dodge minivan, Pete's Jeep, and Paul's Chevy truck, pulled into the farm's parking area outside of Duke's office. As they got out of their vehicles, the smell of the hog farm was overwhelming. Jayne was taken back by it immediately. She softly murmured her displeasure at what she smelled to Chick. "Oh, my goodness! This is horrible! How could anyone stand this smell all day?"

Chick, an educated country boy, but one who had been raised on a dairy farm in western South Carolina, just looked at her. "What smell?"

Standing next to his SUV, Duke's loud voice boomed from across the other side of the large parking lot. "Looks like you brought the whole dang team with you!"

As they walked across the parking lot towards each other, it was Paul who spoke first. "Duke, I'm Paul Waring, thanks for calling me and for agreeing to meet with us. We're excited about the possibility of finding such an important historical location right here on your farm." He then introduced Duke to the others. As they exchanged some small talk with each other, Paul advised Duke they were planning on making a documentary film on the discovery he made. He also told Duke they hoped to make a connection between the remains of the soldier he found to the remains they hoped to find in the grave on his property. "We'd like to include your farm and the gravesite in our video if we can make the proper connections between all of these remains." Duke initially expressed his reluctance to allow the gravesite to be disturbed, but soon convinced by Paul's promise to treat the grave with respect and dignity; he gave his consent for them to proceed with their plans. "Duke, even from our brief conversations, I can sense how important this site is to you and your family. We promise to treat it with the respect it deserves. Nothing is going to be desecrated, I won't let that happen."

Even with that said, Paul could tell some of Duke's concerns still lingered in his mind about allowing the site to be disturbed. "Duke, if we find any remains in the grave, and we expect to based on the clues I have in my possession, I promise you we'll work with your local historical society, with the North Carolina Historical Society, with you, and with whomever else we have to, to find a proper resting place for these soldiers. We believe, as we're sure you likely do as well, these brave soldiers deserve a proper resting spot and a fitting ceremony to honor them for their service to the Confederacy. We'd be honored to have you be a part of this with us." Duke simply nodded his head at what Paul said to him.

With Bobby Ray and Jayne's help, Pete unloaded some of his video equipment from his Jeep as Paul and Chick spoke with Duke about the history of the Johnson farm. As they talked, they learned more about Duke's father and granddaddy, and about the original wooden cross which had marked the gravesite. As they stood talking in the parking lot, Pete started to film the small talk which started their relationship with Duke. Jayne also documented this first meeting by taking digital pictures with her Nikon camera.

"You folks are serious about this, ain't you? Taking these here pictures and videotape and all." Duke said as he alternated stares at Jayne and Pete hard at work.

"Duke, we just want to put together a storyline for our documentary; part of this story is meeting you for the first time. We thought we'd start by taking some shots of us just talking and getting to know each other."

"Sounds like a plan. How do y'all want to start from here?"

"Can we start by seeing the wooden cross you told us about?" Paul asked as he tried to guess which of Duke's barns the cross was in.

Duke led the way to one of his large red painted wooden barns. It housed a great deal of the equipment needed to run his large hog farm. In the barn were tractors, backhoes, bags of feed and grain, and other similar supplies, as well as a small office Duke used when he needed to get away from the business end of the operation each day. As they entered the barn through two large sliding doors, Paul noticed Duke had already taken the wooden cross off the wall. It was lying on top of three sheets of plywood which sat on the barn's concrete floor. "I kinda figured you folks would want to see this so I got it ready for y'all to look at."

As Pete and Jayne documented what they were looking at with videotape and photos, Paul and Chick knelt down to examine the cross and its carved letters up close. After examining it for several minutes, and after running his fingers over each of the letters roughly carved into the wood so many years ago, Paul looked up at Duke. "This is a very special piece of American history, very special. We're honored to have the chance to see it. Do you have any idea what kind of wood this is?"

"It's hand cut rough-hewn pine which probably was harvested from pine trees grown in Virginia or North Carolina. I imagine the wood was likely cut at a family run sawmill. My family has suspected for years the wood may have originally been part of a wagon of some kind as you can see some holes where bolts were in place at one point." After they spent close to an hour looking at the cross, Paul asked Duke to take them to where it had once stood. Bobby

Ray had just finished a rough drawing of the cross and with Chick's help they added several measurements to it

"We're going to drive to where the cross is, so load up what you can into my Ford. The rest of the gear will have to go in your truck. The minivan won't make it back there as the ride is kind of a rough, but y'all can bring the Jeep along if you want."

Paul rode with Duke as they drove the short distance to the fifty plus acres the Johnson family had kept as hunting and fishing spots. As he did, he could not help feeling it was like they were travelling back in time as this part of Duke's farm was a place time had forgotten about it. It was a stunning piece of property. "Duke, this is absolutely beautiful back here. Someone in your family made a great decision to preserve this."

As they were driven back to the gravesite by Chick, Pete and Jayne took the opportunity to document the beauty of the farmland and to put into perspective where the site was situated on the farm. Pete's video camera and the still shots taken by Jayne captured the beauty of the property through the pictures they took.

Driving slowly across Duke's fields, the metal cross finally came into view. "See here, there's the cross my granddaddy done stuck in the ground years ago to replace the wooden cross you just seen."

Seeing the cross, Paul asked for a favor. "Duke, stop here away from the site for a few moments. We want to make sure we document the beauty of the site before we start walking around it. We don't want to spoil the beauty of the field by having tire tracks running through it when people see the video footage. I want it to look like we are seeing it now, almost as if human hands had never touched the property."

"No problem. The cross is something to see up close though. My family believes this is a special place to visit."

Before they approached the grave site, Paul had Pete set up several tripods so the area could be filmed from many different angles. Because of his experience in documenting crime scenes, Paul assigned Bobby Ray to work with Chick so they could draw a somewhat detailed map of the area around the metal cross. As they worked on the map, Paul yelled a thought to them. "Make sure you leave some room on your map so we can pencil in some details once we get to work."

Once all of this was done, Duke led them closer to where the metal cross had stood for years in his field. As they stood a few feet away, Paul was touched by the beauty of the simple cross. "Duke, I don't mean to sound corny, but I'm taken back by the kind act your granddaddy did so many years ago to honor someone who was buried here. That simple act made sure their burial spot would not be forgotten by time. When others see our documentary, I'm sure they will also feel the same way. It's a gesture of kindness which I cannot properly describe. What a thoughtful act!"

Standing near the cross, Paul could see Duke's eyes teared up when he heard his granddaddy described like that. He could tell Duke's granddaddy obviously still held a special place in his heart. "That was just my granddaddy being him. He was a great man!"

Almost finished with their map, Chick and Bobby Ray now took a few quick final measurements to accurately place the cross on it. With the aid of a compass, they also plotted the direction of north on the map so they could have a true sense of direction for any later needs.

Paul then gathered all of them together near Duke's Ford. "I've waited for the right time to tell you about this and now the time is perfect, thanks to Duke." Reaching into his shirt pocket, he unfolded a copy of the roughly drawn map he had found within one of the bottles. "When I first found the letters, I also found this map with them. Take a look at it and tell me if this map is not the same location as what you see here in Duke's field. It certainly looks like it is to me. When you look at the map, you'll see it doesn't tell you much, but there's the cross and the small pile of large rocks." Paul said as he pointed to the two locations on the map.

Looking at the map, the others saw the cross and the pile of rocks which had been crudely drawn on it many years ago. "Why do you think there are no measurements or any other signs on the map to show where the money was buried?" It was a question Jayne asked, but one Paul was glad Duke had not heard. He did not want him to know about the money that was possibly buried by the cross until they knew for sure it was there. Fortunately for them, Duke had walked back to his vehicle to retrieve a pair of sunglasses when Jayne had asked her question. Due to their law enforcement experience, Bobby Ray and Paul both had the answer for Jayne's question. It was Bobby Ray who answered for them.

"When you draw a map to remind you where you have hidden something, you don't have to put in all of the details because you know where you've hidden it. You just want the map to help you with your bearings. If you put too much detail on the map and then it gets lost or misplaced, you've just told someone where to find what you've hidden in the first place. Make sense?"

Jayne still did not completely understand what Bobby Ray told her. "So it's more of a guide or a reference than it is a true map?"

"Exactly."

By now Duke had rejoined them. After a few more minutes of speaking with him about the history of his property and taking in the beauty of the scene in front of them, they started to excavate the ground around where the metal cross stood. As they did, Pete constantly checked and rechecked his video cameras to make sure they were capturing what was occurring. After digging down just over three feet below the surface, and in a complete circle around the cross, Chick and Jayne scanned the hole with the two metal detectors they had rented for their needs. The metal detectors gave off no readings of anything metallic being buried in the area around the cross.

Somewhat disappointed, and just as perplexed, Jayne wiped the sweat of the afternoon's work off her brow as she stood in the hole they had dug. The heat of the North Carolina summer afternoon had the day's temperature close to ninety-five degrees. The humidity was just as high. "Perhaps we need to dig deeper because the metal detectors are not showing anything on their display screens."

Leaning on a shovel and catching his breath from digging, Paul was equally disappointed by the lack of any immediate success. "OK, let's dig down another three feet or so and then we'll see what that brings us." As they started taking turns digging again, Paul noticed Duke had walked back to his Ford and was now driving back towards the barns. "Perhaps he has something else to be doing?" It was the only reason he could think of as to why Duke had left.

As they continued to dig, they could hear the noise of some kind of vehicle being driven in the field. Soon the noise became louder as it moved closer to them. Stopping momentarily to see what the noise was, they saw Duke had gone back to his barn and was returning to the gravesite driving a yellow John Deere 310D backhoe. It was a machine equipped with both a front-end bucket and a backhoe. After parking the still running machine near the other vehicles, Duke climbed down off the backhoe wearing a smile on his face. "I thought this might make it easier on you folks!" Collectively they all smiled at him as they knew he had just made their digging far easier.

In moments, Duke was back in the machine. Following Paul's hand gestures, he carefully scraped the soil away from within the circle where they had been digging. Three complete passes around the circle, with the cross still standing in the middle, enlarged the hole another four feet in diameter. It was now almost seven feet in depth. Still they found nothing. After signaling Duke to turn the backhoe off, Paul had the others take a break to rest.

As they took a break from working under the hot sun for almost two hours, Bobby Ray pulled out the large cooler of bottled water Chick had packed in Paul's truck. The cool water was a welcome relief from their thirst, but it did little to ease the frustration they each felt over finding nothing to indicate they had been digging in the proper location. After taking a long swig of cold water, Chick stood looking at the area they had excavated. "I would have thought we would have found some indication of a grave by now. I wouldn't think a grave that had been hand dug by soldiers would have been dug this deep, especially if they were being pursued by Yankee soldiers. Perhaps they did, but I cannot imagine why."

Paul had moved off a short distance from the cross and was quenching his thirst while seated on a large rock. He sat wondering if he had been wrong about where the money had actually been buried. "Is this another wild goose chase we are part of? Are we chasing the legend of the Confederate gold and silver which may not have ever existed?" Deep down, he did not think so, but he was already questioning himself.

As he sat there, Jayne walked over carrying a bottle of water and one of the metal detectors. Sitting down on another large rock next to where Paul sat, she swapped out the batteries as the icon on one of the metal detector's electronic screen showed the batteries were running low. After she was finished, she sat there cooling down. "Paul, do you think we're in the right spot?"

"I hope so, but I guess we need to either dig deeper or we need to expand the width of the area we're excavating. If we don't find anything after our next attempt we'll try another spot, but I still believe the money is here. It's far too early to get too discouraged."

As Jayne prepared to get back to digging, she grabbed the metal detector she had laid against the rock she was sitting on. Doing so caused the metal detector to give off a faint beep.

"What was that?" Paul asked, taking notice of the beep from where he was sitting.

"I don't know, possibly from metal in the rock I was sitting on perhaps?"

"Maybe or maybe from something else."

Seeing the metal detector so close to the rock Jayne had been sitting on caused Paul to realize he had missed an obvious clue the map had left for them. He kicked himself for wasting time digging by the cross when the map had clearly told him where the money was actually buried. Calling the others over to where Jayne and he had been sitting, he told them Jayne's metal detector had registered a faint beep when she stood up. Slowly, Jayne now made another pass directly over the spot where the metal detector had sat, but this time nothing metallic was detected. She then made a couple of other passes over the ground adjacent to where she had been sitting. Again the metal detector gave no indication of anything metallic being present.

"Perhaps it was a small amount of metal contained within a rock in the ground the metal detector made a slight detection of or perhaps it was just a false positive anomaly which popped up?" Chick was grabbing for answers for what had caused the sound they heard.

"Perhaps, but explain this to me first." Paul said as he tried sorting through several thoughts running through his head. "Tell me why in the area we're digging in . . . within this beautiful meadow . . . why are there no other rocks lying around like these four? Why are they just here? One of Francis' letters spoke about four rocks, and I completely forgot about them because I was so focused on digging by the cross. I'm wondering if these are the rocks his letter talked about being by the gravesite? They have to be the same ones we looked at when we examined the map. Perhaps he used the cross as a reference point so he would see it from a distance when he returned to the area and the rocks are actually on top of the grave? Perhaps they were put there to keep animals from digging up the bodies? I don't know though, I'm just thinking out loud."

Paul quickly got them moving again. "Let's find out what's under these rocks, but first, Chick and Bobby Ray, you need to make sure these rocks are on your map. Make sure the map shows how far they're spaced apart. The map also needs to show their relationship to where the cross is. Jayne, you and Pete need to document these rocks carefully with some more photos and videotape. Make sure you show the rocks with the cross in some of your photos and make sure a segment of your video shows the same thing. Even give some thought to having Duke lift you up in the bucket of the backhoe for an elevated type of photo, just for a different type of view of the scene. However you decide to do it, just make sure you get some good shots of these rocks. Duke, we'll need to carefully move these rocks with your backhoe when the others are done with their tasks."

With all of the tasks soon completed, Paul grabbed a shovel and took away several shovelfuls of soil from the area Jayne had been sitting in. "OK, Jayne, try the metal detector again over where I just dug. Let's see what happens."

Jayne had barely placed the metal detector over the small hole when it gave a loud and steady beep, a beep which got everyone's attention. "It's obvious something's in the ground here, something very large by the size of the icon on the metal detector's screen." Jayne said as she stared at the small hole Paul had dug. "The screen's icon is bouncing back and forth between metal and coins so it's hard to figure out what it's registering." Realizing she had used the word coins in front of Duke, Jayne looked to see what kind of reaction it had gotten. From his facial expressions, she could tell he had not picked up on what she had just said.

"We digging?" Duke asked eagerly as he climbed back up on his John Deere.

"We're digging, but gently, Duke, gently. If I give you the signal to stop, stop immediately and we'll finish it by hand. We don't want to damage anything with that heavy piece of equipment of yours."

Watching as Duke started up his machine, Paul yelled over the noise of the machine to Jayne and Pete without looking at them. "You guys getting this on video and with your cameras?"

Pete was moving one of his tripods from one location to another when Paul hollered to him. "Yeah, but give me one minute. I need Bobby Ray to help me with a video camera I have set up on a tripod. Then I want to turn on my small video camera so I can move about freely while he's digging. I just need a minute."

When Pete gave the sign he was ready, Duke carefully moved the four large rocks away from where they had sat. From his years of experience in running machines like his backhoe, he then began to gently scrape away the soil that had been under the rocks. He had only been working for a couple of minutes when Paul, who was standing next to the bucket as Duke worked the ground around him, waved frantically for him to stop. "You found something! Back the machine away and turn it off for a while until we see what we've got."

With Chick's help, Paul cleared the soil away from the object he saw protruding from the ground. First with shovels and then carefully with their hands, they cleared the remaining soil away. As they did, Bobby Ray shoveled the soil into the bucket of Duke's backhoe so it could be moved away from where they were working.

"It's some kind of cloth, perhaps a shirt or maybe even a blanket."

After two bucket loads of soil had been taken away, it was easy for Paul to see the object in the ground was actually the remnants of two sets of blankets. The blankets had been rolled up and were over five feet in length. "Chick, we've got some remains in here for sure. It appears to be two separate sets of remains. It looks like whomever is here has been carefully wrapped in these blankets. The blankets are in bad shape so we have to be careful. We need to slide a tarp under them as carefully as possible so we can lift the remains out of the grave without damaging them."

Down on their hands and knees, Paul, Chick, and Bobby Ray carefully worked for almost two hours slowly threading a large black plastic tarp under the remnants of the blankets they had found. Paul made them work slowly so neither the blankets nor the soldier's remains were harmed. Anxiously, Duke watched as they worked.

When they finally finished, and after Paul was satisfied nothing had been damaged, he gave the OK for the tarp to be lifted out of the grave. "Let's carefully pick this up and move it out of the grave. Remember folks, we're doing this slowly, and with dignity and respect." With Duke and Jayne's help, Paul and Chick lifted one end of the tarp up to them. Carefully they slowly lifted the remains up and out of the grave. The remains were then carried several feet away from where they had lain for almost one hundred and fifty years. Gently they were laid down on the soft grass within Duke's meadow.

As this was being done, Pete and Jayne documented the removal of the remains everyway they could. After taking numerous digital photos of the process, Jayne walked back towards the gravesite to photograph the now empty grave. She was the first one to see the next object. It was barely noticeable as it protruded ever so slightly out of one of the side walls of the grave they had just excavated. "Guys, I think we have something else here, it looks like another blanket!"

It took almost another painstaking hour of removing the soil by hand to finally clear enough of it from around the third set of blankets. When fully exposed, the object again proved to be two separate blankets. They were very similar in their appearance to those that had been used to wrap the first two sets of remains in. These blankets also appeared to contain the remains of another soldier. After all of the soil was cleared away, and with the same care and respect given to the first sets of remains, the plastic tarp they placed under this set of remains was carefully lifted from the grave. The tarp was slowly carried to where the remains of the first two soldiers had been placed on the ground. It was the first time the remains had felt fresh air in almost one hundred and fifty years.

For several moments they all stood around the blankets they had just removed from the grave. They each tried to comprehend what it was they had just discovered and who it was that had been wrapped in the blankets; wondering at the same time how each of the soldiers had died. As they solemnly stood there, Duke took off his hat and bowed his head to pray. It was a gesture everyone soon took part in. "I just wish my granddaddy was still alive so he could see what had been buried near this cross for all of them years. This was a special place for him."

"Duke, I have a feeling the remains would not be the only thing he would have appreciated seeing." Not understanding what Paul meant by his comment, Duke gave him a quizzical look.

Paul, then Chick, and then the others, with Duke following them, walked back to the grave they had just excavated. Climbing down into the grave and using one of the shovels they had been digging with earlier, Paul quietly dug for several moments. As he dug, the shovel hit something hard in the soil. Stopping his digging, he leaned the shovel against the side of the already chest-deep grave.

"Jayne, hand me one of those metal detectors, please." Paul barely had time to place the metal detector over the area where his shovel had hit something when it immediately gave a strong beep. The presence of coins came up on the metal detector's electronic display screen. Seeing the reading on the display screen caused him to realize they had found what so many others had spent years looking for. When he looked up from where he was standing in the grave, Chick saw a big smile on Paul's face. It was the biggest smile he had ever seen.

The object he located was still approximately four inches under the soil according to the reading he saw on the display screen. Kneeling down in the grave, and again using his hands to slowly scrape away the soil which still hid the object from view, Paul soon determined what the object was. "I think it's a wooden barrel. The top is decayed and appears to have a hole in it, but I can feel one of the metal hoops still around the top part of the barrel. It appears to be in decent shape considering how long it's been here." As he worked the soil away from the top of the barrel, Pete documented the find with his cameras.

Giving him a couple of moments to clear away more of the soil, Chick asked the question the others had patiently waited for someone else to ask. "Is it what we're looking for?" The smile on Paul's face was all Chick needed for an answer.

"I haven't looked inside of it, but I think we found what we had hoped to find!"

As Paul climbed out of the grave, the rest of them were exchanging high fives and back slaps with each other. The only exception was Duke. He was still unaware of what they had found. "Can you believe it has been found after all of these years? And we found it! We found it, not anyone else!" The smiles on their faces added to the confusion Duke was experiencing. He could tell something special had happened, but he was not sure what it was that now made the others so happy.

After a few moments of celebration, Paul calmed them down. "Hey, everyone, listen up for a minute. Take some more video of what we just found and take some digital photos as well, and Chick, plot the wooden barrel on the map for our future needs, but all of you stay out of the grave. I need to talk to Duke for a few minutes."

Walking Duke away from the gravesite, Paul could see from his face he still did not understand what was going on with what they had just found. Now it was time to tell him what had been buried on his property for all of these years. "Duke, when I discovered the remains of the Confederate soldier it was more than just a discovery of the soldier's remains and a few relics from the war I accidently found. It has proved to be much more than that. The relics I found are all priceless in their own way, and the discovery of the soldier, well . . . let's just say that's not something that happens everyday. Those items have proved to be just small pieces of an even bigger find, one we have partially found here today. When I found the soldier's remains I also found clues which ultimately have led us here. We hope other clues will lead us to other places very soon. Are you following me on this so far?"

Still somewhat overwhelmed by the remains of three Confederate soldiers being found on his property, Duke was even more confused by what Paul found in the grave after the remains had been removed. "I'm trying to stay with you, but I'm confused about what y'all think is still in the grave. You said something about a barrel being in the grave, is that right?"

"Duke, let me ask you a question. Being Southern born and bred, you've probably about the legend of the missing Confederate gold and silver from the Civil War, correct?"

"Sure have. My granddaddy and daddy spoke about the legend on many occasions. The money went missing during the war. From what little bit I know about it, it ain't ever turned up yet."

Paul could not help but smile. "Duke, I think it just did!"

"What!"

"The soldier I found appears to be the Confederate officer who was charged with moving the gold and silver out of Richmond. He was likely moving it to either Atlanta or to someplace in Mississippi, but I'm not sure of the exact location at this time. What the location was really doesn't even matter. What matters is I . . . I mean we . . . we don't believe for a moment that he stole the money like some others have suspected he did. What we think happened is that along the way he encountered some difficulties, like three of his men dying here on your property . . . probably from gunshot wounds after being ambushed or from a fate quite similar to that. We also think because some of his men had died, he may have had trouble finishing his mission so he chose to bury some of the money right here. He may have done the same in a couple of other places as well. He likely did this so he could travel faster to where he hoped to get the rest of the money to. That's all a guess on our part, but it makes sense if you think about it. He probably was the person who made the map I showed you before, and quite likely the one who drew the wooden cross and rocks on it. The same cross your granddaddy cared for. Most likely, he planned on using the cross as a reference point for when he felt it was safe to come and dig the money up. The CSA that's carved in the wooden cross did not stand for 'Old Charley', it stood for the Confederate States of America. Duke, what the soldier I found did before he died was to leave clues for someone like me to find. If he had stolen the money then I doubt he would have left any clues behind for the money to be found."

The magnitude of Paul's news was an obvious shock to Duke. "Are y'all telling me what we just found, really what y'all just found, is the missing Confederate gold and silver?"

"Some of it is. We think it's at least part of it."

Already overwhelmed by what had been found on his property earlier, Duke was now stunned after learning about the lost Confederate treasury being located in one of his fields. It was found on the piece of property his granddaddy held sacred for so many years. Standing quietly for a few moments, Duke gently shook his head from side to side as he tried comprehending what he saw and heard. The excitement soon caused him to pace back and forth for several additional moments as he processed all that had happened in just one afternoon.

"I don't believe it. I just don't believe it!" Calming down, he asked the question Paul had been waiting for. "So whose money is it? Seeing that it's buried here on my land, is it mine?"

"Duke, I understand how you could think that way, and to some regard you have a strong argument to make that it is yours. But as we've come to realize, and we were the ones to find it, the money is not ours to lay claim to. You and I don't know each other very well yet, but what I do know about you is that in your heart I believe you already know this money is not yours either. We found it with your help and with your permission, but after you think about it, it's not yours. I'm sure your granddaddy would tell you the same thing. I didn't have the pleasuring of knowing him, but the way you've talked about him and the way he helped raise you, I believe he would tell you the same as I just did. I have him pictured as an honest and humble man, one who would likely tell you the money still belongs to the people of the Confederacy. I also believe he would tell you the money does not belong to one family or to one person, but rather it belongs to a larger group of people. My guess is he would want it shared by that large group of people, most likely Southern people. Am I right?"

Looking down at the ground as he stood silently for a couple of moments, Duke then looked at Paul. "You already know my granddaddy pretty well, don't you?"

Smiling at Duke's comment, Paul shared his thoughts with him. "Duke, I have a plan for the money. I assure you that you're a part of this plan. Like I said, we don't know each other very well yet, but I hope you'll trust me to do the right thing here."

"Paul, I'm a country boy, a simple country boy who still believes in a man's word. You give me your word and we shake on it, then I guess we have to trust each other, don't we?"

In front of Chick, who walked over to where they were talking, Paul and Duke shook hands. It was the time-tested way of doing business between friends. It would be the start of a friendship which would last for many years.

"Duke, before you go and dig this wooden barrel up for us, we're going to ask two more things of you. We believe this is the first of at least two, possibly three locations where the missing gold and silver was hidden, so what we find here today is just the start of our hunt for the rest of it. We know it will be hard for you to do, but it will be just as hard for us to do the same thing. What I'm trying to say is we need you to keep this as close to the vest as possible. Please don't make any mention of this to any reporters. It will only hurt our efforts to find the rest of the missing money. You have my word when we find the next location, and we will, I'll call you before we do any digging. We want you to be there when we do."

Duke nodded his head at Paul's comments. "We shook hands a couple of minutes ago so you have my word I will keep this quiet. You know, I would like to be there when y'all find the next place you think the money has been buried, so please call me. But you said there were two things y'all needed. What's the second?"

"Oh, right. Do you have anything we could make a large screen out of? Just in the event we've missed something, I'd like to build a sifting screen so we could run the soil from the grave through it. I'd like to sift the soil for coins and other items. After that is done, I want to place the remains temporarily back into the grave for now. I'd like the screen to be in the shape of a square, about four to five feet in size so we could set it on blocks, you know concrete blocks or even wooden blocks. It would be easier to sift the soil if the screen was elevated up a few feet off the ground. Can you make something like that up for us?"

"Sure, no problem. I'll call the guys on my cell phone and have them put it together with some metal screening we use for the hog pens. I'll have it framed with wood. I also have plenty of concrete blocks to set the screen on. They can call me when it's ready and I'll pick it up with the backhoe, this way they won't know what's going on down here." It took only a few seconds for Duke to get one of his foremen on the phone, describing to him what he wanted built.

Chick and Bobby Ray had spread out a blue plastic tarp on the ground so the barrel could be set down on top of it after Duke lifted it from the hole with the backhoe. Now following Paul's guidance, Duke carefully removed the rest of the soil from around the wooden barrel. As the soil was being removed, Pete filmed the barrel being unearthed. With the soil being removed from the grave, it was easy to see the barrel had not remained as intact as Paul first thought. The sides were now somewhat rotted from the years it had been in the ground. It was obvious that it was far too fragile to try and move in one piece. Paul quickly made the decision to take the barrel apart by hand. Before they did, Chick took some rough measurements for documentation purposes.

In several pieces the barrel easily came apart, with only the metal hoops standing up to the test of time. As Paul took the barrel apart, he handed the pieces up to Chick so they could be laid out on the tarp. After exposing one side, they saw what was left of several cloth bags, bags which once contained gold and silver coins. Reaching into one of the rotted bags, Paul picked up an 1861 Liberty Head gold dollar coin and held it up for the others to see. "We found it. We found the money just like we thought we would!" Looking up, he saw Duke sitting in the backhoe clapping his hands, happy at what they had just found.

Using six white plastic buckets they had brought with them, Paul and Chick carefully began scooping the gold and silver coins out of the rotted barrel. As they filled each bucket with coins of several different denominations, they set the filled heavy buckets within the backhoe's bucket for Duke to lift out of the grave. It took two of them to place the buckets into the backhoe as the weight of each bucket was significant. Over the next hour, they completely filled five of the six buckets with gold and silver coins. They filled the sixth bucket with the remaining handfuls of coins they found within the rotted barrel.

As the last bucket of coins was handed out of the grave, Bobby Ray was looking at the other buckets of coins they had already excavated. Looking at them, he asked Paul what he thought the value of the coins were worth. "Haven't even thought about it to be honest; I've been too concerned about leaving some of the coins behind in the grave. I don't even know what we have here, but I'm sure it's worth plenty. It's likely worth a lot more now than it was back then. But you know what? For me, the hunt is now on for the rest of the Confederate treasury; the hunt is what it's all about. I could care less what the coins are worth. I just want to find the rest of the treasury." Paul knew they would be hard-pressed to find the rest of the money, but he also knew he was not giving up the hunt. After finding this portion of the missing treasury, no matter how hard it was going to be to find the rest of it, he was going to find it. Putting handcuffs on bad people was a satisfaction Paul had always enjoyed; partially solving the legend of the missing Confederate treasury was a feeling he never experienced before. He now wanted to experience that feeling again.

The buckets of coins had carefully been transferred from the backhoe to the blue tarp. Like kids in a candy store, Paul and the others knelt down next to the buckets, sifting through the Double Eagles, the Half Eagles, the gold dollar coins, and the other types of coins they had found. Excitedly they showed each other the coins they found and the years minted on them. Unlike the wooden barrel, the coins had stood up well despite the number of years they had been buried.

After several minutes of looking at the coins, they were back to work. Jayne ran one of the metal detectors over the entire gravesite as Chick and Bobby Ray began placing the six buckets of coins into Paul's truck. Just before they loaded the coins into the truck, Paul reached into one of the buckets and randomly pulled out an 1862 silver dollar. Just as casually as a young school boy would do to a nickel, he flicked the silver coin in the air to Duke. "That's a gift for you. It's a way for you to remember your granddaddy's good deed, a deed done for these three soldiers." The simple gesture Paul made to Duke again caused him to bow his head in remembrance of his granddaddy. That gesture, and Duke's subsequent head bow, was fortunately caught on videotape by Pete.

Three years later, that simple gesture would bring thousands of people to tears when they watched the premier of Paul's documentary air on South Carolina's ETV affiliates for the first time.

By now darkness had almost descended upon them and they still had not viewed the remains of the three soldiers. They now decided, out of respect to the soldiers, to spend the night in the meadow until they could view the remains the following day. As the others started collecting the tools and the other items they had used during the day, Chick hollered out a thought to them. "I'll get another tarp and we can use it to cover the remains with. That way if it happens to rain nothing will be damaged." With Bobby Ray's help, Paul and Chick soon covered the remains with a large plastic tarp. Over the next couple of hours they took turns, two at a time, staying in the field in shifts while the others showered and ate a cold supper in one of Duke's barns.

Before falling asleep in their vehicles, they sat talking for a few hours next to a small campfire they built away from the gravesite. They each talked of what they had found, at what the experience meant to them, and what they had to do to find the rest of the lost Confederate treasury. As he listened to them talk, Paul knew they had just become as passionate about the hunt for the rest of the missing money as he had been all along.

* * * * * *

The next morning Duke drove out to the field early, bringing with him hot coffee and donuts to a tired group of people who had not slept in a car for years. Soon the smell of hot coffee helped them forget about what little sleep they had actually gotten. As they drank their coffee and ate their relatively simple breakfast, Chick wondered if their experience in waking up to a simple breakfast was similar to one the three Confederate soldiers had experienced in the meadow before being killed. "Who knows, maybe they enjoyed their last cup of coffee right here?" The question he posed to his friends caused them to pause from drinking their coffee and to wonder if his thought might actually have been possible.

As the morning's rising sun quickly warmed the meadow, Paul had Duke and Bobby Ray set up the metal sifting screen which Duke's men had built the day before. They soon started sifting the soil that had been removed from the grave. Next they planned to sift the loose soil remaining in the bottom of the grave. As this was being done, Paul and Chick carefully started unwrapping the tarps and blankets from around the remains of the three soldiers. As the blankets were being peeled back to reveal what was wrapped inside of them, Pete turned on one of his video cameras he had set up on a tripod. Now he carefully filmed the proceedings with his hand held video camera as well.

Slowly unwrapping what was left of the decaying blankets, blankets which had been wrapped around the soldiers so many years ago, the skeletal remains of what appeared to be three young soldiers were seen for the first time. Remarkably their remains were still partially covered by the tattered remnants of three gray Confederate uniforms. Within the blankets, Paul pointed out a belt buckle that one of the soldiers had worn. The same soldier's feet were still wearing his crudely made boots. One other soldier was found not to be wearing any boots. Chick and Paul both thought this was odd, but Pete quickly offered a logical explanation to what they had found.

"Perhaps one of their fellow soldiers needed the boots more than he did. Boots and shoes were precious commodities during the war. As you both likely know, the Battle of Gettysburg was preceded by some of Lee's troops actually looking for shoes there."

Resuming their work, they confined the inspection of the remains to a visual one, electing not to look for any type of identification which may have been buried with the soldiers. Paul's visual scan of the three sets of remains showed nothing of any obvious historical or military value within the blankets. He knew it was not the time or place to be looking for any such items.

With Jayne's help, Duke and Bobby Ray screened all of the soil as Paul and Chick examined the contents of the blankets. They found little when they sifted the soil, finding only a couple of nails and a rusted metal spoon, but found no other coins. Finished with that task, they moved to help with the inspection of the soldier's remains.

After finishing their inspection, and with the same dignity displayed when they removed the remains from the grave, the soldiers' remains, now wrapped in individual blue plastic tarps to protect them from further water damage, were carefully placed back into the grave. The remains were soon covered with the same soil which had previously been in the grave.

Paul stood quietly while Duke used his backhoe to finish filling in the grave. After the four stones were placed back on top of the grave, Duke walked to where Paul and the others were standing. "Duke, I think for now the best thing for us to do is to let these three soldiers rest in peace as they had been." Paul said as he looked at the gravesite. "We have some additional clues we want to work out and hopefully those clues will lead us to the next place where some of the money is buried. When we're done finding the money, we'll all meet with the proper authorities to decide where these soldiers, along with the soldier I found, should be buried."

As the group remained standing next to the grave site, Paul said a short prayer for the soldiers. He was not an overly religious person in any formal sense, but he asked God to continue to watch over them as he already had since the day they had died. Dropping down to one knee, Duke grabbed a handful of loose dirt and gently tossed it on top of the grave. "Amen," was his only comment to what Paul had asked God for.

After thanking Duke for his friendship, and for his faith and trust in them, Paul first, and then the others, said their goodbyes to him. Paul promised to call him soon so he knew how they were making out deciphering the next set of clues.

Driving home, Bobby Ray soon fell fast asleep in Paul's truck, a truck now containing gold and silver coins from the Confederacy. Coins they had found and others had not. Making his way back into South Carolina, Paul tried to remember what the clues were Francis had left in his letter to President Davis. "I remember he said he left some of the money with the children of Governor Allston, but why? Why would he leave the money with his children?" After a few moments of trying to think things out, he knew he was too tired to make any sense of it. His thoughts turned to seeing Donna and to taking a hot shower. He would resume the hunt tomorrow. For now, sharing a meal with his wife, grabbing a hot shower, and then getting some much needed sleep were far more important issues to him than a few more pails of gold and silver coins were. That would all change the following day.

Fall, 1863

22

Charleston.

"Yea, though I walk through the valley of the shadow of death, I will fear no evil; for Thou art with me ..."
The 23rd Psalm

The morning following Sgt. Griffin's death proved to be a tough way to start a difficult day for Francis and his men. As they woke, the humidity was already becoming excessive and they all knew the rising sun would soon make travelling a brutally hot day to endure. Their early thoughts of both the loss of their friend and of the hot day they would be facing made them a disagreeable bunch. The lingering effects of drinking two bottles of spirits the previous night also did not help their moods. Even the early morning coffee they had before they started out did little to make the day look anymore promising to them.

As they started out, Francis was forced to drive one of the wagons on their five-day leg of the mission from Georgetown to Charleston. It was the first time he had driven a wagon since he had been back home a few years ago. Before climbing aboard their wagons, Francis told his men he would feel much safer once they reached the outskirts of the city.

The city of Charleston was rich and prosperous compared to most Southern cities, and one strongly aligned with the Confederate cause. It was a place where Francis knew they could relax far more than they were able to during any other part of their journey. He had promised his men that once they got to Charleston he would give them a couple of days to rest as a reward for making it there with their precious cargo. It was not much, but his promise had the men's spirits soaring high during the hot morning. They each knew they now had something to look forward to. For Francis, once in Charleston he would finally learn how he would complete his mission; hoping it would either be by train or by a Confederate blockade runner. As his men were, he was also now tired of the slow moving wagons which seemed to expose them to all types of problems. Just like those he commanded, he was also looking forward to a couple of days of rest. Besides the physical strain they endured during their journey, he had been forced to deal with the loss of several of his men. Those losses had begun to take an emotional toll on him.

After weighing his options, Francis chose to travel to Charleston by taking a route fairly close to the South Carolina coast. He did so as he thought such a route would steer them away from any Union cavalry troops who might be scouting the area. He wanted to avoid any fights with the Yankees as he knew his men could not hold off any good size group of Union soldiers for long. As he drove his wagon south, he had but one thought about the Yankees at this time. "You leave me alone and I will leave you alone." He hoped his thought would play out just this once. While he knew it would benefit both sides, he knew it would benefit his side far more as they had the gold and silver with them. It would prove to be the only time during the war where he hoped to avoid an encounter with any Union troops. It simply was not in his makeup to avoid a fight, but this time he hoped they could. It would mean they would survive to fight another day.

As they moved along the coast, navigating in and around the physical hazards God and Mother Nature placed in their way, Francis had no way of knowing his route of travel would someday be the same one vacationers would take when visiting the South Carolina coast. It was a coastal stretch of land running from Myrtle Beach to Charleston. The tourists would navigate this stretch far easier, far cooler, and far quicker than the several long hot days it would take Francis and his men to finally reach Charleston.

Despite the loss of Griffin, and despite the oppressively weather, they travelled a good distance during their first day. On each of the following days they travelled without experiencing any problems, but the travel on each of those days began to take an even bigger toll on them. On each successive day, the sun seemed hotter than the previous one. They worked hard, ate little, and barely found enough fresh water to survive on. Now on the fifth day, Francis looked at his pocket watch and saw it was just before noon when they finally reached the outskirts of Charleston.

Knowing he would need a safe place to hide the wagons in the city while they rested and while he got the answers to the questions he had about how they would move their precious cargo further south, Francis decided to rest the men for the rest of the afternoon. He would go and scout Charleston alone. He hoped he could find a safe hiding spot for them inside the city.

Before leaving, he explained his intentions to his men. "If at all possible, I want to enter the city with the wagons under the cover of darkness. Once I find a place to hide them, I'll come back and get you. Please men, be careful while I'm gone as I cannot afford to lose any more of you. I need each and every one of you dearly. Keep a keen eye out for trouble while I'm gone."

With Odom volunteering to take the first watch, Francis rode off to Charleston while the rest of the men moved the wagons into the protective cover of some pine and magnolia trees on the northwest side of the city. As he silently prayed for a day without any encounters with Union troops, his men also prayed they could avoid skirmishing with Union troops of any sort. With a few days of rest was just hours away, they wanted nothing to come between them and that rest. Individually they all prayed for Francis to return quickly so they could enter the city as soon as possible. Like their captain, none of them had ever been to the bustling city of Charleston.

As Francis entered the city for the first time in his life, he saw why it had been talked about so favorably across the South. The city had been laid out well, with many large private homes lining several streets. Several of the city's finest homes were ones which looked out over the harbor directly at Fort Sumter. Stopping near the end of the city, on South Battery Road, he climbed off his horse and gazed out at the fort for the first time. As he looked out at the tiny speck of land in the middle of the harbor, Francis knew the importance of what he was looking at. "This small insignificant little fort, on such a tiny little piece of land, is where this terrible war started. What a sight the first early morning must have been, watching the rockets and mortars fly through the darkness towards the fort and the fort's cannons answering back by firing their rounds repeatedly throughout the battle. The noise alone must have scared the folks in the city out of their wits." Francis pictured the Napoleon and Dahlgren cannons, as well as the Parrott rifles, firing throughout the night, indiscriminately hitting targets at the fort and in the city itself. "Why did all of this have to happen?" He soon found himself shaking his head at the madness of stubborn old men who had failed to reach a compromise between the Southern states and the federal government, a failure which had led to so many lives being wasted far too early in life.

As he rode along the harbor on South Battery Road, Francis saw some of the homes still showed damage from the cannons being fired at the city from the fort, but most of what he saw was relatively minor. Stopping his horse briefly in front of one damaged home, he was surprised by what he saw. While war raged on in other parts of the South, some of the damaged homes were already in various stages of repair. "War has yet to visit Charleston," he thought as he watched workers on scaffolds repairing a damaged roof to the nearby stately looking home. Continuing his ride through the city, whose economy had been ravaged by the effects of the war, he saw some shops and businesses were still open despite the economic impact the war had upon them.

After dismounting his horse in the city's business district, Francis walked the short distance back to South Battery Road, again losing himself in his thoughts about the events that had started the war. As he paused again to look out at Fort Sumter, he was startled from his thoughts by someone he never heard approaching.

"Hello, captain, admiring the view?" asked Colonel Harold Hodges. "Are you here on business or are you just travelling through to your next assignment?"

Francis spun to see who had startled him. He quickly saluted the Confederate officer sitting on his horse. He was wearing a colonel's insignia on his uniform. "Sir, I am indeed here on business. Please allow me to introduce myself. I am Captain Judiah Francis of the Army of Northern Virginia."

"Pleased to meet you, captain. I am Colonel Harold Hodges. I am the commanding officer of the various shore batteries and artillery units in and around Charleston. I'm taking a brief break this morning before I set off to make sure we're ready for the arrival of the Union navy. I'm afraid they're rumored to be headed our way. I have no doubt they will try and bomb us into submission. Likely, I would surmise, for their incorrect belief that it was South Carolina who started this war. Obviously the United States government and I have a different position on who actually started this war. Nevertheless, I want to make sure we have a grand welcome prepared for them. This is why I'm out inspecting each of the shore batteries around the city. I do not like surprises. I like to be prepared when we fight."

"Sir, I do appreciate your concern, but begging your pardon, my men and I have been travelling for several weeks now. We've pretty much been out of contact with news about the war. So please excuse my ignorance, but the Union navy is expected to threaten Charleston and her defenses?"

"That's the word we've been given by some of our spies up north. They've recently alerted us to the position of the Union navy. As of last night a large number of their ships were only four days sailing from here at the most. They may sail south of us, but we've been expecting them for some time now. As I already mentioned, we know the North wants to punish the Confederacy . . . especially Charleston and South Carolina . . . for allegedly starting the war, but we'll have a surprise or two ready for them when they arrive. They want to repay us, in a very unfortunate way mind you, for the damage we inflicted upon their tiny little fort out there. We'll repel them, for that I'm sure, but I want to check on our defenses today to make sure we're well prepared for their arrival." Then Hodges told Francis about one of the steps the Confederacy had taken to prepare for an attack by the Union navy. "We've set buoys out in the harbor to mark off certain distances for our guns. By doing so, we'll know the exact distance of their ships to our cannons. I'm proud to say it was actually my idea to do so. I'm quite confident our guns will inflict some serious damage to their ships. Hopefully it will be enough to keep them from away from Charleston for some time."

Francis looked out towards the entrance of the harbor; picturing the Union navy firing their guns at the city as they sailed further into the harbor. It was not a picture he enjoyed seeing flashing through his mind. "Colonel, like many people, I also hope you are ready for their ships when they arrive. I wish you good luck."

"We will be ready. When the war first started we used fifteen of our shore batteries to fire on Fort Sumter. Those same batteries, plus a few other ones, will punish the Union navy when they try to enter the harbor. If we can inflict substantial damage on a fort sitting roughly fifteen hundred yards out in the harbor, then we can do the same to their ships as they sail even closer to our batteries. They may hurt us somewhat, but when it's over with we'll prevail." Francis liked Hodges' optimism, but he hoped he was not being too overconfident in his predictions.

For a few moments they both thought about the damage such a battle could do to the city. Francis soon interrupted their thoughts. "Colonel, again I'm likely showing my ignorance about the recent events of the war, but what are my chances of getting a ship, perhaps a blockade runner, to sail my men and I further south?"

"Captain, it does seem you have been out of touch with the news of the war. I'm afraid you have no chance at all for that to occur. The last captain who risked running the blockade sailed two days ago and we still don't know if he made it past the Union navy or not. Now the rest of the ship's captains are too damn afraid of losing their boats in any fight with Lincoln's navy. Cannot say I blame them though, we've already lost one of our own blockade runners just outside the harbor's entrance earlier this year. The SS Georgiana I believe she was called. She was scuttled on her maiden voyage so she would not fall into the hands of the Union navy. We cannot afford to lose any more like her."

"Oh, my!" The Georgiana being scuttled was news Francis had not heard before now. As he thought about the loss of the ship, Colonel Hodges pointed out the general location where the Georgiana had been scuttled.

"Captain, you've not told me your business here in Charleston. Exactly what business is it that brings you here?"

Francis hesitated before answering Hodges' question as he did not want to offend him. He could not think of any other way to answer him besides telling Hodges the truth. "Colonel, I mean no disrespect to you, but on orders I have been given I cannot tell you why I am here." Then quickly realizing Colonel Hodges might be someone who could assist him with his needs, he reached inside his blouse. As he handed Hodges the envelope containing his two important letters of introduction, he hoped they would satisfy Hodges' curiosity about why he was in Charleston. "Sir, please read these letters. I believe you will then understand the significance of my assignment."

Hodges was not accustomed to junior officers refusing to give him the answers to questions he asked of them. At first, he was taken aback by the response he had received from Francis. He quickly relaxed his stance after reading the letters written on behalf of Francis by President Davis and Secretary Memminger. Finished reading the letters, Hodges handed them back to the young captain now standing on the side of the road. After doing so, he dismounted from his horse and stood next to him.

"Two fine letters of introduction, captain. I now understand and respect your position. Is there anything I can do to assist you during your stay here in Charleston, for whatever reason that might be?"

Francis knew he had found the help he needed. "Sir, my men and I need a few good hot meals, some much needed sleep, and we need a building, perhaps a warehouse, one big enough to store our four wagons and horses in while we're here. It has to be a building big enough to house both the wagons and my men while we're here as I cannot afford to separate my men from the wagons. We also need some grain or feed for our horses. Can you help us with any of those needs?"

"Captain, not too far from where we are standing, around the corner on King Street in fact, I have a warehouse where we have stored several of our various makes of damaged cannons. We had hoped to ship them down to Savannah so they could be repaired and then put back into service, but with the Union naval blockade being as effective as it is, I doubt that will happen anytime soon. There is plenty of room still left in the warehouse for both your wagons and your men. Behind the warehouse is a small stable and corral we have used in the past. We have not used them for some time now as we have moved the horses closer to our fortifications down by the harbor. The stable and corral should suit your needs during your stay. I will have one of my men unlock the warehouse later this afternoon for you and then it is yours to use during the balance of your stay here in Charleston. I will also have my cooks deliver a hot meal to you and your men tonight around 7 pm. Sometime today my men will leave some feed in a corner of the warehouse for your horses. One of my sergeants will stop in on you each morning to see to your needs. Feel free to tell him what meals and other needs you have. If you have been sent here by President Davis, then I aim to see you are well taken care of. Shall I post a guard around the warehouse for you?"

"Colonel, you are most kind. Please know I shall eagerly mention your name and the assistance you have lent us to President Davis, Mr. Memminger, and to General Lee when I report back to them after my assignment. The details you have mentioned are excellent. My men and I are most appreciative. We shall not need a guard posted for us as I would rather not draw any attention to our presence at this time. Nor do I care to be an additional burden upon you and your men. We have had a long and difficult journey since we started out; we simply need food and rest before we start out again. Sir, I am in debt to you for your kindness. It is my hope to someday repay the kindness you have shown to us."

Francis saluted Hodges and then shook his hand. After they shook hands, Hodges directed him to where the warehouse was located, promising Francis he would try to stop and check in on him in the next day or two. "Captain, I pray for good luck for you and your men. My men are at your disposal if they can be of any help to you. All you have to do is to tell them what you need. I will tell them today to assist you with any needs you have." Knowing he had done what he could to help Francis, Hodges rode off to make his inspections of the shore batteries around Charleston's harbor.

Francis mounted his horse, turned him in the direction Hodges had pointed and slowly rode to where the warehouse stood. A warehouse he would happily call home for the next few days. He could not help thinking how nice it was going to be to finally sleep indoors again. They would have a few nights of sleep where they did not have to worry about being attacked by Union troops as they slept.

After briefing inspecting the exterior of the warehouse, Francis rode back through the city, stopping at a small tavern he found along the way. Silently he thanked Hodges for his support as he ate a small meal of oysters and rice at the tavern on Tradd Street. He briefly gave thought to how he would move the gold and silver further south from Charleston, but the taste of his meal, coupled with the additional thought of his men and he being safe and well fed for a few days, quickly drove the first thought out of his mind. Now he focused on simply enjoying a quiet meal.

By late afternoon, Francis arrived back to where his men had been waiting for him. As he was elated to see nothing had happened to them while he was gone, his men were overjoyed at the news he brought them. Like all soldiers, his men did not ask for much, but the prospect of a few good meals and sleeping with a roof over their heads for the next couple of days made their spirits soar. As is often the case, with good news also comes bad news.

"We have a place to hide the wagons and to get some much needed rest. We also will have some hot meals delivered to us over the next couple of days. I'm hopeful some food for our horses will be delivered as well. I have seen the warehouse where we'll be staying and it will more than suit our needs. The bad news is I'm not confident we'll be able to move further south by train, and the prospect of moving by boat is likely not possible either. The Union naval blockade is keeping our ships in the harbor and no ship's captain will now dare try to run it. I certainly cannot risk running the blockade with the gold and silver as it is far too important to our cause than to risk losing it at sea. We may be forced to continue to move it by wagons after we rest for a few days. For now, we will just rest. I will continue to look for another means to move the money during that time."

While the news was a disappointment to his men as they had hoped for a better way to finish their mission than being forced to again move with the gold and silver over land, for now they focused on the positive news Francis brought them. News of a few good hot meals, a safe place to sleep, and perhaps after that maybe even a bath, made the bad news bearable. They had endured many hardships over the past few weeks, especially losing some of their friends. They each had also lost weight, slept too little, and travelled in all kinds of weather, but mostly they all had been affected in some way by the loss of a friend along the way. They would deal with the adversity the future would present to them, but for right now, on this unusually hot late October afternoon, they just wanted to eat and sleep. Like Francis would do, they also would deal with their problems when they were confronted by them.

It was early evening when they entered the city. As they did, most of the city's residents had already eaten their suppers and finished up their chores for the day. The streets were quiet and free of most people, even though the heat of the afternoon had dissipated. The breeze off the harbor made it a pleasant evening to be outside. Francis had wanted to enter the city under the cover of darkness so as not to draw any attention to his men and their wagons, but he could not refuse Colonel Hodges' offer of a hot meal for his men. Reluctantly he entered the city earlier than he had wanted, but was soon pleased to see the streets were strangely deserted so early in the evening.

Still ever cautious, Francis had his men enter the city through the Goose Creek section of town, not far from where the Washington Race Course stood off of Grove Street; away from the busier section of the city. Constantly reminding them to move as quietly as they could, they slowly moved down the King Street road; his men doing their best to keep the horses quiet. Moving south, parallel to the South Carolina Railroad lines, they made a right turn onto Warren Street, then pushed southwest through the Radcliffe Borough of the city, then onto Wentworth Street, and then back onto the King Street road. Francis knew they could have made their way directly to the warehouse once they were on the King Street road, but he chose to take the streets he had seen earlier in the day. As they moved along, he purposely steered them away from some of the busier intersections so prying eyes did not see them as they moved towards the warehouse. He also did so to make sure no one was following them, pausing several times where streets intersected to make sure no one was.

Once back on the King Street road they proceeded to South Battery Road, a road running close to where the Ashley and Cooper Rivers merge with Charleston Harbor. Off to their east sat Castle Pinckney, one of the first Union pieces of property the Confederacy seized near the start of the war. Close by in the harbor sat Fort Sumter. Francis had the men halt briefly so he could point out the two locations to them. As his men took a few minutes to look at where the war had started, he also found himself briefly looking out at the fort. Then he turned and focused his attention on his men as they looked out at the fort. He thought about why he had stopped there on the street. "They deserve to see where this has all started. They have sacrificed so much for our cause. Those who have died along the way have sacrificed even more. These men who are here with me can at least now tell their families they saw where the war started for all of us."

Slowly they moved along King Street, soon pulling up in front of the warehouse Colonel Hodges had unlocked for them. They had just slid open the two large wooden doors to the warehouse when a sergeant assigned to one of Hodges' artillery units arrived driving a buckboard wagon. Still seated, the sergeant saluted as Francis walked up to the wagon.

"Sir, I assume you are Captain Francis?" Francis could tell from the young sergeant's question that he was somewhat nervous as he spoke to him

"Yes, sergeant, I am Captain Francis."

"I see y'all found the place OK. Hope the warehouse suits your needs for the time y'all are here. I had my men drop off some grain and hay earlier for your horses. Them broken cannons inside, we dun lined them up against one of the walls so y'all would have plenty of room to store them wagons y'all got with ya. You can lock the doors from the inside if y'all need to, but ain't no one gonna bother y'all down here. I got your hot grub here in the wagon. Colonel Hodges done arranged a right fine spread for y'all. I'll bring the wagon inside and your men can unload it there."

"Thank you, sergeant! Please extend our thanks to Colonel Hodges. Also, please tell him we would appreciate the same courtesy tomorrow evening as well. I expect we will be here for at least three days. We appreciate your efforts as well."

"Happy to oblige, captain. I'll have one of my boys bring y'all some biscuits and hot coffee in the morning as well."

By now Francis' men had opened the back doors of the large warehouse, one which had stored cotton and tobacco prior to the war. They were routinely stored there before being shipped to Europe and Mexico. Soon fresh air off the harbor circulated throughout the building, clearing the stale and musty air from inside the warehouse. Standing off to the side, the men closely eyed the food in the wagon as it was driven into the warehouse to be unloaded. Knowing Francis would not let them eat until they had moved the wagons safely inside, and had taken care of the horses, the men now worked quickly to accomplish those tasks.

"Sergeant, I need one more favor from you." Francis stated as the food was being unloaded from the wagon. "Can you leave me your wagon? You can take the horses with you, but I may have the need for a smaller wagon while we're in town for a few days."

"Sir, Colonel Hodges told me personal like to make sure y'all got what ya need while y'all are with us. So if y'all need this here wagon, then I guess it's yours to use. No need to return it, just leave it here in the warehouse and I'll come back to fetch it when you're gone."

As Francis shook hands with the sergeant, the men turned the horses out into the small corral behind the warehouse. Soon they were fed and watered; the men getting fresh water for the horses and for themselves from a hand-cranked water pump they found inside the warehouse. With those tasks finally completed, they knew it was their time to eat.

Moving the food closer to the opened wooden doors in the rear of the warehouse to both enjoy the fresh air and to use the remaining light to eat under, they gorged themselves on the food Hodges had sent over for them. They ate far too much, and far too fast, but after weeks of limited food they each surrendered to their cravings for fresh food.

Shortly after they had eaten, they again checked on the horses. Seeing the horses were well taken care of, they secured the doors to the warehouse and quickly fell fast asleep. They slept soundly and together for the first time in several weeks as no one had to ride guard duty during the night. They were now inside a secure warehouse and inside a fairly secure Confederate city. With their bellies full and after a good night's sleep they would almost feel like new men the next morning.

23

A Cemetery's Treasures.

*"...we cannot dedicate, we cannot consecrate, we cannot hallow this ground.
The brave men, living and dead, who struggled here, have consecrated it, ..."
President Abraham Lincoln's Gettysburg Address, 19 November 1863*

The white plastic pails holding the gold and silver coins had been hidden under a folding table draped with a white drop cloth in Paul's garage. Next to the table sat Paul, Chick, and Bobby Ray, and several empty cans of Coors Light. On the table was a bottle of Jack Daniels which Bobby Ray and Chick had put a good dent in after arriving back at Paul's home from North Carolina. Tired from their two days up in North Carolina, they had just looked forward to sitting in the garage and relaxing over a couple of drinks. The drinks had become more than a couple as they celebrated their successful find at Duke's hog farm. They toasted each other and everything else as they talked about what they had found.

Paul had not called Donna to tell her what they found as he wanted to surprise her in person. Now it was almost time to do just that. It was almost six pm when she arrived home. With Chick and Pete's vehicles in the driveway, as well as Paul's two vehicles, Donna was forced to park at the end of the driveway. After carrying a few of her belongings into the house, she walked into the impromptu celebration being held in her garage. As she did, she misread seeing them drinking as a sign of their bad luck over the past couple of days. Her first comment was the one they had each hoped for.

"Drowning your sorrows I see. Guess you adventure seekers didn't find what you had hoped to find. Hey, it was your first time looking, maybe you'll do better next time. Give me a minute to change my clothes. I'll come out and drown your sorrows with you."

"Hey, hon, do me a favor before you go inside." Paul asked while doing his best to keep a straight face. "Bobby Ray put a six pack under the table in a white bucket. I'm too sore from all the digging to reach for it. Will you grab it for us? The cooler here is just about empty."

Donna gave Paul the *Are your legs broken* look as he was sitting closer to the table than where she stood, but being the good hostess she walked over to get the beer for him. Still staring at Paul, she reached under the table feeling for the bucket of beer. Touching the bucket, she instinctively reached for its handle before trying to pull it out from under the table. "Gees, what do you have in this thing, rocks?" She could not budge it.

"Here, honey, let me help you."

Almost like they had rehearsed it, Chick quickly grabbed the half full bottle of Jack Daniels off the table so it didn't spill as Paul stood up and lifted the small folding table up and out of the way. As he did, Donna's eyes fell on the five full buckets of gold and silver coins the table had hid from her view.

"I, I thought you said ...." Unable to finish her thought, Donna simply stared at the buckets of coins in front of her.

"Donna, we didn't say a thing. You assumed we hadn't found anything because we had put on our gloomy faces to trick you. From how it played out it looks like our little devious plan worked! We thought we'd surprise you with what we found. From the look on your face, I'm guessing we did that. So, what do you think?"

Donna continued to stare at the coins as Bobby Ray and Chick, fueled by fatigue, beer, and Jack Daniels, laughed uncontrollably like two school boys who had played a dirty trick on a friend. Pete, who had not drank nearly as much as Chick and Bobby Ray, sat somewhat amused by what he watched unfold in the garage.

Regaining her composure, Donna turned her attention first to Bobby Ray who had been laughing the loudest at the joke they had played on her. "Bobby Ray, you son of a bitch! You think giving me a heart attack is funny? Just you wait. And Chick, you went along with these two fools on this? You're never going to be my friend! And you, telling me a lie to make me feel sorry for you and then pulling this stunt on me, well ..." She stopped herself in mid-sentence as a more important thought entered her mind. "Whose money is this anyways? Is it ours?" The anger Donna feigned at each of them only made them laugh louder than they had been, but when she asked them whose money it was her question then made each of them laugh even louder. Her kneeling down to examine the coins made them completely lose it. Their laughter was uncontrollable for several moments.

Donna ignored their laughs and looked at coins by the handful, closely examining the types of gold and silver coins she now held. The dates minted on the coins were ones she had never come across in her banking career. Most of the types of coins she was looking at were ones she had also never seen before. "If only these coins could talk, telling us where they had been and who had owned them. Wouldn't that be amazing?"

The comment Donna blurted out now caused the others to quiet down and reflect on what she had just said. They each seemed to realize if the people who had handled the coins from the time of the Civil War could talk to them or if just Captain Francis and his men could talk to them about what life was like during that period of time, perhaps they all would have a better appreciation for what life blesses us with these days.

"OK guys, I liked you better when you were laughing and drinking. I didn't mean to throw a damper on the party with my comment. So what are the plans for all of these coins?"

Paul had been smiling as he watched Donna examine the coins and now he put his beer down on the table. Reaching behind his chair, he showed her the last bucket of coins. It contained the few handfuls the other buckets could not hold. "Well, to start with, after you feed us with one of your famous home cooked meals, we're going to bag these coins up and get them ready to take to the bank tomorrow. Chick is going to spend the night in one of the guest rooms and tomorrow morning we'll get the coins to the bank. Don't be mad, but I didn't want to get you mixed up in any of this by drawing attention to you when your husband went into your bank asking for seven safety deposit boxes, so I called Kristy Thomas and asked her if they had any large boxes available. When I told her I needed seven of them, she asked me if I had just robbed a bank. She doesn't know why we need them, but she saved us seven of them. We just hope we can get all of these coins in them."

Donna had gotten up to get a glass of wine and now sat down on a chair Pete had gotten for her. Taking a sip, she placed her drink down next to the buckets of coins so she could look at them while they all talked. After a couple of moments, she said, "I cannot imagine what these coins are worth in today's market. My goodness, it has to be millions!"

After Donna had been told about the discovery of the coins and about all of the other details regarding the discovery of the Confederate soldiers' remains, a story which lasted until most of the beer was gone; she served her guests one of her special meals in the garage. The pizza which was delivered from Pizza Hut never tasted as good as it did when it was eaten with several pails of gold and silver coins sitting next to them.

* * * * * *

The following morning, after the coins had been safely stored away in the seven safety deposit boxes of the Murrells Inlet National Savings and Loan, Paul went home and began the hunt for the next portion of the missing Confederate treasury. He started by reading and rereading the letter Captain Francis had written to President Davis. He was confident this letter contained the clues he was looking for, clues which would hopefully direct him to the rest of the missing money. But despite knowing the remainder of the missing money had apparently been hidden in two separate locations in South Carolina, some with the children of the late Governor Allston, Paul struggled in his attempts of deciphering the letter's hidden clues. Despite his lack of any immediate success, he read and reread each line of the letter over and over again, hoping to pull the clues he desperately needed from the words Francis had written.

After reading the letter several times, Paul thought a Google search of Governor Allston might be a means of unlocking some vague clue hidden within the Francis letter. Easily finding Allston's name when he Googled it, he learned Allston had served as South Carolina's governor during the years of 1854 to 1858.

From his search for information, both on his computer and from a trip he made later in the day to the Socastee library, Paul found an additional wealth of information on Governor Allston. It was information beyond what he already knew about the governor. Besides being governor, he also learned Allston had been a well-respected businessman, both prior to and after the Civil War. Allston had also served in both the South Carolina Senate and the House of Representatives. Paul also learned Allston had been a West Point graduate, serving as a colonel in the South Carolina militia for a period of time.

Paul's research also showed Allston, who had been born in 1801, had fathered nine children before he died in 1864. He had been buried in Prince George's Courtyard in Georgetown, South Carolina. The information regarding Allston helped him learn about his background, but his search went cold regarding the whereabouts of Allston's children. Sitting at a table in the library, he could feel his frustration rising. "But which of his children had the gold and silver been left with? And what happened to these children? What did Francis mean when he wrote *'they are resting comfortably with the money'*? Why can't I figure this out?"

After returning some of the books he had been reading to the library cart so they could be placed back on the shelves, Paul again focused his attention on the part of the letter regarding Allston's children. Despite his short time living in South Carolina, he had recognized the Allston name when he first read the letter, realizing the name must have belonged to a prominent family from years gone by.

Over the course of the next several days, sometimes with Donna accompanying him, Paul made visits to the greater Georgetown area, including a visit to the gravesite of Governor Allston. He hoped those visits might lead him to clues regarding the whereabouts of the governor's children. He also made a visit to the Allston family estate which was now open to the public to visit. They also made visits to the historical societies in several adjoining communities around Georgetown. During these visits he continued to learn more on Allston's life, but learned little else regarding the governor's children. Despite his efforts, he came away without the one clue he needed to get him started. Paul did not know what the clue was he needed, but he believed it would only take one to make the other clues become obvious. He knew breaking those clues would lead him to at least some of the missing Confederate treasury.

When his search had finally frustrated him enough after several days, Paul knew he needed a break from his hunt. After sleeping late on Sunday morning, Donna and Paul enjoyed a leisurely brunch at an *Eggs Over Easy* restaurant in Murrells Inlet. They had eaten breakfast at this local chain of restaurants on several occasions. It was a nice way to spend a lazy morning. After brunch they stopped to pick up the morning paper, a few groceries, and then headed home, planning on spending a casual day doing nothing.

When they returned home, Paul noticed the light was flashing on their answering machine. "Hey, y'all, it's Sara, your favorite realtor. Stephen and I are going out on the boat this afternoon. Want to join us for some beers and fun? Call me on my cell if you want to join us. I'm headed out to pick up some adult beverages and I want to make sure I get enough. Call me back. See ya!"

Donna had walked into the kitchen as the message played. "Paul, you need to have some fun and I need a day in the sun, so let's go! We can relax, have some beers, and just enjoy the day with them. You game?"

"Sounds good to me! You call Sara and tell her we're in. I'll go pack the cooler. Find out where and when we're meeting them, and we're out of here!"

Donna quickly called Sara and made arrangements to meet at the Reserve Marina, in Pawleys Island, at 2 pm. "When you get to the security gate just tell the guard you're meeting us at the public boat launch. They know we have our boat stored there. We're thinking of heading down river to Georgetown for a late lunch. That work for y'all?"

"Sara, that works great for us. See you guys in a bit!"

The day was turning out just to be what Paul had needed as it gave him a break from the hunt for the missing Confederate treasury. It was a hunt that was starting to consume all of his energies.

With Sara and Stephen, Paul and Donna enjoyed a great day out on the river. After driving down to Georgetown on their boat, they enjoyed a late lunch at *El Dorado*, an Italian restaurant on Front Street. They had eaten there twice before and it had become their favorite restaurant since moving south. The meal they enjoyed, as well as the company of two of their newest friends, turned the day into one they thoroughly enjoyed. It never took much for Paul and Donna to enjoy themselves and this day was proving to be one of the most enjoyable ones they had since moving to South Carolina.

Early that afternoon, Paul had made a comment to all of them about needing a day to clear his head of several thoughts. Sara and Stephen had interpreted his comment as meaning he did not want to talk about his recent discovery of the soldier. They both had been great about not bringing the subject up, except for one question Sara had asked him. For the rest of the day they talked about everything but Paul's discovery. It was just what he had needed, a day of mental relaxation. Now as they made their way back up the Waccamaw River, Paul closed his eyes and allowed the sun to warm his face. As he relaxed during the boat ride, he silently thanked Sara and Stephen for not pestering him for any details regarding his discovery. "Good friends realize when certain subjects are not to be broached. I appreciate them not bombarding me with questions about the soldier. I owe them for that."

As they arrived back at the marina, Stephen deftly maneuvered his boat into the small public boat launch area, easily steering around a large pontoon boat leaving the marina with a group of several couples. As he pulled alongside one of the wooden docks, Paul jumped onto the dock and grabbed the boat's bow line to keep the boat from banging into the dock. As he did, Stephen cut the engine to the boat. Holding the boat close to the dock, Donna began unloading the coolers and towels they had all brought with them for the day. As she did, Sara walked to the parking lot to get her Jeep and the boat's trailer so the boat could be towed out of the water. Stephen had made arrangements for the boat to be serviced the following day and then placed back inside the marina's large boat house for safe keeping.

After helping Stephen fasten the boat to the trailer, Paul looked down the dock to check on Donna. By now she had gathered up their belongings and was walking to where he was waiting for her. As she did, Paul's eyes casually scanned the grounds of the marina as this was only the second time he had been there. As he looked around, his eyes focused on two large black wrought iron gates and their accompanying brick walls. They appeared to form a large rectangle off to the far right side of the marina. Somehow he had not seen this area adjacent to the marina's property before now. Looking at where the brick walls sat, he saw they were partially shielded from view by several large moss covered pine trees, as well as by a few large Southern Live Oaks. Wondering why he had not seen the brick walls before now, he quickly figured the large trees had likely blocked his view in the past. While the brick walls were a distance away from where he stood, Paul could still easily see through the large wrought iron gates. He saw what appeared to be several large stones that had been erected within this small plot of land.

As Sara returned from parking her Jeep, she started to help Donna carry all of their gear back to the top of the boat ramp. Curious about what he was looking at, Paul hollered to his friend.

"Hey, Sara, what's that I'm looking at over there? Are they monuments of some kind or what?"

Turning around to see what Paul was pointing at, she stopped and answered him before making her way to her Jeep. "I believe that's some old family cemetery, but I'm not sure. Don't know, never really paid any attention to it. What's the interest in that anyhow?"

"No reason, just my morbid curiosity I guess. Hey, Donna and I are going to take a look at whatever that is before we leave. Thanks for the great afternoon! Next time we'll take my boat." Saying their goodbyes to Sara and Stephen, they promised each other they would get together for dinner soon. Collecting their belongings, they gave a quick wave to Sara and Stephen as they drove out the parking lot. After putting their cooler and towels in the back of his truck, Paul dragged a protesting Donna over to look at the area which had been fenced in by the brick walls and the black wrought iron gates.

As they got closer to the brick walls, Paul could tell it was a small cemetery. Moving closer, he could also see the two black wrought iron gates were locked by a thick steel chain and a large brass lock. Standing by the wrought iron gates, he could see several soft sandstone headstones, some of which dated back to around the time of the Revolutionary War. Even from where he stood, Paul could see that some of the wording on the headstones had been partially erased by time. While it was difficult to read what was engraved in several of the headstones, he managed to make out the names on a couple of them. Besides the several weather-beaten headstones, he also saw a few small burial vaults that had been built above ground. They appeared to have been made of the same red brick and mortar used to construct the walls of the cemetery. As the headstones were, the burial vaults had also been worn by time as well. Several of the bricks had begun to crumble from their long exposure to the elements.

As he stood by the locked entrance, Paul had somehow not noticed the small sign displayed on the cemetery's brick wall. It was mounted to the left of the two gates. Stepping back to inspect the exterior walls of the cemetery, he finally noticed the sign. It caught him completely off guard.

The sign was the one clue Paul had been looking for. Now he found it by sheer luck. He had almost missed it, even though it had been hanging there for him to see. As he started to read the sign, he had no idea of what it would soon lead him to regarding his search for the rest of the missing Confederate treasury. Slowly he read the sign out loud as a somewhat tired and obviously bored Donna stood near the cemetery gate. *"Turkey Hill Plantation, Allston Family Cemetery, 1780 – 1847."* Reading the first part of the sign caused him to momentarily stop from reading the rest of it. Silently now, he quickly reread what he had just read out loud.

"Donna, did you hear what I just said? The sign says this is the Allston family cemetery!" Paul excitedly glanced back and forth between his tired wife and the sign. Then he quickly read the rest of the sign which greeted visitors to this old family cemetery and to its place in American history. The sign told of the Allston family receiving Land Deeds from King George of England prior to the American Revolution. It also told those who read it who was buried in the cemetery. As he came to the end of what he was reading, the sign ended with the clue he had been looking for. *"Among those family members buried here are children of Governor R.F.W. Allston."* Paul could not help reacting to what he just read. "What!" His loud and unexpected outburst startled Donna. It also caused others who were sitting on the marina's nearby dock to turn and look at him. In a matter of moments their attention returned to what they had been doing and they ignored Paul as he continued to stare at the sign in front of him.

Standing in silence, Paul stared at what he had just read. "Have I just found the children of Governor Allston who Francis referred to in his letter? But what about the gold and silver, what did they do with it?"

"You OK, Paul? It looks like you just saw a ghost in there." Donna was not sure what had startled her husband.

"Maybe I did, maybe I did. Just give me a minute. Just be quiet for a minute, please."

Silent as he walked around the perimeter of the small cemetery, Paul strained to recall exactly what Francis had written in his letter about leaving some of the gold and silver with the children of Governor Allston. His brain could not seem to focus on one single point as it repeatedly bounced back and forth between the contents of the letter, to the discovery he made of the soldier's remains, and to the sign he just read. "Why can't I concentrate?" He quietly asked himself this as he tried recalling the words Francis had used in his letter.

As she stood nearby, Donna could sense Paul was struggling with something, but she remained quiet. She now allowed him time to work out whatever it was he was trying to figure out without disturbing him. She had learned to recognize when he needed his own time and now she could tell this was one of those times.

It took a few minutes, but then the fog which had clouded Paul's brain lifted and he remembered exactly what the words were Francis had used in his letter. *'Those assets were secured within their compound for safe protection. They rest comfortably NW with the money.'* Remembering what he had recently read so many times in the letter over the course of the past week, he quickly walked past Donna, walking back to the locked black gates of the cemetery. Again he stared at the grave markers. The sign he had just read identified the children's grave stones as being the smallest ones present in the cemetery. Now his eyes quickly located them. Softly he muttered his thought out loud. "I wonder which grave stone is marked with the letters NW as his letter makes reference to?"

"Paul, I'm sorry, I didn't hear what you said."

Excited by what he had just learned, and by the connection his new find had with the Francis letter, Paul turned and started to run back to his truck. "Donna, let's go!" By now he knew the importance of what he had just found.

Not yet figuring out what had caused her husband to get so excited, Donna struggled to catch up to him as he jogged towards his pickup truck in the marina's parking lot. Making his way towards his truck, Paul's mind continued to put the connections together. Reaching the truck before Donna, his mind continued to race, thinking of both the descriptions laid out in the Francis letter and what he had just read from the sign on the cemetery wall. "The family gravesite was the *'compound'* the letter referred to and the lines in his letter about *'the children resting comfortably with the money'* meant the children had already been dead and buried. Francis had buried the money near one of their graves, the grave marked with the letters NW. Now it makes sense! The Allston cemetery is also on the way to Charleston from North Carolina where Francis was last seen. This has to be the spot where he has left some of the money." As a somewhat winded Donna finally caught up to him at his truck, Paul tossed her the keys so she could drive them home. As she did, he began to explain the clues he had just put together.

"Oh, my goodness! You think he buried some of the money there thinking no one would look for it in a cemetery?"

"Not sure, perhaps he just stumbled on the cemetery and he needed a spot to hide some of the money. I doubt we'll ever know that answer."

"Very weird, but a great place to hide something if someone wanted to." Then it came to her; almost driving off the side of Willbrook Boulevard as she turned to look at her husband. "Wait, you aren't going to dig in a cemetery are you?" When Paul did not answer her, she quickly knew the answer to her question. "You are, aren't you?"

Soon after they arrived home, Paul was burning the phone lines to Chick and Bobby Ray, trying to get them to meet him at the diner in the morning. They asked him why, but he refused to tell them. He just told them he had solved one of the clues he had discovered in one of the letters. He told them by the time they met the next morning he hoped to have all of the answers he needed. Before hanging up the phone with each of them, Paul promised he would fill them in with the rest of the details over breakfast. "Chick, get in touch with Jayne, and tell Pete to bring one of his small video cameras. I don't want him attracting too much attention when I show you what I think I've found."

While Chick told Paul he and the others would meet him at the diner, Bobby Ray told him he would have to catch up with them later in the day as he had an arrest warrant to serve early the next morning. "Bobby Ray, call me on my cell when you're done and I'll tell you where we are so you can meet us."

* * * * * *

Paul arrived at the Waccamaw Diner early the next morning. Entering the diner, Betty could not resist the opportunity to needle him again. "Here he comes, the world famous finder of dead bodies! We haven't seen you here for days, just where have y'all been?" Expecting some smart comment from her as he walked through the door, he simply gave her a smile and a brief wave as he made his way to his favorite booth in the back of the diner.

"Betty, I'll take some coffee please. That's of course when you can find time to do some work around here!" His comment drew a couple of quick laughs from those who were seated at the nearby lunch counter.

As Betty brought over his coffee, Paul looked around the diner and was relieved to see neither Chubby, nor Swamp, were in the diner. "Good," he thought, "two less people I have to deal with this morning."

"So where y'all been? I haven't seen you for some time now. Y'all doing OK?" Betty asked Paul more than he wanted to share with her, but he knew she was just making conversation with him. He had far too much going on his mind to have much of a conversation with her.

"Just been up in North Carolina visiting old friends. All is good with the world though, thanks for asking." Paul smiled at his comment about visiting old friends. He wished the three Confederate soldiers had been friends of his.

"That's good. You still plan on telling me about your big discovery someday?"

"Told you I would. I keep my promises, but I don't have time to talk about it today. Just so you know, some of my friends are going to be joining me here in a few minutes."

Betty smiled at what Paul told her. Too many men in her life had not kept their promises to her, but for some reason she trusted he would. "Sounds good. Now what can I get ya for breakfast, some grits maybe?" She knew he detested the taste of grits, but it made her laugh each time she asked him if he wanted them.

Somewhat irritated by her grits joke, Paul gave her a sarcastic response back. "No thanks! I'll pass on them *forever*, but thanks for asking *again*. I'll just have some blueberry pancakes. You can also bring me a side of bacon and a small OJ as well."

"Coming up!"

Engrossed with his breakfast and with the day's *USA Today*, he did not notice the others until they began to sit down in the booth with him. "Too hungry to wait for us?" Jayne looked a bit miffed as she sat down next to him.

Paul had wanted to get his meal out of the way so he could tell them about the clues he deciphered. "I could have waited, but once I started telling you about what I have uncovered, I did not want to be chewing and talking at the same time. What I have to tell you is going to be kind of freaky, so I hope you both are up for it."

"In that case, thanks for eating first." Jayne said as she sipped her coffee.

After Betty refilled Paul's coffee cup, she took the other breakfast orders. After she left to place their orders, Paul told them what he had uncovered the previous day.

After hearing what Paul had to say, Chick was the first one to speak. "But if he had nine children and only a couple of them are buried there, what makes you think the gold and silver is with them?"

"I don't know, but what I do know is they were already dead and buried by the time Francis came through the area. We don't know, at least not yet we don't, where the other children are buried. But like I've told you, the letter makes reference to Governor Allston's children sleeping with the money in the compound. There's a pretty good chance I've found the right spot. I'm just disappointed that it took me this long to figure it out. I mean the darn cemetery is right there in plain view and it has the Allston name all over it. It was begging to be found. I guess when I was looking for answers to the questions I had, I just kept asking the wrong questions before I accidently found what I was looking for. I guess dumb luck is just as good as good luck is."

Jayne had almost finished her breakfast as Paul answered Chick's question about the Allston children. "Paul, you've done a remarkable job so far. I would not worry about fretting away a couple of weeks over this. Others have spent years on this and have found nothing."

Always the quietest one of the group, Pete was sitting across from Paul in the booth. Paul was grossed out as he watched him eat his breakfast of yellow grits, hash, and scrambled eggs. As he ate, Pete paused to ask the obvious question. "So what's the plan?"

Paul had spent part of the previous night working on a plan for visiting the cemetery. He was ready with his plan when the question was asked. "Here is my idea, tell me what you think. This morning we'll drive over to the cemetery and I'll show you the spot where I think the money has been buried. I've got to tell you, this cemetery was well respected when someone developed the area around it. The adjacent property now includes a small marina, a public boat launch, and an upscale neighborhood. Both Governor Allston and Francis would be proud of how the cemetery has been maintained. It's truly a beautiful setting." Then he told them the rest of his plan. Soon they were driving to the cemetery.

As they drove up to the security booth outside the Reserve Marina, Jayne, a natural worrier in life, started worrying their reason for being at the cemetery was going to be discovered by the elderly part-time security guard manning the booth. As Chick put the driver's window down in his van, Paul leaned across the front seat. He saw the security guard was wearing the typical white short sleeve shirt with embroidered arm patches which read *Security Officer*. The white shirt, which had coffee stains across the left breast pocket, had a name badge on it. The badge identified the guard's first name as Jerry.

"Good day, sir! How can I help you?"

"Hey, Jerry, a good morning to you also! My friends and I are just headed down to the marina for a short time."

Exiting the booth, Jerry wrote down Chick's license plate number and the time they arrived at the security booth on the daily *Visitor's Log* attached to his clipboard. Then he handed Chick a parking pass for his vehicle. "Good day for it, enjoy yourselves!"

Taking the opportunity to needle Jayne, Paul turned around from where he was sitting in the right front seat to look at her. "You can relax now. Jerry hasn't broken our secret plans to excavate the cemetery." His sarcastic comment drew smirks from both Chick and Pete, and even Jayne had to laugh at her own nervousness.

Chick soon found a parking spot under a couple of large pine trees off in the left front corner of the marina's parking lot. Pete had asked him to try and park in the shade so his camera equipment could stay somewhat cool while it remained in the van. It was already a warm morning by the time they arrived at the marina.

"Pete, I'll take you guys for a walk down to where the cemetery is. This way you can see which camera you might want to use. Then you can casually walk back to the van and grab whatever you need. Jayne's bringing her camera with her so we'll just need one of your video cameras to capture what the cemetery looks like. I figure it might attract a little less attention if we make it look like we're just taking a walk at first."

The walk to the cemetery took them across the marina's parking lot, across the public boat launch area, and then down a wooden walkway. The walkway, which ran along the right side of the small marina, also continued alongside the small inlet off the river. It continued out as far as the Waccamaw River. It was an ideal spot to fish from and to watch the passing traffic on the river. The walkway also had a separate section which led up towards the small cemetery. As they walked, they had a chance to look at several good size boats tied up along the docks. To those boat owners and their guests who were enjoying themselves on this sunny morning, Paul and his friends looked like typical visitors to the marina. No one could have suspected why they were there.

As they made their way along the walkway, Paul stopped their walk on a couple of occasions to make it look like they were admiring the boats that were present. He intentionally did so as he wanted the others to see where the cemetery was located off to the right of the marina's property. He wanted them to put the cemetery in perspective from a distance, along with the rest of the marina's property, for their visit back there later that night. It was going to be almost pitch-dark when they came back.

"Paul, you were right, this is a beautiful setting. I can only hope I'm so lucky to have such a beautiful resting place when it's my time."

"You are very weird sometimes! Even a goofball on occasion, do you know that? We're here to scope out a spot where the gold and silver is likely buried and you're thinking about planning your own funeral!" Besides the barb he directed at her, Chick also shot Jayne a puzzled look after her comment about her final resting place. Now he just shrugged his shoulders at Paul. Chick never saw the expression she gave him behind his back after he had snapped at her, but it was one which made Pete laugh.

As they got closer to the black wrought iron gates which had been chained shut on his first visit to the cemetery, Paul now noticed they were swung wide open. Inside they observed an elderly male caretaker raking the accumulated pine cones and pine needles which blanketed some of the graves. A small push mower waiting to be used sat off to the right of the gates.

"Excuse me, sir!" It took Paul three attempts to get the caretaker's attention, but he finally got it.

"This is private property. You folks cannot come in here, sorry."

"Sir, could we just talk to you for one minute?"

As the elderly caretaker walked towards them, Chick had an idea. "Paul, let me do the talking."

Chick warmly shook hands with the caretaker while introducing himself. He quickly learned the caretaker's name was Woody. "My given name is Woodrow, but most folks call me Woody. I guess Woodrow is too formal for most folks."

"Woodrow it is then! Thanks for taking the time to talk to me. I'm a history professor at the University of South Carolina and these are some of my graduate students. They are helping me with some research for a book I'm writing regarding prominent South Carolina folks. One of those folks we're going to be including in the book is Governor Allston; he was quite a prominent person in his day. I would be grateful if you could allow us to have ten minutes or so to look at the Allston graves that are here. I promise you we will be very respectful of those who are buried here. It would be a big help to the research we are doing if you could assist us."

"You folks know the governor ain't buried here, just his kin is. He's down in Georgetown."

"Yes, we know. But his family history is also going to have a role in my book. That's why we're here today."

"Well, I ain't supposed to let no folks in here, but seeing you are writing a book, can't see no harm in letting you look around for a few minutes. Just mind where the graves are."

"We will, thanks Woodrow!"

Jayne was quickly snapping away with both her Nikon digital camera and an older model Canon 35mm camera she occasionally still used. She took photos of every gravestone and of each burial site within the small cemetery. Once finished taking those pictures, she took interior and exterior real estate type photos showing the layout of the cemetery. She even took a picture of Woody standing next to the sign posted outside of the cemetery. Knowing the importance of the small gravestones, she took her time taking photos of the Allston children's weather-beaten gravestones. They were ones time and weather had impacted harshly. As Paul had noticed the day before, Jayne also saw some of the names and dates were now hard to read.

As she took the photos, Paul walked from gravestone to gravestone with her, carefully looking to see which one bore the initials NW. Softly he whispered into Jayne's ear so Woody, who was standing nearby, did not hear him talk to her as she finished taking the last few photos of the children's graves. "I didn't see the initials NW on any of them, did you?"

Jayne just shook her head to let Paul know she had not seen them either.

"It's not here!" Paul now questioned whether he had misinterpreted what he read the previous day from the sign hanging outside the cemetery. As they stood near the small gravestones, Chick joined them. Retrieving a copy of the Francis letter from his pocket, Paul showed them the letter for the first time. "Here, I made a copy of the letter Captain Francis wrote to President Davis. I was going to show it to you later today. Part of the letter describes the children's graves."

Chick read the letter which Paul had blown up in size when he had it copied at Office Depot. "I don't see what's missing. What are you not seeing here?"

"Look at the end of this one line. See how Francis made a reference to the letters *(NW)* there. Do you see a gravestone with a name that has the letters NW included on it? I don't. That's what is missing!"

"Yeah, you're right."

The three of them stood in silence for a couple of minutes as they each tried to solve the mystery now confronting them. Frustrated at first, Paul suddenly broke their silence. "The letters NW, you know maybe I've had a case of tunnel vision thinking they were associated with a gravestone when really they were not someone's initials after all. Maybe what he is trying to tell us with this clue is that he buried the gold and silver in the northwest corner of the cemetery. Get it? *Northwest* has the two letters in it that we're looking for."

"Sounds logical to me. Inside or out?"

"I'm thinking inside, Chick. He likely would have used the brick walls to hide behind so no one could see him when he buried the money."

By now Pete had returned to the cemetery with his video camera. As Chick and Jayne kept Woody occupied for a few extra minutes, Paul had Pete film the entire interior of the cemetery. "Make sure you get some video of the exterior also, especially around the northwest corner, just in case we're wrong about where we think he buried it."

Pete had only been filming the interior for a few minutes when Bobby Ray, who had called Paul on his cell phone just after they arrived at the cemetery, came strolling through the opened gates with a stern look on his face.

Flashing his badge as he walked towards Woody, Bobby Ray asked a question somewhat loudly. "OK, people, who's in charge here?"

Softly, Woody answered the question. "I guess I am, sir."

Despite being dressed in civilian clothes, Bobby Ray was very official looking as he had his Motorola portable radio and gun displayed on his belt. Wearing dark aviator sunglasses, he walked up to a now very nervous Woody. "Did you let these people in here? This is private property you know!" Not getting a reply to his comments, Bobby Ray sensed the elderly caretaker had not yet caught on that he was just having fun at his expense. He quickly let Woody in on the joke he was playing on him.

"Gees, I thought someone had complained. I was worried that I had just lost my job."

"No, sir, that ain't never happening. These folks here are my friends. Thanks for helping them out. They are all good people, just like you."

"You bet! You folks need a little more time? As long as the cops are here I guess no one is gonna bother us now. Take all the time y'all need." Woody said, somewhat relieved to learn Bobby Ray had just been joking with him.

"Woody, we need about another fifteen more minutes and then we'll be done. Is that OK?"

"That's fine, just fine. I'll keep talking to this here pretty young girl while you fellas finish up whatever it is you're doing. Fellas my age generally don't get to talk to pretty girls too often." From the smile she was wearing, Chick could tell Jayne appreciated Woody's compliment.

Bobby Ray then walked over to where Paul and Chick were standing near the northwest corner of the cemetery. "Standing here alone in the corner like y'all are, are you guys in time out or what?"

"Yeah, something like that." Paul laughed at the funny comment Bobby Ray made about them standing in the corner of the cemetery, but then questioned him about the joke he played on the elderly caretaker. "Why'd you have to do that for? You nearly scared the old man half to death with that act of yours!"

"He's fine, forget about it. So, what's the deal with this place?"

"Bobby Ray, I need you to help Chick draw a map of the cemetery. We don't want to attract too much attention, but can you help him get this done so we can get out of this place before someone starts asking questions. When we get back to the parking lot I'll clue you in with the rest of the details. Basically we think we've found the second of the three locations where the gold and silver has been buried. But for now get moving, please!"

Bobby Ray was somewhat stunned by the little bit of information he had been given. "Are you kidding me? Paul, my house is maybe two miles from here as the dang crow flies. You're telling me that I've lived here for over twenty years near a damn fortune in gold and silver?"

"Yep, hell of a deputy sheriff you are! Not start drawing . . . and fast!"

After finishing what needed to be done, they each thanked Woody for his help and then started back to their vehicles. As they walked, Paul told them what he wanted to do. "Tell you what, just so we don't attract any more attention than we already have, let's get out of here. We can meet down in Pawleys Island at the *Sonic Drive-In*. I need something to drink and we can talk down there without people wondering what we're up to."

* * * * * *

As she munched on her ketchup laden French fries, Jayne agreed with the conclusion Paul and Chick had earlier arrived at. "I'm with you guys that NW means the northwest corner of the cemetery. That's the back corner and it's the area where the children are buried. I think he buried the money right there. We need to go for it."

"For what my two cents are worth, I agree with what Jayne just said. Let's go for it. Couple of things though, documenting the dig on video is going to be tough as we cannot light up the place like I would like, too many people down on the boats would likely see something was going on. We'll also have to keep the noise level from digging and talking to a minimum, but you probably have already been thinking along those lines." Pete had raised several good points for them to consider. They all knew they would somehow have to mask any noise they would make to avoid others seeing and hearing them dig so close to where the boats were moored.

Sitting on the tailgate of Paul's truck, Bobby Ray just sat there taking in the conversation as he munched away on a Sonic double cheeseburger. Finishing his burger, he offered up another point to be considered. "One more thing, we can't leave the ground all dug up like we did at Duke's place. If we do, someone is going to start asking questions and likely Old Woody would spill the beans about us all being there and poking around. We don't need that kind of attention. When we leave, we need to make it look like we were never even there."

"All good points," Chick acknowledged, "this one is going to be a little harder than the first one."

Paul listened to them talk while he was on the phone with Duke, fulfilling his promise to call him when they learned the location of the second site. "Duke is not coming down, but I could tell he appreciated the heads up on what we found. He just wants a call after we get done in the cemetery."

After quickly wolfing down a cheeseburger and draining part of his Coca-Cola, Paul told the others what his plan was. "We have to do this tonight. The forecast I saw this morning has the next two days being pretty much being all rain and we don't want to be leaving shoeprints all over the place in the soft ground. Besides, if we get in there and dig before it rains; the rain will help cover up our tracks to some degree. We'll need some setup time, but let's hope the folks staying on the boats are asleep by midnight because we're going to have shovels in the ground by 1 a.m." Paul took another long sip of his drink and then directed his next comment to Bobby Ray.

"Bobby Ray, I know you have to work in the morning, but we need you to flash your badge to the security guard at the gate so we can get into the marina at that time of night. Come up with some kind of story to make it sound good to the guard, OK?"

"OK, I'll be there. Won't be worth much at work tomorrow, but I'll be there."

* * * * * *

As planned, they all met in the Waffle House parking lot on Highway 17, in Murrells Inlet, just before midnight. After grabbing some coffee to go, and after making sure they had all turned their cell phones to the vibrate mode, they packed their gear into Chick's van and Paul's truck for the short ride to the marina.

Approaching the Reserve Plantation's Security Booth, they could see the security gate was down across the driveway entrance. Pulling up to the booth, Paul rolled down his driver's door window and waited for the security guard to great them. After waiting several moments, Paul was tempted to blow the truck's horn to get the guard's attention but quickly dismissed that thought as he did not want to attract any unnecessary attention despite the late hour of the day. Impatiently, he waited for the guard to appear. "Where the heck is this guy? In the bathroom or what?"

After waiting a few more moments, with still no sign of the guard, Bobby Ray got out of Paul's truck and walked over to the booth. As he did, he saw through the propped open door that the guard was sitting in his chair. Inside the booth a small fan was circulating the evening's hot air and a small color television had the late edition of the local news playing. In moments, the security gate went up and both vehicles quickly entered the complex.

As he got back into the truck, Paul asked Bobby Ray why the guard had not come outside to greet them. "That was quick. What did you tell him?"

"Hell of a security guard, I didn't have to tell him anything. He had the screen door to the booth propped open, the TV on, and he was fast asleep in his chair. I just held the button to the gate until y'all got past it. He never even woke up. Hell of a service that man is providing to these folks who live here! I'm gonna get a job like that when I retire."

Driving slowly down the driveway to the marina, Paul smirked at Bobby Ray's comment about getting a security job when he retired. "Think you can meet the qualifications?"

After parking their vehicles in the back section of the parking lot, they waited a few minutes before starting their walk to the cemetery. Paul wanted to see if anyone had heard them drive in. Seeing no one, he gave them the signal to start moving. The walk to the cemetery was not going to be as easy as the one they had taken earlier in the day. Now they were just not laden down with equipment needed to dig with, but Paul had them take the long way around the marina's repair barn to get to the cemetery. By doing so, he hoped they could avoid being seen by anyone down by the boats. It was a difficult walk to make in the dark, but they made it to the cemetery without being seen and without making too much noise.

As they reached the cemetery, Paul gave out the first assignment of the night. "Jayne, you're the lookout for us. Pick a spot over by the gates so you can see if anyone is up and about down by the docks. Let us know if we're making too much noise."

"Good luck!" She quickly drifted off into the shadows near the cemetery's locked entrance.

Pete and Bobby Ray were quickly up and over the fairly low rear section of the brick wall surrounding the cemetery; climbing over it close to where they were planning on digging. Chick was soon perched on top of the wall handing them down the gear that Paul handed up to him from outside the cemetery. Pete and Bobby Ray stacked the gear near the northwest corner of the cemetery.

After Paul climbed over the wall, Pete and Bobby Ray unfurled a large ten by ten foot black plastic tarp, fastening one end to the several broken bricks on top of the brick wall. After fastening plastic zip ties to the grommet holes in the tarps, they fastened two other similar sized tarps to the first tarp. Soon four two-by-fours were standing on edge with the tarps fastened to them. Paul had gotten the two-by-fours earlier in the afternoon at Home Depot and had drilled holes in the wood boards so they could easily fasten the tarps to the boards with zip ties. They now had a place to work under. The small lean-to style tent they constructed was one which allowed them to use small lights while they dug. As space was limited under the tarps, they knew they would have to take turns rotating in and out from under it. On the left side of the tent, the side closest to the cemetery's entrance, they fastened a smaller black tarp to prevent as much light from escaping from the area they would be working in.

As Pete and Bobby Ray were finishing putting the tarps around their work area, Paul and Chick fastened another black tarp to the inside of the cemetery's two wrought iron gates. Using four zip ties they quickly fastened the tarp in place as another means of hiding what they were trying to do from anyone up late on one of the nearby boats. After letting Jayne know the tarp was in place, she was able to see from the outside that it looked like the cemetery was in complete darkness. From down by the boats no one could have known a black plastic tarp was blocking their view of the inside of the cemetery.

The first pass over the northwest corner with one of the metal detectors gave no indication over the metal detector's headphones that any metallic objects were buried there. After a second pass confirmed the results, Paul told the others he was not surprised by what the metal detectors told them. "OK, so let's do some digging and we'll see if that makes any changes to the readings after we dig down a foot or so. Try to cut the sod carefully so we can put it back in place when we're done."

As Chick and Pete began digging up the sod, Paul crawled out from beneath the tarps carrying the second metal detector in his right hand. In his left hand he had the headphones that went with it. Standing up, he handed the metal detector and the headphones to Bobby Ray. "Sweep the area around the tarps and see if you get any readings. This thing is pretty much idiot proof to use so that's why I'm having you do this for us."

"Thanks for recognizing my level of competency. I appreciate that!"

Crawling back under the tarp, Paul helped to dig out some of the loose soil from the area where Chick and Pete had been digging. They dug out an area almost four feet square and almost a foot deep, placing the loose soil on another tarp that had been placed nearby. Soon finished with their digging, Chick again put the headphones on. They were being used to eliminate the possibility of someone hearing the metal detector if it pinged after registering something metallic buried in the ground. Slowly he moved the metal detector across the area they had dug out. As he did, Paul could see he was focusing on a small area on the very left side of the hole. They were barely five feet away from one of the young children's graves as they dug.

Without saying a word, Chick motioned for them to dig further to the left in that one area. Now down on his knees, Paul used a small garden shovel to dig out three more healthy shovelfuls of soil and sand from the hole. As he put the shovel into the hole for the fourth time, the shovel hit something hard. From the look he saw in Paul's face, Chick knew they had found something. He had barely placed the metal detector in the enlarged hole when he heard the loud ping in his headphones. It told him something metallic had been buried there. Pushing the headphones down around his neck, he looked at them with a smile on his face. "The metal detector is pinging like crazy, something's buried here!"

Making sure the tarps were pulled as tight to each other as possible so no light escaped, Chick shined a small flashlight down into the shallow hole as Paul scooped up some of the remaining loose soil with his hands. As he did, his left hand felt the object his shovel had just struck, it was a large rock. It took a couple more minutes of digging, but quickly they realized the rock had been placed on top of a wooden lid. It was a lid to a wooden barrel, one very similar to the kind they had found buried in North Carolina. Digging out a few more shovelfuls of soil soon enlarged the hole enough so they could clearly see both the rock and the barrel's lid. A few more cleared away enough soil so they could see the top third of the barrel. Chick and Paul grinned at each other as they shook hands. "We're turning out to be quite the treasurer hunters, aren't we?"

Crawling out from under the tarps, Paul went to find Jayne. When he found her by the two locked gates, she was standing near the outer edges of where light from a nearby overhead light met the night's darkness. The overhead light sat close to the marina's sidewalk, barely fifty feet away from where she stood. Quietly approaching her, he saw the pose she had taken was one like that of a cop trying to conduct a surveillance in the middle of the night without being seen.

Somewhat startled when she first heard it, Jayne quickly turned to see what made the noise behind her. Paul had been about fifteen feet away from her when she first heard him. "Jayne, its Paul, hope I didn't scare you too badly. We found it! I just wanted you to know what was going on. It looks like the money is in a wooden barrel, just like in North Carolina." Turning to leave without giving her a chance to say anything, he saw she already had a smile on her face. Even the faint light could not hide her distinctive smile.

Bobby Ray was finishing up with the metal detector when Paul found him. Softly he whispered the good news to him. "Bobby Ray, you can stop now. It looks like we found it where we were digging."

"That's good, but if y'all did, then what's this beeping noise I'm getting here? I've been working this here thing almost ten to twelve feet away from where y'all are."

"What? Show me!"

Bobby Ray passed the metal detector over the area where he had heard the pings. Hearing them again, he handed the headset to Paul to listen to as he passed the metal detector over the patch of ground. The pings were strong and loud, clearly something was buried in the ground by their feet. Paul quickly realized whatever was there had been buried very close to the surface.

Handing the headset back to Bobby Ray, Paul was at a loss for what they had just found. "I didn't expect this, so I don't know what you've found. There aren't any grave markers in this area of the cemetery, and I didn't see any depressions in the ground earlier today to indicate someone was buried here without the grave being marked. For now, just mark the spot with something and we'll come back to it when we get done with what we're working on right now. When you get done marking the spot, we need some large rocks, more dirt, or whatever you can find. Besides the gold and silver, we're likely taking the barrel with us as well. We need to fill the hole with something. Maybe there's an old stone wall just outside the cemetery or something like that. Let me know if you need help and I'll send someone out to help you."

Crawling silently back under the tarps, Paul let Chick and Pete in on what Bobby Ray had found. "Hey, listen to this. Bobby Ray's been playing around with the metal detector out there and it looks like he found another spot where something might be buried. Could there be two spots where the money is buried?"

Chick and Pete had both stopped to listen to what Paul told them, but without saying a word they quickly went back to work excavating the sandy soil from around the entire wooden barrel. As they did, they could see this barrel had remained in far better shape than the one they uncovered on Duke's property. Finishing with their digging, Pete unpacked his camera so they could document the discovery of the barrel while it was still in the ground. As he got ready, Paul began to crawl outside from under the tarps, ones that hid them from prying eyes. "Let me know when you're ready to take a picture and I'll let you know if the flash is something which might give us away to someone down on the dock. I'll let you know if it was that noticeable from outside."

The first picture was quickly taken; the light from the flash barely escaped the tent. Coming back inside the tarps, Paul gave Pete the green light to continue and another nine digital photos were taken to document their find. With Chick holding a flashlight, and from light given off by a small work light Paul wore on a headband, Pete used his hand held video camera to further document what they had just found.

After setting aside the rock, Paul carefully pulled and pried the wooden top off of the barrel. His small work light giving some illumination into the hole while he worked. Reaching into the barrel for the first time, his left hand grabbed the first cloth bag he saw. As he tugged at the bag, he was surprised to see it did not tear from the weight of the coins. Slowly and carefully he lifted the bag of coins out of the barrel and gently placed it inside one of the same plastic buckets they had used in North Carolina. Using both of his hands, he then lifted another bag of coins from inside the barrel with the same results. But the next two cloth bags ripped as he attempted to remove them and soon he was scooping loose coins out of the barrel with his hands.

After several minutes of work, Pete relieved Paul and soon he began scooping the loose coins into a bucket Chick held near the barrel. After almost an hour of work they had filled three of the plastic buckets with gold and silver coins. They had to pause at one point so Chick could grab another empty bucket for them to put more coins in. As he waited for the next bucket, Pete moved closer so his arms could extend further down inside the barrel.

As he did, his right hand touched something other than the loose coins he had been scooping up. "Hey, what's this?" Softly he whispered that something other than coins was hidden in the barrel. "There's something else in here, something wrapped in cloth and it's heavy!" As he grabbed the cloth bag to pull it up, the bag tore and everything inside it dropped back to the bottom of the barrel. Only one object remained tangled up in the bag. After pulling the object free of the bag, Pete wiped the accumulated sand and soil away from it. It was not until Paul moved closer, with the light from his work light now shining down on the object, that they recognized what the crudely made object actually was. "It's a gold bar, a solid gold bar," Pete softly shrieked, "and there's more of them in there!" As he moved back closer to the barrel, Chick and Paul alternated looks of disbelief between the gold bar and each other. Holding the bar for the first time, they each were at a loss for words for a few seconds.

"What have we found?" It was all Chick could muster at the moment.

Pete then alternated between removing several more handfuls of coins and six more bars; three gold and three silver. With the barrel soon emptied of most of the precious contents it had held for so long, they carefully pulled it from the soft sandy soil. Outside of one board, which fell out when they lifted it from the hole, the barrel stayed intact. With the barrel on its side and still hidden from view under the tarps, Pete used his hands to scrape out the remaining few coins. He placed them in one of the plastic buckets they had almost filled with other coins.

Briefly they took a moment to look at what they had freed from the ground. As Chick and Paul finished examining the barrel, Pete ran the metal detector over the hole. He quickly located three gold coins which had fallen out of the barrel when they lifted it from the hole. Patting him on the back, Paul complimented him on what he had done. "That was good thinking on your part, Pete. I would have hated to have left them behind."

While they had been digging up the barrel, Bobby Ray had located a small stone wall running through a wooded area on the backside of the marina's property. It took him a few trips, but with Chick's help they soon had enough large rocks to fill the void left in the ground by the removal of the barrel.

Leaving Pete alone under the tarps to fill in the hole with the rocks and soil, and to replace the sod over the hole, Chick and Paul went to investigate the spot Bobby Ray had found with his metal detector.

"Chick, we only have a couple of hours left before it starts getting light. We don't have time to set up the tarps. Let's just dig and see what we find."

"Sounds like a plan!"

As they started digging the second hole, the clear night they had been working under began to cloud over. The smell of rain was now in the air. Paul sensed the change that was occurring and he prayed it would rain, but not until they finished with everything they needed to get done.

After Bobby Ray had set a tarp on the ground, Chick and Paul cut the sod away and placed it on the tarp. Soon they quietly started digging the second hole. As they had with the soil they removed from the first hole, they also placed the sandy soil from the second hole on the tarp to minimize any signs that someone had been digging in the cemetery. Like the first hole, they again dug up several inches of soil and then ran the metal detector over the hole they were digging.

The strong ping Bobby Ray and Paul heard earlier was now loud and steady; a clear indication something metallic was buried in the ground. Before arriving at the cemetery, Paul had placed black electrical tape over the electronic screens of each metal detector. He had done this to minimize any light from the screens giving away their location to someone who might be in the area. Again they were forced to dig blindly, not knowing how deep the object was buried or what the object was.

Using a small gardener's trowel to dig with, Paul was on his hands and knees removing soil from the hole when the trowel hit a metallic object buried roughly six inches below the surface. Using his hands, he scooped several handfuls of soil from the hole until he could feel the object. Leaning into the shallow hole, he turned the small work light on that he was still wearing around his head. Peering into the hole, he prayed it would not be a coffin or something equally as morbid he would be looking at. Hesitating for a moment, he backed away from the hole. Turning off the small work light, he looked up at Chick. "What if we've found a rotted out coffin or someone's remains? I don't mind telling you this is getting very creepy!"

Regaining his courage, Paul turned his small light on as he moved back closer to the hole. After removing more soil away from the object, he saw it was made of leather. Softly he whispered to Chick and Bobby Ray a brief description of what they had found. "I don't know what it is yet, but whatever it is it has a leather strap on it and I can see it has a metal buckle as well. That's what probably set the metal detector off." Working for several more minutes, he moved more soil away from the edges of the object. Forcing his fingers into the soft sandy soil around the leather object, he yanked at it to try and free it from where it had rested for so many years. As he did, the leather object tore in half as it came free of the soil, dislodging far easier than he had expected. As he tugged to free the object from the soil, Paul had clutched part of the object in his hands and now he fell backwards; his momentum causing him to come to rest in an awkward prone position on the ground. He had expected far more resistance from the object when he tried freeing it from the soil.

Even in the partial darkness, the sight of Paul falling backwards when the object had come free was too much for both Bobby Ray and Chick not too laugh at. They did their best to stifle their laughter as their friend struggled to get back up onto his knees from where he had landed. "I'm glad you both are finding humor in this at my expense. What the heck happened here?"

Standing up while still clutching the object he had freed from the ground, Paul's work light quickly identified it to be the remnants of a small saddlebag, its pouch still strapped shut by a small leather strap. It only took a minute for Chick to realize what the object was. "That's the type of saddlebags a cavalry soldier would have used!"

Placing the torn off portion of the saddlebags on the ground where he now knelt down, Paul unbuckled the leather pouch. Opening the pouch revealed a collection of additional gold and silver coins of several different denominations. "What is going on here? These coins have to be part of the Confederate treasury, but why were they buried ten feet away from what we found already?"

Seeing Paul had only pulled half of a complete set of saddlebags from the hole, Chick then knelt back down to find the other half. After digging with his hands for a couple of moments, he began pulling the other half of the saddlebags from the hole. As he lifted the remaining portion out of the ground, the rotted leather pouch split wide open. Close to two hundred gold and silver coins spilled back into the hole.

The saddlebag splitting open cost them almost another half-hour in time. With daylight approaching, the three of them worked quickly on their knees to recover all of the spilled coins. They were forced to wrap the coins up in a Murrells Inlet sweatshirt Bobby Ray had been wearing as all of their plastic buckets were now completely filled with what they had already retrieved from the barrel.

As the saddlebags were being unearthed, Pete was carefully filling in the first hole they had dug. As he did, he carefully replaced the sod over the top of the hole. Soon finished with that task, he now ran the metal detector over the second hole to see if they had missed anything or had dropped any coins. The metal detector remained quiet. Satisfied he had scanned the second area thoroughly, he placed the metal detector on the ground and now went to work filling in the second hole. As he did, Bobby Ray and Chick carried the heavy buckets of coins to the cemetery's back wall. After resting for a moment, they handed the buckets over the wall to Paul. He was already standing on the outside of the cemetery packing up some of their other gear. After the buckets of coins were safely over the wall, they handed him the two buckets containing the gold and silver bars. Soon Bobby Ray's sweatshirt, now filled with coins from the saddlebags, was also handed over the wall. The last item over the wall was the empty barrel.

After stacking the pails and other items, Paul climbed back over the wall to where Chick and Bobby Ray were catching their breath. "Bobby Ray, you help Pete finish filling in the hole and then both of you double-check the areas around the two holes so it looks like we were never here. Do what it takes to get rid of any extra soil from the two holes, but just get rid of it. Chick, you start collecting our tools and breaking down the tarps. I'm going to get Jayne so we can get out of here as soon as possible. I want to start loading all of this stuff back into our vehicles before anyone sees us. I'll be right back to help you guys."

Jayne had been standing guard alone for several hours when Paul approached her to tell her to come help them finish up. She was relieved to see him as she had become bored by her necessary, but unexciting task. "Well, are you going to tell me? Did you find what we hoped to find?"

"Oh, yeah! But we don't have time for you look at it now. You need to help us police the area where we've been working. We need to get our stuff back to the vehicles quick, daylight will soon be here."

As soon as they finished filling in the second hole, Bobby Ray and Pete swept the two areas where they had been digging for any tools Chick had not seen. Paul did the same and they found nothing had been missed. The areas around the two holes were also free of any extra soil and sod. They had all done what they could to police the area.

Pointing out the two areas where they had been digging, Paul gave Jayne a task to complete to make sure they had not missed anything. "The rest of us are going to start loading everything back into our vehicles. I want you to take one of the metal detectors and run it over the entire area where we were working just to make sure nothing has been missed. Make sure you wear the headset in the event the detector pings so it's not heard by anyone else. I'll come get you when we are done."

The others had already started carrying the now heavy and full plastic buckets of coins, and some of their other gear, back towards the parking lot when Paul caught up to them. He was carrying the plastic tarps and some of the tools they had been digging with. He quickly moved past them as they struggled carrying the heavy buckets. As he did, he urged them to work quickly so they were not delayed in getting away from the marina. Soon he had the tarps and the tools packed away in his truck by the time the others reached the parking lot. Now he helped them place the buckets into the bed of his truck. It took them two trips back and forth from the cemetery to the parking lot, but soon they had everything loaded back into their vehicles. Finally done putting everything away, they realized just how tired they were. They had been up all day, had worked through the night, and had just finished carrying the heavy buckets of coins, the gold and silver bars, and all of their gear back to their vehicles. Tired, but happy at what they had found, Chick leaned against his van to catch his breath. "Paul, we need to hire some younger guys to do the grunt work for us. This is way too much for us old guys."

"Amen to that brother, amen." Bobby Ray was also clearly tired from a long night of work. Unlike the others, in less than three hours he had to be at work.

Dropping down to one knee to catch his breath, Pete looked up at Chick. "When I signed up for this gig you told me I wouldn't have to dig in any sewers, but you never told me I would have to be digging in a bone yard at night. You know that you people are very sick, don't you?"

Pete's comment made them laugh and in some way they each realized what they had just done was beyond what was normal for them to be doing. Before yesterday, none of them had ever thought about digging for gold in a cemetery at night.

After resting for a few moments, Paul jogged back to the cemetery to get Jayne. As he pulled himself up on the cemetery's rear wall, he could see she was still running the metal detector over the areas where they had been working. Looking up, she saw Paul had turned on his small work light to get her attention. Turning off the metal detector, she quickly walked over to where he was on the wall.

"Jayne, let's go!" Paul helped her to the top and then jumped down outside the wall. Jayne jumped to the ground still holding onto the metal detector. "How are we looking in there? Did we leave anything behind?"

Reaching out and grabbing Paul's left hand, Jayne whispered to him. "Just this! I found it on the ground by where the buckets had been stacked by the wall."

Kneeling down behind the brick wall, Paul turned the work light on. Shining the light into his left hand, he saw Jayne had found an 1860 ten-dollar gold coin on the ground. "What the heck, that's no big deal, it's likely only worth a couple of thousand dollars these days." Jayne knew Paul's remark had been made sarcastically and she quietly laughed at the comment.

"Anything else?"

"Nope, we're good to go."

"OK, then let's get out of here, but let's just play it safe. Casually sweep the ground with the metal detector as we make our way back to the parking lot."

They had just started driving back towards the security booth when it started to rain, lightly at first then heavier. "Let's hope it rains for a day or two. It will help cover our tracks and it will also keep our friend Woody from working in there." Paul looked for a response from Bobby Ray, but saw he had already fallen asleep, worn out from an evening of manual labor.

* * * * * *

It did not take long for them to drive back to Paul's house. Backing his truck up towards his garage, Paul could see in his rearview mirror that Donna had seen them pulling into the driveway. She had hit the button to open the garage door for them and now the door finished opening as the truck came to a stop only a couple of feet away from the garage. Now awake from his ten-minute power nap, Bobby Ray jumped out of Paul's truck carrying his rolled up Murrells Inlet sweatshirt with him.

Walking up to Donna, who was standing in the garage wearing her bathrobe, Bobby Ray handed her the dirty sweatshirt. It was still holding some of the coins they had found. Looking at her, he jokingly told her what he wanted done with it. "Wash and iron this for me, no starch please, and keep the change!" Donna had not expected anything but a dirty sweatshirt being handed to her. She nearly doubled over from the unexpected weight of the coins.

"What is in this sweatshirt? What have you guys found tonight?"

Placing the dirty sweatshirt down on the folding table in the garage, she unfolded it. The loose coins spilled out across the table. "Oh, my. I guess you guys found what you were looking for!"

Looking up from the table, Donna saw the full buckets of coins now being carried into the garage. She was about to say something when Jayne came in carrying the plastic Rubbermaid container they had packed the seven gold and silver bars in after leaving the cemetery. Handing Donna one of the gold bars, Jayne introduced herself to her as they had yet to meet each other before now. "We found seven of these, four gold and three silver."

"Oh, Lord! I never would have imagined this. That poor soldier died for all of this."

"You know, I don't think he was the only one who died over this money. I bet several others probably did as well." Jayne said as she wiped dirt from the cemetery off her hands.

"Probably so, probably so."

After carrying the wooden barrel and the torn saddlebags into the garage, Paul closed the garage door. He did not want any of his neighbors to see what they were doing so early in the morning inside his garage.

Standing guard while the others had been working, Jayne now saw the fruits of their labor for the first time. "This is way more than what we found in North Carolina and that doesn't even factor in the gold and silver bars. I can only imagine what these bars themselves are worth. Wow!"

Before starting to examine what they found, Pete documented their find on videotape. Jayne soon followed his lead by taking several digital photos of the coins and bars as well. They had not taken pictures of the saddlebags or of the coins which had spilled out of them at the cemetery as Paul had not wanted to risk having photos taken while they worked without the protection of the tarps. He had been concerned about the camera flash being seen by others.

After documenting what they found, Paul emptied the part of the saddlebag still containing coins. Donna and Jayne soon filled another small plastic bucket with the 196 gold and silver coins that portion of the saddlebags had held for so many years.

Finished counting the coins with Jayne, Donna brought out two six-packs of Coors Light from the kitchen. Thirsty from their hard work, they all stood there enjoying the cold beer as they admired what they had found. Soon Bobby Ray was enjoying his second beer as he sat in plastic lawn chair examining the gold and silver bars which had been spread out on the folding table.

Jayne had started cleaning off the accumulated sand and soil from one section of the saddlebags when she asked Paul to confirm what the soldier's name was he had found.

"Captain Judiah Francis. Why?"

"I'm guessing these are his saddlebags then. The initials *'J.F.'* have been embroidered into them."

Looking at the embroidered initials made the find of the money, as well as the other items, much more personal for Paul. He could not explain it to the others, nor did he try, but somehow he felt a connection to Captain Francis.

"This certainly appears to tie Francis to the coins, doesn't it? This also explains why all of the money was not found in the same spot. The barrel and the saddlebags were likely buried at two different times. His letter tells us that, but until Jayne noticed the initials I had no way of making the connection. His letter clearly spoke of his saddlebags being stuffed with coins. I wonder if he buried them because he was being chased or because he had been shot and knew he was dying. Think about it, the graveyard and the place where I found his remains are not that far apart from each other."

Paul then went into the house, returning a few minutes later carrying a copy of each of the letters he had found. "These are copies of the four letters.

I guess it's time I showed them all to you at one time. You deserve that and more for all of the hard work you've done. I'm sorry I haven't shown them to you before this."

As Donna and Paul had done when they read the letter Francis had written to his father, the others, even Bobby Ray, soon had tears in their eyes as well. Even though she had read the letter before, Jayne began to cry after reading it again. Soon she was wiping away her tears with the sleeve of her dirty sweatshirt. "Paul, now we know what has driven you to find this money. Thanks for allowing us to be a part of it." As Paul already felt, now Jayne also wished she could have met Judiah Francis.

"These letters are worth as much as the money is to me. They are priceless." Chick had read many Civil War era letters during his career, but he told the others the letter Francis had written was the most touching he ever read. "Very personal, truly a touching letter. I'm honored to have had a chance to read it."

As Donna gathered up the letters, everyone else began cleaning off the coins of their accumulated sand and soil. They needed a decent cleaning before they could be taken to the bank later in the morning. Still seated at the folding table, Bobby Ray began wiping down each of the gold and silver bars with a white towel.

After working for another an hour, Paul called a halt to their efforts. "I'm sure you all are as tired as I am. I know Bobby Ray has to be at work soon, but I need the rest of you to help me package all of this up so we can put it under lock and key later this morning. Go home and get a couple of hours of sleep. Be back here by eleven." Handing Jayne a fifty dollar bill, Paul instructed her to buy as many Tupperware containers as she could find. Containers which later that morning would be filled with gold and silver coins before being placed in the safety deposit boxes he planned on renting.

With their work finally done they sat down to enjoy another beer, surrounded by piles of gold and silver coins that a few weeks ago they never would have imagined finding. Soon the others left Paul and Chick to fall asleep in the garage, protecting the money until they returned in a few hours to help move it to the bank.

* * * * * *

Later in the morning, after they had packaged all of the money up into the Tupperware containers, Paul would fulfill his promise and call Duke on the phone. He always kept his promises. Soon both a waitress and a librarian would be pleased that he did.

24

No Way Out.

"It is well that war is terrible, else we grow fond of it."
General Robert E. Lee, at the Battle of Fredericksburg

A noisy carriage rushing down the street outside the warehouse woke Judiah Francis up early in the morning. Lying on his bed of straw on the wooden warehouse floor, he could hear the various sounds a city makes as it wakes up each morning. He could hear people talking outside as they walked by the warehouse, he heard horses pulling wagons on the cobblestone street, and he heard people, perhaps even soldiers, arguing about something down the street. It was far more noise than he was accustomed to since leaving Richmond several weeks ago. He tried falling back asleep, but soon realized it was a futile effort. Sitting up, Francis looked at his men who were still fast asleep on the floor around him. He marveled at their ability to stay asleep despite the noises which had woken him up. "Why are they still sleeping so soundly and I am not?"

After taking care of his personal morning necessities, and after pushing open the two large wooden doors in the back of the warehouse, Francis made a small fire in one of the several fireplaces. It only took him a few minutes to warm up the remaining coffee from last night's dinner. After pouring himself a cup, he walked around the interior of the large warehouse. He had been too hungry and too tired to do so the previous evening. As he did, he came across the various types of damaged cannons Colonel Hodges had told him about. They had been damaged, some even captured, in various battles across Virginia and North Carolina. The cannons had been transported to Charleston by both trains and wagons in the hopes of getting them shipped further south to be repaired. The hopes of getting them repaired and returned to fight again in future battles was now remote.

Francis knew from speaking with Colonel Hodges that the Confederacy, now crippled by the Union naval blockade and still without the support they had hoped would come from Europe, did not have the skilled labor to repair these damaged cannons. They also did not have the raw materials or the factories to produce new ones. While the North continued to produce cannons for their armies, the lone cannon factory in the South, the Tredegar Iron Works, in Virginia, was no longer operational. The South now had little choice but to stockpile these damaged cannons in this warehouse, hoping they could find a way to have them repaired. The priority now was not to repair these damaged cannons, but rather it was trying to keep their armies staffed with enough men to continue the war. Francis also knew trying to maintain the few remaining railroads in the South was another important priority for the Confederacy.

The Confederacy had little choice but to roll the dice, hoping their armies, victorious in so many battles early in the war, could continue to supply them with cannons they seized from the Union army. Their only other hopes for cannons were ones they could purchase from Europe, but these were few and far between because of the naval blockade.

"Captain, it's too bad about these here cannons. Instead of them just sitting here broke and all, our boys should be using them to fight with." Sgt. Odom's comments startled Francis as he had not heard Odom walking towards him. Now he watched as Odom walked around the damaged cannons. Still startled by Odom walking up behind him without making a noise, Francis he knew that was a skill acquired from back home. It was learned from years of hunting in the woods.

Finished with his thoughts regarding Odom's hunting skills, Francis responded to what his sergeant said about the damaged cannons. "Yes, you're right, sergeant. I'm told we have neither the men nor the proper material to fix them fast enough so they haul them here waiting for when the time is right to repair them. Just like you do, I also hope the time comes soon so we can start repairing these cannons. As you said, our boys who are fighting could surely use them. If that does not happen we'll need to keep stealing them from the Yankees.

Francis then pointed to a particular Napoleon style cannon. He told Odom it looked very similar in its damage to one he had seen at the Battle of Ball's Bluff. "I wonder if it is indeed the same one? It would be very ironic if both of us ended up in this same warehouse. Don't you think?"

Deep in his own thoughts, Odom just nodded his head. He was thinking of some of the battles he had fought in and how scared he had been during his first real fight. The noise from the cannons terrified him the first time he heard them roar; firing repeatedly at the Yankee troops charging across the battlefield that morning. Now a veteran of many battles, he chuckled to himself as he recalled being so startled when the cannons had fired for the first time. He had dropped his rifle as he tried covering his ears with his hands to block out the cannons' loud noise. Dropping his rifle was something his fellow soldiers teased him about for several weeks. The noise of cannons being fired was a noise Odom knew he would never forget. It was noise a country boy from the woods of Alabama had never heard the likes of. Like all soldiers, he would never forget the first fight he was in during the war.

By now the others were stirring across the warehouse and starting to move. Sitting down with his men as they drank the rest of the coffee he had left near the fire, Francis told them he was going to try one more time to arrange for them to sail south. "I'm not sure any boat captain will risk losing his boat for us, but I have to try one more time." For a couple of minutes they drank their coffee in silence as Francis thought more on how he could get them further south.

"I'll likely be gone for a while and while I'm gone I want two of you here at all times to guard the wagons. If y'all want to take turns looking out at Fort Sumter or to walk around the nearby streets that is fine with me, but two of you are here at all times. If anyone asks why we're in town, tell them whatever y'all want, except of course the real reason. Don't tell anyone where we're staying as I don't want visitors here. No one, and I mean no one, comes into the warehouse. Understood?"

Collectively his still tired group of soldiers nodded their heads at Francis. "Good," he said as he looked back at them, "y'all should be getting some fresh coffee and biscuits soon. Enjoy them as y'all deserve that and much more for all of your hard work these past few weeks."

As he prepared to leave them for a few hours, Francis stopped and walked back to where the men still sat on the warehouse floor drinking coffee. "Men, one more thing. I'm going to try and find some mortar mix. If I do, I'll arrange for it to be delivered here today. Somehow find a tub for us to mix it in when I get back. I'll give y'all the rest of the details later."

The news of Francis trying to find some mortar mix confused the men as none of them could figure out what he planned on using it for. During the time he was gone they tried to guess what he planned on doing with it. They would all guess wrong.

Francis spent the morning and part of the afternoon trying to find a ship to take them and their precious cargo further south. Despite his efforts, he could not convince any of the ship's captains he talked to into risking their ships by running the blockade. Individually they each told him they had heard about too many other ships being sunk by the Union navy for them to chance running the blockade. One of the captains he talked to, Captain Thomas Henry Neugebauer, told him of the effectiveness of the blockade. "We cannot even chance running it at night anymore. Those Union ships fire all different types of colored flares when they see a ship they do not recognize out there at night. The rest of their ships then converge in the area, firing their cannons at any ship that does not come to a stop after it's signaled to do so. Too many boats and ships have been sunk, and too many men have died, for me to risk trying it. I'd like to as there is good money in trying it, but I just can't risk losing my ship."

After a few hours of speaking with captains of several ships, Francis was frustrated that no captain would risk running the blockade. Soon he realized they were protecting their ships just as he was protecting the gold and silver in his possession. While knowing they were right about protecting their ships, he still had hoped one of them would have risked running the blockade. As he walked along the waterfront, he wondered what he would have done if he had found a ship's captain willing to take such a risk. "If one of them had said they would do it, would I have taken that risk? Our cause would certainly not be helped if we risked moving the gold and silver by ship and then it ended up on the ocean floor. The cause would certainly be doomed then."

Francis then turned his efforts to trying to find a way to move the gold and silver south by rail, but news of the rail lines still in operation was sketchy. He could find no one with accurate information on what trains, if any, were still running. Even his efforts to find out such information at the Charleston telegraph office proved fruitless as Union troops had caused havoc with the telegraph lines coming into the city. As he met roadblock after roadblock, and as he already knew he could not risk moving the gold and silver by ship, he now realized he also could not risk moving the money by railroad either. Chancing to move the money by railroad might also lead to it being lost as well, this time to the advancing Union army instead of to the bottom of the ocean. Frustrated by what he learned, he sat down on a bench outside the small telegraph office. "I would rather lose the money to the bottom of the ocean than to have it fall into the hands of the Yankees."

Leaving the telegraph office, Francis started walking back in the direction of the warehouse. He was disappointed he had failed to find another means to move the gold and silver by. Now he walked slowly, upset that his hopes of getting the money to Atlanta by either boat or rail had been dashed. While he had done what he could to find an alternate means of travel, now he was resigned to the fact that he would be forced to once again travel with the money hidden in the slow moving wagons. "I will need fresh supplies and some new men, but this is the safest way to move the money. I cannot risk losing the money, just as I cannot fail those men who have put their trust in me. I will have to tell my men the news I had hoped not to tell them." Before returning to the warehouse Francis sought out Colonel Hodges. He wanted to thank him for his hospitality, and to verify one piece of information Hodges had already told him.

As he looked for Hodges, Francis learned he was expected to be on South Battery Road later in the afternoon before making his daily rounds of the facilities within his command. Hodges was going to be evaluating the Charleston shore batteries, specifically the Fort Johnson Battery, the Oblique Battery, and Battery Number One, as they practiced firing at an old ship the

Confederacy had moored in the harbor. By three in the afternoon, he finally located Hodges as he rode up to watch the firing accuracy of the shore batteries. Francis waited until Hodges dismounted before walking over to him; saluting him as his rank deserved. "Colonel, good afternoon! My men and I are most grateful for the fine meal you sent over to us last evening. The warehouse is also working out for us very well. Again, you have my thanks for that as well. Sir, my men and I are in your debt."

"Captain, it was my pleasure, no problem at all. Will you and your men require a similar meal tonight as well?"

"Sir, I hate to impose further upon you, but if you could possibly arrange another meal for us, well . . . well, we certainly would not refuse your gracious hospitality."

Hodges could not help laughing over how Francis had phrased his request for another meal. "Consider it done, Judiah, no problem at all. I will have your meal delivered to you around six this evening. Now, captain, you must excuse me. I need to make sure these three batteries are ready for the Union navy when they arrive. We want to give them that special welcome I told you about."

"Colonel, I beg your time for just another moment or two. Sir, if I may ask, the damaged cannons in the warehouse we're using, how likely is it they will be moved in the near future?"

"Captain, I'm not sure why you ask that question, but I'm sure you have your reason. However, the answer to your question is not likely at all. They've already been there for several months and I don't see them being moved any time soon because of that damn Union naval blockade. Our resources are too thin right now to spend time and money on fixing damaged cannons, especially when we can simply get other ones from the Yankees when we keep beating them on the battlefields. I'm afraid the damaged cannons will likely remain in the warehouse until the end of the war. Are they in your way? Do I need to move them to another location?"

"No, no sir, they are fine where they are. Colonel, my men and I are leaving in the morning for the Georgetown area. With your permission I would like to have the warehouse locked when we leave as I need to leave a few things behind. I expect to be back in five or six days. Do I have your permission to place locks on the warehouse doors?"

"Captain, the letters you showed me yesterday proved to me you are completing an assignment for men far more important than I am. I trust you have your reasons for wanting locks on the doors. You may use the warehouse for as long as you need it as I don't have an immediate need for it. If I should need it, I promise you and I will talk first before I take it back. I will have locks and keys delivered to you this evening with your meal. Anything else?"

Francis stepped back and saluted Hodges again. They then exchanged handshakes as if they were old friends saying goodbye to each other. "Colonel, as I mentioned to you yesterday, you have my word President Davis and General Lee will both be told of your significant support and hospitality. I will be honored to personally tell them of your assistance. Again, my personal thanks to you for your kindness and for the support you have shown to me and my men."

"Captain, I wish you the best of luck with whatever it is you are doing. Someday, perhaps when this terrible insanity is finally over with, you will tell me what it was you were doing here in Charleston. Regardless, good luck to you and your men!" With that, and with his horse being attended to by one of his aides, Hodges walked away to start his evaluation of the nearby shore batteries.

As Francis walked back towards the warehouse, his horse in tow, he stopped again to look out over Charleston Harbor and at Fort Sumter. It was hot for a November afternoon, but one being cooled by a breeze blowing in off of the harbor. As he enjoyed a rare tranquil late afternoon, he knew in other places across the South that men, both young and old, blue and grey, were dying for their respective causes, causes wise old men should never have allowed to escalate this far. As he started walking back to his men, he shuddered at the thought of so many men already dying in the war. "What a terrible waste of so many lives."

As he walked along, Francis momentarily stopped again to look out over the harbor. Doing so, he felt for the pocket watch he carried in his blouse. His fingers instinctively felt for the engraved initials on the cover before withdrawing it from his pocket. It was nearly four pm. After spending a few more moments enjoying the view, he headed back to the warehouse where he knew his men were waiting for word on how they would continue with their mission.

* * * * * *

Back at the warehouse, with his men gathered around him by the fenced in corral, Francis told them of his failed efforts in trying to arrange transportation by both ship and rail. "We would have to make our way all the way back to Wilmington, North Carolina, where I have learned some of the boat captains there are risking running the blockade because of the profits they can make if they successfully slip through it. I'm afraid that's not feasible at this point in time as it would mean risking the gold and silver far too much. We'll have to move it south in the wagons as I cannot justify moving it any other way at this time." The disappointment in their faces was obvious to Francis after delivering the news to them, but like most soldiers he could tell they were still committed to finishing their mission.

Francis then cheered them up with two more pieces of information. First, he told them he had arranged for another hot meal to be delivered that evening. Then he told them they had to be ready to move out early the next morning. His plan was to retrieve the money they had buried in the cemetery and then return back to Charleston. "Hopefully it will be an easy trip to make. Then we'll come back to rest here for another day or two."

"How are we going to get the wagons up there, captain? Seems we got too many wagons and not enough of us to drive them all." Davis asked out of concern.

"We're only going to bring one of the wagons with us, the rest are staying here."

The men exchanged confused looks with each other. Then Sgt. Stine asked the question that was on each of their minds. "Begging your pardon, sir, but whose going to stay and look after our gold and silver?"

Pointing to the cannons on the other side of the warehouse, Francis offered a simple reply. "They are."

The men again exchanged confused looks with each other, wondering if Francis had lost his mind that afternoon or whether he had been drinking.

"Did the mortar get delivered?"

Again it was Stine who spoke up. "Yes, sir. We got it piled up inside by the side door over yonder." Francis looked to where Stine was pointing and saw the small pile of mortar mix sitting there. Motioning for his men to follow him inside, he led them over to where the damaged cannons sat on the far side of the warehouse.

"Tomorrow we'll head back north, past Georgetown, to retrieve what we buried there and then we'll bring it back here. After we get here, I will seek some additional help before we travel back to North Carolina to retrieve what we've buried there. Before we finally leave this place I want to try and contact Richmond to see how they want us to proceed, but first I want all of the money to be here. The battles currently being fought in Virginia and North Carolina, as well as the Union naval blockade, will influence to some degree our ability to get safely back to where we first buried the money. I'll make the decision on how we're going to get back there after we retrieve the money from the cemetery."

"Captain, you know we're with you and all, but if we ain't bringing these here wagons with us, ain't you afraid someone is gonna find the gold and silver that's hidden in them?" Like his fellow soldiers, Davis had grown to feel personally responsible for the safety of the Confederacy's treasury. It was now their personal responsibility to protect the money they had been entrusted with.

"No, I'm not, because the gold and silver won't be in the wagons, it will be hidden in these cannons."

Still confused the men again stared at each other, not comprehending what Francis had already carefully planned out in his mind.

"Men, the damaged cannons here in the warehouse are more than likely ones which will never be repaired or even be moved to another location for many reasons. To take all of the wagons back with us to the cemetery would slow us up and cost us precious time, time we do not have. I want to move quickly and return back here even quicker. To do so, we're going to leave the rest of the wagons here in the warehouse; just like we're going to do with the gold and silver. No one will even know what's in here. When our dinner is delivered here tonight, locks and keys will also be delivered for the warehouse doors. We will lock the warehouse when we're gone and take the keys with us. Colonel Hodges is also going to have two guards placed on duty here until we return."

Francis could sense his men did not like the idea of leaving the gold and silver behind. They had fought hard to protect it since leaving Richmond with it. Doing so, they had seen their fellow soldiers die protecting it. They had also seen several others die over it as well. They now considered it their duty to protect it. "We're going to leave the gold and silver behind, but we're not going to leave it in the wagons for someone to find. We're going to hide it, and those cannons are going to defend it for us."

The only one to catch on to what Francis was trying to tell them was Sgt. Banks. He saw the smile that slowly crossed Banks' face as he finally figured out what Francis had planned. "Captain, with no disrespect intended, but I thought you, well ya know, had gone plumb crazy and all. But now I've got it, at least I think I do." The others still had not figured it out.

"Men, we're going to take the gold and silver coins, as well as the bars of gold and silver, and the bag of jewelry, and we're going to place all of those items in the barrels of some of those cannons. Then we are going to seal the ends of the cannons with the mortar I had delivered here today. I ask each of you, would you think to look in the barrels of damaged cannons for gold and silver? Would you?"

Chewing on a piece of straw as he listened to Francis tell them his plan, Sgt. Davis had taken off his hat and was now scratching his head as he visualized what had been planned for the gold and silver. He stared blankly at the cannons for a couple of minutes. "I got to give ya that one, captain. Ya done got me. I know I'd never be looking there for it." Francis smiled as he had gotten the response he had been hoping for.

"Alright, I want to move the cannons away from the wall and then we'll start mixing the mortar." Francis said before assigning his men to their specific tasks. "Stine, you and Odom start unloading the wagons of all the gold and silver. Banks and Davis will help me move the wagons away from the walls. Once we're done with all of that we'll load the barrels with the gold and silver. Let's get this done before they deliver our dinner as I don't want anyone seeing what we're doing."

Working with a team of horses they had moved into the warehouse, Banks and Davis moved all of the cannons out into the center of the large warehouse. From the collection of cannons, Francis selected a few Napoleons, two Sea Coast guns, a mortar, two Griffin guns, and two older Dahlgren cannons as the ones he wanted the gold and silver to be hidden in. His plan was to hide the gold and silver in these cannons, cap the end of the barrels with a few inches of mortar, and then place the cannons against the back wall of the warehouse. He would then attempt to hide what they had done by placing several of the other damaged cannons directly in front of them.

As they filled the barrels with the gold and silver coins, some of the smaller bags of coins went in as full bags, while the bigger bags had to be split open and dumped in as those bags would not fit. At first, Francis did not like the thought of having to split the bags open, but then realized by doing so they could hide more coins in the barrels when they were loose and not in bags. Within the cannon containing the gold and silver bars, Francis placed the cloth bag of valuable jewelry that so many Southern ladies had contributed their prized earrings, rings, and necklaces to. When they were finished filling the eight cannon barrels, they were left with only a few hundred coins they could not fit into any of the barrels. Francis had the remaining coins placed inside his saddlebags. Filling one of the cannons with so few coins, compared to what the rest of the cannons now held, made little sense to him. As the men loaded his saddlebags with the remaining coins, he told them his next plan. "We'll keep these coins with us. When we return here with the money we retrieve from the cemetery, we'll place all of it in a few of the other cannons just like we've already done."

Francis then selected four other cannons from the ones they had not filled with any of the gold and silver. "Men, these four cannons, fill them with whatever you can find. Use empty coin bags, rags, sticks of wood, or whatever you have, just leave enough room so we can fill the ends of the barrels with mortar."

As the others grabbed whatever they could find from within the warehouse to fill the four cannons Francis had selected, Odom and Stine started mixing the mortar with water in an old horse trough they found behind the warehouse. With the mortar almost ready, Francis pried a large nail from one of the warehouse beams.

Francis first had Banks wet the inside of each cannon barrel with water so the mortar would properly adhere to the sides. Then they began to pack the mortar into the ends of the barrels. They packed each of the twelve cannons with mortar twice; the second time filling up a few voids that occurred when the mortar started to set. Soon they were finished with the mortar. After the mortar had a few minutes to setup, Francis went to each cannon with the nail he pulled from the warehouse beam. As he walked from cannon to cannon, he carefully inscribed C.S.A. into the still drying mortar. Then he inscribed an even number under the C.S.A. inscription for each cannon packed with the gold and silver; randomly choosing the numbers 2, 6, 8, 10, 12, 16, 18 and 30. For the four cannons which had been sealed with mortar like the others, but packed with only the various items they found within the warehouse, Francis inscribed an odd number under his C.S.A. inscription. For those numbers he randomly chose 3, 7, 9 and 11.

"OK, men, let's give the mortar time to dry. Then we'll move the cannons back into place. You now know another part of the secret regarding a good part of our treasury. You knew where it was when we moved it out of Richmond, you knew where it was during our trip, and now you know where it's hidden. Not too many people can lay claim to knowing what y'all do. I want to personally thank each of you for your service to the Confederacy. I'm proud of each of you. Let's get cleaned up for dinner, later we'll move the cannons back into place after we eat."

Soon their dinner was delivered, as were the locks for the warehouse. As the men cleaned up at the water pump, it was Francis who took the time to lay out the meal for the men, just as they had done throughout the mission for him. It was an attempt on his part to show them the respect he had developed for them. It was a gesture his men would not overlook.

As they ate their meal, a meal of cold fried chicken, oysters, corn on the cob, fresh baked bread, and coffee, the men joked with each other about hiding the gold and silver in the cannon barrels. It was Odom who directed one comment to Francis. "Captain, I ain't nearly as smart as y'all so it took me a spell to figure out what y'all done here with these cannons and all; meaning that writing you put into the end of them thar cannons. Tell me something, will ya?" Odom now pointed at the cannons from where he sat eating his meal. "Them thar four cannons . . . y'all put odd numbers on them . . . and the others y'all done put even numbers on them. Again, I ain't the smartest man here, but them cannons with them odd numbers, are them decoys or something?"

"Very perceptive of you, Sgt. Odom. Well done!"

After finishing their meal, and after taking a few minutes to share one of the few remaining cigars they had, Francis had the men push the cannons into place against the far wall of the warehouse. He had the cannons inscribed with even numbers lined up against the wall and then had the four cannons with the odd numbers placed in front of them. When they were done, it looked like the cannons had never been moved.

As his men spent the rest of the evening winding down from the day, Francis poured himself a cup of coffee and then climbed up on the wagon they would be taking with them the next day. He needed to be alone, away from his men, as he had one more task to complete before shutting his eyes for the night.

With the loss of each of his men, Francis had realized his mission was becoming more difficult to complete. He had known when they left Richmond that they would face problems along the way, but the problems he encountered, like the number of men who had died, was beyond what he or anyone else could have expected. Now he knew for many reasons, such as the problems he was encountering with both the blockade and the railroads, that the chances of his mission failing had become a strong possibility. The trips he planned to make back to North Carolina and to the Georgetown area only added to the likelihood of his mission failing. Sitting in the wagon thinking this all out, he knew he and his men would fight to the end to deliver the money, but now his confidence had started to fade. He had to prepare for the worst.

Working with the light a single small candle gave out, Francis wrote his first letter in many months. It started as *Dear President Davis*. Finishing the letter, he let the ink dry on the paper while he took a sip of his now tepid coffee. "I hope this letter will never have to be delivered to President Davis. If it is, it will mean I have failed him. Most likely, it will also mean that I am dead." It was a somber thought he reflected on for several minutes.

As he sat in the wagon finishing his coffee, Francis spied two empty liquor bottles in the bed of the wagon. They had been full when he had been given them by James Wood. Seeing the empty bottles brought back sad memories of the terrible afternoon in Georgetown. Holding the bottles up to the candle's flame, he could see the insides of the bottles were now dry. After removing the small cork from the end of one of the bottles, he rolled up his letter to President Davis and the rough map of the field in North Carolina where they had buried some of the gold and silver. Then he placed them inside the bottle. After replacing the cork, he placed the bottle into one side of his saddlebags; ones sitting next to him in the wagon. "At least I know the letter is protected from the weather for now." Sitting in the wagon as tears slowly rolled down his face, Francis knew the chances of seeing his mother and father, and his home in Virginia, were dwindling. He still held out hope he would see them again, but his heart was telling him otherwise. Reaching for the second empty liquor bottle, he now placed one of the letters from both President Davis and Secretary Memminger inside. After putting the cork back in the neck, he carefully placed the bottle inside the other section of his saddlebags so the two bottles would not break.

Blowing out the candle, Francis laid down on a blanket in the bed of the wagon. Even though the warehouse was still warm that evening, he wrapped himself up in another blanket to fight off the chill he felt from the letter he had just written. Soon he fell asleep. While he could not possibly have known it, it would be one of his last comfortable nights of sleep here on earth.

He was correct about the letter he had written to President Davis.

25

Strong Black Friends.

*"Well, I wish some of you would tell me the brand of whiskey that Grant drinks.
I would like to send a barrel of it to my other generals."*
President Abraham Lincoln

After Bobby Ray, Pete, and Jayne left to go home, Paul closed his overhead garage door, set the alarm to his house and went to bed instead of sleeping in the garage with the money they had found. Chick and he both needed a couple of hours of sleep before the others returned back to the house later in the morning to package up what they had found at the cemetery so it could be brought to the bank. Later in the morning as she prepared to leave for work, Donna assured her very tired husband that she would reset the alarm as she left the house.

Separated by only the thin sheetrock wall between Paul's bedroom and the guest bedroom Chick had crashed in, they each spent a restless few hours trying to fall asleep. It proved to be a wasted effort for both of them as they were far too excited about what they had found at the cemetery. The fact they had finally gotten to bed when the sun was just starting to make its presence known through the bedroom windows did not help their efforts in catching some much needed sleep.

Tired from their lack of sleep and tired of trying to fall asleep, Chick and Paul had just made their way back into Paul's garage with their first cup of coffee when Jayne pulled into the driveway. The back seat of her Honda Accord was loaded with the Tupperware containers she had just purchased at Wal-Mart. As they were helping her unload her car, Pete also arrived. As Paul carried the last few containers, Chick helped Pete carry his camera gear into the garage. He surprised them by bringing a dozen assorted donuts from Dunkin' Donuts with him. "I figured a little sugar would help our tired bodies get going this morning."

After they had gotten everything into the garage, Paul closed the garage door from the prying eyes of any of his neighbors. "If any of them are on the ball they would have to think with all of the traffic that's been coming and going from here at all hours lately that we're selling drugs or something. If only they knew."

As they ate their donuts and drank the coffee Paul made for them, they started to talk about their successful trip to the cemetery. As they talked about what they had found, Paul remembered he owed Duke a phone call.

"Duke, good morning, it's Paul."

"Hey, partner, how did y'all make out last night? Any luck?"

"Listen, I don't want to talk on the phone about this. You never know who might be listening, OK?"

"Oh, yeah, I understand. I'll call you at your house tonight when I get back home. But y'all can't leave me wondering all day about what happened. Just give me a hint."

"Duke, more, much more than we got when we visited with you."

"Seriously?"

"Extremely."

"Whoa! I'm with you on the next one. Partner, please tell me there is gonna be one more!"

"Hope so, but we'll talk about that tonight. Sound OK?"

"Sounds like a plan. I'll call you around nine. Y'all have a good one!"

Sitting in the garage, they excitedly talked for several more minutes about what they found at the cemetery, but soon the sugar from the donuts wore off and the fatigue of the previous day kicked in. Before being able to catch up on their sleep they still needed to package up what they had found. After cleaning off more of the accumulated sand and soil, they packed each of the containers Jayne had purchased with loose coins. After filling them, they placed the plastic containers inside several of Paul's empty cardboard moving boxes. They also used another moving box to hide the container which held the gold and silver bars. Paul wanted to use the cardboard boxes so no one could see what the containers held when they wheeled them into the bank in a couple of hours.

As the others continued to pack the cardboard boxes, Paul called his bank and put a hold on the last ten large safety deposit boxes they had available. "If my neighbors think we're selling drugs out of the garage, then the bank has to think we're keeping our drug profits with them." His comments brought a collective laugh from the tired group.

After they finished packing the coins into the containers, Chick took a moment to clean off the exterior of the wooden barrel the coins and bars had been found in. "Paul, look at this. It's not much, but it tells us a little more about the barrel."

Carefully cleaning away some of the accumulated grime with a soft brush, Paul and Chick were able to read some of the faint stenciling still remaining on one side of the barrel. "This word here clearly appears to be the word *flour*, but I cannot make out the words before and after it. Near the bottom I can make out the words *Richmond, Virginia*, but I cannot figure out what any of the other stenciled words are, can you?"

Paul grabbed a magnifying glass off his workbench, one he used when he first read the letters he found, but even with the help of the magnifying glass he could not make out any of the other words. Time spent in the ground had faded the rest of the stenciling to both the naked eye and the magnifying glass.

While they were examining the barrel, Pete again documented their findings by videotaping what they found. As he did, Paul held up each of the seven gold and silver bars so they could be filmed. At the same time, Chick held up a ruler alongside each of the bars to document their individual sizes. On average, each bar was approximately ten inches in length, three inches in width and almost two inches in diameter. "That's a lot of coins, jewelry, silver teacups, or whatever, to melt down to make those bars. I can only imagine what each of those bars is worth in today's market." Pete's comment caused the others to think about what had been melted down to make up each of the bars they found.

* * * * * *

As Paul, Chick, and Jayne drove to the bank with their precious cargo hidden inside several cardboard moving boxes, Pete drove back to the cemetery to do a final walk around the perimeter to make sure they had not left anything behind. The day's rainstorm made it an easy task to complete as no one was visiting the old cemetery on a rainy day.

Arriving at the bank and using a hand truck borrowed from one of his neighbors, Paul and Jayne stacked several boxes of coins onto it while Chick guarded the rest of the coins still in his van.

"Back again, Paul? Based on the number of safety deposit boxes you've rented, your visits are becoming very mysterious. The girls behind the teller line, especially Paula and Barbara, have a bet going. They're all trying to guess what it is you're putting in them. But I doubt you're going to tell them, and you don't have to . . . it's none of their business anyhow. One thing though, please tell me it's not drug money or anything else illegal, that's all I want to make sure of. I hate it when the damn state auditors start asking me questions." Holly McNamara had been only half-kidding when she asked her question.

"You have nothing to worry about, Holly. In fact, you and the other girls, like many others, will soon know what it is we're putting into these boxes, but until then you'll have to keep guessing. Now, can I have the keys for the boxes and the use of one of your private rooms? We have to transfer a few items from these packing boxes into the safety deposit boxes and we need some privacy."

Handing Paul the keys, Holly then signed them into the bank's Safety Deposit Room. "Holly, just one more thing before you leave. Jayne is going to stay with these boxes for a couple of minutes while I fetch the rest of them from our van. One of our friends will be joining us as well. His name is Chick Mann, just for your record keeping and all. I'll be right back."

In a small room the bank had designated as their Safety Deposit Room, one which afforded privacy for the renters of the bank's safety deposit boxes, the three of them filled the secure metal drawers with the coins and bars they found in the cemetery. Some of the smaller plastic containers fit perfectly into the metal drawers, but the larger containers had to be emptied so the coins could fill some of the voids caused by other containers. Emptying a few of the small containers also allowed them to place more loose coins into the boxes. It took some time, but eventually they filled each of the ten safety deposit boxes to near capacity with what they found.

When they completed the transfer of the coins and bars to the safety deposit boxes, Paul waved to Holly to get her attention. Giving them the privacy they needed, she had returned to her desk while they worked behind closed doors. Now she walked to where Paul was waiting for her so they could return the safety deposit boxes to the bank's secured vault. After the vault was opened, Paul and Chick struggled to lift the heavy metal drawers back into their respective slots. Holly could not help noticing how heavy they were to lift. "What in heaven's name do y'all have in there? Wait, I don't want to know . . . I don't want to know. Don't tell me! Forget I asked!"

After securing the safety deposit boxes in the vault, Holly handed Paul his set of keys. Then she initialed each of the Safety Deposit Box Access Cards for the boxes he had rented. The records noted what time they left the vault area for the day. As she walked with them to the bank's lobby, Holly jokingly asked Paul if he wanted her to contact the bank's Myrtle Beach office to see what they had available for similar size safety deposit boxes.

"That's a good idea, Holly. Call me when you find out and I'll tell you what we need." She had only been joking with Paul, but hearing his response told her he had not been.

"Are you really serious about needing more?" Stunned by Paul's answer, Holly stared at him over the top of her glasses for a brief moment. "Do y'all really need more of them?"

"Yes, ma'am, the big ones preferably."

As they walked out the bank's front door, Holly was left standing alone in the lobby. She had one thought as she watched them walk across the parking lot. "What in the world is going on here I wonder?"

* * * * * *

Outside of speaking with Duke on the phone that evening and telling him about their discovery, Paul focused his efforts on catching up with his sleep. He was so tired he quickly fell into a deep sleep. He dreamt of nothing that night, not even of the rest of the gold and silver which was still out there waiting to be found.

The next afternoon, Paul played a round of golf at *The Links* with Chick and Bobby Ray. It was hard not to talk about what they had found, but they made a promise to each other not to talk about the gold and silver. It would be a day to just relax and have fun. Despite struggling with their golf game, they enjoyed the sun and each other's company as they made their way around the course in Pawleys Island. With no place to be after they finished, they each enjoyed a few cocktails during their casual round; tipping the cart girl rather liberally for the generous drinks she fixed for them. As the round progressed, they almost made it through the entire eighteen holes without talking about it, but that would have been impossible for them to do.

After finishing a rather unremarkable round of golf, they sat in the shade on the clubhouse porch enjoying a couple of afternoon cocktails. Each of them struggled not to break their promise, but it was Chick who finally started talking about what they had found.

"I know we promised not to talk about this, but where do we go from here?"

"Home, I guess." Bobby Ray never passed up the opportunity to fit a joke into a conversation.

Chick gave Bobby Ray a frown as they relaxed in oversized green wicker rocking chairs on the side porch of the clubhouse. "You know what I mean, Bobby Ray. What's the next part of this adventure for us?"

Setting down his half empty glass of Jack and Coke, Paul looked over at his friend who was working at adding up their golf scores. "Bobby Ray, anyone asking questions about this down at the Sheriff's Office?"

"No, not really. They all know you and I are buddies, but no one is asking me any questions and I haven't been asking any either. I'm trying to fly below the radar if you catch my drift."

"Good idea, Bobby Ray."

After they each had one more Jack and Coke, they walked to their cars and prepared to head for home, agreeing to meet for lunch the following day at the diner. Carrying his Nike golf bag as he walked back to his truck, Paul made a mental note to give Steve a call. "Gosh, it's been over two weeks since I spoke to him. I need to call him."

Opening the door to his truck, Paul turned to see Chick was changing his shoes in the parking lot. "Chick, it's up to you about Pete, but try and get Jayne down to lunch tomorrow. I want her opinion on where we go from here."

* * * * * *

The following morning, Chick phoned two of his friends who taught United States history at two different colleges in North Carolina. Like him, they also had a passion about the Civil War; both being far more versed in certain areas about the war than he was. He called to ask them what they each knew about the legend of the missing Confederate treasury.

To his surprise, Chick found both of them believed the treasury had actually been moved out of Richmond during the war. Perhaps even more to his surprise, and independent of each other, he learned neither of them believed in any conspiracy theories about the money being stolen by Union troops, crooked Southern politicians, or by those charged with moving it. Each of them was of the opinion the money was still out there, probably buried for some unknown reason by those who were charged to get it to Atlanta, Mississippi, or to wherever.

Professor Jeffrey Brandau had attended college with Chick and had become a well-respected Civil War author, lecturer, and researcher prior to joining the staff at the University of North Carolina. Over the phone he told Chick his opinions. Brandau believed the treasury was still likely buried somewhere between lower North Carolina and Georgia. "I know for a fact from my research the money did exist and that it had been moved out of Richmond before the Union army advanced on the city. From what I've learned, it was comprised mostly of gold and silver coins. It may have also included some crudely made gold and silver bars, and perhaps even some Mexican currency, but I'm not positive on all of that. I do know the South had been selling cotton to Mexico during that period of time so it would be safe to bet the treasury included some type of Mexican currency." Brandau pressed him on why he was calling about the Confederate treasury, but Chick easily avoided answering the question by moving on with the conversation.

Professor Timothy Baughman, of the University of Wilmington, had met Chick through a series of Civil War lectures they both attended a few years back. Through their mutual interests in the Civil War and in the game of golf they had become good friends. While speaking with Baughman, Chick learned he had similar thoughts as Brandau regarding the treasury. The only difference being Baughman was of the opinion those charged with moving the money south from Richmond had hidden the money for a certain reason. "They probably buried it because they were being chased by others, perhaps it was even by Union or Confederate soldiers who wanted to steal the gold and silver." He told Chick his thinking was whoever had buried the money could not find it when they went back to retrieve it. Baughman was also of the opinion that whoever had buried the money perhaps had been killed during the war before they could get back to where they buried it. "Chick, we likely will never know the whole story, but I do know I'd like to be there when the money is found." He also told Chick he felt the money had been buried or hidden somewhere north of Georgia. "That would have been a tough trip to make and I doubt the money ever made it as far south as Georgia. While I know the Confederacy was afraid of Union troops capturing it, I'm quite sure that never happened. I've always felt it never made it to Georgia. My guess is it's in your neck of the woods, likely the Charleston area, but who knows where it might be. Somebody is going to find it by accident someday I suspect." As they talked, Chick mentioned what Brandau's opinions were regarding the missing treasury. Baughman ended their conversation by telling him he felt his theory about the missing treasury was the more likely scenario than the one their mutual friend had previously shared with him. "Unfortunately for Jeff, his golf game is as bad as his knowledge of the Civil War is!" Chick laughed when he heard this as he knew Baughman was joking with him regarding their friend's opinion of the missing money.

Later, as they ate lunch at the diner, Chick told the others about the conversations he had with his two friends. "They both felt something likely happened along the way and the money had been buried for one reason or another. In fact, they both still think it's out there someplace."

Paul had listened as Chick summarized what his two friends had told him. Halfway through his BLT, Paul told him what he thought about his friends read on the missing Confederate treasury. "Chick, you know some pretty smart guys, especially that Baughman guy. The money was out there just like they said. Perhaps your buddy is correct. Maybe the rest of the missing gold and silver is in Charleston. Who knows though?"

As they ate their lunch, Paul handed each of them copies of the letter Francis had written to President Davis. "Look at the wording in his letter. It's obvious he was trying to give Davis some clues about where he left the money. We just have to figure out the clues no one else has been able to do. It's simple really. All we need to do is figure out what he was trying to tell President Davis and then we go and find the rest of the treasury."

Chick smirked at Paul's attempt to minimize the difficulty of the problem they were now facing. "If only it was going to be that easy."

Several minutes later, and after a few more bites of her turkey club sandwich, Jayne pointed out one of the obvious clues the letter contained. "The letter, if it's real, was apparently written in Charleston as it shows the date and the location at the top of the page. But then it confusingly speaks of him trying to get back to Charleston. Which is it? But I do think we need to focus our efforts in Charleston as the letter also speaks of a warehouse there, one on the King Street road. I think we need to hit those clues hard." She was soon pleased to hear Chick agreed with her.

"I agree, I think we need to start there also. Besides what my friends told me on the phone this morning, and as Jayne has already pointed out, I also believe Charleston is the place we should start. It was a Confederate stronghold and it had a busy harbor. Perhaps he was trying to get the rest of the money there so he could ship it further south. But let me ask you one question. If the letter was written in Charleston, why does he say they are going to ride north into South Carolina if he is already there?"

"That's a good point, Chick." Paul offered. "I think it's just one of several clues he's left for someone to figure out. But I also think we already know what he meant by that one clue. I believe he was trying to tell President Davis or whoever read the letter that he buried some of the money north of Charleston, probably the money we've just found in the cemetery."

Chick thought for a moment about the clue and about Paul's response to his point. "Yeah, you're probably right. I missed that one. That's what he was doing, especially when he also talked about leaving the money with the Allston children. I totally missed that one."

Paul then told them which clue had him stumped. "I'm with both of you that Charleston needs to be the next place we start looking. What I cannot figure out from the letter is when he talks about the *'battered and broken, these strong, solid black friends of ours, who have served us so well since Fort Sumter.'* The obvious thought is that he was talking about black slaves, but I'm not so sure the slaves served the South well enough for him to have trusted them with the treasury, at least what was left of it. I'm not convinced he was referring to slaves. What do you think he means by this section of his letter?"

Jayne had not been able to get past thinking Francis was talking about slaves with that one reference. "Paul, I think he is referring to slaves in his letter. Many slaves remained loyal to their owners during the war, even after Lincoln emancipated them. Remember, not every slave owner was a bastard as it's often portrayed these days. But I have to admit, this section of the letter has got me also."

Paul looked at Bobby Ray who was sitting in the corner of the booth eating his lunch, but adding very little to the conversation. "How about you, Bobby Ray? I'm dying to hear your thoughts on this."

Putting down his bacon double cheeseburger, Bobby Ray paused a moment to wipe his face with his napkin before answering the question. "I'm with y'all so far, but I'm totally convinced the money is in Charleston. We've got us some work to do down there, but it's there, I'm telling y'all that right now. That one clue y'all have been talking about hasn't yet convinced me he was talking about leaving the money with slaves."

"What do you think he meant by that reference then?" Paul asked as Chick and Jayne stared at Bobby Ray.

"Look here, in the second to last paragraph. The letter refers to *'the black friends'*. Then it says *'I could not force them to protect what they could not'*. To me it means the slaves didn't have the guns needed to protect any money he left with them. If that's the case, and if he did leave the money with them, I don't suspect the slaves of that time would have written down what they would have done with the money, but it sure enough would have been talked about in later years. No one could have kept a secret like that for long, not white nor black folks. He may be talking about slaves in his letter, but I doubt he left the money with them. Hell, you had two bureaucratic governments fighting each other and they didn't leave us any records of the missing money. You can't expect regular folks to have done that for us. I've been living here my whole life, and while I've heard a bunch of different stories about this missing money, I haven't ever heard any rumors or stories coming from black folks or white folks over the years about the money being left with slaves. I can tell you with great confidence the money was not left with any slaves. I'm not sure what he meant by the term *'the black friends'*, but it sure in hell was not slaves he was referring to. No Confederate officer would have risked leaving the treasury of the Confederacy with slaves. Not in those days they wouldn't! It's sure confusing and all, but I'm telling y'all one thing for sure. The money is in Charleston. For sure it is."

Paul stared blankly at his friend for a few seconds, trying as he did to figure out what Bobby Ray, in his own unique Southern style, had just told them. He had complicated the obvious parts of the Francis letter and minimized the most important parts. Paul was now more confused over the clues in the letter than he was before his friend had spoken. Politely he responded back. "I'll buy some of that logic of yours. What he was describing in his letter is confusing, but I'm also very confident he was not talking about slaves."

They sat in the diner's booth for another hour talking about the various clues which had been left in the Francis letter. As they did, they put together a plan of what to do next in their efforts to solve the mystery facing them. When they finished talking, Paul assigned each of them one clue to follow up on. Before they broke for the day, they agreed to meet early next Tuesday morning at Paul's house for their first trip to Charleston. "Who knows, maybe we'll get lucky and find something." They all knew it was too big of a wish to hope for.

* * * * * *

The following Tuesday, without Bobby Ray and Pete as they had other matters to attend to, Jayne, Chick, and Paul started the leisurely two hour trip down Highway 17 from Murrells Inlet to Charleston. After making a brief stop in Georgetown, they each talked about what they had been able to find out from the clues left in the Francis letter.

"Amazingly, I did find a website which listed our soldier, Captain Judiah Francis, as being a member of the Confederate army. He served in the Army of Northern Virginia, in the Fourth Cavalry Unit's Company C to be precise. That cavalry unit was one which fell under the command of the well-known General Jeb Stuart. The records on the website, if they are accurate, show Francis appeared to have joined the army in 1861. The same records show he enlisted in Roanoke, Virginia. Any other information, such as promotions, demotions, or even if he had been injured while fighting during the war, is information I can't find as yet. I'll keep poking for more on him when I can." Paul knew what he told them offered little help to what they were trying to find in Charleston.

"The only other news I learned was regarding the injury the minie ball likely caused when it got lodged into Francis' left femur. I called a doctor friend of mine back in Connecticut and vaguely asked him about what kind of an actual injury would have occurred from that type of a gunshot. He told me while the minie ball being stuck in the bone was serious in itself, the soft tissue injury and possibly the rupturing of one of the blood vessels in his leg would have been the most devastating injuries Francis sustained. That's especially true since either the loss of blood or blood poisoning, septicemia is what the medical folks call it, coupled with the lack of medical care, could have led to his death very soon after the injury was sustained. Who knows how bad it was for him, but it was obviously bad."

Chick and Jayne took time to absorb what Paul told them before Jayne passed on what she had learned. "My news is not much better, but I did find some information regarding the King Street road. It's the road Francis talked about in his letter. In fact, it still exists today. The upper part of the road, while still called King Street, is also known as US 78 where it runs through North Charleston down towards Charleston Harbor. It may be the place we want to start our search today. Perhaps the warehouse he spoke about in his letter still exists today in some shape or form."

Paul nodded at the news he just heard. "It's as good as any place to start, I guess."

Jayne also told them she had contacted the Charleston Civil War Historical Group, and the Charleston Slave Museum, to learn what roles slaves played in supporting the Confederate cause during the war. "I wish I had something of substance to tell you, but like Paul said, either the records don't exist or I need to get down there and do some research on my own. They did tell me that while many slaves remained loyal to their owners, little record was kept of the actual support given to the Confederacy by those slaves."

* * * * * *

It was almost noon by the time they reached Charleston. To their surprise, Chick quickly found a parking place along busy Murray Boulevard. They parked adjacent to the harbor and close to where the city of Charleston years ago had built a small park known as White Point Gardens. The view from the park looked directly out over the harbor at Fort Sumter, and at nearby Castle Pinckney. While walking through the park, they took the time to notice the many historical markers and Civil War era cannons located there. The area around White Point Gardens was bustling with tourists taking advantage of a beautiful sunny afternoon. As a group of female joggers dodged the many horse-drawn carriages that were present, several construction workers were enjoying their lunch break from the work they were performing on two nearby Civil War era homes. Looking at the homes being worked on, Paul wondered if they had been damaged during the battle over Fort Sumter.

As the three of them walked along on South Battery Road, then onto King Street, and then back onto East Battery and East Bay streets, they noticed the many fine homes and small businesses in the area, but they found nothing closely resembling an old warehouse. Even venturing further up to where Broad Street and Ashley Avenue intersect on the city's lower west side produced nothing resembling an old warehouse. Stopping to chat with several area residents and shopkeepers also produced no one who could remember such a building being present for some time.

Chick then told them something he had not thought of until now. "Perhaps we can't find this warehouse because it doesn't exist any longer. A good part of Charleston was destroyed around the time of the war by both accidental and intentionally set fires. Perhaps the warehouse was one of those buildings burnt up during one of those fires. Maybe the Union army had the place torn down for some reason when they occupied Charleston for a period of time."

Paul thought about what Chick had said for several moments. "Well, so much for finding a warehouse loaded with clues to make the hunt for the rest of the money come easy. All we have here are some fancy homes, a few with a good deal of history to them, but far too many which mean nothing to us. This whole area is nice, especially the areas near King Street and Tradd Street, as these homes, many which date back to the Revolutionary War and before, have been well taken care of. I have to give the city and the owners of these homes a pat on the back for preserving them so well, but it's a damn shame the other nearby areas have not been preserved better than they have. This part of the city played a big role in shaping our nation's history. These neighborhoods look directly out at Fort Sumter, but further down this same street, what is it now? It's nothing but a neighborhood full of yuppies and fancy homes, far too many restaurants, boat clubs, and tourist trap locations, all which look out over the harbor. Hell, half of the people living and working along this one street likely couldn't point Fort Sumter out to you even if you showed them where it was. The other half probably doesn't have any idea of what the historical importance of Fort Sumter, Castle Pinckney, and Fort Moultrie are. I don't like it, not one bit!"

As a Civil War buff, Paul could never understand why so many towns and cities, and corporate greed, had been allowed to encroach on areas of historical significance. He was old school in his thoughts about historical preservation and a strong believer in our country's history needing to be preserved for future generations of Americans to enjoy. He had been of this opinion for several years. His opinion was that far too many burger joints, gas stations, souvenir shops, and other businesses, as well as too many neighborhoods, had encroached upon our nation's historic battlefields and other similar sites. "It's a damn shame we've allowed this to happen. A damn shame!" Silently, Chick and Jayne both agreed with his position about the urban sprawl now threatening far too many of the country's historical locations along the east coast.

The rest of the day was spent trying to track down answers to the clues they had. While they stopped and read the many historical markers in and around the city, and stopped at other locations seeking answers to their clues, they still could not break the remaining clues Francis had left in his letter. Even stopping at places like the Charleston Visitor's Center kiosks, at the main branch of the Charleston Public Library, and at the famous Robert Mills Fireproof Building, which was now the home of the South Carolina Historical Society, did little to help break any of the clues.

Even on their ride home, as they read through the many pamphlets, books, and handouts they had picked up during their various stops, they still were no closer to solving the clues. As he had done countless times before now, Paul read and reread the Francis letter as they drove home. Whether he read it silently or out loud, neither way proved to be any help to them.

* * * * * *

Over the course of the next week they spoke to each other on the phone every time they felt they had broken one of the clues, but each phone call always ended with disappointment when someone else quickly dismissed a thought with a logical argument against it. As the week came to a close, the phone calls became fewer in number between them. Paul could sense frustration entering the picture and he knew the others had temporarily lost some of their focus. To some degree, he knew he had as well.

After a weekend spent doing nothing except for chores around the house, as well as spending parts of those same two afternoons on the beach with Donna at nearby Huntington State Park, Paul knew he had to recapture his focus. After Donna left for work on Monday morning, he spread out on a table in his garage, and nearby on the garage floor, the saddlebags, the old and new maps of Charleston and Georgetown he had, the flour barrel, the gold coins he found with Francis' remains, and the Francis letters. He hoped spreading these items out would help him find a connection between them. Such a connection would help break down the wall which was keeping him from seeing the obvious connection to at least one clue he held. Sitting at the table as he tried to find a connection to one of the clues Francis had left in his letter, Paul grew even more frustrated than he had been over the past few days. "It's here, I know it is, but why can't I work this out?" Even taking a break later in the day to grab something to eat did little to help his efforts in finding the one connection he needed.

Despite his best efforts, including spending several hours poring over what information he had available to him, Paul continued to struggle to make the tiniest connection he needed to get on with the hunt for the rest of the missing Confederate treasury. He was beyond frustrated with his lack of progress. "Am I that blind, or perhaps that stupid, that I cannot figure out what it is he is trying to tell me in the letter he wrote to President Davis. Why can't I figure this out?" Soon frustrated to no end, he packed the items back up he had been working with and put them away.

Later that same night, still frustrated by the lack of progress he was making, Paul made a spontaneous decision to revisit Charleston the next morning without the others so he could work without any interruptions.

The next morning he was up early preparing to leave when Donna surprised him. "Paul, I'm taking a mental health day and I'm coming with you. I haven't been to Charleston yet, and I promise I won't get in your way, but I'm coming. Tell me if you need my help when we get there, but otherwise I just want to see the sights while you do whatever it is you have to do."

"No problem here, I'm glad you're coming. I'm sure I can put you to work once we get there. Who knows, maybe I'll even bounce a few ideas off you."

Paul dragged Donna around Charleston at a fast pace later that morning and into the early afternoon as he wanted to seek answers to the clues he had at as many places as possible. Early in the afternoon they grabbed a taxi and he took her with him when he spoke with a few staff members at the Charleston Confederate Museum. He had contacted them the previous day and arranged to meet with two of the museum's staff members regarding Charleston's role in the Civil War. Despite his frantic pace, Donna kept up with him. As promised, she did not interfere with his efforts to break any of Francis' clues. But like the phone calls between Paul and the others, calls which had recently accomplished little, his trip to Charleston was also accomplishing little as well.

Despite several hours of crisscrossing the city and speaking to several Civil War experts, Paul had nothing positive happen to improve his chances of finding the balance of the treasury. It was nearly 3 pm when he gave up hopes of finding any new information regarding the clues he had. After ignoring the many hints Donna had dropped to him over the past hour, he finally relented and they stopped for a late lunch at a small restaurant on Calhoun Street. It was located immediately around the corner from the College of Charleston.

Disappointed by the results of the day, Paul ate only a small portion of his lunch before they finally started making their way back to their car. As they walked back on Meeting Street, he patiently waited outside as Donna browsed through several shops and boutiques. Standing outside one of the shops, he unfolded a copy of the letter Francis had written to President Davis. Slowly he reread the letter to himself. "I know he's not referring to slaves in his letter when he talks about *'our black friends, while strong and solid'* as it just doesn't make sense. They were fighting a war in which slavery was one of the principle issues, especially here in the South. The letter was too polite, almost too complimentary, for a Confederate officer to write in those days about slaves. So, if it wasn't slaves he was talking about, what was it and why can't I figure this out?"

Done with her late afternoon shopping, they casually walked back to their car, cutting through White Point Gardens located at the end of Meeting Street. The park was just around the corner from where they had parked their car. Despite the cool breeze blowing in off the harbor, the sun warmed them as they walked hand in hand. Walking across Murray Boulevard, Paul stopped briefly to admire the view of Fort Sumter lying far out in Charleston Harbor. "What it must have been like that first morning when the Confederates were shelling the fort. If only the fort could speak."

Donna had kept on walking down the sidewalk, but stopped when she heard his voice. "What's that, Paul?"

"Nothing, just thinking out loud."

Walking back across the street, they stopped to take a closer look at a monument the city of Charleston had erected in White Point Gardens. They saw it was one dedicated *'To the Defenders of Charleston'*, those Confederate soldiers who had served the city so well during the Civil War. As they started to walk back towards the car, Paul stopped to ponder a thought he had. Again, Donna kept walking without him. Realizing he was not behind her; she stopped and turned to look at him. "Paul, are you coming?"

"Yeah, in a minute." Frustrated by the lack of progress, he sat down on a nearby park bench and took the Francis letter out of his pocket to read again. Pausing before reading the letter, Paul hollered down the sidewalk to his wife. "Donna, I just need a couple of minutes. Just let me think something out and then we'll get going."

"OK, I'll just take a walk around the park for a couple of minutes, but then we have to get going. It's going to be late by the time we get back home."

"What? Yeah, OK." Paul tried one more time to decipher the Francis clues.

Fifteen minutes later Donna was back from her stroll through the park. Taking off her sunglasses as she sat down on the bench next to him, she asked him if he had made any progress deciphering the clues. "Any luck?"

"Nope! No pun intended, but I don't have a clue as to what he is trying to tell us. Not a darn clue!" Standing up, Paul refolded the letter and placed it back inside his shirt pocket. "I know as much now as I did before my two trips down to this fine city. It's here, but I'll be darned if I can figure it out. OK, let's go, I need to get you home. Thanks for being so patient."

Donna was silent for a couple of moments as they started walking to their car, but then she asked her husband a question. "Paul, some of those cannons I saw in the park have numbers on them. Why is that?"

Lost in his own thoughts, Paul was at first confused by what Donna asked him. "Numbers? What numbers? I don't know, probably serial numbers put on them by the manufacturers when the cannons were made."

Donna laughed at his answer. "I doubt that!"

"OK, so maybe it's not a serial number, maybe it's something else, but what's so funny?"

"Paul, it can't be a serial number. How would the cannons be able to fire if the number was there? I mean, you know, with the concrete and all that's there."

Immediately Paul stopped walking, his brain instantly bombarded with thoughts and questions racing through his mind. Grabbing Donna by the arm, he spun her around on the sidewalk, quickly walking her back in the direction they had just come from. "Show me!"

"Paul, it's probably nothing. I just saw the numbers and the letters, and I thought you might know what they meant."

"Perhaps it's nothing, perhaps it's everything. Where'd you see it? Show me!"

Donna quickly pointed to one of the park's Seven Inch Banded Brooks Rifle, a cannon still pointing out at Fort Sumter after all of these years since the war. Like the other cannons in the park, it had been permanently mounted on a display for tourists to have their pictures taken next to. A brass plate on the ground below each mounted cannon told visitors the types of cannons they were looking at. As Paul walked towards the cannon, two other cannons known as Columbiad cannons - 'Confederate Rodmans' - sat off to his right. Like the Brooks Rifle, the Columbiads were still pointed out at the fort, poised to fire their next shot. Donna watched from the sidewalk as he slowly walked over to the cannon she had pointed out.

First looking at the barrel end of the cannon, he saw it looked like most cannons that had been put out on public display. It had been painted with several coats of black paint to protect it from the elements. Like the others, the cannon had been placed on a concrete mount and the barrel had been filled with some type of mortar. In the past, Paul had always thought these types of historical cannons had likely been filled to keep rain water from damaging the interior of the barrel. Now as he stared at the mortar, his eyes saw the small inscription. Carefully inscribed, and still visible after so many years, were the letters C.S.A.. Also still visible was the number 10. The number had been inscribed directly below the letters. Instantly he knew they were the clues he had been looking for.

"You idiot!" Paul screamed out loud to no one but himself. His sudden outburst drew puzzled and concerned looks from several nearby tourists in the park. Standing only a few steps away, Donna burst out laughing as she knew her innocent observation had caused him to finally find what he had been looking for. The smile that crossed his face confirmed to her something special was soon to happen.

Quickly they retreated to a quieter section of the park. Sitting down on one of the benches near the King Street section of the park, Paul leaned over and gave his wife a long and passionate kiss. Softly, so others walking nearby could not hear him, he whispered to her. "You found it, Donna! You found it!"

"Paul, I know you're excited about what I just found, and excuse my ignorance, but what is it I just found that has gotten you so excited? And one more thing, back there when you yelled 'you idiot', you were talking about yourself, correct?"

Excited by what they had just found, he could not help laughing at what Donna just asked him. "Correct. I'm the idiot I was referring to. I spent so much time looking at the cannons themselves, and everything else, that I missed the obvious clue that was staring me in the face. But you didn't, you saw it!" Paul leaned over and gave her another long kiss.

Almost whispering so others nearby in the park could not hear him, Paul explained to Donna the meaning of the clues the Francis letter held and what the inscriptions in the cannon meant. "This cannon, and several more like it, were used by Francis to hide the remaining gold and silver in."

"You mean this cannon is ….."

Quickly he put his hand over Donna's mouth before she could finish her thoughts, most importantly, before she could let everyone else in the park know what it was they had just found. After taking his hand off of her mouth, Paul gave her another kiss as a way to show her his appreciation for what she had just found.

Donna was completely taken back by the totally out of character public display of affection Paul showed her, but she enjoyed it. "Gees, with all this kissing going on, I hope we can figure out some other clues here today as well. I'm starting to like this."

Paul laughed again and as he did he could feel the tension from the last two weeks leave his body. He was back to being himself at last. But as fast as his body relaxed, his mind started racing, thinking of the steps he needed to take.

"Donna, you know what this means, right?"

"I think it means I'm probably driving home by myself tonight and you're staying down here. Am I correct?"

"Yes, you are. Are you OK with that? I mean, I have to figure out a few more things, make a few phone calls to get the others down here and then start looking for the other cannons. We figured out the last piece of the puzzle, but there's still a lot of work to do yet."

"If I said no would you be happy with that answer? Of course you wouldn't. I want you to be happy and I want you to figure this all out. I'm amazed at what you've found so far. I know when you're ready you are going to rock the world with the story you're going to tell them. So no, I don't mind you staying down here, go find the rest of it and get it done."

"Thanks for understanding all of this for me. I appreciate it."

"I know you do. Tell you what, tell Chick to stop by the house when you call him. When I get home, I'll pack a bag with some fresh clothes for you for a couple of days."

Walking her to her car, Paul kissed her again and then they said their goodbyes. "Call me when you get home so I know you got there safely."

As Paul watched her drive down the street, his head was already spinning. It was busy trying to figure out what his next step was going to be. Among his many thoughts was how he was going to locate the other cannons that had the same markings as the one they just found. Donna had not even reached the end of the street and he was already on the phone to Chick.

"Hello?"

Still far too excited from what he just discovered with Donna, Paul skipped the usual telephone pleasantries and got right to the point. "Chick, I need Jayne and you to get down to Charleston right now."

"Right now? What's so important that it cannot wait until tomorrow?"

"How about the missing clue we've been looking for. I found it. Well, actually Donna found it, but she didn't know what she found until she told me about it. Get down here and then I'll put the remaining pieces of the puzzle together for you and ... can you just get Jayne and get down here? I'll fill you in some more when you get here."

"Paul, how can you be so confident about what you've found? We've been striking out for the past couple of weeks and all of a sudden you think you've solved the mystery because your wife told you about something." Not totally convinced that his friend had found the clue they needed to move forward with their search, Chick was hesitant to believe Paul.

"Chick, the letter our friend wrote, in it he talks about *'the strong black solid friends of ours who have served us well since Fort Sumter'*. He also makes a reference to the letters CSA. He wasn't talking about slaves, he was talking about cannons. But listen; whether he was talking about slaves, cannons, or what the price of tea in China was at the time . . . I'm not talking about this on the cell anymore as I don't know who might be listening. Get Jayne and get down here tonight. I'll give you the rest of the story when you get here. You both are going to be amazed at what I've discovered. I still don't have all of the answers yet, that's why I need you guys down here. I need your help. You coming or not?"

"OK, OK, I trust you. Get a couple of hotel rooms ready for us. I'll get Jayne and we'll call you when we're just outside of the city. You want me to get Pete and Bobby Ray down there also?"

"No, not yet. We still have some work to do before we need them here. Listen, before you come down, stop at my house first. Donna is going to pack a bag of clean clothes for me for a couple of days, grab them for me. You guys better pack for a couple of days as well. Call me when you're close to Charleston and I'll let you know where we're staying. Chick, I promise this is going to be the best one yet. Hey, make sure you bring a flashlight."

After ending the phone call, Paul walked a few blocks until he got to the Charleston Holiday Inn – Mills House. He had seen the hotel on Meeting Street earlier in the day. Once there, he reserved three hotel rooms for the next three days. As he finished making the reservation, he hoped they would find what they were looking for before the hotel reservations expired.

* * * * * *

Four hours later Chick and Jayne were finally pulling into Charleston. They barely had time to check into the Holiday Inn before Paul was dragging them down to where the cannons silently stood in the park off of South Battery Road.

As they neared the park, both Chick and Jayne could sense the tone of excitement in Paul's voice over the discovery he had made. Despite their best efforts at prying the big surprise from him, he resisted their efforts, waiting instead for them to see in person what it was that had made him so excited.

"There she is!" Smiling, Paul proudly pointed at the Banded Brooks cannon which held the clue he hoped would soon lead them to other cannons in the city. Other cannons hopefully with similar markings to the ones he now showed Chick and Jayne.

"OK, we see the cannon. So what's this got to do with you being so excited and dragging us down here in the middle of the night? I cannot believe one old cannon has gotten you so excited!" Chick still did not grasp what the connection was between the clues and the cannon he was looking at.

"This cannon, hopefully like the other ones we're going to find in the city are the *'strong solid black friends of ours'*. Like I told you on the phone, Francis was talking about cannons, not slaves. He also talked about the cannons being, and I quote, *'even in number, remain loyal protectors of our C.S.A. assets. I am confident that you will find them in excellent shape, even in years to come.'* Get it? He knew the cannons would hold their shape, staying strong and hard even years after he wrote the letter. If he was talking about slaves, just like any other group of people they would get old and tired, even die off, but the cannons are still in great shape, even after all of these years of sitting here in this park."

"So you're saying, what?"

"OK, come take a closer look. Give me the flashlight."

Handing him the flashlight, Chick and Jayne moved closer to the cannon behind where Paul stood. "Look closely at the end of the cannon. See here, somewhat crudely inscribed in the mortar are the letters CSA. Under the letters is the number 10. Come look at this next cannon." Walking several yards to where the next cannon sat permanently mounted on a stand in the park, Paul showed them the same inscription in the mortar. It was an inscription just like the previous one, one which had been scratched into the cannon's mortar many years ago. "See, this inscription also reads CSA. Look under the letters, the number 16 has been inscribed into the mortar. Are you getting it yet?"

"Well?" Chick stood there scratching his head.

Excited by what he had figured out, Paul could not help but laugh as he sensed Chick's frustration at not understanding what the inscriptions meant. "OK, let's look at the next cannon."

"Paul, are you trying to tell us the rest of the Confederate gold and silver has been hidden in these cannons for all of these years?" Jayne was just now starting to catch on.

"Yep, but not in this one. Look closely at this inscription. It's similar to the other two, but it has the number 11 inscribed in it. Let's go back to the letter for a moment. We know Francis wrote about something protecting the CSA assets. We now know he was talking about cannons and not slaves. He also wrote they were *'even in number'*. He repeats the word *'even'* in the next sentence, and in both sentences the word *'even'* is underlined. It's the only word in the entire letter which has been underlined. He did that to stress his point. I think only the cannons with an even number under the CSA inscription have gold and silver in them. The odd numbers, and at this point who knows how many there are of them, were likely just cannons possibly made to blend in with the others; others which have been marked with even numbers. You know, decoys or something like that."

A puzzled look now on her face, Jayne looked back at the cannon displaying the odd number in the mortar. "A decoy?"

"I'm not sure, but yes, that's my guess. Look, the letter talks about the assets being secured within a Confederate warehouse on the King Street road. That would have been right around the corner from here. In fact, the road over there is King Street. We tried looking for the warehouse when we came down here recently, remember? I'm confident now that Francis spent time in a warehouse and these cannons were there also. For some reason our soldier felt trapped, or possibly it was for some other reason, but he saw these cannons as being his only way of keeping the gold and silver out of the hands of the advancing Union army. Who knows, perhaps the cannons were damaged ones or perhaps the warehouse was a repair facility, but think of it, what an ingenious way to hide the gold and silver. Who would ever think to hide gold and silver coins within a cannon barrel? For that matter, who would even think to look for gold and silver coins in a cannon barrel? I know I wouldn't. When the war was over the cannons weren't needed any longer and they were later placed in parks, perhaps around the entire city, as a means to honor those men who served the Confederacy so well. By the way, the answer to my previous question is apparently no one!"

Chick barely said a word the entire time he was being shown the inscriptions in the cannons. Instead, he chose to just listen as Paul attempted to convince them what he uncovered earlier in the day was the clue they had been searching for. He finally started to speak, but waited a couple of minutes until some nearby residents, out for an evening walk with their dog, had gotten out of earshot.

"Paul, I disagree with you. You said no one would ever think to look in these cannons for the missing money. But I think the correct answer is one person would and that's you. And now, and without speaking for Jayne, I think the number is three. Like I have been, I suspect she also has been convinced the cannons hold the rest of the missing money. Convince us some more."

"Hopefully I can tomorrow. I have one more thing for you to think about tonight though. The Francis letter says in the last paragraph, and again I quote, *'while even in number'*. It also talks about money being held in his saddlebags. The letter also says he *'could not force them to protect what they could not'*. We found his saddlebags, right? Jayne, you were the one who found his initials on the saddlebags. What I'm saying is that he likely put the money in up to twelve cannons and then marked some of them with even numbers and some with odd numbers. His letter has the number twelve in it. We just don't know yet what the combination of the twelve numbers is. We know we have to find twelve cannons, but we don't know how many have odd numbers inscribed into them and how many have even numbers with similar inscriptions. Hopefully we will know that answer tomorrow. I'm also guessing what he couldn't fit into those cannons he put in his saddlebags. Those were the gold and silver coins we found in the saddlebags buried in the cemetery. The letter tells us he was planning on going back to retrieve the gold and silver he had already buried in South Carolina. That was the money he left with the children of Governor Allston. He likely went back to get the money, got shot, and was perhaps dying when he buried the saddlebags a few feet away from the first pile of money they had buried in the flour barrel. That explains why he never came back to get the money out of the cannons. He and his men were probably killed before they could return to get the money. He got back to the cemetery and buried his saddlebags, but then he apparently died after being shot. Is this making any sense to either of you?"

"Paul, you've convinced us, now all we have to do tomorrow is to find the other cannons." Jayne and Chick exchanged excited smiles with each other at the thought of finding the rest of the missing Confederate treasury. They knew they were very close to finding it.

As they walked back to their hotel, it was Chick's turn to ask Paul one last question for the night. "Just tell me we are not going to jackhammer the concrete out of these cannons in the middle of the night."

"We aren't, at least not yet we aren't, but I like your way of thinking though. We'll figure it out, but not tonight, I'm too tired."

Before returning to the hotel they shared a late dinner together at a small restaurant on Wentworth Street. It was one which specialized in Southern fried chicken. After returning to the hotel, they agreed to meet in the hotel's restaurant the following morning to decide upon a strategy to search for the remaining cannons. As they waited in the lobby for the elevator to take them to their rooms, Jayne clasped Paul's hands with hers. "Paul, you did it. The money has to be in those cannons, it has to be."

"Let's hope so. Thanks for coming down here tonight on such short notice. You and Chick have been a big help."

* * * * * *

First to arrive at the restaurant the following morning, Paul was pleased to see he had a few minutes to himself. Waiting for Chick and Jayne before ordering his breakfast, he sat in one of the booths drinking his first cup of coffee and reading the morning's *USA Today*. He had been reading the paper for almost twenty minutes when they both came into the restaurant.

"Morning, Paul!" Unrehearsed, they both greeted him at the same time.

"Morning back at you!" Paul did not even look up from the article he was reading as they both slipped into the other side of the booth.

"Something good in the paper that's got your attention this morning?"

"I'm reading this article which talks about so many cities and towns across the country that are facing tough economic times. It talks about budget deficits and budget cuts, both of which have resulted in so many communities being forced to cut back on services they have routinely provided in the past to their residents. So many communities are being forced to cut services so they can maintain their budgets to some extent. It's kind of ironic that one of the cities they're referencing in the article is Charleston."

More interested in looking over the breakfast menu than listening to what Paul was saying, Chick only casually listened to what was being said. "So what's so different about Charleston compared to all of those other communities and what's so interesting about this particular article? These stories are in the papers and on the television news everyday it seems. Frankly, I cannot bear to read any more of these articles as all they do is tell us more and more bad news about the economy. Between the television news and the newspapers, I'm tired of reading and hearing about it, it's just so damn depressing."

Paul finished reading the article and then put the newspaper down before he answered Chick's question about Charleston being mentioned. "The difference is not every city in 2011 can host an anniversary celebration. It's a year which happens to be, as you esteemed instructors of American History know, the one hundred and fiftieth year of the start of the Civil War. A war, I remind you both, which started darn close to the same street where I showed you the three cannons last night. Two of those cannons are sitting there still packed with some of the missing Confederate treasury. Think of the magnitude of such an anniversary. To me, something celebrating its one hundred and fiftieth anniversary must be a fairly important event to remember as we don't seem to celebrate insignificant events in history. The newspaper article talks about Charleston being forced to cancel the city's big celebration they were planning for the sesquicentennial anniversary of the Civil War because of budget problems. That historic anniversary is what separates Charleston from the other cities being talked about in the article."

Realizing he had been talking too loud, Paul quickly turned around in the booth to see if anyone had heard him. Fortunately the restaurant was not very busy. The two waitresses who were working were busy chatting up the restaurant manager on the other side of the room. He was relieved to see no one had heard him.

Chick just stared at Paul for a moment before he spoke. "The what anniversary? How did you know that?"

"Sesquicentennial, it means one hundred and fifty years. Chick, tell me you didn't know that?"

"I hate to show my ignorance, but …."

"I know what it means!" Interrupting Chick, Jayne briefly smiled as she looked at Paul. The twinkle in her eye told him she was about to say something sarcastic. She then told both of them what she knew about the term sesquicentennial. "I would have thought Chick would have known what sesquicentennial meant as well. Maybe he needs to expand his areas of knowledge a bit before he even contemplates going on Jeopardy." It was her attempt at a good natured jab at her mentor. The jab worked as Chick now stared at her in disbelief, not sure if she actually knew what sesquicentennial meant or if she was just pulling his leg.

After ordering their breakfast, Jayne asked Paul what the game plan was for the day regarding the cannons they hoped to find.

"Well, I was not prepared for this to happen when I left the house with Donna yesterday so all my maps of Charleston are back at home. I guess to start with we need to find a few new ones so we can each work off the same style of map. Then we can split up so we can cover the parks and some other areas where the cannons might be located in the city. The Visitor's Center has a good map and I know it has the city's parks displayed on it. We can stop there first and pick up a few copies to work with. While we're there we might as well pick their brains for any other possible locations to check. How's that sound?"

Between bites of his toasted cinnamon raisin bagel, Chick answered Paul. "Sounds good to us. We just have to hope we can find the other cannons somewhere in the city. If we don't, who knows where they might be after all of this time."

Over their breakfast and a second cup of coffee, Paul worked out the final details of the search with them. "I'll keep a record of where we find the cannons. You guys just call me each time you find one and tell me the number inscribed in the mortar. Tell me the location where you find it as well and then I'll call the other person so we aren't wasting time checking places we've already looked at. Try not to venture out of the area you're covering so we aren't stepping on each other's toes."

As they finished up their breakfast, the waitress brought over the bill. Paul thanked her and asked for a large black hazelnut coffee to go. "I'll take care of breakfast today. It's the least I can do to show you my appreciation for coming down here on such short notice." After paying the bill, he grabbed his coffee to go. They were off to locate Francis' strong black friends.

Walking along Ann Street to one of the Visitor Center kiosks, Jayne asked Paul a question similar to the one Chick had posed last night. "Once we locate the cannons we still have to find a way to retrieve the gold and silver from them. Have you figured that out yet?"

"I've got some of the details worked out in my head, but not all of them. I think I'm going to have the mayor of this fine city do some of the dirty work for us."

Jayne laughed at his answer, at first thinking he was joking with her. Looking at his face as they continued to walk along on the sidewalk, she quickly realized he had not been joking with her. "The mayor? He's going to think we're nuts when we tell him what we want to do. Why would he want to help us?"

"I don't believe for a moment that he's going to think we're nuts at all. I have no doubts at all that he's going to help us. In fact, I know he's going to help us, seeing that we're going to indirectly help him with his upcoming campaign for the vacant United States senate seat he's seeking."

Paul's comment caused Chick and Jayne to stop dead in their tracks as they turned onto Ann Street. "We're going to help him with what?" The incredulous look from Chick made Paul laugh as he knew neither of them could possibly have known what angle he had lined up in his head. But then they had not read the story in the newspaper. It was a story he knew would soon help them get the cannons opened so they could get to the gold and silver hidden within them.

"Listen, do you think Mayor William Davis wants to be remembered as the mayor who cancelled the Civil War's 150th Anniversary Celebration in the city where it all started? Personally, I don't think he wants to be remembered this way. Cancelling the celebration means too much to the hotels, to the restaurants, and to all of the other businesses who make their living off the dollars tourists spend here in Charleston. Look around you, the Civil War is still a big historical event to people across the South . . . Charleston included . . . the negative political exposure in cancelling such an event is far too great for a senatorial candidate to expose himself to. The fact that Charleston, like many other municipalities across the country, is facing budget problems doesn't matter. People will equate the cancellation of the anniversary celebration to him and their disappointment in the celebration being cancelled will be remembered at election time. The mayor will not want to incur their wrath at the polls, so he'll help us. He just doesn't know it yet, but when we present it to him this way he'll help us. He may think in his own way that we're nuts, but all politicians like money and votes. When he hears we're going to give him the money Charleston needs to pay for the anniversary celebration, he's going to very quickly see the positive side of helping us get the cannons opened. Opening those cannons for us is going to be a huge help for his political campaign. It's a simple math formula if you think really about it. His help, plus the money Charleston gets from us, equals votes."

Chick stared at Paul as he listened to what he had planned for the mayor. He continued to stare at him even after he finished talking. "You know, you scare me."

"I what? How do I do that?" Paul could not help but smile at what Chick had just said to him.

"Yesterday, without anything to help you except a casual remark your wife made about the markings she saw on a cannon, you quickly figured out the clues regarding the cannons. You figured out what the inscriptions left on the cannons meant and all of that. You made all of those connections in a very short period of time. Then this morning, in about twenty minutes tops after reading a simple newspaper article, you calculated a way to get the mayor of Charleston to help us so it would benefit his future political career. Last night I was struggling to keep up with you when you showed us the markings on the cannons and when you were telling us what they all meant. Hell, I was even struggling to figure out what I wanted for breakfast this morning. Now you have the rest of the details pretty much worked out to make this work to our advantage. You know, I consider myself to be an educated man and a pretty intelligent one as well, but your brain definitely works differently than mine does. I do wish I had your reasoning skills. That, my friend, is how you scare me."

Giggling to herself at first, Jayne suddenly burst out laughing, unable to hold it any longer. Her laughter drawing smiles from those walking by on the sidewalk. "Paul, you know Chick's right. He and I have talked about this since we were digging back in North Carolina. You seem to have a special talent at seeing through the fog which surrounds all of these clues you've uncovered. It's almost like you know what the important details are and which ones are the superfluous ones. I want to know how you do it."

"Don't know what to tell you. I didn't know I was doing anything different than what you two were doing. Maybe being a state cop for all of those years makes me look at things differently. Who knows?"

"Maybe."

They soon got back on track and walked the short distance to a nearby tourist kiosk. There Paul obtained three colored maps of the city, the same ones tourists often use when they're trying to find the various Civil War sites, museums, restaurants and shops spread out across Charleston. They were fortunate enough to have obtained the maps from a longtime resident of the city. She was able to tell them a handful of locations to check for cannons which had been put on display. "Seems everywhere you go in Charleston we have cannons. Tourists like you folks love them. Hope you find the right one to have your picture taken next to."

Sitting down on a bench at one of the city's bus stops, Paul pulled a blue Sharpie pen from his pants pocket and dissected each of the maps into three fairly equal sections. He did so by drawing blue lines across the maps. "Chick, you take this piece of the pie, the piece up around Park Circle and south as far as Cosgrove Avenue; Jayne you take the middle piece, the piece which starts with Cosgrove as the northern most point and go south as far as where Hampton Park is on the west side of the city and as far east where Highway 17 enters the city. I'll take the last piece, from where Jayne stops here at Hampton Park; I'll finish down by the harbor. Call me when you find something and I'll keep a running tally on what we find. I'll call you both later and we'll meet somewhere for a late lunch or whatever."

Walking the short distance back down Meeting Street, Paul decided he would start back at the park where he and Donna located the three cannons the previous day. He wanted to start there so he could make sure in the previous day's excitement he had not missed any other cannons in the area. Walking through the park, he could not help noticing the tourists who were having their pictures taken next to the three cannons. The very same cannons inscribed with the markings Donna had accidently found for him. A large church group held up a small sign identifying their church as they stood next to the cannon inscribed with the number sixteen. The church group was all smiles as their pastor took several photos of them surrounding the cannon. Nearby, the cannon marked with the number ten was patiently letting three young children sit on it as their father documented their visit to Charleston by taking pictures of their smiling faces. Filling in the sheet of paper he was working with to log the locations of the cannons they found, he could not help smiling at the sight of the cannons being used as props in the tourist's pictures. "If only they knew how much money they were standing next to. They all would be amazed."

Paul soon left the park after finding he had not missed any other cannons the previous day. Now he started to search his section on the map for any others. He walked around for almost two hours trying to find any types of cannons, but found none. As he walked, he took a moment to stop at a neighborhood deli on Queen Street to use the bathroom and to buy a bottle of water to quench his thirst. Taking his first sip of water, his cell phone announced an incoming call from Chick.

"Chick, talk to me!"

"I found two, one good and one bad. I found one marked with the number eighteen and one marked with the number three." Chick described the locations where he found them. They were in a small park near the east side of the city, just off of Oakwood Avenue.

"Nice work, but listen." Paul said, somewhat excited by Chick's find. "I know we talked about telling me where you find them, but now that I've thought about it, don't do that. Just tell me the numbers you find on them. I know what it is you're after. I don't mean to sound paranoid, but you never know who might be listening. Let's not tip our hands to someone who might be. And one more thing, just keep some rough notes on where you find them. Later in the day we'll compare notes with each other. From now on just call me with the numbers you find."

"OK, I've got you. Good idea."

"Chick, number three is not a bad one. The way I look at it, it's one we wanted to find no matter what. Now we only need to find seven more. Any number is a good number for us, but I know what you meant when you said a bad one."

"Understand. Hey, did you hear from Jayne yet?"

"Nope, not yet. Keep hunting and I'll talk to you soon. Hey, nice find with those two. Good job!"

For the next forty-five minutes, Paul scoured several places on his section of the map. He had just finished checking two nearby city parks for the still to be found cannons when he found cannons number seven and twelve by pure accident. He noticed them as he was walking to another nearby park. The two cannons stood guard at the entrance to a small private cemetery located near the intersection of Broad and Logan Streets. It was obvious they had been there for many years. The cemetery was one which had been neglected for far too long as it was easy to see the grounds had not been cared for recently. Throwing a couple of dead tree branches out of the way made it possible for him to read the inscriptions on the barrels of the two Napoleon style cannons. After logging the cannons on his form, he walked a short distance into the cemetery to survey the neglect. "I guess this place has either fallen victim to budget cuts or else no one buried here is important enough to have someone care for its upkeep." In the brief time he spent in the cemetery, he saw several headstones marking the graves of men and women who had served the United States in several different wars. "I'll make sure we take care of this problem real soon."

As excited as Chick was when he called with the news of the cannons he found, Paul found himself just as excited when he phoned Chick and Jayne with the news of the two cannons he found. "We're down to five we have to find. We're doing fabulous so far."

As Paul gave Jayne the good news, she also gave him equally good news. It was news he misunderstood at first. "Paul, we really only need to find four more."

"Jayne, is your math that bad? We had twelve we needed to find. We reduced the number by three from the ones Donna and I found yesterday, so that's nine left to find. Chick and I have found a total of four more this morning so that means we have five left to find. What's so hard to figure out?"

"Paul, when you called me I was just about to call you. I found another one. It's been marked with the number thirty, it's on ....."

Quickly he cut her off, explaining to her why he had. "Jayne, I'm sorry for doubting your math skills, I apologize. Guess I just got caught up in the moment. Listen, I should have called you earlier about this, but just tell me the numbers you find and you keep notes on where they are. I'll explain the rest later, OK?"

"OK, I think I know what you mean, but I got it for now. Something like loose lips sink ships, correct?"

"Exactly. Hey, what kind of shape is it in?"

"Looks fine, strong and black just as he said it would. Right now a young mother is holding her child on it while daddy takes their picture. If only they knew, huh? I'll go tell them not to dent it while they are having their pictures taken."

"Yeah, do that. Nice find by the way, I'll call you later." Finished speaking, Paul quickly jotted down the information Jayne told him about the cannon she had found.

By mid-afternoon, Paul had not found any of the four other still to be located cannons; neither had Jayne or Chick. At least not ones he had been told about as his cell phone had not rung to tell him any more good news. Taking a break after being in the sun for most of the day, he sat in the shade provided by a small maple tree in front of one of the many restaurants in the city's entertainment district. It was one of the neighborhoods the city had revitalized several years ago. Now tourists flocked to the area to spend their vacation dollars on overpriced sweatshirts and expensive dinners. Sitting in the shade, he called Jayne on her cell phone for an update.

"Hey, Paul."

"I take it no news is bad news. Am I correct?"

"Unfortunately you are. I've checked everywhere I could think and then some, but no dice. I don't know where else to check in my section. What's the plan from here?"

"I'll call Chick and tell him we're done for the day. Let's meet back in front of the hotel and then we can pick one of the bars near there to have a beer at. I'm hot and thirsty, I need a beer. I'll see you there."

"Sounds good to me. I'll be there in a few." Jayne was pleased to learn the hunt was being called off for the rest of the day.

Calling Chick to give him the news, Paul found he was as tired as they both were when he answered the call. "If you hadn't called me, I was stopping for a beer without you. My feet are killing me from all of this walking. I'll be there in about fifteen minutes, don't start without me!"

After meeting back in front of their hotel, the first order of business was to sit and rest. They did so at The Blue and Grey Saloon, an upscale neighborhood bar close to their hotel. Hot and thirsty, they each quickly drained two ice cold mugs of PBR. Drinking their beers, they exchanged notes on where they had found the cannons. "Here are some photos of the one I found, it looks like it could fire a cannon ball right now. It's still in great shape." Donna showed them the digital photos she had taken with her Nikon camera.

After taking a strong hit from his third beer, Paul set the frosted glass mug down on the bar. It was a long wooden bar which had been lacquered with far too many coats of polyurethane. The saloon, like its name implied, was designed to cater to the hordes of tourists who came to Charleston to visit Fort Sumter and the other Civil War attractions in the area. In both the bar and dining area hung numerous paintings and pictures of what Fort Sumter looked like after the cannon firing had ceased upon the tiny fort. Several facsimile Civil War uniforms and other curios decorated both areas of the saloon.

"Well, we made some progress today, but we didn't find all of them. Let's try it again tomorrow and see what happens, then we'll make our move to the mayor's office." Chick nodded his approval as he downed his last mouthful of PBR from the mug he had been drinking from. Trying to get the barmaid's attention so she could order another round of beers for them, Jayne briefly looked at Paul before nodding her approval as well. Still tired and hot from a long day of walking, she was ready to relax in the air conditioned saloon for the balance of the evening. Her companions offered no protest when she told them she was not planning on moving from her bar stool for a while. Her plan had just become their plan as well.

* * * * * *

They had become pretty comfortable sitting around and just talking after chasing down Civil War cannons on a warm November afternoon. They had not relaxed like this together since first teaming up to hunt for the missing money. It was a moment which was far overdue.

26

The Yankees Are Coming.

"Let me beseech you to lay aside all rancor and bring about a
consummation devoutly to be wished – a reunited country."
Confederate President Jefferson Davis, CSA, 1888

The next morning Francis and his men had barely woken up when Confederate soldiers galloping through the city streets first sounded the alarm. Their cries warned everyone, soldiers and residents alike, that Union troops had been found camped twenty-five miles north of Charleston and just southwest of Georgetown. Charleston had lived in fear of Union reprisals since the start of the war and now the residents feared the worst was about to happen to them.

Hearing the news, Francis quickly gathered his men together in the warehouse and prepared them for the return trip to the Allston family cemetery. They needed to try and retrieve the money they had buried there. He knew he was taking a risk making the trip, but his options were limited. As risky as it was to travel back to retrieve the money, it was even riskier leaving the rest of the gold and silver hidden in the damaged cannons. Now they had to move quickly or risk being trapped in Charleston. Before leaving the warehouse, he quickly inspected the cannons one last time. He prayed the money would remain safe until he could return to move it further south.

As he pushed his men towards the outskirts of the city, Francis knew the trip to the cemetery would now be a difficult one to make because of the presence of Union soldiers in the area. He also knew the return trip to Charleston would likely be an even riskier trip to make as their slow moving wagon would be loaded down with gold and silver from the cemetery. He now worried about being overrun by Union cavalry and the money being lost. "I have to risk it. I have no other choice."

As they reached the outskirts of the city, Francis impulsively called them to a halt. "Men, this is going to be a difficult trip to make. I fully expect we'll be attacked at some point. Somehow, and at all costs, we need to get the money we've buried in the cemetery back to the warehouse. Now listen carefully to what I have to say. If something should happen to me, I have written a letter to President Davis. It's in one my saddlebags, within a liquor bottle that has a likeness of President Washington on it. Also, in my saddlebags are letters written by President Davis and Treasury Secretary Memminger, they are in a second bottle. Extra copies of those two letters are within two envelopes inside my saddlebags as well. If I should die, or if I'm no longer able to travel with you, take all of those letters with you as they will give you free and unobstructed passage across the South. Most importantly though, make sure the letter gets delivered to President Davis with my sincere apologies for not delivering it in person to him. If you get the money back to Charleston without me, I want you to hide the money from the cemetery in the cannons like we did with the rest of the money. Hide it just like we did last night. My letter to President Davis explains how we have protected it and where it is stored. Don't worry about me if I shall fall injured or dead; just worry about protecting the gold and silver. Promise me you will do so!"

His remaining men, Sgts. Stine, Davis, Banks, and Odom, now truly realized the seriousness of the danger they faced. They had come to admire Francis as he had done everything they had done and even more. As they had worked in the heat, so had he; if they went without food, so had he. Other leaders they served under would never have endured the same hardships with them as he had. Collectively they nodded their heads to show him they understood his orders, but individually each of them knew they would not let him fall into the hands of the hated Yankees. Injured or dead, he was their leader. They were determined not to fail him or to lose him.

Riding northeast again, they rode together at first as they left the outskirts of Charleston. Sgt. Odom now drove the single wagon they were bringing back to the cemetery. His horse, a four year old grey stallion, trotted along behind the wagon, securely tied to the back of it. At first, they all rode their horses near the wagon as they were still close to the relative safety that Charleston afforded them. Shortly after leaving the area around the city, Francis sent Stine out on their west flank, Banks out in front of them, and Davis off to the east as they made their way towards Georgetown. As an experienced cavalry officer he knew what tactics to employ to protect his main body. On this occasion it was to protect the wagon they would need to bring the gold and silver back to Charleston in. He had always felt safer with scouts out protecting his main body, but in this case it was especially important to do for the overall safety of his small group of men. Three sets of eyes riding away from the wagon would give them a chance to make a stand and fight. It would also give them time to hide. The strength of any Union troops they encountered would decide which it would be. "The first sign of trouble you need to get back to us as soon as you can. We'll have a much better chance of winning a fight and staying alive if we're all together. Now ride, but be alert!"

The three sergeants had been out protecting their advance towards Georgetown for almost four hours when Odom heard Banks' distinct whistle. Almost at the same time, Davis and Stine could be seen approaching at a fast gallop. They each had seen the threat approaching them.

"Captain, Yankees!" Banks yelled, trying to catch his breath. "Yankees, four or five of them on horses, headed right this way, no more than two miles from here. They's headed this way, but right casually mind you. They don't look like they's fixin' to fight as they's just riding along right casually, but they's coming this way. I looked, but I didn't see no others following after them."

Banks had just finished giving Francis the news of the approaching Union soldiers when Davis rode up next to them. "Captain, I ain't one to run away from a fight, but I know what ya want to get done with the gold and silver. I seen an old road, not much more than a path really, over yonder off to the east a bit. If we hurry we can get down in there and make use of the pine trees to hide from view. It's a thick stand of trees, there's enough to give us some good cover."

Francis did not hesitate for a moment. "Take us there!"

In minutes, Davis led them to the stand of trees. Odom quickly drove the wagon as deep into the tree line as possible to get it out of view of the passing Union soldiers. They had only been hidden for a couple of minutes when Stine saw the soldiers approaching. They watched quietly, hidden behind the pine trees and scrub brush that was present, as the four Union soldiers casually approached near them. As they passed by, Francis and the others did their best to keep their horses quiet.

As the Union soldiers passed by their hiding spot, Stine carefully followed them a short distance. He was now on foot and staying within the tree line. He watched until the soldiers had ridden well out of sight. After watching for several more minutes to make sure they had not doubled back towards them, he returned to where the others still hid in the woods. "Captain, they rode off south, almost like they were headed towards Charleston. I hope they keep going that way for a long spell."

"Did they see our tracks we left? Any good soldier would certainly have seen the wagon tracks we had to have left in the ground."

"If they did, they didn't bother to stop and check them out. They just kept riding along and talking to each other just as y'all seen them do here."

Francis waited several more minutes before he moved the men out. He wanted to make sure the Union soldiers had not decided to double back towards their position. Soon satisfied he had waited long enough, they started moving northeast again. As they moved along, with Stine, Banks, and Davis again keeping a close eye out for Union troops, Francis rode his horse to the left of where Odom sat driving the wagon towards their destination.

Riding next to each other, Francis and Odom talked about the war, about the slavery issue, and on other matters related to the war. "Big Ed, for us to win this war, which in my opinion has always been a long shot due to the strength and power of the North, we must convincingly win the battles we fight against the Union armies. We cannot just injure them. We must devastate them with large losses of men. Doing so would likely effect the morale of their folks back home and put pressure on Lincoln to end the war. Who knows, he might not even be their President after the next election if things keep going badly for the North. But at the same time we must be able to sustain our own economy, that is one reason why protecting the gold and silver is so important. We must be able to sustain our own economy and our armies. Doing so will hopefully cause England to join us in our fight. Then, and only then, we would be able to defeat the Yankees. I also believe we need to take the war to the Yankees, just as they have done to us. We need to fight them on their own soil like we did at Gettysburg. That would likely influence the opinion Northern folks have on this war."

Odom took all of this in as he drove the wagon north, but sat quietly for several minutes as he thought about what Francis had just said. "Captain, I'm just a simple country boy doing my part, but I didn't think it was all that complicated. I just thought we had to kill more of them than they did of us and then it would be over."

Francis smiled at the simplistic way Odom had put things in perspective. "That's how it's supposed to work, but it's much more complicated than that I'm afraid."

Expecting a response back, Francis turned in his saddle to see Odom fall forward out of the wagon's seat and onto the ground. Stunned by what happened, Francis quickly realized he had been riding close to the noisy wagon as it moved along and had not heard the noise of the gunshots until the second shot was fired. The second shot hit the back of the seat where Odom had just been seated.

Now turning to face the direction from where the shots had been fired, Francis saw three Union soldiers at first, and then the fourth, as they charged towards him and the now stopped and driverless wagon. Odom's lifeless body rested on the ground not far from where the wagon had stopped. Francis then turned to see where the others were. As he located them, off to his sides and to his north, he incorrectly sensed in the stress of the moment that they just sat on their horses watching for what seemed like minutes before moving to assist him.

Instinctively, Francis dismounted his horse, running to check on Odom. He was dead, killed by a well-aimed or perhaps lucky rifle shot through the base of his skull. One minute they had been talking about the war and the next minute Odom was dead on a rough South Carolina trail. He hadn't even had time to defend himself.

Standing up, Francis ran back to the wagon. Reaching over the left side of the Conestoga wagon, he felt blindly for his Morse carbine rifle as his eyes remained focused on the fast charging Union soldiers. Finding the rifle with his left hand, he knelt down by the left rear wheel of the wagon as the Union cavalry soldiers rapidly approached his position. He now had no time to look to see where his men were. "Stay calm, just load the rifle and make the shot count, but stay calm." He knew the others would soon be there to help him, but for now he tried to calm himself as he took aim at the lead rider approaching him. It only took a couple of seconds to steady the rifle against the wagon and fire his first shot. As he did, first Stine, then Davis, raced by him to intercept the approaching cavalry soldiers, now one soldier less from the shot he had fired.

Francis had aimed well and the cavalry officer fell from his saddle, bouncing along the trail for several feet after hitting the ground. Now Stine and Davis both charged at the cavalry soldier on their right. He was now separated from the others by the void in their ranks caused by Francis shooting the lead soldier. It only took a few seconds for Stine and Davis, with their acquired marksmanship and riding skills, both learned from years of country living, to quickly shoot and kill the next cavalry soldier.

As they turned their horses around to race back towards Francis, the remaining two Union cavalry soldiers each fired a shot at him, but both shots missed their intended target. As Stine raced back towards his captain, the cavalry officer who Francis had shot staggered to his feet. Despite bleeding heavily from a gunshot wound to his left shoulder, he began running towards Francis who was now focused on the two remaining cavalry soldiers. The two mounted soldiers posed the bigger immediate threat to him.

Spurring his horse to move faster, Stine's horse quickly closed the distance between them and the injured cavalry officer. In seconds, Stine was upon him, knocking him to the ground while still seated on his horse. As Stine dismounted from his horse, the injured cavalry officer, a young lieutenant, again rose to his feet to resume the fight. This time Stine knocked him to the ground with a strong right punch. With the fight now knocked out of him, the Union lieutenant offered no further resistance as Stine grabbed him and pulled him to his feet. Grabbing a large dagger from his boot, Stine pressed the knife to the left side of the lieutenant's throat for the other two cavalry soldiers to now see. He had quickly realized the Union lieutenant was better alive to them than dead and now he gambled his bluff would work. "Keep on coming ya blue belly bastards and I'll stick this lieutenant of yours through the throat so dang hard his eye balls will pop out! Try me if ya don't believe me!"

Now dismounted and standing near Francis, Banks walked closer to where Stine had the Union lieutenant by the back of the neck. He pointed his rifle at the two mounted Union soldiers as he moved closer to support his friend. "I hope you Yankee boys give it a go as it will give me a chance to shoot at least one of you! Which one it is I ain't figured out yet."

"Don't listen to them, shoot them I tell you, shoot them!" Just as he finished speaking, Stine punched the right side of the lieutenant's face, knocking him out cold. Kneeling down next to him, Stine now placed the dagger at the edge of the lieutenant's right ear, threatening to plunge it into his skull. Smiling as he looked up at the two Union soldiers, he challenged them to try something foolish. "Y'all think I'm joking, don't ya?"

Francis now approached Stine as he held the dagger against the lieutenant's head. Carrying his pistol in his right hand, he yelled at the two cavalry soldiers as he walked closer to where they jockeyed their horses in front of Stine and their injured lieutenant. "You men, you just killed one of my men! We weren't looking for a fight with you today, but if you want to try and finish it then we aim to oblige you. But I promise you we will be the ones who will be left standing and this lieutenant of yours will be the first one to die. I promise you that and I promise you will die also. If you want to live I suggest you leave, but he's staying with us until I know you are gone. You have my word that no further harm will come to him unless you come at us again. If you do, he will die before anyone else does and it will be a painful death. As God is my witness that man will die and it will be because you will have tried something foolish. It's your choice, stand and fight or leave now, but decide quickly or we will make that unfortunate decision for you."

Still mounted on their horses and still holding their rifles, the two Union soldiers looked at each other, both realizing without saying a word they were powerless to do anything except save their own lives. Nearby they saw Davis was pointing another rifle at them. Turning their horses around, they paused to look down at their still unconscious lieutenant lying on the ground. "Johnny Reb, you won this here fight, but hell is just a moment away if you harm that man. That's our brother lying there. Hurt him and like you promised, I promise you will die. Maybe not today and maybe not during this here war, but I will find you and I will kill you. You hear me?"

"I hear you and you heard me. He will not be harmed. Now get or I'll have a third ear carved into his head!"

Beaten this time, but with a rage burning inside of them as their brother was now a Confederate prisoner, the Union soldiers rode off. As they did, they looked back over their shoulders at Francis with disdain.

With the Union soldiers soon out of sight, Francis gave the men their next order. "Men, get a hole dug so we can bury Sgt. Odom. I'll tie up our prisoner and treat his shoulder wound a bit. We need to move out before they come back with more men."

"What about the dead Yankee?"

Francis did not look up from where he knelt down next to the lifeless body of his friend. Angrily he yelled back at the question asked of him. "What about him!"

The men knew what the response meant. They would only have to dig one grave. It was not a time to be smiling as one of their friends had just been killed, but the men appreciated how harshly Francis dealt with the Yankee cavalry soldiers. Now he refused to have them dig a hole for the dead Yankee soldier. They had come to learn when Francis was challenged he would not back down. Today he had been challenged and he had won.

After the men wrapped Odom in a blanket and placed him in the shallow grave they had dug, Francis joined them. With tears in his eyes, he said a few words as he stood at the edge of Odom's grave. "Lord, this was a good man, a gentle man and a servant of yours. Right or wrong, he died serving the country he loved. Lord, take him to heaven to be with you and absolve him of his sins. Amen." Finishing his brief prayer, he grabbed a handful of dirt and threw it down on top of the blanket covering his friend. Perhaps because he survived longer than some of the others who had also died during this mission, or because of his friendliness, or because of his willingness to do whatever needed to be done, he had developed a fondness for Odom. It hurt him to lose such a fine soldier. As he stood over the grave, Francis knew he had one more task to complete for his friend. "I will have to write his folks when I get the time. It's the least I can do for such a fine man."

As the men finished filling in the grave, and with tears and anger still in his eyes, Francis finished treating the lieutenant's wound. The fifty caliber bullet had gone clean through his shoulder, but the wound was not life threatening. As he treated the wound, the young stocky blond hair lieutenant regained consciousness and identified himself. He told Francis his name was Lt. John Mannion. Whether it was due to the pain he was experiencing from his shoulder wound or from the frustration of now being a Confederate prisoner, he said little else. The only other information he provided was that he was from Pennsylvania.

"Lieutenant, I understand this is war and with war comes death. I don't know which one of you killed our friend today, but you have taken a fine soldier from us. I promised your brothers we would not harm you. I honor my promises, but take heed of my warning. If you should try something foolish, it will be me who shoots you dead where you stand. You're probably a fine man and perhaps in a life without war we might have been friends if we had ever met, but now this terrible war prevents that from occurring. I shall find no pleasure in shooting you if you go against us, but I will shoot you. I hope you understand what I'm saying."

Mannion was sitting on the ground looking up at Francis as he spoke to him. Now he just hung his head between his knees. He did not speak, choosing instead to just nod his head to show he understood what he had been told.

Stine stood close to where Mannion sat on the ground. He had been the closest to Odom and now he waited for their prisoner to try something foolish so he could hurt him. "What now, captain? We turning around or moving on?"

"We're still moving on. We're going after what we started out for."

"Whose gonna drive the wagon then?"

Looking down at their injured prisoner who was still seated on the ground, Francis surprised them with his answer as he kicked Mannion's feet. "He is."

Looking up, Mannion saw Francis had been talking about him. "Sir, I'm injured. It hurts real bad. I don't think I can drive a wagon."

Without a lick of sympathy, Francis glared down at Mannion. "You're injured? My man now lies in the ground dead. You can drive the wagon or you can join Sgt. Odom where he lies, except you won't be getting buried. Which is it?"

Mannion slowly struggled to his feet, his hands still tied behind his back. After retying his hands in front of him so he could drive the wagon, Banks and Stine roughly lifted him onto the wagon's seat. "Men, ride out like you were doing so we know what lies in front of us. I'll follow behind the wagon. If you hear a shot, Lt. Mannion will be dead because of something foolish he tried."

* * * * * *

It took them almost three more full days of riding before they finally reached Georgetown. When they did, Francis allowed his men a day to rest so they could get cleaned up. He also arranged for them to get a couple of meals in them before they started out again. As they rested, Francis still mourned the death of Odom. While he realized Mannion had been doing what was expected of a soldier, he still directed his contempt at him.

On the morning after they arrived in Georgetown, Francis allowed a local doctor to treat Mannion's injury. He also saw to it that he was fed a meal after being treated. His responsibilities as an officer dictated he do so. He hoped his fair treatment of a Union soldier might someday result in a captured Confederate soldier being treated well somewhere down the line. "He's probably scared crazy, wondering what we're going to do to him," Francis thought as he watched Mannion eat his meal. "It's good that he does, it will keep him from trying something foolish. Because I will shoot him if he does." But deep down he wondered if he could shoot an unarmed man. "I'd probably be thinking about escaping as well. It's a soldier's duty to at least try."

After resting for almost a full day, they started moving north again. The rest served them well as it also allowed them time to mourn the loss of Odom.

But now as they drew closer to where the money was buried, Francis set a fast pace for them under the hot sun.

By late afternoon they had put almost sixteen miles between them and Georgetown when Francis called a halt so they could rest near a small stream. Like his men, the horses also needed to cool off for a spell under some nearby oak trees. The cool fresh water which flowed in the stream was a welcome relief to all of them, including their horses. After resting by the stream for several minutes, and with Banks guarding Mannion, Davis and Stine enjoyed a brief catnap in the shade provided by the trees.

Francis had used his map to push them to where they now rested. From his map he could see it would be a short ride to the narrowest point of the river where he hoped they could cross without further incident. Studying the map, he saw Stine and Davis had fallen asleep. He knew he could easily succumb to doing the same after riding so hard, but the goal was almost in sight and he would have time to sleep later. "OK, men, it's time to move out." As they all stood up and prepared to move out, Francis stopped Mannion from climbing back onto the wagon.

"Lieutenant, this is as far as you go with us. I'm sure you will be able to find one of your units someplace near here. But watch out as you do, folks in these here parts don't take kindly to men wearing blue uniforms these days. Make sure you tell your people we treated you well. Tell them I kept my promise about not harming you. I hope you feel the same way."

"Captain, I'm obliged to how you treated me. This here war is indeed terrible. While I'm not sorry for what happened when we first met, I'm not proud of what happened to your man either. I keep thinking about what you said to me that day, that perhaps we might all have become friends if this war hadn't happened. Who knows if that would have happened, but I'll keep it as a good thought. I don't bear any ill will against you or your men. You are just doing what I was doing, my duty. I hope you can respect that."

"That's why no harm came to you, lieutenant. You were only doing what was expected of you as a soldier. Now you best be on your way before I change my mind. Good luck to you."

Mannion raised his right hand and weakly saluted Francis, nodding his head to the others as he began to walk away. He had fully expected to be sent to a prisoner camp or held in some other manner until he could be exchanged in a swap of prisoners, but now he was free. He walked away counting his blessings. He also tried to count how many days it would be until he could see his family again, but stopped counting after realizing it was far too many. After walking a short distance, he stopped to look back at where Francis and the others had been. They were already gone. Out of sight and gone without making a bit of noise.

With Banks now driving the wagon, they quickly moved off towards the river. His horse and Odom's were tied to the rear of it as it moved along. Davis lingered behind for several minutes until he was confident Mannion was not trying to follow them. Stine rode out in front of the others, his eyes scanning the woods for trouble. Francis did the same a short distance off to the west.

As Francis rode along his thoughts drifted back to the day he was summoned to meet with General Lee and given this assignment. "I knew this was not going to be an easy assignment to complete, but who knew it would come to this. Only four of us are now left and there is still so much to accomplish. God have mercy upon us."

They moved another eight miles during the hot afternoon before making camp near the river. Still seated on his horse, Francis gave the men some instructions. "Boys, no fire tonight, we don't know what kind of trouble lies out there. It makes no sense letting the Yankees know where we are with our smoke. Take care of the horses and wagons; I'm going to take a ride to make sure we're not being watched."

Francis was gone for almost an hour before he returned to where they were camped for the night. Riding around the perimeter of the camp had made him feel uneasy the entire time; stopping on a couple of occasions to just listen to the noises the woods made. While sitting on his horse, he had not seen or heard anything unusual, but his training and experience told him he was being watched. Now, as he dismounted, both Stine and Banks could see the look of alarm in his face. Taking advantage of the time Francis had been away scouting the area, Davis was taking a nap in the back of the wagon.

Grabbing his rifle, Stine walked over to where Francis stood looking into the trees. "Captain, I can see it in your eyes, what did you see out there?"

"Nothing, just nothing and that's what scares me. I've got a bad feeling we're being watched. I know you've had the same feeling before. Yours proved right that night a couple of weeks ago. I've got the same feeling now. I'd like to keep moving, but it soon will be dark and I don't want us riding into a trap that might be set for us. Let's just keep a close eye out. We'll take turns sleeping later. Hopefully I'm wrong about this, but I don't think so."

"Captain, let's set a trap for them instead of riding into one."

Francis looked at his sergeant for a moment. Stine was a soldier just like he was, never afraid of a fight and never afraid of bringing the fight to the Yankees he despised. "So what's your plan, sergeant?"

"Well, you dun said no fire, so maybe we just make a little bit of noise to see if they's out there. If they is . . . well I guess then they will know where we are, won't they. Out here in these woods I'm thinking only a deaf man might not be able to find us. It's almost too dang quiet out here." Stine paused to consider what he had just said. He didn't like the thought of Union soldiers hunting them. He liked it even less after realizing they would almost be telling the Yankees where to find them by the noises they would make. Finished with his thoughts, he described the rest of his plan to Francis. "Then we all make up our bedrolls so it looks like we is all sleeping, but we ain't. We's just waiting fer them right thar in the tree line. Gonna be a full moon tonight, the moon will let us know when company is here. We'll be ready for them blue bellies when they get here."

"OK, let's try it. But first, let's eat some of those cold biscuits so we have something in our bellies. As it starts to get dark we'll follow your plan. The tree line is a good spot to hide in. Good idea you had." Francis patted Stine on the back as they started to walk over to where the wagon had been left. It had been a simple gesture of appreciation by Francis, but to Stine it meant everything. Then they woke Davis up, telling Banks and he of the trap they intended to set.

Keeping their attention directed at the woods, they ate their cold biscuits and talked for a short period of time as it began to get dark. Then they put Stine's plan into action. One by one they crept back into the tree line to take up their positions. Now they just sat and waited to see if Francis' uneasy feelings had been real.

* * * * * *

They would have to wait several hours before catching anything in the trap they set, but what they would trap would soon lead to the beginning of the end of their journey. It would be an ending they could not possibly have seen coming.

27

The Cannons Reveal Their Secrets.

"God gave us Lincoln and Liberty, let us fight for both."
General Ulysses S. Grant, USA

The early start they had wanted to give to the following morning never happened. The previous day's heat caused the beer to flow into the late evening hours and had impacted their good intentions for an early start. Now it was almost ten when Jayne, followed closely by Chick, finally joined Paul in the hotel restaurant. Slumping against the back it when she first sat down, her head rested against the red vinyl headrest of the booth. Greeted this morning by a throbbing headache, she quickly closed her eyes to prevent the morning's bright sunlight from adding to the pain she was already experiencing. Paul could not help smiling at her condition as he had been there several times in the past. "Do you at least feel worse than you look?" It was just a small jab, but it made him laugh when he said it to her.

"I don't know, I think it's a tie. I haven't drank that many beers in a long time. The two shots of tequila Chick talked me into seemed like a good idea at the time, but now I'm not so sure it was. I'm definitely out of shape when it comes to drinking."

Chick sat in the booth next to Jayne with his eyes closed as well. Soon he put his sunglasses on to cut down on the light streaming into his eyes. A comment he made about the morning seeming to be an unusually bright one, was one Paul quickly laughed at. "Perhaps it's the tequila which has made your eyes so sensitive this morning?" He was getting great pleasure out of the fact that his two friends were having such a difficult and painful start to their day.

"We have a busy day in front of us, you two gonna be OK?"

"Yeah, I'll be fine. I just need some coffee, a light breakfast, six more hours of sleep, and I'll be good to go." Paul chuckled at Jayne's response.

Despite their late start to the day, Chick and Jayne soon followed Paul out the front of the hotel after finishing their breakfast. He led the way down Meeting Street to the South Carolina Historical Society building. Entering the lobby they spied Ellen Johnson, one of the two volunteer staff members greeting visitors to the building. She had supplied them with some of the names of the parks they visited yesterday when they were on the hunt for the cannons.

"Hey, Ellen! Paul Waring, I'm not sure if you remember me, but my friends and I were in yesterday. You gave us some tips on where to find Civil

War cannons here in the city. That was a big help you gave us, thanks for the assistance."

"Oh, sure, I remember. How did you make out? Did you get the photos you wanted of the cannons?"

"We did OK, but we're hoping to take a few additional photos today of some similar cannons which might be in and around the city. We'd like to include as many photos as possible in the book we are thinking of doing and we'd like to take pictures of as many different cannons as possible. Would you know of any other cannons in the city that perhaps you might have forgotten to mention to us yesterday?" Paul did not like the fact that he was being less than honest with her as to why they were still looking for Civil War era cannons, but more than anything he wanted to find the ones they still needed to locate. He knew stretching the truth a bit might help them find the ones they were still looking for.

"No, I don't think so. There aren't any other parks in the city with Civil War cannons in them. I believe I told you about all of them yesterday, at least I think I did. The Confederate Soldier's Cemetery has a few cannons there, but you specifically asked about our parks yesterday. You didn't say anything about wanting to visit cemeteries, so I didn't tell you about those."

Suddenly the dull headache Jayne had from drinking too much the previous evening disappeared. She could not believe Ellen had not told them about these additional cannons yesterday. The tone of her voice indicated her displeasure at not being told about this information before now. "This cemetery, they have cannons on display there?"

"Yes, they do. If I remember correctly they have at least four, maybe even six or eight."

"Ellen, do you know what kind they are?" The tone in Jayne's voice, as she asked a follow-up question, still showed her annoyance with her.

"What kind they are? Big old black ones, that's what I know them as. I must admit, I have no idea what kind they are. It's been a while since I was there. To be honest, I don't have much of an interest in cannons. I can tell you folks do though."

Paul had been busy looking at his map while Jayne and Ellen were talking. Not being able to locate the Confederate Soldier's Cemetery, he now slid the map across the glass countertop separating Ellen's work space from the public area of the building. "Ellen, the cemetery, can you show us where it is on the map?"

* * * * * *

After getting Chick's van out of the hotel's valet parking garage, they were soon on their way to the cemetery. "Can you believe she didn't tell us about these cannons yesterday? Like we only wanted to see cannons that were in city parks. Unbelievable!" Jayne was far more upset about this than her two partners were.

Paul was giving Chick directions from where he sat in the right front seat. As he did, Jayne continued to fume in the backseat about Ellen. "Jayne, I'm with you on that, but at least we have a place to look this morning. According to the map we should be there in just a couple of minutes."

Driving up to the cemetery, they saw two large black Napoleon cannons sitting just inside the main entrance. They were situated next to each other, their barrels angled slightly away from each other. Between the two cannons stood three flagpoles which proudly bore the American flag, the South Carolina state flag, and the flag of the Confederacy. The neatly manicured twenty-five acre cemetery held the remains of several hundred Confederate soldiers, most of whom were from South Carolina. Inside the main gate stood a black granite *Roll of Honor* monument, it listed the names of each of the soldiers who had been buried in the cemetery. The monument also listed the regiment or company each soldier had served with.

Surveying the grounds of the cemetery from where he stood, Paul could not help noticing how well the grounds were being maintained. It pleased him to see the care being given to the final resting place of so many brave soldiers. It was being cared for far better than the cemetery he had visited yesterday.

"Are those the ones?" Chick's question was one Paul and Jayne had no answer to as they had been standing away from the two cannons admiring the various monuments erected to honor those men who had died fighting for the Confederacy.

"If they're not the ones, perhaps those are." Paul pointed at two other cannons he saw on display near a side entrance to the cemetery. "Or maybe those are." Scanning the cemetery grounds, his eyes had located the last two cannons on display. They were further down the main driveway. The last two cannons sat there with their barrels facing to the north. From how those cannons had been positioned, it looked as if they were ready to fire upon the advancing Northern invaders should they come again.

Jayne and Paul each walked to two different sets of cannons, the two by the main entrance and the two by the side entrance. They soon found neither sets of cannons had the even numbered markings they were anxiously searching for. But one of them, one which was sitting by the cemetery's side entrance, had been inscribed with the number nine. The cannon sitting next to it had been filled with mortar, but had none of the markings they were after.

After taking time to examine cannon number nine, and to document its location, Paul and Chick paused for a moment to inspect a map they were using. As they did, Jayne walked off to check the next two cannons further down the cemetery's driveway. In a matter of moments she yelled back to them. "Guys, come here, I found one!"

As they rushed to look at the cannon she found, Paul looked over at Chick. "Perhaps she could have announced it just a little louder. I'm not sure everyone in Charleston heard her."

Paul's comment caused Chick to laugh as they jogged to where Jayne was standing by the cannons. "She's just excited. No one else is here, so we're OK."

"Look, it has the CSA inscription on it and the number eight under the lettering. We found another one. Now we only have two left to find!" Excited by what she found, Paul could see that any lingering effects Jayne experienced from the previous night's festivities had long since disappeared. So had her frustration with Ellen.

Chick looked at the inscriptions in the mortar to satisfy his own curiosity. "Yep, that's one of the ones we want. Do you two see any others around?"

Taking her Nikon camera out of its case so she could document the inscription at the end of the barrel and its overall condition, Jayne did not bother to look at Chick when she started taking her pictures. "I haven't seen any others, have you?"

As she finished taking the pictures of the cannon, a white Ford Ranger pick-up truck drove up to where they were. It was being driven by one of the cemetery's employees. The driver's door had *Maintenance Division* written in black block style letters on it. A small Craftsman lawn mower, its tires covered with fresh wet grass which had just been mowed, and two Craftsman weed trimmers were in the bed of the truck.

"Morning! Got family here or y'all just visiting?" The driver of the truck wore a rolled up long sleeve green work shirt. His first name was embroidered on the left side of the shirt just above the front pocket. It was easy to see his shirt was already soaked with sweat from cutting grass in the day's warm temperature.

"Hey, Ken, good morning to you. My name is Paul and this is Chick and Jayne. We're doing a book of photographs on military cemeteries here in South Carolina to coincide with the upcoming anniversary of the Civil War. We're thinking of including a few photographs of the Civil War cannons that are here in your cemetery."

"Sounds like a good idea for a book! Our cannons are all still in pretty good condition despite their age, except for 'Old Number Six' that is. She's down in the shop as we're fixing to give her a new paint job. The damn salt air wreaks havoc on these cannons after a while."

Ken's statement immediately got their attention. "What's 'Old Number Six'? I'm not sure what you mean by that," Paul asked Ken Barton, the cemetery's maintenance foreman. As the question was asked, Chick and Jayne moved closer to where Ken still sat in his truck. They hoped to hear the answer they wanted him to tell them.

"Old Number Six? Why that's another cannon just like the one right there that's on display. We call it 'Old Number Six' because someone scratched the number six in the mortar when they filled in the barrel years ago. Must have been an inventory number of some kind at some point, but no one knows for sure. Mortar is still in good shape, the cannon itself just needs a paint job. We've got it down in the shop like I said. Care to see it?"

Not wanting to sound too eager, Paul waited a moment before answering. "Sure, if you don't mind?"

"Ain't no problem at all. The painter ain't even here today so you folks won't be in the way at all."

They soon were looking at 'Old Number Six'. It sat mounted on wooden blocks in the Maintenance Building waiting for the new coat of black paint to be applied. It was the largest of the cannons they found so far.

"Ken, OK if we take a couple of pictures?" Jayne cautiously asked.

"Sure, snap away. Ain't no problem at all."

As Paul and Chick inspected the cannon, they saw the markings they were looking for as Jayne took her digital pictures. When she was finished, Paul shook Ken's hand as they started walking back to Chick's van. "Ken, thanks for letting us see how you folks take care of these cannons, it was very interesting." Nervously, he then asked Ken one final question. "So you don't replace the mortar in the barrels when you repaint them?"

"Nope, no need to unless it's cracked real bad. In fact, we haven't had to change out the mortar in any of the cannons in the years I've been here. Whoever mixed the mortar that was placed in these cannons knew what he was doing. We'll just give 'Old Number Six' a couple of coats of paint and put her back on display right where she was."

"Thanks again for your time. We'll get out of your way, I'm sure you're a busy man. Take care!"

"You're welcome! Y'all come back anytime!"

As they walked back to where Chick's van was parked, Paul whispered under his breath. "We are coming back and won't Ken be surprised when he finds out what's inside the cannon he's about to have painted."

Getting into the van, Chick looked at Paul and asked him what the plan was. "Where to now?"

"I saw a Costco not too far from here when we driving this way earlier. Let's head over there so we can have Jayne's photographs developed and blown up. Then we're going to call the mayor of this fine city and make an appointment to see him. After that, I have a couple of other calls to make."

"But what about the last cannon?" Jayne asked from the van's back seat.

"We'll find it, relax. For now, let's get moving on the photos."

* * * * * *

Late that afternoon, after having several eight by ten photographs made up of the cannon inscriptions Paul had chosen, he dialed the office of Charleston's mayor, the Honorable William Davis. After being put on hold a couple of times, and after speaking with two members of the mayor's secretarial staff, Paul finally was able to speak with Edwin Henion. He was responsible, among other things, for who did and who did not get to see the mayor.

"Mr. Henion, my name is Paul Waring. My two friends and I would like to make an appointment to see the mayor. We would only need fifteen to twenty minutes of his time."

"Mr. Waring, may I ask what you wish to speak to the mayor about?"

"We'd like to speak with him regarding the cancellation of the Civil War Anniversary Celebration."

"I'm sorry, Mr. Waring, but the celebration had to be cancelled due to budgetary issues. Our struggling local economy, as well as our rising operating costs, has forced us to cancel the celebration so we can continue providing our residents with the services they expect the city to provide. The celebration's cost was an expense we simply could not justify at this time. We even tried to host it with private funding, but our fundraising efforts fell far short of what we would have needed to raise. I'm sorry."

"Probably a very unpopular and tough decision the mayor had to make. I would suspect it might have an adverse impact on his upcoming campaign for the senate seat my friends and I know he's seeking."

"We've discussed that. It probably will have some negative impact, but the mayor hopes his constituents will remember the many other good things he's done for them and Charleston when it comes time to vote."

"Mr. Henion, my friends and I want this Civil War celebration to be held. What if I was to tell you we have the means for the mayor to pay for this celebration; can you get us this meeting?"

"I would need to know more about how you believe we could pay for this event. We've gone over the budget several times. We've even gone over our available discretionary funding a few times as well. We just cannot find any such means for the city to pay for this event."

"Mr. Henion, all we need is twenty minutes tops. You give us that time and we'll give the mayor the means to pay for the celebration. All of this is legal and all of it is above board; it comes with no ethical problems at all. The best part for you is we don't want anything in return. And one more thing, we have a funding source that's not part of your budget. That source will pick up the tab for the cost of the entire celebration. How's that sound?"

"You have my attention." Henion replied, his interest in hearing more about Paul's plan increasing as the conversation continued.

"It's really a simple formula. The mayor makes the celebration happen with the money the city will soon have. That makes him a hero to the people and a hero, perhaps most importantly, to your local business community as they, like the city, will benefit from the additional influx of tourist dollars. As you'll soon learn, he will not only have found a way for the city to host this celebration, but at the same time he'll have found a way to put tourist dollars in the pockets of your local business owners. Something we believe they'll remember when it comes time to cast their votes. Besides being able to fund the celebration, we probably are also going to show him how he can pay to maintain a few of your parks and cemeteries better than you folks have been doing, again at no cost to the city. You're smart enough to know this will all equate to votes in his upcoming election. From that election he gets the job he wants and you get to ride his coattails in Washington for as long as you like."

"Want to tell me anything else?"

"Yes, just two things. Neither my friends nor I are crazy. We'll deliver proof to you in the twenty minute meeting where the money will come from to fund these projects. Interested?"

"Anything else?" Henion cautiously asked.

"Not until we meet with the mayor. I hope we can get a chance to meet each other as well. The mayor only has to make one promise to me and it's an easy one for him to make. I can assure you of that."

"Always a catch, isn't there? But OK, I'll take a chance and I'll give you your twenty minutes. The schedule for tomorrow is tight, but how about ten-fifteen in the morning? We can meet right here at city hall?"

"Thanks for your help. We promise you a big surprise. See you then."

After giving the news to Chick and Jayne about their meeting with Mayor Davis, Paul called Donna to give her the good news about finding the cannons. "I'm happy for you, Paul. I know this means a lot to you. I guess I'm going to be living with a celebrity, huh?"

"What? I always thought I was a celebrity in your eyes." Paul teased her as she had been the celebrity back home, the one who had gotten her picture in the local paper on so many occasions when her bank had sponsored charity functions in town. She had been the face of the bank with so many people and civic organizations. They talked on the phone for another ten minutes about a few other pending issues at home, but as they talked he made sure Donna knew it was her casual observation of the inscription in the cannon's mortar which made the final portion of the discovery possible.

"Paul, I wish I could be there, but I'm just glad you found what you were looking for. Call me tomorrow when you are done."

"I will, but I've got to go now. I have a couple of calls to make before the big day tomorrow. I'll call you tomorrow when we get done with everything."

"Paul, wait, I've got a surprise for you. Guess who surprised us by showing up here today?"

"Hopefully it's Brian and Sean?"

"Yep! They kept reading about their father becoming a big time treasure hunter and they wanted to come down to see what you have found. I guess their timing could not have been better, seeing what you have just found over the last two days."

Paul talked to his boys on the phone for the next half hour; briefly filling them in on what had been going on over the last two days. Then, with some reluctance on Donna's part because she was going to be left out due to work commitments, he made plans for the boys to drive down to Charleston the following morning to meet him after he got done with meeting with the mayor. "Guys, I'll call you after the meeting and we'll figure out where to meet. It will be great to have you here for this. I'll see you tomorrow!"

Finished with his phone call, Paul had Chick contact Bobby Ray and Pete while he made his last two calls. "Tell those two to get their butts down here tonight . . . tell them it's important. You can also tell them dinner is on me. That will get them down here for sure. I'm quite confident it will get Bobby Ray down here as he never misses out on a free meal."

The next phone call Paul made was to his good friend, Steve Alcott, the person indirectly responsible for the remains of Captain Francis being found. "Steve, the meeting is all set for tomorrow. Can you have him here by ten? The meeting is at City Hall. I'll meet you both in the lobby by ten."

"We'll be there by ten. I'll have him with me, even if I have to drag him there. Paul, you've done a fabulous job with all of this. I'm proud of you!"

Paul then joked with Steve about what he had discovered. "All of this was made possible because of that lousy boat you sold me! Honestly, it was simply a lucky find which anyone could have made. I just happened to find him, that's all."

"I'm not so sure about that. I'll see you in the morning."

Then Paul made his last phone call before calling it quits for the day. He wanted to get back to the hotel to take a shower and relax before dinner, but he had made a promise to a friend that he would call him. After dialing the number, the phone rang twice before it was answered. "Duke, it's Paul, we've got some great news for you. Hey, but listen, just to play it safe I want this conversation to be a simple one because we're talking on cell phones. You need to come down to Charleston tomorrow for the day and perhaps even for the following day as well. It's important for you to be here and to be a part of it. Understand what I'm telling you?"

"Paul, I'll be there, but I'm afraid it won't be until sometime late in the afternoon. I've got a meeting already set up with a buyer and I can't change it, it's too important for our company's future."

"No problem, we understand. But you need to be here for this. I want you to meet some people, so get here as soon as you can."

"I'll see if my buddy will fly me down on his Cessna. He flies into Charleston all the time so it shouldn't be a problem. I'll let you know. Hey, tell me, did you get it?"

"Tomorrow we will. It's probably yours and the cemetery combined, at least."

"Well, I'll be! You done good for a Yankee! I'll see you folks tomorrow sometime." Paul laughed as he ended the call with Duke. He looked forward to seeing his new friend.

* * * * * *

The following morning could not come quick enough for the three of them as they each spent a restless night tossing and turning in their hotel beds after their second long day of cannon hunting. Awake early and eager to get started, they entered the lobby of Charleston City Hall a few minutes before ten.

Already waiting for them in the lobby was Steve Alcott. With him was the guest he had been asked to bring. Paul first greeted his friend, thanking him for being able to make it on such short notice. He greeted Steve's guest next. "Good morning, Your Honor. My name is Paul Waring; it's a pleasure to meet you. These are my good friends, Chick Mann and Jayne Ewald."

"Mr. Waring, I'm not sure how I can be of assistance to you, but as a favor to my good friend I'm here with you today. I guess I'm also here out of my own curiosity and because Steve told me you were going to fuel my passion for the Civil War with some kind of announcement. I'm eager to hear what you have to say."

"Your Honor, we're going to do so very soon, I promise. You will also understand very shortly why I've asked for you to be here. What my friends and I are going to tell the mayor will make all of this very clear. But first, I'm going to ask Steve and you for one more favor. Let us get into see the mayor first and then I'll come out to get you both. Steve, is that OK?"

"That's fine. Just remember our guest has other obligations later this morning."

After taking the elevator up to the second floor they found the mayor's office. The hallway door was marked *Office of the Mayor*. On the door above the black painted letters was a painted seal of the city of Charleston. Within minutes they were introducing themselves to Edwin Henion, the mayor's Chief of Staff. Soon he escorted the three of them into one of the small wood paneled conference rooms which sat off the mayor's main office.

On the walls of the small conference room hung several paintings of Charleston's past mayors. Small brass plates on the picture frames identified the mayors by name and by the dates they had served in office. Henion interrupted Paul as he looked at the photos of the previous mayors. "I have to tell you, Mr. Waring, the mayor and I are very interested in hearing what you have to say. The mayor has a busy day ahead of him, but you will have his full attention while he's here. Before he comes in, do you have anything else to tell me beyond what we have discussed already?"

Paul just smiled at the attempt Henion made to gather some additional information from him. "I think its best we discuss the rest of what we have to say with the mayor present."

It took a couple of minutes, but soon Mayor William Davis entered the room. Immediately he was shaking hands with the three of them. It almost seemed as if the mayor was making a campaign stop seeking their votes. Paul could quickly tell the mayor was a high energy person who tried to dominate the room with his personality. "Good morning, folks. I'm pleased to meet each of you. Edwin tells me you may have a partial remedy to some of our financial concerns. For the record, I want the Anniversary Celebration for the Civil War to be held and I want it held here in Charleston, but I'm afraid we just cannot afford it right now. I'm all ears though, so tell me how you can help us. Please, have a seat." Mayor Davis directed them to several leather chairs seated around a large oak conference table.

"Mayor, I promise you we are going to show you how you can host this celebration without spending any city dollars. But first, I need a minute, please excuse me." After being seated for only a few moments, Paul stood up from the table and walked to a door that led directly out into the main hallway outside the conference room. Opening the door, he saw Steve and the Judge seated on a bench in the hallway. Quickly he motioned for Steve and his guest to join them.

As soon as the three of them entered the conference room, Mayor Davis stood up; immediately recognizing his good friend, Steve Alcott, as he walked into the room. As they greeted each other with warm smiles and firm handshakes, it was apparent to Paul that Steve and the mayor were as good of friends as he had mentioned they were. Previously he had told Paul that several years ago they had been partners in a few small real estate ventures before the mayor moved back to Charleston to run for office, taking advantage of his family name which was still quite prominent there. While the Davis name was a common old Southern name, to the dismay of Mayor Davis and his family they had found no blood connection to the former President of the Confederacy.

"Steve, good morning! It has been far too long since we've seen each other. Edwin didn't tell me you were going to be here. Obviously you are going to be part of this meeting, but I'm not sure why. My guess is that it will be made clear to me soon enough."

"Yes, it will. You will be very pleased by what you hear, but I'll let Paul and his friends, who are all good friends of mine, explain it to you. I suggest you listen closely to what they have to tell you. But first, I need to introduce a good friend to you. Mr. Mayor, this is Judge Howard Nathan Morgan, of the United States Court of Appeals for the Fourth Circuit. Judge Morgan is here as a favor to Paul and I. I hope you don't mind?"

"Of course not! Your Honor, it is indeed a pleasure. I've heard your name mentioned many times by several friends of mine who are members of the South Carolina Bar. I can assure you that you're held in the highest regard by each of them. I have to assume many of them are mutual friends of ours, but that is for us to discuss another time perhaps. Judge Morgan, Steve, please, have seats at the table next to where I'm sitting. My interest is piqued even more about this meeting now that both of you are here."

As Paul pulled out chairs for Judge Morgan and Steve to sit in, he caught the mayor and Edwin Henion exchanging puzzled looks at each other. "Mr. Mayor, I apologize for not telling Edwin that Judge Morgan and Steve were going to be here, but I needed to keep that close to the vest until today. I assure you that no disrespect was intended."

As he sat down, Paul could see the faint smiles which now crossed the faces of Chick and Jayne. They knew he had just shown the mayor two of his high cards. The mayor would soon have to abide by what Judge Morgan would tell him; if he didn't his chances for the senate seat he coveted so badly were likely going to be doomed. Paul had realized by having Steve and Judge Morgan present for the meeting their presence would add some much needed credibility to the presentation he was about to make.

"Nice touch introducing Judge Morgan into the meeting," Chick thought to himself. "Now he has him." As hard as he tried, he could not make the faint smile disappear from his face.

Paul got things moving by addressing Mayor Davis. "Mr. Mayor, thanks again for taking time from your busy schedule to meet with us. I'm not sure if you have ever heard my name before, but recently my friends and I have received a fair amount of unwanted media attention from several news stories that talked about the remains of a Civil War soldier I recently found up in Murrells Inlet. I found the soldier's remains inside a large oak tree alongside the Waccamaw River. A discovery my good friend here deserves some credit for, whether directly or indirectly I'm not sure yet, but that's only part of the reason why we asked to meet with you today." Paul had given a nod of his head in Steve's direction as he spoke with the mayor.

"Yes, yes, I knew I recognized your name from some place. A very fascinating story, I followed it very closely in the papers. Is this why we are meeting here today?" As expected, Mayor Davis' interest increased significantly after realizing who Paul was.

"Yes, it is."

Paul saw he also now had the close attention of Judge Morgan as he noticed him shifting slightly forward in his chair so he could hear every word being said. For the next several minutes, Paul painted a picture of what he found on his trips to the site where he had found the soldier's remains. He intentionally did not tell them all of the details, but he did tell them about the letters he found from both President Davis and Secretary Memminger. He also told them about the letter Captain Francis had written to his father. He purposely did not tell them about the letter Francis had written to President Davis or about the clues the letter contained as he had yet to receive the commitment he was seeking from the mayor.

"Mr. Mayor, are you aware of the legend, or the myth, or perhaps even the story, it depends on how you want to describe it I guess, regarding the Confederate treasury which disappeared during the Civil War after it had been moved out of Richmond?"

"Of course I am! Every person, at least those my age, who has been born in the South has heard that story. No one knows for sure whatever happened to the money or if the story is even true, but it's a well-known story that's for sure."

"It's not a story, it really happened."

Paul was looking directly at Mayor Davis as he answered him, but he quickly glanced back at Judge Morgan. The Judge now leaned back in his chair waiting for the discussion to continue. His years of courtroom experience had taught him when to interrupt a conversation and when to sit and listen. Now was a time to just listen.

Somewhat taken back by the confident tone Paul had given to his response about whether the Confederate treasury had actually existed; Mayor Davis was at a loss for words momentarily. "Well, Mr. Waring, maybe so, but I would need some sort of proof before I could say for sure the treasury disappeared like folks believe it did. Do you have such proof?"

Smiling, Paul nodded to Jayne. As she stood up to hand out the photographs they had blown up, he continued with his presentation.

"Mayor, to answer your question, yes we do. These photos are ones my friends and I have taken over the past few weeks. They're photos we took when we recovered approximately two-thirds of the missing Confederate gold and silver, money which disappeared almost one hundred and fifty years ago. The two locations where we found the money will not be discussed here today, but they will be in the future. I will tell you that neither location was here in Charleston." Standing up, Paul slid two identical pristine 1861 gold Liberty Head ten-dollar coins across the table. They were for the mayor and Judge Morgan to first look at.

Looks of amazement were exchanged between Mayor Davis and Judge Morgan as they looked at the coins and the photographs for the first time. Those same looks were soon shared with Steve and the mayor's aide. No one spoke for a few moments as they simply alternated their stares between the coins and the photographs now spread out across the table. The photographs included pictures of Paul and the others digging up the gold and silver coins at Duke's farm, of the recovered coins sitting in the plastic buckets, and photos of the coins they recovered at the cemetery. "Mayor, this last photograph here, under the tarp you see are the remains of three Confederate soldiers we found. They had been buried with the gold and silver in North Carolina. It was quite the find." Judge Morgan had already moved out of his seat to get a better look at the photographs that were spread out on the table. With his reading glasses perched low on his nose, he alternated looks of disbelief at Paul and at the photographs. Having difficulty believing what he was hearing, he looked at Steve for some type of confirmation. The slight nod of Steve's head Steve told the Judge what he was hearing and seeing was the truth.

Holding one of the gold coins in his right hand as he examined the photographs, Mayor Davis quietly spoke to his aide. "Edwin, I think you had better clear my schedule for the rest of the day. I believe we need to hear what Mr. Waring is going to tell us without rushing him. Please have someone arrange for some refreshments for our guests." Hearing this, Paul could not help but to exchange smiles with Chick and Jayne. His smile told them they would soon be opening the cannons to recover the rest of the missing gold and silver.

"Mr. Waring, you and your friends have made an amazing discovery, simply amazing, but I have a feeling you have more to tell us. I don't believe you had us meet here today to just tell us a great story. Am I correct?"

"Yes, Your Honor, you are. We mean ...."

"Paul, I'm sorry for interrupting you, but what you've already found, well, where is it? And, if I might ask, how much did you already find?" Mayor Davis now sat on the edge of his seat, obviously intrigued by what he already heard. It was not what he expected to hear during this meeting.

"To answer your first question, what we've already found is safely tucked away. No disrespect, but that's not something my friends and I are going to discuss here today. To answer your second question, we don't know. We have yet to count or itemize what we've found, but conservatively in today's market we think a safe guess is that we've probably found at least twenty million dollars, give or take a million or two."

Mayor Davis dropped the gold coin he had been holding when he heard what Paul had just told him. The coin rattled on the large conference table for a couple of seconds before it came to rest face up. It had been the only noise made in the room as it rattled on the table. "Twenty million dollars? Is that what you just said?" The dollar amount he heard caused the mayor to rise out of his chair in disbelief. Now he stood with his hands on the edge of the conference table waiting to hear more. Judge Morgan and Edwin Henion sat staring at Paul, hoping to hear him confirm what they had just heard him say.

"Yes, sir, and there's more to find. That's why we're here today."

Steve sat in his chair smiling as the mayor's question was answered. He knew Paul was about to tell all of them something even better than what he had already told them.

Shocked at the dollar amount Paul had already given them, Mayor Davis was now even more shocked to hear there was still more gold and silver waiting to be found. "Wait a minute, you mean you know where the rest of the money is? Is it here in Charleston?"

"Well, before I answer your question I need an answer from you, Mr. Mayor. It's more of a promise, I guess. That's why I've asked Judge Morgan to be here today. Mayor, I mean no disrespect by this, but plenty of folks, politicians included, seem to do crazy things when money is involved, especially when big money is involved. I suspect many people, including several states, and perhaps even the federal government, will soon file claims against this money when we make it public what we have found. What we want from you today, Mr. Mayor, is for you, as the city's chief executive officer, to raise your right hand and to solemnly swear in front of Judge Morgan that you will promise not to seize, or to interfere, or to attempt to hold in anyway, any of the remaining money we may find. We also want you to promise to abide by the court's final say in how the money is to be disbursed. Mr. Mayor, to answer your question, yes, the rest of the money is hidden here in Charleston."

It was Edwin Henion who was the first to speak. The others were still too taken back by what Paul had told them. "Mr. Waring, correct me if I'm wrong. What you're saying is that you would expect Charleston to receive a portion of the found money, hopefully a generous portion, and this money would then enable the city to pay for the Civil War's Anniversary Celebration. Your thinking is Charleston might receive enough to cover the cost of the celebration so it would not have an adverse impact upon the city budget. That's what you were alluding to on the phone yesterday, correct?"

"Correct. I would suspect Charleston will likely be able to pay for the Anniversary Celebration and at least one other obligation the city currently has. We've found a lot of money already and we're going to find a lot more as well. It will be up to others to decide who gets what, but I'd be shocked if Charleston didn't receive a portion of the recovered money."

Mayor Davis did not say a word. He just sat there digesting what Paul had told them. He now wondered how Charleston, as well as his own political career, could benefit from this infusion of money. Now he looked to Judge Morgan for advice. It was just what Paul had hoped he would do. "Judge, what he's asking me to do here today, can he do that? Is it legal?"

"It is if I say it is and from what I know right now it's legal. Mr. Mayor, I'm not your attorney, but over thirty-five years of practicing law tells me you would be very foolish not to agree to what Mr. Waring is asking of you. Charleston is likely going to reap a huge financial benefit at little, if any, expense to the city. I would also offer to you that the positive media attention for the city and to your administration is another added bonus you cannot put a price tag on. You certainly don't have to agree to what Mr. Waring is requesting of you, but if you don't, he's also not obligated to tell you where the rest of the money is. I would think you would rather be a so-called partner with Mr. Waring and his associates rather than declining his offer."

Mayor Davis looked at his aide who was seated next to him and saw he was nodding his head in agreement with what Judge Morgan had just said. "Mayor, this is a homerun in every way possible. I would strongly recommend you accept the conditions Mr. Waring has asked of you."

Before he could respond, Paul had Jayne slide a piece of paper across the table to Mayor Davis. "Mayor, besides your verbal promise, I'd appreciate you signing this agreement that we typed up last night. It's just what we talked about, but it's also now in writing. You sign it, I'll sign it, and perhaps Judge Morgan will sign it as a witness. Then I'm sure Mr. Henion can find someone here in the building to notarize it for us, just to make it official and all. You can have a copy for your records and I'll keep the original."

As he took in all that was being said, Judge Morgan smiled to himself as he realized Paul had just told the mayor he did not trust his verbal promise to not try and seize the money they hoped to find later in the day. He then looked at Paul. "Mr. Waring, seems you have thought of everything, haven't you?"

"I've tried to, Judge."

After reading the one-page document Jayne had slid across the table to him, Mayor Davis signed his name to it. He then passed it across the table to Judge Morgan to endorse as a witness to his promise. Then he raised his right hand for all to see, promising neither he nor the city would attempt to seize any of the money. It took several minutes to complete the notary process, but soon it was and copies of the document were given to the mayor and to Judge Morgan. "OK, what's next, Mr. Waring?"

Paul suggested to Mayor Davis that he take Edwin Henion, Steve, and Judge Morgan out to lunch so he and the others could have time to get done what they needed to get done before he showed them where the gold and silver was hidden. He then made a couple of requests of the mayor so the gold and silver could be taken out of the cannons. First, he requested the mayor arrange to have the Charleston Public Works Department contacted so three of their heavy duty flatbed wreckers could be made available to him. "Please tell them we need them here as soon as possible, and please tell them we're going to need a large part of their garage to work in later this afternoon. They'll need to clear an area for us to use. Oh, and we are also going to need two police cars to escort us around the city for a few hours."

Looking at his aide, Mayor Davis directed him to contact the Public Works superintendent and the police chief's office. "Tell them they are to give Mr. Waring anything he needs today." After giving Henion his marching orders, the mayor looked back at Paul. "Anything else?" Henion paused to hear the answer before leaving the conference room.

"Yes, three more things as well. Please make sure the Public Works Department has an air compressor and an air chisel, or a chipping hammer, and at least twenty-five large clean tote bins ready for us when we get there. Oh, one last thing. Yesterday when we walked by City Hall, I noticed a Loomis armored car parked out in front of the building. Does the city use Loomis as a courier for your bank transactions?"

Edwin Henion, who had walked back towards the conference table, answered for the mayor, first by nodding his head. "I'm not really sure why you are asking, Mr. Waring, but to answer your question, yes we do. May I ask why you asked that question?"

"Because I expect in a very short time we're going to find a few million dollars in gold and silver. I'd like you to make arrangements with Loomis to have them loan us one of their armored cars. We'll need to have the armored car meet us at the Public Works garage, say around four this afternoon. It's going to take us a couple of hours to get to the gold and silver, so no sense having them stand around in the heat waiting for us to get to it. Tell them we should be ready around then, but we'll need that vehicle for a few hours after that as well. We'll have one more stop to make after we get done at the garage."

Edwin Henion looked over at Mayor Davis. He again nodded his approval to Paul's request.

Listening to Paul tell the mayor what he needed him to do caused Steve, as hard as he tried not to, to laugh out loud. "I cannot wait to see what he's going to ask for next! A very remarkable and brazen young man he is, very remarkable!" He had not directed his comments to anyone in particular, but they drew a chuckle from Judge Morgan. Soon even Mayor Davis had to laugh at Steve's comment.

Still smiling at Steve's comment, Judge Morgan walked over to a nearby side table where a large pot of coffee had been brought into the room. After pouring himself a cup, he picked up the phone sitting at the far end of the table. Phoning his law clerk, he directed her to cancel his schedule for the rest of the day. Picking up his cup of coffee, he turned to look at the others who were still seated around the table. "This is going to be something I want to see. I'm not going to miss out on this opportunity."

As Paul looked over at Mayor Davis, he could see the look of concern in his face. "Mr. Mayor, I know this is confusing. While we haven't given you all of the details, we soon will, I promise. As I suggested, take the others to lunch and we'll meet you at the Public Works garage at three this afternoon. We promise you won't regret this." Gathering up the photos and the original agreement the mayor had signed; Paul again directed a comment to Mayor Davis. "Mr. Mayor, you can keep those two gold coins for now. Consider them part of the down payment on the cost of the anniversary celebration."

Followed by Chick and Jayne, Paul soon exited the elevator and walked out into the lobby of city hall. As they did, Chick stopped them so they could talk for a moment. "Well, that went too smoothly. I expected some resistance, perhaps reluctance might be a better word, to cooperate with us, but I'm glad it went well. One thing though, isn't it strange that neither the mayor, nor his aide, asked us where the money had been hidden in the city. I would have thought that would have been one of the first questions they might have asked."

"So did I," Paul replied, "but they likely realized we weren't going to tell them, so they didn't ask. Who knows, but we got what we needed so let's get moving. I'll see you two later at the garage. Good luck!"

The two police officers assigned to Chick and Jayne for the afternoon were already there waiting for them in the lobby of city hall. As the four of them left, Paul stayed behind to call Bobby Ray on his cell phone.

"What's up, bro?"

"Bobby Ray, we've got no time for games right now. I need you and Pete to meet me at the city's Public Work garage by two. Tell Pete I want his cameras set up and ready to film the cannons when they're being delivered to the garage. And do me a favor, Brian and Sean are driving down here to see this thing unfold. Call them on Brian's cell and give them directions to the PW garage. Try to get them there by two." In his excitement, Paul realized he had unintentionally referred to the garage by the abbreviation used by most cops when referring to Public Works departments. The abbreviation made radio transmissions shorter and easier to understand.

"We'll be ready. See you then, amigo!"

Over the next two hours, while Paul went to meet with the Public Works superintendent, Jayne and Chick, with help from the two Charleston police officers, guided the wreckers around the city. Their assignment for the afternoon was to pick up the cannons from where they had sat in the city's various parks. One had sat in a neglected cemetery for many years. After being loaded onto the flatbed wreckers, the cannons would be brought to the Public Works garage.

As they drove around the city in the lead police car, Jayne rode in the back seat, while Chick sat in the front seat with Officer Lonnie Mo. "Officer Mo, this is the first time Jayne has ridden in the back seat of a police car. Well, the first time not wearing handcuffs that is."

"Jackass!"

Jayne's quick response caused Chick and Officer Mo to laugh. Jayne had led a quiet life, almost a boring one, surrounded by mostly her books and her research. A member of a religious order stood a far better chance of being placed in the back of a police car under arrest than she had. Chick soon turned around to look at her and saw she was now smiling at the comment he had made.

Just before three, they were all back at the Public Works garage. All of the cannons were lined up in one section of the twenty bay garage. Each now resting on large bundles of heavy wooden railroad ties. The ties were being used to protect the garage's concrete floor from damage and to hold the weight of the heavy cannons. The cannons sat roughly four feet off the floor of the large garage. Cannons number eight, nine, and 'Old Number Six' were the only ones not there. Paul and the others had decided they would deal with them at the end of the day as they knew those three cannons were not going anywhere between now and then. Before the others arrived at the garage, Paul instructed Chick and Jayne not to mention anything about the one cannon they had not located. "What they don't know won't hurt them, plus it will buy us another few days to try and find it before someone else does."

Having already photographed them, Pete just finished videotaping the cannons when the mayor and the others arrived with sirens wailing. They had been personally escorted there by Charleston's police chief and Officer Mo. Seeing the circus that was about to unfold in front of him, just like it had in the marina's parking lot the day he told Bobby Ray about finding the remains of Captain Francis, Paul had his friend run interference with the Charleston police officers who were now present. He hoped the bond between fellow police officers would make them understand that all was on the level. In short order, Bobby Ray soon had the Charleston officers off to the side of the garage telling them his jokes and listening to theirs.

Watching as the mayor climbed out of his city vehicle, Paul saw he had brought someone with him who he did not recognize. Now he walked to intercept them before they could get inside of the garage. Mayor Davis quickly saw the concerned look on his face.

"Paul, this is Mr. James Randall, he's the unofficial historian for the city of Charleston. The unofficial part means we work him hard and he does not get paid for his services. I want him to witness part of our city's past coming to life here today. I hope you don't mind?"

"Nope, no problem at all, just no photos please." Paul then introduced his two sons to Mayor Davis. "They're going to be our laborers for the day. I get to work them hard as well, except I have to pay them for their services, usually by way of an expensive dinner bill."

Followed by the others, Mayor Davis walked into the Public Works garage half expecting to see gold and silver piled up in front of him. What he saw was only a semi-circle of old black cannons sitting in front of him. In the semi-circle were a combination of Napoleon cannons of several different types, including an 1841 Seacoast gun, one 1841 twelve pounder and one 1857 twelve pound smoothbore cannon. With them sat two Griffin guns, made by the Phoenix Iron Company, in Phoenixville, Pennsylvania. Also present was one Parrott rifle, the Banded Brooks Rifle, and one Dahlgren cannon.

"What's all this? What are these cannons doing here and where's the gold and silver you told us all about?" Nearby the mayor saw twenty-five blue tote bins. They were neatly stacked by the cannons, but were also void of any riches.

"Mayor, when I found the soldier's remains I also found clues he had left behind in a letter regarding the Confederate gold and silver. It took luck and determination to figure out what the clues exactly meant, but we have. The clues he left regarding the money hidden here in Charleston were the hardest ones to figure out."

Mayor Davis still did not understand what the connection was to the cannons. "Why the cannons?"

As Paul answered the mayor's question, and as he had done earlier without interrupting to ask any questions, Judge Morgan listened in quietly. "For around one hundred and fifty years these cannons have been here in Charleston. Some of them likely fired upon Fort Sumter to start the Civil War. In fact, some of them may have even defended Charleston when the Union navy later sailed into your harbor. Certainly all of them have allowed scores of young children to climb on them so their parents could take their pictures. Since the summer of 1863, based on one of the letters I found, they have held the balance of the missing Confederate gold and silver. Captain Judiah Francis, the Confederate soldier whose remains I found, for some unknown reason chose these cannons to hide the gold and silver in. As I told you earlier today, he was the soldier charged by both President Jefferson Davis and General Lee to move the money south out of Richmond. The money was being moved so it could be kept out of the hands of the advancing Union army. Somehow Francis had made his way to Charleston and for some yet to be determined reason he decided to hide the money in these cannons. Who knows why he came here? Perhaps it was to rest, but more than likely it was to move the treasury further south by boat or perhaps by the railroad, but he never did. Again, he chose to hide the gold and silver here in these cannons for reasons we may never know. It's been here ever since, just waiting to be found. There are other details to tell you, but we can save them for another time. Let's go see what Captain Francis cleverly hid so many years ago."

Almost dumbfounded by what he had just been told, Mayor Davis first sought a clarification from Paul. "Let me get this straight. You're telling us that these here cannons, the ones sitting right here under our noses while on display in our own parks, have held part of the missing Confederate treasury for all of these years? The money has been right here the whole time?"

"Yes, sir. That's what the clues are telling us."

"But what if the cannons he had hid the gold and silver in were later assigned to units in the field? The money would certainly have been found then."

"Our thinking is these cannons were likely damaged or they had been taken out of service for some other reason. Francis would certainly not have risked putting the gold and silver in new or serviceable cannons as the money would easily have been found. Not him, he would not have done that."

"Paul, it sounds like you have gotten to know this Captain Francis fellow pretty well."

"Mr. Mayor, I think I've actually gotten to know him very well over the past few weeks since I found him. I believe he was quite the person. He had to have been if President Davis and General Lee trusted him enough to move a significant part of the Confederate treasury for them. He had to have been a very special person." Mayor Davis and Judge Morgan both nodded their heads in agreement to Paul's comments about Captain Francis.

"Mr. Waring, I'm not a Missouri boy, I'm a born and proudly raised South Carolinian, but you are going to have to show me you are right. I hope you are, but right now I'm pretty skeptical of the story you're trying to sell me on. It sounds more like a storyline for a movie than it does anything else."

"Mr. Mayor, I can understand your reluctance to believe me, really I can."

Paul walked with Mayor Davis, Judge Morgan, James Randall, Edwin Henion, and Chief Walter Barber, Charleston's police chief, over to where the cannons were lined up. As he did, Pete filmed what was transpiring in the garage. Chick and Jayne followed the group to where the cannons sat. As the group stood talking by the cannons, Jayne also documented what was taking place by taking photos of them with her camera.

"Gentlemen, look at the end of this cannon, specifically at the mortar and tell me what you see."

It was James Randall who answered for the group now assembled by the barrel end of cannon number seven. "I can see someone has inscribed C.S.A. and the number seven into the mortar. What's that mean?" Randall even took time to point out the periods which followed each of the three letters.

"Tell you what, let's find out. But remember what was inscribed into the mortar." Paul then gave the Public Works staff the signal to drill out the century old plus mortar from within the barrel of cannon number seven.

As Pete's video cameras had captured Paul standing near the cannon inscribed with the number seven, and as the cameras had captured him explaining what the inscription meant at the end of the barrel to Mayor Davis and the others, they now continued to capture what was unfolding in the large garage. As the cameras caught the Public Works staff preparing to drill out the mortar from within the cannon barrel, they also caught the anxious facial expressions of all who were present. The cameras caught everything, even the tension and hopes which filled the large garage.

The portable two-tone colored *Sullair 375* air compressor had sat quiet outside one of the large garage bay doors. It had been towed into place by one of the Public Works department's Chevy pickup trucks. As quietly as it had sat there, it quickly became loud and noisy as the compressor's diesel engine fired up after Stephen 'Tiny' Cochran, the Public Works superintendent, signaled the department's Lead Mechanic, Gary Montano, to start it up. Montano quickly had the air compressor fully charged and ready to go to work.

Despite sitting almost sixty feet away, the noise from the diesel engine startled Mayor Davis and several others when it fired up. They cringed at the loud noise even from where they stood within the garage. The black smoke that came from the diesel engine when it fired up, while thick and foul smelling at first, soon dissipated. Only the noise of the loud diesel engine was left to reverberate throughout the large garage.

In moments, the long single three-eighth inch green rubber hose running from the air compressor into the garage was charged with air. The chipping hammer attached to the other end of the air hose vibrated as it sat on the garage floor. The vibrations caused by the compressed air signaled it was ready to go to work.

Some of those present within the garage moved further away from where the air compressor sat as they hoped the few extra feet would somehow quiet the loud noise they now heard. Paul and Judge Morgan just stood there, simply donning the eye and ear protection Tiny had issued to all of them. All of their eyes were focused on the end of the cannon barrel as they watched Montano use the chipping hammer to quickly break through the roughly six inches of old mortar. After the mortar crumbled under the pounding it had taken from the modern chipping hammer, Tiny motioned for the air compressor to be shut off. Soon the garage was quiet again. A slight trace of mortar dust momentarily lingered in the air until the large ceiling fans in the garage pushed it away from where they all stood.

Anxiously, Paul spoke first. "OK, let's see what we found."

With his two boys holding the ends of one of the large tote bins, Paul first pulled out pieces of the broken up mortar. Tossing them into the tote bin, he reached into the barrel and pulled out pieces of rotted wood, remnants of what appeared to be old cloth bags, and various items of torn and tattered clothing. With the help of the public works staff, he used a small metal hoe to rake the rest of the contents out of the barrel. The contents fell onto a blue plastic tarp which had been spread out on the floor. To the surprise of many, nothing of value fell out. A quick check of the cannon's interior by Chick, who used a portable spotlight to see inside the barrel, showed it contained nothing else.

Mayor Davis quickly uttered a sarcastic comment after Chick confirmed the barrel was empty. Paul had anticipated the comment and was ready for it. "I don't see any lost Confederate money as you claimed there would be. All I see is old junk, perhaps precious in some way to Mr. Randall's trained eyes, but nothing that's of real use to the city. You said the cannons contained the missing gold and silver."

"Yes, I did, but I didn't say this particular cannon did." Paul said as he pointed at the cannon they had just cleaned out. "Come look at these other cannons and tell me what's different about the mortar in the ends of those barrels compared to the one we just drilled."

Walking to where the next cannon stood, Mayor Davis was quick to launch another disgusted barb at Paul. "Nothing, I don't see anything different. Just like the first cannon these other cannons have the same etching in the mortar as the first one did. If something is different, I don't see it!"

"Well, I do," offered Judge Morgan. Unlike the mayor, he took time to look at each of the other cannons before speaking. "The rest of these cannons all have even numbers inscribed in the mortar, the first one had an odd number. Mr. Waring, is that what you wanted us to see?"

"Precisely, Judge. One of the clues we were able to figure out, a clue which Captain Francis left us, was only the cannons which have even numbers inscribed in the mortar contain the gold and silver he had hidden. We believe the odd numbered cannons were probably decoys; perhaps used to make the others blend in with them. Pretty ingenious we thought."

"I would have liked to have met this Captain Francis fellow. He sounds like he was an interesting character."

"Me too, Judge, me too."

Turning back towards Mayor Davis, Paul offered the mayor the next pick. "Mayor, pick an even number you see inscribed in one of these cannons and we will drill that one next."

Briefly the mayor looked over the choices he had in front of him. "Let's try number ten as I hope we find ten million dollars hidden in these cannons."

As with the first cannon they drilled, the century old plus mortar quickly crumbled from the pounding it took from the chipping hammer. As Gary Montano, with help from a couple of other Public Work employees, dragged the long air hose out of the way, Paul told Brian and Sean to grab two tote bins. With his sons again holding one of the tote bins in place directly under the end of the barrel, a fairly large piece of mortar was removed from within the cannon. As it was being removed, Paul could see five coins had become set in the once wet mortar when it dried in the barrel so many years ago. He smiled when he saw the coins encrusted in the mortar as he felt a sense of relief that he had been right. It had taken a casual observation by his wife to see the markings in the mortar, but he had correctly figured out the remaining clues Francis left in his letter.

First showing Chick and Jayne what he pulled out from inside the cannon, he then held the mortar in his hands for another minute so Pete could film what they had found. As he turned around to show the others what the cannon had held for so many years, Paul asked Mayor Davis a question before handing him the dried piece of mortar. "Mr. Mayor, now do you believe us?" The mortar had dried with three silver coins and two gold coins encrusted in it. Mayor Davis proudly showed the others what he now held in his hands.

"Pete, Jayne, are you both getting this?" Paul asked with a smile on his face.

"The cameras are rolling. We're getting it."

After marveling at what had been handed to him, Mayor Davis looked at Paul. "I must confess I had my doubts, especially after you found nothing in the first cannon, but now it looks like you folks have correctly deciphered the clues your soldier left you. My apologies for doubting you. What other secrets does this cannon hold for us?"

With the first chunk of mortar placed into the tote box, Paul reached into the barrel of the cannon and quickly withdrew two handfuls of coins. As the coins hit the bottom of the tote bin, he laughed to himself. He was thinking the mayor was likely already calculating Charleston's cut of the gold and silver. After a few more handfuls of coins were scooped out of the cannon, two Public Works employees helped Chick as he used the hoe to rake the rest of the coins out of the roughly six foot barrel. The cannon held gold and silver coins of several different denominations. Soon the two tote bins were so full that the coins in the last tote bin began to overflow onto the blue plastic tarp. As the last of the coins tumbled out the end of the barrel, one fell out of the already overflowing tote bin and rolled off the tarp a short distance away onto the garage floor. Mayor Davis moved quickly to catch up to the coin as it rolled away. As he did, the others had a laugh at his expense as the sight of the city's mayor chasing the loose coin proved quite comical to watch.

"Hey, this gold dollar coin could be worth a few thousand dollars in today's market. I don't care how funny it looked. I'll chase any coin worth that kind of money." To his credit, he soon joined them in their laughter, realizing he probably had looked funny chasing the loose coin. "I know you folks are filming all of this, but I don't think we need to show the mayor chasing down a loose coin in the finished video!" His comment made them all laugh louder than they already had been.

After the laughter died down, the garage became strangely quiet as all who were present just stood there staring at the two tote bins full of gold and silver coins. They were transfixed by what they had just found in the barrel of one cannon. Edwin Henion, who had knelt down for a closer look at the coins, soon looked up at Paul. "I think your previous estimate of twenty million dollars has just increased."

As he was dragging the air hose towards the next cannon they were going to open, Tiny Cochran stopped momentarily to look at the coins Henion still knelt next to. "You know, I'm a Charleston resident my whole life. I still have a picture of my mom holding me when I was young, sitting on one of the cannons looking out at Fort Sumter. Some of you, or perhaps your own kids, might have even sat on one of those same very cannons. How could we have ever known we were sitting on so much money?" Tiny's comment caused several of them to nod their heads as they reflected back on similar experiences from their youth.

As Pete and Jayne documented what the cannon had held, Paul asked Tiny for several sheets of paper and a Sharpie pen. After receiving them, he wrote the number ten down on three sheets of paper, placing one sheet in each of the two tote bins of coins and placing the third sheet partway into the end of the barrel of cannon number ten. "This way we can still identify what cannon was what number and what each cannon contained before we emptied it."

Seeing what his friend was doing caused Steve Alcott to offer a comment regarding his observations. "Paul, your law enforcement training is showing. I'm guessing you have used all of your skills with this adventure."

Handing the rest of the paper and the Sharpie to Bobby Ray, Paul figured he probably had. "Steve, I hadn't thought about it, but I guess you're right. Came in handy without me even thinking about it."

As they had with cannon number ten, they slowly emptied the next cannon of its contents, having similar results and similar thrills when the coins were freed from the black cannon that had held them for so long. The only change they made to their procedure in emptying the coins from the cannons was one they made after emptying cannon number ten.

They had not realized how heavy the filled tote bins were going to be until they struggled to lift the heavy bins onto wooden pallets after emptying cannon number ten. Placing the bins on the pallets was done to make the loading of the armored car easier. It was Tiny's idea to move a fork lift into place under each cannon so the bins could be filled while they sat on a wooden pallet directly under the end of the barrel. "Work smarter, not harder" was the comment Tiny made as he drove the fork lift into place under cannon number twelve.

As the mortar was cleared away from the end of the barrel of cannon number twelve, they received another surprise. As Chick reached inside the barrel, he expected to find more loose coins. Quickly he withdrew his right hand as it touched something his hand had not sensed as being coins. Peering into the cannon's dark barrel, he asked for a light of some kind.

"This work?" Bobby Ray asked him as he handed Chick a small black flashlight he sometimes wore on his belt. Twisting the end of the flashlight so it turned on, Chick soon had the inside of the barrel illuminated for the first time in many years. In moments, he handed the flashlight back to Bobby Ray.

"Chick, what did y'all find in there?" Even the usually low-key Bobby Ray was now excited over the events of the afternoon. His excitement had grown as he knew something else besides loose coins had been hidden inside the barrel.

"Not sure yet, but it's proving tough to grab. Whatever it is it's made of cloth. I can sense it's tearing a bit as I tug on it."

It took a few more gentle tugs and tears in it, but soon Chick pulled out a decaying cloth bag of coins. After placing the bag of coins into one of the tote bins, he reached back into the barrel and grabbed onto another full bag of coins. As he began pulling the bag out, the decaying cloth bag ripped wide open and he withdrew just the ripped bag from inside the cannon. Only two silver dollars remained caught up inside the decaying bag. "Well, at least we know where the rest of the coins are." Emptying the rest of the bags of coins out of the barrel proved difficult as they had partially adhered to the inside of the cannon. Extracting the bags and their precious coins took time to complete, but soon they had the barrel cleaned out.

The next cannon they emptied had been marked with the number thirty. Like the others, this cannon also yielded another surprise for them. After Paul removed the broken up mortar, he found the cannon did not contain either loose or bagged coins, but rather it held a combination of twenty-eight gold and silver bars. They were soon found to be similar to the ones they had found in the cemetery a couple of weeks earlier.

While the gold and silver bars alone had captured everyone's attention, it was the first item Paul pulled out of the cannon which really surprised all of them. After the mortar had been cleared from the barrel, a decaying cloth bag was removed from inside the cannon. It was the bag of jewelry Francis had placed in the cannon. The bag contained some of the finest jewelry Southern women had ever worn at the time of the war. After it was opened, all who were present were stunned by what they found.

"This is totally unexpected. No one has ever mentioned this as being part of the Confederate treasury that I know of." For Chick, the person who knew the most about the Civil War among those standing around him, it was a find which caught him totally off-guard. "This had to be a great sacrifice to make for so many ladies. The donation of their jewelry, while likely difficult to part company with for some women, had to have been a personal sacrifice they were willing to make to show their support for the Confederacy. I would suspect this jewelry was among their most prized possessions. This jewelry has just caused this find to be an even more special one than we expected as it shows the personal sacrifices these women made. Some likely donated their jewelry in hopes it would be used to buy food or medical supplies their loved ones might have benefitted from. Money is money, but this collection of jewelry shows how personal the Southern cause had become to them and how much they wanted the Confederacy to succeed. Wow!"

After spending several minutes examining the jewelry, Paul handed one of the gold bars to the mayor so he and Judge Morgan could examine it. As he turned the gold bar over and over in his hands, Mayor Davis was overwhelmed by what they had just found within this one cannon. "These bars are magnificent, crudely made, but magnificent. What do you think they were made from?"

"Not sure, but I'm guessing they were likely made from people's silverware, perhaps even from jewelry similar to what we've just found. All melted down to support the Confederacy." As he held one of the gold bars in his hands, Paul tried imagining what had been melted down to make the bar he now held. "Doesn't really matter though, they're likely worth a whole lot more than the coins are. We've already found seven similar bars, found them at our last site. They look just like these do."

"You found more of these already?" Mayor Davis was surprised to learn other similar looking bars had already been found by Paul and his friends.

"Yes, we did. They surprised us when we found them there also, just as we're surprised by finding these. A nice surprise though, a very nice surprise."

The remaining cannon was then opened and emptied of its coins. On average, the contents of each cannon contained between three and four full tote bins of coins. When they had emptied the five even numbered cannons of their hidden assets, a total of fourteen tote boxes had been almost completely filled with gold and silver coins. Two additional tote boxes held the twenty-eight gold and silver bars they found in one of the cannons. They had found even more than Paul hoped they would.

As Mayor Davis stood with Paul near the emptied out cannons, they could not help staring at the three wooden pallets stacked with tote bins full of gold and silver. The bins now held several million dollars worth of valuables. Paul could not help but needle the mayor while they looked at what they had just found. "Think we have enough to pay for that Anniversary Celebration of yours yet?"

"Yes, Paul, I think we do. So what's your guess on the worth of what you've found here today?"

Paul called Chick to come over to where he stood with the mayor. As he walked over to join them, Judge Morgan and the mayor began speaking to each other. As they spoke, Paul and Chick briefly talked between themselves for a few minutes, roughly trying to calculate what they had found. "Mayor, it's a very rough guess, but we feel we can add another six to eight million, perhaps up to ten, to what we've found already. Conservatively we're probably looking at somewhere between six to ten million sitting here in front of us. Not a bad days work and we aren't even done yet."

"You mean there's more?" The excitement of the afternoon caused Mayor Davis to forget Paul had earlier mentioned they would be moving to another location after finishing up at the garage.

"Let's get together with Chief Barber so we can get to the other two cannons as soon as possible." As Paul, Mayor Davis, Judge Morgan and Chief Barber talked, Steve stood nearby listening to what was being discussed. Meanwhile, Chick and Jayne, with help from Bobby Ray and Paul's two sons, supervised the loading of the now filled tote bins into the armored car. As they did, Pete filmed the process to its end. When they were finished, Chick put eight empty tote bins into his van for their needs at the cemetery.

After speaking with Chief Barber and after the armored car had been loaded, Paul called everyone together in the garage. He then addressed Judge Morgan. "Your Honor, I hope what you and the others have seen here today gives all of you even more of an appreciation for the Civil War than what I know you already have. It certainly has done just that for my friends and me. We have no ownership of this money and we will not be making a claim for any of it as we realize it still belongs to others and not to us. Our motivation has simply been about our passion for the war. It has also been about solving the clues Captain Francis left behind for us. I guess you could say it was the thrill of the hunt which kept us going. We haven't mentioned this today as we've been kind of busy, but we plan on making a documentary of what we've found as we think it's a great story that needs to be told." Paul paused a few moments to collect his thoughts. "Very soon we're going to secure the tote bins with lids and with security tags we've had made up. The tags are tamper resistant. How does all of this sound to you so far?"

"Where do you plan on securing this armored truck?" It was a question asked by Judge Morgan.

"With the mayor's approval and with Chief Barber's as well, I would like to secure it within the Impound Lot next to the Charleston Police Department's parking garage. I have briefly looked at the lot already. Between the well-secured gate, the ten foot high privacy fence, the security cameras, and the razor wire on top of the fencing, I believe it's a secure enough location for now. Mr. Henion confirmed to me earlier the folks at Loomis have graciously allowed us the use of their armored car until we can get this all figured out. To me, it makes the most sense to keep the money stored within the armored car for now. Perhaps we can take the added precaution of disabling the truck mechanically so it cannot be easily moved if someone wants to try and steal it. I know the Impound Lot is monitored by a fairly sophisticated video and audio surveillance system. The system is similar to one we used back in Connecticut. I also know the system will allow for additional monitoring at little expense, so I would like to have the means to monitor the audio and video feeds on both my laptop and on my Blackberry. Mr. Mayor, is this acceptable to you? I'm trying to show you the same trust you showed in us here today by leaving the money with you."

"I'll have Chief Barber make it happen. If Judge Morgan has no problems with your suggestions, then it's acceptable to me."

Listening to what had been said, Judge Morgan thought for a moment before speaking. "Mayor, I believe the proper safeguards are in place for the city to protect this money for the immediate future, but I will likely instruct the United States Marshal for South Carolina to come take possession of this money within the next week. Until then it is your responsibility to protect this money and this part of our history." Judge Morgan then looked at Chief Barber. "Chief, I'm holding you personally responsible for this money. Put a plan together to protect this money around the clock; I don't care what it costs, just to do it. If I learn of any tampering to the armored car or to any of its contents . . . well, let's just say you don't want that to happen. For if it does, you'll be standing before me in open court and you won't be having a good day. Understood?"

"I do, Judge. We'll protect the money. Sir, you have nothing to worry about. I may not be sleeping too well over the next few days, but I hear you loud and clear." Chief Barber knew Judge Morgan had nothing to worry about regarding the safety of the recovered coins and other valuables. He knew it would be himself who would be doing all of the worrying for the next few days.

Paul then excused himself, asking the others to give him a moment with Judge Morgan. The two of them walked a short distance away from the others, standing near the now empty cannons as they talked. "Judge, one more thing. We have two more cannons to open today. I don't want to wait until tomorrow to do so as I'm afraid once the word gets out everyone in the world will be looking for gold inside of ceremonial cannons from here to who knows where." Pausing, Paul then directed his next comment directly at Morgan. "Your Honor, with all due respect, I don't think you should be there when we open those two cannons. What I'm going to propose to the mayor is that we open those cannons with the whole world watching us. I dislike publicity which is directed at me, always have, but I think opening those cannons with the media present gets this story out in the open and a great story starts to get told today. I believe in transparency and being upfront about what I'm doing, that's why I want to open the cannons today. In my opinion, the money still belongs to the people of the South. I just think they should see and hear about it as soon as possible. Doing so would also likely give the people of Charleston an opportunity to feel good about themselves. It would also give Mayor Davis, who has been great about all of this, a pat on the back for his cooperation and for agreeing to safeguard all that we have found here today. But for you, I would again suggest you not be there. Your position needs to be protected, separated from all of the publicity this story is likely to generate."

"Paul, I appreciate you looking out for my concerns. I have no interest in being in front of any television cameras as I'm not made to do that kind of work. You certainly don't need my permission to host a media event as I have no authority at this time on matters like that. That's an issue the mayor and you have to iron out. But I want you to know I appreciate your position on who the money belongs to. The world needs a few more people like you folks."

"Judge, I appreciate your kind comments. We all thank you for being here as your presence certainly gave some dignity to the events of the day. I will have Steve call you later so you know how we made out when we opened the last two cannons." They shook hands with each other before Judge Morgan left to say goodbye to the others. Soon Paul left with the others to finish their day by opening the two cannons that waited for them at the cemetery.

* * * * * *

At six pm, with Duke Johnson now present, along with representatives from every local television station and print media organization from across South Carolina, cannon number eight was opened. Mayor Davis, with help from Tiny Cochran and Gary Montano, symbolically helped to empty the gold and silver from the cannon on the grounds of Charleston's Confederate Soldier's Cemetery. The television film crews and the newspaper photographers could not take enough photos of the three tote bins filled with gold and silver coins from the cannon. Next to the tote bins stood two burly Charleston police officers as Chief Barber was already heeding the stern warning Judge Morgan had given him earlier in the afternoon.

As the public part of the event concluded, and after most of the media had left to prepare their follow-up stories for their eleven pm broadcasts and for the morning editions of their newspapers, the gold and silver was loaded into the armored car. As this happened, Mayor Davis took Paul off to the side and away from the few remaining newspaper reporters who were still present. "Paul, I want to thank you for what you have done for Charleston. On a personal note, I appreciate the touch you suggested regarding the media event. It got me some free and much needed publicity. I won't forget that."

"Mayor, it was a pleasure. Thanks for your help today. I'm glad it all worked out. I'm looking forward to attending the Anniversary Celebration."

"So am I, so am I."

The mayor was still basking in the glow of knowing his face was already being shown on all of the local television stations that evening. In one form or another, the residents of the city would soon learn their mayor played an instrumental role in helping to discover the missing Confederate gold and silver which had been hidden in Charleston for all of these years. He knew the positive effects from this story would likely carry over to the voting booths in a few months. *Senator William Davis* had a nice ring to it he thought as he walked back to where his aide waited for him.

As they walked back to where cannon eight was still on display, Paul stopped for a moment. "As the famous philosopher Alice Zerbola often said, 'Ironic, isn't it?'"

"What's ironic, Paul?"

"Mayor, don't you see the irony in all of this? Here is Charleston, the birthplace of where the fighting first started in that terrible war; it's a city located in the state which was the first to secede from the Union. Now Charleston and South Carolina will likely be among those who benefit the most from the money we have found. As Alice often said, 'Ironic, isn't it?'"

"Yes, I guess it's just that, very ironic. Say, who is this Alice person you are referring to? I've never heard her name before."

Paul started to walk away, but turned and looked over his shoulder at Mayor Davis. "She was my mother-in-law, a nice lady who I miss."

In a few short minutes, with Paul and his friends present, as well as Mayor Davis and his aide, along with Paul's two sons, and the crew from the Charleston Public Works garage, Ken Barton, the cemetery's superintendent, opened the large overhead door to the cemetery's maintenance building. Duke Johnson, who had not had the chance to privately see one of the cannons opened up, now saw the last one being opened. After the mortar had been removed from 'Old Number Six', Paul looked over at Duke. He was still smiling from what he had just witnessed. "Duke, it's the last one. It's all yours to empty out, go for it!"

An hour later they were all done. The last of the blue tote boxes, almost totally full of gold and silver coins from the last two cannons, had now been packed away inside the white colored Loomis armored car. Four Charleston police vehicles, three police motorcycles, the Charleston police department's helicopter, and Officer Lonnie Mo, who was riding shotgun in the back, escorted the armored car safely back to the Charleston Police Department. It would be safe there until United States Marshals took possession of the money three days later.

Paul had not mentioned to Mayor Davis that one other Confederate cannon had yet to be located. He hoped they could locate it before someone else did. But not tonight, it was time to rest and time to call Donna with the news of the day.

28

The Mission Dies.

"I am going fast now. I am resigned; God's will be done."
Major General J.E.B. Stuart, CSA

They waited patiently, hidden in the tree line and within the many large shrubs which were mixed in amongst the trees. It was almost as if they were back home hunting, waiting for deer to come out to forage for their nightly meal. Tonight it would be different as it was Yankee soldiers they waited for, soldiers who were hunting them as well. As the night wore on they entertained themselves with their own thoughts to stay awake.

Waiting quietly on the far right side of the tree line, Sgt. Stine had loaded Odom's rifle to use besides his own. As he waited to see if his trap would work, he spent time recalling the various battles he had fought in before being selected for this assignment. He had been wounded twice, scared more than that, and yet he could not wait to get back to the war. He missed being with the folks he grew up with, most of them fighting in the same company with him. More than a few of the men he had served with were dead already, killed in some of the war's earliest battles. Despite that he longed to get back to those who were still alive as they were the only friends he had known in life. If he was to die in this war, Stine wanted to die fighting alongside his friends and fighting to defend Virginia.

Sgt. Davis occupied the time daydreaming of home and listening to the sounds which came from the woods around him. He had heard the same noises so many times back home and had hunted many of the same animals making noises this night. Day or night, nice weather or bad weather, he always felt the most comfortable in the woods. Even on this night he was comfortable as he listened closely for the unmistakable sound a man makes when he is trying to be quiet in the woods. Davis longed to return to the woods and mountains of Virginia as he had long ago grown tired of this senseless war.

Sgt. Banks had not thought of his family or of the war while he waited in the woods. He was fast asleep. Fighting a fever the last few days, the lack of sleep, as well as the lack of clean drinking water, had affected him greatly. He had fallen asleep in the woods trying to regain his strength, comfortable knowing his fellow Virginians were protecting him as he did.

As the others did, Francis also had thoughts of home. He spent several minutes thinking of his parents and sister, but spent most of the time thinking of the young and pretty Rita Margaret Lyman who lived near his family's farm in Virginia. He hoped to make her his wife when the war was over. They had known each other for many years, having first met at the church their families attended on Sunday mornings when they were young children. Over the years they had become friends; developing a fancy for each other during their early teenage years. As he thought of her, Francis thought about the question he would ask her the next time they saw each other. "I hope she will say yes when I ask her to marry me."

The noise of a heavy foot stepping on a dry fallen tree branch snapped each of them back from where they had been in their thoughts of being home with their family and friends. Hearing the noise, Francis kicked Banks as quietly as possible, waking him from the deep and restful sleep he had been enjoying. Quickly he was awake and scanning the wood line in front of him for Union soldiers.

While they quickly focused on the area where they had spread out their bedrolls, their experiences from being in the woods back home and from serving in the army had taught them not to just focus on the obvious. Now their eyes also scanned the entire area around them, making sure danger was not sneaking up on them in other places besides the obvious one. Francis had reminded them of that again when they first hid in the woods. He had also told them he would be the one to pay attention to the areas away from where the shooting started. They would deal with the obvious threat they saw and he would deal with the danger lurking elsewhere.

The first noise had come from off to their right, close to where Stine was hiding in the woods. Now he crouched down behind a pine tree, partially hidden from view by a Palmetto bush which grew near the tree he was hiding behind. Stine first, and then Davis, saw the figure slowly creep towards their bedrolls from the woods off to the right. As their eyes followed this figure, they also saw a second figure appear from the woods directly in front of them. Both figures were less than forty feet from where they hid. The light from the moon was now their ally as it allowed them to watch the figures move closer to the trap they had set for them.

Quickly two other Union soldiers came running out of the woods off to the left of where Francis and Banks now knelt low in the tree line; the two running ran as fast as they could without making too much noise. Francis and Banks watched as the soldiers sprinted the last few feet to the bedrolls which no longer contained any sleeping men. Raising their rifles, with bayonets fixed, the Union soldiers repeatedly stabbed the empty bedrolls several times before realizing they had been fooled.

Almost as if it had been choreographed, the Union soldiers stopped their attack on the empty bedrolls. As they turned to see the rifles of Francis' men light up the night as the powder in the rifles burned, the burning powder sent two minie balls racing towards them. It was now too late for the soldiers to react to what they saw as Davis and Stine had already fired at them. The Union soldiers had been too close for two experienced Confederate soldiers to miss. Quickly two Union soldiers fell dead.

First firing McKinney's rifle, Francis struck his target with a shot to the soldier's stomach. The Union soldier dropped to his knees as he clutched his burning stomach, then falling to the ground on his back, the pain too intense for him to continue on with the fight.

Standing up, Francis fired the last two shots from his pistol. Missing with the first, he struck the fourth soldier in the upper left arm with the second shot. Picking up Odom's rifle, Stine also fired at the soldier who had been shot in the arm. The hastily fired shot struck the soldier in the upper right thigh. Despite being shot twice, the soldier still did not fall and he recklessly fired his rifle at Francis, but the shot was high and it harmlessly flew into the woods. Dropping his empty rifle, the soldier hobbled off into the woods as fast as his injuries allowed.

Stine then moved forward to check on the first two intruders they had shot. He quickly saw both were dead. As he moved toward the soldier Francis had shot in the stomach, one who was now trying to crawl off into the woods, a shot was fired from the woods. Mortally wounded, Stine fell to the ground just after yelling *"Look out!"* He had seen the last soldier firing his rifle as he charged towards them.

Reacting to Stine's warning, Francis spun around to see the fifth and last Union soldier charging at him, his empty rifle poised to crush the side of Francis' head with a deadly blow. But before the soldier could swing his rifle, Francis reacted first. Without a wasted movement, he quickly ran his saber into the charging soldier's upper chest. Now injured and down on the ground, neither of the surviving soldiers saw what ended their lives. Their time on earth ended when a Confederate saber was run through each of them. The attack was over, but Stine was dead. His death enraged Francis as he had lost another man.

Despite killing two Union soldiers with his saber, and despite having hung other men during this mission, Francis was not a violent man. However, when challenged to defend his men and himself, he had the ability many other men did not have. It was the ability to deal the final savage blow to end a threat. As he felt after having his men hang those who had tried to sneak up on them that night in the barn, he also had no regret this night for what he had done. "Now I'm going to go find that last Yankee bastard and I'm going to kill him also! Damn him!" As he started into the woods, Davis called to him.

"Captain, not now, it's too dangerous. We don't know who else might be out there."

The words of caution caused Francis to pause and think. "Davis is right. Now is not the time to pursue anyone." He turned and walked back to where his two remaining men stood. By now Banks had reloaded all of their rifles. He had also checked on Stine, but he was dead.

Like Francis, Davis now mourned the loss of a fellow Virginian, one he had come to love as much as he loved his own brothers who were still back home. Burying the others had always been hard on him, but now digging the grave for his friend was almost too much for him to handle. As he finished burying his friend, he seethed hatred at the Yankees, vowing to extract revenge on them for taking the life of someone he thought of as a brother. "I shall curse the damned Yankees until the day I die." Lying nearby were the bodies of the dead Union soldiers. Davis angrily yelled at the dead soldiers as he threw the shovel in their direction. "Dig your own graves, damn you!"

Francis checked the bodies of the dead soldiers for anything he and his men might be able to use, but he found nothing except a small amount of tobacco and a homemade pipe. "Not like Union soldiers to attack at night. They must have thought they could take us or else they thought we had more food than we do." Collecting their own gear, he and his two remaining men prepared to move out before they could be attacked again. As they did, Davis took the saddle and reins from Stine's horse and placed them in the rear of the wagon. Stine's horse was left to wander off on his own.

Davis now drove the single wagon, his horse and Odom's tied to the rear of it as they pushed northeast. As they moved along they kept the Waccamaw River to their right. With Francis keeping a sharp eye out for sudden movements in the tall river grass, Davis kept a close lookout in the direction of where several large rice fields stood. In the distance, lights from the main house of a nearby plantation could be seen across the narrowing river.

The moon's bright light and the events of the evening combined to play tricks on Francis' tired mind as they pushed slowly onward. The tall river grass caused him to stop on several occasions as a soft gentle wind pushed the tall grass in directions his tired mind perceived to be the shapes of Union soldiers dancing nearby. Despite what had just happened, he sensed the extreme fatigue he was beginning to feel. Looking at Davis, he could see he was also struggling to stay awake as he drove the wagon. In his head he played out the few options he still had as they slowly moved along. "We need to get some sleep, but we cannot stop now. We need to cross the river first and then we can sleep." They moved even slower over the next hour due to their fatigue and due to being overly cautious. In a hushed but fatigued voice, Francis finally called them to a stop, knowing they needed to sleep. It would be the first fatal mistake he made during the entire mission.

As Davis pulled the wagon to a stop, he looked up at the bright full moon which had helped them navigate their way. Still seated, he took a long sip of water from his canteen. Standing up from where he had sat on the wagon's hard wooden seat, he took a moment to stretch his arms and legs in the autumn's warm early morning hours. As he stood there stretching his tired body, Francis rode up slowly along the left side of the wagon. Without the slightest bit of warning, two shots rang out from the woods off to their left and Davis fell dead, shot through the left side of his neck. Francis instinctively turned to where the loud noise of the rifle shots had come from. As he did, he heard footsteps running nearby in the woods.

Hearing the ugly sound a minie ball makes when it strikes flesh, Francis then turned to look at Davis, but he was already dead. His lifeless body had fallen awkwardly across the seat of the wagon. Turning in his saddle, he looked for Banks who had been riding out in front of them. As almost if on cue, Banks' riderless horse trotted slowly back in the direction of where Francis still sat on his horse. He realized Banks had likely been killed by Union soldiers who had quietly ambushed him.

Reacting to the noise of footsteps running through the brush towards him, Francis withdrew his saber from his scabbard. Doing so caused the scabbard's worn leather strap to break and it fell harmlessly to the ground. Then he heard the voices of the soldiers who had just shot Davis and ambushed Banks. "We got two of them, let's get the last one! He's all alone now!" From the protective darkness of the woods where they had been, he saw two Union soldiers charge at him on foot. He was fortunate to see them as they ran from the woods into a small clearing the moon had illuminated. As the first soldier grabbed the reins to his horse, the other tried desperately to knock Francis out of his saddle.

With his saber in his right hand as he fought to maintain control of the reins in his still weak left hand, Francis spurred his horse with his right foot as the Union soldier pulled on his left leg. Confused by the command given him, and by the soldier yanking on the reins at the same time, the horse quickly moved to its left; the quick movement nearly throwing Francis out of the saddle. As his horse turned, it stepped on the left foot of the soldier grabbing at the reins. Screaming out in pain, the soldier let go of the reins as he fell to the ground, his foot broken from the horse's weight.

Free of the soldier who had been grabbing at the reins, Francis' horse lurched forward. As it did, Francis hacked twice at the soldier who had been trying to knock him out of his saddle. The second slash of his saber caused the fatal wound to the soldier's neck. The pain the soldier felt caused him to scream out in agony, a scream that was likely heard for some distance. Momentarily giving thought to dismounting from his horse so he could end the life of the soldier who was rolling on the ground with a broken foot, Francis chose to flee as other trouble likely lurked in the darkness.

Darting away and riding low in the saddle, Francis was surprised to hear the sound of two musket shots being fired at him. The first shot whizzed by the left side of his head as it flew off into the woods out in front of him. But then he felt the hot sting in his left leg and he knew he had been shot. "Damn it!" He cried out not because he had been shot, but because he immediately knew the wound would impact his ability to finish what he had been charged with. "It will be alright, I will have it taken care of. It will be alright." Francis pushed his horse hard to move away from the threat they faced, while at the same time trying to convince himself that he would be fine. He was only successful in moving further away from the Union soldiers, deep down he knew he was in trouble.

He pushed his horse as hard as he could for almost another hour before finally stopping to rest. They both needed a drink of water and Francis knew he needed to treat his wound before he bled to death. He now had little to use except his hands and his bayonet. Along with the wagon, the rest of his supplies had been abandoned when the soldiers charged at him from the woods.

After drinking a few handfuls of water from a small stream which fed into the Waccamaw River, Francis sat down and leaned back against a large Live Oak tree, catching his breath before treating his wound. "If only I could rest here for a spell, everything would then be fine." Then the pain in his leg began to throb and he knew it had to be attended to. Taking his boot off, Francis cut his pant leg so he could see the wound the minie ball had caused. Trying several times to stick a finger into the wound to feel for the minie ball, the pain was too intense and he nearly passed out from his attempts.

Taking off the bandana he wore around his neck to catch his sweat; he crawled back to the stream and drenched it in the cool running water. Ripping a small piece of cloth off the bandana, Francis gingerly placed it in the wound to stem the flow of blood. It hurt to do, but doing so slowed the flow of blood. Using the rest of the bandana as a tourniquet, he used a small piece of a tree branch, turning and twisting it several times to further stem the flow of blood. Satisfied after several minutes that he had done what he could, he again leaned back against the tree and drifted off to sleep. He was alone now, his men all dead. Now he was hurt and being hunted by the Union army. For the moment, he was too tired and too hurt to care.

Francis had only been asleep for twenty minutes when a flock of ducks flying overhead loudly made their presence known. Their noises startled him awake as he saw them land nearby in the river. Waking up, he was confused at first as he had lost sense of where he was, but the pain from his leg quickly reminded him what had happened and where he was. Reaching for his pocket watch, he saw it was twenty after six in the morning.

Believing his pursuers had to be closing in on him, Francis struggled to get up. He used all of his strength and the support of the Live Oak tree to finally stand up. He tried keeping his weight off his injured left leg, but when he mounted his horse he was forced to put some it on his injured leg; doing so quickly caused intense pain to flow throughout his body. Sitting on his horse as he waited for the pain to subside, he looked down at the bandana covering his wound. It had practically stopped the flow of blood from the wound. "Thank goodness for small miracles!"

Francis realized unless he could find a doctor to remove the minie ball from his leg he was not going to be strong enough to dig up the money he had buried in the cemetery. "That should not be a big task for any person to do on their own, but now with this ball in my leg I do not have the means to do the work alone." Now his thoughts turned to getting back to the cemetery for another reason. It was no longer to dig up what he had buried there, now it was to bury his saddlebags. They contained the rest of the gold and silver coins that he could not hide in the cannons back in Charleston. "I will bury the saddlebags near the rest of the money until I can return to get all of it at one time. If I can bury the saddlebags there, I'll have a better chance of getting back to Charleston for help. I'll be able to travel lighter and faster, and I'll be at peace knowing the money is at least safe for now."

Besides his wounded leg and the Union soldiers pursuing him, Francis faced one other obstacle, crossing the Waccamaw River. Sizing up the river as he rode along its western bank, he knew he had to find the narrowest point to cross due to his wounded leg. He realized he would have to pick a time when the river was quiet. He knew when the river's tides changed that would be when it was at its calmest. South of where he now was, the river's brackish water met the Atlantic's salt water in Winyah Bay, just outside of Georgetown. Looking at the banks of the river, he could tell the depth of the river changed significantly with each change of the ocean's tides. Finding a spot that afforded him the best chance of crossing the river safely, Francis waited for the current to slow. As he did, he started to feel both the painful effects of the lodged minie ball in his leg and weakness from not having had much to eat. "I have to cross the river now or I'll never be strong enough to do so."

Nearby, Francis spied an oak tree sitting all alone next to the river, a single large tree towering over the chest high river grass. Riding closer to the tree, long since dead from a lighting strike years ago, he could see a section had snapped partway off the tree's main trunk. It had likely snapped when the tree was either hit by lightning or when it died shortly afterwards. Arriving at the tree, he quickly saw the large limb as his means of crossing the river. The river was far too deep to risk crossing on his horse and getting stuck in the deep mud on the banks of the river would only serve to panic his horse. Abandoning his horse was a huge risk, but he had to get back to the cemetery sitting on the other side of the river. It was a risk he knew he had to take. "Hopefully I can find another horse at one of the plantations I come across." Getting down off of his horse, he saw the large tree limb was almost six feet in length. As it bobbed in the brackish water, he could see it was roughly twenty inches in diameter. It was barely attached to the tree.

Leaning against his horse to keep his weight off his injured leg, Francis removed his gold pocket watch from his uniform blouse and placed it inside one of his saddlebags. After removing the saddlebags from his horse, he carefully protected them as he slowly slid down the river bank towards the dead tree. Reaching the tree limb, he set the saddlebags down on the bank of the river. "I have to keep the saddlebags dry because of my watch and because of the letters they contain. I cannot allow them to get wet." After taking a few minutes to inspect the tree limb, he was somewhat confident he could use it as a way to cross the river. Moving slowly and painfully, he crawled and climbed his way back up the bank to where he had left his horse.

Exhausted by the time he got back to his horse, Francis lay on the ground for several minutes trying to muster his strength to finish what had to be done. Finally able to stand again, he made the painful short walk to where his horse stood quietly, watching as its owner made his way over to him. "It's OK old friend, it's OK. It's just time for us to say goodbye to each other, that's all. You have served me well old friend and I shall miss you." Patting him on the neck, he then gave his horse a hug. He had owned his horse since before the war had started. Grabbing his bayonet from where he kept it by his saddle, he now placed it within his right boot. Unbuckling his saddle, but without the strength to lift it off his horse, he gave it a gentle push, allowing it to fall to the ground. Removing the bit from the horse's mouth, he allowed the reins to also fall to the ground. Saying his final goodbye to his friend, he gently slapped the horse on its backside, urging the dark brown horse he called *Warrior* to leave him. After walking a short distance away, his horse stopped to eat some of the grass growing on the side of the river, unaware his owner would never ride him again. "I have just lost my last friend from this mission," Francis thought as he painfully stooped to pick up his blanket. Tears filled his eyes as he looked back at his horse one last time. Struggling because of his injured leg, he placed the reins on top of his saddle in a neat pile. Then he limped away without looking back.

Slowly sliding back down the river bank, Francis again made his way to the tree limb, and to the saddlebags he had left by the side of the river. It took him several attempts, but finally he was able to free the limb from the main trunk of the tree. Lying on the bank nearby was another dead tree limb, longer and skinner in size than the first one. Using his bayonet, he cleaned away the small dead starter shoots on the limb. "Hopefully I can use this to help me keep my balance and to help push me across the river."

Straddling the large dead tree limb, Francis placed his saddlebags and blanket over his left shoulder; adjusting himself to allow for the weight of the heavy saddlebags. At first, the cool river water actually made his injured leg feel better for a moment, but then the brackish water began to sting as it entered his wound. "I need to get across the river quickly," Francis thought, "this muddy water cannot be doing my leg any good." He then secured his empty pistol by pushing it further down into his waistband.

Using the small tree limb as a pole to push away from the shore, Francis took a moment to make sure no one was watching him from the banks of the river or from any small boats that might be nearby. Sensing he was alone, outside of the several hawks and egrets that watched him as they hunted for their breakfast, he pushed himself further out into the fairly calm river until the pole could no longer feel the bottom. The relief he had first felt from the water now caused him to feel sick to his stomach, the nausea almost causing him to lose his balance. "Stay focused and keep your balance, don't let the river get the best of you!" He made himself talk out loud as it forced him to concentrate on maintaining his balance as he slowly moved across the river. As he focused on maintaining his balance, he also kept reminding himself to use both his good leg and the pole to make his way to the other side of the river.

The river showed its mercy to him as it soon allowed him to make it to the eastern side without incident. Out of sheer luck he reached a section of the river with both a sandy bottom and a long but gradual grade to the top of the river bank. Reaching the top of the grade was a struggle due to the pain he now felt in his leg; Francis was utterly exhausted by the time he got there. Despite the hunger pains he also felt, he was far too exhausted to eat any of the peaches hanging from several well-kept peach trees. Fatigue had won out over hunger.

Lying there for several minutes as he caught his breath, Francis rested with his head propped up by his saddlebags. As he rested, he could smell a fire burning nearby. The smell came from the chimney of a nearby rice plantation whose peach trees he now lay under. Nearby he could hear singing, likely from slaves working in the nearby rice fields. He had seen the rice fields along the river earlier in the morning. Now too tired and too injured to care about eating or being found, he quickly fell asleep in the shade provided by the peach trees.

Francis had been asleep for almost about two hours when he was woken by the sounds of children's voices. Opening his eyes, he looked up to see five young children staring down at him. The children, both white and black, were two young boys and three slightly older girls. They had been playing in the peach orchard when they found him asleep. Now as he woke, one of the young girls, a white girl, ran off screaming to her father. "Papa, papa, come see what we all have found!" Her voice trailing off the further away she got from where he still rested on the ground.

"Hey, mista, is you a soldier man?" Francis looked at the young black boy who had asked him the question.

"Yes, I am. I . . . I need some water. Can you help me?" None of the children moved to help him. He was the first real soldier they had ever seen up close.

Francis soon heard the voice of the young girl who had run off to find her father. Her voice was coming closer to him now. "Over here, papa, he is over here!" He saw her first and then her father as he followed her to where she now stood next to the other children. Francis' first impression was he was too old to be the young girl's father as his hair was very grey, but then he saw the man's facial features were still those of a fairly young man. It was not the age of this man which concerned him, it was the rifle he was carrying that now concerned him. Behind the girl's father, two black men followed at a cautious distance.

"Scoot you kids, move out of the way!" The girl's father said in a gentle voice.

Francis was defenseless as he lay on the ground. He was entirely at the mercy of this stranger who now had his rifle pointed somewhat in his direction. "You a Confederate soldier?"

Weak and extremely thirsty, Francis answered him. "Yes, sir. My name is Captain Judiah Francis, I'm from Virginia. The Yankees shot me last night, got a Yankee minie ball stuck here in my left leg. I'm hurt pretty bad. Sir, I need some water, I'm darn thirsty. Can you please have someone get me some water?"

"Whatcha all doing down in these parts if ya are from Virginia as ya say ya are? Don't sound right to me."

"Sir, President Davis and General Lee, well they both assigned me and my men to take care of something for them. It's something kind of important for the entire Confederacy. That's why I'm down here. My men are all dead, killed by Union soldiers or by accidents. I'm the only one left."

Hearing General Lee's name being mentioned excited the girl's father, but he still stared hard at Francis. "You know General Lee . . . personal like I mean?"

Francis struggled to raise himself partway off the ground, finally making it to a sitting position. "Yes, sir, I know the general fairly well. He is a fine general and an even better person. I know he would express his appreciation personally to you if he knew you had taken care of me. I sure could use some water. Please, sir, may I have some?"

Thomas Daly stood silent for the next few moments as he stared down at the injured soldier helplessly lying on the ground before him. Sizing the situation up, he saw the pistol tucked into Francis' pants. He also saw his saber nearby on the ground. Standing there, he nodded his head as he pondered what Francis had just told him. After thinking over what now confronted him in his peach orchard, Daly glanced over his left shoulder at one of the two slaves standing behind him. "Moses, get on up to the well. Bring this here soldier some cool water to drink. Be quick about it!"

"Yes, suh, Mr. Tom."

Daly then knelt down next to Francis and looked at his wounded leg. "We ain't got no doctor in these parts now, the two we had are both off doctoring you soldier boys someplace. Closest doctor is down in Charleston. My wife and Big Ned's wife are both real good at doctoring things back together. We'll get you up there to see them after you have some water."

"Thank you, sir! Bless you. May I ask you your name?"

"My name is Thomas Daly. My family and I own this plantation, got over two thousand acres now. We named this place Rice Fields, named it after one of the crops we grow here. My family came here from Ireland many years ago. Right proud to be in this fine country, it's our home now." Daly turned to the other slave who stood quietly off to the side, one who had never taken his eyes off of Francis. "Big Ned, get up to the barn and fetch the buckboard down here. Tell Miss Diana we got a man hurt real bad down here. You best tell Josalee the same news as Miss Diana is gonna be needing her help. Tell them to be ready to do some doctoring on this soldier. Hurry now!"

"Yes, suh, I'll tell them about this soldier man!"

Francis collapsed back onto the ground; relieved help was on the way. "Thank you, Mr. Daly. Thank you!"

Soon Francis found himself lying on a large wooden table in what appeared to be a room off the plantation's kitchen. The room was mostly bare except for a few plates and glassware sitting on a small table on one side of the room. Nearby on a wall hung a likeness of George Washington, resplendent looking in his uniform. Even from the starkness of the room he could sense it was the home of a wealthy plantation owner.

Diana Daly had introduced herself to Francis when she first saw him being carried into the room by Moses and Big Ned. Soon she was telling him to prepare for the pain he was going to feel when she removed the boot from his injured leg. She had already tried to comfort him by cleaning his dirty face with a cool wet towel and by giving him two small glasses of bourbon to help dull the pain, but Francis writhed in pain when she took his boot off. The pain was one he had never experienced in life before.

As his pain momentarily subsided, Big Ned's wife, Josalee, a large woman with a warm friendly face, entered the room carrying a large white ceramic bowl filled with hot water, and with rags torn from old bed sheets. Never looking at him, Josalee directed all of her attention to the wound in his leg. By this time Diana had removed his boots, his left sock, and had ripped most of his left pant leg up past his knee. Doing so allowed the small round hole in his leg to be easily seen against his otherwise almost pale white leg. From the looks he soon saw in the faces of Diana and Josalee, Francis could tell the wound was bad.

"Mrs. Daly, I can tell from your expressions the wound must be bad. If you cannot get the minie ball out, then all I can ask of you is to clean the wound as best you can. Whatever you can do for me is most appreciated, but please do your best as I must get back to Charleston, both to see a doctor and to complete what is expected of me. Please know I'm most grateful for your kindness."

Diana then gave Francis a larger glass of bourbon to drink. With Josalee's help, she then went to work on his leg while Big Ned and Moses held him down on the table. The sting of the bourbon she poured directly into the leg wound was in itself almost too much pain for him to bear, but as she poked around in his leg trying to find the minie ball with a large pair of tweezers the pain was now unbearable. "Please, I beg you, please stop!" Diana ignored his cries as she had finally found the minie ball, but despite her best efforts over the next few minutes she could not free it from where it was lodged in his leg. After Francis passed out from the pain he felt, she again attempted to free the stubborn minie ball. Her efforts again failed to free the stubborn ball from his leg.

When Francis finally came to, Diana was again cleansing his face with a cool towel. It did little to help dull the pain he still felt. "Son, we tried our best, but we could not get the minie ball out. You need to see a doctor as soon as possible if you want to save your leg. I'm afraid if you don't that soon an infection will set in and you'll likely lose your leg. I'm sorry I could not do more for you."

Still groggy from the bourbon and the pain, Francis patted Diana on the left hand, thanking her for her help. Then he fell asleep again.

* * * * * *

Waking up three hours later, Francis found himself alone in the same room and still lying on the table. Propping himself up on his elbows, he looked for his saddlebags, hoping they had not disappeared. He soon saw they had been placed in a corner of the room. Next to the saddlebags sat his still wet boots, his pistol, and his saber. Looking down at his injured leg, he saw his wound had been bandaged with clean white pieces of cloth. The pain was still intense, but it was far more manageable than it was when Diana had been poking around inside of it earlier.

As he sat propped up on the table, Diana entered the room carrying a small tray of food. Josalee soon followed her into the room carrying a large glass of warm cider. She quietly walked to where Diana now stood. "We don't have nearly as much food as we had before the war started, but we have enough to be thankful for and to share with you. We probably would do the same for a Yankee soldier who was hurt just like you are. It makes no sense not to be compassionate when someone is hurt."

Francis quickly ate the meal that had been prepared for him, realizing as he finished how fast he had eaten everything which had been set in front of him. The warm cider had been his first real treat in several weeks. He was now somewhat embarrassed by how fast he had eaten his meal. "Sorry, Mrs. Daly, I guess my table manners are a bit rusty these days."

"Nothing to apologize for, my boy use to eat like that also. He was a big eater, just like you. At least I know you like our cooking. I'll get you some more food later, you just rest for now." As they left the room, Thomas Daly came into the room to check on Francis.

"Mr. Daly, I'm most appreciative of the hospitality your family has shown me. I shall never forget how kindly I was treated. I hope I can someday repay the kindness to your family."

Francis then told Daly of his plan to soon leave so he could try and make his way back to Charleston. "Mr. Daly, I need to borrow a horse to finish what General Lee has assigned me to do. I fear I'm going to fail him, but I must try to complete what is expected of me. For me to do so I must have a horse, but as an honest man I must tell you I don't know when, or if, I can ever return your horse to you. Sir, I must again ask you for your help. Can you lend me a horse so I can at least try to finish what my men have already died for?"

Thomas Daly was silent for a few moments as he thought about what Francis had just asked of him. "Captain, I'm not a born Southerner like you and like many of my neighbors are. Perhaps it's for that reason that I cannot make sense of this terrible war. This is a war where men from the same country, who just a few short years ago fought side by side to defeat the Red Coats, now fight and kill each other. All of this, especially the killing, just makes no sense to me."

"Mr. Daly, I also have difficulty understanding it at times myself. I don't know if that gives you any comfort, but many of us share your concerns as well. I agree with the senselessness of this war and that it needs to end before we're all dead, but like my fellow Virginians I will continue to defend my home from those who want to tell us how to live. All we want is to be free and independent . . . free from any type of government which tries to tell us how to live our lives. But I do agree with you, there is no reason we cannot live in peace amongst each other."

"Judiah, you appear to be a bright young man, a dedicated idealist perhaps, but a fine man. I will be happy to lend you the horse you need and I hope whatever it is you need to do that you can finish it. I can sense it is important for you to do so. Whether I get the horse back or not is of little concern to me. What is of concern to me is I fear what you are trying to finish is soon going to kill you. That, my friend, will cause me great sorrow. I won't try to dissuade you from your responsibilities, but I am afraid I shall never see you again."

Daly excused himself, coming back several minutes later when Francis had just finished putting his boots back on. Making sure the cork was tight on the bottle, he handed Francis a small bottle of bourbon. He also handed him an envelope containing several sheets of writing paper, a quill, and a small bottle of ink. "Judiah, the bourbon is for the pain. The pen and paper is because I would like to hear from you so I know you are safe. When I receive your letter, I hope it will tell me you have seen a doctor and your leg is healing. Please, I beg you, get to a doctor soon!" Tears soon welled in the eyes of both men as in their own hearts they both knew Daly's prediction of Francis dying was a strong likelihood.

Soon climbing onto the horse Daly had lent him, Francis expressed his appreciation to both Thomas and Diana for their kindness. "Remember not to worry about the horse, Judiah, consider him a gift." Sitting on the borrowed horse, he smiled at them as he patted the satchel of food they had prepared for him. He promised he would see them again, but as he rode away he knew that would likely not happen in this lifetime. Diana now had tears in her eyes as she watched him ride away. They had just met a few short hours ago, but she had already lost one son to the war and now she feared she would lose their new friend to the war as well.

* * * * * *

It was dusk by the time Francis finally reached the Allston cemetery. Nearing the cemetery, he took time to briefly scout the surrounding area, making sure he was alone. Reaching the back wall of the cemetery, he carefully dismounted his horse. His leg was now throbbing from both the minie ball still inside it and from enduring the ride back to the cemetery from the Daly plantation. "Whatever good they had done to my leg, I now fear I've set that good deed back because of this painful ride. I must get this money buried and be on my way to Charleston."

Being careful to protect his injured leg, Francis was forced to drag the heavy saddlebags behind him for most of the way. He was exhausted from the ride and from the leg wound which had sapped his strength. Tired and confused, he struggled to find the location where they had previously buried some of the gold and silver. It took him several minutes to get his bearings, but finally he was convinced he was close to the original location. Using just his hands at first, and then a broken brick which had once been part of the cemetery's wall, he scraped away at the soft sandy soil. Soon he had dug a shallow hole, one slightly deeper than he needed to bury his saddlebags.

Before burying them, Francis removed his gold watch and the two glass bottles from inside the saddlebags. One of the bottles contained the letter he had recently written to President Davis. They also contained the two letters he had been handed at the start of his mission. Placing the saddlebags within the hole, he quickly filled it with loose soil, doing his best to make it look like no one had been there. Still fearing someone would see where he had been digging, he managed to find a few handfuls of pine needles. He scattered them on top of the small hole in a further attempt to hide what he had just buried inside the small family cemetery.

Even without the heavy saddlebags to carry, he struggled to make his way back to where he had tied up his horse. Trying to climb up onto his borrowed horse just as he had effortlessly done so many countless times before with his own horse; Francis fell twice. Weak and tired, the wound to his left leg bleeding again, he gasped for air on this warm evening after falling to the ground. As he did, he sensed a fever beginning to invade his body, likely from an infection that had settled into his leg. Summoning all of his strength, he made it up onto the horse on his third attempt. Exhausted, he paused for a moment to catch his breath before slowly moving off in the direction of the Waccamaw River.

As he rode back towards the river, Francis tried eating from the satchel of food Diana had made for him, but his fever now diminished his appetite. After riding for only a couple of miles, most of the time slumped forward in the saddle and barely conscious, he fell from the horse, unable to hang onto the reins any longer. Falling asleep where he landed, he made no effort to crawl into the safety of the nearby woods. Utterly exhausted from the events of the day, he cared little about anything except fulfilling his need for sleep. As he slept his borrowed horse wandered off, leaving him truly alone.

The stars were shining brightly in the clear night sky when Francis finally came to. His clothes were now damp from sleeping in the dew covered meadow grass that he had landed in after falling off his horse. Lying there on this peaceful night, he could hear the sound of the river as it flowed nearby. It was the only sound he heard; the woods and adjoining meadows remarkably quiet this clear bright night. His leg now throbbed. Touching it only intensified the pain he felt as he realized his bandages had become soaked with blood. Then he smelled the rancid odor coming from his wounded leg. "Gangrene has set in! I must get to a doctor or I'm surely going to lose my leg! My God, my God, what has happened to me?" Seriously injured and with no one to help him, Francis felt alone and scared. Less than two days ago he had been strong and confident, now he was barely able to care for himself.

Looking for his borrowed horse for several moments, he soon realized it was gone. Lying on the ground, Francis collapsed into tears. He now knew he was likely facing the final days of his life. With his horse now gone, he also knew his chances of reaching a doctor and saving his leg, and possibly his life, was now unlikely. For nearly an hour he allowed himself to wallow in self-pity, picturing how and where he would soon die.

After forcing himself to finally sit up, he contemplated his next move. As he did, he forced himself to eat the rest of the food Diana had prepared for him. Eating soon caused his determination to momentarily return to him. "I will make it to the river and somehow I will make my way back to the Daly plantation. They will help me!" Lying back on the ground as he waited for a moment of severe pain to pass, Francis was determined to move on, but still exhausted he again fell asleep in the meadow's damp grass.

Soon waking up more feverish than he had been, he was momentarily confused as to where he was because of the infection which had set in. After clearing his head, he looked at his pocket watch before heading out. From the light of the moon, he could see it was almost four in the morning. Concentrating on standing up, Francis finally began making his way towards the river.

Reaching the river just after daylight, he stumbled upon a wooden dock. Tied up to the dock was a small wooden flat bottom boat, one very similar he thought to the one Johnny Lincoln was in the day they had met. The boat was one used by slaves as they worked in the nearby rice fields lining the river. Francis had been told by Thomas Daly that his plantation was surrounded by three other large rice plantations, each one stretching from the South Carolina coast back to where the land met the Waccamaw River. "Finally a little bit of luck," Francis thought as he crawled into the small boat.

Barely having the strength to push away from the dock, Francis found the river's current to be stronger than it was when he crossed it the first time. He struggled in his weakened condition to steer the boat, but now the current was stronger than he was and it carried him away from the Daly plantation. It also carried him further away from where he had buried the gold and silver. As he struggled with his attempts to steer the boat, he heard voices come from the same side of the river he had just left.

"There he is, there he is! Look in the boat, that's the reb we were told about!" Another angry voice yelled out. "Get him! Shoot that son of a bitch!" The three Union soldiers fired their muskets at him several times, but the distance between them and the boat caused the minie balls to fall far short of their intended target and they splashed harmlessly in the river.

Out of range of the muskets being fired at him, Francis momentarily became lucid and strong. Frantically he steered the small boat to the opposite shore. Across the river and downstream from where he had climbed into the boat, he was quickly out of sight of the Union soldiers. In electing to row the small boat to the opposite side of the river, he now made his second mistake. It was a mistake which would soon prove to be a costly one. Still weak and exhausted, his temperature spiked even higher from the infection which had begun to invade his body, Francis' decision making skills now started to falter. In a moment of bad judgment, he had steered the small boat towards shore. Staying in the boat would have taken him down the river towards the relative safety of Georgetown and perhaps, just perhaps, things might have gone differently for him.

Struggling to climb out of the boat, his pistol fell from his waistband into the shallow murky water. Not stopping to look for it, Francis summoned some of his remaining strength to pull the wooden boat up onto a small sandbar along the bank of the river. Finally getting the boat onto the sandbar, he then did his best to hide it within the branches of a tall pine tree which had recently fallen alongside the river. While he knew the boat was his only way out of the area, and while he also knew he needed to keep it from being found by anyone who might be searching for it, his confused mind won out over logic. Instead of telling him to stay in the boat, something which afforded him some safety and comfort for his injured leg, his confused mind told him to hide in the woods from the soldiers who were hunting him. As he finished hiding the boat, he spied a length of rope which had been left in it. Grabbing the rope, he slowly limped away. It was a spontaneous thought to take the rope with him, but it was one which would soon help hide him.

As he limped along the river's sandy shore, a few gold coins fell from his pockets. Picking them up, he placed them back into one of the pockets of his blouse and then moved as quickly as he could out of sight into the woods. Slumping against a large tree, Francis thrust his saber into the ground to help slowly lower himself to a seated position. Thirsty, and now in significant pain, he reached into his blouse and pulled out the small bottle of bourbon Thomas Daly had given him. Dismissing any notion of pouring some of it on his wound, he drank the bourbon in three quick swigs. From where he sat slumped against the tree, Francis had a clear view of the river. As he rested, he watched to see if any soldiers or anyone else approached his position. After resting for almost two hours, he realized he was safe for now. He also now realized if he was threatened by anyone there was little he could do to protect himself except to possibly hide from being captured. The thought of hiding and not making a stand to fight was against his principles, but with few other choices he knew he would hide in order to survive. While he rested in the humidity of an already hot morning, he found himself alternating between being feverish and having the chills. His weakened condition soon caused him to fall asleep again.

Waking up almost two hours later, Francis at first felt somewhat better as his fever seemed to have lessened for the time being. After sitting up, and after unwrapping the bandages around his wounded leg, he saw the infection which had set in around his wound. The foul smell of dying tissue was sickening. "I'm dying," he thought, "and no one is here to help me."

Francis briefly thought about surrendering to any Union soldiers who might find him, but he immediately dismissed the idea as it went against everything he stood for. "If I'm to die I will die on my own terms, not in some intolerable Yankee prisoner camp and certainly not missing a leg. I may die, but I will have my dignity and my honor intact." The thought soon cleared from his tired mind, he crawled down to the water to wash his leg, hoping at the same time for some miracle to occur from the powers of the river.

After washing himself, Francis put his uniform blouse back on. As he did, he took the time to go over the letter he had written to President Davis. Playing the letter over and over in his head, he knew he had failed to complete his mission. He paused to look back on all that went wrong. "Perhaps the assignment was doomed from the beginning."

Sitting down, Francis took the folded up paper from the envelope Thomas Daly had given him. He also took the quill and the small bottle of ink out of his blouse. Then he started to write a letter, but it was not addressed to Daly. It was a letter he addressed to his father. As he started to write, tears flowed down his cheeks as he knew he would never again see his parents or the home in Virginia he loved.

Folding up the letter, Francis inserted it into the same bottle containing the letter he had written to President Davis. In the same bottle was the small map of the field where he had buried some of the gold and silver in North Carolina. Reaching into his blouse pocket, he pulled out the second bottle which contained the letters President Davis and Secretary Memminger had written for him. As he stared at the folded up pieces of paper inside the bottle, he thought back to the day he had met both Davis and Memminger. "If only it could have worked out differently. I have failed them and myself."

As he went to place the two bottles back inside his blouse, Francis could not find the cork to the bottle which contained the letters he had written to President Davis and to his father. The cork had fallen into the thick layer of dead leaves blanketing the ground he sat on. Despite frantically searching for it, he could not find it. Ripping a piece of cloth off of his dirty bandana, he placed the cloth within the neck of the bottle in an attempt to try and keep the letters dry. Then he placed the small bottle in the inside left front pocket of his uniform blouse. The other inside pocket now held the other bottle containing the letter to President Davis. "At least if I should die the letters will survive me. Hopefully someone will read my letter to President Davis and deliver the gold and silver to a place I was not able to reach, for I have failed to complete a mission that was entrusted to me." Even as injured as he was, Francis was upset that he had failed the men who trusted him. Briefly he thought of the men who had died during this mission. He knew he had failed them as well.

From off in the distance, Francis could now hear voices. Soon he could tell they were across the river, but moving closer to him. While he knew he was not in any immediate danger, he painfully stood up, looking to see where the voices came from. As he tried to determine how close the soldiers were to him, he tightened the worn leather belt holding his pants up. Because he had lost so much weight, his uniform was now far too big for him. It simply hung on him. As he dressed, his thoughts took him back to the day he had his picture taken wearing his uniform. It had been the only picture ever taken of him. He smiled as he thought about the picture as he had looked so proper in his uniform. As he looked back, he hoped his parents had received the single photograph he sent them several months ago. "At least they will have something to remember me by."

Finished getting dressed, Francis threw the quill, the bottle of ink, the bottle which had contained the bourbon he just drank, and the envelope Daly had given him into the river so nothing was left behind for Union soldiers to find. After ripping them up, he did the same with the extra copies of the letters President Davis and Secretary Memminger had written for him. Then he moved away from the river several hundred feet, hoping as he did that he would not be seen by an alert Yankee soldier. Stopping soon to again rest from the exhaustion and hunger pains he felt, he sat down on an old moss covered tree stump, his saber drawn and ready. "If they come it shall be over quick for me as I'm too weak to defend myself." Bowing his head, he silently prayed. "Please, God, when the time does come, please have mercy upon me. Please let my death come quick."

Drifting in and out of consciousness, his leg quickly ravaged by the infection inside of it, Francis remained seated on the tree stump within a group of large Live Oaks. In one of his remaining lucid moments, he spied a nearby Live Oak tree with a large opening in its base. It was an opening large enough for a man to hide in. His will to survive still with him, he crawled his way to the large tree to investigate the opening at the base of the tree. As he crawled to the tree, Francis could see the clear early afternoon sky had quickly grown darker. A thunderstorm was rapidly approaching; lightning and thunder already announcing the storm's fast-paced arrival, one which would soon drench the woods with heavy rains.

Even though he was dying, Francis still paused at the opening at the base of the tree to make sure no animals were hiding inside. "I'm hurt enough already, I don't need to be bitten by a coon or by some other animal." Poking his saber around inside the opening, he was soon relieved to find no one had yet made the inside of the Live Oak their home.

The thunderstorm was soon upon him, but like most afternoon storms hitting the Carolinas, it lasted only two hours, dumping a great deal of rain before clearing out. While taking refuge inside the large tree, Francis was able to catch a few handfuls of rain as it cascaded down the outside of the Live Oak. "How can something as simple as rainwater taste so good?" It tasted better to him that afternoon than it ever had before. His thirst quenched by the captured rainwater, he soon drifted in and out of consciousness. Hidden inside the massive Live Oak, he remained there for several hours.

The next morning he was awake early. After crawling out from inside the tree, Francis realized how weak he had gotten and how stronger the foul smell was that came from his injured leg. He knew the end was likely near. Second guessing himself as he sat on the ground, he wondered if he should have stayed at the Daly plantation due to his injury. At the same time, he also wondered if he should have tried making it to Georgetown in the small boat he found. As he found himself questioning what he had done, he also told himself if he had stayed at the Daly plantation he would have wondered if he should have tried to finish his mission.

"I'm a soldier and I did what soldiers are ordered to do, I tried to finish my mission. I will not fault myself for trying." Deep down, he wished he had stayed with the Daly's. "If I had, perhaps I would have had a chance to see mother and father one more time." Francis briefly thought about trying to make it back to the small boat, but it was only a brief thought as he was now too weak to even attempt it. He again heard the voices of the Union soldiers who continued to hunt for him. Now he could tell some of the soldiers had crossed the river looking for him. He knew they would soon find him if he did not hide.

Despite the effects of the infection which continued to sap his strength, Francis continued to fight the brave fight. "I may be dying, but I'm still going to make it hard for the Yankees to find me." Mustering all of his remaining strength, he got to his feet and staggered over to where a rock sat several feet from the Live Oak he had sought shelter in. Weakened greatly by the infection, the rock now looked to him like it weighed a thousand pounds. In normal times he could have picked it up and carried it with little effort. Summoning his remaining strength, he first carried, then rolled, and then pushed the rock until it was positioned within the base of the deformed Live Oak tree. The simple task of moving the rock inside the tree, one he could have completed within five minutes if he was healthy, took him over an hour to now complete.

Finished positioning the rock, he rested for several minutes as the effort of moving it to where he wanted it had nearly done him in.

Knowing he was fading fast, Francis again crawled back into the base of the tree after catching his breath. Steadying himself by holding onto the tree's interior, he painfully stood up on the rock. Using deformities he found within the tree, he used them as hand and footholds to climb several feet higher. As he climbed slightly higher, splintered sections of the tree's interior caught on his clothing, badly scratching his hands and legs at the same time. Ignoring the sharp edges of the splintered wood, he climbed high enough within the cavity of the tree until he was satisfied no one could see him from the outside.

Using the rope he found within the small boat, Francis now strung the thick rope across the middle of the tree's interior. He tied the rope to two opposite and splintered sides of the tree. The badly splintered sides allowed him to securely fasten the rope to them. He was able to run the length of rope easily across the tree's narrow interior twice. Using the rest of the remaining length of rope, he fastened himself to the two sections he had strung across the inside of the tree. Finished tying the rope around his chest, he slowly leaned against the rope to make sure it would hold his weight. "This rope will help me keep my balance. It should also hold me for some time if I should lose consciousness and fall onto it. Even if I lose my balance, I'm high enough in the tree that no one will see me." The tree's interior had grown tight where he fastened the rope, but it served the purpose he was looking for. For a time, it would hide him from Union soldiers.

Francis had held his saber between his knees as he tied off the rope. Now he placed the saber's handle around a curled up section of dead splintered wood within the Live Oak. The tree's interior looked far worse than the outside of the tree had. As he worked, he wondered if this Southern Live Oak had also been struck by lightning in the past. Reaching into his boot, he pulled his bayonet out and jammed it into the tree close to where he hung his saber.

Now almost unconsciousness from the infection in his leg and from the fever that was again running high, Francis carefully pulled his gold watch from his pocket. He had one last task to complete. As he had done countless times before, he slowly ran his fingers over the outside of the watch for the last time, feeling for his initials engraved into the cover. Barely able to read the time because of the lack of light within the tree, he saw the watch read ten minutes to five, it was almost mealtime back home he thought. Ignoring his pain, he closed the face of the watch and fastened the gold chain around another small piece of splintered wood inside the tree. Wanting his final thought to be of home, and wanting his watch to be the last thing he would see as he left this world, he purposely fastened it at the same height as his head. Grabbing the watch as it hung from the tree, he held it for the last time. As he did, he softly kissed the watch. After letting it slowly slide out of his hand, it swayed from side to side within the small opening of the tree he now hid within. "Goodbye mother, goodbye father. I love you both!" Tears of sadness now streamed down both of his cheeks. Judiah knew the end was near.

His chores now completed, Francis leaned back against the tree's interior. As he carefully stood on a deformity within the tree, his left hand held onto the rope to help him keep his balance. Now he intentionally wedged his right arm inside a splintered section of the tree. Doing so would take some of his weight off the ropes when he fell unconscious. Then he closed his eyes to rest.

In minutes, Francis lost consciousness for the last time. Falling forward, with his left arm and upper torso now suspended over one side of the rope, and with the rest of his body suspended on the other side, the rope did what he wanted it to do. With the rope supporting his weight and with his right arm still purposely wedged within the splintered interior of the tree, he accomplished what he had been determined to do. He had hid from the Yankees and he would die on his own terms. Soon he took his last breath. He would remain hidden until a transplanted Yankee found him many years later.

Inside the closed watch Francis had loved so dearly, the time read 6:23 pm. Its owner now dead, the watch soon would be also.

* * * * * *

Over the many years following his death, the saber continued to hang within the tree where Francis had placed it. But time also causes death to parts of trees, just as it does to people. Years after it finally died, the tree's splintered wood gave way and the saber fell. When it did it got caught in the uniform pants hanging next to it. The bayonet had fallen to the ground inside the tree years earlier. Over time the cloth blouse, as well as the pants Francis had worn, rotted somewhat and spilled the gold coins from the pockets where they had been placed. As the bayonet had, the coins also fell to the ground inside the tree. They would become buried under layers of leaves that fell over many years. But for some reason the rope Francis found in the small boat held him up for many years, suspended in place inside the Live Oak tree until it was time for him to be found.

He would have liked the person who finally found him. They would have made great friends.

* * * * * *

The war would rage across different parts of the country until both sides finally met in early April, 1865. At Appomattox Court House in Virginia, on April 9th, General Robert E. Lee and General Ulysses S. Grant would meet to discuss the terms of the South's surrender. Three days later, on April 12th, the same day the Confederacy had opened fire upon Fort Sumter four years earlier, the South formally surrendered.

On April 14th, exactly four years surrendering Fort Sumter to the Confederacy, General Robert Anderson raised the American flag back to the top of the fort's flagpole. That same evening President Lincoln would be shot at Ford's Theatre. He would die the following morning.

As Francis had not seen the war end, Lincoln would not see the country heal itself.

29

The Southern States Fight Again.

'I wish I was in the land of cotton,
Old times there are not forgotten;
Look away! Look away! Look away, Dixie Land!"
'I Wish I Was In Dixie', Confederate Civil War song.

In the days and weeks following the announcements of the discovery of the long lost Confederate treasury, Paul and his friends became the focus of many national and local news stories. The country, once divided by a terrible war, now could not get enough of the story surrounding the discovery of the gold and silver.

Comparisons soon followed which likened Paul to those who had made previous startling discoveries of gold and silver, some while diving on shipwrecks in the nearby Atlantic Ocean. He detested the comparisons and he quickly let others know that he did. It was soon too much attention for all of them and after enduring it for almost ten days they did their best to deflect as much of the media attention away from them as possible. Paul had promised Greg Masterson, the writer who threatened to expose him as a fraud if he did not come through with the promises he had made, an interview after they had talked at the end of the staged press conference in North Carolina. It was the only one-on-one interview he immediately consented to after the money had been found. It was done to fulfill a promise he had made. Their collective efforts at ignoring the media only intensified the public's curiosity about them as Paul had made one early statement which soon made them all so attractive to the public.

The day after opening the cannons in Charleston, the first organized press conference was held there to tell the media about what they had found. Paul was asked a question by a *Fox News* reporter about how the millions of dollars in gold and silver would change their lives because of their new found wealth.

Paul shocked the world with his answer when he told the reporter the money was not theirs to keep. In his response to the question, he told everyone present they had always pursued the hunt for the money ". . . *just for the thrill of finding it. In our opinion, the money still belongs to the people of those states who had formed the Confederacy. It does not belong to us."* That simple response immediately made them the darlings of the media. As the media now would not let go of the story, nor would the public. It seemed as if the entire country could not get enough information about what they had found. That single statement charmed everyone who saw or read the stories containing his comment. But the comment now also caused many civic and historical groups, as well as each of the states who had comprised the Confederacy, and the federal government, to soon lay claim to the found money. For many skewed reasons, several private citizens also filed claims as well.

Paul and his friends were further rewarded with the public's affection when news of Duke Johnson's family was told. When the story was told how Duke's granddaddy had unknowingly cared for the gravesite of three Confederate soldiers for so many years, the public's appetite for more news on the story simply intensified. Their appetite was additionally fed when later news stories reported the Johnson family, as a tribute to the soldiers who had been buried on their property for almost one hundred and fifty years, had donated the land where they had been buried to the state of North Carolina so it could be made into a state park. In the years which followed, even though the soldiers had been finally interred elsewhere, the park would remain a popular Civil War site for the public to visit.

By late October, the early unofficial estimates of what the value of the gold and silver were worth proved to be substantially higher than what Paul had first suggested to Mayor Davis. Judge Morgan, of the United States Court of Appeals for the Fourth Circuit, who was present when some of the money had been found, recused himself from any further official proceedings due to ethical reasons. In doing so, he recommended the United States District Court for the Eastern District of North Carolina be assigned jurisdiction for the final distribution of the found Confederate gold and silver. Shortly after Judge Morgan made his recommendation, the Wilmington office of the Eastern District court was assigned jurisdiction of the case.

Initially the court ordered the United States Marshal's Service to only take possession of what had been found in Charleston, but then Paul was ordered to surrender all of the gold and silver he had stored in the safety deposit boxes back in Murrells Inlet. At the same time, he also surrendered the saber, the bayonet, and the clothing he found with the remains of Captain Francis.

The court further ordered that the collection of gold and silver, the jewelry, and the other surrendered items, were to be examined by a panel of three independent examiners whose backgrounds were in numismatics and Civil War artifacts. It took almost three months for the independent examination to run its course, but in late January the examiners announced to the court the estimated value of the discovery was thirty-two million dollars. When the news was made public it caused another round of media attention to be directed at Paul and his friends. They again did their best to avoid speaking to the media, but soon realized they had become unwanted celebrities for a period of time. Deep down they wished for their fifteen minutes of fame to finally be up.

The independent examiner's estimate of what the gold and silver was worth caused one of Paul's earlier predictions to unfortunately come true. When they had met with Mayor Davis the day they opened the cannons, Paul had told all who were present that money makes people *"seem to do crazy things."* Now he was being proven right.

Several Southern states, most notably those who had been part of the Confederacy from the very beginning, had already filed suit in court seeking a portion of the money. In one state's skewed logic they sought all it. When word got out in follow-up stories as to what the final estimated value had come in at, all of the states who were once part of the Confederacy filed suits seeking immediate disbursement of the found money. The governors of most of those states, as well as several state Attorney Generals, amped up pressure on the court through a flurry of letters and other political maneuvers. In doing so, they urged the court to quickly decide what to do with the money. As the states did, so did the federal government. In addition to the several states who sought part of the found money, so did several agencies of the federal government. They all now did their best to justify to the court their reasons why they should receive a substantial portion of the proceeds. In doing so, they all now acted like Paul had told Mayor Davis they would. Paul's previous career had taught him that greed often rears its head in many different ways.

In early February, the court sent letters to the governors of several former states of the Confederacy who had sought some or all of the money which had been found. The court chose not to send letters to any former Confederate states west of Louisiana and Arkansas or to the governors of any states who land had been former United States territories at the time of the Civil War, specifically those territories who supported the Confederacy. As each of the governors of the former Confederate states received a letter from the court, so did the National Park Service. They were all directed to attend a meeting at the United States District Courthouse in Charleston to discuss what should occur with the found money. The letter advised all of the parties involved that this meeting was the court's single attempt to mediate a solution on how the money should be disbursed. The letter also strongly recommended to the states, and to the National Park Service, that they come up with a mutually agreed upon plan regarding the disbursement of the money prior to the meeting date. The letter warned them if they did not the case would likely languish on the court's docket for several more months. Each of the plaintiffs was also directed by the court to provide a list of proposed projects they would fund if the court granted them any part of the found assets.

The letter further advised the parties that Judge Howard Nathan Morgan, despite his superficial involvement in the discovery of the gold and silver in Charleston, would be the initial mediator in this matter. This was based on an agreement reached by the United States District Courts in Virginia, North Carolina, and South Carolina. After attempting to mediate a fair and equitable disbursement of the found money, Judge Morgan would then make known his recommendations to the United States District Court for the Eastern District of North Carolina for their review. The letter also advised everyone the court was not bound to follow any of the recommendations made by Judge Morgan. The letter concluded by stating the court hoped this meeting would prevent future prolonged and expensive legal hearings from occurring. The court's letter expressed hope that this meeting would result in a disbursement of the funds to the satisfaction of everyone.

Prior to the meeting date, Judge Morgan extended written subpoenas mandating Paul, Chick, and Jayne be present for this meeting. After receiving his subpoena, and through a request Paul made to Judge Morgan through the judge's law clerk, similar subpoenas were also sent to Mayor Davis, Bobby Ray, Pete, and to Duke Johnson, mandating they be present as well.

On the morning of Tuesday, February 17th, representatives from ten former Confederate states, as well as from the National Park Service, and the court's guests, met for the first time with Judge Morgan to start discussions on how the found money should be disbursed. Early on it was apparent the states had not been able to agree upon a plan to disburse the money amongst themselves. Paul had been right again, greed had clouded the ability of three states to reach a mutual agreement with the remaining states. The Confederacy was at war again, but this time it was with each other and it was over money. Early on in the proceedings, Judge Morgan quickly let everyone present know of his displeasure.

For the rest of the day, with a court stenographer, a court clerk, and two Deputy United States Marshals present, Judge Morgan allowed each of the ten states who had filed motions seeking a portion of the money to demonstrate to the court their justification for laying claim to a portion of the Confederate gold and silver. The Park Service was also given the same opportunity at the conclusion of the state presentations. Previously, the court directed three private citizens, as well as several other civic and historical groups who had filed claims against the found money to submit written responses to the court justifying their positions.

After listening to each of the presentations, each state was given an additional five minutes to summarize the reasons why they felt they were entitled to a portion of the found money. The Park Service summarized their reasons after the state presentations had concluded. After listening to each of the summaries, Judge Morgan recessed the meeting for the day, instructing the representatives to return at ten the following morning.

* * * * * *

In his opening comments the following morning, Judge Morgan started by briefly summarizing the proceedings of the previous day. Then, in a move which surprised all present, he allowed one more speaker to address the group.

"Last evening I took the time to reflect back on each of your presentations. I also gave a thorough review to the notes I had made throughout the day. As I did, I realized I had not allowed one person to speak. While not representing any of the states gathered here today, or the federal government, Mr. Paul Waring is the person most responsible for this meeting being held. It is he, along with the assistance of those colleagues of his, whose efforts, some made of pure luck and others by their sheer determination, have led to the discovery of the long lost Confederate treasury. Without their efforts, I suspect we would all be doing something else today. I'm quite certain we would not be meeting here. I believe we owe him the opportunity to present his opinion on how the money should be disbursed. Do any of you have an objection to him speaking to the court and to you?"

Raising his hand, Devin Stilson, the Attorney General for the state of Mississippi, asked one question of the court. "Your Honor, the state of Mississippi is grateful to Mr. Waring and to his colleagues for their dedicated efforts in finding the lost gold and silver. It is truly a remarkable discovery. However, I do have one question for the court. How much influence does Mr. Waring's voice have with the court in deciding how the money is to be disbursed?"

Taking a moment to remove his glasses, Judge Morgan placed them on the desk he was sitting at before answering Attorney Stilson's question. "How can I answer your question when I have yet to hear what he has to say? I will remind the state of Mississippi, as I will also remind all of you, that in my entire career as a jurist no one has ever personally influenced any of my decisions. My decisions are influenced solely by the facts which have been presented, not by the individuals who have presented them. Does that answer your question, sir?"

"Yes, it does, Your Honor. I meant no disrespect to you or to the court with my question."

"None has been taken. I understand the point you have raised."

Then Judge Morgan invited Paul to stand and address the others who were present.

"Thank you, Your Honor. My friends and I sincerely appreciate being invited to attend these proceedings and to address the court with our thoughts. First, we want to again make it clear to everyone that we, either as a group or as individuals, are making no claim to any of this money as it is simply not ours to keep in any manner. The recent comparisons the media has made, some of which have labeled us as treasurer hunters, are both unfair and inaccurate as we have not done this for any financial reward or for any other type of personal gain. However, we do have our opinions on how we believe the money should be disbursed.

We were somewhat upset by what we heard yesterday from each of the state presentations. We were equally upset by the presentation which was made by the National Park Service. Actually it is what we did not hear that is upsetting. While all offered plans on how they would use the funds to build new schools, new roads, or for other similar needs, no one said they would use the money to preserve any of the Civil War sites which are located within their respective jurisdictions. Nor was there any mention of the funds being used to acquire privately held property which has historical value attached to it from the Civil War. Nor did any of the presenters suggest they would use any portion of the funds to preserve Civil War monuments which currently exist. My friends and I heard no mention of using any part of the money to fund educational programs related to the war. For what it is worth, we believe it is important for us to remember our past, especially since the financial means to do so are now available.

Your Honor, thirty-two million dollars is a great deal of money. While we firmly believe the money belongs to the people of the United States, we also believe it primarily belongs to the people of those states who were part of the Confederacy. It was their relatives, their friends, and their states whose money likely created a portion of the funds that comprised the treasury of the Confederacy. The same treasury we are meeting here to discuss.

My friends and I would like to see this money divided up amongst those states who are here today, the states who truly were the states of the Confederacy. However, certain states like Virginia, North Carolina, South Carolina, and Georgia, possibly Mississippi as well; they deserve a larger portion of the found money than the other former Confederate states do. It was those states I have mentioned who had the most prominent roles, the most battles fought in them, and who had the largest burdens placed on their civilian populations than the other states did during the war. We just think they should get a bigger slice of the pie than the other states, but everyone should get something.

Your Honor, we are meeting here in Charleston, the city which most historians, if not all, cite as being the place where the first hostile shot of the Civil War was fired. As you may know, Charleston has recently had to cancel its plans to host the one hundred and fiftieth anniversary celebration of the start of the Civil War. Like so many cities and towns across our country, Charleston is facing tough economic times. They had to cancel the anniversary celebration so essential city services could still be provided to the city's residents. Your Honor, no matter what anyone's position is on the Civil War, whether someone believes it was good or bad is not the issue. We all know too well the horrors of war and we all know slavery was an embarrassing blemish on our past, but the Civil War has a significant place in our country's history. As my friends and I believe the states represented here today should receive a portion of the money which has been found, we also believe the court should allocate a portion of the money to the city of Charleston. Some of the money we have found was money hidden in likely the very same cannons that fired the first shots of the war. In our opinion, Charleston should be given a portion of the money so it can properly host the anniversary celebration of our nation's most tragic war. That celebration is not just for the people of Charleston to take part in; it's one for everyone to take part in."

Pausing for a moment, Paul saw Mayor Davis nod his head at him. It was a nod silently thanking him for going to bat for the city and for the mayor's political future as well.

Before he could continue, Judge Morgan asked Paul a question. "Mr. Waring, am I correct in hearing that you believe the court should come up with some simple formula and then, just as simply perhaps, divide the money between the states who are represented here? Am I also correct in hearing you believe this formula should somehow allow for a greater disbursement to the states you just mentioned? Is that what you are saying?"

"Yes, Your Honor. Each of these states made a conscious decision to leave the Union so they could support the Confederacy. Each state made their own sacrifices to the war and as they each shared in the Confederacy's defeat, they would have also shared in the victory with the other states if they had won. If victories and defeats are to be shared, so then should the found Confederate treasury. Besides those states I have mentioned and the unique roles they each played in the war for the Confederacy, we see no real reason to complicate the distribution of part of this money. Trying to figure out which state gets what percentage of the found money based on how many battles were fought in each state, or deciding who gets what based on how many soldiers each state contributed to the cause, would be a ridiculous task to try and undertake. My friends and I believe as each of the states equally shared in the bitter defeat of the Confederacy, they should also equally share their found treasury. It's a simplistic approach to a complex problem, but one we believe is a fair one. However, we hope the court would impose stipulations on those states who receive some of the money. It's also our hope the court will consider a couple of other allocations we would like to see made."

Taking notes as Paul talked, Judge Morgan quickly put his pen down, interrupting the presentation being made. "Mr. Waring, did I hear you correctly? Did you say *stipulations*? And what other allocations would you be referring to? The majority of the states that comprised the Confederacy are here today, who else might you be referring to?"

"Yes, sir, those states are all here, except for Texas of course. I did use the term stipulations and I promise I will clarify that point in a moment. But I . . . I mean we . . . we also believe the federal government deserves to be compensated for its losses."

Ronald Nihill, an Assistant Attorney General for the state of Louisiana, stood up and waited for the court to recognize him. After being recognized, he questioned Paul on his position regarding compensating the federal government with a portion of the found Confederate treasury. "Mr. Waring, why should the court consider compensating the federal government with some of this found money? It was not theirs to start with."

"Sir, I beg to differ. Some of it, in fact, likely a very large portion, was very much their money."

"How so?"

"Well, if I remember my history correctly, I seem to remember it was just after Louisiana seceded from the Union that a group of Confederate soldiers, secessionists, Southern patriots, or whatever they were called, and likely with a few other men from Louisiana mixed in with them, seized the United States Mint located in New Orleans and made off with a bunch of money. I seem to remember they appropriated somewhere around $20,000,000 in cash, bonds, and notes. This was all done for the benefit of the Confederacy. The money they seized was the property of the United States government. A good portion of it was in the form of gold and silver coins, some of which may be the same very coins my friends and I have recently found. To take the point even further, I seem to recall a rather prominent Confederate general, perhaps the same one who led the attack on Fort Sumter, helped coordinate the raid on the mint."

"Well... I..."

"To take it a step further, I also seem to remember a certain Confederate state, in fact, the same one we are meeting in today, started the hostilities of the Civil War by firing their cannons at a fort. It was Fort Sumter to be precise, a fort also owned by the United States government. Seems I remember learning about that fort and a couple of others just like it sustaining some pretty heavy damage from Confederate cannons being fired at them. I also seem to remember these forts were all located in the South." Paul paused for a moment to look at Attorney Nihill's reaction to his comments before continuing. "In this case it's a pot of money, but it seems we should be fair when the pie is being sliced up. Fair is fair, at least that's what I've always been told."

"Sir, the United States government has enough money already, don't y'all think?" Nihill asked.

"Perhaps so, but if they do it seems they, just like the states sitting here, would likely be doing a better job at preserving Fort Sumter and so many other important Civil War sites across the South. As far as I can tell, they're not doing a great job at it, and I suspect your states are not either. Probably comes down to a lack of money all across the board, for them and for you."

Judge Morgan tried, but he could not help but chuckle at Paul's comments. He knew the points raised were valid ones. They were also ones the state representatives could not logically argue against as both time and many historians had well-documented the facts now being spoken about.

"Sir, we are not saying the United States government is the only entity besides you folks who should get a portion of the money. Nor are we saying they should get more than you. We believe a site in Pennsylvania should also get a portion of the money as well. Brave men from both sides died fighting for the causes they believed in at a place called Gettysburg. We as a nation, likely from a speech President Lincoln gave there, consider that to be hallowed ground. It is all of that and more. Seems to us we should be doing a better job of caring for that piece of property than we currently are so that future generations of Americans can appreciate the terrible battle which took place there. At the same time, perhaps we should also consider buying some of the adjacent land surrounding the Gettysburg battlefields, land where many a brave young Confederate soldier died while fighting for your cause. Those properties need to be preserved as much as the other sites there already have been. Especially now because we have the funding available to do so without burdening the taxpayers even more than they already are."

Paul paused for a moment to reflect on the points he had just raised and to gather his thoughts on the points he still wanted to address.

"My friends and I are not proposing we give any money directly to the United States Treasury or to Pennsylvania. Instead, we're suggesting the court should consider allocating a portion of the funds directly to the National Park Service, with a mandate these funds are to be used exclusively for the upkeep of both Fort Sumter and Gettysburg. The mandate, in our opinion, should limit the use of these funds for three specific needs. The Park Service should be told these funds are only available for use to preserve these two locations, for use in funding continuing education programs at both locations, and for future property acquisitions which are adjacent to the Gettysburg battlefields."

Seated as Paul had spoken, Attorney Nihill stood up from his chair to make a follow up response to Paul's comments, but then quietly sat down. He passed on an opportunity to speak when Judge Morgan asked him if he had anything else to say.

Paul then continued with his presentation. "Your Honor, the court is in the unique position of not only being able to allocate a portion of the found money to the states which comprised the Confederacy and to the Park Service so they can care for the two national parks we have already mentioned, but the court also has the opportunity to make one more important allocation to the Park Service. This additional allocation is one which will benefit the public and not the Park Service per se. We strongly urge the court to do so. Doing so will also recognize another important anniversary in our nation's history. As we hope Charleston will be awarded a portion of the money so the city can properly host the upcoming historic anniversary of the start of the Civil War, we also hope the court will award the Park Service a portion of the money so they can prepare our national parks for the upcoming one hundredth anniversary of our first national park. We would like to see our parks receive some much needed maintenance before this anniversary arrives. Currently the Park Service does not have the funding for completing this maintenance. We hope the court will honor our national parks with an additional allocation of money needed to restore some of them to the condition they should be in."

Raising his right hand to indicate he had a comment to make, Virginia's Attorney General, Robert Tolomeo, waited until Paul finished with his comments. "Your Honor, the state of Virginia, the state where the capitol of the Confederacy was proudly located, and the home of Captain Judiah Francis, is proud to support the recommendation Mr. Waring has just made. He makes a very logical argument for a portion of the funds being granted to the federal government, specifically to the National Park Service." In short order, the representatives of Alabama, Georgia, and North Carolina, joined Virginia in supporting Paul's recommendation regarding the Park Service being granted a portion of the assets which once were part of the Confederate treasury. The comment made by Attorney Tolomeo gave Paul some hope that his points were being taken seriously.

"Your Honor, our friend Duke Johnson is with us today. I believe everyone here now knows about the rich history of the Johnson property in North Carolina. It is also now well-known that his granddaddy, as did Duke's father, and as Duke himself has also done, cared for a grave on their property for many years. It was not the grave of family members they were caring for, but rather a grave which has turned out to be the resting place of three Confederate soldiers for so many years. They did so not because they knew they were tending the grave of Confederate soldiers, but rather they did so because they knew another human being had been buried there. They simply wanted the grave to be cared for. To me and my friends, as it hopefully does to all of you, the Johnson family epitomizes what Southern families, what all American families stand for, and that is caring about others. Recently his family has donated a part of their special tract of land to the state of North Carolina so it can be converted to a state park; the work is being done as we speak. It's the same land where those soldiers were buried. Your Honor, my friends and I, and without Duke knowing about this before now, believe the Johnson family should be compensated for their generous donation of that piece of land which North Carolinians and others will soon enjoy for many years to come."

Without a moment of hesitation, North Carolina's Attorney General, Anthony Cummings, rose to address those who were present. "I would like to thank Mr. Waring and his friends for recognizing the Johnson family and for recognizing the generous donation of some of their land so another beautiful North Carolina state park can be built. Your Honor, as Virginia has done before us on a previous recommendation of Mr. Waring's, the state of North Carolina, in grateful appreciation to the Johnson family, who are long and proud members of our fine state since before the Civil War, recommends this suggestion of Mr. Waring's also be given serious consideration and approval. North Carolina believes the Johnson family should be compensated for their donation of not only the land they have given to our great state, but also for the time their family has spent caring for the grave of three brave Confederate soldiers. Thank you."

Judge Morgan paused momentarily to reflect on the comments Mr. Cummings had made. "Mr. Cummings, the point raised by Mr. Waring regarding the Johnson family, and your subsequent support of his recommendation, will be so noted. The previous comments made by Mr. Tolomeo, which received support from you and from two other states, have already been so noted. Thank you for your comments."

After being sure Judge Morgan had finished speaking, Paul then continued with his presentation. "Your Honor, as I have mentioned my friends and I are not filing any claims against this money despite the fact we were directly responsible for finding nearly thirty-two million dollars in gold and silver. As you all are aware, this money had been lost for years and was money no one else could find. However, I do have two requests for a small portion of this money." Nervously, Paul paused for a brief moment before continuing. "We're requesting the court allocate one hundred thousand dollars to me and my friends for a project we're undertaking. Chick Mann and Jayne Ewald, both of whom are educators here in South Carolina, and Pete Cater, a professional videographer who has been working with us, along with me and my other colleagues, are planning on making a documentary film on what we've found during our hunt for the missing Confederate treasury. We believe this video will help preserve our nation's history. We also believe it's simply a great story which needs telling."

Absorbing what he just heard, Judge Morgan asked Paul a follow-up question. "Mr. Waring, say your documentary becomes a profitable venture for your group of friends and you, have you discussed what you would do with any profits that are generated by this film?"

"Yes, we have, Your Honor. After all expenses are paid, any profits will be distributed to various veterans' hospitals across the states, both in the North and in the South, who had soldiers participate in the Civil War. We would like to think the soldiers of the Civil War, who were often treated so poorly for their wounds due to the medical practices of that time, would be proud to know the story we want to tell about them might make some money to help care for our soldiers who have been injured while defending our country today. My friends and I are willing to operate under any financial guidelines set by the court to monitor the use of such funds. When the documentary starts to show any form of a profit we'll be happy to demonstrate to the court, as well as to others, anytime the court requests, how any profits have been allocated. Judge, this is a self-serving statement, but we promise we will not embarrass the court in any way if this request is approved."

Judge Morgan, as did several others in the room, nodded their heads in silent approval at the project Paul and his friends planned to undertake. It was obvious to Paul they were pleased how profits from the film project would benefit today's wounded soldiers.

"Your Honor, I'm somewhat embarrassed to ask the court for this last request I have, but seeing what the final sum was of the gold and silver we found, well, um ... I ... Your Honor, what I'm trying to say is our search took us to three different locations to find the money. To get the search moving we had to host a press conference and um . . . I . . . Your Honor, what I'm still trying to say is I personally spent slightly over twenty-five hundred dollars during the course of the search for the money. I have some receipts and some I don't have, but ...."

"Excuse me, Mr. Waring, but are you asking the court to consider reimbursing you for the expenses you incurred during your searches?"

"Yes, sir, I am. Twenty-five hundred dollars would cover just about most of it. I hope the court would trust me on the amount. It's not a lot of money to most people, but to a retired state trooper it's a fair piece of change. Again, I'm embarrassed to ask this of the court."

"Mr. Waring, the court will consider this request. For the record, the court has complete trust in you. You have nothing to be embarrassed about by asking the court to consider this request of yours."

Still somewhat embarrassed by the personal request he had made, Paul acknowledged Judge Morgan's comments. "Thank you, sir."

Raising his hand, North Carolina's Attorney General Anthony Cummings again rose from his chair. He waited for the court to recognize him before speaking.

"Mr. Cummings?"

"Your Honor, seeing Mr. Waring and his associates have likely generated a few million dollars of unexpected income for us, the state of North Carolina would be pleased to pick up the check for his expenses. Seeing what he has done for all of us, it seems like the least we could do for him."

"Thank you, Mr. Cummings. The court will take notice of your generosity on Mr. Waring's behalf. Seems to me all of the states should make some kind of an effort to reimburse him for this rather paltry sum of money, but we will figure it out." Paul nodded his head in appreciation to Cummings.

"Your Honor, as I mentioned, my friends and I are aware of what the three independent auditors have been put the value of our find at. It's a staggering amount of money, at least to us it is. We understand the gold and silver will likely be sold in one way or another to reach that estimated dollar value. We have no concerns with that process. However, my friends and I are also aware that included in those thirty-two million dollars was an estimated value of the saber which once belonged to Captain Francis. My understanding is the estimate also included the historical value of his uniform and of a few other items as well. We would hope the court would order that those items are not to be auctioned off to raise any money. We're of the opinion these items are irreplaceable; they belong in a museum for the public to see. They shouldn't simply be auctioned off so they can be put on display in someone's private collection. Your Honor, as we feel about those items, we also feel the same about these items."

Paul then bent over and picked up the small moving box he stored some of the items in that he had found. Walking over to where Judge Morgan sat, he set the box down on a small table next to him. "Your Honor, and with the court's permission, I would like to show all of you a couple of items I have found."

"We're all eager to see what you have in the box, Mr. Waring."

As he donned a pair of white cloth gloves, Paul explained the historical importance of the items stored within the simple cardboard box to everyone present.

"Your Honor, with the remains of Captain Francis, I also found two letters he had written. These same letters helped us find the gold and silver we're discussing here today." Reaching into the box, Paul handed Judge Morgan a pair of white cloth gloves to put on. Allowing him time to put the gloves on, he then handed Morgan the original letter Francis had written to President Davis. Next, he placed down on the table the original letter Francis had written to his father. "Your Honor, these two original letters are irreplaceable. They are important parts of our nation's history. You can see the one you're holding was written by Captain Francis; it was addressed to President Jefferson Davis. That letter contains the hidden clues which my friends and I were able to decipher. It was those very same clues which led us to the gold and silver Francis had taken great pains to protect by hiding it so well. The second letter was also written by Captain Francis. It was addressed to his father; we believe it was likely written when Francis was near death. Neither of them should be any place but in a museum for the public to enjoy. We believe everyone here today, after they have had a chance to read them, will agree with our recommendations regarding the two letters." Then Paul showed those present the two bottles he found the letters in, describing to them how he and Donna had removed the letters.

Chick and Jayne began passing out copies of both letters to everyone in the room as the presentation regarding the two bottles was taking place. As those present soon finished reading the letter a dying Judiah Francis had written to his father, Paul could see the emotions of sorrow which appeared in the faces of the state representatives. The same emotions appeared in the face of Mayor Davis.

Paul glanced at Judge Morgan as he finished reading the letter Francis had written to his father. Putting the letter down on his desk, he swiveled his chair so the back of it now faced the others in the room. Somewhat shielded by his chair, Judge Morgan wiped his eyes with his handkerchief. Several others in the room had the same reaction after reading the letter. It was just as powerful a letter to them as it had been to he and Donna when they first read it. The reactions Paul saw in the room made him smile as he now knew Francis would be remembered by all of them as well.

Then Paul reached into the cardboard box one more time. "Your Honor, the same applies to this gold watch and to the collection of jewelry we found when we opened the cannons in Charleston. I found this gold watch with the remains of Captain Francis. Like his remains, this watch also survived being hidden within a tree for almost one hundred and fifty years. Sir, if you look closely you will see it still has his initials engraved in it. The watch and the jewelry, like all of the other items, are all irreplaceable. They deserve to be seen by the generations which follow ours. Your Honor, we hope the court will come to the same conclusion we have come to, one which mandates all of these items are to permanently stay together. They tell a story about Captain Francis and the ordeal he went through to protect the treasury of the Confederate States of America. Your Honor, not to be repetitive, but these items deserve to stay together forever. Sir, if we may be so bold to make this next suggestion to the court. Seeing these items were recovered here in South Carolina, we would like to suggest that a good place to display these items from the start would be the South Carolina Confederate Relic Room and Military Museum. We believe this museum would be a great place to first display these priceless artifacts, especially now as we celebrate a significant anniversary of the Civil War. After the items are displayed there, we believe it would be most fitting if they were then placed on display in a museum in Virginia, the state which Captain Francis called home."

After taking a few minutes to personally examine the items Paul produced from the cardboard box, and after allowing the various state representatives time to examine them as they sat on the table adjacent to where he sat, Judge Morgan acknowledged Paul's presentation to the court.

"Very well, Mr. Waring, the court will take your recommendations under advisement. The court wants you to retain possession of the letters, the gold watch, and the other items for now. You may use them in the documentary film you are making, but keep them safe as I am holding you responsible for their safety."

"Yes, Your Honor." As he packed the items back into the cardboard box, Paul held out hope he had gotten his points across to the court.

Looking up from where he sat, Judge Morgan saw most of those who were present were shaking their heads in silent agreement to what Paul had just recommended. "From what I'm seeing from each of you it appears the ten states seated before me, as well as the National Park Service, agrees with Mr. Waring's recommendations regarding the letters and the other items he has shown us. Does any state, or the Park Service, not agree with that assessment of mine? Speak now if you do." The lack of any opposition to Paul's recommendations was noted by Judge Morgan. It was also noted in the official transcript of the day's proceedings.

"Now, Mr. Waring, is there anything else you wish to offer to the court?"

"There is, Your Honor. I would like to speak to the court regarding the stipulations we would like to see imposed on those states and the Park Service if they are granted any portion of the found money. We would like to make a brief recommendation on that."

"Please explain to the court what you mean by the term *stipulations*."

"Your Honor, we would like the court to mandate this money, money which was either seized during the Civil War or donated to the Confederate cause by citizens of the Confederacy, be used for the preservation of Civil War sites or for the acquisition of additional properties which are now currently privately owned. My friends and I simply define these additional properties as being those locations where significant Civil War battles were fought. It is land which has yet to be preserved for our future generations to visit. We're hoping the court will restrict the usage of the money solely for the purposes I have mentioned here today. We also hope the court will mandate these funds cannot be used for any other reasons, such as administrative costs or for other projects. The money, as I have already suggested, belongs to the people. They deserve to see it used to remember and to protect our past. Our past is now our nation's history; the sacrifices so many young men made during that terrible war are an important part of our history."

Paul paused for a moment as he knew the emotions of the moment had started to effect his presentation. Gathering himself, he continued. "Your Honor, we found two cannons in a small cemetery here in Charleston, a cemetery which obviously has been neglected over the years for one reason or another. It's quite likely the neglect occurred because of a lack of funding. If mandates are to be placed upon the states, and if Charleston is to receive a portion of the money, we would like to see Charleston mandated to care for that cemetery. It's the final resting spot for several military veterans; men and women who answered the call to duty when our country needed their services. We believe their final resting spot deserves better care than what it's currently receiving." Taking another moment to collect his thoughts, and to make sure he had spoken on all of the points he discussed with Chick and Jayne earlier, Paul spoke for the final time. "Your Honor, my friends and I appreciate you allowing us to address the court today. Thank you." After he finished speaking, the large courtroom remained quiet for several moments as the others in the room digested the many recommendations he had made. The silence was soon broken by Judge Morgan.

"A very impressive presentation you have made today, Mr. Waring. You and your friends have done great things recently. Today you have raised several valid points for the court to consider. Well-thought-out. Thank you." As they listened to Judge Morgan's comments, Jayne and Chick both realized there had not been any objections voiced to the court regarding Paul's recommendations.

"Before I adjourn this meeting for the day, I would like to offer each of you one last opportunity to make any final comments to the court." It was quiet in the courtroom for several seconds before Mayor Davis motioned to Judge Morgan.

"Your Honor, if I may?"

"Please do, Mr. Mayor."

"Sir, as you know I represent the city of Charleston, not the state of South Carolina. While I don't have a say in how the money is to be disbursed, I would like to offer to the court the city of Charleston supports each of the recommendations made here today by Mr. Waring. As the city's mayor, I hope the court will set aside a portion of the available funds for Charleston due to the unique role we had in the Civil War. However, whether or not the court allocates us any portion of the found money, I promise the court and Mr. Waring that we will make sure the cemetery he has mentioned gets cared for better than it has been. It no longer matters whether it's privately owned or a city cemetery. We will start to take better care of those who once took care of us. I would also like to publicly commend Mr. Waring and his colleagues for their position regarding the found money. I'm not sure many people these days would have taken such a position. It is refreshing to know people with such strong convictions still exist. Thank you, Your Honor."

Virginia's Attorney General rose to address the court again.

"Yes, Mr. Tolomeo?"

"Your Honor, if I may. The state of Virginia has a long and proud history of fighting for our freedom. Our forefathers fought bravely in both the Revolutionary War and the Civil War; today is no different. Today it is our sons and daughters who continue to protect our freedoms by serving in our armed forces. We're a state whose soldiers and residents endured so much during the Civil War. Like many states here today, Virginia was a state who lost so many of its fine young men during that terrible war. As we have fought without hesitation in the past for our freedoms, today Virginia again does not hesitate to support all of the recommendations made by Mr. Waring. To be honest, I'm somewhat embarrassed our presentation was not as thoughtful or as well-presented as his was. I now believe my fellow representatives and I would be foolish not to collectively support Mr. Waring's recommendations. If we do not, then I fear this matter will be tied up in the courts for possibly years and then the courts will have the final say in what to do with the money. Mr. Waring has offered fair and sensible solutions here today for the disbursement of the money. Virginia sees no reason not to accept his recommendations. As a former member of the Confederacy, Virginia will be pleased to just receive a fair share of the treasury that was once partially ours. I promise that our fine state will obey any mandates the court imposes regarding the use of the money. I urge all of you to do the same. Thank you."

Two other states, Georgia and North Carolina, who earlier followed Virginia's lead in supporting Paul's initial recommendations, again supported Virginia's position on accepting the other recommendations that he had made. Soon, Mississippi and Alabama joined them; concurring with the comments Mr. Tolomeo made. Each of these states strongly recommended that immediate approval be given to all of Paul's recommendations.

As Judge Morgan prepared to end the meeting, he asked South Carolina's Attorney General, Carol Lemieux, if she would also support the recommendations Paul had made.

"Your Honor, while the state of South Carolina does not object to any of Mr. Waring's recommendations, we will, as it seems to be our history, not go along with the popular vote at this time. However, we will go along with whatever distribution of this money the court decides upon. I promise the court that South Carolina will not lead another insurrection over this matter as we are still smarting from the first one we led."

Her comments drew laughter from all in the room. Soon Judge Morgan concluded the meeting. As he did, he promised he would make his recommendations known to the Wilmington office of the United States District Court for the Eastern District of North Carolina within two weeks.

* * * * * *

In the days following the meetings in Charleston, Paul and his friends met on two occasions to begin the planning of their documentary film. Plans were soon put into place to conduct the research needed for the documentary and to start the shooting of the exterior scenes. Those scenes would be shot in both North Carolina and South Carolina once spring began. They all agreed Jayne, Chick, and Paul would be responsible for writing the script for the documentary. The decision was made to start this part of the project by the end of the April.

On March 26th, the United States District Court for the Eastern District of North Carolina announced their decision on how the gold and silver was to be divided between the various states and the National Park Service. Before the decision could be made public, it had been leaked to a reporter in North Carolina by an employee of the court. The announcement was first made known to Paul and his colleagues, and to Mayor Davis, almost a week later. It was made known to them through a special meeting Judge Morgan arranged at the United States District Court on Broad Street in Charleston. On the day Paul and his colleagues learned how the gold and silver was to be disbursed; several newspapers ran stories in their morning editions regarding the court's decision.

In their decision, the court first wrote it had taken notice of the fact that several states had voiced their support of the recommendations Paul had made. The court also noted no states voiced any objections to the recommendations that had been made. The court also wrote they concurred with several recommendations Judge Morgan had made.

The court did make one significant change to how everyone thought the money would be disbursed. Because of the historical value of both the coins and the gold and silver bars, the court elected to have Paul and his colleagues assist the three independent examiners with the disbursement of the found assets. The assets would be evenly shared between those states that had comprised the Confederate States of America. This was done as the court, through Judge Morgan, had reached out to Paul to determine if he and his colleagues would assist the examiners with making the disbursement to the states. In agreeing to do so, Paul, Chick and Jayne declined the court's offer of a small stipend for their services. By doing so they had remained true to their word. They would not profit in any way for finding the Confederate treasury.

The court specifically ordered only those states that had been present at the meeting in Charleston were to receive portions of the found money. The court's decision also advised that Judge Morgan would conduct a final review of the money's disbursement to the states and to the Park Service. This would be done to assure the disbursement had been done equitably. As the court awarded similar shares of the found money to each of the states, the court also awarded a similar share to the United States government, specifically to the Park Service. The court's decision dismissed any and all other claims which had been filed against the found money.

While the court's decision mandated disbursement of the assets to ten states who had once been part of the Confederate States of America, The National Park Service, like Charleston, would be the only other governmental agency to receive any other portion of it. Sharing of the assets was to occur after Paul and his colleagues had disbursed equal shares of the first million dollars to the states of Virginia, North Carolina, South Carolina, Georgia, and Mississippi. That initial disbursement would be followed by a similar disbursement of two million dollars to the Park Service. The court's decision agreed with Paul's logic about maintaining the nation's national parks for the generations that followed. Both the Gettysburg National Military Park and the Fort Sumter National Monument would each receive one million dollars in funding for repairs, maintenance, and continuing education programs. The Park Service also was granted permission to use a portion of the money for land acquisitions in and around the Gettysburg National Military Park. To the surprise of almost everyone, the court also agreed with Paul's comments concerning the upkeep of our national parks. Citing the upcoming one hundredth anniversary of the nation's first national park, the court awarded the Park Service an additional one million dollars. The Park Service was directed to dedicate these funds solely for repairs and improvements to the ten busiest national parks across the country.

For their efforts in finding the gold and silver, and for their services in helping to disburse the found money, the court awarded Paul and each of his four colleagues a token gesture of three gold Liberty Head dollars, two gold Liberty Head twenty-dollar coins, five gold Liberty Head ten-dollar coins and two Seated Liberty silver dollars. It came as a complete surprise to them that the court had granted them any of the Confederate treasury, but as he had with the previous clues, Paul soon figured out it had been based on a recommendation Judge Morgan made in his writings to the court. Paul was also pleased to learn the court awarded him three thousand dollars for his out-of-pocket expenses incurred during the hunt for the missing money.

The court's decision also awarded the city of Charleston one hundred and seventy-five thousand dollars so the city could host the Civil War's Anniversary

Celebration. From that allocation, Charleston was mandated by the court to set aside twenty-five thousand dollars and place it in a special fund. Those funds were to be specifically earmarked for the maintenance and upkeep of the city's public and private cemeteries where Civil War and other war veterans had been buried.

The court also took time to give special recognition to Duke Johnson's family. The court's decision spoke at length about the compassion the Johnson family had given to the grave site of the three Confederate soldiers for so many years. The court also recognized the Johnson family for their generous donation of a parcel of their farmland so a North Carolina state park could be built. Citing those two points, the court awarded the Johnson family one hundred and fifty thousand dollars. After hearing about the court's decision, Duke joked with Paul that his family had been paid around one thousand dollars per year for maintaining the gravesite for the past one hundred and fifty years.

The court ignored Paul's request for one hundred thousand dollars to be set aside to help fund the documentary film they wanted to make regarding the story of Captain Francis and the lost Confederate gold and silver. Instead, the court ordered the project to be funded with two hundred thousand dollars. The court mandated that any profits from the documentary were to be used for *'the benefit of our sailors and soldiers injured while defending our freedoms'*. The court wrote in their decision the documentary was *'indeed a story that needs to be told to America'* and also wrote *'our nation's history, whether good or bad, has to be preserved for the generations that followed'*.

The decision of the court to disburse the recovered Confederate assets directly to the states and to the Park Service was partially due to the historical value of the items that comprised the treasury. This part of the court decision surprised Paul and several others as they expected the court would simply conduct an auction of those items and then disburse the monies raised to the parties involved. In explaining the reason for doing so, the court's opinion echoed what Paul had said regarding some of the personal belongings of Captain Francis. The court concurred that the gold and silver coins, as well as the gold and silver bars, were irreplaceable. The decision reflected how uncomfortable the court had felt in auctioning off a part of the country's history. The decision would now leave it up to the states to do what they wished with the assets they would soon receive. Each state would be free to either sell off the coins or to put them on display in their museums.

Lastly, the court again agreed with Paul and ordered the items which had once belonged to Judiah Francis, including the four letters, to be kept together *'forever and for a day'* so the public could experience what life and death had been like during the final days of his life. The court further ordered that while the items were to stay together, they were to be shared amongst those states who expressed an interest in displaying them for their citizens to view. The belongings of Captain Francis would first be displayed at the South Carolina Confederate Relic Room and Military Museum. They would remain there until the end of April, 2015. By then the one hundred and fiftieth anniversary of the end of the Civil War would be over. After that time period, the items would be put on display in Richmond for the balance of 2015. The court's decision assigned the Park Service the responsibility of monitoring the sharing of these items among the fifty states after leaving Richmond.

Several states grumbled when they heard the restrictions that had been placed on the use of their newly acquired funds, but none raised any formal complaints to the court. By now, the media had run several stories on the court's decision; lauding the court for earmarking the funds for the benefit of the public. Collectively the states decided to remain silent regarding the court's decision. None of the states made any backdoor attempts at trying to modify the court's decision on how they could spend the money as they all were afraid of the negative media backlash they would receive if they criticized the court's disbursement of the funds. Publicly the states took the position they were pleased the court's decision allowed them some leeway in how the money could be used to care for their Civil War sites. Privately they had hoped the funds could have been used for other means as well.

For Mayor Davis the court's decision was news he had hoped for and he quickly reorganized his anniversary celebration committee so Charleston could finally host the event during the month of April. The historic celebration would become a focal point in the documentary film Paul and his friends would soon make.

Overall everyone, including the Park Service, came out a winner as they would soon share in a pot of money that was roughly twenty-seven and a half million dollars after all of the other disbursements had been made. Any frustration the states might have felt quickly dissipated after the court's decision had been read. Since the last cannon had been opened at the cemetery, Paul and his colleagues scoured the city trying to find the last missing cannon. It took some effort, but they finally found the last one. It was inscribed with the number two on it.

It had taken them several frustrating days to find it, but after Chick suggested they should expand their search off the peninsula section of Charleston, where they had found the other cannons, they found the last cannon at Fort Moultrie Historic Park, on Sullivan's Island. It was a relief to them to find the old cannon as now they knew it was they who had found the last part of the missing Confederate gold and silver and not someone else. Paul and the others wanted all of the lost money to be shared by everyone who had already received a portion of the other money. Their final wish would now be granted. The remaining gold and silver coins were found in an old Garrison mortar, one they almost missed the day they visited Fort Moultrie.

After the court's decision had been read that morning, Paul advised Judge Morgan of the last cannon being found. Two days later, under Paul's supervision, and with the assistance of both the city of Charleston and the National Park Service, the last cannon was opened. It revealed no additional surprises, just gold and silver coins. The coins were soon determined to be among the rarest and most valuable from that time period. Their estimated value, at almost seven hundred thousand dollars, made those who had shared in the initial disbursement even more pleased to hear their original allocations would be slightly increased.

After leaving the United States District Court on the day the decision was first read, Paul and his friends stopped to celebrate the court's favorable decision on how the money was to be split up.

At the Charles Towne Pub, located a short walk from the hotel they were staying at, Chick raised his first bourbon of the afternoon and proposed a toast in Paul's honor. The simple toast recognized him for the discovery he made and for the adventure he had led them on. Graciously accepting the compliment, he joined the others by raising his frosted mug of Coors Light. Then Paul stood and again raised his mug of beer, somberly offering the next toast. "Perhaps the person we should be toasting today is the friend we never had a chance to meet, Captain Judiah Francis. Here is a toast to him, to his men, and to what they were tasked with doing. Most importantly, it's a toast to how they all died. For now we know they died serving their country. While proudly serving their country, they each deserved a fate far better than what they received."

They all stood quietly for a moment, holding their drinks in a salute to Francis and his men. "Hear, hear!" They finally yelled in unison before sitting down. Remarkably none of them took a sip of their drinks. There would be time for that later.

30
A Final Tribute.

"Let the tent be struck."
Dying words of General Robert E. Lee, CSA

On the morning of April 3rd, a red Ford dump truck, towing one of Duke's Low Boy trailers with a green John Deere backhoe on it, slowly entered the driveway of Duke Johnson's hog farm in Maple Hill. Escorted by four North Carolina Highway Patrol vehicles, two black funeral hearses closely followed the dump truck onto the property. Paul, Chick, Jayne, and Duke, along with several of his employees, were standing in the driveway waiting for them. Soon they all made their way to the meadow where Duke's granddaddy had placed the steel cross so many years ago. Already in place was a new freshly paved driveway which soon would take visitors to the newest state park in North Carolina.

Near the steel cross now stood the original wooden cross, it had been gingerly taken there from the barn so it was present for the ceremony. Close to the two crosses stood Honor Guards from the North Carolina National Guard, the North Carolina Highway Patrol, the South Carolina Highway Patrol, the Charleston Police Department, from various North and South Carolina chapters of the Veterans of Foreign Wars, and from the Sons of the Confederacy. Their various flags, including the flags of the United States, the North Carolina state flag, the South Carolina state flag, the flag of the Confederacy, and the POW/MIA flag, waved in the gentle breeze which blew across Duke's field on a beautiful sunny spring morning.

Standing near the Honor Guards were several local and state politicians, including North Carolina's governor, Beatrice Downs, and Mayor William Davis. Also present were dozens of Civil War reenactors representing various units from both the North and the South. Next to the reenactors stood nearly two hundred proud military veterans. These veterans were from World War Two, the Korean War, and the Vietnam War. Proudly standing with them were several active duty members from each branch of the nation's military. These active duty military members were soldiers, Marines, Air Force, and navy personnel who had recently returned home from serving overseas. It was an impressive sight to see.

Off to the side were satellite trucks from several news stations. Close to them stood a large contingent of television reporters and print media representatives from various national and local media outlets.

Standing proudly near the gravesite in their uniforms was the Maple Hill High School band and choral group.

With the assistance of both Jayne and Bobby Ray, Pete captured the events of the morning on three video cameras. The video they shot that morning, as well as several still photographs taken by Jayne, would later win them acclaim when it was included in the documentary film they all would soon collaborate on. Their documentary would later win three East Coast Independent Film Association awards, including one for cinematography.

After brief comments from Governor Downs, Duke Johnson, and Paul, the remains of the three Confederate soldiers were respectfully removed from their resting places and placed into identical dark maple wooden caskets. As the last Confederate soldier was being placed into his casket, the Maple Hill High School band softly played *Dixie*. That song, followed by a rendition of *America the Beautiful*, one sung by the Maple Hill High School chorus, and coupled with what was taking place with the remains of the long dead Confederate soldiers, brought tears to the faces of many people who were present. As the third casket was closed and was being carried to where the first two caskets were waiting to be placed into the hearses, the ceremony paused as a single bugler from the North Carolina National Guard played Taps. As the bugler finished, a command was given to *Present Arms*. The military and law enforcement personnel present, including those veterans from several generations of our nation's wars, came to attention; holding their salute until the caskets had been placed in the two hearses. When the doors to the hearses were finally closed, the command was given to *Order Arms*. Overhead three National Guard Sikorsky UH-60 Black Hawk helicopters flew by in formation as a tribute to the fallen Confederate soldiers.

The ceremony soon over, the hearses carried the soldiers to be reunited with their leader, Captain Judiah Francis.

* * * * * *

Three days later, in the shadows of the Confederate Monument and just outside of Jackson Circle, in a ceremony which would have awed them, the remains of Captain Judiah Francis, Sgt. Mark Foster, Sgt. Daniel Sturges, and Sgt. Gerald Rickert were laid to rest on the property once owned by General Robert E. Lee's wife's family, now the hallowed ground known as Arlington National Cemetery. It was a ceremony which was carried as the lead story on most local and national news networks across much of the country later that evening. After almost one hundred and fifty years they were now back together, their mission now finished. Now they could rest in peace.

* * * * * *

A few days arriving back home, with the attention and focus of the media now on someone else, Paul went to have breakfast at the Waccamaw Diner for the first time in several weeks. Betty saw him as soon as he walked through the door; running up to him she gave him a big hug. "I cannot believe what I've read about you recently. You've done something so special. Your wonderful story has touched so many lives just here in the Inlet. So many of the Inlet's families, families who first settled this area and who still have kin living around here, had relatives that served in the Confederate army. Everyone is talking about what you've found." As Betty let go of him, he could see the tears in her eyes.

She smiled back at him, wiping her tears away with her apron. "Y'all having breakfast with us this morning?"

"Sure am. How about some blueberry pancakes, a side of sausage, a glass of OJ and some coffee."

As Paul walked to his favorite booth, Betty yelled to him. "You made me a promise, remember?"

"I remember. Bring me my breakfast and I'll tell you all you want to know!" Paul smiled as he slid into the booth with the day's edition of *USA Today*.

As he ate his breakfast, Betty asked him every question she could think of. Patiently he answered every one of them for her. He had taken a liking to her since the first time they had met. She was a hard working country girl who had always made him feel welcome at the diner.

After his third cup of coffee, with his breakfast long since finished, Paul could not wait to get it over with. "OK, I'm done, Betty. I've got to go." As he picked up the bill from the table, she thanked him for taking the time to tell her all about what he had found. After hugging him one more time, he handed her eight dollars to cover the cost of his breakfast. Finally saying goodbye to her, he started to leave, but then stopped and walked back to the booth where he had eaten his breakfast. Betty had just begun to clear away his dirty dishes. "Hey, I'm not sure I left you enough for a tip. Here take this." He said, placing the additional tip in her right hand. Then he turned and left.

Betty's hands were full of dirty dishes when Paul had given her the extra tip. Placing the dishes down on a nearby table, she looked to see what he had given her. It took a moment for her to realize what he had given her, but as he walked across the diner's parking lot to his truck Paul heard the scream she let out. It was the first 1861 three-dollar gold coin she had ever received as a waitress.

After eating breakfast, Paul went to the Socastee Public Library to bring back some long overdue books he had signed out. Walking into the library, he looked over at the Reference Desk and saw Caren was busy working with someone. He had been to the library on several occasions seeking answers to the clues Francis had left in his letter. On several of those occasions, she had assisted him with his research needs. As she finished with her customer, Caren looked up and saw Paul walking over to her desk.

"Remember me?"

"Sure I do, you're the guy I joked with the first day I saw you here. You needed help with some research. If my memory serves me right, I helped you on a couple of other occasions after that, right?"

"Good memory."

"Hey, wait a minute! Aren't you the guy I saw on television and in the newspapers as well? You're the one who found the dead soldier and all of the Confederate money, aren't you?"

"Good memory, again."

"Well, I'll be. Hey, I think I joked with you about sharing some of the gold with me after you found what you were looking for. I did, didn't I?"

"Yes, you did. I'm just here today because I wanted to return the books I had taken out and while I was here I wanted to thank you for all of your help."

Extending his hand to her, they shook hands. As they talked for a couple of minutes, Paul answered a few of her questions regarding what he found, but soon told her he needed to get going. "I'm glad I was able to help you a little bit. This is something I won't forget for some time."

"Me either, Caren, me either."

As Paul started to walk away, he saw she was still looking at him. Stopping, he turned to look back at her. "Sorry, Caren. I almost forgot. Here you go!"

Caren reached up with both hands and caught what Paul tossed to her. It was an 1862 gold dollar coin. Watching her expression as she examined the coin, Paul could tell she was surprised by what he tossed her. "I promised I would share what I found with you!"

Still smiling from the expression he saw on Caren's face, Paul walked out the double sliding front doors of the library and across the sun-drenched parking lot to his truck. He had fulfilled the promises he had made.